THE NEW ANNOTATED

H. P. LOVECRAFT

BEYOND ARKHAM

Howard Phillips Lovecraft (1890–1937),
pictured here at age forty-four.

THE NEW ANNOTATED

H. P. LOVECRAFT

BEYOND ARKHAM

Howard Phillips Lovecraft

Edited with a Foreword and Notes by

LESLIE S. KLINGER

with additional research by Janet Byrne

INTRODUCTION BY VICTOR LaVALLE

Liveright Publishing Corporation
A Division of W. W. Norton & Company
Independent Publishers Since 1923

For information about permission to reproduce selections from this book,
write to Permissions, Liveright Publishing Corporation, a division of
W. W. Norton & Company, Inc., 500 Fifth Avenue, New York, NY 10110

For information about special discounts for bulk purchases, please contact
W. W. Norton Special Sales at specialsales@wwnorton.com or 800-233-4830

Manufacturing by Transcontinental
Book design by JAM Design
Production manager: Anna Oler

ISBN 978-1-63149-263-1

Liveright Publishing Corporation, 500 Fifth Avenue, New York, N.Y. 10110
www.wwnorton.com

W. W. Norton & Company Ltd., 15 Carlisle Street, London W1D 3BS

1 2 3 4 5 6 7 8 9 0

Contents

Introduction

by Victor LaValle

1

I COME NOT to bury Lovecraft, but to praise him.

Such a thing—my praise, this book—would have seemed wild as hell to Lovecraft himself. Unimaginable, really. After all, the man died thinking himself a failure. He published a handful of short stories in small magazines that catered to readers of the weird and fantastical. The man certainly never made enough money with his writing to support himself—hardly enough to pay one utility bill. And now here I am writing an introduction to the *second* volume of his stories, published in this gorgeous, oversized hardcover and filled with insightful annotations by Leslie S. Klinger.

What an afterlife.

Being a writer myself I am inclined to cheer for any one of us who achieves such success, even if the author himself isn't alive to enjoy it. Makes me think of Melville, who died believing *Moby-Dick* had been a failure, or Emily Dickinson, who could never have imagined how many souls she spoke for in her poems, the majority of which went unpublished in her life.

So I am here to praise Lovecraft, to celebrate him and his mighty works. But I'm going to take the long way to get there. If you're dying to get to his stories, please feel free to jump ahead. I couldn't blame you; those stories are the reason we're all here.

But if you did stick with me, well, I'm happy to have you. In order to talk about Howard I'm going to take a detour that leads to upstate New York, and, for a little while, I'm going to talk about Mary Shelley's *Frankenstein*. But bear with me. Here, all roads lead to Lovecraft, eventually.

2

THE HASTINGS INSTITUTE sits half an hour's drive north of New York City. It's an independent bioethics research institute in a town called Garrison. I'd been invited there to join a panel titled "What Can *Frankenstein* Teach Us about Living in the Genetics Age?" It rained on the way up, and the sky became a stone gray that suited an evening spent discussing Mary Shelley's classic Gothic novel. Her work has obviously endured, 2018 being the two hundredth anniversary of its publication. And since I'm writing this introduction, it should be clear that H. P. Lovecraft's fiction has endured, too—not quite a hundred years for Lovecraft yet, though he's getting there. But why? What keeps one writer's creation alive while another's decays just as surely as his flesh?

There were three of us on the panel that evening. Myself, Charlotte Gordon—a historian who wrote a riveting biography of Mary Shelley and her mother, Mary Wollstonecraft—and Josephine Johnson, the director of research for the Hastings Center. The house packed quickly. Who knew so many would be drawn to a discussion of genetics and *Frankenstein*? If I'm honest, I felt a little overmatched. Professor Gordon is a historian who won the National Book Critics Circle Award for Biography in 2015 and Ms. Johnson is listed as "an expert on the ethical, legal, and policy implications of biomedical technologies, particularly as used in human reproduction, psychiatry, genetics, and neuroscience."

I, by comparison, make up stories.

Ms. Johnson's talk focused, as you'd imagine, most clearly on the biomedical end of the conversation. In particular she talked about an innovation called CRISPR, which stands for "clusters of regularly interspaced short palindromic repeats." CRISPR is a technology that allows scientists to edit genomes. That sounds simple, but please let your head explode as you consider this: A handful of scientists have figured out how to rewrite the genetic code of a living thing in order to deactivate certain traits. For example, CRISPR can be used to modify mosquitos so they can't transmit diseases like malaria. Eventually, human genetic codes might be rewritten so that diseases like cancer could be, basically, deactivated. A Chinese geneticist has already claimed he's achieved this in two infant girls.

At this point science fiction risks being outpaced by science.

3

NOW THIS WILL sound strange, but while learning about CRISPR I thought of one Lovecraft story in particular, the famed novella *At the Mountains of Mad-*

ness. In that story a race of alien beings called the Elder Things created a race of creatures called shoggoths; the shoggoths were treated as slave labor by the Elder Gods. The real point, here, is about the ideas of scientific discovery and genetic experimentation—that Lovecraft had been toying with ideas not that far off from CRISPR long before any of the scientists who created it were even born. While Lovecraft is often categorized as a horror or supernatural writer, one of the bed-rocks of his artistic vision is that he was, from a young age, curious about the world, an amateur scientist. We know this, in part, because he shared his insights with his friends through his correspondence.

Lovecraft, famously, lived in his letters. Friends and admirers wrote to him, and he wrote and wrote and wrote back. He's often depicted as a kind of shut-in, afraid of the outside world, but I wonder if it would be more accurate to say that in his younger years he explored the world with his intellect, only his body stayed home—a kind of astral projection.

It's no surprise that the sciences would be embedded in the man's conscious-ness, considering his life spanned some of the great milestones of modern science: Darwin's theory of evolution, Einstein's theory of general relativity, to name just two you may have heard about. And perhaps most of all he fell in love hard with astronomy and the study of space. When he was younger, he self-published *The Rhode Island Journal of Astronomy*, for God's sake.

He showed an equal hunger for the past, the more distant the better. The Egypt of "Under the Pyramids," for instance, is a fine example of how much you can glean about a part of the world, and a civilization, that you damn sure never went any-where near. Even the Antarctica of Lovecraft's imagination showed an intimacy with the best knowledge available to him at that time. From a young age, it was clear that he wanted to know and understand this world.

And yet . . .

There's a common mistake many of us make, thinking that intelligence eradi-cates ignorance. Henry Ford introduced the Model T to the world and mass pro-duction of the automobile. He also helped spread the gospel of a truly evil text: *The Protocols of the Elders of Zion*. Hell, Henry Ford actually gets a name check in *Mein Kampf*! Hitler calls himself a "great admirer" of Ford.

Brilliance never saved anyone from bigotry.

4

I FELL IN love with H. P. Lovecraft when I was ten. In 1982 Del Rey published his stories in a series of paperbacks with these beautiful, lurid painted covers. In one, a monk has pulled open his black robes to reveal his body is . . . a skeleton! Maybe this sounds cheesy now, but I fell hard for it when I was kid. (I still do, honestly.)

I snapped up those paperbacks for the covers more than the author. Maybe I'd heard the name Lovecraft here or there, Stephen King name checking him in *Danse Macabre* perhaps. But he didn't mean anything more to me than that. "The Strange High House in the Mist," collected in this volume, is the first story I remember making me reel. I didn't even make it through the first paragraph before I felt my wig blown back. It took only three sentences:

> In the morning mist comes up from the sea by the cliffs beyond Kingsport. White and feathery it comes from the deep to its brothers the clouds, full of dreams and dank pastures and caves of leviathan. And later, in still summer rains on the steep roofs of poets, the clouds scatter bits of those dreams, that men shall not live without rumour of old, strange secrets, and wonders that planets tell planets alone in the night.

That last bit—"secrets, and wonders that planets tell planets alone in the night"—gave me the serious shivers. It's something similar, in mood, to the famous opening paragraph of Shirley Jackson's *Haunting of Hill House*. That's how it read to me. Lovecraft is dinged for being a bit purple with his prose, but what emotional register would *you* use when discussing the secrets planets share?

Ten-year-old me was here for all of it: the high anxiety, waves of madness, and the terror of human insignificance. Certain writers must be encountered at a young age or else their spell will never be cast properly. Some people would say this is because an older reader has matured out of the appeal such pulp provides, but I call bullshit on that. Instead, I would say that as a child the aperture of your imagination is wide open. In adulthood we call its closure "maturity," but that hardly seems like a triumph to me. Instead, I still try to embrace the bravery of such openness, though I admit it does get more difficult. But back then nothing imaginative was alien to me.

All this is to say I felt smitten with Howard Phillips Lovecraft and his work.

I'm hardly the only one.

He didn't become a foundational author of the modern horror canon by accident. And my love remained pure until age fifteen or so. Something strange happened when I reread him at that stage. There were aspects of his writing that I simply hadn't noticed before, but as a (slightly) more mature reader I couldn't ignore them anymore.

I realized that H. P. Lovecraft had been a racist.

A perfect example can be found in this volume: "The Rats in the Walls." The narrative could be summed like this: No one should look too deeply into his family past, terrible truths are hiding there; a not uncommon theme in the Lovecraft oeuvre. At ten years old, I'd enjoyed this story just fine, but this time I wasn't a child. And at fifteen I actually registered the name of the narrator's cat: Nigger-Man.

What?

What. The. Fuck?

I remember, distinctly, closing the book and looking at the old Del Rey cover, wondering if somehow my old copy had been switched out. That couldn't have always been the name of the cat. I couldn't possibly have overlooked it. Especially since the name comes up, by my count, nineteen damn times!

By the end of the tale I felt pummeled. I hardly noticed the plot or the language or the mood of the tale. This time the only horror in the story was that cat. And now, when I read *At the Mountains of Madness*, I couldn't help noticing that the shoggoths, the race of genetically engineered slaves, were not who the narrator empathized with. Instead, he seemed to sympathize with the Elder Gods, whose chattel, at some point long ago, had risen up and resisted their enslavement. My sense of betrayal felt as deep as the catacombs beneath the home in "The Rats in the Walls."

Soon after I came across a piece of Lovecraft juvenilia, an early poem. It's called "On the Creation of Niggers."

Yeah.

So at fifteen I stopped reading H. P. Lovecraft.

If you've ever loved an author, felt the effect of his or her imagination right down in your DNA, you'll know what it means to reject a beloved writer entirely. You'll understand the heartache I felt as I threw away those Del Rey paperbacks.

5

OBVIOUSLY, I RETURNED to reading the man again. But the journey to get here took me decades. I remained disdainful of Lovecraft even as I devoured the work of his acolytes: Fritz Leiber, Robert Bloch, and Ramsey Campbell, to name three of my favorites. Much of the old master's influence was visible in their fiction, but not all of it. Not the worst of it.

Soon I read the writers inspired by those three giants. And on and on, until eventually I became one of them, too, a writer within this tradition. Even if I hadn't read Lovecraft's fiction in decades its imprint was impossible to miss. In a way I embodied one of Lovecraft's oldest tropes: a man with a tainted lineage, a flaw at the root of the family tree. But when faced with the truth of Lovecraft's flaw, I deviated from the old storyline. I wasn't driven mad by the knowledge, not anymore.

Still get angry about it though.

This brings me back to the Hastings Center, the lecture on CRISPR technology. CRISPR has been touted, rightly, as one of the most significant breakthroughs in scientific history. The ability to edit life-threatening conditions out of our genomes can't be overstated as a triumph of human intelligence. I imagine Lovecraft would be awed by such innovation.

And yet this technology will undoubtedly give rise to "designer babies." Children with bespoke genomes, selected off a checklist by their parents before the kids are born. Which attributes will be prized, and which will be erased? And how many human flaws have turned out to be a godsend? I'm thinking now of genres as a living organism—one that continues to live and grow and change for as long as there are writers practicing it, keeping it vital.

One way to deal with a writer like Lovecraft is to, effectively, CRISPR him out of the canon. Cut him from the Cosmic Horror corpus. Aside from the impossibility of the idea, let's consider what we would lose: "From Beyond," "The Outsider," "The Music of Erich Zann," "Pickman's Model," and *The Dream-Quest of Unknown Kadath*. And that's just to name a handful of the tales in this volume. That doesn't even touch on the Mythos stories. So, okay, let's admit he can't be deactivated.

But don't get it twisted, I'm not saying the fiction is so worthwhile that we just have to shrug our shoulders and live with the rest. It's easy to tell people to "get over it" when you're not the one being wounded. So if we can't CRISPR him, if we reject a designer literary tradition, then what is the alternative?

Include Lovecraft's tales, and a healthy critique of them, too.

Lovecraft will never be canceled, but the folks who dismiss, or try to drown out, any criticism of the man and his work are as preposterous as climate change deniers. Both are telling you to disbelieve your lying eyes.

But I'm here to assure you that no such choice is necessary. You can love something, love someone, *and* criticize them. That's called maturity. *The New Annotated H. P. Lovecraft: Beyond Arkham* holds to the high standard set by the previous volume, and Leslie Klinger's context is half informative, half wildly fun. This should come as no surprise to anyone who knows Klinger's work.

Lovecraft's stories will last for as long as we are drawn to them. Who *we* are is such a diverse cast of readers that Howard himself would probably never believe it possible. Let this be the highest compliment one can pay to a writer, and to the work: that its appeal and influence far outstrip the artist's wildest expectations.

Foreword

by Leslie S. Klinger

More than eighty years after his death at the age of forty-seven, Howard Phillips Lovecraft continues to exert a hold on American popular and literary culture. A semiannual convention, NecronomiCon, held in his beloved Providence, Rhode Island, celebrates Lovecraft's enduring legacy and the weird fiction he championed. More and more of the thousands of letters he wrote to a wide range of family and friends have been published, and a massive variorum edition of his fiction, edited by S. T. Joshi, appeared in 2016, allowing scholars to read the versions that Lovecraft himself favored. Books inspired by his writing—and in the case of Paul La Farge's 2017 novel *The Night Ocean*, his life—populate best-seller lists. Providence has mounted a plaque honoring its native son, and plans to erect a statue of HPL have been launched.

Yet Lovecraft's legacy is as complex as ever: In 2016, the World Fantasy Awards dropped the use of his likeness because his racist views and perorations were offensive to many awardees. Lovecraft's racial attitudes are on full display in many of the stories included here, including "The Terrible Old Man" and "The Horror at

H. P. Lovecraft Memorial Square,
at the intersection of Angell and
Prospect Streets, Providence, 2015.
Photograph courtesy of Donovan K. Loucks

Red Hook," both of which characterize early twentieth-century immigrant populations unfavorably. A cat owned by the narrator of "The Rats in the Walls" has a racially offensive name, and "Facts concerning the Late Arthur Jermyn and His Family" treats racial intermixing, about which Lovecraft expressed revulsion. It is important to acknowledge Lovecraft's racism, not only because it reflects all too common views of the era in which he was writing but also because the power of certain of his stories is derived, in part, from his deep-seated fear of miscegenation.

Just as significantly, his worldview was shaped by his remove from the world. A tale such as "The Outsider," probably the most psychologically compelling of all of his work, or "The Music of Erich Zahn," an achingly beautiful story about people isolated from society, may be seen as reflecting Lovecraft's own personal sense of isolation. A student of the life of Lovecraft, however, will quickly learn that the man was much more nuanced than the prevailing view of him might suggest. He is dismissed by some as a recluse and a misanthrope—uneasy with American modernity and with the country's progression toward a more diverse and scientifically advanced state. As to his reclusiveness, while he never traveled to the western United States or left North America, he made frequent visits to friends and distant towns on the East Coast and in the South, as well as a trip to Quebec, and his network of correspondents was vast.

Nor was Lovecraft wholly misanthropic: He clearly cherished a large circle of friends, among them a few Jews, although he was known to excoriate "the Jewish race." Briefly married to Sonia Greene, a Jewish tradeswoman, and close friends with the poet and critic Samuel Loveman, also a Jew, Lovecraft was capable of maintaining relationships with Jews who had *assimilated* into society and did not assert their religious differences. Yet some of his political and philosophical ideas, such as supporting eugenics and rejecting the intermixing of ethnic groups, sounded like those of the Nazi Party, and Lovecraft's letters clearly reveal a narrow point of view and little tolerance for people of color or unassimilated ethnicity. Stories such as "The Horror at Red Hook" and "He" reek of Lovecraft's abhorrence of New York, where he was surrounded by masses of such people.

As may be expected, Lovecraft's positions changed over time, and these changes are reflected in his fiction. While he was never going to be comfortable in a multicultural city like New York—his two-year exile there ended in a triumphant shout of "I AM PROVIDENCE!"—he ultimately seemed to have recognized that homogeneous populations could breed weakness as well as strength. This is evident from his later fiction, such as *At the Mountains of Madness,* in which the demise of the Old Ones may be seen as a sign of the weakness of the slave system their culture instituted.

Lovecraft's reactions to advances in science seem to have altered over time as well. Initially, he feared the chaos and the horrors inherent in the newly discovered verities of astronomy and physics, and a story such as "From Beyond" may be seen as a warning of the risks of scientific advancement. But he eventually saw the power of the new theories expressed by Einstein and others, and "The Dunwich Horror" and *At the Mountains of Madness*, for instance, imply a confidence in scientists, if not the views of the scientific establishment.

Lovecraft was born in 1890 in Providence, the only child of Winfield Scott and Sarah Susan Phillips Lovecraft. His father was committed to a local asylum in 1893—probably due to dementia caused by syphilis—and Lovecraft was raised by his mother, aunts, and grandfather in shabby gentility. Though he attended public schools, HPL was a precocious child, studying classics at an early age and fascinated by science. The earliest known examples of his fiction are from the age of seven; he wrote his first *salable* fiction when he was fifteen, although it was not published until 1918. In 1906, he began writing an astronomy column for the local newspaper, and his first published verse appeared in another newspaper in 1912. Yet he never achieved any financial success as a writer. His early stories, published before 1923, appeared in amateur journals, and it was not until 1923 that he began selling pieces to *Weird Tales*, a pulp magazine that paid little but whose audience was exactly suited to Lovecraft's themes. He became the magazine's biggest star, and in 1924, he was offered its editorship.

Lovecraft's father had died in 1898; in 1919, his mother was institutionalized in the same asylum that had housed his father. After Sarah's death, in 1921, Lovecraft's horizons broadened. He met his future wife, Sonia Greene, at an amateur press convention in Boston, moved with her to New York after they married in 1924. The experience was immediately disastrous—Lovecraft was a "fish out of water" in New York, unable to find work and completely uncomfortable with his environs. These views are expressed in the story "He," below. With HPL's career foundering, Sonia moved to Cincinnati a year later for business, and they never lived together again as husband and wife. By 1926, Lovecraft moved back to Providence, sharing a home with his aunt. When she died in 1932, he moved in with another aunt, with whom he lived until he died of cancer, in 1937.

Over thirty years, Lovecraft produced scores of stories, including three novellas, dozens of poems, and thousands of letters. Yet at his death his writing was virtually unknown outside the circle of his friends and readers of *Weird Tales*. One or two tales had been published in mainstream anthologies, and one of his stories was published in a limited-edition pamphlet. No collection of his work appeared until 1939, when his friends the prolific writer August Derleth and the editor and science fiction writer Donald Wandrei formed Arkham House and published *The Outsider and Others*. Yet Lovecraft's writing was far richer—and weirder—than the tropes of hollow-eyed monsters, anguished strongmen, nude women in serpentine bondage, and cloaked alien beings that populated the covers of *Weird Tales* and with which he has become associated. As Arkham House began to publish more and more of HPL's work in book form in the 1940s and 1950s, critics began to take notice of his writing and the genre of weird fiction, and by the 1990s, appreciation of his work had spread far beyond the little band of his devotees. Perhaps the zenith of his reputation was marked in 2005, with publication of a Library of America edition of his collected fiction, edited by the best-selling horror writer Peter Straub.

The decision on the part of W. W. Norton to include a volume of Lovecraft's fiction in its celebrated series of annotated classics was another high-water mark. *The New Annotated H. P. Lovecraft*, published in 2014 and embraced widely both by the Lovecraft community and by a general readership, included twenty-two stories that focused on the fictional town of Arkham, Massachusetts, the river valley of the Miskatonic, and the activities of Miskatonic University. The stories included in that volume also fit neatly into Lovecraft's so-called Cthulhu Mythos, the invention of the circle of friends and admirers who surrounded him and that was perpetuated in "Lovecraftian" tales by imitators.

But there are many other Lovecraft stories worthy of attention, including HPL's personal favorites. During his abbreviated career, Lovecraft penned seventy-one tales, some only fragments, listed in Appendix 2.[1] He also contributed to a number of "revisions," collaborations with other authors.[2] This volume collects another twenty-five of Lovecraft's stories, omitted from the first volume only because they make no mention of Arkham or the Miskatonic River (or its university). Some are early versions of ideas that he would develop in more detail as he matured. Others reflect his search for his own style of writing. Several reflect experiments of recording, to the best of his recollection, vivid dreams.

The stories in this volume were the products of the first half of Lovecraft's career. The first, "The Tomb," written in 1917, may be said to be his first mature tale, written when he was twenty-seven; the last, *The Dream-Quest of Unknown Kadath*, written in 1926–27, was never published during his lifetime and represents his last serious effort at fantasy. After *Dream-Quest*, Lovecraft's writing became more focused on what would later be seen as early science fiction, exploring his ideas of "cosmic horror." Over the ten-year span covered by this book, we see Lovecraft experimenting with and mastering his craft. He wrote "Dunsanian" or

---

1. Appendix 2 is arranged chronologically. An alphabetical list of Lovecraft's fiction is Appendix 5 of this editor's previous volume, *The New Annotated H. P. Lovecraft* (New York: Liveright, 2014).

2. See Appendix 6 of the previous volume for a complete list.

"dreamland" tales such as "Polaris" and "Celephaïs," which bear a strong—and, as it happens, entirely coincidental—resemblance to the fantasy stories of Lord Dunsany, whose work he discovered after he had produced his own efforts. He also wrote tales such as "The Temple" and "Cool Air," in which he deliberately copied the style of Edgar Allan Poe, whose work he greatly admired. HPL's output included pseudo-scientific stories including "From Beyond"—now viewed as early science fiction—and tales of pure whimsy such as "The Cats of Ulthar" and "The Other Gods." This was an evolving artist, broadening his palette.

There are works of genius here. August Derleth thought "The Outsider" to be Lovecraft's finest creation, and many critics agree that the psychological complexity and depth of its almost entirely mute narrator (not the only unspeaking Lovecraft character) make it one of HPL's greatest achievements. "The Music of Erich Zann" was one of Lovecraft's two favorites, along with "The Colour Out of Space" (found in the previous volume). "The Horror at Red Hook," despite its nasty racial overtones, and "Pickman's Model," evocatively set in bohemian Boston, with their focus on ghouls and other denizens of an unknown and unknowable underground, have inspired legions of fans of dark fantasy. "The Rats in the Walls" is regarded by some as Lovecraft's finest work of pure horror, following in the footsteps of two of the writer's favorites, M. R. James and Arthur Machen.

A more detailed review of Lovecraft's life, literary career, and critical reception can be found in the foreword to the previous volume of *The New Annotated H. P. Lovecraft*. The stories in these two volumes provide the reader with a virtually complete picture of Lovecraft's achievements in fiction. I hope that together, these two volumes will help the reader to understand, in the words of Joyce Carol Oates, Lovecraft's "incalculable influence on succeeding generations of writers of horror fiction."[3]

3. Joyce Carol Oates, "The King of Weird," *New York Review of Books*, October 31, 1996.

Editor's Note

The first volume of *The New Annotated H. P. Lovecraft* was based on a "definitive" text prepared by S. T. Joshi and published in the 2001 Barnes & Noble edition of Lovecraft's *Complete Fiction*. Subsequently, Joshi has edited a "variorum" edition, showing in great detail every variant to the "definitive" text in numerous sources. This variorum edition compares Lovecraft's autograph manuscripts, typescripts, the first published appearances, reprints in *Weird Tales*, and in some cases Lovecraft's own revisions of the stories in preparation for reprinting. Sadly, because none were collected in book form during HPL's lifetime, he did not create his *own* definitive text, but the text in this volume (except where noted) reflects a best guess as to his intentions. Many thanks are due to Mr. Joshi, not only for sharing the text in electronic form but also for continued correspondence about many small textual issues in presenting these stories.

As additional aids to the reader, this volume includes an outline of Lovecraft's life, a chronological table presenting his fiction in the order it was written, and a unique gazetteer, listing each geographical place-name referenced in his fiction (including, of course, many invented places). Although new Lovecraftian comic books and films have appeared since 2014, the appendices in the previous volume of *The New Annotated H. P. Lovecraft* covering those subjects have not been updated. However, a supplemental bibliography is appended here.

The stories in this collection, over ninety years old, reflect a long-departed era. Furthermore, Lovecraft deliberately employed an antiquarian, even archaic style of writing. Accordingly, as in the previous volume, I have provided notes in three categories: glossary, historical and cultural background, and inconsistencies in the story narrative. While some of the stories included here have been annotated previously by the inestimable Mr. Joshi, I have gone to sources that span the breadth of the Lovecraft community to consider different points of view. However, the reader will not find the kind of scholarship that more academic Lovecraft scholars such as Donald R. Burleson, Dirk W. Mosig, Robert H. Waugh, and Gavin Callaghan have undertaken. I have resisted the urge to apply psychoanalytic or deconstructive techniques to Lovecraft's work, preferring to approach the tales as thrilling entertainment.

My aim is, as always, to enhance the reader's experience of the author's labors. I have posed questions regarding the narratives, where the meaning is obscure, and, where I can, provided explanations designed to make the author's intentions more understandable. H. P. Lovecraft does not need my help to succeed in terrifying the reader, but if I am able to bring new visitors into his chamber of cosmic horrors, I am delighted.

THE
STORIES

The Tomb[1]

"The Tomb" is the first story written by HPL as an adult. Some view it as the earliest of his "mind-transference" tales (later examples include "Beyond the Wall of Sleep," The Case of Charles Dexter Ward, *and "The Thing on the Doorstep"); others argue that we are meant to believe only that it is a depiction of insanity. Betraying Lovecraft's fascination with the England of a bygone era, the story builds powerfully to an intriguingly ambiguous conclusion.*

Sedibus ut saltem placidis in morte quiescam.

—VIRGIL[2]

In relating the circumstances which have led to my confinement within this refuge for the demented, I am aware that my present position will create a natural doubt of the authenticity of my narrative. It is an unfortunate fact that the bulk of humanity is too limited in its mental vision to weigh with patience and intelligence those isolated phenomena, seen and felt only by a psychologically sensitive few, which lie outside its common experience. Men of broader intellect know that there is no sharp distinction betwixt the real and the unreal; that all things appear as they do only by virtue of the delicate individual physical and mental media through which we are made conscious of them; but the prosaic materialism of the majority condemns as madness the flashes of super-sight which penetrate the common veil of obvious empiricism.

My name is Jervas Dudley, and from earliest childhood I have been a dreamer and a visionary. Wealthy beyond the necessity of a commercial life, and temperamentally unfitted for the formal studies and social recreations of my acquaintances, I have dwelt ever in realms apart from the visible world; spending my youth and adolescence in ancient and little-known books, and in roam-

1. Written in June 1917, and HPL's first story since 1908, it was published in *The Vagrant* 14 (March 1922), 50–64. It subsequently appeared in *Weird Tales* 7 (January 1926), 117–23.2.

2. "At any rate in death I may rest in peaceful abodes." *Virgil's Aeneid,* Book VI, line 371, trans. Frederick Holland Dewey (New York: Translation Publishing Company, 1917), 281. Dewey, however, rearranges the Latin to read *"ut saltem in morte quiescam placidis sedibus,"* a literal arrangement of the words in the order of the English translation ("*sedibus*" means "abodes"), while in the more traditional 1863 edition published by John Conington (London: Whittaker and Co.), the Latin appears in the form quoted by HPL.

Palinurus, Aeneas's helmsman, fell overboard on a voyage, his body never recovered. Meeting Aeneas on the occasion of his master's visit to the underworld, he begs him to bury him so that he might cross the Styx and find peace.

3. A nymph or fairy that inhabits a tree, usually an oak tree.

4. That is, in the mid-nineteenth century, if we take this story to be a narrative contemporary with its publication.

5. Either placed in urns (said of ashes) or buried.

The Dryad, by Evelyn De Morgan (1884–85).

ing the fields and groves of the region near my ancestral home. I do not think that what I read in these books or saw in these fields and groves was exactly what other boys read and saw there; but of this I must say little, since detailed speech would but confirm those cruel slanders upon my intellect which I sometimes overhear from the whispers of the stealthy attendants around me. It is sufficient for me to relate events without analysing causes.

I have said that I dwelt apart from the visible world, but I have not said that I dwelt alone. This no human creature may do; for lacking the fellowship of the living, he inevitably draws upon the companionship of things that are not, or are no longer, living. Close by my home there lies a singular wooded hollow, in whose twilight deeps I spent most of my time; reading, thinking, and dreaming. Down its moss-covered slopes my first steps of infancy were taken, and around its grotesquely gnarled oak trees my first fancies of boyhood were woven. Well did I come to know the presiding dryads[3] of those trees, and often have I watched their wild dances in the struggling beams of a waning moon— but of these things I must not now speak. I will tell only of the lone tomb in the darkest of the hillside thickets; the deserted tomb of the Hydes, an old and exalted family whose last direct descendant had been laid within its black recesses many decades before my birth.

The vault to which I refer is of ancient granite, weathered and discoloured by the mists and dampness of generations. Excavated back into the hillside, the structure is visible only at the entrance. The door, a ponderous and forbidding slab of stone, hangs upon rusted iron hinges, and is fastened *ajar* in a queerly sinister way by means of heavy iron chains and padlocks, according to a gruesome fashion of half a century ago.[4] The abode of the race whose scions are here inurned[5] had once crowned the declivity which holds the tomb, but had long since fallen victim to the flames which sprang up from a stroke of lightning. Of the midnight storm which destroyed this gloomy mansion, the older inhabitants of the region sometimes speak in hushed and uneasy voices; alluding to what they call "divine wrath" in a manner that in later years vaguely increased the always strong fascination which I had felt for the forest-darkened sepulchre. One man only had perished in the fire. When

the last of the Hydes was buried in this place of shade and stillness, the sad urnful of ashes had come from a distant land; to
which the family had repaired when the mansion burned down.
No one remains to lay flowers before the granite portal, and
few care to brave the depressing shadows which seem to linger
strangely about the water-worn stones.

I shall never forget the afternoon when first I stumbled upon
the half-hidden house of death. It was in mid-summer, when
the alchemy of Nature transmutes the sylvan landscape to one
vivid and almost homogeneous mass of green; when the senses
are well-nigh intoxicated with the surging seas of moist verdure
and the subtly indefinable odours of the soil and the vegetation. In such surroundings the mind loses its perspective; time
and space become trivial and unreal, and echoes of a forgotten
prehistoric past beat insistently upon the enthralled consciousness. All day I had been wandering through the mystic groves
of the hollow; thinking thoughts I need not discuss, and con-
versing with things I need not name. In years a child of ten, I
had seen and heard many wonders unknown to the throng; and
was oddly aged in certain respects. When, upon forcing my way
between two savage clumps of briers, I suddenly encountered
the entrance of the vault, I had no knowledge of what I had
discovered. The dark blocks of granite, the door so curiously
ajar, and the funereal carvings above the arch, aroused in me
no associations of mournful or terrible character. Of graves and
tombs I knew and imagined much, but had on account of my
peculiar temperament been kept from all personal contact with
churchyards and cemeteries. The strange stone house on the
woodland slope was to me only a source of interest and speculation; and its cold, damp interior, into which I vainly peered
through the aperture so tantalisingly left, contained for me no
hint of death or decay. But in that instant of curiosity was born
the madly unreasoning desire which has brought me to this hell
of confinement. Spurred on by a voice which must have come
from the hideous soul of the forest, I resolved to enter the beckoning gloom in spite of the ponderous chains which barred my
passage. In the waning light of day I alternately rattled the rusty
impediments with a view to throwing wide the stone door, and
essayed to squeeze my slight form through the space already pro-

6. Plutarch's *Lives of the Noble Greeks and Romans*, also known as *Parallel Lives* or *Plutarch's Lives*, written over a period of two decades and probably completed around 100 CE. It was translated from the original Greek into Latin in 1470 and issued in Rome by the printer Ulrich Han, of Ingolstadt and Vienna. Jacques Amyot's 1559 translation into French became the basis for the first English translation, by Sir Thomas North (1579), long recognized as important source material for William Shakespeare (particularly *Coriolanus* but also *Julius Caesar* and other plays—see Lance Morrow, "Plutarch's Exemplary Lives," *Smithsonian*, July 2004). Early translations into Italian include those by Donato Acciaioli (1478) and Lodovico Domenichi (1560), the latter known for producing accessible renderings into the vernacular; Domenichi's range was vast: from Pliny to books of jokes—see George W. McClure, *The Culture of Profession in Late Renaissance Italy* (Toronto: University of Toronto Press, 2004). Later translations of *Parallel Lives* into English include one signed by the poet John Dryden in 1683 (and later revised by Arthur Hugh Clough): Bernadotte Perrin, translator of Harvard's Loeb Classical Library edition, noted in his introduction that Dryden in fact wrote only the preface and the life of Plutarch, the rest having been furnished by an uncredited team of translators (Plutarch, *Lives* [Bury St. Edmunds, Suffolk, UK: St. Edmundsbury Press, 1914]), xviii. Perrin also provides a useful summary of the seminal translations through the ages, and enumerates their various features and failings.

7. Plutarch writes,

> Aegeus afterwards, knowing her whom he had lain with to be Pittheus's daughter, and suspecting her to be with child by him, left a sword

vided; but neither plan met with success. At first curious, I was now frantic; and when in the thickening twilight I returned to my home, I had sworn to the hundred gods of the grove that *at any cost* I would some day force an entrance to the black, chilly depths that seemed calling out to me. The physician with the iron-grey beard who comes each day to my room once told a visitor that this decision marked the beginning of a pitiful monomania; but I will leave final judgment to my readers when they shall have learnt all.

The months following my discovery were spent in futile attempts to force the complicated padlock of the slightly open vault, and in carefully guarded inquiries regarding the nature and history of the structure. With the traditionally receptive ears of the small boy, I learned much; though an habitual secretiveness caused me to tell no one of my information or my resolve. It is perhaps worth mentioning that I was not at all surprised or terrified on learning of the nature of the vault. My rather original ideas regarding life and death had caused me to associate the cold clay with the breathing body in a vague fashion; and I felt that the great and sinister family of the burned-down mansion was in some way represented within the stone space I sought to explore. Mumbled tales of the weird rites and godless revels of bygone years in the ancient hall gave to me a new and potent interest in the tomb, before whose door I would sit for hours at a time each day. Once I thrust a candle within the nearly closed entrance, but could see nothing save a flight of damp stone steps leading downward. The odour of the place repelled yet bewitched me. I felt I had known it before, in a past remote beyond all recollection; beyond even my tenancy of the body I now possess.

The year after I first beheld the tomb, I stumbled upon a worm-eaten translation of Plutarch's *Lives*[6] in the book-filled attic of my home. Reading the life of Theseus, I was much impressed by that passage telling of the great stone beneath which the boyish hero was to find his tokens of destiny whenever he should become old enough to lift its enormous weight.[7] This legend had the effect of dispelling my keenest impatience to enter the vault, for it made me feel that the time was not yet ripe. Later, I told myself, I should grow to a strength and ingenuity which might enable me to unfasten the heavily chained door with ease; but until then I would do better by conforming to what seemed the will of Fate.

Accordingly my watches by the dank portal became less persistent, and much of my time was spent in other though equally strange pursuits. I would sometimes rise very quietly in the night, stealing out to walk in those churchyards and places of burial from which I had been kept by my parents. What I did there I may not say, for I am not now sure of the reality of certain things; but I know that on the day after such a nocturnal ramble I would often astonish those about me with my knowledge of topics almost forgotten for many generations. It was after a night like this that I shocked the community with a queer conceit about the burial of the rich and celebrated Squire Brewster, a maker of local history who was interred in 1711, and whose slate head-stone, bearing a graven skull and crossbones,[8] was slowly crumbling to powder. In a moment of childish imagination I vowed not only that the undertaker, Goodman[9] Simpson, had stolen the silver-buckled shoes, silken hose, and satin small-clothes of the deceased before burial; but that the Squire himself, not fully inanimate, had turned twice in his mound-covered coffin on the day after interment.

But the idea of entering the tomb never left my thoughts; being indeed stimulated by the unexpected genealogical discovery that my own maternal ancestry possessed at least a slight link with the supposedly extinct family of the Hydes. Last of my paternal race, I was likewise the last of this older and more mysterious line. I began to feel that the tomb was *mine,* and to look forward with hot eagerness to the time when I might pass within that stone door and down those slimy stone steps in the dark. I now formed the habit of *listening* very intently at the slightly open portal, choosing my favourite hours of midnight stillness for the odd vigil. By the time I came of age, I had made a small clearing in the thicket before the mould-stained facade of the hillside, allowing the surrounding vegetation to encircle and overhang the space like the walls and roof of a sylvan bower. This bower was my temple, the fastened door my shrine, and here I would lie outstretched on the mossy ground, thinking strange thoughts and dreaming strange dreams.

and a pair of shoes, hiding them under a great stone that had a hollow in it exactly fitting them; and went away making her only privy to it, and commanding her, if she brought forth a son who, when he came to man's estate, should be able to lift up the stone and take away what he had left there, she should send him way to him with those things with all secrecy, and with injunctions to him as much as possible to conceal his journey from every one. . . . Theseus displaying not only great strength of body, but equal bravery, and a quickness alike and force of understanding, his mother Aethra conducting him to the stone, and informing him who was his true father, commanded him to take from thence the tokens that Aegeus had left, and sail to Athens. He without any difficulty set himself to the stone and lifted it up. (*Plutarch's Lives,* The Translation Called Dryden's, Corrected from the Greek and Revised by A. H. Clough, vol. 1 [Boston: Little, Brown, 1906], 3–5)

8. Lovecraft drew inspiration for this description—and for the 1917 genesis of "The Tomb"—from a visit in June of that year with his aunt Lillian D. Clark to the grave of a distant relative, Simon Smith. Smith died on March 4, 1711, and was buried in Warwick, Rhode Island. His body was subsequently disinterred and transferred to Swan Point Cemetery, in Providence, where Lovecraft and Clark saw this tombstone iconography, probably from a replacement of the 1711 stone (Letter to the Gallomo [Alfred Galpin and Maurice W. Moe], January 1920, quoted in H. P. Lovecraft, *Lord of a Visible World: An Autobiography in Letters,* ed. S. T. Joshi and David E. Schultz [Athens: Ohio University Press, 2000], 67; see also H. P. Lovecraft, *The Thing on the Doorstep and Other Weird Stories,*

ed. with an introduction and notes by S. T. Joshi [New York: Penguin, 2001], 368). However, Lovecraft leaves the geographical setting for the tale ambiguous, and the Hyde family holdings could be anywhere in New England.

9. E. Cobham Brewer's *Dictionary of Phrase and Fable* (Philadelphia: Henry Altemus, 1898) defines "goodman": "A husband or master is the Saxon *guma* or *goma* (a man), which in the inflected cases becomes guman or goman. In *St. Matt.* xxiv. 43, 'If the goodman of the house had known in what watch the thief would come, he would have watched.' Gomman and gommer, for the master and mistress of a house, are by no means uncommon." The courtesy title was commonplace in New England in pre-Revolutionary days.

10. In the winter of 1636, Roger Williams was banished from the Massachusetts Bay Colony and acquired the land from the Indians that he named Providence Plantation (eventually becoming Providence, Rhode Island). By 1640, the colony was well established, but what attracted Sir Geoffrey to leave England to come to America will never be known.

The night of the first revelation was a sultry one. I must have fallen asleep from fatigue, for it was with a distinct sense of awakening that I heard the *voices*. Of those tones and accents I hesitate to speak; of their *quality* I will not speak; but I may say that they presented certain uncanny differences in vocabulary, pronunciation, and mode of utterance. Every shade of New England dialect, from the uncouth syllables of the Puritan colonists to the precise rhetoric of fifty years ago, seemed represented in that shadowy colloquy, though it was only later that I noticed the fact. At the time, indeed, my attention was distracted from this matter by another phenomenon; a phenomenon so fleeting that I could not take oath upon its reality. I barely fancied that as I awoke, a *light* had been hurriedly extinguished within the sunken sepulchre. I do not think I was either astounded or panic-stricken, but I know that I was greatly and permanently *changed* that night. Upon returning home I went with much directness to a rotting chest in the attic, wherein I found the key which next day unlocked with ease the barrier I had so long stormed in vain.

It was in the soft glow of late afternoon that I first entered the vault on the abandoned slope. A spell was upon me, and my heart leaped with an exultation I can but ill describe. As I closed the door behind me and descended the dripping steps by the light of my lone candle, I seemed to know the way; and though the candle sputtered with the stifling reek of the place, I felt singularly at home in the musty, charnel-house air. Looking about me, I beheld many marble slabs bearing coffins, or the remains of coffins. Some of these were sealed and intact, but others had nearly vanished, leaving the silver handles and plates isolated amidst certain curious heaps of whitish dust. Upon one plate I read the name of Sir Geoffrey Hyde, who had come from Sussex in 1640[10] and died here a few years later. In a conspicuous alcove was one fairly well-preserved and untenanted casket, adorned with a single name which brought to me both a smile and a shudder. An odd impulse caused me to climb upon the broad slab, extinguish my candle, and lie down within the vacant box.

In the grey light of dawn I staggered from the vault and locked the chain of the door behind me. I was no longer a young man, though but twenty-one winters had chilled my bodily frame. Early-rising villagers who observed my homeward progress looked at me strangely, and marvelled at the signs of ribald revelry which they saw in one whose life was known to be sober and solitary. I did not appear before my parents till after a long and refreshing sleep.

Henceforward I haunted the tomb each night; seeing, hearing, and doing things I must never recall. My speech, always susceptible to environmental influences, was the first thing to succumb to the change; and my suddenly acquired archaism of diction was soon remarked upon. Later a queer boldness and recklessness came into my demeanour, till I unconsciously grew to possess the bearing of a man of the world despite my lifelong seclusion. My formerly silent tongue waxed voluble with the easy grace of a Chesterfield[11] or the godless cynicism of a Rochester.[12] I displayed a peculiar erudition utterly unlike the fantastic, monkish lore over which I had pored in youth; and covered the flyleaves of my books with facile impromptu epigrams which brought up suggestions of Gay,[13] Prior,[14] and the sprightliest of the Augustan wits and rhymesters.[15] One morning at breakfast I came close to disaster by declaiming in palpably liquorish accents an effusion of eighteenth-century Bacchanalian mirth; a bit of Georgian playfulness never recorded in a book, which ran something like this:

Come hither, my lads, with your tankards of ale,
And drink to the present before it shall fail;
Pile each on your platter a mountain of beef,
For 'tis eating and drinking that bring us relief:
   So fill up your glass,
   For life will soon pass;
When you're dead ye'll ne'er drink to your king or your lass!

Anacreon[16] had a red nose, so they say;
But what's a red nose if ye're happy and gay?
Gad split me! I'd rather be red whilst I'm here
Than white as a lily—and dead half a year!
   So Betty, my miss,
   Come give me a kiss;
In hell there's no innkeeper's daughter like this!

11. Chesterfield, properly Philip Dormer Stanhope, fourth earl of Chesterfield (1694–1773), wrote but did not condone (or live to see) publication of *Letters to His Son on the Art of Becoming a Man of the World and a Gentleman* (1774). The volume, issued due to an inelegance and breach of etiquette in Chesterfield's disposition of his estate, was ironically to become fashionable as an etiquette manual.

The book had its origins in Chesterfield's deep attachment to his illegitimate son, Philip Stanhope, the product of an affair with a governess, Madelina Elizabeth du Bouchet, when Chesterfield was serving as British ambassador to Holland. Chesterfield began writing the teenaged Philip letters of life instruction, penned in several languages (including Latin) expressly for the purpose of giving the boy a smattering of each. The letters, which warned against coarseness, themselves sometimes advocated certain forms of coarseness, but their "easy grace" proved captivating: Meant for Philip's eyes only, they were collected and sold to a publisher by Philip's destitute widow, Eugenia Stanhope, following his sudden death of dropsy (edema) in his late thirties. Chesterfield died five years later, pointedly making no provision in his will for Eugenia but creating annuities for Philip and Eugenia's two boys. Portions of the will, demonstrating that he had shamed himself by providing for his illegitimate grandsons—then considered a truer breach of etiquette than his stinginess to his daughter-in-law—were printed in *The Gentleman's Magazine* around the time of publication of *Letters to His Son on the Art of Becoming a Man of the World and a Gentleman*, ensuring strong sales. The book remained in print for at least a century—both Eugenia's sole means of support in the last decades of her life and the only thing anyone now remembers Chesterfield for.

12. The Earl of Rochester, John Wilmot (1647–1680), celebrated for his bawdy verse.

13. English poet/playwright John Gay (1685–1732) is best remembered for *The Beggar's Opera* (1728), immortalizing Polly Peachum (based on eighteenth-century soprano Faustina Bordoni, whose onstage fights with the character Lucy Lockit lampoon the professional rivalry between Bordoni and fellow soprano Francesca Cuzzoni, which itself had been exploited

John Gay.

the year before the opera's composition by pamphleteers and satirists claiming that the singers resorted to ripping out each other's hair onstage and clawing each other's faces) and Polly's husband, Captain Macheath, in song; the music was arranged by the Berlin-born Johann Christoph Pepusch, a near-contemporary of George Frideric Handel whose precocity led to his leaving home at fourteen to take professional positions at the Prussian court and later in Holland and England, where he obtained a doctorate at the University of Oxford and, in London,

Young Harry, propp'd up just as straight as he's able,
Will soon lose his wig and slip under the table;
But fill up your goblets and pass 'em around—
Better under the table than under the ground!
  So revel and chaff
  As ye thirstily quaff:
Under six feet of dirt 'tis less easy to laugh!

The fiend strike me blue! I'm scarce able to walk,
And damn me if I can stand upright or talk!
Here, landlord, bid Betty to summon a chair;
I'll try home for a while, for my wife is not there!
  So lend me a hand;
  I'm not able to stand,
But I'm gay whilst I linger on top of the land![17]

About this time I conceived my present fear of fire and thunderstorms. Previously indifferent to such things, I had now an unspeakable horror of them; and would retire to the innermost recesses of the house whenever the heavens threatened an electrical display. A favourite haunt of mine during the day was the ruined cellar of the mansion that had burned down, and in fancy I would picture the structure as it had been in its prime. On one occasion I startled a villager by leading him confidently to a shallow sub-cellar, of whose existence I seemed to know in spite of the fact that it had been unseen and forgotten for many generations.[18]

At last came that which I had long feared. My parents, alarmed at the altered manner and appearance of their only son, commenced to exert over my movements a kindly espionage which threatened to result in disaster. I had told no one of my visits to the tomb, having guarded my secret purpose with religious zeal since childhood; but now I was forced to exercise care in threading the mazes of the wooded hollow, that I might throw off a possible pursuer. My key to the vault I kept suspended from a cord about my neck, its presence known only to me. I never carried out of the sepulchre any of the things I came upon whilst within its walls.

One morning as I emerged from the damp tomb and fastened

the chain of the portal with none too steady hand, I beheld in an adjacent thicket the dreaded face of a watcher. Surely the end was near; for my bower was discovered, and the objective of my nocturnal journeys revealed. The man did not accost me, so I hastened home in an effort to overhear what he might report to my careworn father. Were my sojourns beyond the chained door about to be proclaimed to the world? Imagine my delighted astonishment on hearing the spy inform my parent in a cautious whisper *that I had spent the night in the bower outside the tomb;* my sleep-filmed eyes fixed upon the crevice where the padlocked portal stood ajar! By what miracle had the watcher been thus deluded? I was now convinced that a supernatural agency protected me. Made bold by this heaven-sent circumstance, I began to resume perfect openness in going to the vault; confident that no one could witness my entrance. For a week I tasted to the full the joys of that charnel conviviality which I must not describe, when the *thing* happened, and I was borne away to this accursed abode of sorrow and monotony.

I should not have ventured out that night; for the taint of thunder was in the clouds, and a hellish phosphorescence rose from the rank swamp at the bottom of the hollow. The call of the dead, too, was different. Instead of the hillside tomb, it was the charred cellar on the crest of the slope whose presiding daemon beckoned to me with unseen fingers. As I emerged from an intervening grove upon the plain before the ruin, I beheld in the misty moonlight a thing I had always vaguely expected. The mansion, gone for a century, once more reared its stately height to the raptured vision; every window ablaze with the splendour of many candles. Up the long drive rolled the coaches of the Boston gentry, whilst on foot came a numerous assemblage of powdered exquisites from the neighbouring mansions. With this throng I mingled, though I knew I belonged with the hosts rather than with the guests. Inside the hall were music, laughter, and wine on every hand. Several faces I recognised; though I should have known them better had they been shrivelled or eaten away by death and decomposition. Amidst a wild and reckless throng I was the wildest and most abandoned. Gay blasphemy[19] poured in torrents from my lips, and in my shocking sallies I heeded no law of God, Man, or Nature. Suddenly a peal of thunder,

worked with Gay at Lincoln's Inn Fields Theatre. A work of satire, *The Beggar's Opera* references real-life debtors' prison inmate and government consultant Jonathan Wild, who was eventually hanged for robbery; Jack Sheppard, a folk hero, also eventually hanged, who was raised in a workhouse and was known for fencing stolen goods and for being a prison escape artist; and the charismatic Robert Walpole, chancellor of the exchequer and lord of the treasury, who assumed the mantle of prime minister before the title was actually in use in England and was equally a frequent target of charges of corruption and the beneficiary of important titles and lavish gifts, including the house now known simply as 10 Downing Street—today the prime minister's official residence. The opera was reworked by Bertolt Brecht into *The Threepenny Opera* (1928) and also spawned the popular song "Mack the Knife" (comp. Kurt Weill), introduced by Louis Armstrong in 1956.

Kurt Weill.

14. Matthew Prior (1664–1721) was an English diplomat and poet.

15. The English poets of the first half of the eighteenth century, dominated by Alexander Pope; the poets took the name from the (Caesar) Augustan period of Roman literature, which included the work of Ovid, Horace, and Virgil.

16. A Greek lyric poet (ca. 582 BCE–ca. 485 BCE), often referred to as "the singer from Teos," whose compositional range included odes and hymns and whose love not only of drink but of beauty, male and female, was cited by Horace: "Thus soft Anacreon for [the flautist and kitharist] Bathyllus burn'd / And of his love he sadly mourn'd / He to his harp did various griefs rehearse / And wept in an unlabour'd verse." See John Broderick Roche, *The First Twenty-Eight Odes of Anacreon: In Greek and in English; in Both Languages, in Prose as Well as in Verse, with Variorum Notes, a Grammatical Analysis, and a Lexicon* (London: Sherwood, Gilbert, and Piper, 1827), 66–69; and William Armstrong Percy III, *Pederasty and Pedagogy in Ancient Greece* (Urbana and Chicago: University of Illi-

Anacreon, ca. 475 BCE.

Shutterstock.com

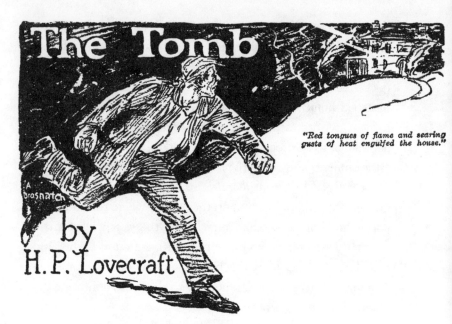

"Red tongues of flame and searing gusts of heat engulfed the house."
Weird Tales (January 1926) (artist: Andrew Brosnatch)

resonant even above the din of the swinish revelry, clave the very roof and laid a hush of fear upon the boisterous company. Red tongues of flame and searing gusts of heat engulfed the house; and the roysterers, struck with terror at the descent of a calamity which seemed to transcend the bounds of unguided Nature, fled shrieking into the night. I alone remained, riveted to my seat by a grovelling fear which I had never felt before. And then a second horror took possession of my soul. Burnt alive to ashes, my body dispersed by the four winds, *I might never lie in the tomb of the Hydes!* Was not my coffin prepared for me? Had I not a right to rest till eternity amongst the descendants of Sir Geoffrey Hyde? Aye! I would claim my heritage of death, even though my soul go seeking through the ages for another corporeal tenement to represent it on that vacant slab in the alcove of the vault. *Jervas Hyde* should never share the sad fate of Palinurus![20]

As the phantom of the burning house faded, I found myself screaming and struggling madly in the arms of two men, one of whom was the spy who had followed me to the tomb. Rain was pouring down in torrents, and upon the southern horizon were flashes of the lightning that had so lately passed over our heads. My father, his face lined with sorrow, stood by as I shouted my demands to be laid within the tomb; frequently admonishing my captors to treat me as gently as they could. A blackened circle on the floor of the ruined cellar told of a violent stroke from the heavens; and from this spot a group of curious villagers with lanterns were prying a small box of antique workmanship which the thunderbolt had brought to light. Ceasing my futile and now objectless writhing, I watched the spectators as they viewed the treasure-trove, and was permitted to share in their discoveries. The box, whose fastenings were broken by the stroke which had unearthed it, contained many papers and objects of value; but I had eyes for one thing alone. It was the porcelain miniature of a young man in a smartly curled bag-wig,[21] and bore the initials "J. H." The face was such that as I gazed, I might well have been studying my mirror.

On the following day I was brought to this room with the barred windows, but I have been kept informed of certain things through an aged and simple-minded servitor, for whom I bore a fondness in infancy, and who like me loves the churchyard. What I have dared relate of my experiences within the vault has brought me only pitying smiles. My father, who visits me frequently, declares that at no time did I pass the chained portal, and swears that the rusted padlock had not been touched for fifty years when he examined it. He even says that all the village knew of my journeys to the tomb, and that I was often watched as I slept in the bower outside the grim facade, my half-open eyes fixed on the crevice that leads to the interior. Against these assertions I have no tangible proof to offer, since my key to the padlock was lost in the struggle on that night of horrors. The strange things of the past which I learnt during those nocturnal meetings with the dead he dismisses as the fruits of my lifelong and omnivorous browsing amongst the ancient volumes of the family library. Had it not been for my old servant Hiram, I should have by this time become quite convinced of my madness.

But Hiram, loyal to the last, has held faith in me, and has done that which impels me to make public at least a part of my story. A week ago he burst open the lock which chains the

nois Press, 1996), 159–60. Percy provides a modern translation of the Horace ode: "Not otherwise, they say, did Anacreon of Teos burn for Samian Bathyllus: often with hollow lyre he sang his sad song of love in no elaborate meter" (ibid., 159).

17. "History has not been kind to Lovecraft's verse," remarks Will Murray, in "A Probable Source for the Drinking Song from 'The Tomb,'" *Lovecraft Studies* 15 (Fall 1987): 77–80. "His eighteenth-century effusions are all but dismissed by even his more ardent admirers." But this poem, Murray points out, "is unlike any other poem Lovecraft ever wrote. Indeed, with its unabashed praise for drinking and wenching and living for the moment, it is utterly unlike the sedate Lovecraft" (77). Murray suggests somewhat unconvincingly that HPL may have imitated a poem titled "The Songe," by Thomas Morton, in *New English Canaan*, also titled *New Canaan* (Amsterdam: Jacob Frederick Stam, 1637), 134; an 1883 version of the Morton works, with introductory matter and notes by Charles Francis Adams Jr., was published in Boston by John Wilson and Son in 1883 (https://archive.org/stream/newenglishcanaan00mort/newenglishcanaan00mort_djvu.txt). One other possible source for the Lovecraft verse is suggested in S. T. Joshi and David E. Schultz, *An H. P. Lovecraft Encyclopedia* (Westport, CT: Greenwood, 2001), 272.

18. Donald R. Burleson points out that Jervas leads the villager here "at a time when Jervas was supposedly *keeping* his entire connexion with the house and the tomb secret" (*H. P. Lovecraft: A Critical Study* [New York: Greenwood, 1983], 21. Emphasis added).

19. This is the first use in HPL's tales of one of his favorite words, "blasphemy" (often used in adjectival form, "blasphemous").

In 1927, in his masterwork "Supernatural Horror in Literature" (reprinted in *Dagon and Other Macabre Tales*, corrected seventh printing, ed. S. T. Joshi [Sauk City, WI: Arkham House Publishers, Inc., 1965], 365–436), HPL explained that the true weird tale must contain at least a hint of "that most terrible conception of the human brain—a malign and particular suspension or defeat of those fixed laws of Nature which are our only safeguard against the assaults of chaos and the dæmons of unplumbed space" (368). This is the concept of "blasphemy" in its biblical sense, the opposite of holiness, which requires that individuals conform to the class to which they belong and that the categories of creation be kept distinct. See Robert M. Price's "Lovecraft's Concept of Blasphemy," *Crypt of Cthulhu* 1 (Hallowmas 1981): 6.

20. See note 2, above.

21. An eighteenth-century style of wig, in which the long hair at the back, often arranged in a braid or ponytail (both of which were called "queues"), was placed in a black silk bag. Ribbons attached to the bag for the purpose of cinching the whole bundle were usually pulled to the front and tied in a bow, known as a "solitaire," over the stock (a high, stiff collar decorated with buckles), and sometimes a rosette was affixed at the back.

A bag-wig.

door of the tomb perpetually ajar, and descended with a lantern into the murky depths. On a slab in an alcove he found an old but empty coffin whose tarnished plate bears the single word *"Jervas"*. In that coffin and in that vault they have promised me I shall be buried.

Polaris[1]

HPL weaves his knowledge of astronomy into a tantalizing puzzle inspired by a dream of his own: Who is the dreamer, and who is the dream? Lovecraft's style here bears an uncanny resemblance to that of Lord Dunsany (Edward Plunkett [1878–1957]), whose work so impressed HPL, though he did not read it until the fall of 1919. Both Lovecraft and Dunsany were likely influenced by Edgar Allan Poe's "Shadow—A Parable" (1835) and "Silence—A Fable" (1838), "assuredly poems in every sense of the word save the metrical one," HPL wrote, "[which] owe as much of their power to aural cadence as to visual imagery."[2]

nto the north window of my chamber glows the Pole Star[3] with uncanny light. All through the long hellish hours of blackness it shines there. And in the autumn of the year, when the winds from the north curse and whine, and the red-leaved trees of the swamp mutter things to one another in the small hours of the morning under the horned waning moon, I sit by the casement and watch that star. Down from the heights reels the glittering Cassiopeia[4] as the hours wear on, while Charles' Wain[5] lumbers up from behind the vapour-soaked swamp trees that sway in the night-wind. Just before dawn Arcturus[6] winks ruddily from above the cemetery on the low hillock, and Coma Berenices[7] shimmers weirdly afar off in the mysterious east; but still the Pole Star leers down from the same place in the black vault, winking hideously like an insane watching eye which strives to convey some strange message, yet recalls nothing save that it once had a message to convey. Sometimes, when it is cloudy, I can sleep.

Well do I remember the night of the great Aurora,[8] when over the swamp played the shocking coruscations of the daemon-light. After the beams came clouds, and then I slept.

And it was under a horned waning moon that I saw the city for the first time. Still and somnolent did it lie, on a strange pla-

1. Probably written in the late spring or early summer of 1918, it first appeared in *The Philosopher* 1, no. 1 (December 1920), 3–5. It was eventually reprinted in *Weird Tales* 30, no. 6 (December 1937), 749–51, 759.

2. Lovecraft, "Supernatural Horror in Literature," 399.

3. Alpha Ursae Minoris, commonly known as Polaris or the polestar, is actually a "multiple star"—three stars, Polaris Aa, Polaris Ab, and Polaris B, in tight orbits around each other, the brightest point in the constellation known as Ursa Minor, the Little Bear or Little Dipper. It currently sits almost motionless in the sky above the north polar axis of the Earth. (Its motion is limited to a sphere about 1.5 degrees wide, which it travels every twenty-four hours around the true pole.) This has not always been so: 4,800 years ago, the polestar was Thuban, in the constellation Draconis, and in another 8,000 years it will be Deneb, in the constella-

tion Cygnus (Ian Ridpath, ed., *Norton's Star Atlas* [New York: Pearson Education, 2004)], 5). Over a period of about 26,000 years the axis of the pole traces a hypothetical circle in the heavens, so that eventually Alpha Ursae Minoris will again be the polestar. (Jean Meeus, in *Mathematical Astronomy Morsels*, calculates the period of precession to be 25,770 years [Richmond, VA: Willmann-Bell, 1997)], chapter 50.) See note 16, below.

4. An easily recognizable constellation in the northern sky in the shape of the letter *W*.

5. Charles's Wain—reportedly from "churl's waggen," meaning the farmer's wagon, as contrasted with the women's wagon (or "fallen woman") Ursa Minor—is an Old English name for Ursa Major, the Big Bear or Big Dipper, which forms the shape of a wheelbarrow and is often used as a pointer to the polestar. Thus some philologists find the source of "Charles's" in the medieval word "carle," meaning farmer, rather than in any association with King Charles. However, Richard Hinckley Allen, in his comprehensive *Star Names and Their Meanings* (New York and London: G. E. Stechert, 1899), concludes instead that the name Charles (Charlemagne, Charles the Great) arose "out of the verbal association of the star-name *Arcturus* with *Arturus* or Arthur, and the legendary association of Arthur and Charlemagne; so that what was originally the wain of Arcturus [Bear Watcher or Bear Guardian, and the brightest star in the kite-shaped constellation Böotes] or Böotes [Herdsman or Plowman] . . . became at length the wain of Carl or Charlemagne" (428).

6. The fourth-brightest star in the sky after Sirius, Canopus, and Alpha Centauri, and the brightest in the northern celestial hemisphere. It is classed as a "red

teau in a hollow betwixt strange peaks. Of ghastly marble were its walls and its towers, its columns, domes, and pavements. In the marble streets were marble pillars, the upper parts of which were carven into the images of grave bearded men. The air was warm and stirred not. And overhead, scarce ten degrees from the zenith, glowed that watching Pole Star.[9] Long did I gaze on the city, but the day came not. When the red Aldebaran,[10] which blinked low in the sky but never set, had crawled a quarter of the way around the horizon, I saw light and motion in the houses and the streets. Forms strangely robed, but at once noble and familiar, walked abroad, and under the horned waning moon men talked wisdom in a tongue which I understood, though it was unlike any language I had ever known. And when the red Aldebaran had crawled more than half way around the horizon, there were again darkness and silence.

When I awaked, I was not as I had been. Upon my memory was graven the vision of the city, and within my soul had arisen another and vaguer recollection, of whose nature I was not then certain. Thereafter, on the cloudy nights when I could sleep, I saw the city often; sometimes under that horned waning moon, and sometimes under the hot yellow rays of a sun which did not set, but which wheeled low around the horizon.[11] And on the clear nights the Pole Star leered as never before.

Gradually I came to wonder what might be my place in that city on the strange plateau betwixt strange peaks. At first content to view the scene as an all-observant uncorporeal presence, I now desired to define my relation to it, and to speak my mind amongst the grave men who conversed each day in the public squares. I said to myself, "This is no dream, for by what means can I prove the greater reality of that other life in the house of stone and brick south of the sinister swamp and the cemetery on the low hillock, where the Pole Star peers into my north window each night?"

One night as I listened to the discourse in the large square containing many statues, I felt a change; and perceived that I had at last a bodily form. Nor was I a stranger in the streets of Olathoë,[12] which lies on the plateau of Sarkis, betwixt the peaks Noton and Kadiphonek.[13] It was my friend Alos who spoke, and his speech was one that pleased my soul, for it was the speech of a true man and patriot. That night had the news come of Daikos' fall, and of the advance of the Inutos;[14] squat, hellish, yellow fiends who five years ago had appeared out of the unknown west to ravage the confines of our kingdom, and finally to besiege our towns. Having taken the fortified places at the foot of the mountains, their way now lay open to the plateau, unless every citizen could resist with the strength of ten men. For the squat creatures were mighty in the arts of war, and knew not the scruples of honour which held back our tall, grey-eyed men of Lomar from ruthless conquest.

Alos, my friend, was commander of all the forces on the plateau, and in him lay the last hope of our country. On this occasion he spoke of the perils to be faced, and exhorted the men of Olathoë, bravest of the Lomarians, to sustain the traditions of their ancestors, who when forced to move southward from Zobna before the advance of the great ice-sheet (even as our descendants must some day flee from the land of Lomar), valiantly and victoriously swept aside the hairy, long-armed, cannibal Gnophkehs that stood in their way. To me Alos denied a warrior's part, for I was feeble and given to strange faintings when subjected to stress and hardships. But my eyes were the keenest in the city, despite the long hours I gave each day to the study of the Pnakotic manuscripts[15] and the wisdom of the Zobnarian Fathers; so my friend, desiring not to doom me to inaction, rewarded me with that duty which was second to nothing in importance. To the watch-tower of Thapnen he sent me, there to serve as the eyes of our army. Should the Inutos attempt to gain the citadel by the narrow pass behind the peak Noton, and thereby surprise the garrison, I was to give the signal of fire which would warn the waiting soldiers and save the town from immediate disaster.

Alone I mounted the tower, for every man of stout body was needed in the passes below. My brain was sore dazed with excitement and fatigue, for I had not slept in many days; yet was my purpose firm, for I loved my native land of Lomar, and the marble city of Olathoë that lies betwixt the peaks of Noton and Kadiphonek.

But as I stood in the tower's topmost chamber, I beheld the horned waning moon, red and sinister, quivering through the vapours that hovered over the distant valley of Banof. And

giant" for its age, although it is not particularly red in color but rather orange-yellow to the naked eye. According to Allen, *Star Names and Their Meanings*, "Arcturus has been an object of the highest interest and admiration to all observant mankind from the earliest times, and doubtless was one of the first stars to be named" (98).

7. A small, not very bright constellation near Ursa Major, Berenice's Hair, named after Berenice II of Egypt (267 or 266–221 BCE), although probably first called Ariadne's Hair, according to Allen, *Star Names and Their Meanings*.

8. The aurora borealis (the northern lights), giant swirls of spectacular color, are a phenomenon caused by electrical discharges of Earth's magnetic field as protons and electrons from the sun collide with it in the ionosphere. The greatest geomagnetic storms ever recorded began on August 28, 1859. However, the *Boston Evening Transcript* for March 22, 1918, reported: "One of the most brilliant displays of Aurora Borealis seen in Boston in many years occurred last evening. The display exhibited all the colors of the rainbow. At times the entire heavens were filled with kaleidoscopic light, and the eastern and southern skies were as brightly illuminated as was the north" (reprinted in the *Los Angeles Times* for March 22, 1918, http://www.solarstorms .org/NewsPapers/1918g.pdf). This substorm must have occurred just before the events of this tale were recorded.

9. The polestar is directly overhead only when at the North Pole. "Scarce ten degrees from the zenith" is nearly overhead. The city is therefore quite far north, observes Donald R. Burleson, though "[t]he air was warm and stirred not" (*H. P. Lovecraft: A Critical Study*, 25). This supports the later revelation that the vision is in the distant past,

when apparently a different climate held in the far north.

There have long been suggestions of a Golden Age (and its location has been termed "Atlantis" by some) situated in the far north in the distant past, though there is no evidence extant that such a civilization existed. The topic is covered in detail in *The New Annotated Frankenstein* (New York: Liveright, 2017), p. 14, note 7, by this editor.

10. Aldebaran, Alpha Tauri, is the brightest star in the constellation Taurus (the Bull) and one of the brighter stars in the northern sky. Orange-yellow in color, it is a red giant in age. According to *Allen*, the name means "the follower." "Aldebaran was the divine star in the worship of the [pre-Islamic Arab] tribe Misām, who thought that it brought rain, and that its heliacal rising unattended by showers portended a barren year" (384).

11. This is not a sight seen with the naked eye; a bright sun that does not set appears on cloudy nights. The observer is presumably seeing an alternate world or dimension. Note that a similar phenomenon is recorded in Philip Pullman's *His Dark Materials* (1995–2000), where the aurora are portals to alternate worlds that can be glimpsed through the lights.

12. This is the first mention of this mythical city; it reappears in "The Quest of Iranon" (pp. 89–96, below), *The Dream-Quest of Unknown Kadath* (pp. 329–432, below), and "The Mound" (see note following).

13. These are all locations in the land of Lomar, mentioned below. In "The Mound," a story cowritten by Lovecraft and Zelia Bishop in late 1929 and early 1930 (but not published until 1940), the land is said to be near the North Pole.

through an opening in the roof glittered the pale Pole Star, fluttering as if alive, and leering like a fiend and tempter. Methought its spirit whispered evil counsel, soothing me to traitorous somnolence with a damnable rhythmical promise which it repeated over and over:

> *"Slumber, watcher, till the spheres*
> *Six and twenty thousand years*
> *Have revolv'd, and I return*
> *To the spot where now I burn.*[16]
> *Other stars anon shall rise*
> *To the axis of the skies;*
> *Stars that soothe and stars that bless*
> *With a sweet forgetfulness:*
> *Only when my round is o'er*
> *Shall the past disturb thy door."*

Vainly did I struggle with my drowsiness, seeking to connect these strange words with some lore of the skies which I had learnt from the Pnakotic manuscripts. My head, heavy and reeling, drooped to my breast, and when next I looked up it was in a dream; with the Pole Star grinning at me through a window from over the horrible swaying trees of a dream-swamp. And I am still dreaming.

In my shame and despair I sometimes scream frantically, begging the dream-creatures around me to waken me ere the Inutos steal up the pass behind the peak Noton and take the citadel by surprise; but these creatures are daemons, for they laugh at me and tell me I am not dreaming. They mock me whilst I sleep, and whilst the squat yellow foe may be creeping silently upon us. I have failed in my duty and betrayed the marble city of Olathoë; I have proven false to Alos, my friend and commander. But still these shadows of my dream deride me. They say there is no land of Lomar, save in my nocturnal imaginings; that in those realms where the Pole Star shines high and red Aldebaran crawls low around the horizon, there has been naught save ice and snow for thousands of years, and never a man save squat yellow creatures, blighted by the cold, whom they call "Esquimaux."[17]

And as I writhe in my guilty agony, frantic to save the city whose peril every moment grows, and vainly striving to shake off this unnatural dream of a house of stone and brick south of a sinister swamp and a cemetery on a low hillock; the Pole Star, evil and monstrous, leers down from the black vault, winking hideously like an insane watching eye which strives to convey some strange message, yet recalls nothing save that it once had a message to convey.

14. In *The Dream-Quest of Unknown Kadath*, HPL records that "the hairy cannibal Gnophkehs overcame many-templed Olathoe and slew all the heroes of the land of Lomar." See the following paragraph, which contains contradictory information. The Gnophkehs are also mentioned in "The Mound" (see preceding note). Note that the fiends are "yellow" (see "Nyarlathotep," in *The New Annotated H. P. Lovecraft* (hereafter referred to as the previous volume), pp. 30–34, note 9, by this editor, and "He," pp. 277–89, note 13, below.

15. See "The Whisperer in Darkness," pp. 388–456, of the previous volume, note 63, and Appendix 3 of that volume.

16. The poem refers to the cycle of nearly 26,000 years that will bring Polaris (and any other star) back to its status of reigning polestar. See note 3, above. Thus the narrator suggests that he is experiencing a past life and not merely a dream.

17. The term "Eskimo" is obsolete today, the result, in part, of genetic forensics: A 2014 study of DNA fragments from ancient hair and teeth collected in Siberia, Alaska, Canada, and Greenland has yielded clues to the ancestry of the modern-day Inuit, suggesting that they are descendants not (as previously thought) of Paleo-Eskimos (also known as the Dorset), a culture that thrived for more than four thousand years, but of an entirely distinct culture, the Thule. The Thule swept into the region about seven hundred years ago, but there is no evidence of interbreeding between the Thule and the Paleo-Eskimos. Rather, the Paleo-Eskimos simply vanished. The exact reasons for their disappearance remain unclear, though climate change or medical problems seem to be likely candidates. See Maanasa Raghavan et al., "The Genetic Prehistory of the New World Arctic," *Science* 345 (August 29, 2014), 1255832-1–1255832-9.

The Transition of Juan Romero[1]

This story remained unpublished during Lovecraft's lifetime, probably by choice. Lovecraft does not seem to have shown it to anyone until 1932, when he allowed his fourteen-year-old friend (and, later, literary executor) R. H. Barlow[2] to type it. In these very early stories, including "Dagon" and "Beyond the Wall of Sleep" in the first volume, we see HPL experimenting with styles. Here, he continues to test the idea of presenting a supernatural thread in a larger realistic tapestry—an idea that he would execute to perfection in "The Call of Cthulhu" and At the Mountains of Madness.

1. Written in 1919, the story was not published until 1944, when it was collected in the Arkham House volume entitled *Marginalia*, edited by August Derleth and Donald Wandrei. It was subsequently included in the Arkham House collection *Dagon and Other Macabre Tales*, published in 1965 with an introduction by Derleth. A 1986 edition of *Dagon and Other Macabre Tales* is a revision and reissue, with new introductions by S. T. Joshi and T. E. D. Klein replacing Derleth's.

2. Robert Hayward Barlow (1918–1951), from 1948 to 1951 chair of the anthropology department at Mexico City College, with a specialty in indigenous Mesoamerica, often found himself in a kind of mutual tutelage with older writers. He counted among his students William Burroughs, four years his senior; in 1950, then in Mexico on the GI Bill, the future author of *Naked Lunch* took Barlow's class on the Mayan codices.

The writer Paul La Farge describes Lovecraft and Barlow's first meeting, in

Of the events which took place at the Norton Mine on October 18th and 19th, 1894, I have no desire to speak. A sense of duty to science is all that impels me to recall, in these last years of my life, scenes and happenings fraught with a terror doubly acute because I cannot wholly define it. But I believe that before I die I should tell what I know of the—shall I say transition—of Juan Romero.

My name and origin need not be related to posterity; in fact, I fancy it is better that they should not be, for when a man suddenly migrates to the States or the Colonies,[3] he leaves his past behind him. Besides, what I once was is not in the least relevant to my narrative; save perhaps the fact that during my service in India[4] I was more at home amongst white-bearded native teachers than amongst my brother-officers. I had delved not a little into odd Eastern lore when overtaken by the calamities which brought about my new life in America's vast West—a life wherein I found it well to accept a name—my present one—which is very common and carries no meaning.

In the summer and autumn of 1894 I dwelt in the drear expanses of the Cactus Mountains,[5] employed as a common labourer at the celebrated Norton Mine; whose discovery by an aged prospector some years before had turned the surrounding region from a nearly unpeopled waste to a seething cauldron of sordid life. A cavern of gold, lying deep below a mountain lake, had enriched its venerable finder beyond his wildest dreams, and now formed the seat of extensive tunnelling operations on the part of the corporation to which it had finally been sold. Additional grottoes had been found, and the yield of yellow metal was exceedingly great; so that a mighty and heterogeneous army of miners toiled day and night in the numerous passages and rock hollows. The Superintendent, a Mr. Arthur, often discussed the singularity of the local geological formations; speculating on the probable extent of the chain of caves, and estimating the future of the titanic mining enterprise. He considered the auriferous cavities the result of the action of water, and believed the last of them would soon be opened.

It was not long after my arrival and employment that Juan Romero came to the Norton Mine. One of a large herd of unkempt Mexicans attracted thither from the neighbouring country, he at first commanded attention only because of his features; which though plainly of the Red Indian type, were yet remarkable for their light colour and refined conformation, being vastly unlike those of the average "Greaser" or Piute of the locality.[6] It is curious that although he differed so widely from the mass of Hispanicised and tribal Indians, Romero gave not the least impression of Caucasian blood. It was not the Castilian conquistador[7] or the American pioneer, but the ancient and noble Aztec,[8] whom imagination called to view when the silent peon would rise in the early morning and gaze in fascination at the sun as it crept above the eastern hills, meanwhile stretching out his arms to the orb as if in the performance of some rite whose nature he did not himself comprehend. But save for his face, Romero was not in any way suggestive of nobility. Ignorant and dirty, he was at home amongst the other brown-skinned Mexicans; having come (so I was afterward told) from the very lowest sort of surroundings. He had been found as a child in a crude mountain hut, the only survivor of an epidemic which had stalked lethally by. Near the hut, close to a rather unusual rock fissure, had lain two skeletons, newly picked by vultures, and presumably forming the sole remains of his parents. No one recalled their identity, and

1934, when the writer paid an extended visit to the young man's small-town home, in DeLand, Florida, named after a New York philanthropist and manufacturer of the chemical leavener saleratus, used in baking powder:

Barlow hadn't mentioned his age, and he was reluctant to send along a photo of himself, because, he said, he had a "boil." Lovecraft was surprised to discover, when he got off the bus in DeLand, that Barlow had just turned sixteen. Lovecraft was forty-three.

So there they were, the older writer, in a rumpled suit and with a face "not unlike Dante," according to Barlow; and the young fan, slight and weasel-faced, with slicked-back black hair and glasses with thick round lenses. Barlow's father was visiting relatives in the North, and Lovecraft ended up staying with Barlow and his mother for seven weeks. (Paul La Farge, "The Complicated Friendship of H. P. Lovecraft and Robert Barlow, One of His Biggest Fans," *The New Yorker*, March 9, 2017)

Robert H. Barlow, probably some time in the late 1940s in Mexico.

La Farge reports that as literary executor Barlow was unfairly thwarted at every turn by Lovecraft acolytes envious that he had been thus designated by HPL.

3. "The Colonies" and "the States" seem to both refer to the United States, with the former phrase meaning the pre-Revolution American colonies. In this context, however, it is more likely that the narrator meant *the Australian* colonies, which did not confederate until 1901 and shared the same reputation as the United States as a place for a person from the Continent to start over without the burden of a reputation or history.

4. The narrator does not reveal his age, though he does speak of his Indian experiences as a "closed chapter" of his life, suggesting that some years—perhaps ten or fifteen—have passed since his military service. It is pleasant to imagine that he was an officer of the 5th (Northumberland Fusiliers) Regiment of Foot (the "Northumberland Fusiliers" after 1881), a British infantry force serving in India in 1881, to which was attached one John H. Watson, MD, as its assistant surgeon. However, it is more likely that he was an officer of the Corps of Royal Engineers and learned mining skills in that service. His military career must have taken some sharp turns for him to descend from the lofty post of a British army officer to the job of common laborer.

5. Nevada's Cactus Range lies in Nye County. The definitive history of the district is Shawn Hall's *Preserving the Glory Days: Ghost Towns and Mining Camps of Nye County, Nevada* (Reno: University of Nevada Press, 1999, rev. ed.), which lavishly and lovingly catalogues every claim, grubstake, camp, promotional scam, ranch settlement, platting, post office, and stage line from the 1880s onward and includes hundreds of photo-

they were soon forgotten by the many. Indeed, the crumbling of the adobe hut and the closing of the rock fissure by a subsequent avalanche had helped to efface even the scene from recollection. Reared by a Mexican cattle-thief who had given him his name, Juan differed little from his fellows.

The attachment which Romero manifested toward me was undoubtedly commenced through the quaint and ancient Hindoo[9] ring which I wore when not engaged in active labour. Of its nature, and manner of coming into my possession, I cannot speak. It was my last link with a chapter of life for ever closed, and I valued it highly. Soon I observed that the odd-looking Mexican was likewise interested; eyeing it with an expression that banished all suspicion of mere covetousness. Its hoary hieroglyphs[10] seemed to stir some faint recollection in his untutored but active mind, though he could not possibly have beheld their like before. Within a few weeks after his advent, Romero was like a faithful servant to me; this notwithstanding the fact that I was myself but an ordinary miner. Our conversation was necessarily limited. He knew but a few words of English, while I found my Oxonian Spanish[11] was something quite different from the patois of the peon of New Spain.

The event which I am about to relate was unheralded by long premonitions. Though the man Romero had interested me, and though my ring had affected him peculiarly, I think that neither of us had any expectation of what was to follow when the great blast was set off. Geological considerations had dictated an extension of the mine directly downward from the deepest part of the subterranean area; and the belief of the Superintendent that only solid rock would be encountered, had led to the placing of a prodigious charge of dynamite. With this work Romero and I were not connected, wherefore our first knowledge of extraordinary conditions came from others. The charge, heavier perhaps than had been estimated, had seemed to shake the entire mountain. Windows in shanties on the slope outside were shattered by the shock, whilst miners throughout the nearer passages were knocked from their feet. Jewel Lake,[12] which lay above the scene of action, heaved as in a tempest. Upon investigation it was seen that a new abyss yawned indefinitely below the seat of the blast; an abyss so monstrous that no handy line might fathom it, nor any lamp illuminate it. Baffled, the excavators sought a conference with the Superintendent, who ordered great lengths of rope to be taken to the pit, and spliced and lowered without cessation till a bottom might be discovered.

Shortly afterward the pale-faced workmen apprised the Superintendent of their failure. Firmly though respectfully they signified their refusal to revisit the chasm, or indeed to work further in the mine until it might be sealed. Something beyond their experience was evidently confronting them, for so far as they could ascertain, the void below was infinite. The Superintendent did not reproach them. Instead, he pondered deeply, and made many plans for the following day. The night shift did not go on that evening.

At two in the morning a lone coyote on the mountain began to howl dismally. From somewhere within the works a dog barked in answer; either to the coyote—or to something else. A storm was gathering around the peaks of the range, and weirdly shaped clouds scudded horribly across the blurred patch of celestial light which marked a gibbous moon's[13] attempts to shine through many layers of cirro-stratus vapours. It was Romero's voice, coming from the bunk above, that awakened me; a voice excited and tense with some vague expectation I could not understand:

"¡Madre de Dios!—el sonido—ese sonido—¡oiga Vd! ¿lo oye Vd?[14]—Señor, THAT SOUND!"

I listened, wondering what sound he meant. The coyote, the dog, the storm, all were audible; the last named now gaining ascendancy as the wind shrieked more and more frantically. Flashes of lightning were visible through the bunk-house window. I questioned the nervous Mexican, repeating the sounds I had heard:

"¿El coyote?—¿el perro?—¿el viento?"[15]

But Romero did not reply. Then he commenced whispering as in awe:

"El ritmo, Señor—el ritmo de la tierra[16]—THAT THROB DOWN IN THE GROUND!"

And now I also heard; heard and shivered and without knowing why. Deep, deep, below me was a sound—a rhythm, just as the peon had said—which, though exceedingly faint, yet dominated even the dog, the coyote, and the increasing tempest. To

graphs of abandoned sites, with maps and detailed present-day driving directions. There were dozens, if not hundreds, of gold mines in Nye County, but there is no record of a Norton Mine, celebrated or uncelebrated, though Hall notes, "By the summer of 1869 [the small townsite] Grant City [along the Grant Range] had a population of more than 100 and contained a number of businesses including a saloon, a blacksmith shop, and George Norton's assay office. Norton had some claims just to the south of Grant City" (96). There was a Norton *Ranch* in northern Nevada (usually referred to as Norton's Ranch; for its precise location, see Ronald Wilden, *General Geology of the Jackson Mountains, Humboldt County, Nevada*, Geological Survey Bulletin 1141-D, Prepared in Cooperation with the Nevada Bureau of Mines and the Department of the Interior [Washington, DC: U.S. Government Printing Office, 1963], 35), near the Jackson Mountains and the small town of Sulphur, but the narrator is very definite in identifying the Cactus mountains. We may perhaps conclude that the narrator conferred on the mine a slightly more formal name than any of George Norton's claims may have possessed, or that he altered the name of the mine, not the place.

6. "Greaser" is a derogative term for Mexicans, dating back to its first recorded usage in 1855. The Piutes (more properly, Paiutes) are Native Americans of two Shoshonean peoples (northern Paiute and southern Paiute). The northern Paiutes were traditionally found in eastern California, western Nevada, and southeast Oregon, while the southern Paiute inhabited the Colorado River basin and Mojave Desert in northern Arizona and southeastern California including the Owens Valley, southern Nevada and southern Utah. Early explorers thought that the southern Paiutes looked more

like Mexicans than Native Americans. The modern languages of the Paiutes are indeed derived from Aztecan roots but blend in Ute elements.

7. The Spanish explorers who conquered much of the Americas in the sixteenth century.

8. The "ancient and noble" Aztecs (or Mexica) were an empire that thrived from the thirteenth to the sixteenth century in Central America, arising out of migrations of the Nahua (indigenous people of Mexico and El Salvador) as early as the sixth century CE. The Spanish explorer Hernando (or Hernán) Cortés, allied with the Aztecs' enemies in Tenochtitlan, brought down the empire in 1521. Perhaps the best-known and most deeply contested aspect of the culture is the practice of ritual sacrifice. It has been estimated—implausibly, it has also been argued—that as many as eighty thousand prisoners were jettisoned down a wall or staircase of the Templo Mayor at Tenochtitlan, which effectively served as a chute of carnage in a four-day period in 1487, on the occasion of the reconsecration of the sacred site. Ross Hassig, in *Aztec Warfare: Imperial Expansion and Political Control* (Norman: University of Oklahoma Press, 1995), suggested that "[a] reported 80,400 men . . . from Huexotzinco, Tlaxcallan, Atlixco, Tliliuhqui-Tepec, Cholallan, Tecoac, Zacatlan, Xiuhcoac, Tozapan, Tlappan, and the Huaxtec area" (205) were offered for sacrifice, although he later revised his estimate to "between 10,000 and 80,400 people." See his "El Sacrificio y las Guerras Floridas," *Arqueología Mexicana* 11 (2003): 47. The BBC reduced the number to four thousand: See Jonathan Glancey, "The Templo Mayor: A Place for Human Sacrifice," BBC, February 27, 2015. The colonial historian Fernando de Alva Cortés Ixtlilxóchitl, author of *Codex*

"The Conquistadors," from Margaret Duncan Coxhead, *Romance of History: Mexico; With 12 Reproductions in Color of Original Drawings by J. H. Robinson*, Romance of History series, J. Lang, ed. (New York: Frederick A. Stokes Company, 1909).

seek to describe it were useless—for it was such that no description is possible. Perhaps it was like the pulsing of the engines far down in a great liner, as sensed from the deck, yet it was not so mechanical; not so devoid of the element of life and consciousness. Of all its qualities, *remoteness* in the earth most impressed me. To my mind rushed fragments of a passage in Joseph Glanvill which Poe has quoted with tremendous effect—

"—the vastness, profundity, and unsearchableness of His works, *which have a depth in them greater than the well of Democritus.*"[17]

Suddenly Romero leaped from his bunk; pausing before me to gaze at the strange ring on my hand, which glistened queerly in every flash of lightning, and then staring intently in the direction of the mine shaft. I also rose, and both stood motionless for a time, straining our ears as the uncanny rhythm seemed more and more to take on a vital quality. Then without apparent volition we began to move toward the door, whose rattling in the gale held a comforting suggestion of earthly reality. The chanting in the depths—for such the sound now seemed to be—grew in volume and distinctness; and we felt irresistibly urged out into the storm and thence to the gaping blackness of the shaft.

We encountered no living creature, for the men of the night shift had been released from duty, and were doubtless at the Dry Gulch settlement[18] pouring sinister rumours into the ear of some drowsy bartender. From the watchman's cabin, however, gleamed a small square of yellow light like a guardian eye. I dimly wondered how the rhythmic sound had affected the watchman; but Romero was moving more swiftly now, and I followed without pausing.

As we descended the shaft, the sound beneath grew definitely composite. It struck me as horribly like a sort of Oriental ceremony, with beating of drums and chanting of many voices. I have, as you are aware, been much in India. Romero and I moved without material hesitancy through drifts and down ladders; ever toward the thing that allured us, yet ever with a pitifully helpless fear and reluctance. At one time I fancied I had gone mad—this was when, on wondering how our way was lighted in the absence of lamp or candle, I realised that the ancient ring on my finger was glowing with eerie radiance, diffusing a pallid lustre through the damp, heavy air around.

It was without warning that Romero, after clambering down one of the many rude ladders, broke into a run and left me alone. Some new and wild note in the drumming and chanting, perceptible but slightly to me, had acted on him in startling fashion; and with a wild outcry he forged ahead unguided in the cavern's

Ixtlilxóchitl (written in the early seventeenth century), estimates that one in five children of slaves were killed annually. In "Malinalco: An Expression of Mexica Political and Religious Dominance in a Subject Territory" (PhD diss., University of Texas at Austin, 2012), Virginia Walker King warns that "Ixtlilxóchitl was writing an indigenous history in Spanish for a Spanish audience" and that his text was composed "more than eighty years and two generations after the Conquest" and thus "reflects a subsequent bias" (41). For more on Fernando de Alva Cortés Ixtlilxóchitl's "Europeanization" of Aztec history, see Galen Brokaw and Jongsoo Lee, *Fernando de Alva Ixtlilxochitl and His Legacy* (Tucson: University of Arizona Press, 2015). The *Codex* is online at http://www.famsi.org/research/graz/ixtlilxochitl/index.html. In "The Enigma of Aztec Sacrifice," *Natural History* 86, no. 4 (April 1977): 46–51, ethnologist Michael Harner, citing demographer Woodrow Borah, asserted that 1 percent "of the total population [of central Mexico]," or as many as 250,000 persons per year, were sacrificed by the Aztecs in the fifteenth century. Inga Clendinnen, in *Aztecs: An Interpretation* (Cambridge: Cambridge University Press, 1991), now in its tenth printing, is an original, nuanced, and highly readable treatment of the culture that also serves as a useful compendium of prior research; while speaking sensationally of "kindergartens of doomed infants" (137) and other victims, Clendinnen reassesses many prior claims.

9. An archaic reference to Hinduism, the third largest religion in the world, practiced by a majority in India. Its primary denominations are Shaivism, Shaktism, Vaishnavism, and Smartism.

10. Presumably in Sanskrit, suggests Leigh Blackmore, in "Some Notes on

Lovecraft's 'The Transition of Juan Romero,'" *Lovecraft Annual* 3 (2009), 163.

11. It is implied that the narrator acquired the Spanish language in the course of his studies at Oxford University—another indication of the length of his fall from grace. Spanish would have been an unusual field of study in the mid-nineteenth century; while the university's first Teacher of Spanish, Lorenzo Lucena, was appointed in 1858, the sub-faculty of Spanish, which falls under the Faculty of Medieval and Modern Languages, was not established until 1969. However, in 1895, Oxford's Taylor Institution Library received a major bequest from Williamina Mary Martin, a woman identified in all subsequent histories only by her name: one thousand books in Spanish and Portuguese that, in addition to editions of *Don Quixote*, also included works by the Golden Age playwrights Pedro Calderón de la Barca (1600–1681), or simply Calderón, and Lope Félix de Vega Carpio (1562–1635), known as Lope de Vega and author of, among other works, the verse play *Fuenteovejuna* (1619). Availing himself of this trove, the narrator may have acquired Spanish in the course of reading Cervantes and other well-known writers rather than by applying himself wholly to the language alone. He may have gone up to Oxford but not put himself under a tutor, or he may never have attended Oxford but learned his Spanish from an Oxonian. It was not until some three decades after the events of our narrative that, in 1927, a capital campaign in London raised £25,000 for the dual purpose of founding the King Alfonso XIII Professorship of Spanish and the Spanish Departmental Library.

12. There is no extant record of a Jewel Lake in Nye County, Nevada, though there is one in northern California (cre-

gloom. I heard his repeated shrieks before me, as he stumbled awkwardly along the level places and scrambled madly down the rickety ladders. And frightened as I was, I yet retained enough of perception to note that his speech, when articulate, was not of any sort known to me. Harsh but impressive polysyllables had replaced the customary mixture of bad Spanish and worse English, and of these only the oft repeated cry *"Huitzilopotchli"*[19] seemed in the least familiar. Later I definitely placed that word in the works of a great historian—and shuddered when the association came to me.

The climax of that awful night was composite but fairly brief, beginning just as I reached the final cavern of the journey. Out of the darkness immediately ahead burst a final shriek from the Mexican, which was joined by such a chorus of uncouth sound as I could never hear again and survive. In that moment it seemed as if all the hidden terrors and monstrosities of earth had become articulate in an effort to overwhelm the human race. Simultaneously the light from my ring was extinguished, and I saw a new light glimmering from lower space but a few yards ahead of me. I had arrived at the abyss, which was now redly aglow, and which had evidently swallowed up the unfortunate Romero. Advancing, I peered over the edge of that chasm which no line could fathom, and which was now a pandemonium of flickering flame and hideous uproar. At first I beheld nothing but a seething blur of luminosity; but then shapes, all infinitely distant, began to detach themselves from the confusion, and I saw—was it Juan Romero?—*but God! I dare not tell you what I saw! . . .* Some power from heaven, coming to my aid, obliterated both sights and sounds in such a crash as may be heard when two universes collide in space. Chaos supervened, and I knew the peace of oblivion.

I hardly knew how to continue, since conditions so singular are involved; but I will do my best, not even trying to differentiate betwixt the real and the apparent. When I awaked, I was safe in my bunk and the red glow of dawn was visible at the window. Some distance away the lifeless body of Juan Romero lay upon a table, surrounded by a group of men, including the camp doctor. The men were discussing the strange death of the Mexican as he lay asleep; a death seemingly connected in some way with the terrible bolt of lightning which had struck and shaken the mountain. No direct cause was evident, and an autopsy failed to shew any reason why Romero should not be living. Snatches of conversation indicated beyond a doubt that neither Romero nor I had left the bunkhouse during the night; that neither had been awake during the frightful storm which had passed over the Cactus range. That storm, said men who had ventured down the mine shaft, had caused extensive caving in, and had completely closed the deep abyss which had created so much apprehension the day before. When I asked the watchman what sounds he had heard prior to the mighty thunderbolt, he mentioned a coyote, a dog, and the snarling mountain wind—nothing more. Nor do I doubt his word.

Upon the resumption of work Superintendent Arthur called on some especially dependable men to make a few investigations around the spot where the gulf had appeared. Though hardly eager, they obeyed; and a deep boring was made. Results were very curious. The roof of the void, as seen whilst it was open, was not by any means thick; yet now the drills of the investigators met what appeared to be a limitless extent of solid rock. Finding nothing else, not even gold, the Superintendent abandoned his attempts; but a perplexed look occasionally steals over his countenance as he sits thinking at his desk.

One other thing is curious. Shortly after waking on that morning after the storm, I noticed the unaccountable absence of my Hindoo ring from my finger. I had prized it greatly, yet nevertheless felt a sensation of relief at its disappearance. If one of my fellow-miners appropriated it, he must have been quite clever in disposing of his booty, for despite advertisements and a police search the ring was never seen again. Somehow I doubt if it was stolen by mortal hands, for many strange things were taught me in India.

My opinion of my whole experience varies from time to time. In broad daylight, and at most seasons I am apt to think the greater part of it a mere dream; but sometimes in the autumn, about two in the morning when winds and animals howl dismally, there comes from inconceivable depths below a damnable suggestion of rhythmical throbbing . . . and I feel that the transition of Juan Romero was a terrible one indeed.

ated in 1921) and another in Colorado. In fact, according to the U.S. Census Bureau's 2010 gazetteer files (https://www2.census.gov/geo/docs/maps-data/data/gazetteer/counties_list_32.txt), Nye County has only about 17 square miles of water, compared with over 18,000 square miles of land.

13. The first published version of the story included the following:

*AUTHOR'S NOTE: Here is a lesson in scientific accuracy for fiction writers. I have just looked up the moon's phases for October, 1894, to find when a gibbous moon was visible at 2 a.m., and have changed the dates to fit!!

14. "*Oiga Vd*" is another way of saying "*Oiga usted*," meaning "Hey, you, listen!" "*Lo oye Vd?*" means "Do you hear it?"

15. "A coyote? A dog? The wind?"

16. "The rhythm (beat), Señor—the rhythm of the earth."

17. The epigram is at the head of Poe's "A Descent into the Maelström," first published in *Graham's Magazine* 18 (May 1841), 235–41. It is drawn from Joseph Glanvill's essay "Against Confidence in Philosophy, and Matters of Speculation": "The *ways* of God in *Nature* (as in *Providence*) are not as *ours* are: Nor are the models that we frame [in] any way commensurate to the vastness and profundity of his Works; which have a *depth* in them greater than the *Well of Democritus*" (*Essays on Several Important Subjects in Philosophy and Religion* [London: Baker, 1676]). In *The Vanity of Dogmatizing* (London: Printed by E. C. for Henry Eversden, 1661), published under at least one other title, Glanvill, one of the most prolific seventeenth-century popularizers of natural science and surely one of its

more prolix, famously argued that words had no fixed meaning.

18. F. B. Weeks, in "Geology and Mineral Resources of the Osceola Mining District, White Pine County, Nev.," *U.S. Geological Survey Bulletin 340-A* (1908): 117–33, notes that from 1877 to 1907, in Dry Gulch settlement in White Pine County, adjacent to Nye County, placer mining—manually separating the eroded mineral from gravel and sand (as distinct from hard rock mining)—yielded nearly two million dollars' worth of gold. In the same period, the settlement's lodes yielded just under a quarter-million dollars' worth. While labor-intensive, placer mining required no machinery, only a prospector's pan, sluice boxes, and a penstock and steel sectional pipe for hydraulicking. Steam- and diesel-powered gold dredges were not used until at least a decade and a half after the events recorded by the narrator.

A. H. Koschmann and M. H. Bergendahl, in *Principal Gold-Producing Districts of the United States*, Geological Survey Professional Paper 610 (Washington, DC: U.S. Government Printing Office, 1968), note that gold placers were found in 1865 in a New Mexico settlement also called Dry Gulch—near Nogal Peak in the Sierra Blanca Range (207).

19. More commonly spelled *Huitzilopochtli*, the solar deity and god of war of the Aztecs. One of the two temples at Tenochtitlan (see note 8, above) was named for him. The "great historian" mentioned by the narrator may be Daniel Garrison Brinton, MD, who edited the *Library of Aboriginal American Literature*, which included the volume entitled *Rig Veda Americanus: Sacred Songs of the Ancient Americans, with a Gloss in Nahuatl* (1890; New York: Mythik Press, 2015), containing numerous references to Huitzilopochtli; or it may be William H. Prescott, whose *History of the Conquest of Mexico* (New York: Harper and Brothers, 1843) also fits the bill.

Huitzilopotchli.

The Doom That Came to Sarnath[1]

By late 1919 Lovecraft had attended a lecture by Lord Dunsany and began to read widely in his work. Some dismiss this story as an imitation of Dunsany's fantasies, but Lovecraft's efforts have gained a far larger audience than Dunsany's originals. As in "Polaris," Lovecraft created a rich tapestry of gods, lands, and peoples and eventually wove them firmly into his elaborate "dreamland."

There is in the land of Mnar[2] a vast still lake that is fed by no stream and out of which no stream flows. Ten thousand years ago there stood by its shore the mighty city of Sarnath,[3] but Sarnath stands there no more.

It is told that in the immemorial years when the world was young, before ever the men of Sarnath came to the land of Mnar, another city stood beside the lake; the grey stone city of Ib,[4] which was old as the lake itself, and peopled with beings not pleasing to behold. Very odd and ugly where these beings, as indeed are most beings of a world yet inchoate and rudely fashioned. It is written on the brick cylinders of Kadatheron[5] that the beings of Ib were in hue as green as the lake and the mists that rise above it; that they had bulging eyes, pouting, flabby lips, and curious ears, and were without voice. It is also written that they descended one night from the moon in a mist; they and the vast still lake and grey stone city Ib. However this may be, it is certain that they worshipped a sea-green stone idol chiselled in the likeness of Bokrug, the great water-lizard; before which they danced horribly when the moon was gibbous. And it is written in the papyrus of Ilarnek,[6] that they one day discovered fire, and thereafter kindled flames on many ceremonial occasions. But not much is written of these beings, because they lived in very ancient times, and man is young, and knows but little of the very ancient living things.

1. "The Doom That Came to Sarnath" was written in December 1919 and was first published in *The Scot* 44 (June 1920), 90–98. It was reprinted in *Weird Tales* 31, no. 6 (June 1938), 742–46.

2. Mnar reappears in "The Nameless City" (probably written in January 1921) and in *At the Mountains of Madness* (1931).

3. There is another Sarnath, a city in the state of Uttar Pradesh in India. The city is often visited as the site of the first teachings of the Buddha and is named after the deer park there (the Sanskrit "*Sāranganātha*" means Lord of the Deer).

4. This is the earliest mention of Ib in Lovecraft's work. For others, see "The Nameless City" (80–93), in the previous volume, where it is said to have been built before mankind existed, and *At the Mountains of Madness* (457–572), where it is called a "pre-human blasphemy."

5. Kadatheron reappears in "The Quest of Iranon," pp. 89–96, below, written on

February 28, 1921, and in *The Dream-Quest of Unknown Kadath*, pp. 329–432, below.

6. A city on the river Ai, mentioned also in "The Quest of Iranon" and in *The Dream-Quest of Unknown Kadath*.

7. Thraa reappears in "The Quest of Iranon" and in *The Dream-Quest of Unknown Kadath*.

After many aeons men came to the land of Mnar; dark shepherd folk with their fleecy flocks, who built Thraa,[7] Ilarnek, and Kadatheron on the winding river Ai. And certain tribes, more hardy than the rest, pushed on to the border of the lake and built Sarnath at a spot where precious metals were found in the earth.

Not far from the grey city of Ib did the wandering tribes lay the first stones of Sarnath, and at the beings of Ib they marvelled greatly. But with their marvelling was mixed hate, for they thought it not meet that beings of such aspect should walk about the world of men at dusk. Nor did they like the strange sculptures upon the grey monoliths of Ib, for those sculptures were terrible with great antiquity. Why the beings and the sculptures lingered so late in the world, even until the coming of men, none can tell; unless it was because the land of Mnar is very still, and remote from most other lands both of waking and of dream.

As the men of Sarnath beheld more of the beings of Ib their hate grew, and it was not less because they found the beings weak, and soft as jelly to the touch of stones and spears and arrows. So one day the young warriors, the slingers and the spearmen and the bowmen, marched against Ib and slew all the inhabitants thereof, pushing the queer bodies into the lake with long spears, because they did not wish to touch them. And because they did not like the grey sculptured monoliths of Ib they cast these also into the lake; wondering from the greatness of the labour how ever the stones were brought from afar, as they must have been, since there is naught like them in all the land of Mnar or in the lands adjacent.

Thus of the very ancient city of Ib was nothing spared save the sea-green stone idol chiselled in the likeness of Bokrug, the water-lizard. This the young warriors took back with them to Sarnath as a symbol of conquest over the old gods and beings of Ib, and a sign of leadership in Mnar. But on the night after it was set up in the temple a terrible thing must have happened, for weird lights were seen over the lake, and in the morning the people found the idol gone, and the high-priest Taran-Ish lying dead, as from some fear unspeakable. And before he died, Taran-Ish had scrawled upon the altar of chrysolite with coarse shaky strokes the sign of DOOM.

After Taran-Ish there were many high-priests in Sarnath, but never was the sea-green stone idol found. And many centuries came and went, wherein Sarnath prospered exceedingly, so that only priests and old women remembered what Taran-Ish had scrawled upon the altar of chrysolite. Betwixt Sarnath and the city of Ilarnek arose a caravan route, and the precious metals from the earth were exchanged for other metals and rare cloths and jewels and books and tools for artificers and all things of luxury that are known to the people who dwell along the winding river Ai and beyond. So Sarnath waxed mighty and learned and beautiful, and sent forth conquering armies to subdue the neighbouring cities; and in time there sate upon a throne in Sarnath the kings of all the land of Mnar and of many lands adjacent.

The wonder of the world and the pride of all mankind was Sarnath the magnificent. Of polished desert-quarried marble were its walls, in height three hundred cubits and in breadth seventy-five, so that chariots might pass each other as men drave them along the top. For full five hundred stadia[8] did they run, being open only on the side toward the lake; where a green stone sea-wall kept back the waves that rose oddly once a year at the festival of the destroying of Ib. In Sarnath were fifty streets from the lake to the gates of the caravans, and fifty more intersecting them. With onyx were they paved, save those whereon the horses and camels and elephants trod, which were paved with granite. And the gates of Sarnath were as many as the landward ends of the streets, each of bronze, and flanked by the figures of lions and elephants carven from some stone no longer known among men. The houses of Sarnath were of glazed brick and chalcedony, each having its walled garden and crystal lakelet. With strange art were they builded, for no other city had houses like them; and travellers from Thraa and Ilarnek and Kadatheron marvelled at the shining domes wherewith they were surmounted.

But more marvellous still were the palaces and the temples, and the gardens made by Zokkar the olden king. There were many palaces, the least of which were mightier than any in Thraa or Ilarnek or Kadatheron. So high were they that one within might sometimes fancy himself beneath only the sky; yet when lighted with torches dipt in the oil of Dothur their walls shewed vast paintings of kings and armies, of a splendour at once inspiring and stupefying to the beholder. Many were the pillars

8. An ancient unit of length; although it meant different lengths in different cultures, a stadion (the singular form) was between 575 and 650 feet (175 and 210 meters) long.

[31]

of the palaces, all of tinted marble, and carven into designs of surpassing beauty. And in most of the palaces the floors were mosaics of beryl and lapis-lazuli and sardonyx and carbuncle and other choice materials, so disposed that the beholder might fancy himself walking over beds of the rarest flowers. And there were likewise fountains, which cast scented waters about in pleasing jets arranged with cunning art. Outshining all others was the palace of the kings of Mnar and of the lands adjacent. On a pair of golden crouching lions rested the throne, many steps above the gleaming floor. And it was wrought of one piece of ivory, though no man lives who knows whence so vast a piece could have come. In that palace there were also many galleries, and many amphitheatres where lions and men and elephants battled at the pleasure of the kings. Sometimes the amphitheatres were flooded with water conveyed from the lake in mighty aqueducts, and then were enacted stirring sea-fights, or combats betwixt swimmers and deadly marine things.

Lofty and amazing were the seventeen tower-like temples of Sarnath, fashioned of a bright multi-coloured stone not known elsewhere. A full thousand cubits high stood the greatest among them, wherein the high-priests dwelt with a magnificence scarce less than that of the kings. On the ground were halls as vast and splendid as those of the palaces; where gathered throngs in worship of Zo-Kalar and Tamash and Lobon, the chief gods of Sarnath, whose incense-enveloped shrines were as the thrones of monarchs. Not like the eikons of other gods were those of Zo-Kalar and Tamash and Lobon, for so close to life were they that one might swear the graceful bearded gods themselves sate on the ivory thrones. And up unending steps of shining zircon was the tower-chamber, wherefrom the high-priests looked out over the city and the plains and the lake by day; and at the cryptic moon and significant stars and planets, and their reflections in the lake, by night. Here was done the very secret and ancient rite in detestation of Bokrug, the water-lizard, and here rested the altar of chrysolite which bore the DOOM-scrawl of Taran-Ish.

Wonderful likewise were the gardens made by Zokkar the olden king. In the centre of Sarnath they lay, covering a great space and encircled by a high wall. And they were surmounted by a mighty dome of glass, through which shone the sun and moon and stars and planets when it was clear, and from which were hung fulgent images of the sun and moon and stars and planets when it was not clear. In summer the gardens were cooled with fresh odorous breezes skilfully wafted by fans, and in winter they were heated with concealed fires, so that in those gardens it was always spring. There ran little streams over bright pebbles, dividing meads of green and gardens of many hues, and spanned by a multitude of bridges. Many were the waterfalls in their courses, and many were the lilied lakelets into which they expanded. Over the streams and lakelets rode white swans, whilst the music of rare birds chimed in with the melody of the waters. In ordered terraces rose the green banks, adorned here and there with bowers of vines and sweet blossoms, and seats and benches of marble and porphyry. And there were many small shrines and temples where one might rest or pray to small gods.

Each year there was celebrated in Sarnath the feast of the destroying of Ib, at which time wine, song, dancing, and merriment of every kind abounded. Great honours were then paid to the shades of those who had annihilated the odd ancient beings, and the memory of those beings and of their elder gods was derided by dancers and lutanists crowned with roses from the gardens of Zokkar. And the kings would look out over the lake and curse the bones of the dead that lay beneath it. At first the high-priests liked not these festivals, for there had descended amongst them queer tales of how the sea-green eikon had vanished, and how Taran-Ish had died from fear and left a warning. And they said that from their high tower they sometimes saw lights beneath the waters of the lake. But as many years passed without calamity even the priests laughed and cursed and joined in the orgies of the feasters. Indeed, had they not themselves, in their high tower, often performed the very ancient and secret rite in detestation of Bokrug, the water-lizard? And a thousand years of riches and delight passed over Sarnath, wonder of the world and pride of all mankind.

Gorgeous beyond thought was the feast of the thousandth year of the destroying of Ib. For a decade had it been talked of in the land of Mnar, and as it drew nigh there came to Sarnath on horses and camels and elephants men from Thraa, Ilarnek, and

9. The vale of Pnath, a vast, lightless valley in the dreamland, also appears in *The Dream-Quest of Unknown Kadath* and is the subject of a story by Robert Blake, who appears in the last story Lovecraft wrote, "The Haunter of the Dark"; see the previous volume, pp. 779–806.

10. Another geographical feature mentioned in "The Quest of Iranon."

Kadatheron, and all the cities of Mnar and the lands beyond. Before the marble walls on the appointed night were pitched the pavilions of princes and the tents of travellers, and all the shore resounded with the song of happy revellers. Within his banquet-hall reclined Nargis-Hei, the king, drunken with ancient wine from the vaults of conquered Pnath,[9] and surrounded by feasting nobles and hurrying slaves. There were eaten many strange delicacies at that feast; peacocks from the isles of Nariel in the Middle Ocean, young goats from the distant hills of Implan, heels of camels from the Bnazic desert,[10] nuts and spices from Cydathrian groves, and pearls from wave-washed Mtal dissolved in the vinegar of Thraa. Of sauces there were an untold number, prepared by the subtlest cooks in all Mnar, and suited to the palate of every feaster. But most prized of all the viands were the great fishes from the lake, each of vast size, and served up on golden platters set with rubies and diamonds.

Whilst the king and his nobles feasted within the palace, and viewed the crowning dish as it awaited them on golden platters, others feasted elsewhere. In the tower of the great temple the priests held revels, and in pavilions without the walls the princes of neighbouring lands made merry. And it was the high-priest Gnai-Kah who first saw the shadows that descended from the gibbous moon into the lake, and the damnable green mists that arose from the lake to meet the moon and to shroud in a sinister haze the towers and the domes of fated Sarnath. Thereafter those in the towers and without the walls beheld strange lights on the water, and saw that the grey rock Akurion, which was wont to rear high above it near the shore, was almost submerged. And fear grew vaguely yet swiftly, so that the princes of Ilarnek and of far Rokol took down and folded their tents and pavilions and departed for the river Ai, though they scarce knew the reason for their departing.

Then, close to the hour of midnight, all the bronze gates of Sarnath burst open and emptied forth a frenzied throng that blackened the plain, so that all the visiting princes and travellers fled away in fright. For on the faces of this throng was writ a madness born of horror unendurable, and on their tongues were words so terrible that no hearer paused for proof. Men whose eyes were wild with fear shrieked aloud of the sight within the king's banquet-hall, where through the windows were seen no longer the forms of Nargis-Hei and his nobles and slaves, but a horde of indescribable green voiceless things with bulging eyes, pouting, flabby lips, and curious ears; things which danced horribly, bearing in their paws golden platters set with rubies and diamonds containing uncouth flames. And the princes and travellers, as they fled from the doomed city of Sarnath on horses and camels and elephants, looked again upon the mist-begetting lake and saw the grey rock Akurion was quite submerged.

Through all the land of Mnar and the lands adjacent spread the tales of those who had fled from Sarnath, and caravans sought that accursed city and its precious metals no more. It was long ere any traveller went thither, and even then only the brave and adventurous young men of distant Falona dared make the journey; adventurous young men of yellow hair and blue eyes, who are no kin to the men of Mnar. These men indeed went to the lake to view Sarnath; but though they found the vast still lake itself, and the grey rock Akurion which rears high above it near the shore, they beheld not the wonder of the world and pride of all mankind. Where once had risen walls of three hundred cubits[11] and towers yet higher, now stretched only the marshy shore, and where once had dwelt fifty millions of men now crawled only the detestable green water-lizard. Not even the mines of precious metal remained, for DOOM had come to Sarnath.

But half buried in the rushes was spied a curious green idol of stone; an exceedingly ancient idol coated with seaweed and chiselled in the likeness of Bokrug, the great water-lizard. That idol, enshrined in the high temple at Ilarnek, was subsequently worshipped beneath the gibbous moon throughout the land of Mnar.

11. Again, an ancient measure of length that varied from culture to culture—between 18 and 21 inches (450 and 525 millimeters), said to be the length of the forearm. The *Jewish Encyclopedia* notes that all early measurements were based upon body parts—which are variable, requiring standardization: into such units as the "ell," of which there were two, of different lengths: the first equal to a cubit (six handbreadths) and the second to a cubit plus a handbreadth.

The Terrible Old Man[1]

The first story by HPL explicitly set in New England, in the invented town of Kingsport, the tale combines certain Dunsanian elements (for example, robberies gone wrong) with hints of magic and mythology. Although it is the shortest of any of Lovecraft's significant stories, the figure of the Terrible Old Man is powerful and reappears in later work. It also unsubtly expresses Lovecraft's twisted desire for the ethnic cleansing of New England.

1. Written in early 1920, the story first appeared in *The Tryout* 7, no. 4 (July 1921), 10–14. It was reprinted in *Weird Tales* 8, no. 2 (August 1926), 191–92.

2. Note that the names are Italian, Polish, and Portuguese, respectively.

3. "Locating whatever might have been Lovecraft's model for the Terrible Old Man's House in Marblehead [Kingsport], however, presents a problem," writes Philip A. Shreffler, in *The H. P. Lovecraft Companion* (Westport, CT, and London: Greenwood Press, 1977).

> There is indeed a Water Street in Marblehead, and it is "near the sea" (and the Boston Yacht Club!). But actually Water Street is nothing more than a dead-end circle at the end of Front Street, which runs along the Marblehead harbor; Water Street itself is only about 150 feet long and has on it only one house, which is not particularly evocative. . . . However, if we can assume . . . that Lovecraft applied the name of one street to its own extension, then Front Street becomes

t was the design of Angelo Ricci and Joe Czanek and Manuel Silva[2] to call on the Terrible Old Man. This old man dwells all alone in a very ancient house in Water Street near the sea,[3] and is reputed to be both exceedingly rich and exceedingly feeble; which forms a situation very attractive to men of the profession of Messrs. Ricci, Czanek, and Silva, for that profession was nothing less dignified than robbery.

The inhabitants of Kingsport[4] say and think many things about the Terrible Old Man which generally keep him safe from the attentions of gentlemen like Mr. Ricci and his colleagues, despite the almost certain fact that he hides a fortune of indefinite magnitude somewhere about his musty and venerable abode. He is, in truth, a very strange person, believed to have been a captain of East India clipper ships[5] in his day; so old that no one can remember when he was young, and so taciturn that few know his real name. Among the gnarled trees in the front yard of his aged and neglected place he maintains a strange collection of large stones, oddly grouped and painted so that they resemble the idols in some obscure Eastern temple. This collection frightens away most of the small boys who love to taunt the Terrible Old Man about his long white hair and beard, or to break the small-paned windows of his dwelling with wicked missiles; but there are other things which frighten the older and more curious folk who sometimes steal up to the house to peer in through the dusty panes. These folk say that on a table in a bare room on the ground floor are many peculiar bottles, in each a small piece of lead suspended pendulum-wise from a string. And they say that the Terrible Old Man talks to these bottles, addressing them by such names as Jack, Scar-Face, Long Tom, Spanish Joe, Peters, and Mate Ellis, and that whenever he speaks to a bottle the little lead pendulum within makes certain definite vibrations as if in answer. Those who have watched the tall, lean, Terrible Old Man in these peculiar conversations do not watch him again. But Angelo Ricci and Joe Czanek and Manuel Silva were not of Kingsport blood; they were of that new and heterogeneous alien stock which lies outside the charmed circle of New England life and traditions,[6] and they saw in the Terrible Old Man merely a tottering, almost helpless greybeard, who could not walk without the aid of his knotted cane, and whose thin, weak hands shook pitifully. They were really quite sorry in their way for the lonely, unpopular old fellow, whom everybody shunned, and at whom all the dogs barked singularly. But business is business, and to a robber whose soul is in his profession, there is a lure and a challenge about a very old and very feeble man who has no account at

The Pirate's Hideout, 116 Front Street, Marblehead, Massachusetts, 2017. In his *H. P. Lovecraft Companion*, Philip A. Shreffler proposes that this building was Lovecraft's inspiration for the home of "The Terrible Old Man." However, Lovecraft wasn't familiar with Marblehead at the time he wrote the story.

Photograph courtesy of Donovan K. Loucks

transformed into the fictional Water Street. And this theory seems particularly attractive because of one small single-room building about halfway down Front Street. Nestled sideways into the hillside incongruously among the large Federal houses of the area is the Pirate's Hideout, which is also variously known as the fisherman's shack and the cordwainer's shop. . . . Several legends surround this tiny hut, which stands just back from what is locally called Oakum Bay. Some say that pirate treasure was exchanged for goods there, while another tale maintains that on certain nights a person standing near the Pirate's Hideout may hear, borne on the east wind, the terrified screams of a woman murdered by pirates and buried in the lower marshes. . . . Although there are only a couple of gnarled trees near the Pirate's Hideout, and no curiously painted stones at all, there is the maritime connection and legends macabre enough to make the place stick in Lovecraft's imagination. (97–98)

It should be noted that this is all probably wishful thinking at best; HPL did not visit Marblehead until 1922.

4. A fictional seaport of New England, about which more is revealed in "The Festival," written in October 1923. All that can be discerned here is that it is a "little town" on the coast of the Atlantic, containing the probably roughly parallel Ship Street and Water Street (probably roughly parallel because the property of the Terrible Old Man had its front gate on Water Street and its back gate on Ship Street). Water Street is described below as "near the sea." In 1931, HPL expressly stated that Kingsport was a disguised version of Marblehead, Massachusetts (see "The Picture in the House," in the previous volume, pp. 35–44, note 7), but there are similarities to Salem as well (see "The Festival," pp. 103–13, note 11, in the same volume).

5. The "clipper ships" were square-rigged wooden (and, after the 1860s, sometimes iron ore) sailing ships, with three or more masts and a length five times their width. The East India Company, known colloquially as the John Company, traded between England, India, and China and, operating nearly as a nation unto itself, maintained an army and printed and used a proprietary currency. By the last quarter of the eighteenth century, one of the principal commodities exported from India (mainly from Rangpur, in Bengal Province) to China by the British was opium, used as payment for highly sought-after goods (including silk, tea, and porcelain) from China then brought to the West. Widespread addiction to opium forced a ban on its importation, whereupon the East India Company subcontracted distribution to private shipowners who operated in the so-called country trade (purchasing the drug at auctions in Kolkata and Mumbai). These country traders then sold to Chinese smugglers plying the waters of the South China Sea and the Shiziyang (the upper channel of the Pearl River estuary), from whom they received payment in silver and gold. "The Chinese coast from Macao to Chusan is now the constant cruising ground of twenty opium ships. The waters of Canton are converted into one grand rendezvous for more than thirty opium boats," reported the *Chinese Repository*, a Protestant missionary periodical, in 1838. Five years later, the Rev. W. M. Lowrie, en route to Amoy, recorded in his diary that the three main "opium depots" were at Tongshan (or Tongsan) Harbor, in Howtowshan (How-tow-shan) Bay, and on Namoa Island. See Zheng Yangwen, *The Social Life of Opium in China* (Cam-

the bank, and who pays for his few necessities at the village store with Spanish gold and silver minted two centuries ago.

Messrs. Ricci, Czanek, and Silva selected the night of April 11th for their call. Mr. Ricci and Mr. Silva were to interview the poor old gentleman, whilst Mr. Czanek waited for them and their presumable metallic burden with a covered motor-car in Ship Street, by the gate in the tall rear wall of their host's grounds. Desire to avoid needless explanations in case of unexpected police intrusions prompted these plans for a quiet and unostentatious departure.

As prearranged, the three adventurers started out separately in order to prevent any evil-minded suspicions afterward. Messrs. Ricci and Silva met in Water Street by the old man's front gate, and although they did not like the way the moon shone down[7] upon the painted stones through the budding branches of the gnarled trees, they had more important things to think about than mere idle superstition. They feared it might be unpleasant work making the Terrible Old Man loquacious concerning his hoarded gold and silver, for aged sea-captains are notably stubborn and perverse. Still, he was very old and very feeble, and there were two visitors. Messrs. Ricci and Silva were experienced in the art of making unwilling persons voluble, and the screams of a weak and exceptionally venerable man can be easily muffled. So they moved up to the one lighted window and heard the Terrible Old Man talking childishly to his bottles with pendulums. Then they donned masks and knocked politely at the weather-stained oaken door.

Waiting seemed very long to Mr. Czanek as he fidgeted restlessly in the covered motor-car by the Terrible Old Man's back gate in Ship Street. He was more than ordinarily tender-hearted, and he did not like the hideous screams he had heard in the ancient house just after the hour appointed for the deed. Had he not told his colleagues to be as gentle as possible with the pathetic old sea-captain? Very nervously he watched that narrow oaken gate in the high and ivy-clad stone wall. Frequently he consulted his watch, and wondered at the delay. Had the old man died before revealing where his treasure was hidden, and had a thorough search become necessary? Mr. Czanek did not like to wait so long in the dark in such a place. Then he sensed a soft tread or tapping on the walk inside the gate, heard a gentle fumbling at the rusty latch, and saw the narrow, heavy door swing inward. And in the pallid glow of the single dim street-lamp he strained his eyes to see what his colleagues had brought out of that sinister house which loomed so close behind. But when he looked, he did not see what he had expected; for his colleagues were not there at all, but only the Terrible Old Man leaning quietly on his knotted cane and smiling hideously. Mr. Czanek had never before noticed the colour of that man's eyes; now he saw that they were yellow.[8]

Little things make considerable excitement in little towns, which is the reason that Kingsport people talked all that spring and summer about the three unidentifiable bodies, horribly slashed as with many cutlasses, and horribly mangled as by the tread of many cruel boot-heels, which the tide washed in. And some people even spoke of things as trivial as the deserted motor-car found in Ship Street, or certain especially inhuman cries, probably of a stray animal or migratory bird, heard in the night by wakeful citizens. But in this idle village gossip the Terrible Old Man took no interest at all. He was by nature reserved, and when one is aged and feeble one's reserve is doubly strong. Besides, so ancient a sea-captain must have witnessed scores of things much more stirring in the far-off days of his unremembered youth.[9]

bridge: Cambridge University Press, 2005), 105.

6. Toward the end of the nineteenth century, as the area around Providence industrialized, the immigrant population changed from largely English, Irish, German, and Swedish to eastern European, southern European, and Mediterranean.

7. The moon was in its third quarter on April 11, 1920; however, on April 11, 1919, the previous year, the moon was nearing fullness (the full moon was April 15). But April 11, 1920, was a Sunday night, an appealing day for the criminals to carry out their attack because the streets would not be busy; April 11 was a Friday in 1919.

8. Donald R. Burleson, in "'The Terrible Old Man': A Deconstruction," *Lovecraft Studies* 15 (Fall 1987), 65–68, suggests that the man here represents a god reborn. Carl Buchanan explores this and the mythic foundations of the story in detail in "'The Terrible Old Man': A Myth of the Devouring Father," *Lovecraft Studies* 15 (Fall 1987), 19–31.

9. Peter Cannon writes, "Altogether the Terrible Old Man, however much Lovecraft meant the reader to sympathize with the 'victim' of the tale rather than the thieves, comes off as an unpleasant creature, not really human" ("Lovecraft's Old Men," *Nyctalops* 3, no. 2 [March 1981], 13).

The Cats of Ulthar[1]

In this Dunsanian tale of the justice of the gods, one of Lovecraft's favorites, he shares some of his own love of cats. He weaves a story set in what would become part of his fictional landscape, the outliers of his dreamland, with characters who would reappear in later tales. Some have tried to incorporate this story into the so-called Cthulhu Mythos, but the gods who appear here seem only distant relations of the terrible figures found in tales such as "The Call of Cthulhu" and "The Haunter of the Dark."

1. "The Cats of Ulthar" was written in June 1920 and published that year in *The Tryout* 6, no. 11, 3–9. It was reprinted in *Weird Tales* 7, no. 2 (February 1926), 252–54, and again in *Weird Tales* 21, no. 2 (February 1933), 259–61. The story was later republished as a booklet under the imprint of the Dragon-Fly Press, in Florida, an extremely limited printing by HPL's friend Robert Barlow in 1935. It would not have been overlooked by HPL that the Latin "*ultor*" means "avenger."

2. The town of Ulthar reappears in "The Other Gods," pp. 106–10, below, and in other stories.

3. Presumably this refers to the Latin name for Egypt, rather than the ruler Aegyptus, who in Greek mythology was an early ruler of Egypt and the twin brother of Danaus.

4. Since antiquity, Meroë has been described variously as a region, a "commercial state," and a city. It is located south of the confluence of the Atbarah

It is said that in Ulthar,[2] which lies beyond the river Skai, no man may kill a cat; and this I can verily believe as I gaze upon him who sitteth purring before the fire. For the cat is cryptic, and close to strange things which men cannot see. He is the soul of antique Ægyptus,[3] and bearer of tales from forgotten cities in Meroë[4] and Ophir.[5] He is the kin of the jungle's lords, and heir to the secrets of hoary and sinister Africa. The Sphinx is his cousin, and he speaks her language; but he is more ancient than the Sphinx, and remembers that which she hath forgotten.

In Ulthar, before ever the burgesses forbade the killing of cats, there dwelt an old cotter[6] and his wife who delighted to trap and slay the cats of their neighbours. Why they did this I know not; save that many hate the voice of the cat in the night, and take it ill that cats should run stealthily about yards and gardens at twilight. But whatever the reason, this old man and woman took pleasure in trapping and slaying every cat which came near to their hovel; and from some of the sounds heard after dark, many villagers fancied that the manner of slaying was exceedingly peculiar. But the villagers did not discuss such things with the old man and his wife; because of the habitual expression on the withered faces of the two, and because their cottage was so small and so darkly hidden under spreading oaks at the back of a neglected yard. In truth, much as the owners of cats hated these odd folk, they feared them more; and instead of berating them as brutal assassins, merely took care that no cherished pet or mouser should stray toward the remote hovel under the dark trees. When through some unavoidable oversight a cat was missed, and sounds heard after dark, the loser would lament impotently; or console himself by thanking Fate that it was not one of his children who had thus vanished. For the people of Ulthar were simple, and knew not whence it is all cats first came.

One day a caravan of strange wanderers from the South entered the narrow cobbled streets of Ulthar. Dark wanderers they were,[7] and unlike the other roving folk who passed through the village twice every year. In the market-place they told fortunes for silver, and bought gay beads from the merchants. What was the land of these wanderers none could tell; but it was seen that they were given to strange prayers, and that they had painted on the sides of their wagons strange figures with human bodies and the heads of cats, hawks, rams, and lions. And the leader of the caravan wore a head-dress with two horns and a curious disc betwixt the horns.

There was in this singular caravan a little boy with no father or mother, but only a tiny black kitten to cherish. The plague had not been kind to him, yet had left him this small furry thing to mitigate his sorrow; and when one is very young, one can find great relief in the lively antics of a black kitten. So the boy whom the dark people called Menes smiled more often than he wept as he sate playing with his graceful kitten on the steps of an oddly painted wagon.

On the third morning of the wanderers' stay in Ulthar, Menes could not find his kitten; and as he sobbed aloud in the market-place certain villagers told him of the old man and his wife, and of sounds heard in the night. And when he heard these things his sobbing gave place to meditation, and finally to prayer. He stretched out his arms toward the sun and prayed in a tongue no villager could understand; though indeed the villagers did not try very hard to understand, since their attention was mostly taken up by the sky and the odd shapes the clouds were assuming. It was very peculiar, but as the little boy uttered his petition there seemed to form overhead the shadowy, nebulous figures of exotic

and Nile Rivers, about 150 miles (240 kilometers) northeast of Khartoum; writing in the fifth century, Herodotus estimated it to be "two months' journey south of Aswan" (see Stanley M. Burnstein, "Herodotus and the Emergence of Meroë," *Journal of the Society for the Study of Egyptian Antiquities* 11 [1978]: 4). When an Egyptian army overran Napata in 590 BCE, Meroë became the capital of the kingdom of Kush (Nubia) and the location of its court. For a useful brief summary of Meroë's politics, its trade and technology, its stelae, baths, and pyramids, its language and script, its matriarchal tradition, and its sacking and fall in 350 CE by an army from the kingdom of Axum, or Aksum (present-day Ethiopia), see Helen Chapin Metz and LaVerle Berry, eds., *Sudan: A Country Study*, with illustrations from the Thomas Leiper Kane Collection in the Library of Congress Hebraic Section (Washington, DC: Federal Research Division, Library of Congress, 1992; rev. 2015), 5–9.

The Meroë pyramids in Sudan.
iStock.com

5. Ophir is a region mentioned in Genesis but of uncertain location, variously placed in India, Africa, Israel, and elsewhere. It figures in Lovecraft's friend Robert E. Howard's tales of Conan the Cimmerian (most often referred to as "the Cimmerian" or "the barbarian" in the stories, the first of which was written in 1932, and known largely as Conan the

Barbarian since the 1982 film of the same name, directed by John Milius and starring Arnold Schwarzenegger in the title role; for a profile of Milius, see Thomas H. Green, "John Milius: The Craziest Man in Hollywood?," *Telegraph*, November 1, 2013). The Howard stories are set in a mythical past twelve thousand years ago. David McIntee, in *Fortune and Glory: A Treasure Hunter's Handbook* (London: Bloomsbury, 2016), tells the story of Edgar Rice Burroughs's earlier use, in *The Return of Tarzan* (1913), of the fictional place-name Opar, derived from the biblical Ophir, or Sophir, presumed to have been the site of King Solomon's gold (31–34). (HPL was an early fan of Burroughs, expressing effusive praise in a letter published in the March 7, 1914, issue of *All-Story* magazine.) McIntee places Solomon's mines squarely in Kudiramalai, Sri Lanka (39–41).

6. A tenant given the use of a cottage in exchange for labor, cash, or cloth. Adrienne D. Hood, in *The Weaver's Craft: Cloth Commerce, and Industry in Early Pennsylvania* (Philadelphia: University of Pennsylvania Press, 2003), notes the prevalence of the practice in the early eighteenth century in Northern Ireland, Scotland, and Germany, and its importation to America (26–27).

7. Cf. Lord Dunsany's "Idle Days on the Yann," first published in 1910: "And the Wanderers were a weird, dark tribe, that once in every seven years came down from the peaks of Mloon." HPL likely read the tale before composing "The Cats of Ulthar."

8. Atal has become a priest by the time of "The Other Gods," pp. 106–10, below, and an old man by the time of *The Dream-Quest of Unknown Kadath*, pp. 329–432, below.

things; of hybrid creatures crowned with horn-flanked discs. Nature is full of such illusions to impress the imaginative.

That night the wanderers left Ulthar, and were never seen again. And the householders were troubled when they noticed that in all the village there was not a cat to be found. From each hearth the familiar cat had vanished; cats large and small, black, grey, striped, yellow, and white. Old Kranon, the burgomaster, swore that the dark folk had taken the cats away in revenge for the killing of Menes' kitten; and cursed the caravan and the little boy. But Nith, the lean notary, declared that the old cotter and his wife were more likely persons to suspect; for their hatred of cats was notorious and increasingly bold. Still, no one durst complain to the sinister couple; even when little Atal, the innkeeper's son,[8] vowed that he had at twilight seen all the cats of Ulthar in that accursed yard under the trees, pacing very slowly and solemnly in a circle around the cottage, two abreast, as if in performance of some unheard-of rite of beasts. The villagers did not know how much to believe from so small a boy; and though they feared that the evil pair had charmed the cats to their death, they preferred not to chide the old cotter till they met him outside his dark and repellent yard.

So Ulthar went to sleep in vain anger; and when the people awaked at dawn—behold! every cat was back at his accustomed hearth! Large and small, black, grey, striped, yellow, and white, none was missing. Very sleek and fat did the cats appear, and sonorous with purring content. The citizens talked with one another of the affair, and marvelled not a little. Old Kranon again insisted that it was the dark folk who had taken them, since cats did not return alive from the cottage of the ancient man and his wife. But all agreed on one thing: that the refusal of all the cats to eat their portions of meat or drink their saucers of milk was exceedingly curious. And for two whole days the sleek, lazy cats of Ulthar would touch no food, but only doze by the fire or in the sun.

It was fully a week before the villagers noticed that no lights were appearing at dusk in the windows of the cottage under the trees. Then the lean Nith remarked that no one had seen the old man or his wife since the night the cats were away. In another week the burgomaster decided to overcome his fears and call at the strangely silent dwelling as a matter of duty, though in doing so he was careful to take with him Shang the blacksmith and Thul the cutter of stone as witnesses. And when they had broken down the frail door they found only this: two cleanly picked human skeletons on the earthen floor, and a number of singular beetles crawling in the shadowy corners.

There was subsequently much talk among the burgesses of Ulthar. Zath, the coroner, disputed at length with Nith, the lean notary; and Kranon and Shang and Thul were overwhelmed with questions. Even little Atal, the innkeeper's son, was closely questioned and given a sweetmeat as reward. They talked of the old cotter and his wife, of the caravan of dark wanderers, of small Menes and his black kitten, of the prayer of Menes and of the sky during that prayer, of the doings of the cats on the night the caravan left, and of what was later found in the cottage under the dark trees in the repellent yard.

And in the end the burgesses passed that remarkable law which is told of by traders in Hatheg and discussed by travellers in Nir;[9] namely, that in Ulthar no man may kill a cat.[10]

9. Hatheg and Nir are mentioned again in "The Other Gods" and *The Dream-Quest of Unknown Kadath.*

10. Duncan Norris, in "Lovecraft and Egypt: A Closer Examination," *Lovecraft Annual* 10 (2016), 8, notes that Diodorus Siculus, in his *Bibliotheca Historica,* claimed that he had personal knowledge that "when one of the Romans killed a cat and the multitude rushed in a crowd to his house, neither the officials sent by the king to beg the man off nor the fear of Rome which all the people felt were enough to save the man from punishment, even though his act had been an accident" (Loeb Classical Library, §1.83, trans. C. H. Oldfather).

Facts concerning the Late Arthur Jermyn and His Family[1]

A regular theme of Lovecraft's fiction is the inexorable weight of heredity and ancestral sins on the present generation. Lovecraft certainly feared the taint of his own parents' madness (both died, it will be recalled, in the same asylum), and he was compelled to write again and again, in tales such as "The Rats in the Walls" and The Case of Charles Dexter Ward, *of the crushing burden of the past. Here he combines the theme with another that he would express masterfully in "The Call of Cthulhu": Sometimes it is better to remain ignorant!*

1. The story was written in 1920 and first published in *The Wolverine* (March 1921), 3–11, and (June 1921), 6–11. It was republished in *Weird Tales* 3, no. 4 (April 1924), 15–18, under the title "The White Ape," and in *Weird Tales* 25, no. 5 (May 1935), 642–48, as "Arthur Jermyn."

2. Likely the theories of Charles Darwin regarding evolution. Lovecraft is said to have read, if not Darwin, then Hugh Elliot (who had translated the early evolutionist Jean-Baptiste Lamarck) and Ernst Haeckel, thereby arriving at an imperfect—or distorted—understanding of natural selection. At this period in his career, he is also said to have been skeptical about Einstein's theory of relativity. In an April 1920 letter to the Gallomo (*Letters to Alfred Galpin*, edited by S. T. Joshi and David E. Schultz [New York: Hippocampus Press, 2003], 75), he referred to Einstein's own view that only twelve living men could fully compre-

I.

LIFE IS A hideous thing, and from the background behind what we know of it peer daemoniacal hints of truth which make it sometimes a thousandfold more hideous. Science, already oppressive with its shocking revelations,[2] will perhaps be the ultimate exterminator of our human species—if separate species we be—for its reserve of unguessed horrors could never be borne by mortal brains if loosed upon the world.[3] If we knew what we are, we should do as Sir Arthur Jermyn did; and Arthur Jermyn soaked himself in oil and set fire to his clothing one night. No one placed the charred fragments in an urn or set a memorial to him who had been; for certain papers and a certain boxed *object* were found, which made men wish to forget. Some who knew him do not admit that he ever existed.

Arthur Jermyn went out on the moor and burned himself after seeing the boxed *object* which had come from Africa. It was this *object*, and not his peculiar personal appearance, which made him end his life. Many would have disliked to live if possessed of the peculiar features of Arthur Jermyn, but he had been a poet and scholar and had not minded. Learning was in his blood, for his great-grandfather, Sir Robert Jermyn, Bart., had been an anthropologist of note,[4] whilst his great-great-great-grandfather, Sir Wade Jermyn, was one of the earliest explorers of the Congo region,[5] and had written eruditely of its tribes, animals, and supposed antiquities. Indeed, old Sir Wade had possessed an intellectual zeal amounting almost to a mania; his bizarre conjectures on a prehistoric white Congolese civilisation earning him much ridicule when his book, "Observations on the Several Parts of Africa," was published.[6] In 1765 this fearless explorer had been placed in a madhouse at Huntingdon.[7]

Madness was in all the Jermyns, and people were glad there were not many of them.[8] The line put forth no branches, and Arthur was the last of it. If he had not been, one cannot say what he would have done when the *object* came. The Jermyns never seemed to look quite right—something was amiss, though Arthur was the worst, and the old family portraits in Jermyn House shewed fine faces enough before Sir Wade's time. Certainly, the madness began with Sir Wade, whose wild stories of Africa were at once the delight and terror of his few friends. It shewed in his collection of trophies and specimens, which were not such as a normal man would accumulate and preserve, and appeared strikingly in the Oriental seclusion in which he kept his wife. The latter, he had said, was the daughter of a Portuguese trader whom he had met in Africa; and did not like English ways. She, with an infant son born in Africa, had accompanied him back from the second and longest of his trips, and had gone with him on the third and last, never returning. No one had ever seen her closely, not even the servants; for her disposition had been violent and singular. During her brief stay at Jermyn House she occupied a remote wing, and was waited on by her husband alone. Sir Wade was, indeed, most peculiar in his solicitude for his family; for when he returned to Africa he would permit no one to care for his young son save a loathsome black woman from Guinea. Upon coming back, after the death of Lady Jermyn, he himself assumed complete care of the boy.

But it was the talk of Sir Wade, especially when in his cups, which chiefly led his friends to deem him mad. In a rational age like the eighteenth century it was unwise for a man to talk

"The White Ape," as "Facts concerning the Late Arthur Jermyn and His Family" was titled.
Weird Tales (April 1924)
(artist: William Fred Heitman)

hend the theory. By 1923, when observations of a total solar eclipse provided support for Einstein's theory, HPL began to work his understanding of relativity into his broader philosophy, stating, "All is chance, accident, and ephemeral illusion. . . . All the cosmos is a jest, and fit to be treated only as a jest, and one thing is as true as another" (Letter to James F. Morton, May 26, 1923, in *Selected Letters, 1911–1924*, ed. August Derleth and Donald Wandrei [Sauk City, WI: Arkham House, 1965], 231; hereafter *Selected Letters*, I). Only slowly did he come to the realization that the frightening prospects of the effects of chance and chaos could be limited to the subatomic world. See S. T. Joshi's "Topical References in Lovecraft," 40, for a discussion of HPL's assimilation of Einstein's theories.

The greatest antagonist, however, Lovecraft contended, was *change*: "Change is the enemy of everything really worth cherishing. It is the remover of landmarks, the destroyer of all which is homelike and comforting, and the constant symbol and reminder of decay and death" (Letter to Helen V. Sully, October 28, 1934, in H. P. Lovecraft, *Selected Letters, 1934–1937*, ed. August Derleth and James Turner [Sauk City, WI: Arkham House Publishers, 1976], 50; hereafter *Selected Letters*, V).

3. The narrator of "The Call of Cthulhu" (in the previous volume, pp. 123–57) expresses a similar sentiment: "The most merciful thing in the world, I think, is the inability of the human mind to correlate all its contents. We live on a placid island of ignorance in the midst of black seas of infinity, and it was not meant that we should voyage far. The sciences, each straining in its own direction, have hitherto harmed us little; but some day the piecing together of dissociated knowledge will open up such terrifying vistas of reality, and of our frightful position therein, that we shall either go mad from the revelation or flee from the deadly light into the peace and safety of a new dark age."

4. For the early history of anthropology (or protoanthropology) as a field of study, see Andrew Curran, "Anthropology," in *Cambridge Companion to the French Enlightenment*, ed. Daniel Brewer (Cambridge: Cambridge University Press, 2014), 29–43.

5. Founded in the late fourteenth century by Lukeni lua Nimi, the kingdom of Kongo once encompassed much of present-day Angola, Cabinda, the Republic of Congo, the Democratic Republic of Congo, and Gabon. Its capital was Mbanza. The earliest European contact occurred long before Sir Wade's explorations, in the summer of 1482, when the Portuguese explorer Diego Cão placed a stone marker at the mouth of the uncharted Congo River at what is

about wild sights and strange scenes under a Congo moon; of the gigantic walls and pillars of a forgotten city, crumbling and vine-grown, and of damp, silent, stone steps leading interminably down into the darkness of abysmal treasure-vaults and inconceivable catacombs. Especially was it unwise to rave of the living things that might haunt such a place; of creatures half of the jungle and half of the impiously aged city—fabulous creatures which even a Pliny[9] might describe with scepticism; things that might have sprung up after the great apes had overrun the dying city with the walls and the pillars, the vaults and the weird carvings. Yet after he came home for the last time Sir Wade would speak of such matters with a shudderingly uncanny zest, mostly after his third glass at the Knight's Head;[10] boasting of what he had found in the jungle and of how he had dwelt among terrible ruins known only to him. And finally he had spoken of the living things in such a manner that he was taken to the madhouse. He had shewn little regret when shut into the barred room at Huntingdon, for his mind moved curiously. Ever since his son had commenced to grow out of infancy he had liked his home less and less, till at last he had seemed to dread it. The Knight's Head had been his headquarters, and when he was confined he expressed some vague gratitude as if for protection. Three years later he died.

Wade Jermyn's son Philip was a highly peculiar person. Despite a strong physical resemblance to his father, his appearance and conduct were in many particulars so coarse that he was universally shunned. Though he did not inherit the madness which was feared by some, he was densely stupid and given to brief periods of uncontrollable violence. In frame he was small, but intensely powerful, and was of incredible agility. Twelve years after succeeding to his title he married the daughter of his gamekeeper, a person said to be of gypsy extraction, but before his son was born joined the navy as a common sailor, completing the general disgust which his habits and mesalliance had begun. After the close of the American war[11] he was heard of as a sailor on a merchantman in the African trade, having a kind of reputation for feats of strength and climbing, but finally disappearing one night as his ship lay off the Congo coast.

In the son of Sir Philip Jermyn the now accepted family peculiarity took a strange and fatal turn. Tall and fairly handsome, with a sort of weird Eastern grace despite certain slight oddities of proportion, Robert Jermyn began life as a scholar and investigator. It was he who first studied scientifically the vast collection of relics which his mad grandfather had brought from Africa, and who made the family name as celebrated in ethnology as in exploration. In 1815 Sir Robert married a daughter of the seventh Viscount Brightholme and was subsequently blessed with three children, the eldest and youngest of whom were never publicly seen on account of deformities in mind and body. Saddened by these family misfortunes, the scientist sought relief in work, and made two long expeditions in the interior of Africa. In 1849 his second son, Nevil, a singularly repellent person who seemed to combine the surliness of Philip Jermyn with the hauteur of the Brightholmes, ran away with a vulgar dancer, but was pardoned upon his return in the following year. He came back to Jermyn House a widower with an infant son, Alfred, who was one day to be the father of Arthur Jermyn.

Friends said that it was this series of griefs which unhinged the mind of Sir Robert Jermyn, yet it was probably merely a bit of African folklore which caused the disaster. The elderly scholar had been collecting legends of the Onga tribes[12] near the field of his grandfather's and his own explorations, hoping in some way to account for Sir Wade's wild tales of a lost city peopled by strange hybrid creatures. A certain consistency in the strange papers of his ancestor suggested that the madman's imagination might have been stimulated by native myths. On October 19, 1852, the explorer Samuel Seaton[13] called at Jermyn House with a manuscript of notes collected among the Ongas, believing that certain legends of a grey city of white apes ruled by a white god might prove valuable to the ethnologist. In his conversation he probably supplied many additional details, the nature of which will never be known, since a hideous series of tragedies suddenly burst into being. When Sir Robert Jermyn emerged from his library he left behind the strangled corpse of the explorer, and before he could be restrained, had put an end to all three of his children; the two who were never seen, and the son who had run away. Nevil Jermyn died in the successful defence of his own two-year-old son, who had apparently been included in the old man's

now Shark Point, Angola, thereby staking Portugal's claim to the territory; see "Into Africa: Who Was Diego Cão?," *Smithsonian*, July 5, 2010. Cão made a second voyage in 1485: See University of Amsterdam ethnographer and anthropologist Johannes Fabian's fascinating *Remembering the Present: Painting and Popular History in Zaire* (Berkeley: University of California Press, 1996), 22–23, which features 101 paintings and a narrative by the contemporary Zairean artist Tshibumba Kanda-Matulu. Sir Wade may have been one of the earliest *English* explorers of the region; European exploration of southern and central Africa was very limited until the nineteenth century.

6. S. T. Joshi points out that this detail is often overlooked by scholars: Sir Wade is not merely guilty of miscegenation; rather, he discovered the "true fount of all white civilization," and the white ape is itself a result of miscegenation. "By marrying this white ape, Sir Wade has, as it were, given his descendants an 'extra dose' of the blood of this corrupt race, producing the physiognomic and temperamental anomalies of the Jermyn line" (160). The existence of this "corrupt race," then—and not merely the fact that Sir Wade married the white ape—is the basis for the generalized statement of horror expressed in the opening paragraph of the tale. See S. T. Joshi, "What Happens in 'Arthur Jermyn,'" in *Primal Sources: Essays on H. P. Lovecraft* (New York: Hippocampus Press, 2003), 159–61.

7. Huntingdon, in Cambridgeshire, England, was the birthplace of Oliver Cromwell. S. T. Joshi states, in his annotated collection of Lovecraft, *The Call of Cthulhu and Other Weird Stories* (New York: Penguin, 1999), that "there was no insane asylum in the town of Huntingdon . . . at this time" (366, note 4). While

that may be true, in the sense of a public institution, of which there were very few and even fewer of which were available to nonpaupers, there may well have been several private madhouses in Huntingdon. By the middle of the eighteenth century, there were numerous private madhouses in England, though official information regarding the locations, owners, and so forth is not available for periods prior to 1774. Many madhouses were unlicensed, and many licensed facilities made no official reports. See William Ll. Parry-Jones, *The Trade in Lunacy: A Study of Private Madhouses in England in the Eighteenth and Nineteenth Centuries* (Abingdon, Oxfordshire, UK: Routledge, 2013; 1st ed., 1972), 29. It is not surprising, then, that there is no record of the Huntingdon madhouse in which Sir Wade was placed.

8. The family of Jermyn of Rushbrook, in the county of Suffolk, was, according to the *Herald and Genealogist*, vol. 5 (1870), "though perhaps not so ancient as some other East-Anglian families, was from early times highly allied as well as knightly and considerable." The pedigree of the family begins with Robert Jermyn of Woodton and Hempnall (Norfolk), who died in 1720 and was likely the father of Sir Wade, but the branch of Sir Wade has— not surprisingly, given this history—been omitted from the family tree.

9. Gaius Plinius Secundus (Pliny the Elder), described by Cambridge University classics professor and bestselling writer Mary Beard as "the extraordinary Roman polymath now best remembered as the one celebrity victim of the eruption of Vesuvius in 79 CE" (*SPQR* [New York: Liveright, 2015], 120), is perhaps at least as well known for his *Naturalis Historia* (published ca. 77–79 CE), a casually subversive thirty-seven-volume encyclopedia whose primary value, Beard

madly murderous scheme. Sir Robert himself, after repeated attempts at suicide and a stubborn refusal to utter any articulate sound, died of apoplexy in the second year of his confinement.

Sir Alfred Jermyn was a baronet before his fourth birthday, but his tastes never matched his title. At twenty he had joined a band of music-hall performers, and at thirty-six had deserted his wife and child to travel with an itinerant American circus.[14] His end was very revolting. Among the animals in the exhibition with which he travelled was a huge bull gorilla of lighter colour than the average; a surprisingly tractable beast of much popularity with the performers. With this gorilla Alfred Jermyn was singularly fascinated, and on many occasions the two would eye each other for long periods through the intervening bars. Eventually Jermyn asked and obtained permission to train the animal, astonishing audiences and fellow-performers alike with his success. One morning in Chicago, as the gorilla and Alfred Jermyn were rehearsing an exceedingly clever boxing match,

Barnum & Bailey poster, 1900.

the former delivered a blow of more than usual force, hurting both the body and dignity of the amateur trainer.[15] Of what followed, members of "The Greatest Show on Earth"[16] do not like to speak. They did not expect to hear Sir Alfred Jermyn emit a shrill, inhuman scream, or to see him seize his clumsy antagonist with both hands, dash it to the floor of the cage, and bite fiendishly at its hairy throat. The gorilla was off its guard, but not for long, and before anything could be done by the regular trainer the body which had belonged to a baronet was past recognition.

II.

ARTHUR JERMYN WAS the son of Sir Alfred Jermyn and a music-hall singer of unknown origin. When the husband and father deserted his family, the mother took the child to Jermyn House; where there was none left to object to her presence. She was not without notions of what a nobleman's dignity should be, and saw to it that her son received the best education which limited money could provide. The family resources were now sadly slender, and Jermyn House had fallen into woeful disrepair, but young Arthur loved the old edifice and all its contents. He was not like any other Jermyn who had ever lived, for he was a poet and a dreamer. Some of the neighbouring families who had heard tales of old Sir Wade Jermyn's unseen Portuguese wife declared that her Latin blood must be shewing itself; but most persons merely sneered at his sensitiveness to beauty, attributing it to his music-hall mother, who was socially unrecognised. The poetic delicacy of Arthur Jermyn was the more remarkable because of his uncouth personal appearance. Most of the Jermyns had possessed a subtly odd and repellent cast, but Arthur's case was very striking. It is hard to say just what he resembled, but his expression, his facial angle, and the length of his arms gave a thrill of repulsion to those who met him for the first time.

It was the mind and character of Arthur Jermyn which atoned for his aspect. Gifted and learned, he took highest honours at Oxford and seemed likely to redeem the intellectual fame of his family. Though of poetic rather than scientific tem-

suggests, may be as a work of cultural criticism detailing Roman opulence, social inequality, and depredations caused by or carried out by rulers. Book 36, section 24, contains a chilling, almost offhand reference to mass suicides of laborers who broke under the strain of construction of the Cloaca Maxima, a massive sewer that still today carries Romans' bathroom waste. To halt the contagion of suicide, "the king devised a strange remedy that was never contrived except on that one occasion. He crucified the bodies of all who had died by their own hand, leaving them to be gazed at by their fellow-citizens and also torn to pieces by beasts and birds of prey" (*Pliny's Natural History*, trans. H. Rackham. W. H. S. Jones, and D. E Eichholz [Cambridge, MA, and London: Harvard University Press and William Heinemann, 1949–54], http://www.masseiana.org/pliny.htm/#BOOK XXXVI.

10. There is no longer any trace of this tavern, in Suffolk or elsewhere.

11. Based on the date of Sir Wade's institutionalization in 1765, Wade's son Philip must have served in the British navy during the (American) Revolutionary War (1775–1783). This also fits with the marriage of Philip's son, Robert, in 1815. Robert must have been born just before Philip enlisted in the navy, between 1775 and 1780. The recital of his history as an ethnologist suggests that he married later in life, by this reckoning between ages thirty-five and forty. His second son, Nevil, would have been born in the period 1817–1825, when Robert was in his forties to mid-fifties, making Nevil somewhere between twenty-four and thirty-two when he ran off with the "vulgar dancer." Nevil's son, Arthur, was born in 1850, according to the narrative describing Arthur as two years old in 1852. Sir Robert must have been quite a vigorous man, despite being in his sev-

enties in 1850, to have strangled Samuel Seaton as well as the three adult Jermyn children. Perhaps this vigor was attributable to his genetic makeup.

12. The Tonga, an ethnic and linguistic group centered in the Zambezi basin, live principally in southern Zambia (1.38 million today, comprising 12 percent of the population), northern Zimbabwe (where in the 1950s forcible relocation of sixty thousand residents to make way for construction of the Kariba Dam led to severe food and water deprivation), the Inhambane Province of southeast Mozambique, and other parts of southern Africa, including Malawi and Botswana. The language, Chitonga, of Bantu origin, began to be taught in elementary schools only in 2005; previously, Shona and Ndebele, now spoken by 10 million and 1.6 million, respectively, of the total population of 14.5 million in Zimbabwe (which has sixteen languages), were imposed.

Jermyn may have misunderstood the *T* to be a prefix denoting "the Ongas" and so originated the misnaming. As is evident from W. A. Elmslie's "The Orthography of African Names and the Principles of Nomenclature," *Scottish Geographical Magazine* 7, no. 7 (July 1891), 370–75, there was a great deal of confusion and misunderstanding of the naming principles at work in the various African languages.

13. It is not possible to identify this explorer. Two well-known traveler-explorers, the American John Lloyd Stephens and the British-Australian George William Evans, both died in 1852, but neither under mysterious circumstances; nor did they report any African journeys.

14. That is, in 1886. As will be seen shortly, it was Barnum & Bailey's circus that Jermyn joined.

perament, he planned to continue the work of his forefathers in African ethnology and antiquities, utilising the truly wonderful though strange collection of Sir Wade. With his fanciful mind he thought often of the prehistoric civilisation in which the mad explorer had so implicitly believed, and would weave tale after tale about the silent jungle city mentioned in the latter's wilder notes and paragraphs. For the nebulous utterances concerning a nameless, unsuspected race of jungle hybrids he had a peculiar feeling of mingled terror and attraction; speculating on the possible basis of such a fancy, and seeking to obtain light among the more recent data gleaned by his great-grandfather and Samuel Seaton amongst the Ongas.

In 1911, after the death of his mother, Sir Arthur Jermyn determined to pursue his investigations to the utmost extent. Selling a portion of his estate to obtain the requisite money, he outfitted an expedition and sailed for the Congo. Arranging with the Belgian[17] authorities for a party of guides, he spent a year in the Onga and Kaliri country,[18] finding data beyond the highest of his expectations. Among the Kaliris was an aged chief called Mwanu, who possessed not only a highly retentive memory, but a singular degree of intelligence and interest in old legends. This ancient confirmed every tale which Jermyn had heard, adding his own account of the stone city and the white apes as it had been told to him.

According to Mwanu, the grey city and the hybrid creatures were no more, having been annihilated by the warlike N'bangus[19] many years ago. This tribe, after destroying most of the edifices and killing the live beings, had carried off the stuffed goddess which had been the object of their quest; the white ape-goddess which the strange beings worshipped, and which was held by Congo tradition to be the form of one who had reigned as a princess among those beings. Just what the white ape-like creatures could have been, Mwanu had no idea, but he thought they were the builders of the ruined city. Jermyn could form no conjecture, but by close questioning obtained a very picturesque legend of the stuffed goddess.

The ape-princess, it was said, became the consort of a great white god who had come out of the West. For a long time they had reigned over the city together, but when they had a son all three went away. Later the god and the princess had returned, and upon the death of the princess her divine husband had mummified the body and enshrined it in a vast house of stone, where it was worshipped. Then he had departed alone. The legend here seemed to present three variants. According to one story nothing further happened save that the stuffed goddess became a symbol of supremacy for whatever tribe might possess it. It was for this reason that the N'bangus carried it off. A second story told of the god's return and death at the feet of his enshrined wife. A third told of the return of the son, grown to manhood—or apehood or godhood, as the case might be—yet unconscious of his identity. Surely the imaginative blacks had made the most of whatever events might lie behind the extravagant legendry.

Of the reality of the jungle city described by old Sir Wade, Arthur Jermyn had no further doubt; and was hardly astonished when, early in 1912, he came upon what was left of it. Its size must have been exaggerated, yet the stones lying about proved that it was no mere negro village. Unfortunately no carvings could be found, and the small size of the expedition prevented operations toward clearing the one visible passageway that seemed to lead down into the system of vaults which Sir Wade had mentioned. The white apes and the stuffed goddess were discussed with all the native chiefs of the region, but it remained for a European to improve on the data offered by old Mwanu. M. Verhaeren, Belgian agent at a trading-post on the Congo, believed that he could not only locate but obtain the stuffed goddess, of which he had vaguely heard; since the once mighty N'bangus were now the submissive servants of King Albert's government,[20] and with but little persuasion could be induced to part with the gruesome deity they had carried off. When Jermyn sailed for England, therefore, it was with the exultant probability that he would within a few months receive a priceless ethnological relic confirming the wildest of his great-great-great-grandfather's narratives—that is, the wildest which he had ever heard. Countrymen near Jermyn House had perhaps heard wilder tales handed down from ancestors who had listened to Sir Wade around the tables of the Knight's Head.

Arthur Jermyn waited very patiently for the expected box from M. Verhaeren, meanwhile studying with increased dili-

15. Gavin Callaghan, in "A Reprehensible Habit: H. P. Lovecraft and the Munsey Magazines," in *Lovecraft and Influence: His Predecessors and Successors*, ed. Robert H. Waugh (Lanham, Toronto, and Plymouth, UK: Scarecrow Press, 2013), points out the strong resemblance to the frequent dangerous boxing matches between Akut, the ape-friend of Korak, and Tarzan's son Korak, in *The Son of Tarzan* (1915), by Edgar Rice Burroughs (77).

16. (P. T.) Barnum & (James A.) Bailey's circus, founded in 1871, billed itself as "The Greatest Show on Earth."

17. In the late nineteenth century, the Belgian king Leopold II established his own personal colony in what is now the Democratic Republic of Congo (the name it acquired in 1960), known after 1885 as the Congo Free State. Leopold's exploitation of the country and its inhabitants for the purposes of harvesting rubber took the form of, among other acts of violence, mutilation: children and adults who failed to work hard enough had their right hand chopped off. Public outcry included publication of Joseph Conrad's *Heart of Darkness* (1899); a scathing report by British consul Roger Casement (1903); the unstinting activities of the Congo Reform Association, founded in 1904 and led by Edmund Dene Morel, Dr. Henry Grattan Guinness; and Casement; and Arthur Conan Doyle's *The Crime of the Congo: An Exposé of Belgian Abuses in Africa* (1909), which followed the Belgian government's takeover of the colony in 1908 and its renaming ("the Belgian Congo").

18. "*Kaliri*" is a Swahili verb meaning "to memorize" or "to remember." The Dung Kaliri are a clan in Mongalla Province in South Sudan (northeast Africa) and, according to L. F. Nalder, ed., *A Tribal Survey of Mongalla Province* (London:

Oxford University Press, 1937), members of the larger Bekat clan (120–22). Nalder cites Charles Gabriel Seligman and Brenda Zara Salaman Seligman's *Pagan Tribes of the Nilotic Sudan* (London: George Routledge & Sons, 1932) as the foremost early twentieth-century anthropological and ethnographic authority on the Nilotic cultural history of South Sudan. Two of the Seligmans' principal subjects of study were South Sudan's two largest ethnic groups, the Dinka and the Nuer—descendants of whom sixty years later, fleeing civil war, would famously walk hundreds of miles to northwestern Kenya, where the United Nations' Kakuma Refugee Camp was established for ten thousand "Lost Boys of Sudan." Ranging in age from eight to eighteen, they represented slightly less than half the number who had attempted the flight to safety, some of the latter toddlers valiantly shepherded by children only slightly older than themselves. The survivors arrived at Kakuma (and other refugee camps) having witnessed their charges drowned, starved, shot, even devoured by crocodiles. Among the numerous records of their now-famous struggle are *What Is the What: The Autobiography of Valentino Achak Deng*, a novel by Dave Eggers (San Francisco: McSweeney's 2006) and the feature-length documentaries *Lost Boys of Sudan* (2004), directed by Megan Mylan and Jon Shenk, and *The Lost Boys* (2002), directed by Clive Gordon.

19. According to W. A. Elmslie, note 12, above, the use of the apostrophe is incorrect—the correct tribal name would be Nbangus. There is no record of such a tribe.

20. King Albert I of the Belgians reigned from 1909 to 1934, succeeding Leopold II (his uncle) upon his death.

gence the manuscripts left by his mad ancestor. He began to feel closely akin to Sir Wade, and to seek relics of the latter's personal life in England as well as of his African exploits. Oral accounts of the mysterious and secluded wife had been numerous, but no tangible relic of her stay at Jermyn House remained. Jermyn wondered what circumstance had prompted or permitted such an effacement, and decided that the husband's insanity was the prime cause. His great-great-great-grandmother, he recalled, was said to have been the daughter of a Portuguese trader in Africa. No doubt her practical heritage and superficial knowledge of the Dark Continent had caused her to flout Sir Wade's talk of the interior, a thing which such a man would not be likely to forgive. She had died in Africa, perhaps dragged thither by a husband determined to prove what he had told. But as Jermyn indulged in these reflections he could not but smile at their futility, a century and a half after the death of both of his strange progenitors.

In June, 1913, a letter arrived from M. Verhaeren, telling of the finding of the stuffed goddess. It was, the Belgian averred, a most extraordinary object; an object quite beyond the power of a layman to classify. Whether it was human or simian only a scientist could determine, and the process of determination would be greatly hampered by its imperfect condition. Time and the Congo climate are not kind to mummies; especially when their preparation is as amateurish as seemed to be the case here. Around the creature's neck had been found a golden chain bearing an empty locket on which were armorial designs; no doubt some hapless traveller's keepsake, taken by the N'bangus and hung upon the goddess as a charm. In commenting on the contour of the mummy's face, M. Verhaeren suggested a whimsical comparison; or rather, expressed a humorous wonder just how it would strike his correspondent, but was too much interested scientifically to waste many words in levity. The stuffed goddess, he wrote, would arrive duly packed about a month after receipt of the letter.

The boxed object was delivered at Jermyn House on the afternoon of August 3, 1913, being conveyed immediately to the large chamber which housed the collection of African specimens as arranged by Sir Robert and Arthur. What ensued can best be gathered from the tales of servants and from things and papers later examined. Of the various tales that of aged Soames, the family butler, is most ample and coherent. According to this trustworthy man, Sir Arthur Jermyn dismissed everyone from the room before opening the box, though the instant sound of hammer and chisel shewed that he did not delay the operation. Nothing was heard for some time; just how long Soames cannot exactly estimate, but it was certainly less than a quarter of an hour later that the horrible scream, undoubtedly in Jermyn's voice, was heard. Immediately afterward Jermyn emerged from the room, rushing frantically toward the front of the house as if pursued by some hideous enemy. The expression on his face, a face ghastly enough in repose, was beyond description. When near the front door he seemed to think of something, and turned back in his flight, finally disappearing down the stairs to the cellar. The servants were utterly dumbfounded, and watched at the head of the stairs, but their master did not return. A smell of oil was all that came up from the regions below. After dark a rattling was heard at the door leading from the cellar into the courtyard; and a stable-boy saw Arthur Jermyn, glistening from head to foot with oil and redolent of that fluid, steal furtively out and vanish on the black moor surrounding the house. Then, in an exaltation of supreme horror, everyone saw the end. A spark appeared on the moor, a flame arose, and a pillar of human fire reached to the heavens. The house of Jermyn no longer existed.

The reason why Arthur Jermyn's charred fragments were not collected and buried lies in what was found afterward, principally the thing in the box. The stuffed goddess was a nauseous sight, withered and eaten away, but it was clearly a mummified white ape of some unknown species, less hairy than any recorded variety, and infinitely nearer mankind—quite shockingly so. Detailed description would be rather unpleasant, but two salient particulars must be told, for they fit in revoltingly with certain notes of Sir Wade Jermyn's African expeditions and with the Congolese legends of the white god and the ape-princess. The two particulars in question are these: the arms on the golden

21. The Royal Anthropological Institute of Great Britain and Ireland is the result of the 1871 merger of the Ethnological Society (founded in 1842 and itself a successor to the Aborigines Protection Society, founded in 1837) and the Anthropological Society. The Institute was granted the right to add the word "Royal" in 1907.

locket about the creature's neck were the Jermyn arms, and the jocose suggestion of M. Verhaeren about a certain resemblance as connected with the shrivelled face applied with vivid, ghastly, and unnatural horror to none other than the sensitive Arthur Jermyn, great-great-great-grandson of Sir Wade Jermyn and an unknown wife. Members of the Royal Anthropological Institute[21] burned the thing and threw the locket into a well, and some of them do not admit that Arthur Jermyn ever existed.

The Temple[1]

Like "Dagon," this story combines the setting of the Great War with Lovecraft's suggestions of a far-distant history of humankind (and perhaps other species). Also as in "Dagon," Lovecraft here combines a realistic-seeming series of events with an insidious element of the supernatural. Though some find the portrait of the Prussian naval officer heavy-handed, Lovecraft deftly creates a compelling narrator whose very rigidity empowers the story's unexpected conclusion.

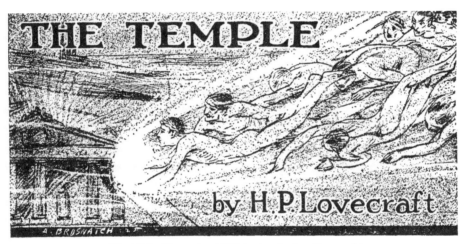

Weird Tales (September 1925) (artist: Andrew Brosnatch)

(Manuscript found on the coast of Yucatan.)[2]

On August 20, 1917,[3] I, Karl Heinrich, Graf von Altberg-Ehrenstein, Lieutenant-Commander in the Imperial German Navy[4] and in charge of the submarine U-29,[5] deposit this bottle and record in the Atlantic Ocean at a point to me unknown but probably about N. Latitude 20°, W. Longitude 35°,[6] where my ship lies disabled on the ocean floor. I do so because of my desire to set certain unusual facts before the public; a thing I shall not in all probability survive to accomplish in person, since the circumstances surrounding me

1. "The Temple" was written in the autumn of 1920, before "Celephaïs" (early November 1920), but not published until it appeared in *Weird Tales* 6, no. 3 (September 1925), 329–36, 429–31. It was reprinted in *Weird Tales* 27, no. 2 (February 1936), 239–44, 246–49.

2. The Yucatán peninsula of Mexico is over three thousand nautical miles from the place where the narrator records depositing the bottle.

3. Although it was Lovecraft's birthday, very little of note occurred in the Great War on this date: On the western front, there was a slight advance of British forces north of Ypres, and the French forces, conducting their third offensive, carried enemy defenses north of Verdun, taking five thousand prisoners. On the eastern front, Russian forces were retiring, while in the south, Italian forces prevailed. Seesawing back and forth until the fall of 1918, when the Allied offensive was successful and the German forces exhausted, the war ended on November 11, 1918, with an armistice.

4. The relatively short-lived Imperial Navy (Kaiserliche Marine) was created out of an existing coast guard (Norddeutsche Bundesmarine) and Prussia's navy; its ships were scuttled at the end of the Great War, in 1919, but in World War II a thousand or more new U-boats would be built.

In the First World War, the navy began with a rather small fleet of about forty *Unterseeboote*, or U-boats, quadrupling the number by 1917. There were roughly three times as many as that by war's end, with construction of an additional two hundred or more said to be underway in the shipyards. While most were designed for deep-sea use, the balance were used in coastal areas, for coastal attacks and minelaying.

There was no such rank as lieutenant-commander in the navy; the ranks were Leutnant zur See (second or sublieutenant at sea), Oberleutnant zur See (senior lieutenant or simply lieutenant at sea), Kapitänleutnant (captain lieutenant), and Kapitän zur See (captain at sea). U-boats were commanded by a captain; perhaps the original captain of the "U-29" died, and a senior officer took command.

5. The last commander of the actual SM (Seine Majestät) *U-29* was the highly

Wittenbergplatz Station, Berlin, Germany.

are as menacing as they are extraordinary, and involve not only the hopeless crippling of the U-29, but the impairment of my iron German will in a manner most disastrous.

On the afternoon of June 18,[7] as reported by wireless to the U-61,[8] bound for Kiel,[9] we torpedoed the British freighter *Victory*,[10] New York to Liverpool, in N. Latitude 45° 16', W. Longitude 28° 34';[11] permitting the crew to leave in boats in order to obtain a good cinema view for the admiralty records. The ship sank quite picturesquely, bow first, the stern rising high out of the water whilst the hull shot down perpendicularly to the bottom of the sea. Our camera missed nothing, and I regret that so fine a reel of film should never reach Berlin. After that we sank the lifeboats with our guns and submerged.[12]

When we rose to the surface about sunset a seaman's body was found on the deck, hands gripping the railing in curious fashion. The poor fellow was young, rather dark, and very handsome; probably an Italian or Greek, and undoubtedly of the *Victory's* crew. He had evidently sought refuge on the very ship which had been forced to destroy his own—one more victim of the unjust war of aggression which the English pig-dogs[13] are waging upon the Fatherland. Our men searched him for souvenirs, and found in his coat pocket a very odd bit of ivory carved to represent a youth's head crowned with laurel. My fellow-officer, Lieut. Klenze, believed that the thing was of great age and artistic value, so took it from the men for himself. How it had ever come into the possession of a common sailor, neither he nor I could imagine.

As the dead man was thrown overboard there occurred two incidents which created much disturbance amongst the crew. The fellow's eyes had been closed; but in the dragging of his body

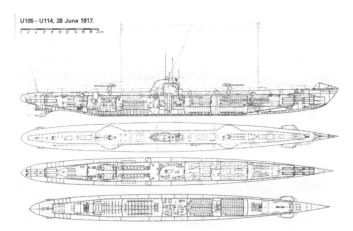

Plans for the German *U-29* submarine?

to the rail they were jarred open, and many seemed to entertain a queer delusion that they gazed steadily and mockingly at Schmidt and Zimmer, who were bent over the corpse. The Boatswain[14] Müller, an elderly man who would have known better had he not been a superstitious Alsatian swine,[15] became so excited by this impression that he watched the body in the water; and swore that after it sank a little it drew its limbs into a swimming position and sped away to the south under the waves. Klenze and I did not like these displays of peasant ignorance, and severely reprimanded the men, particularly Müller.

The next day a very troublesome situation was created by the indisposition of some of the crew. They were evidently suffering

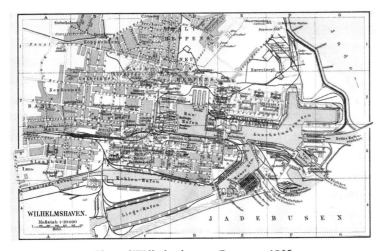

Plan of Wilhelmshaven, Germany, 1905.

decorated thirty-three-year-old Kapitän-leutnant Otto Weddigen. Commissioned in August 1914, the *U-29* had a short length of service, going down with all hands, including Weddigen, on March 18, 1915, in the Pentland Firth, a strait in the north of Scotland, as a result of ramming by HMS *Dreadnought*. (Captain Weddigen had himself sunk eight ships in the war, the first four in 1914, as commander of the SM *U-9*.) The identity of Lovecraft's *U-29* is unknown.

6. About 1,000 nautical miles west of the coast of Africa and about 600 miles west-northwest of the Cape Verde Islands, south of the Tropic of Cancer. The U-boat traveled about 1,450 nautical miles from the site of the attack on the *Victory*.

7. This was a week before the first U.S. troops to take part in the war arrived in France.

8. The *U-61*, after taking part in three patrols, resulting in the sinking of two ships, was struck by a mine (laid by HMS *E51*) on November 29, 1917, and sank with the loss of all hands. It was commanded by Oberleutnant Theodor Schultz, age twenty-nine. A comprehensive accounting of U-boat activity in the two world wars may be found at www.uboat.net.

9. Capital of the state of Schleswig-Holstein and the headquarters of Germany's Baltic Naval Station, Kiel was one of two main commands of the Kaiserliche Marine during the Great War; the second was at Wilhelmshaven, home of the North Sea Naval Station, which hosted the High Seas Fleet. The navy's profusion of bases and complicated command structure served as "a recipe for bureaucratic rivalry" and "confusion in the implementation of policies," argues

Graham Watson, former lecturer in history at the University of Wales at Cardiff, in "Organisation of the Imperial German Navy, 1914–1918," http://www.naval-history.net/XGW-GermanNavy1914-1918.htm. This was borne out in late 1918, when Admiral Reinhard Scheer, head of a "Supreme Command" established only months earlier, advanced a largely secret plan to have the High Seas Fleet take on the Royal Navy in an all-out pitched battle. The German sailors perceived the order to put to sea as suicidal: The fleet was greatly outgunned. Concluding that the war was already lost, they refused to leave port. Scheer's plan was abandoned, but unrest spread from Wilhelmshaven to Kiel and elsewhere. The mutiny sparked a revolution that overthrew the imperial monarchy and established the Weimar Republic. *The Wilhelmshaven Revolt: A Chapter of the Revolutionary Movement in the German Navy, 1918–1919*, a firsthand account by helmsman and frequently jailed activist Ernst Schneider, writing as "Icarus," was published in England in 1943.

10. There is no record of a British (or American) freighter named *Victory* operating in the Great War. Many of the "British" freighters used in the war were built by American shipyards. In America, after 1942, an entire class of expanded versions of the early "Liberty" freighters was named "Victory" and many ships were christened with "Victory" as part of their name.

11. These coordinates mark a spot in the North Atlantic Ocean that is about 360 nautical miles northeast of the Central Group of the Azores and 840 nautical miles southwest of the Irish coast. It is quite near the underwater peak named the Olympus Knoll (N 45°25′, W 27°40′).

Photograph of the German *U-1* submarine.

from the nervous strain of our long voyage, and had had bad dreams. Several seemed quite dazed and stupid; and after satisfying myself that they were not feigning their weakness, I excused them from their duties. The sea was rather rough, so we descended to a depth where the waves were less troublesome. Here we were comparatively calm, despite a somewhat puzzling southward current which we could not identify from our oceanographic charts. The moans of the sick men were decidedly annoying; but since they did not appear to demoralise the rest of the crew, we did not resort to extreme measures. It was our plan to remain where we were and intercept the liner *Dacia*,[16] mentioned in information from agents in New York.

In the early evening we rose to the surface, and found the sea less heavy. The smoke of a battleship was on the northern horizon, but our distance and ability to submerge made us safe. What worried us more was the talk of Boatswain Müller, which grew wilder as night came on. He was in a detestably childish state, and babbled of some illusion of dead bodies drifting past the undersea portholes; bodies which looked at him intensely, and which he recognised in spite of bloating as having seen dying during some of our victorious German exploits. And he said that the young man we had found and tossed overboard was their leader. This was very gruesome and abnormal, so we confined

Müller in irons and had him soundly whipped. The men were not pleased at his punishment, but discipline was necessary. We also denied the request of a delegation headed by Seaman Zimmer, that the curious carved ivory head be cast into the sea.

On June 20, Seamen Bohm and Schmidt, who had been ill the day before, became violently insane. I regretted that no physician was included in our complement of officers, since German lives are precious; but the constant ravings of the two concerning a terrible curse were most subversive of discipline, so drastic steps were taken. The crew accepted the event in a sullen fashion, but it seemed to quiet Müller; who thereafter gave us no trouble. In the evening we released him, and he went about his duties silently.

In the week that followed we were all very nervous, watching for the *Dacia*. The tension was aggravated by the disappearance of Müller and Zimmer, who undoubtedly committed suicide as a result of the fears which had seemed to harass them, though they were not observed in the act of jumping overboard. I was rather glad to be rid of Müller, for even his silence had unfavourably affected the crew. Everyone seemed inclined to be silent now, as though holding a secret fear. Many were ill, but none made a disturbance. Lieut. Klenze chafed under the strain, and was annoyed by the merest trifles—such as the school of dolphins which gathered about the U-29 in increasing numbers, and the growing intensity of that southward current which was not on our chart.

It at length became apparent that we had missed the *Dacia* altogether. Such failures are not uncommon, and we were more pleased than disappointed; since our return to Wilhelmshaven[17] was now in order. At noon June 28 we turned northeastward, and despite some rather comical entanglements with the unusual masses of dolphins were soon under way.

The explosion in the engine room at 2 p.m. was wholly a surprise. No defect in the machinery or carelessness in the men had been noticed, yet without warning the ship was racked from end to end with a colossal shock. Lieut. Klenze hurried to the engine room, finding the fuel-tank and most of the mechanism shattered, and Engineers Raabe and Schneider instantly killed. Our situation had suddenly become grave indeed; for though the

12. Such atrocities were not limited to the Germans. On August 19, 1915, in retaliation for the sinking, in May of that year, of Cunard liner RMS *Lusitania*, which had resulted in more than a thousand passenger casualties, Lieutenant-Commander Godfrey Herbert, commander of the Royal Navy's decoy, or Q-ship, *Baralong*, deceived Kapitänleutnant Bernd Wegener, the commander of the *U-27*, as the latter attacked the British freighter *Nicosian*. Flying a false American flag (America was then neutral), the *Baralong* approached to "rescue" the crew of the *Nicosian*. When it got into close proximity to the *U-27*, it reverted to British colors and fired at point-blank range, sinking the submarine. Lieutenant-Commander Herbert ordered his men to kill the survivors of the sunken U-boat, including those unarmed and swimming in the water, regardless of their attempts to surrender. Reports of the incident were suppressed by the Royal Navy. Despite the German government's call for Herbert to be tried for murder, he received a commendation and a promotion. See Liam Nolan and John E. Nolan, *Secret Victory: Ireland and the War at Sea, 1914–1918* (Blackrock, Ireland: Mercier Press Ltd., 2009), 126–28. HPL made clear his opinion of the sinking of the *Lusitania* in the 1915 poem "The Crime of Crimes":

> Craz'd with the Belgian blood so lately shed,
> The bestial Prussian seeks the ocean's bed;
> In Neptune's realm the wretched coward lurks
> And on the world his wonted evil works.
> Like slinking cur, he bites where none oppose;
> Victorious over babes, his valour grows.

13. "*Schweinehund*" (pig-dog) is said to be a mortal insult to Germans and was frequently used in movies and comics depicting World War II.

14. Boatswain's mates, as they are called in the U.S. Navy, were enlisted men charged with care of the structural components of a ship. The rank or rating did not exist in the German navy; the equivalent rank would be that of a petty officer.

15. The Alsace region in eastern France passed back and forth between French and German control; an Alsatian therefore was not a "real" German, in the eyes of the narrator.

16. Dacia, an ancient land on the Black Sea, included a part of the Carpathian Mountains. There was no ocean liner named *Dacia*. (Two Peninsular and Oriental Steam Navigation Company and Cunard liners had half-rhyming names: *Mongolia* and *Laconia*.) Only hours before the *Baralong* incident (see note 12, above), the *U-24* sank the White Star Line's *Arabic*, bound for the United States, with the loss of forty to forty-four passengers and crew (accounts differ). Three of the casualties were American, which led to vociferous protests by the U.S. government. In all, nineteen Allied ships were sunk by U-boats in August 1915.

Eight days after the sinking of the *U-27* and the *Arabic*, on August 27, Kaiser Wilhelm II, advised by Chancellor Theodore von Bethmann-Hollweg, ordered that passenger ships could only be sunk after warning and the saving of passengers and crews. However, in January 1917, Germany announced a return to its previous policy of unrestricted naval warfare—that is, it would again attack civilian ships as well as military. See "Dagon," in the previous volume, pp. 3–10, note 4.

chemical air regenerators[18] were intact, and though we could use the devices for raising and submerging the ship and opening the hatches as long as compressed air and storage batteries might hold out, we were powerless to propel or guide the submarine.[19] To seek rescue in the lifeboats would be to deliver ourselves into the hands of enemies unreasonably embittered against our great German nation, and our wireless had failed ever since the *Victory* affair to put us in touch with a fellow U-boat of the Imperial Navy.

From the hour of the accident till July 2 we drifted constantly to the south, almost without plans and encountering no vessel. Dolphins still encircled the U-29, a somewhat remarkable circumstance considering the distance we had covered. On the morning of July 2 we sighted a warship flying American colours, and the men became very restless in their desire to surrender. Finally Lieut. Klenze had to shoot a seaman named Traube, who urged this un-German act with especial violence. This quieted the crew for the time, and we submerged unseen.

The next afternoon a dense flock of sea-birds appeared from the south, and the ocean began to heave ominously. Closing our hatches, we awaited developments until we realised that we must either submerge or be swamped in the mounting waves. Our air pressure and electricity were diminishing, and we wished to avoid all unnecessary use of our slender mechanical resources; but in this case there was no choice. We did not descend far, and when after several hours the sea was calmer, we decided to return to the surface. Here, however, a new trouble developed; for the ship failed to respond to our direction in spite of all that the mechan-

An American-built warship, the USS *Lake Forest*, later commissioned the SS *War Fox* by the British navy.

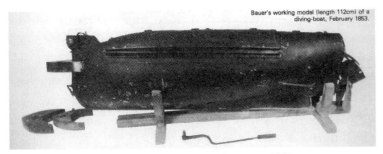
Bauer's working model (length 112cm) of a diving-boat, February 1853.

Working model of Bauer's submarine, 1853.

ics could do. As the men grew more frightened at this undersea imprisonment, some of them began to mutter again about Lieut. Klenze's ivory image, but the sight of an automatic pistol calmed them. We kept the poor devils as busy as we could, tinkering at the machinery even when we knew it was useless.

Klenze and I usually slept at different times; and it was during my sleep, about 5 a.m., July 4, that the general mutiny broke loose. The six remaining pigs of seamen, suspecting that we were lost, had suddenly burst into a mad fury at our refusal to surrender to the Yankee battleship two days before; and were in a delirium of cursing and destruction. They roared like the animals they were, and broke instruments and furniture indiscriminately; screaming about such nonsense as the curse of the ivory image and the dark dead youth who looked at them and swam away. Lieut. Klenze seemed paralysed and inefficient, as one might expect of a soft, womanish Rhinelander.[20] I shot all six men, for it was necessary, and made sure that none remained alive.

We expelled the bodies through the double hatches and were alone in the U-29. Klenze seemed very nervous, and drank heavily. It was decided that we remain alive as long as possible, using the large stock of provisions and chemical supply of oxygen, none of which had suffered from the crazy antics of those swine-hound seamen. Our compasses, depth gauges, and other delicate instruments were ruined; so that henceforth our only reckoning would be guesswork, based on our watches, the calendar, and our apparent drift as judged by any objects we might spy through the portholes or from the conning tower. Fortunately we had storage batteries still capable of long use, both for interior lighting and for the searchlight. We often cast a beam around the ship, but saw only dolphins, swimming parallel to our own drifting course.

17. See note 9, above.

18. Wilhelm Bauer, the first German submarine engineer, designed a ship in 1864 that, propelled by a single-drive internal combustion engine, would have a capacity of 100 hp on the surface (230 hp when submerged) and an underwater speed of eight to nine knots. It would be safe to a depth of nearly 100 feet (30 meters) and was to be armed with five guns designed to fire while submerged. Bauer estimated that the ten-man crew could survive for twenty-four hours without renewing the air, but he also included a purification system that used oxygen and potash to allow an additional twenty-four hours' survival.

A largely self-taught turner's apprentice, Bauer was said to have come up with the idea for a sub by watching seals play in the Baltic (*Engineering: An Illustrated Weekly Journal* 20 [July 30, 1875], 96). When the first model he designed and extensively sea-tested, *Brandtaucher* (German for "fire-diver"), developed a leak and sank on its tenth voyage, in February 1851, he devised a way to release himself and the vessel's two other crew members aboard by shooting them all to the surface like "so many corks of champagne bottles." Another model of Bauer's was subsequently commissioned by Grand Duke Konstantin Nikolayevich (1827–1892), tasked with reforming the Russian navy. Bauer died at fifty-three of complications from gout.

The first full-scale German submarine actually built before 1900, the invention of the torpedo engineer Karl Leps, was primitive and had no air-renewal or ventilation system. The first air-renewal system (developed by Dräger of Lübeck, utilizing caustic potash, or lye) appeared in the U-2, commissioned in 1908. It had previously been used in mining, in "the Dräger breathing apparatus, 1907 type." Under the direction of Hans Techel, the best-known German submarine engineer of the day, the U-5 through U-8 vessels were projected to be built with the same air-purification system. The system (which used an improved version of Bauer's idea, sucking air by means of fans through caustic potash filters while enriching the remaining air with oxygen) proved its worth when the U-3 nearly sank in 1911. The men trapped in the ship were suffering from a concentration of carbon dioxide and chlorine gas, but the purification system allowed them to last for twenty-seven hours awaiting rescue. In fact, the specifications claimed that the system would allow a twenty-four-man crew to breathe for seventy-two hours, and it was a staple of the U-boat throughout the Great War. See Eberhard Rössler, *The U-Boat: The Evolution and Technical History of German Submarines* (London: Cassell, 2002). Similar systems are still in use today, in such places as the International Space Station, although zeolites (naturally occurring porous minerals that are now largely synthetically produced) have generally replaced potash as the absorbent material. See https://ntrs.nasa.gov/archive/nasa/casi.ntrs .nasa.gov/20050210002.pdf.

19. The narrator has omitted certain details here: The *Unterseeboote* of the era usually had two different propulsion systems, kerosene- or diesel-fueled engines for surface travel and *electrical* motors for underwater travel. Very few U-boats were designed with single-propulsion systems, although the batteries for the electrical motors (and the lights and other systems) were charged by running the kerosene- or diesel-powered generators on the surface. Even if the surface engines were damaged, the electrical engines would continue to operate so long as battery power remained. Therefore, if the boat truly couldn't move, the damage must have been to the drive trains or else both the

I was scientifically interested in those dolphins; for though the ordinary *Delphinus delphis* is a cetacean mammal, unable to subsist without air, I watched one of the swimmers closely for two hours, and did not see him alter his submerged condition.

With the passage of time Klenze and I decided that we were still drifting south, meanwhile sinking deeper and deeper. We noted the marine fauna and flora, and read much on the subject in the books I had carried with me for spare moments. I could not help observing, however, the inferior scientific knowledge of my companion. His mind was not Prussian, but given to imaginings and speculations which have no value. The fact of our coming death affected him curiously, and he would frequently pray in remorse over the men, women, and children we had sent to the bottom; forgetting that all things are noble which serve the German state. After a time he became noticeably unbalanced, gazing for hours at his ivory image and weaving fanciful stories of the lost and forgotten things under the sea. Sometimes, as a psychological experiment, I would lead him on in these wanderings, and listen to his endless poetical quotations and tales of sunken ships. I was very sorry for him, for I dislike to see a German suffer; but he was not a good man to die with. For myself I was proud, knowing how the Fatherland would revere my memory and how my sons would be taught to be men like me.

On August 9, we espied the ocean floor, and sent a powerful beam from the searchlight over it. It was a vast undulating plain, mostly covered with seaweed, and strown[21] with the shells of small molluscs. Here and there were slimy objects of puzzling contour, draped with weeds and encrusted with barnacles, which Klenze declared must be ancient ships lying in their graves. He was puzzled by one thing, a peak of solid matter, protruding above the ocean bed nearly four feet at its apex; about two feet thick, with flat sides and smooth upper surfaces which met at a very obtuse angle. I called the peak a bit of outcropping rock, but Klenze thought he saw carvings on it. After a while he began to shudder, and turned away from the scene as if frightened; yet could give no explanation save that he was overcome with the vastness, darkness, remoteness, antiquity, and mystery of the oceanic abysses. His mind was tired, but I am always a German, and was quick to notice two things: that the U-29 was standing the deep-sea pressure splendidly, and that the peculiar dolphins were still about us, even at a depth where the existence of high organisms is considered impossible by most naturalists. That I had previously overestimated our depth, I was sure; but none the less we must still be deep enough to make these phenomena remarkable. Our southward speed, as gauged by the ocean floor, was about as I had estimated from the organisms passed at higher levels.

It was at 3:15 p.m., August 12, that poor Klenze went wholly mad. He had been in the conning tower using the searchlight when I saw him bound into the library compartment where I sat reading, and his face at once betrayed him. I will repeat here what he said, underlining the words he emphasised: "_He_ is calling! _He_ is calling! I hear him! We must go!" As he spoke he took his ivory image from the table, pocketed it, and seized my arm in an effort to drag me up the companionway to the deck. In a moment I understood that he meant to open the hatch and plunge with me into the water outside, a vagary of suicidal and homicidal mania for which I was scarcely prepared. As I hung back and attempted to soothe him he grew more violent, saying: "Come now—do not wait until later; it is better to repent and be forgiven than to defy and be condemned." Then I tried the opposite of the soothing plan, and told him he was mad—pitifully demented. But he was unmoved, and cried: "If I am mad, it is mercy! May the gods pity the man who in his callousness can remain sane to the hideous end! Come and be mad whilst _he_ still calls with mercy!"

This outburst seemed to relieve a pressure in his brain; for as he finished he grew much milder, asking me to let him depart alone if I would not accompany him. My course at once became clear. He was a German, but only a Rhinelander and a commoner; and he was now a potentially dangerous madman. By complying with his suicidal request I could immediately free myself from one who was no longer a companion but a menace. I asked him to give me the ivory image before he went, but this request brought from him such uncanny laughter that I did not repeat it. Then I asked him if he wished to leave any keepsake or lock of hair for his family in Germany in case I should be rescued, but again he gave me that strange laugh. So as he climbed the ladder I went to the levers, and allowing proper time-intervals operated

diesel engines and the electrical motors were damaged. "Raising" and "lowering" the ship would have been accomplished by means of filling or emptying the ballast tanks, controlled by electrical motors. Again, see Rössler, _The U-Boat_.

20. The Prussian kingdom dominated the German confederation, and its Junkers, landowning nobility, became the de facto ruling class of Germany. Though the Rhineland—the regions on the west and east banks of the Rhine River—were controlled by Prussia, the Rhinelanders were not "true" Prussians; hence the narrator's slur.

21. Strown. HPL loved the archaic flavor of this form of the past participle of "strew" and used it frequently.

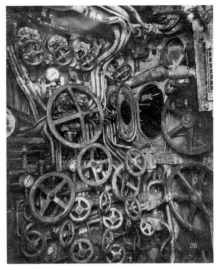

Control room of the German _U-110_ submarine.

the machinery which sent him to his death. After I saw that he was no longer in the boat I threw the searchlight around the water in an effort to obtain a last glimpse of him; since I wished to ascertain whether the water-pressure would flatten him as it theoretically should, or whether the body would be unaffected, like those extraordinary dolphins. I did not, however, succeed in finding my late companion, for the dolphins were massed thickly and obscuringly about the conning tower.

That evening I regretted that I had not taken the ivory image surreptitiously from poor Klenze's pocket as he left, for the memory of it fascinated me. I could not forget the youthful, beautiful head with its leafy crown, though I am not by nature an artist. I was also sorry that I had no one with whom to converse. Klenze, though not my mental equal, was much better than no one. I did not sleep well that night, and wondered exactly when the end would come. Surely, I had little enough chance of rescue.

The next day I ascended to the conning tower and commenced the customary searchlight explorations. Northward the view was much the same as it had been all the four days since we had sighted the bottom, but I perceived that the drifting of the U-29 was less rapid. As I swung the beam around to the south, I noticed that the ocean floor ahead fell away in a marked declivity, and bore curiously regular blocks of stone in certain places, disposed as if in accordance with definite patterns. The boat did not at once descend to match the greater ocean depth, so I was soon forced to adjust the searchlight to cast a sharply downward beam. Owing to the abruptness of the change a wire was disconnected, which necessitated a delay of many minutes for repairs; but at length the light streamed on again, flooding the marine valley below me.

I am not given to emotion of any kind, but my amazement was very great when I saw what lay revealed in that electrical glow. And yet as one reared in the best *Kultur* of Prussia I should not have been amazed, for geology and tradition alike tell us of great transpositions in oceanic and continental areas. What I saw was an extended and elaborate array of ruined edifices; all of magnificent though unclassified architecture, and in various stages of preservation. Most appeared to be of marble, gleaming whitely in the rays of the searchlight, and the general plan was of a large city at the bottom of a narrow valley, with numerous isolated temples and villas on the steep slopes above. Roofs were fallen and columns were broken, but there still remained an air of immemorially ancient splendour which nothing could efface.

Confronted at last with the Atlantis[22] I had formerly deemed largely a myth, I was the most eager of explorers. At the bottom of that valley a river once had flowed; for as I examined the scene more closely I beheld the remains of stone and marble bridges and sea-walls, and terraces and embankments once verdant and beautiful. In my enthusiasm I became nearly as idiotic and sentimental as poor Klenze, and was very tardy in noticing that the southward current had ceased at last, allowing the U-29 to settle slowly down upon the sunken city as an aëroplane settles upon a town of the upper earth. I was slow, too, in realising that the school of unusual dolphins had vanished.

In about two hours the boat rested in a paved plaza close to the rocky wall of the valley. On one side I could view the entire city as it sloped from the plaza down to the old river-bank; on the other side, in startling proximity, I was confronted by the richly ornate and perfectly preserved facade of a great building, evidently a temple, hollowed from the solid rock. Of the original workmanship of this titanic thing I can only make conjectures. The facade, of immense magnitude, apparently covers a continuous hollow recess; for its windows are many and widely distributed. In the centre yawns a great open door, reached by

22. The lost civilization of Atlantis was a popular topic of the day. William Scott-Elliot's eighty-seven-page *The Story of Atlantis: A Geographical, Historical, and Ethnological Sketch* was published in 1896 by the Theosophical Publishing Society and reprinted in 1925 in a combined revised edition with his *The Lost Lemuria* (1904), accompanied by six detailed maps of the world's configuration at different periods. See "The Call of Cthulu," in the previous volume, pp. 123–57, note 16.

Wreck of the German *U-118* submarine.

23. A temple or shrine.

an impressive flight of steps, and surrounded by exquisite carvings like the figures of Bacchanals in relief. Foremost of all are the great columns and frieze, both decorated with sculptures of inexpressible beauty; obviously portraying idealised pastoral scenes and processions of priests and priestesses bearing strange ceremonial devices in adoration of a radiant god. The art is of the most phenomenal perfection, largely Hellenic in idea, yet strangely individual. It imparts an impression of terrible antiquity, as though it were the remotest rather than the immediate ancestor of Greek art. Nor can I doubt that every detail of this massive product was fashioned from the virgin hillside rock of our planet. It is palpably a part of the valley wall, though how the vast interior was ever excavated I cannot imagine. Perhaps a cavern or series of caverns furnished the nucleus. Neither age nor submersion has corroded the pristine grandeur of this awful fane[23]—for fane indeed it must be—and today after thousands of years it rests untarnished and inviolate in the endless night and silence of an ocean chasm.

I cannot reckon the number of hours I spent in gazing at the sunken city with its buildings, arches, statues, and bridges, and the colossal temple with its beauty and mystery. Though I knew that death was near, my curiosity was consuming; and I threw the searchlight's beam about in eager quest. The shaft of light permitted me to learn many details, but refused to shew anything within the gaping door of the rock-hewn temple; and after a time I turned off the current, conscious of the need of conserving power. The rays were now perceptibly dimmer than they had been during the weeks of drifting. And as if sharpened by the coming deprivation of light, my desire to explore the watery secrets grew. I, a German, should be the first to tread those aeon-forgotten ways!

I produced and examined a deep-sea diving suit of joined metal, and experimented with the portable light and air regenerator. Though I should have trouble in managing the double hatches alone, I believed I could overcome all obstacles with my scientific skill and actually walk about the dead city in person.

On August 16 I effected an exit from the U-29, and laboriously made my way through the ruined and mud-choked streets to the ancient river. I found no skeletons or other human remains, but gleaned a wealth of archaeological lore from sculptures and coins. Of this I cannot now speak save to utter my awe at a culture in the full noon of glory when cave-dwellers roamed Europe and the Nile flowed unwatched to the sea. Others, guided by this manuscript if it shall ever be found, must unfold the mysteries at which I can only hint. I returned to the boat as my electric batteries grew feeble, resolved to explore the rock temple on the following day.

On the 17th, as my impulse to search out the mystery of the temple waxed still more insistent, a great disappointment befell me; for I found that the materials needed to replenish the portable light had perished in the mutiny of those pigs in July. My rage was unbounded, yet my German sense forbade me to venture unprepared into an utterly black interior which might prove the lair of some indescribable marine monster or a labyrinth of passages from whose windings I could never extricate myself. All I could do was to turn on the waning searchlight of the U-29, and with its aid walk up the temple steps and study the exterior carvings. The shaft of light entered the door at an upward angle, and I peered in to see if I could glimpse anything, but all in vain. Not even the roof was visible; and though I took a step or two inside after testing the floor with a staff, I dared not go farther. Moreover, for the first time in my life I experienced the emotion of dread. I began to realise how some of poor Klenze's moods had arisen, for as the temple drew me more and more, I feared its aqueous abysses with a blind and mounting terror. Returning to the submarine, I turned off the lights and sat thinking in the dark. Electricity must now be saved for emergencies.

Saturday the 18th I spent in total darkness, tormented by thoughts and memories that threatened to overcome my German will. Klenze had gone mad and perished before reaching this sinister remnant of a past unwholesomely remote, and had advised me to go with him. Was, indeed, Fate preserving my reason only to draw me irresistibly to an end more horrible and unthinkable than any man has dreamed of? Clearly, my nerves were sorely taxed, and I must cast off these impressions of weaker men.

I could not sleep Saturday night, and turned on the lights regardless of the future. It was annoying that the electricity should not last out the air and provisions. I revived my thoughts of euthanasia, and examined my automatic pistol. Toward morning I must have dropped asleep with the lights on, for I awoke in darkness yesterday afternoon to find the batteries dead. I struck several matches in succession, and desperately regretted the improvidence which had caused us long ago to use up the few candles we carried.

After the fading of the last match I dared to waste, I sat very quietly without a light. As I considered the inevitable end my mind ran over preceding events, and developed a hitherto dormant impression which would have caused a weaker and more superstitious man to shudder. *The head of the radiant god in the sculptures on the rock temple is the same as that carven bit of ivory which the dead sailor brought from the sea and which poor Klenze carried back into the sea.*

I was a little dazed by this coincidence, but did not become terrified. It is only the inferior thinker who hastens to explain the singular and the complex by the primitive short cut of supernaturalism. The coincidence was strange, but I was too sound a reasoner to connect circumstances which admit of no logical connexion, or to associate in any uncanny fashion the disastrous events which had led from the *Victory* affair to my present plight. Feeling the need of more rest, I took a sedative and secured some more sleep. My nervous condition was reflected in my dreams, for I seemed to hear the cries of drowning persons, and to see dead faces pressing against the portholes of the boat. And among the dead faces was the living, mocking face of the youth with the ivory image.

I must be careful how I record my awaking today, for I am unstrung, and much hallucination is necessarily mixed with fact. Psychologically my case is most interesting, and I regret that it cannot be observed scientifically by a competent German authority. Upon opening my eyes my first sensation was an overmastering desire to visit the rock temple; a desire which grew every instant, yet which I automatically sought to resist through some emotion of fear which operated in the reverse direction. Next there came to me the impression of *light* amidst the darkness of dead batteries, and I seemed to see a sort of phosphorescent glow in the water through the porthole which opened toward the temple. This aroused my curiosity, for I knew of no deep-sea organism capable of emitting such luminosity. But before I could investigate there came a third impression which because of its irrationality caused me to doubt the objectivity of anything my senses might record. It was an aural delusion; a sensation of rhythmic, melodic sound as of some wild yet beautiful chant or choral hymn, coming from the outside through the absolutely sound-proof hull of the U-29. Convinced of my psychological and nervous abnormality, I lighted some matches and poured a stiff dose of sodium bromide solution, which seemed to calm me to the extent of dispelling the illusion of sound. But the phosphorescence remained, and I had difficulty in repressing a childish impulse to go to the porthole and seek its source. It was horribly realistic, and I could soon distinguish by its aid the familiar objects around me, as well as the empty sodium bromide glass of which I had had no former visual impression in its present location. The last circumstance made me ponder, and I crossed the room and touched the glass. It was indeed in the place where I had seemed to see it. Now I knew that the light was either real or part of an hallucination so fixed and consistent that I could not hope to dispel it, so abandoning all resistance I ascended to the conning tower to look for the luminous agency. Might it not actually be another U-boat, offering possibilities of rescue?

It is well that the reader accept nothing which follows as objective truth, for since the events transcend natural law, they are necessarily the subjective and unreal creations of my overtaxed mind. When I attained the conning tower I found the sea in general far less luminous than I had expected. There was no animal or vegetable phosphorescence about, and the city that sloped down to the river was invisible in blackness. What I did see was not spectacular, not grotesque or terrifying, yet it removed my last vestige of trust in my consciousness. *For the door and windows of the undersea temple hewn from the rocky hill were vividly aglow with a flickering radiance, as from a mighty altar-flame far within.*[24]

Later incidents are chaotic. As I stared at the uncannily lighted door and windows, I became subject to the most extravagant visions—visions so extravagant that I cannot even relate them. I fancied that I discerned objects in the temple; objects

24. HPL explained his intent in a letter: "My submarine city is a work of man—a templated and glittering metropolis that once reared its copper domes and colonnades of chrysolite to glowing Atlantean suns. Fair Nordick bearded men dwelt in my city, and spoke a polish'd tongue akin to Greek; and the flame that the Graf von Altberg-Ehrenstein beheld was a witch-fire lit by spirits many millennia old" (Letter to Frank Belknap Long, January 26, 1924, *Selected Letters*, I, 287).

both stationary and moving; and seemed to hear again the unreal chant that had floated to me when first I awaked. And over all rose thoughts and fears which centred in the youth from the sea and the ivory image whose carving was duplicated on the frieze and columns of the temple before me. I thought of poor Klenze, and wondered where his body rested with the image he had carried back into the sea. He had warned me of something, and I had not heeded—but he was a soft-headed Rhinelander who went mad at troubles a Prussian could bear with ease.

The rest is very simple. My impulse to visit and enter the temple has now become an inexplicable and imperious command which ultimately cannot be denied. My own German will no longer controls my acts, and volition is henceforward possible only in minor matters. Such madness it was which drove Klenze to his death, bareheaded and unprotected in the ocean; but I am a Prussian and a man of sense, and will use to the last what little will I have. When first I saw that I must go, I prepared my diving suit, helmet, and air regenerator for instant donning; and immediately commenced to write this hurried chronicle in the hope that it may some day reach the world. I shall seal the manuscript in a bottle and entrust it to the sea as I leave the U-29 forever.

I have no fear, not even from the prophecies of the madman Klenze. What I have seen cannot be true, and I know that this madness of my own will at most lead only to suffocation when my air is gone. The light in the temple is a sheer delusion, and I shall die calmly, like a German, in the black and forgotten depths. This daemoniac laughter which I hear as I write comes only from my own weakening brain. So I will carefully don my diving suit and walk boldly up the steps into that primal shrine; that silent secret of unfathomed waters and uncounted years.

Celephaïs[1]

The story of Kuranes, who longs to find the land of dreams, may be dismissed as another Dunsanian tale satisfying HPL's own desires, in which a young man disappears into a fantasy world. A similar theme is expressed in both "The Silver Key," written six years later, featuring Lovecraft's avatar Randolph Carter, and The Dream-Quest of Unknown Kadath, *written just after "The Silver Key," in which both Carter and Kuranes appear. In both of those tales, however, Lovecraft appears to have come to realize that it is not the world of dreams that he desires; rather, as Carter and Kuranes discover, it is lost youth itself.*

In a dream Kuranes saw the city in the valley, and the sea-coast beyond, and the snowy peak overlooking the sea, and the gaily painted galleys that sail out of the harbour toward distant regions where the sea meets the sky. In a dream it was also that he came by his name of Kuranes, for when awake he was called by another name. Perhaps it was natural for him to dream a new name; for he was the last of his family, and alone among the indifferent millions of London, so there were not many to speak to him and remind him who he had been. His money and lands were gone, and he did not care for the ways of people about him, but preferred to dream and write of his dreams. What he wrote was laughed at by those to whom he shewed it, so that after a time he kept his writings to himself, and finally ceased to write. The more he withdrew from the world about him, the more wonderful became his dreams; and it would have been quite futile to try to describe them on paper. Kuranes was not modern, and did not think like others who wrote. Whilst they strove to strip from life its embroidered robes of myth, and to shew in naked ugliness the foul thing that is reality, Kuranes sought for beauty alone. When truth and experience failed to reveal it, he sought it

1. Written in November 1920, it was not published until two years later, in *The Rainbow* 2 (May 1922), 10–12, the amateur journal of Sonia Greene, later HPL's wife. It was reprinted in *Weird Tales* 34, no. 1 (June–July 1939), 129–32.

in fancy and illusion, and found it on his very doorstep, amid the nebulous memories of childhood tales and dreams.

There are not many persons who know what wonders are opened to them in the stories and visions of their youth; for when as children we listen and dream, we think but half-formed thoughts, and when as men we try to remember, we are dulled and prosaic with the poison of life. But some of us awake in the night with strange phantasms of enchanted hills and gardens, of fountains that sing in the sun, of golden cliffs overhanging murmuring seas, of plains that stretch down to sleeping cities of bronze and stone, and of shadowy companies of heroes that ride caparisoned white horses along the edges of thick forests; and then we know that we have looked back through the ivory gates into that world of wonder which was ours before we were wise and unhappy.

Kuranes came very suddenly upon his old world of childhood. He had been dreaming of the house where he was born; the great stone house covered with ivy, where thirteen generations of his ancestors had lived, and where he had hoped to die. It was moonlight, and he had stolen out into the fragrant summer night, through the gardens, down the terraces, past the great oaks of the park, and along the long white road to the village. The village seemed very old, eaten away at the edge like the moon which had commenced to wane, and Kuranes wondered whether the peaked roofs of the small houses hid sleep or death. In the streets were spears of long grass, and the window-panes on either side were either broken or filmily staring. Kuranes had not lingered, but had plodded on as though summoned toward some goal. He dared not disobey the summons for fear it might prove an illusion like the urges and aspirations of waking life, which do not lead to any goal. Then he had been drawn down a lane that led off from the village street toward the channel cliffs, and had come to the end of things—to the precipice and the abyss where all the village and all the world fell abruptly away into the unechoing emptiness of infinity, and where even the sky ahead was empty and unlit by the crumbling moon and the peering stars. Faith had urged him on, over the precipice and into the gulf, where he had floated down, down, down; past dark, shapeless, undreamed dreams, faintly glowing spheres that may have been partly dreamed dreams, and laughing winged things that seemed to mock the dreamers of all the worlds. Then a rift seemed to open in the darkness before him, and he saw the city of the valley, glistening radiantly far, far below, with a background of sea and sky, and a snow-capped mountain near the shore.

Kuranes had awaked the very moment he beheld the city, yet he knew from his brief glance that it was none other than Celephaïs, in the Valley of Ooth-Nargai[2] beyond the Tanarian Hills, where his spirit had dwelt all the eternity of an hour one summer afternoon very long ago, when he had slipt away from his nurse and let the warm sea-breeze lull him to sleep as he watched the clouds from the cliff near the village. He had protested then, when they had found him, waked him, and carried him home, for just as he was aroused he had been about to sail in a golden galley for those alluring regions where the sea meets the sky. And now he was equally resentful of awaking, for he had found his fabulous city after forty weary years.

But three nights afterward Kuranes came again to Celephaïs. As before, he dreamed first of the village that was asleep or dead, and of the abyss down which one must float silently; then the rift appeared again, and he beheld the glittering minarets of the city, and saw the graceful galleys riding at anchor in the blue harbour, and watched the gingko trees of Mount Aran[3] swaying in the sea-breeze. But this time he was not snatched away, and like a winged being settled gradually over a grassy hillside till finally his feet rested gently on the turf. He had indeed come back to the Valley of Ooth-Nargai and the splendid city of Celephaïs.

Down the hill amid scented grasses and brilliant flowers walked Kuranes, over the bubbling Naraxa on the small wooden bridge where he had carved his name so many years ago, and through the whispering grove to the great stone bridge by the city gate. All was as of old, nor were the marble walls discoloured, nor the polished bronze statues upon them tarnished. And Kuranes saw that he need not tremble lest the things he knew be vanished; for even the sentries on the ramparts were the same, and still as young as he remembered them. When he entered the city, past the bronze gates and over the onyx pavements, the merchants and camel-drivers greeted him as if he had never been away; and it was the same at the turquoise temple of Nath-Horthath, where

2. Mentioned again in *The Dream-Quest of Unknown Kadath*, pp. 329–432, below.

3. Also mentioned in *The Dream-Quest of Unknown Kadath*.

4. Alan Lightman's *Einstein's Dreams* (1992) is a lovely novel exploring the idea that time might work differently in different realities (consistent with Einstein's special theory of relativity). There is no doubt that HPL read Einstein's early work and struggled, as many did, to understand his theories. In "Hypnos," written in 1922, HPL makes specific reference to Einstein's theory that "all time and space are relative."

5. A great sea in dreamland, on which Randolph Carter sails for twenty-two days (in *The Dream-Quest of Unknown Kadath*).

6. Also mentioned in *The Dream-Quest of Unknown Kadath*.

the orchid-wreathed priests told him that there is no time in Ooth-Nargai, but only perpetual youth.[4] Then Kuranes walked through the Street of Pillars to the seaward wall, where gathered the traders and sailors, and strange men from the regions where the sea meets the sky. There he stayed long, gazing out over the bright harbour where the ripples sparkled beneath an unknown sun, and where rode lightly the galleys from far places over the water. And he gazed also upon Mount Aran rising regally from the shore, its lower slopes green with swaying trees and its white summit touching the sky.

More than ever Kuranes wished to sail in a galley to the far places of which he had heard so many strange tales, and he sought again the captain who had agreed to carry him so long ago. He found the man, Athib, sitting on the same chest of spices he had sat upon before, and Athib seemed not to realise that any time had passed. Then the two rowed to a galley in the harbour, and giving orders to the oarsmen, commenced to sail out into the billowy Cerenerian Sea[5] that leads to the sky. For several days they glided undulatingly over the water, till finally they came to the horizon, where the sea meets the sky. Here the galley paused not at all, but floated easily in the blue of the sky among fleecy clouds tinted with rose. And far beneath the keel Kuranes could see strange lands and rivers and cities of surpassing beauty, spread indolently in the sunshine which seemed never to lessen or disappear. At length Athib told him that their journey was near its end, and that they would soon enter the harbour of Serannian, the pink marble city of the clouds,[6] which is built on that ethereal coast where the west wind flows into the sky; but as the highest of the city's carven towers came into sight there was a sound somewhere in space, and Kuranes awaked in his London garret.

For many months after that Kuranes sought the marvellous city of Celephaïs and its sky-bound galleys in vain; and though his dreams carried him to many gorgeous and unheard-of places, no one whom he met could tell him how to find Ooth-Nargai, beyond the Tanarian Hills. One night he went flying over dark mountains where there were faint, lone campfires at great distances apart, and strange, shaggy herds with tinkling bells on the leaders; and in the wildest part of this hilly country, so remote that few men could ever have seen it, he found a hideously ancient wall or causeway of stone zigzagging along the ridges and valleys; too gigantic ever to have risen by human hands, and of such a length that neither end of it could be seen.[7] Beyond that wall in the grey dawn he came to a land of quaint gardens and cherry trees, and when the sun rose he beheld such beauty of red and white flowers, green foliage and lawns, white paths, diamond brooks, blue lakelets, carven bridges, and red-roofed pagodas, that he for a moment forgot Celephaïs in sheer delight. But he remembered it again when he walked down a white path toward a red-roofed pagoda, and would have questioned the people of that land about it, had he not found that there were no people there, but only birds and bees and butterflies. On another night Kuranes walked up a damp stone spiral stairway endlessly, and came to a tower window overlooking a mighty plain and river lit by the full moon; and in the silent city that spread away from the river-bank he thought he beheld some feature or arrangement which he had known before. He would have descended and asked the way to Ooth-Nargai had not a fearsome aurora sputtered up from some remote place beyond the horizon, shewing the ruin and antiquity of the city, and the stagnation of the reedy river, and the death lying upon that land, as it had lain since King Kynaratholis came home from his conquests to find the vengeance of the gods.

So Kuranes sought fruitlessly for the marvellous city of Celephaïs and its galleys that sail to Serannian in the sky, meanwhile seeing many wonders and once barely escaping from the high-priest not to be described, which wears a yellow silken mask over its face and dwells all alone in a prehistoric stone monastery on the cold desert plateau of Leng.[8] In time he grew so impatient of the bleak intervals of day that he began buying drugs in order to increase his periods of sleep. Hasheesh[9] helped a great deal, and once sent him to a part of space where form does not exist, but where glowing gases study the secrets of existence. And a violet-coloured gas[10] told him that this part of space was outside what he had called infinity. The gas had not heard of planets and organisms before, but identified Kuranes merely as one from the infinity where matter, energy, and gravitation exist. Kuranes was now very anxious to return to minaret-studded Celephaïs, and increased his doses of drugs; but eventually he had no more

7. The structure Kuranes sees sounds much like the Great Wall of China (the average height of which, however, is only about 6 feet). With a length of about 5,500 miles, the Great Wall can certainly be described as "too gigantic to have been raised by human hands," and there has long been (completely unfounded) speculation that aliens had a part in its construction. Unfortunately, its history is now well documented, and the wall is a testament to the ruthless sacrifice of thousands of soldiers, peasants, and rebels by various rulers.

Great Wall of China, ca. 1907.

8. This is Lovecraft's first mention of the land of Leng, although it is part of the dreamland in *The Dream-Quest of Unknown Kadath*. It is described in "The Hound" (pp. 94–102 of the previous volume), written in October 1922, as part of "Central Asia"; in *At the Mountains of Madness*, the narrator reports that Leng, the "most ancient" of lands, a "fabled nightmare plateau," was likely the lofty range of mountains discovered by the Miskatonic University team (the Miskatonic River and its valley and envi-

rons are first mentioned in "The Picture in the House," in the previous volume, pp. 35–44).

9. Fitz Hugh Ludlow's 1857 *The Hasheesh Eater: Being Passages from the Life of a Pythagorean* (New York: Harper & Bros.), more than even Thomas De Quincey's *Confessions of an English Opium-Eater* (London: Taylor and Hessey, 1821), to which book Ludlow acknowledged a debt, popularly described the agonies and ecstasies of the drug and addiction. "My career . . . ," he wrote, "still ran through lands as glorious, as unfrequented, as weird as [De Quincey's] own, and takes those who would follow it out of the trodden highways of mind" (v). The book went through many editions and was rediscovered in the 1960s. Hashish was freely available in the nineteenth century—there were hundreds of hashish "parlors" in New York, Chicago, and Boston, and it was offered to tourists at the Philadelphia Centennial Exposition in 1876—and it was not until 1906 that the federal government classed it (and marijuana) as a poison. The sale of marijuana for private use was effectively outlawed in 1937 with the passage of the Marihuana Tax Act, championed by William Randolph Hearst and others, ostensibly on moral grounds. Some historians, however, suggest that Hearst's opposition was more likely based on his desire to quash the cultivation of hemp, which threatened the success of nylon, in which Hearst and other businessmen had invested heavily. See Richard J. Bonnie and Charles H. Whitebread, *The Marihuana Conviction: A History of Marihuana Prohibition in the United States* (Richmond: University Press of Virginia, 1974), republished in 1999 as *The Marijuana Conviction: The History of Marijuana Prohibition in the United States* (New York: Lindesmith Center Drug Policy Classic).

money left, and could buy no drugs. Then one summer day he was turned out of his garret, and wandered aimlessly through the streets, drifting over a bridge to a place where the houses grew thinner and thinner. And it was there that fulfilment came, and he met the cortege of knights come from Celephaïs to bear him thither forever.

Handsome knights they were, astride roan horses and clad in shining armour with tabards of cloth-of-gold curiously emblazoned. So numerous were they, that Kuranes almost mistook them for an army, but their leader told him they were sent in his honour; since it was he who had created Ooth-Nargai in his dreams, on which account he was now to be appointed its chief god for evermore. Then they gave Kuranes a horse and placed him at the head of the cavalcade, and all rode majestically through the downs of Surrey and onward toward the region where Kuranes and his ancestors were born. It was very strange, but as the riders went on they seemed to gallop back through Time; for whenever they passed through a village in the twilight they saw only such houses and villagers as Chaucer[11] or men

Geoffrey Chaucer, by an unknown seventeenth-century artist.

before him might have seen, and sometimes they saw knights on horseback with small companies of retainers. When it grew dark they travelled more swiftly, till soon they were flying uncannily as if in the air. In the dim dawn they came upon the village which Kuranes had seen alive in his childhood, and asleep or dead in his dreams. It was alive now, and early villagers courtesied as the horsemen clattered down the street and turned off into the lane that ends in the abyss of dream. Kuranes had previously entered that abyss only at night, and wondered what it would look like by day; so he watched anxiously as the column approached its brink. Just as they galloped up the rising ground to the precipice a golden glare came somewhere out of the east and hid all the landscape in its effulgent draperies. The abyss was now a seething chaos of roseate and cerulean splendour, and invisible voices sang exultantly as the knightly entourage plunged over the edge and floated gracefully down past glittering clouds and silvery coruscations. Endlessly down the horsemen floated, their chargers pawing the aether as if galloping over golden sands; and then the luminous vapours spread apart to reveal a greater brightness, the brightness of the city Celephaïs, and the seacoast beyond, and the snowy peak overlooking the sea, and the gaily painted galleys that sail out of the harbour toward distant regions where the sea meets the sky.

And Kuranes reigned thereafter over Ooth-Nargai and all the neighbouring regions of dream, and held his court alternately in Celephaïs and in the cloud-fashioned Serannian. He reigns there still, and will reign happily forever, though below the cliffs at Innsmouth[12] the channel tides played mockingly with the body of a tramp who had stumbled through the half-deserted village at dawn; played mockingly, and cast it upon the rocks by ivy-covered Trevor Towers,[13] where a notably fat and especially offensive millionaire brewer enjoys the purchased atmosphere of extinct nobility.

10. The beings described in "Beyond the Wall of Sleep," in the previous volume, pp. 18–29, written in 1919, are not explicitly described as gases, but they seem to be bodiless. A sentient gas comes to Earth in "The Colour Out of Space," in the previous volume, pp. 310–42, written much later, in March 1927.

11. Geoffrey Chaucer, the great English poet of the Middle Ages, lived ca. 1343–1400.

12. Note that this Innsmouth is located in England, outside London; in later stories, an Innsmouth appears in New England. Of course, it was common for towns in the New World to bear the same names as towns in the mother country (often with "New" preceding the name, as in "New England"), but this Innsmouth is not to be found in any contemporary gazetteer.

13. In *The Dream-Quest of Unknown Kadath*, Kuranes refers to the Towers as the place "where he was born and where thirteen generations of his forefathers had first seen the light." We may therefore identify Kuranes as a Trevor, a family well-represented in the lineages of England (although the first Baron Trevor was made only in 1880).

From Beyond[1]

In this story, Lovecraft again experiments with "scientific fiction"—early science fiction—at which he first tried his hand in the 1919 tale "Beyond the Walls of Sleep." Based heavily on the author's readings in physics, the story seeks to establish that science can and will reveal universes beyond our conception. At the same time, here we have an early expression of what would become known as Lovecraft's "cosmic horror"—the discovery that the universe is filled with deadly alien creatures that are fundamentally indifferent to humankind. This is the earliest tale of the author's set in Providence, a place chosen perhaps because of its inherently prosaic nature.

1. Written in November 1920, the story did not see print until it appeared in *Fantasy Fan* 1, no. 10 (June 1934), 147–51, 160; it was subsequently reprinted in *Weird Tales* 31, no. 2 (February 1938), 227–31.

Horrible beyond conception was the change which had taken place in my best friend, Crawford Tillinghast. I had not seen him since that day, two months and a half before, when he had told me toward what goal his physical and metaphysical researches were leading; when he had answered my awed and almost frightened remonstrances by driving me from his laboratory and his house in a burst of fanatical rage. I had known that he now remained mostly shut in the attic laboratory with that accursed electrical machine, eating little and excluding even the servants, but I had not thought that a brief period of ten weeks could so alter and disfigure any human creature. It is not pleasant to see a stout man suddenly grown thin, and it is even worse when the baggy skin becomes yellowed or greyed, the eyes sunken, circled, and uncannily glowing, the forehead veined and corrugated, and the hands tremulous and twitching. And if added to this there be a repellent unkemptness; a wild disorder of dress, a bushiness of dark hair white at the roots, and an unchecked growth of pure white beard on a face once clean-shaven, the cumulative effect is quite shocking. But such was the aspect of Crawford Tillinghast on the night his half-coherent message brought me to his door after my weeks of exile; such the spectre that trembled as it admitted me, candle in hand, and glanced furtively over its shoulder as if fearful of unseen things in the ancient, lonely house set back from Benevolent Street.[2]

That Crawford Tillinghast should ever have studied science and philosophy was a mistake. These things should be left to the frigid and impersonal investigator, for they offer two equally tragic alternatives to the man of feeling and action; despair if he fail in his quest, and terrors unutterable and unimaginable if he succeed. Tillinghast had once been the prey of failure, solitary and melancholy; but now I knew, with nauseating fears of my own, that he was the prey of success. I had indeed warned him ten weeks before, when he burst forth with his tale of what he felt himself about to discover. He had been flushed and excited then, talking in a high and unnatural, though always pedantic, voice.

"What do we know," he had said, "of the world and the universe about us? Our means of receiving impressions are absurdly few, and our notions of surrounding objects infinitely narrow. We see things only as we are constructed to see them, and can gain no idea of their absolute nature. With five feeble senses we pretend to comprehend the boundlessly complex cosmos, yet other beings with a wider, stronger, or different range of senses might not only see very differently the things we see, but might see and study whole worlds of matter, energy, and life which lie close at hand yet can never be detected with the senses we have.[3] I have always believed that such strange, inaccessible worlds exist at our very elbows, and now I believe I have found a way to break down the barriers. I am not joking. Within twenty-four hours that machine near the table will generate waves acting on unrecognised sense-organs that exist in us as atrophied or rudimentary vestiges. Those waves will open up to us many vistas unknown to man, and several unknown to anything we consider organic life. We shall see that at which dogs howl in the dark, and that at which cats prick up their ears after midnight. We shall see these things, and other things which no breathing creature has yet seen. We shall overleap time, space, and dimensions, and without bodily motion peer to the bottom of creation."

When Tillinghast said these things I remonstrated, for I knew him well enough to be frightened rather than amused; but he

2. A Providence street. In *The Case of Charles Dexter Ward*, in the previous volume, pp. 171–309, Ward loves to walk in "the gracious southerly realm [of Providence] about George, Benevolent, Power, and Williams Streets, where the old slope holds unchanged the fine estates and bits of walled garden and steep green lane in which so many fragrant memories linger" (183).

3. The idea that the universe has qualities or features (for example, cosmic rays) that cannot be perceived by humans' five senses is set forth in some detail in Hugh Elliot's *Modern Science and Materialism* (London: Longmans, Green and Co. 1919), a work that S. T. Joshi believes was familiar to HPL. See Joshi's *I Am Providence: The Life and Times of H. P. Lovecraft* (New York: Hippocampus Press, 2010), 317–19.

was a fanatic, and drove me from the house. Now he was no less a fanatic, but his desire to speak had conquered his resentment, and he had written me imperatively in a hand I could scarcely recognise. As I entered the abode of the friend so suddenly metamorphosed to a shivering gargoyle, I became infected with the terror which seemed stalking in all the shadows. The words and beliefs expressed ten weeks before seemed bodied forth in the darkness beyond the small circle of candle light, and I sickened at the hollow, altered voice of my host. I wished the servants were about, and did not like it when he said they had all left three days previously. It seemed strange that old Gregory, at least, should desert his master without telling as tried a friend as I. It was he who had given me all the information I had of Tillinghast after I was repulsed in rage.

Yet I soon subordinated all my fears to my growing curiosity and fascination. Just what Crawford Tillinghast now wished of me I could only guess, but that he had some stupendous secret or discovery to impart, I could not doubt. Before I had protested at his unnatural pryings into the unthinkable; now that he had evidently succeeded to some degree I almost shared his spirit, terrible though the cost of victory appeared. Up through the dark emptiness of the house I followed the bobbing candle in the hand of this shaking parody on man. The electricity seemed to be turned off, and when I asked my guide he said it was for a definite reason.

"It would be too much . . . I would not dare," he continued to mutter. I especially noted his new habit of muttering, for it was not like him to talk to himself. We entered the laboratory in the attic, and I observed that detestable electrical machine, glowing with a sickly, sinister, violet luminosity. It was connected with a powerful chemical battery, but seemed to be receiving no current; for I recalled that in its experimental stage it had sputtered and purred when in action. In reply to my question Tillinghast mumbled that this permanent glow was not electrical in any sense that I could understand.

He now seated me near the machine, so that it was on my right, and turned a switch somewhere below the crowning cluster of glass bulbs. The usual sputtering began, turned to a whine, and terminated in a drone so soft as to suggest a return to silence.

Meanwhile the luminosity increased, waned again, then assumed a pale, outré colour or blend of colours which I could neither place nor describe. Tillinghast had been watching me, and noted my puzzled expression.

"Do you know what that is?" he whispered. "That is ultra-violet." He chuckled oddly at my surprise. "You thought ultra-violet was invisible, and so it is—but you can see that and many other invisible things now.

"Listen to me! The waves from that thing are waking a thousand sleeping senses in us; senses which we inherit from aeons of evolution from the state of detached electrons to the state of organic humanity. I have seen truth, and I intend to shew it to you. Do you wonder how it will seem? I will tell you." Here Tillinghast seated himself directly opposite me, blowing out his candle and staring hideously into my eyes. "Your existing sense-organs—ears first, I think—will pick up many of the impressions, for they are closely connected with the dormant organs. Then there will be others. You have heard of the pineal gland?[4] I laugh at the shallow endocrinologist, fellow-dupe and fellow-parvenu[5] of the Freudian. That gland is the great sense-organ of organs—I have found out. It is like sight in the end, and transmits visual pictures to the brain. If you are normal, that is the way you ought to get most of it . . . I mean get most of the evidence from beyond."

I looked about the immense attic room with the sloping south wall, dimly lit by rays which the every-day eye cannot see. The far corners were all shadows, and the whole place took on a hazy unreality which obscured its nature and invited the imagination to symbolism and phantasm. During the interval that Tillinghast was silent I fancied myself in some vast and incredible temple of long-dead gods; some vague edifice of innumerable black stone columns reaching up from a floor of damp slabs to a cloudy height beyond the range of my vision. The picture was very vivid for a while, but gradually gave way to a more horrible conception; that of utter, absolute solitude in infinite, sightless, soundless space. There seemed to be a void, and nothing more, and I felt a childish fear which prompted me to draw from my hip pocket the revolver I always carried after dark since the night I was held up in East Providence.[6] Then, from the farthermost regions of remoteness, the sound softly glided into existence. It was infinitely faint,

4. A small endocrinal gland located in the midbrain. Because of its location deep in the brain, it has long been considered to have metaphysical or mystical significance. René Descartes, for example, credited the pineal gland with effectively housing the soul and speculated that all thought originated there. Its only apparent function is to produce melatonin, critical to the regulation of sleep.

5. A parvenu is a person who has, in this case, attained recognition or fame but not achieved the dignity or manner usually associated with it. Here, Tillinghast is saying that endocrinologists (and Freudians) have been credited with knowing more than they really do. This sentence does not appear in the manuscript of the story, only in the printed versions.

6. This reference to a robbery also does not appear in the manuscript of the story, only in the printed versions. S. T. Joshi comments (in *The Dreams in the Witch House and Other Weird Stories* [New York: Penguin, 2004], 404, note 7) that it is "not clear" whether the reference constitutes evidence that HPL may have personally experienced a robbery, but it is clear that he frequently walked through disreputable neighborhoods in East Providence on his way to visit his friends C. M. Eddy and Muriel Eddy (whom he met in 1923). Lovecraft owned a number of rifles and pistols around 1905 (when he was the gun-toting fifteen-year-old leader of the Providence Detective Agency), but he appears to have disposed of them later in the decade, and there is no evidence that he retained any guns at the time of writing this tale.

subtly vibrant, and unmistakably musical, but held a quality of surpassing wildness which made its impact feel like a delicate torture of my whole body. I felt sensations like those one feels when accidentally scratching ground glass. Simultaneously there developed something like a cold draught, which apparently swept past me from the direction of the distant sound. As I waited breathlessly I perceived that both sound and wind were increasing; the effect being to give me an odd notion of myself as tied to a pair of rails in the path of a gigantic approaching locomotive. I began to speak to Tillinghast, and as I did so all the unusual impressions abruptly vanished. I saw only the man, the glowing machine, and the dim apartment. Tillinghast was grinning repulsively at the revolver which I had almost unconsciously drawn, but from his expression I was sure he had seen and heard as much as I, if not a great deal more. I whispered what I had experienced, and he bade me to remain as quiet and receptive as possible.

"Don't move," he cautioned, "for in these rays we are able to be seen as well as to see. I told you the servants left, but I didn't tell you how. It was that thick-witted housekeeper—she turned on the lights downstairs after I had warned her not to, and the wires picked up sympathetic vibrations. It must have been frightful—I could hear the screams up here in spite of all I was seeing and hearing from another direction, and later it was rather awful to find those empty heaps of clothes around the house. Mrs. Updike's clothes were close to the front hall switch—that's how I know she did it. It got them all. But so long as we don't move we're fairly safe. Remember we're dealing with a hideous world in which we are practically helpless. . . . Keep still!"

The combined shock of the revelation and of the abrupt command gave me a kind of paralysis, and in my terror my mind again opened to the impressions coming from what Tillinghast called "beyond." I was now in a vortex of sound and motion, with confused pictures before my eyes. I saw the blurred outlines of the room, but from some point in space there seemed to be pouring a seething column of unrecognisable shapes or clouds, penetrating the solid roof at a point ahead and to the right of me. Then I glimpsed the temple-like effect again, but this time the pillars reached up into an aërial ocean of light, which sent down one blinding beam along the path of the cloudy column I had seen before. After that the scene was almost wholly kaleidoscopic, and in the jumble of sights, sounds, and unidentified sense-impressions I felt that I was about to dissolve or in some way lose the solid form. One definite flash I shall always remember. I seemed for an instant to behold a patch of strange night sky filled with shining, revolving spheres, and as it receded I saw that the glowing suns formed a constellation or galaxy of settled shape; this shape being the distorted face of Crawford Tillinghast. At another time I felt the huge animate things brushing past me and occasionally walking or drifting through my supposedly solid body, and thought I saw Tillinghast look at them as though his better trained senses could catch them visually. I recalled what he had said of the pineal gland, and wondered what he saw with this preternatural eye.

Suddenly I myself became possessed of a kind of augmented sight. Over and above the luminous and shadowy chaos arose a picture which, though vague, held the elements of consistency and permanence. It was indeed somewhat familiar, for the unusual part was superimposed upon the usual terrestrial scene much as a cinema view may be thrown upon the painted curtain of a theatre. I saw the attic laboratory, the electrical machine, and the unsightly form of Tillinghast opposite me; but of all the space unoccupied by familiar material objects not one particle was vacant. Indescribable shapes both alive and otherwise were mixed in disgusting disarray, and close to every known thing were whole worlds of alien, unknown entities.[7] It likewise seemed that all the known things entered into the composition of other unknown things, and vice versa. Foremost among the living objects were great inky, jellyish monstrosities which flabbily quivered in harmony with the vibrations from the machine. They were present in loathsome profusion, and I saw to my horror that they overlapped; that they were semi-fluid and capable of passing through one another and through what we know as solids. These things were never still, but seemed ever floating about with some malignant purpose. Sometimes they appeared to devour one another, the attacker launching itself at its victim and instantaneously obliterating the latter from sight. Shudderingly I felt that I knew what had obliterated the unfortunate servants, and could not exclude the things from my mind as I strove to observe other

7. The idea that angels and demons swam invisibly in the air, surrounding humankind, was not new. Peter Dendle explains,

> The demonology of the early centuries C.E. is preserved in a considerable body of philosophical, literary, and religious sources, reflecting the intermingling of numerous cultures and traditions throughout the Roman Empire and the Near East. A premise common to or implicit in many of the cosmological systems articulated is that spiritual substances populate the universe as fully as physical substances do, and that nature abhors a vacuum no less in one realm than in the other. . . . Observe the pious thirteenth-century Abbot Richalm of Schönthal, whose sanctity secures him an enhanced percipience, allowing him to see what the common run of mortals cannot: "They ride like motes in the sunbeam; they are scattered everywhere like dust; they come down upon us like rain; their multitude fills the whole world; the whole air, the whole air, I say, is but a thick mass of devils." ("Patristic Demonology and Lovecraft's 'From Beyond,'" *Journal of the Fantastic in the Arts* 8, no. 3 [1997], 282, 284)

The Irish fantasy writer Joseph Sheridan Le Fanu also incorporated this idea, in such tales as "Green Tea" and "The Familiar" (both appeared in *In a Glass Darkly* in 1872).

properties of the newly visible world that lies unseen around us. But Tillinghast had been watching me, and was speaking.

"You see them? You see them? You see the things that float and flop about you and through you every moment of your life? You see the creatures that form what men call the pure air and the blue sky? Have I not succeeded in breaking down the barrier; have I not shewn you worlds that no other living men have seen?" I heard him scream through the horrible chaos, and looked at the wild face thrust so offensively close to mine. His eyes were pits of flame, and they glared at me with what I now saw was overwhelming hatred. The machine droned detestably.

"You think those floundering things wiped out the servants? Fool, they are harmless! But the servants are gone, aren't they? You tried to stop me; you discouraged me when I needed every drop of encouragement I could get; you were afraid of the cosmic truth, you damned coward, but now I've got you! What swept up the servants? What made them scream so loud? . . . Don't know, eh? You'll know soon enough! Look at me—listen to what I say—do you suppose there are really any such things as time and magnitude? Do you fancy there are such things as form or matter? I tell you, I have struck depths that your little brain can't picture! I have seen beyond the bounds of infinity and drawn down daemons from the stars. . . . I have harnessed the shadows that stride from world to world to sow death and madness. . . . Space belongs to me, do you hear? Things are hunting me now—the things that devour and dissolve—but I know how to elude them. It is you they will get, as they got the servants. Stirring, dear sir? I told you it was dangerous to move. I have saved you so far by telling you to keep still—saved you to see more sights and to listen to me. If you had moved, they would have been at you long ago. Don't worry, they won't hurt you. They didn't hurt the servants—it was seeing that made the poor devils scream so. My pets are not pretty, for they come out of places where aesthetic standards are—very different. Disintegration is quite painless, I assure you—but I want you to see them. I almost saw them, but I knew how to stop. You are not curious? I always knew you were no scientist! Trembling, eh? Trembling with anxiety to see the ultimate beings I have discovered? Why don't you move, then? Tired?

Well, don't worry, my friend, for they are coming. . . . Look! Look, curse you, look! . . . It's just over your left shoulder. . . ."

What remains to be told is very brief, and may be familiar to you from the newspaper accounts. The police heard a shot in the old Tillinghast house and found us there—Tillinghast dead and me unconscious. They arrested me because the revolver was in my hand, but released me in three hours, after they found it was apoplexy which had finished Tillinghast and saw that my shot had been directed at the noxious machine which now lay hopelessly shattered on the laboratory floor. I did not tell very much of what I had seen, for I feared the coroner would be sceptical; but from the evasive outline I did give, the doctor told me that I had undoubtedly been hypnotised by the vindictive and homicidal madman.

I wish I could believe that doctor. It would help my shaky nerves if I could dismiss what I now have to think of the air and the sky about and above me. I never feel alone or comfortable, and a hideous sense of pursuit sometimes comes chillingly on me when I am weary. What prevents me from believing the doctor is this one simple fact—that the police never found the bodies of those servants whom they say Crawford Tillinghast murdered.

Ex Oblivione[1]

Judging from his literary fecundity at the time, it is difficult to believe that, at the age of thirty, when Lovecraft likely wrote this prose poem, he shared the narrator's ennui. Yet in his roughly contemporaneous essay "In Defence of Dagon," he wrote, "There is nothing better than oblivion, since in oblivion there is no wish unfulfilled." One must see these rather dire thoughts as those of a man trying out a philosophical point of view. For the first time, Lovecraft was experiencing life outside the pervasive influence of his mother, then hospitalized.

1. Written in 1920 or 1921, "Ex Oblivione" was first published in *The United Amateur* 20, no. 4 (March 1921), 59–60. The Latin title literally means "from oblivion," but its sense here is "lost and forgotten."

2. Shining, illuminated.

When the last days were upon me, and the ugly trifles of existence began to drive me to madness like the small drops of water that torturers let fall ceaselessly upon one spot of their victim's body, I loved the irradiate[2] refuge of sleep. In my dreams I found a little of the beauty I had vainly sought in life, and wandered through old gardens and enchanted woods.

Once when the wind was soft and scented I heard the south calling, and sailed endlessly and languorously under strange stars.

Once when the gentle rain fell I glided in a barge down a sunless stream under the earth till I reached another world of purple twilight, iridescent arbours, and undying roses.

And once I walked through a golden valley that led to shadowy groves and ruins, and ended in a mighty wall green with antique vines, and pierced by a little gate of bronze.

Many times I walked through that valley, and longer and longer would I pause in the spectral half-light where the giant trees squirmed and twisted grotesquely, and the grey ground stretched damply from trunk to trunk, sometimes disclosing the mould-stained stones of buried temples. And always the goal of my fancies was the mighty vine-grown wall with the little gate of bronze therein.

After a while, as the days of waking became less and less bearable from their greyness and sameness, I would often drift in opiate peace through the valley and the shadowy groves, and wonder how I might seize them for my eternal dwelling-place, so that I need no more crawl back to a dull world stript of interest and new colours. And as I looked upon the little gate in the mighty wall, I felt that beyond it lay a dream-country from which, once it was entered, there would be no return.

So each night in sleep I strove to find the hidden latch of the gate in the ivied antique wall, though it was exceedingly well hidden. And I would tell myself that the realm beyond the wall was not more lasting merely, but more lovely and radiant as well.

Then one night in the dream city of Zakarion I found a yellowed papyrus filled with the thoughts of dream-sages who dwelt of old in that city, and who were too wise ever to be born in the waking world. Therein were written many things concerning the world of dream, and among them was lore of a golden valley and a sacred grove with temples, and a high wall pierced by a little bronze gate. When I saw this lore, I knew that it touched on the scenes I had haunted, and I therefore read long in the yellowed papyrus.

Some of the dream-sages wrote gorgeously of the wonders beyond the irrepassable gate, but others told of horror and disappointment. I knew not which to believe, yet longed more and more to cross forever into the unknown land; for doubt and secrecy are the lure of lures, and no new horror can be more terrible than the daily torture of the commonplace. So when I learned of the drug which would unlock the gate and drive me through, I resolved to take it when next I awaked.

Last night I swallowed the drug and floated dreamily into the golden valley and the shadowy groves; and when I came this time to the antique wall, I saw that the small gate of bronze was ajar. From beyond came a glow that weirdly lit the giant twisted trees and tops of the buried temples, and I drifted on songfully, expectant of the glories of the land from whence I should never return.

3. "The image of the wall is a paradox," writes Robert H. Waugh, in "Documents, Creatures, and History in H. P. Lovecraft," *Lovecraft Studies* 25 (Fall 1991), 2–10. "The usual significance of a wall lies in its excluding us from a definite thing on the other side; most of the time it is built because someone wants to go beyond it. . . . But a wall that has no structure . . . endless, extending infinitely without meeting itself, has nothing on the other side and does not define, as a real wall does, an inside and an outside. . . . Confronted by such a wall, we cannot know whether we are inside or outside or whether we want to escape or to enter" (3).

But as the gate swung wider and the sorcery of drug and dream pushed me through, I knew that all sights and glories were at an end; for in that new realm was neither land nor sea, but only the white void of unpeopled and illimitable space.[3] So, happier than I had ever dared hoped to be, I dissolved again into that native infinity of crystal oblivion from which the daemon Life had called me for one brief and desolate hour.

The Quest of Iranon[1]

This is a fundamentally sad story, in many ways the antidote to such hopeful tales as "Celephaïs" and, later, "The Silver Key." Unlike that of Kuranes or Randolph Carter, Iranon's quest—for happiness in a lost land of dreams—fails. Ultimately Iranon loses faith in himself and in his inherent nobility. As in "Polaris," HPL depicts the fantasy world as a place not where bliss is assured but rather where one's true nature will emerge.

Into the granite city of Teloth wandered the youth, vine-crowned, his yellow hair glistening with myrrh and his purple robe torn with briers of the mountain Sidrak that lies across the antique bridge of stone. The men of Teloth are dark and stern, and dwell in square houses, and with frowns they asked the stranger whence he had come and what were his name and fortune. So the youth answered:

"I am Iranon, and come from Aira, a far city that I recall only dimly but seek to find again. I am a singer of songs that I learned in the far city, and my calling is to make beauty with the things remembered of childhood. My wealth is in little memories and dreams, and in hopes that I sing in gardens when the moon is tender and the west wind stirs the lotos-buds."

When the men of Teloth heard these things they whispered to one another; for though in the granite city there is no laughter or song, the stern men sometimes look to the Karthian hills in the spring and think of the lutes of distant Oonai whereof travellers have told. And thinking thus, they bade the stranger stay and sing in the square before the Tower of Mlin, though they liked not the colour of his tattered robe, nor the myrrh in his hair, nor his chaplet of vine-leaves, nor the youth in his golden voice. At evening Iranon sang, and while he sang an old man

1. "The Quest of Iranon" was written on February 28, 1921, and published at last in *Galleon* 1, no. 5 (July–August 1935), 12–20; it was reprinted in *Weird Tales* 33, no. 3 (March 1939), 125–29.

2. Having a glassy appearance.

3. The city of Athens was ruled by nine magistrates known as "archons"; the title was hereditary. An archonship appears to rule Teloth.

prayed and a blind man said he saw a nimbus over the singer's head. But most of the men of Teloth yawned, and some laughed and some went away to sleep; for Iranon told nothing useful, singing only his memories, his dreams, and his hopes.

"I remember the twilight, the moon, and soft songs, and the window where I was rocked to sleep. And through the window was the street where the golden lights came, and where the shadows danced on houses of marble. I remember the square of moonlight on the floor, that was not like any other light, and the visions that danced in the moonbeams when my mother sang to me. And too, I remember the sun of morning bright above the many-coloured hills in summer, and the sweetness of flowers borne on the south wind that made the trees sing.

"O Aira, city of marble and beryl, how many are thy beauties! How loved I the warm and fragrant groves across the hyaline[2] Nithra, and the falls of the tiny Kra that flowed through the verdant valley! In those groves and in that vale the children wove wreaths for one another, and at dusk I dreamed strange dreams under the yath-trees on the mountain as I saw below me the lights of the city, and the curving Nithra reflecting a ribbon of stars.

"And in the city were palaces of veined and tinted marble, with golden domes and painted walls, and green gardens with cerulean pools and crystal fountains. Often I played in the gardens and waded in the pools, and lay and dreamed among the pale flowers under the trees. And sometimes at sunset I would climb the long hilly street to the citadel and the open place, and look down upon Aira, the magic city of marble and beryl, splendid in a robe of golden flame.

"Long have I missed thee, Aira, for I was but young when we went into exile; but my father was thy King and I shall come again to thee, for it is so decreed of Fate. All through seven lands have I sought thee, and some day shall I reign over thy groves and gardens, thy streets and palaces, and sing to men who shall know whereof I sing, and laugh not nor turn away. For I am Iranon, who was a Prince in Aira."

That night the men of Teloth lodged the stranger in a stable, and in the morning an archon[3] came to him and told him to go to the shop of Athok the cobbler, and be apprenticed to him.

"But I am Iranon, a singer of songs," he said, "and have no heart for the cobbler's trade."

"All in Teloth must toil," replied the archon, "for that is the law." Then said Iranon,

"Wherefore do ye toil; is it not that ye may live and be happy? And if ye toil only that ye may toil more, when shall happiness find you? Ye toil to live, but is not life made of beauty and song? And if ye suffer no singers among you, where shall be the fruits of your toil? Toil without song is like a weary journey without an end. Were not death more pleasing?" But the archon was sullen and did not understand, and rebuked the stranger.

"Thou art a strange youth, and I like not thy face nor thy voice. The words thou speakest are blasphemy, for the gods of Teloth have said that toil is good. Our gods have promised us a haven of light beyond death, where there shall be rest without end, and crystal coldness amidst which none shall vex his mind with thought or his eyes with beauty. Go thou then to Athok the cobbler or be gone out of the city by sunset. All here must serve, and song is folly."

So Iranon went out of the stable and walked over the narrow stone streets between the gloomy square houses of granite, seeking something green in the air of spring. But in Teloth was nothing green, for all was of stone. On the faces of men were frowns, but by the stone embankment along the sluggish river Zuro sate a young boy with sad eyes gazing into the waters to spy green budding branches washed down from the hills by the freshets. And the boy said to him:

"Art thou not indeed he of whom the archons tell, who seekest a far city in a fair land? I am Romnod, and born of the blood of Teloth, but am not old in the ways of the granite city, and yearn daily for the warm groves and the distant lands of beauty and song. Beyond the Karthian hills lieth Oonai, the city of lutes and dancing, which men whisper of and say is both lovely and terrible. Thither would I go were I old enough to find the way, and thither shouldst thou go an[4] thou wouldst sing and have men listen to thee. Let us leave the city Teloth and fare together among the hills of spring. Thou shalt shew me the ways of travel and I will attend thy songs at evening when the stars one by one bring dreams to the minds of dreamers. And peradventure it

4. An obsolete usage, meaning "if."

"Beyond the Karthian hills lieth Onai, the city of lutes and dancing."
Weird Tales (March 1939) (artist: Virgil Finlay)

may be that Oonai the city of lutes and dancing is even the fair
Aira thou seekest, for it is told that thou hast not known Aira
since old days, and a name often changeth. Let us go to Oonai,
O Iranon of the golden head, where men shall know our longings
and welcome us as brothers, nor ever laugh or frown at what we
say." And Iranon answered:

"Be it so, small one; if any in this stone place yearn for beauty
he must seek the mountains and beyond, and I would not leave
thee to pine by the sluggish Zuro. But think not that delight
and understanding dwell just across the Karthian hills, or in any

spot thou canst find in a day's, or a year's, or a lustrum's journey.[5] Behold, when I was small like thee I dwelt in the valley of Narthos by the frigid Xari, where none would listen to my dreams; and I told myself that when older I would go to Sinara on the southern slope, and sing to smiling dromedary-men[6] in the market-place. But when I went to Sinara I found the dromedary-men all drunken and ribald, and saw that their songs were not as mine, so I travelled in a barge down the Xari to onyx-walled Jaren. And the soldiers at Jaren laughed at me and drave[7] me out, so that I wandered to many other cities. I have seen Stethelos that is below the great cataract, and have gazed on the marsh where Sarnath[8] once stood. I have been to Thraa, Ilarnek, and Kadatheron on the winding river Ai, and have dwelt long in Olathoë in the land of Lomar.[9] But though I have had listeners sometimes, they have ever been few, and I know that welcome shall await me only in Aira, the city of marble and beryl where my father once ruled as King. So for Aira shall we seek, though it were well to visit distant and lute-blessed Oonai across the Karthian hills, which may indeed be Aira, though I think not. Aira's beauty is past imagining, and none can tell of it without rapture, whilst of Oonai the camel-drivers whisper leeringly."

At the sunset Iranon and small Romnod went forth from Teloth, and for long wandered amidst the green hills and cool forests. The way was rough and obscure, and never did they seem nearer to Oonai the city of lutes and dancing; but in the dusk as the stars came out Iranon would sing of Aira and its beauties and Romnod would listen, so that they were both happy after a fashion. They ate plentifully of fruit and red berries, and marked not the passing of time, but many years must have slipped away. Small Romnod was now not so small, and spoke deeply instead of shrilly, though Iranon was always the same, and decked his golden hair with vines and fragrant resins found in the woods. So it came to pass one day that Romnod seemed older than Iranon, though he had been very small when Iranon had found him watching for green budding branches in Teloth beside the sluggish stone-banked Zuro.

Then one night when the moon was full the travellers came to a mountain crest and looked down upon the myriad lights of Oonai. Peasants had told them they were near, and Iranon knew

5. In the lexicon of ancient Rome, a "lustrum" was a five-year period and the interval between censuses; hence, a wanderer might travel for five years without being assigned to a location. The word also referred to a sacrifice and ceremony performed at the end of each census to mark the cleansing of the city. See *Ancient Rome: An Anthology of Sources*, ed. and trans., with an introduction, by Christopher Francese and R. Scott Smith (Indianapolis, IN: Hackett, 2014).

6. Camel drivers.

7. The archaic past tense of "drive."

8. See "The Doom That Came to Sarnath," pp. 29–35, above.

9. Olathoë and Lomar first appear in "Polaris," pp. 15–19, above.

that this was not his native city of Aira. The lights of Oonai were not like those of Aira; for they were harsh and glaring, while the lights of Aira shine as softly and magically as shone the moonlight on the floor by the window where Iranon's mother once rocked him to sleep with song. But Oonai was a city of lutes and dancing, so Iranon and Romnod went down the steep slope that they might find men to whom songs and dreams would bring pleasure. And when they were come into the town they found rose-wreathed revellers bound from house to house and leaning from windows and balconies, who listened to the songs of Iranon and tossed him flowers and applauded when he was done. Then for a moment did Iranon believe he had found those who thought and felt even as he, though the town was not an hundredth as fair as Aira.

When dawn came Iranon looked about with dismay, for the domes of Oonai were not golden in the sun, but grey and dismal. And the men of Oonai were pale with revelling and dull with wine, and unlike the radiant men of Aira. But because the people had thrown him blossoms and acclaimed his songs Iranon stayed on, and with him Romnod, who liked the revelry of the town and wore in his dark hair roses and myrtle. Often at night Iranon sang to the revellers, but he was always as before, crowned only with the vine of the mountains and remembering the marble streets of Aira and the hyaline Nithra. In the frescoed halls of the Monarch did he sing, upon a crystal dais raised over a floor that was a mirror, and as he sang he brought pictures to his hearers till the floor seemed to reflect old, beautiful, and half-remembered things instead of the wine-reddened feasters who pelted him with roses. And the King bade him put away his tattered purple, and clothed him in satin and cloth-of-gold, with rings of green jade and bracelets of tinted ivory, and lodged him in a gilded and tapestried chamber on a bed of sweet carven wood with canopies and coverlets of flower-embroidered silk. Thus dwelt Iranon in Oonai, the city of lutes and dancing.

It is not known how long Iranon tarried in Oonai, but one day the King brought to the palace some wild whirling dancers from the Liranian desert, and dusky flute-players from Drinen in the East, and after that the revellers threw their roses not so much at Iranon as at the dancers and the flute-players. And day by day that Romnod who had been a small boy in granite Teloth grew coarser and redder with wine, till he dreamed less and less, and listened with less delight to the songs of Iranon. But though Iranon was sad he ceased not to sing, and at evening told again his dreams of Aira, the city of marble and beryl. Then one night the red and fattened Romnod snorted heavily amidst the poppied silks of his banquet-couch and died writhing, whilst Iranon, pale and slender, sang to himself in a far corner. And when Iranon had wept over the grave of Romnod and strown it with green budding branches, such as Romnod used to love, he put aside his silks and gauds and went forgotten out of Oonai the city of lutes and dancing clad only in the ragged purple in which he had come, and garlanded with fresh vines from the mountains.

Into the sunset wandered Iranon, seeking still for his native land and for men who would understand and cherish his songs and dreams. In all the cities of Cydathria and in the lands beyond the Bnazic desert[10] gay-faced children laughed at his olden songs and tattered robe of purple; but Iranon stayed ever young, and wore wreaths upon his golden head whilst he sang of Aira, delight of the past and hope of the future.

So came he one night to the squalid cot of an antique shepherd, bent and dirty, who kept lean flocks on a stony slope above a quicksand marsh. To this man Iranon spoke, as to so many others:

"Canst thou tell me where I may find Aira, the city of marble and beryl, where flows the hyaline Nithra and where the falls of the tiny Kra sing to verdant valleys and hills forested with yath trees?"[11] And the shepherd, hearing, looked long and strangely at Iranon, as if recalling something very far away in time, and noted each line of the stranger's face, and his golden hair, and his crown of vine-leaves. But he was old, and shook his head as he replied:

"O stranger, I have indeed heard the name of Aira, and the other names thou hast spoken, but they come to me from afar down the waste of long years. I heard them in my youth from the lips of a playmate, a beggar's boy given to strange dreams, who would weave long tales about the moon and the flowers and the west wind. We used to laugh at him, for we knew him from his birth though he thought himself a King's son. He was comely, even as thou, but full of folly and strangeness; and he ran away

10. Mentioned previously in "The Doom That Came to Sarnath."

11. In *The Dream-Quest of Unknown Kadath*, Lake Yath is said to be on the large island of Oriab.

12. Why does Iranon suddenly become old? Brian Humphreys, in "Who or What Was Iranon?," *Lovecraft Studies* 25 (Fall 1991), 10–13, argues that the "elder world" mentioned here is the realm of the Great Ones, and that Iranon's apparent youth is the product of his distant relation to the Elder Gods. This relationship is further evidenced by the prayers of the old man who heard him sing and the "nimbus" that appeared over the singer's head. His ancestry, Humphreys contends, explains the otherwise inexplicable "instant ageing" of Iranon when he learns the truth of his origins (12).

when small to find those who would listen gladly to his songs and dreams. How often hath he sung to me of lands that never were, and things that never can be! Of Aira did he speak much; of Aira and the river Nithra, and the falls of the tiny Kra. There would he ever say he once dwelt as a Prince, though here we knew him from his birth. Nor was there ever a marble city of Aira, nor those who could delight in strange songs, save in the dreams of mine old playmate Iranon who is gone."

And in the twilight, as the stars came out one by one and the moon cast on the marsh a radiance like that which a child sees quivering on the floor as he is rocked to sleep at evening, there walked into the lethal quicksands a very old man in tattered purple, crowned with withered vine-leaves and gazing ahead as if upon the golden domes of a fair city where dreams are understood. That night something of youth and beauty died in the elder world.[12]

The Outsider[1]

"The Outsider" is perhaps the single most analyzed story of any of Lovecraft's considerable output. It has been considered from biographical and psychoanlytic angles, as an antireligion polemic, an expression of philosophy, a criticism of progress, and a depiction of "homosexual panic."[2] Yet none of these interpretations is wholly satisfying, and Lovecraft was vague about his intentions. Ten years after the story's creation, Lovecraft dismissed it as nothing more than an imitation of Poe. Yet perhaps because of its very plasticity, many regard it as his finest work of short fiction, and shortly after his death, August Derleth and Donald Wandrei chose it to headline the first published collection of his work, The Outsider and Other Stories *(1937).*

> That night the Baron dreamt of many a woe;
> And all his warrior-guests, with shade and form
> Of witch, and demon, and large coffin-worm,
> Were long be-nightmared.[3]
>
> —KEATS

Unhappy is he to whom the memories of childhood bring only fear and sadness. Wretched is he who looks back upon lone hours in vast and dismal chambers with brown hangings and maddening rows of antique books, or upon awed watches in twilight groves of grotesque, gigantic, and vine-encumbered trees that silently wave twisted branches far aloft. Such a lot the gods gave to me—to me, the dazed, the disappointed; the barren, the broken. And yet I am strangely content, and cling desperately to those sere memories, when my mind momentarily threatens to reach beyond to *the other.*

I know not where I was born, save that the castle was infinitely old and infinitely horrible; full of dark passages and having high ceilings where the eye could find only cobwebs and shadows.

1. Written in the summer of 1921, "The Outsider" was first published in *Weird Tales* 7, no. 4 (April 1926), 449–53.

2. See, for example, Dirk W. Mosig's groundbreaking "An Analytical Interpretation: The Outsider, Allegory of the Psyche." Mosig championed a Jungian interpretation of Lovecraft's work ("Toward a Greater Appreciation of H. P. Lovecraft: The Analytic Approach," *The Miskatonic*, EOD 1 [June 1973]; reprinted in *The Miskatonic: Lovecraft Centenary Edition* [Glenview, IL: The Moshassuck Press, 1991], 2–14, and in *Mosig at Last: A Psychologist Looks at H. P. Lovecraft*

[West Warwick, RI: Necronomicon Press, 1997], 35–42).

3. The quotation is from the last stanza of "The Eve of St. Agnes," lines 372–75, by John Keats, first published in *Lamia, Isabella, The Eve of St. Agnes, and Other Poems* (1820). William Fulwiler, in "Reflections on 'The Outsider,'" *Lovecraft Studies* 1, no. 2 (Spring 1980), 3–4, argues that the point of the epigraph is to tell the reader that the following is a dream. How else to explain, Fulwiler argues, the following unanswerable questions: "Why did the Outsider lose his memory? How did he become reanimated? How did he come to live in a castle with a well-stocked library located in an underground cavern? What was the source of light in the cavern? Why did the Outsider have to travel all the way to Egypt to find tombs to haunt?" (3).

4. Mollie Burleson finds these comments "typical of both a Gothic and a modern woman," concluding that the narrator is "the Outsider, Woman, an outsider in a world dominated by men" ("The Outsider: A Woman?," *Lovecraft Studies* 22/23 [Fall 1990], 22–23).

5. Who taught the narrator to read? Similarly, the creature in Mary Shelley's *Frankenstein* attains the skill without a teacher. See this editor's *New Annotated Frankenstein* (New York: Liveright, 2017), p. 157, note 5, for a discussion of the near-impossibility of such a feat. "In fact," points out Forrest Jackson, in "The Reflection of Narcissus: And How It Applies to Shelley's *Frankenstein* and Lovecraft's 'The Outsider,'" *Crypt of Cthulhu* 13, no. 3 (Lammas 1994), 9–13, "it goes to prove that for Lovecraft and his character, reading carries an objective weight that precludes the necessity of experience" (12). Jackson notes that Peter Cannon, in *H. P. Lovecraft*

The stones in the crumbling corridors seemed always hideously damp, and there was an accursed smell everywhere, as of the piled-up corpses of dead generations.[4] It was never light, so that I used sometimes to light candles and gaze steadily at them for relief; nor was there any sun outdoors, since the terrible trees grew high above the topmost accessible tower. There was one black tower which reached above the trees into the unknown outer sky, but that was partly ruined and could not be ascended save by a well-nigh impossible climb up the sheer wall, stone by stone.

I must have lived years in this place, but I cannot measure the time. Beings must have cared for my needs, yet I cannot recall any person except myself; or anything alive but the noiseless rats and bats and spiders. I think that whoever nursed me must have been shockingly aged, since my first conception of a living person was that of something mockingly like myself, yet distorted, shrivelled, and decaying like the castle. To me there was nothing grotesque in the bones and skeletons that strowed some of the stone crypts deep down among the foundations. I fantastically associated these things with every-day events, and thought them more natural than the coloured pictures of living beings which I found in many of the mouldy books. From such books I learned all that I know. No teacher urged or guided me, and I do not recall hearing any human voice in all those years—not even my own; for although I had read of speech, I had never thought to try to speak aloud.[5] My aspect was a matter equally unthought of, for there were no mirrors in the castle, and I merely regarded myself by instinct as akin to the youthful figures I saw drawn and painted in the books. I felt conscious of youth because I remembered so little.

Outside, across the putrid moat and under the dark mute trees, I would often lie and dream for hours about what I read in the books; and would longingly picture myself amidst gay crowds in the sunny world beyond the endless forest. Once I tried to escape from the forest, but as I went farther from the castle the shade grew denser and the air more filled with brooding fear; so that I ran frantically back lest I lose my way in a labyrinth of nighted silence.

So through endless twilights I dreamed and waited, though

I knew not what I waited for. Then in the shadowy solitude my longing for light grew so frantic that I could rest no more, and I lifted entreating hands to the single black ruined tower that reached above the forest into the unknown outer sky. And at last I resolved to scale that tower, fall though I might; since it were better to glimpse the sky and perish, than to live without ever beholding day.

In the dank twilight I climbed the worn and aged stone stairs till I reached the level where they ceased, and thereafter clung perilously to small footholds leading upward. Ghastly and terrible was that dead, stairless cylinder of rock; black, ruined, and deserted, and sinister with startled bats whose wings made no noise. But more ghastly and terrible still was the slowness of my progress; for climb as I might, the darkness overhead grew no thinner, and a new chill as of haunted and venerable mould assailed me. I shivered as I wondered why I did not reach the light, and would have looked down had I dared. I fancied that night had come suddenly upon me, and vainly groped with one free hand for a window embrasure, that I might peer out and above, and try to judge the height I had attained.

All at once, after an infinity of awesome, sightless crawling up that concave and desperate precipice, I felt my head touch a solid thing, and I knew I must have gained the roof, or at least some kind of floor. In the darkness I raised my free hand and tested the barrier, finding it stone and immovable. Then came a deadly circuit of the tower, clinging to whatever holds the slimy wall could give; till finally my testing hand found the barrier yielding, and I turned upward again, pushing the slab or door with my head as I used both hands in my fearful ascent. There was no light revealed above, and as my hands went higher I knew that my climb was for the nonce ended; since the slab was the trap-door of an aperture leading to a level stone surface of greater circumference than the lower tower, no doubt the floor of some lofty and capacious observation chamber. I crawled through carefully, and tried to prevent the heavy slab from falling back into place; but failed in the latter attempt. As I lay exhausted on the stone floor I heard the eerie echoes of its fall, but hoped when necessary to pry it open again.

Believing I was now at a prodigious height, far above the accursed branches of the wood, I dragged myself up from the floor

(Boston: Twayne Publishers, 1989), "cites the passage as a 'rare admission of the limitations of book learning'" (47).

and fumbled about for windows, that I might look for the first time upon the sky, and the moon and stars of which I had read. But on every hand I was disappointed; since all that I found were vast shelves of marble, bearing odious oblong boxes of disturbing size. More and more I reflected, and wondered what hoary secrets might abide in this high apartment so many aeons cut off from the castle below. Then unexpectedly my hands came upon a doorway, where hung a portal of stone, rough with strange chiselling. Trying it, I found it locked; but with a supreme burst of strength I overcame all obstacles and dragged it open inward. As I did so there came to me the purest ecstasy I have ever known; for shining tranquilly through an ornate grating of iron, and down a short stone passageway of steps that ascended from the newly found doorway, was the radiant full moon, which I had never before seen save in dreams and in vague visions I dared not call memories.

Fancying now that I had attained the very pinnacle of the castle, I commenced to rush up the few steps beyond the door; but the sudden veiling of the moon by a cloud caused me to stumble, and I felt my way more slowly in the dark. It was still very dark when I reached the grating—which I tried carefully and found unlocked, but which I did not open for fear of falling from the amazing height to which I had climbed. Then the moon came out.

Most daemoniacal of all shocks is that of the abysmally unexpected and grotesquely unbelievable. Nothing I had before undergone could compare in terror with what I now saw; with the bizarre marvels that sight implied. The sight itself was as simple as it was stupefying, for it was merely this: instead of a dizzying prospect of treetops seen from a lofty eminence, there stretched around me on a level through the grating nothing less than *the solid ground*, decked and diversified by marble slabs and columns, and overshadowed by an ancient stone church, whose ruined spire gleamed spectrally in the moonlight.

Half unconscious, I opened the grating and staggered out upon the white gravel path that stretched away in two directions. My mind, stunned and chaotic as it was, still held the frantic craving for light; and not even the fantastic wonder which had happened could stay my course. I neither knew nor cared whether my experience was insanity, dreaming, or magic; but was determined to gaze on brilliance and gaiety at any cost. I knew not who I was or what I was, or what my surroundings might be; though as I continued to stumble along I became conscious of a kind of fearsome latent memory that made my progress not wholly fortuitous. I passed under an arch out of that region of slabs and columns, and wandered through the open country; sometimes following the visible road, but sometimes leaving it curiously to tread across meadows where only occasional ruins bespoke the ancient presence of a forgotten road. Once I swam across a swift river where crumbling, mossy masonry told of a bridge long vanished.

Over two hours must have passed before I reached what seemed to be my goal, a venerable ivied castle in a thickly wooded park; maddeningly familiar, yet full of perplexing strangeness to me. I saw that the moat was filled in, and that some of the well-known towers were demolished; whilst new wings existed to confuse the beholder. But what I observed with chief interest and delight were the open windows—gorgeously ablaze with light and sending forth sound of the gayest revelry. Advancing to one of these I looked in and saw an oddly dressed company, indeed; making merry, and speaking brightly to one another. I had never, seemingly, heard human speech before; and could guess only vaguely what was said. Some of the faces seemed to hold expressions that brought up incredibly remote recollections;[6] others were utterly alien.

I now stepped through the low window into the brilliantly lighted room, stepping as I did so from my single bright moment of hope to my blackest convulsion of despair and realisation. The nightmare was quick to come; for as I entered, there occurred immediately one of the most terrifying demonstrations I had ever conceived. Scarcely had I crossed the sill when there descended upon the whole company a sudden and unheralded fear of hideous intensity, distorting every face and evoking the most horrible screams from nearly every throat. Flight was universal, and in the clamour and panic several fell in a swoon and were dragged away by their madly fleeing companions. Many covered their eyes with their hands, and plunged blindly and awkwardly in their race to escape; overturning furniture and

6. These, suggests S. T. Joshi, in *H. P. Lovecraft: Decline of the West* (Berkeley Heights, NJ: Wildside Press, 1990), 120, are the actual descendants of the narrator.

7. A phantom or specter.

stumbling against the walls before they managed to reach one of the many doors.

The cries were shocking; and as I stood in the brilliant apartment alone and dazed, listening to their vanishing echoes, I trembled at the thought of what might be lurking near me unseen. At a casual inspection the room seemed deserted, but when I moved toward one of the alcoves I thought I detected a presence there—a hint of motion beyond the golden-arched doorway leading to another and somewhat similar room. As I approached the arch I began to perceive the presence more clearly; and then, with the first and last sound I ever uttered—a ghastly ululation that revolted me almost as poignantly as its noxious cause—I beheld in full, frightful vividness the inconceivable, indescribable, and unmentionable monstrosity which had by its simple appearance changed a merry company to a herd of delirious fugitives.

I cannot even hint what it was like, for it was a compound of all that is unclean, uncanny, unwelcome, abnormal, and detestable. It was the ghoulish shade of decay, antiquity, and desolation; the putrid, dripping eidolon[7] of unwholesome revelation; the awful baring of that which the merciful earth should always hide. God knows it was not of this world—or no longer of this world—yet to my horror I saw in its eaten-away and bone-revealing outlines a leering, abhorrent travesty on the human shape; and in its mouldy, disintegrating apparel an unspeakable quality that chilled me even more.

I was almost paralysed, but not too much so to make a feeble effort toward flight; a backward stumble which failed to break the spell in which the nameless, voiceless monster held me. My eyes, bewitched by the glassy orbs which stared loathsomely into them, refused to close; though they were mercifully blurred, and shewed the terrible object but indistinctly after the first shock. I tried to raise my hand to shut out the sight, yet so stunned were my nerves that my arm could not fully obey my will. The attempt, however, was enough to disturb my balance; so that I had to stagger forward several steps to avoid falling. As I did so I became suddenly and agonisingly aware of the *nearness* of the carrion thing, whose hideous hollow breathing I half fancied I could hear. Nearly mad, I found myself yet able to throw out a

"To my horror I saw in its eaten-away and bone-revealing outlines a leering, abhorrent travesty on the human shape; and in its moldy, disintegrating apparel an unspeakable quality that chilled me even more."

Weird Tales (April 1926) (artist: Belle Goldschlager)

hand to ward off the foetid apparition which pressed so close; when in one cataclysmic second of cosmic nightmarishness and hellish accident *my fingers touched the rotting outstretched paw of the monster beneath the golden arch.*[8]

I did not shriek, but all the fiendish ghouls[9] that ride the night-wind shrieked for me as in that same second there crashed down upon my mind a single and fleeting avalanche of soul-annihilating memory. I knew in that second all that had been; I remembered beyond the frightful castle and the trees, and recognised the altered edifice in which I now stood; I recognised, most

8. There can be little doubt, argues Paul Monteleone, in "The Inner Significance of 'The Outsider,'" *Lovecraft Studies* 35 (Fall 1996), 9–21, that the figure that greets the narrator here is a corpse. In that revelation, then, the Outsider, who seeks a restoration to life and the passage of time, realizes that behind all life is "a mere corpse, a sprawling heap of dust that dreams the endless and suffering world. This is his inner significance: he is the inner significance of all" (21).

9. It was in 1921 that HPL first referred to "ghouls" in his fiction (they are also mentioned in "The Nameless City," in the previous volume, 80–93). Will Murray argues, in "Lovecraft's Ghouls," *Crypt of Cthulhu* 14 (St. John's Eve 1983), 8–9, 27, that HPL not only drew on the Persian roots of the word (see "Pickman's Model," note 5, below) but also based his idea of ghouls on the myth of Anubis, the jackal-headed Egyptian god who is the guardian of the dead (9).

10. A legendary drug of forgetfulness; "heart's-ease," in Robert Fagles's translation of *The Odyssey* (New York: Penguin, 1999)—see Book 4: The King and Queen of Sparta, 131.

11. Nephren-Ka is also mentioned in *The Case of Charles Dexter Ward*, written in January–March 1927, and "The Haunter of the Dark," written in November 1935. See the previous volume, pp. 171–309, 779–806.

12. Hadoth appears in *The Case of Charles Dexter Ward* as well.

13. Nitokris, reportedly the last ruler of the Sixth Dynasty of Egypt (2345–2180 BCE), is remembered for having invited all of her enemies to a feast at a temple below the Nile and arranging to drown them all. Herodotus mentions this episode in his *Histories*, vol. 2, 100, and Nitokris appears in the writings of the priest and important literary source Manetho (305–285 BCE), who in *Aegyptiaca* chronicled the Egyptian kings through a span of almost three thousand years (from 3100 BCE to 343 BCE), but she is of dubious authenticity. Although HPL was apparently aware of Herodotus's account, he was likely brought to a greater awareness of Nitokris when he heard Lord Dunsany read from his play entitled *The Queen's Enemies* (Letter to

terrible of all, the unholy abomination that stood leering before me as I withdrew my sullied fingers from its own.

But in the cosmos there is balm as well as bitterness, and that balm is nepenthe.[10] In the supreme horror of that second I forgot what had horrified me, and the burst of black memory vanished in a chaos of echoing images. In a dream I fled from that haunted and accursed pile, and ran swiftly and silently in the moonlight. When I returned to the churchyard place of marble and went down the steps I found the stone trap-door immovable; but I was not sorry, for I had hated the antique castle and the trees. Now I ride with the mocking and friendly ghouls on the night-wind, and play by day amongst the catacombs of Nephren-Ka[11] in the sealed and unknown valley of Hadoth[12] by the Nile. I know that light is not for me, save that of the moon over the rock tombs of Neb, nor any gaiety save the unnamed feasts of Nitokris[13] beneath the Great Pyramid; yet in my new wildness and freedom I almost welcome the bitterness of alienage.

For although nepenthe has calmed me, I know always that I am an outsider; a stranger in this century and among those who are still men. This I have known ever since I stretched out my fingers to the abomination within that great gilded frame; stretched out my fingers and touched *a cold and unyielding surface of polished glass.*[14]

Reinhardt Kleiner, November 9, 1919, *Selected Letters*, I, 91–92).

14. The discovery of the reflected image recalls Edgar Allan Poe's "William Wilson" (1839), with which HPL was certainly familiar, and Alfred de Musset's 1835 "December Night," described as "a dialogue between the author and his double" (in the four-poem cycle *Nights* [Ardmore, PA: Fifth Season Press, 1999], trans. Norman Cameron). It also broadly echoes, in certain respects, the central themes of Robert Louis Stevenson's *The Strange Case of Dr. Jekyll and Mr. Hyde* (1886) and Oscar Wilde's *The Picture of Dorian Gray* (1891), both of which were in HPL's library. George T. Wetzel, in "The Cthulhu Mythos: A Study," in *H. P. Lovecraft: Four Decades of Criticism*, edited by S. T. Joshi, 79–95 (Athens: Ohio University Press, 1980), points out the parallel with a story by Nathaniel Hawthorne, "Fragments from the Journal of a Solitary Man" in *The Dolliver Romance and Other Pieces* (Boston: James R. Osgood & Co., 1876), in which the following passage appears:

I dreamed that one bright forenoon I was walking through Broadway, and seeking to cheer myself with the warm and busy life of that far-famed promenade. . . . I found myself in this animated scene, with a dim and misty idea that it was not my proper place, or that I had ventured into the crowd with some singularity of dress or aspect which made me ridiculous. . . . Every face grew pale; the laugh was hushed . . . and the passengers on all sides fled as from an embodied pestilence. . . .

I passed not one step further, but threw my eyes on a looking-glass which stood deep within the nearest shop. At the first glimpse of my own figure I awoke, with a horrible sensation of self-terror and self-loathing. . . . I had been promenading Broadway in my shroud!

Forrest Jackson, note 5, above, observes that like the creature in Mary Shelley's *Frankenstein*, who learns from his reflection in a pool of water that he is a monster, the narrator of "The Outsider" is destroyed by seeing his reflection. Both visions result from being in the company of normal humans. "In the end," writes Jackson, "once monstrosity is established by the process of socialization, only suicide or nepenthe can kill the image of the double and the madness it brings" (12).

The Other Gods[1]

In this simple parable about the wages of hubris, Lovecraft returns to characters and a setting that he had begun to limn in "The Cats of Ulthar" and would explore in much more detail in The Dream-Quest of Unknown Kadath. *Dunsanian in tone, the story is notable for the details of HPL's unique cosmos and his depiction of the insignificance of Earth's own gods.*

1. The story, probably written on August 14, 1921, first appeared in *Fantasy Fan* 1, no. 3 (November 1933), 35–38. It was reprinted in *Weird Tales* 32, no. 4 (October 1938), 489–92.

2. Ngranek and the "carven image" play an important role in *The Dream-Quest of Unknown Kadath*, pp. 329–432, below.

3. Robert M. Price suggests, in "Two Biblical Curiosities in Lovecraft," *Lovecraft Studies* 7, no. 1 (Spring 1988), 12–13, 18, that "Kadath" may have taken its name from the biblical "Kadesh" (Numbers 13:26). This identification is also pointed out by William Neff, in a letter to *Lovecraft Studies* 22/23 (Fall 1990), 66–67, in which he explains that Kadesh was "the doomed city of Egyptian history—the largest northernmost city of the Egyptian Empire (when at its greatest extent). It was heavily fortified and garrisoned (a 'chariot city'). . . . Kadesh was destroyed for rebellion by order of the warrior Pharaoh Thutmose III—was later rebuilt, and destroyed a second time by a fleet of barbarian pirates about 1200 BC" (67).

Atop the tallest of earth's peaks dwell the gods of earth, and suffer no man to tell that he hath looked upon them. Lesser peaks they once inhabited; but ever the men from the plains would scale the slopes of rock and snow, driving the gods to higher and higher mountains till now only the last remains. When they left their older peaks they took with them all signs of themselves; save once, it is said, when they left a carven image on the face of the mountain which they called Ngranek.[2]

But now they have betaken themselves to unknown Kadath[3] in the cold waste where no man treads, and are grown stern, having no higher peak whereto to flee at the coming of men. They are grown stern, and where once they suffered men to displace them, they now forbid men to come, or coming, to depart. It is well for men that they know not of Kadath in the cold waste, else they would seek injudiciously to scale it.

Sometimes when earth's gods are homesick they visit in the still night the peaks where once they dwelt, and weep softly as they try to play in the olden way on remembered slopes. Men have felt the tears of the gods on white-capped Thurai,[4] though they have thought it rain; and have heard the sighs of the gods in the plaintive dawn-winds of Lerion.[5] In cloud-ships the gods are wont to travel, and wise cotters[6] have legends that keep them from certain high peaks at night when it is cloudy, for the gods are not lenient as of old.

In Ulthar,[7] which lies beyond the river Skai, once dwelt an old man avid to behold the gods of earth; a man deeply learned in the seven cryptical books of Hsan,[8] and familiar with the Pnakotic Manuscripts[9] of distant and frozen Lomar. His name was Barzai the Wise, and the villagers tell of how he went up a mountain on the night of the strange eclipse.

Barzai knew so much of the gods that he could tell of their comings and goings, and guessed so many of their secrets that he was deemed half a god himself. It was he who wisely advised the burgesses of Ulthar when they passed their remarkable law against the slaying of cats,[10] and who first told the young priest Atal[11] where it is that black cats go at midnight on St. John's Eve.[12] Barzai was learned in the lore of earth's gods, and had gained a desire to look upon their faces. He believed that his great secret knowledge of gods could shield him from their wrath, so resolved to go up to the summit of high and rocky Hatheg-Kla on a night when he knew the gods would be there.

Hatheg-Kla is far in the stony desert beyond Hatheg, for which it is named, and rises like a rock statue in a silent temple. Around its peak the mists play always mournfully, for mists are the memories of the gods, and the gods loved Hatheg-Kla when they dwelt upon it in the old days. Often the gods of earth visit Hatheg-Kla in their ships of cloud, casting pale vapours over the slopes as they dance reminiscently on the summit under a clear moon. The villagers of Hatheg say it is ill to climb Hatheg-Kla at any time, and deadly to climb it by night when pale vapours hide the summit and the moon; but Barzai heeded them not when he came from neighbouring Ulthar with the young priest Atal, who was his disciple. Atal was only the son of an innkeeper, and was sometimes afraid; but Barzai's father had been a landgrave[13] who dwelt in an ancient castle, so he had no common superstition in his blood, and only laughed at the fearful cotters.

Barzai and Atal went out of Hatheg into the stony desert despite the prayers of peasants, and talked of earth's gods by their campfires at night. Many days they travelled, and from afar saw lofty Hatheg-Kla with his aureole of mournful mist. On the thirteenth day they reached the mountain's lonely base, and Atal spoke of his fears. But Barzai was old and learned and had no fears, so led the way boldly up the slope that no man had scaled

4. An apparently fictional name; the word means "department" or "sector" in Tamil.

5. Lerion (a festival folk dance in the Philippines) is the name of the land that is the source of the river Skai, as revealed in *The Dream-Quest of Unknown Kadath*.

6. Peasant farmers, so named in the Scottish Highlands.

7. The village of Ulthar is mentioned in "The Cats of Ulthar," pp. 40–43, above.

8. "Earth" instead of "Hsan" in other texts. The books reappear in *The Dream-Quest of Unknown Kadath*.

9. See "Polaris," pp. 15–19, above, for the first mention of the land of Lomar and the Pnakotic Manuscripts.

10. See "The Cats of Ulthar."

11. Atal figures as a young boy in "The Cats of Ulthar" and, in *The Dream-Quest of Unknown Kadath*, is a three-hundred-year-old bearded patriarch of the Temple of the Elder Ones, "still very keen of mind and memory."

12. The feast day of St. John the Baptist, traditionally June 23, six months before Christmas.

13. A count; *Landgraf* in German.

since the time of Sansu, who is written of with fright in the mouldy Pnakotic Manuscripts.

The way was rocky, and made perilous by chasms, cliffs, and falling stones. Later it grew cold and snowy; and Barzai and Atal often slipped and fell as they hewed and plodded upward with staves and axes. Finally the air grew thin, and the sky changed colour, and the climbers found it hard to breathe; but still they toiled up and up, marvelling at the strangeness of the scene and thrilling at the thought of what would happen on the summit when the moon was out and the pale vapours spread around. For three days they climbed higher, higher, and higher toward the roof of the world; then they camped to wait for the clouding of the moon.

For four nights no clouds came, and the moon shone down cold through the thin mournful mists around the silent pinnacle. Then on the fifth night, which was the night of the full moon, Barzai saw some dense clouds far to the north, and stayed up with Atal to watch them draw near. Thick and majestic they sailed, slowly and deliberately onward; ranging themselves round the peak high above the watchers, and hiding the moon and the summit from view. For a long hour the watchers gazed, whilst the vapours swirled and the screen of clouds grew thicker and more restless. Barzai was wise in the lore of earth's gods, and listened hard for certain sounds, but Atal felt the chill of the vapours and the awe of the night, and feared much. And when Barzai began to climb higher and beckon eagerly, it was long before Atal would follow.

So thick were the vapours that the way was hard, and though Atal followed on at last, he could scarce see the grey shape of Barzai on the dim slope above in the clouded moonlight. Barzai forged very far ahead, and seemed despite his age to climb more easily than Atal; fearing not the steepness that began to grow too great for any save a strong and dauntless man, nor pausing at wide black chasms that Atal scarce could leap. And so they went up wildly over rocks and gulfs, slipping and stumbling, and sometimes awed at the vastness and horrible silence of bleak ice pinnacles and mute granite steeps.

Very suddenly Barzai went out of Atal's sight, scaling a hideous cliff that seemed to bulge outward and block the path for any climber not inspired of earth's gods. Atal was far below, and planning what he should do when he reached the place, when curiously he noticed that the light had grown strong, as if the cloudless peak and moonlit meeting-place of the gods were very near. And as he scrambled on toward the bulging cliff and litten sky he felt fears more shocking than any he had known before. Then through the high mists he heard the voice of unseen Barzai shouting wildly in delight:

"I have heard the gods! I have heard earth's gods singing in revelry on Hatheg-Kla! The voices of earth's gods are known to Barzai the Prophet! The mists are thin and the moon is bright, and I shall see the gods dancing wildly on Hatheg-Kla that they loved in youth! The wisdom of Barzai hath made him greater than earth's gods, and against his will their spells and barriers are as naught; Barzai will behold the gods, the proud gods, the secret gods, the gods of earth who spurn the sight of men!"

Atal could not hear the voices Barzai heard, but he was now close to the bulging cliff and scanning it for foot-holds. Then he heard Barzai's voice grow shriller and louder:

"The mists are very thin, and the moon casts shadows on the slope; the voices of earth's gods are high and wild, and they fear the coming of Barzai the Wise, who is greater than they. . . . The moon's light flickers, as earth's gods dance against it; I shall see the dancing forms of the gods that leap and howl in the moon-light. . . . The light is dimmer and the gods are afraid. . . ."

Whilst Barzai was shouting these things Atal felt a spectral change in the air, as if the laws of earth were bowing to greater laws; for though the way was steeper than ever, the upward path was now grown fearsomely easy, and the bulging cliff proved scarce an obstacle when he reached it and slid perilously up its convex face. The light of the moon had strangely failed, and as Atal plunged upward through the mists he heard Barzai the Wise shrieking in the shadows:

"The moon is dark, and the gods dance in the night; there is terror in the sky, for upon the moon hath sunk an eclipse foretold in no books of men or of earth's gods.[14] . . . There is unknown magic on Hatheg-Kla, for the screams of the frightened gods have turned to laughter, and the slopes of ice shoot up endlessly into the black heavens whither I am plunging. . . . Hei! Hei! At last! *In the dim light I behold the gods of earth!*"

14. An ordinary lunar eclipse is caused by the earth passing between the sun and the moon, so that the earth's shadow (or its penumbra) falls on the moon's surface. Lunar eclipses are as predictable as clock-work. An *unpredictable* lunar eclipse can only occur when a body *other than the Earth* (and large enough to cast a shadow visible from the Earth) passes between the sun and the moon. Here, the "unfore-told" eclipse could have been caused by the immense body of a god or a ship of the gods passing between the sun and the moon.

15. In Greek myth, a flaming river, one of five in the underworld; also called Pyriphlegethon.

16. Kieran Setiya points out that "[t]hese allusions at least begin to suggest the gulfs of space, and the insignificance of mankind, crystallized in the Mythos fiction of Lovecraft's later career." See "Two Notes on Lovecraft," *Lovecraft Studies* 26 (Spring 1992), 15.

And now Atal, slipping dizzily up over inconceivable steeps, heard in the dark a loathsome laughing, mixed with such a cry as no man else ever heard save in the Phlegethon[15] of unrelatable nightmares; a cry wherein reverberated the horror and anguish of a haunted lifetime packed into one atrocious moment:

"The *other* gods! The *other* gods! The gods of the outer hells that guard the feeble gods of earth! . . . Look away! . . . Go back! . . . Do not see! . . . Do not see! . . . The vengeance of the infinite abysses . . . That cursed, that damnable pit . . .[16] Merciful gods of earth, *I am falling into the sky!*"

And as Atal shut his eyes and stopped his ears and tried to jump downward against the frightful pull from unknown heights, there resounded on Hatheg-Kla that terrible peal of thunder which awaked the good cotters of the plains and the honest burgesses of Hatheg, and Nir, and Ulthar, and caused them to behold through the clouds that strange eclipse of the moon that no book ever predicted. And when the moon came out at last Atal was safe on the lower snows of the mountain without sight of earth's gods, or of the *other* gods.

Now it is told in the mouldy Pnakotic Manuscripts that Sansu found naught but wordless ice and rock when he climbed Hatheg-Kla in the youth of the world. Yet when the men of Ulthar and Nir and Hatheg crushed their fears and scaled that haunted steep by day in search of Barzai the Wise, they found graven in the naked stone of the summit a curious and Cyclopean symbol fifty cubits wide, as if the rock had been riven by some titanic chisel. And the symbol was like to one that learned men have discerned in those frightful parts of the Pnakotic Manuscripts which are too ancient to be read. This they found.

Barzai the Wise they never found, nor could the holy priest Atal ever be persuaded to pray for his soul's repose. Moreover, to this day the people of Ulthar and Nir and Hatheg fear eclipses, and pray by night when pale vapours hide the mountain-top and the moon. And above the mists on Hatheg-Kla earth's gods sometimes dance reminiscently; for they know they are safe, and love to come from unknown Kadath in ships of cloud and play in the olden way, as they did when earth was new and men not given to the climbing of inaccessible places.

The Music of Erich Zann[1]

Like "The Outsider," "The Music of Erich Zann" has been studied and debated extensively. HPL himself rated the story very highly, and it was one of the few for which he was to receive critical acclaim during his lifetime. Partially based on a dream, it has been interpreted as plumbing the depths of Lovecraft's own mind, as the narrator leads the reader across the boundary of a shadowy river into the strange unknown interior of a city. Seen as representing a flight from cosmic horror, and set in a place not even the narrator can identify, its strength lies in its ambiguity.

Weird Tales (May 1925) (artist: Andrew Brosnatch)

I have examined maps of the city with the greatest care, yet have never again found the Rue d'Auseil.[2] These maps have not been modern maps alone, for I know that names change. I have, on the contrary, delved deeply into all the antiquities of the place; and have personally explored every region, of whatever

1. Probably written in December 1921, the story first appeared in *National Amateur* 44, no. 4 (March 1922), 38–40. It was reprinted in *Weird Tales* 5, no. 5 (May 1925), 219–24, and again in *Weird Tales* 24, no. 5 (November 1934), 644–

48, 655–56. In 1936, Lovecraft called it his second favorite story (first place going to "The Colour Out of Space," in the previous volume, pp. 310–42), but he reached this verdict "because it isn't as bad as most of the rest. I like it for what it *hasn't* more than for what it *has*" (Letter to Wilfred Blanch Talman, November 10, 1936, *Selected Letters*, V, 348).

2. A distinctly French-sounding street name, but not one found on any map. Donald R. Burleson, in *H. P. Lovecraft: A Critical Study*, suggests that it may be translated as "of being on the threshold," as in "on the threshold of immense and terrific revelations" (94, note 26). Robert M. Price prefers the word "sill" to "threshold," with reference especially to Zann's window ("Erich Zann and the Rue d'Auseil," *Lovecraft Studies* 22/23 [Fall 1990], 13).

3. Thus, suggests Robert M. Price, in "Erich Zann and the Rue d'Auseil," "It is as if the road carries its traveler through time (backward) as well as space."

name, which could possibly answer to the street I knew as the Rue d'Auseil. But despite all I have done it remains an humiliating fact that I cannot find the house, the street, or even the locality, where, during the last months of my impoverished life as a student of metaphysics at the University, I heard the music of Erich Zann.

That my memory is broken, I do not wonder; for my health, physical and mental, was gravely disturbed throughout the period of my residence in the Rue d'Auseil, and I recall that I took none of my few acquaintances there. But that I cannot find the place again is both singular and perplexing; for it was within a half-hour's walk of the University and was distinguished by peculiarities which could hardly be forgotten by anyone who had been there. I have never met a person who has seen the Rue d'Auseil.

The Rue d'Auseil lay across a dark river bordered by precipitous brick blear-windowed warehouses and spanned by a ponderous bridge of dark stone. It was always shadowy along that river, as if the smoke of neighbouring factories shut out the sun perpetually. The river was also odorous with evil stenches which I have never smelled elsewhere, and which may some day help me to find it, since I should recognise them at once. Beyond the bridge were narrow cobbled streets with rails; and then came the ascent, at first gradual, but incredibly steep as the Rue d'Auseil was reached.

I have never seen another street as narrow and steep as the Rue d'Auseil. It was almost a cliff, closed to all vehicles, consisting in several places of flights of steps, and ending at the top in a lofty ivied wall. Its paving was irregular, sometimes stone slabs, sometimes cobblestones, and sometimes bare earth with struggling greenish-grey vegetation.[3] The houses were tall, peaked-roofed, incredibly old, and crazily leaning backward, forward, and sidewise. Occasionally an opposite pair, both leaning forward, almost met across the street like an arch; and certainly they kept most of the light from the ground below. There were a few overhead bridges from house to house across the street.

The inhabitants of that street impressed me peculiarly. At first I thought it was because they were all silent and reticent; but later decided it was because they were all very old. I do not know how I came to live on such a street, but I was not myself when I moved there. I had been living in many poor places, always evicted for want of money; until at last I came upon that tottering house in the Rue d'Auseil, kept by the paralytic Blandot. It was the third house from the top of the street, and by far the tallest of them all.

My room was on the fifth story; the only inhabited room there, since the house was almost empty. On the night I arrived I heard strange music from the peaked garret overhead, and the next day asked old Blandot about it. He told me it was an old German viol-player,[4] a strange dumb man who signed his name as Erich Zann,[5] and who played evenings in a cheap theatre orchestra; adding that Zann's desire to play in the night after his return from the theatre was the reason he had chosen this lofty and isolated garret room, whose single gable window was the only point on the street from which one could look over the terminating wall at the declivity and panorama beyond.

Thereafter I heard Zann every night, and although he kept me awake, I was haunted by the weirdness of his music. Knowing little of the art myself, I was yet certain that none of his harmonies had any relation to music I had heard before; and concluded that he was a composer of highly original genius. The longer I listened, the more I was fascinated, until after a week I resolved to make the old man's acquaintance.

One night, as he was returning from his work, I intercepted Zann in the hallway and told him that I would like to know him and be with him when he played. He was a small, lean, bent person, with shabby clothes, blue eyes, grotesque, satyr-like face, and nearly bald head; and at my first words seemed both angered and frightened. My obvious friendliness, however, finally melted him; and he grudgingly motioned to me to follow him up the dark, creaking, and rickety attic stairs. His room, one of only two in the steeply pitched garret, was on the west side, toward the high wall that formed the upper end of the street. Its size was very great, and seemed the greater because of its extraordinary bareness and neglect. Of furniture there was only a narrow iron bedstead, a dingy washstand, a small table, a large bookcase, an iron music-rack, and three old-fashioned chairs. Sheets of music were piled in disorder about the floor. The walls were of bare boards,

4. The viol, also known as the viola dagamba (the "leg viol"), although similar to a cello, has a flat back, sloped shoulders, C-shaped sound holes, and five to seven strings. The instrument became popular in the Renaissance and Baroque periods and hence was an unlikely instrument for a musician in a "cheap theatre orchestra" (though he may have played the violin or cello in that orchestra and merely kept the viol for his personal amusement). Despite references to the instrument "screaming" or "shrieking," the viol or viola has never been a name used for the violin; nor are there any indications that Zann held the chosen instrument to his chin. Hence, we must accept that the instrument he played for the narrator actually was a viol, kept in a cloth bag rather than a rigid case. Despite the narrator's thorough inventory of Zann's room, the bookcase or a closet must have concealed another instrument, most likely a violin.

Viola da gamba.
Shutterstock.com

Blandot, who identified Zann as a "viol-player," was likely French (confirmed by the street name); a viol is a "*viole*" in French, a violin a "*violon*." Therefore the instrument misidentification, if it occurred, cannot be blamed on language differences. Presumably Blandot did not mean to convey to the narrator that Zann played the viol *in the orchestra*; rather, that he played it in the house. The sound of the viol is quite a bit deeper than that of the violin.

5. Does this statement—"who signed his name as Erich Zann"—imply that that is not in fact his name but rather a stage name? Carl Buchanan, in his Freudian interpretation of the tale, points out that "Erich" means king (from its Scandinavian roots) and that "Zand" is Dutch for sand—thus the name denotes that the man's true identity is the King of Sleep. See "'The Music of Erich Zann': A Psychological Interpretation (or Two)," in *A Century Less a Dream: Selected Criticism on H. P. Lovecraft*, ed. Scott Connors, 224–29 (Holikong, PA: Wildside Press, 2002), 225.

and had probably never known plaster; whilst the abundance of dust and cobwebs made the place seem more deserted than inhabited. Evidently Erich Zann's world of beauty lay in some far cosmos of the imagination.

Motioning me to sit down, the dumb man closed the door, turned the large wooden bolt, and lighted a candle to augment the one he had brought with him. He now removed his viol from its moth-eaten covering, and taking it, seated himself in the least uncomfortable of the chairs. He did not employ the music-rack, but offering no choice and playing from memory, enchanted me for over an hour with strains I had never heard before; strains which must have been of his own devising. To describe their exact nature is impossible for one unversed in music. They were a kind of fugue, with recurrent passages of the most captivating quality, but to me were notable for the absence of any of the weird notes I had overheard from my room below on other occasions.

Those haunting notes I had remembered, and had often hummed and whistled inaccurately to myself; so when the player at length laid down his bow I asked him if he would render some of them. As I began my request the wrinkled satyr-like face lost the bored placidity it had possessed during the playing, and seemed to shew the same curious mixture of anger and fright which I had noticed when first I accosted the old man. For a moment I was inclined to use persuasion, regarding rather lightly the whims of senility; and even tried to awaken my host's weirder mood by whistling a few of the strains to which I had listened the night before. But I did not pursue this course for more than a moment; for when the dumb musician recognised the whistled air his face grew suddenly distorted with an expression wholly beyond analysis, and his long, cold, bony right hand reached out to stop my mouth and silence the crude imitation. As he did this he further demonstrated his eccentricity by casting a startled glance toward the lone curtained window, as if fearful of some intruder; a glance doubly absurd, since the garret stood high and inaccessible above all the adjacent roofs, this window being the only point on the steep street, as the concierge had told me, from which one could see over the wall at the summit.

The old man's glance brought Blandot's remark to my mind,

and with a certain capriciousness I felt a wish to look out over the wide and dizzying panorama of moonlit roofs and city lights beyond the hilltop, which of all the dwellers in the Rue d'Auseil only this crabbed musician could see. I moved toward the window and would have drawn aside the nondescript curtains, when with a frightened rage even greater than before the dumb lodger was upon me again; this time motioning with his head toward the door as he nervously strove to drag me thither with both hands. Now thoroughly disgusted with my host, I ordered him to release me, and told him I would go at once. His clutch relaxed, and as he saw my disgust and offence his own anger seemed to subside. He tightened his relaxing grip, but this time in a friendly manner; forcing me into a chair, then with an appearance of wistfulness crossing to the littered table where he wrote many words with a pencil in the laboured French of a foreigner.

The note which he finally handed me was an appeal for tolerance and forgiveness. Zann said that he was old, lonely, and afflicted with strange fears and nervous disorders connected with his music and with other things. He had enjoyed my listening to his music, and wished I would come again and not mind his eccentricities. But he could not play to another his weird harmonies, and could not bear hearing them from another; nor could he bear having anything in his room touched by another. He had not known until our hallway conversation that I could overhear his playing in my room, and now asked me if I would arrange with Blandot to take a lower room where I could not hear him in the night. He would, he wrote, defray the difference in rent.

As I sat deciphering the execrable French I felt more lenient toward the old man. He was a victim of physical and nervous suffering, as was I; and my metaphysical studies had taught me kindness. In the silence there came a slight sound from the window—the shutter must have rattled in the night-wind—and for some reason I started almost as violently as did Erich Zann. So when I had finished reading I shook my host by the hand, and departed as a friend. The next day Blandot gave me a more expensive room on the third floor, between the apartments of an aged money-lender and the room of a respectable upholsterer. There was no one on the fourth floor.

It was not long before I found that Zann's eagerness for my company was not as great as it had seemed while he was persuading me to move down from the fifth story. He did not ask me to call on him, and when I did call he appeared uneasy and played listlessly. This was always at night—in the day he slept and would admit no one. My liking for him did not grow, though the attic room and the weird music seemed to hold an odd fascination for me. I had a curious desire to look out of that window, over the wall and down the unseen slope at the glittering roofs and spires which must lie outspread there. Once I went up to the garret during theatre hours, when Zann was away, but the door was locked.

What I did succeed in doing was to overhear the nocturnal playing of the dumb old man. At first I would tiptoe up to my old fifth floor, then I grew bold enough to climb the last creaking staircase to the peaked garret. There in the narrow hall, outside the bolted door with the covered keyhole, I often heard sounds which filled me with an indefinable dread—the dread of vague wonder and brooding mystery. It was not that the sounds were hideous, for they were not; but that they held vibrations suggesting nothing on this globe of earth, and that at certain intervals they assumed a symphonic quality which I could hardly conceive as produced by one player. Certainly, Erich Zann was a genius of wild power. As the weeks passed, the playing grew wilder, whilst the old musician acquired an increasing haggardness and furtiveness pitiful to behold. He now refused to admit me at any time, and shunned me whenever we met on the stairs.

Then one night as I listened at the door I heard the shrieking viol swell into a chaotic babel of sound; a pandemonium which would have led me to doubt my own shaking sanity had there not come from behind that barred portal a piteous proof that the horror was real—the awful, inarticulate cry which only a mute can utter, and which rises only in moments of the most terrible fear or anguish. I knocked repeatedly at the door, but received no response. Afterward I waited in the black hallway, shivering with cold and fear, till I heard the poor musician's feeble effort to rise from the floor by the aid of a chair. Believing him just conscious after a fainting fit, I renewed my rapping, at the same time calling out my name reassuringly. I heard Zann stumble to the window and close both shutter and sash, then stumble to the door, which he falteringly unfastened to admit me. This time his delight at having me present was real; for his distorted face gleamed with relief, while he clutched at my coat as a child clutches at its mother's skirts.

Shaking pathetically, the old man forced me into a chair whilst he sank into another, beside which his viol and bow lay carelessly on the floor. He sat for some time inactive, nodding oddly, but having a paradoxical suggestion of intense and frightened listening. Subsequently he seemed to be satisfied, and crossing to a chair by the table wrote a brief note, handed it to me, and returned to the table, where he began to write rapidly and incessantly. The note implored me in the name of mercy, and for the sake of my own curiosity, to wait where I was while he prepared a full account in German of all the marvels and terrors which beset him. I waited, and the dumb man's pencil flew.

It was perhaps an hour later, while I still waited and while the old musician's feverishly written sheets still continued to pile up, that I saw Zann start as from the hint of a horrible shock. Unmistakably he was looking at the curtained window and listening shudderingly. Then I half fancied I heard a sound myself; though it was not a horrible sound, but rather an exquisitely low and infinitely distant musical note, suggesting a player in one of the neighbouring houses, or in some abode beyond the lofty wall over which I had never been able to look. Upon Zann the effect was terrible, for dropping his pencil suddenly he rose, seized his viol, and commenced to rend the night with the wildest playing I had ever heard from his bow save when listening at the barred door.

It would be useless to describe the playing of Erich Zann on that dreadful night. It was more horrible than anything I had ever overheard, because I could now see the expression of his face, and could realise that this time the motive was stark fear. He was trying to make a noise; to ward something off or drown something out—what, I could not imagine, awesome though I felt it must be. The playing grew fantastic, delirious, and hysterical, yet kept to the last the qualities of supreme genius which I

6. "Zann cannot express himself in terms of our world," observes Robert M. Price, in "Erich Zann and the Rue d'Auseil" (see note 2, above). His written French is "execrable" and his attempt to communicate in German is sucked out of the window by the uncanny wind.

knew this strange old man possessed. I recognised the air—it was a wild Hungarian dance popular in the theatres, and I reflected for a moment that this was the first time I had ever heard Zann play the work of another composer.

Louder and louder, wilder and wilder, mounted the shrieking and whining of that desperate viol. The player was dripping with an uncanny perspiration and twisted like a monkey; always looking frantically at the curtained window. In his frenzied strains I could almost see shadowy satyrs and Bacchanals dancing and whirling insanely through seething abysses of clouds and smoke and lightning. And then I thought I heard a shriller, steadier note that was not from the viol; a calm, deliberate, purposeful, mocking note from far away in the west.

At this juncture the shutter began to rattle in a howling night-wind which had sprung up outside as if in answer to the mad playing within. Zann's screaming viol now outdid itself, emitting sounds I had never thought a viol could emit. The shutter rattled more loudly, unfastened, and commenced slamming against the window. Then the glass broke shiveringly under the persistent impacts, and the chill wind rushed in, making the candles sputter and rustling the sheets of paper on the table where Zann had begun to write out his horrible secret. I looked at Zann, and saw that he was past conscious observation. His blue eyes were bulging, glassy, and sightless, and the frantic playing had become a blind, mechanical, unrecognisable orgy that no pen could even suggest.

A sudden gust, stronger than the others, caught up the manuscript and bore it toward the window. I followed the flying sheets in desperation, but they were gone before I reached the demolished panes.[6] Then I remembered my old wish to gaze from this window, the only window in the Rue d'Auseil from which one might see the slope beyond the wall, and the city outspread beneath. It was very dark, but the city's lights always burned, and I expected to see them there amidst the rain and wind. Yet when I looked from that highest of all gable windows, looked while the candles sputtered and the insane viol howled with the night-wind, I saw no city spread below, and no friendly lights gleaming from remembered streets, but only the blackness of space illimitable; unimagined space alive with motion and music, and having no semblance to anything on earth. And as I stood there looking in terror, the wind blew out both the candles in that ancient peaked garret, leaving me in savage and impenetrable darkness with chaos and pandemonium before me, and the daemon madness of that night-baying viol behind me.

I staggered back in the dark, without the means of striking a light, crashing against the table, overturning a chair, and finally groping my way to the place where the blackness screamed with shocking music. To save myself and Erich Zann I could at least try, whatever the powers opposed to me. Once I thought some chill thing brushed me, and I screamed, but my scream could not be heard above that hideous viol. Suddenly out of the blackness the madly sawing bow struck me, and I knew I was close to the player. I felt ahead, touched the back of Zann's chair, and then found and shook his shoulder in an effort to bring him to his senses.

He did not respond, and still the viol shrieked on without slackening. I moved my hand to his head, whose mechanical nodding I was able to stop, and shouted in his ear that we must both flee from the unknown things of the night. But he neither answered me nor abated the frenzy of his unutterable music, while all through the garret strange currents of wind seemed to dance in the darkness and babel. When my hand touched his ear I shuddered, though I knew not why—knew not why till I felt of the still face; the ice-cold, stiffened, unbreathing face whose glassy eyes bulged uselessly into the void. And then, by some miracle finding the door and the large wooden bolt, I plunged wildly away from that glassy-eyed thing in the dark, and from the ghoulish howling of that accursed viol whose fury increased even as I plunged.

Leaping, floating, flying down those endless stairs through the dark house; racing mindlessly out into the narrow, steep, and ancient street of steps and tottering houses; clattering down steps and over cobbles to the lower streets and the putrid canyon-walled river; panting across the great dark bridge to the broader, healthier streets and boulevards we know; all these are terrible impressions that linger with me.[7] And I recall that there was no

7. "This is plainly a dream-like, poetic line," writes Robert E. Pierson; "where else do we float and fly but in our dreams? Lovecraft is forcing us into a state of confusion—a state in which dream and reality clash and then strangely coalesce." See "High House, Shunned House and a Silver Key," *Nyctalops* 3, no. 2 (March 1981), 6.

wind, and that the moon was out, and that all the lights of the city twinkled.

Despite my most careful searches and investigations, I have never since been able to find the Rue d'Auseil. But I am not wholly sorry; either for this or for the loss in undreamable abysses of the closely written sheets which alone could have explained the music of Erich Zann.

The Lurking Fear¹

Lovecraft wrote this tale in installments to satisfy the demands of the publisher of Home Brew *magazine, where it first appeared. With many of the trappings of a traditional tale of the supernatural—a deserted mansion, a lonely mountain, strange sightings and rumors—the story is another exploration by HPL of his theme of hereditary degeneration, ancient horrors visited upon the present, as related in "Facts concerning the Late Arthur Jermyn and His Family" and "The Rats in the Walls." Like "Beyond the Wall of Sleep," "The Lurking Fear" is set in the Catskills, in the southeastern part of New York State. Though Lovecraft never visited the mountains, his familiarity with the region is evident in the 1919 "Beyond the Wall of Sleep."² The loneliness of the Catskills sparked his imagination, and it became a canvas on which Lovecraft could depict another moralizing example of a family turned by isolation and miscegeny into abominations.*

"The Lurking Fear," *Adventure Comics*, 1991.
Cover art by Cariello

1. Written in November 1922, "The Lurking Fear" first appeared serially in *Home Brew* 2, no. 6 (January 1923),

Home Brew magazine (January 1923).

4–10; 3, no. 1 (February 1923), 18–23; 3, no. 2 (March 1923), 31–37, 44, 48; and 3, no. 3 (April 1923), 35–42. It was illustrated by Clark Ashton Smith. HPL had previously written "Herbert West: Reanimator" (in the previous volume, pp. 45–79) for *Home Brew* in 1922. *Home Brew*, edited by "Missus and Mister George Julian Houtain," billed itself as "America's Zippiest Pocket Magazine" and featured "peppy stories—pungent jests—piquant gossip." The story was reprinted in *Weird Tales* 11, no. 6 (June 1928), 791–804.

2. See "Beyond the Wall of Sleep," in the previous volume, pp. 18–29.

3. There is a Tempest Mountain in Montana (east of Granite Peak), and the highest point on Moreton Island, in Queensland, off the east coast of Australia, is named Mount Tempest, described in the country's travel guides as "the highest stabilized sand dune in the world." There is also a peak named Mount Tempest in Ireland. However, there are no records of a Tempest Mountain in the Catskills. David Haden, in "The Annotated 'The Lurking Fear'" (in *Lovecraft in Historical Context: A Fifth Collection* [self-published, 2014], 46, note 18), suggests that this may be a disguised version of Tremper Mountain, located in the center of the Catskills; below the mountain lies the hamlet originally named Ladew Corners.

"The Shadow on the Chimney."
Home Brew (January 1923) (artist: Clark Ashton Smith; reprinted with permission of CASiana Enterprises, the Literary Estate of Clark Ashton Smith)

I. THE SHADOW ON THE CHIMNEY

THERE WAS THUNDER in the air on the night I went to the deserted mansion atop Tempest Mountain[3] to find the lurking fear. I was not alone, for foolhardiness was not then mixed with that love of the grotesque and the terrible which has made my career a series of quests for strange horrors in literature and in life. With me were two faithful and muscular men for whom I had sent when the time came; men long associated with me in my ghastly explorations because of their peculiar fitness.

We had started quietly from the village because of the reporters who still lingered about after the eldritch[4] panic of a month before—the nightmare creeping death. Later, I thought, they might aid me; but I did not want them then. Would to God I had let them share the search, that I might not have had to bear the secret alone so long; to bear it alone for fear the world would call me mad or go mad itself at the daemon implications of the thing. Now that I am telling it anyway, lest the brooding make me a maniac, I wish I had never concealed it. For I, and I only, know what manner of fear lurked on that spectral and desolate mountain.

In a small motor-car we covered the miles of primeval forest and hill until the wooded ascent checked it. The country bore an aspect more than usually sinister as we viewed it by night and without the accustomed crowds of investigators, so that we were often tempted to use the acetylene headlight[5] despite the attention it might attract. It was not a wholesome landscape after dark, and I believe I would have noticed its morbidity even had I been ignorant of the terror that stalked there. Of wild creatures there were none—they are wise when death leers close. The ancient lightning-scarred trees seemed unnaturally large and twisted, and the other vegetation unnaturally thick and feverish, while curious mounds and hummocks in the weedy, fulgurite-pitted[6] earth reminded me of snakes and dead men's skulls swelled to gigantic proportions.[7]

Fear had lurked on Tempest Mountain for more than a century. This I learned at once from newspaper accounts of the catastrophe which first brought the region to the world's notice. The place is a remote, lonely elevation in that part of the Catskills where Dutch civilisation once feebly and transiently penetrated,[8] leaving behind as it receded only a few ruined mansions and a degenerate squatter population inhabiting pitiful hamlets on isolated slopes. Normal beings seldom visited the locality till the state police were formed, and even now only infrequent troopers patrol it. The fear, however, is an old tradition throughout the neighbouring villages; since it is a prime topic in the simple dis-

4. One of Lovecraft's favorite words, meaning weird or fantastic. See "The Hound" in the previous volume, pp. 94–102, note 2. It appears seven times in the stories in this volume, eighteen times in the previous volume's tales.

5. Acetylene gas lamps burned acetylene (C_2H_2) gas, produced when calcium carbide (CaC_2) reacts with water. Used in Victorian coaches, on trains, and in early Model-T Fords, they were touted as products for the home until electrical lighting supplanted them everywhere. In the early twentieth century, portable acetylene lamps were carried into mines, usually providing the only source of light.

Acetylene lamp.
Shutterstock.com

6. Fulgurites, aptly described as "petrified lightning" (the Latin "*fulgur*" means "lightning"), are tubes of fused quartz (SiO_2), the product of lightning striking mineral deposits such as silica-rich sand or carbonate-rich soil. Rootlike underground deposits, they have no practical value other than as tangible evidence of lightning strikes.

7. Haden, in his "Annotated 'The Lurking Fear,'" suggests a connection to the legends of Catskill gnomes, who brewed a drink that swelled the heads of all who

drank it. See Charles M. Skinner's *Myths and Legends of Our Own Land,* 4th ed. (New York and Philadelphia: J. B. Lippincott & Co., 1896), a book known to HPL.

8. See "Beyond the Wall of Sleep" in the previous volume, pp. 18–29, note 5, for a consideration of the popular view of residents of the Catskills as "degenerate."

"The Martense Mansion."
Home Brew (January 1923) (artist: Clark Ashton Smith; reprinted with permission of CASiana Enterprises, the Literary Estate of Clark Ashton Smith)

course of the poor mongrels who sometimes leave their valleys to trade hand-woven baskets for such primitive necessities as they cannot shoot, raise, or make.

The lurking fear dwelt in the shunned and deserted Martense mansion, which crowned the high but gradual eminence whose liability to frequent thunderstorms gave it the name of Tempest Mountain. For over a hundred years the antique, grove-circled stone house had been the subject of stories incredibly wild and monstrously hideous; stories of a silent colossal creeping death which stalked abroad in summer. With whimpering insistence the squatters told tales of a daemon which seized lone wayfarers after dark, either carrying them off or leaving them in a frightful state of gnawed dismemberment; while sometimes they whispered of blood-trails toward the distant mansion. Some said the thunder called the lurking fear out of its habitation, while others said the thunder was its voice.

No one outside the backwoods had believed these varying and

conflicting stories, with their incoherent, extravagant descriptions of the half-glimpsed fiend; yet not a farmer or villager doubted that the Martense mansion was ghoulishly haunted. Local history forbade such a doubt, although no ghostly evidence was ever found by such investigators as had visited the building after some especially vivid tale of the squatters. Grandmothers told strange myths of the Martense spectre; myths concerning the Martense family itself, its queer hereditary dissimilarity of eyes,[9] its long, unnatural annals, and the murder which had cursed it.

The terror which brought me to the scene was a sudden and portentous confirmation of the mountaineers' wildest legends. One summer night, after a thunderstorm of unprecedented violence, the countryside was aroused by a squatter stampede which no mere delusion could create. The pitiful throngs of natives shrieked and whined of the unnamable horror which had descended upon them, and they were not doubted. They had not seen it, but had heard such cries from one of their hamlets that they knew a creeping death had come.

In the morning citizens and state troopers followed the shuddering mountaineers to the place where they said the death had come. Death was indeed there. The ground under one of the squatters' villages had caved in after a lightning stroke, destroying several of the malodorous shanties; but upon this property damage was superimposed an organic devastation which paled it to insignificance. Of a possible seventy-five natives who had inhabited this spot, not one living specimen was visible. The disordered earth was covered with blood and human debris bespeaking too vividly the ravages of daemon teeth and talons; yet no visible trail led away from the carnage. That some hideous animal must be the cause, everyone quickly agreed; nor did any tongue now revive the charge that such cryptic deaths formed merely the sordid murders common in decadent communities. That charge was revived only when about twenty-five of the estimated population were found missing from the dead; and even then it was hard to explain the murder of fifty by half that number. But the fact remained that on a summer night a bolt had come out of the heavens and left a dead village whose corpses were horribly mangled, chewed, and clawed.

The excited countryside immediately connected the horror

9. The condition is known as heterochromia. David Haden calls this "a visual expression of some miscegenation lurking far back in the Martense ancestry" ("The Annotated 'The Lurking Fear,'" 46, note 18). The Martense name would likely have been known to Lovecraft through his extensive knowledge of the Revolutionary War. The Martenses (among whose family tree were a Jan Martense and a Gerrit Martense) were significant landholders in Brooklyn. Martense Lane (now Border Avenue) was the attack route used by British general James Grant in the Battle of Brooklyn in 1776, the first major battle of the American Revolution. The road itself is mentioned in "The Horror at Red Hook," pp. 249–76, below.

10. In 1660, at the age of only ten or fifteen, Leffert Pietersen van Haughwout emigrated from Holland to Flatbush, then part of Long Island and known as Midwout or Vlacke bos, the latter from a Dutch phrase meaning "wooded plain." He joined the ranks of influential Dutch settlers already in New York, and by the eighteenth century his descendants had adopted his first name as their surname. Although there is no record of a "Lefferts Corner" in the Catskills, Long Island, or Brooklyn (where Flatbush is today located), there is a family museum on Flatbush Avenue, the Lefferts Historic House—once the home of one of Van Haughwout's fourteen children. The Brooklyn Historical Society houses the Lefferts family papers, items from which predate Van Haughwout's arrival in New York by ten years. Prospect-Lefferts Gardens, Brooklyn, is a residential neighborhood situated on land once owned by the Lefferts family.

with the haunted Martense mansion, though the localities were over three miles apart. The troopers were more sceptical; including the mansion only casually in their investigations, and dropping it altogether when they found it thoroughly deserted. Country and village people, however, canvassed the place with infinite care; overturning everything in the house, sounding ponds and brooks, beating down bushes, and ransacking the nearby forests. All was in vain; the death that had come had left no trace save destruction itself.

By the second day of the search the affair was fully treated by the newspapers, whose reporters overran Tempest Mountain. They described it in much detail, and with many interviews to elucidate the horror's history as told by local grandams. I followed the accounts languidly at first, for I am a connoisseur in horrors; but after a week I detected an atmosphere which stirred me oddly, so that on August 5th, 1921, I registered among the reporters who crowded the hotel at Lefferts Corners,[10] nearest village to Tempest Mountain and acknowledged headquarters of the searchers. Three weeks more, and the dispersal of the reporters left me free to begin a terrible exploration based on the minute inquiries and surveying with which I had meanwhile busied myself.

So on this summer night, while distant thunder rumbled, I left a silent motor-car and tramped with two armed companions up the last mound-covered reaches of Tempest Mountain, casting the beams of an electric torch on the spectral grey walls that began to appear through the giant oaks ahead. In this morbid night solitude and feeble shifting illumination, the vast box-like pile displayed obscure hints of terror which day could not uncover; yet I did not hesitate, since I had come with fierce resolution to test an idea. I believed that the thunder called the death-daemon out of some fearsome secret place; and be that daemon solid entity or vaporous pestilence, I meant to see it.

I had thoroughly searched the ruin before, hence knew my plan well; choosing as the seat of my vigil the old room of Jan Martense, whose murder looms so great in the rural legends. I felt subtly that the apartment of this ancient victim was best for my purposes. The chamber, measuring about twenty feet square, contained like the other rooms some rubbish which had once been furniture. It lay on the second story, on the southeast corner of the house, and had an immense east window and narrow south window, both devoid of panes or shutters. Opposite the large window was an enormous Dutch fireplace with scriptural tiles representing the prodigal son,[11] and opposite the narrow window was a spacious bed built into the wall.

As the tree-muffled thunder grew louder, I arranged my plan's details. First I fastened side by side to the ledge of the large window three rope ladders which I had brought with me. I knew they reached a suitable spot on the grass outside, for I had tested them. Then the three of us dragged from another room a wide four-poster bedstead, crowding it laterally against the window. Having strown it with fir boughs, all now rested on it with drawn automatics, two relaxing while the third watched. From whatever direction the daemon might come, our potential escape was provided. If it came from within the house, we had the window ladders; if from outside, the door and the stairs. We did not think, judging from precedent, that it would pursue us far even at worst.

I watched from midnight to one o'clock, when in spite of the sinister house, the unprotected window, and the approaching thunder and lightning, I felt singularly drowsy. I was between my two companions, George Bennett being toward the window and William Tobey toward the fireplace. Bennett was asleep, having apparently felt the same anomalous drowsiness which affected me, so I designated Tobey for the next watch although even he was nodding. It is curious how intently I had been watching that fireplace.

The increasing thunder must have affected my dreams, for in the brief time I slept there came to me apocalyptic visions. Once I partly awaked, probably because the sleeper toward the window had restlessly flung an arm across my chest. I was not sufficiently awake to see whether Tobey was attending to his duties as sentinel, but felt a distinct anxiety on that score. Never before had the presence of evil so poignantly oppressed me. Later I must have dropped asleep again, for it was out of a phantasmal chaos that my mind leaped when the night grew hideous with shrieks beyond anything in my former experience or imagination.

In that shrieking the inmost soul of human fear and agony clawed hopelessly and insanely at the ebony gates of oblivion. I

11. Told by Jesus in one of the four Gospels (Luke 15:11–32), the parable of the prodigal son celebrates the return of a young man who, after living as a wastrel and squandering his inheritance, repents and is celebrated by his father, outraging his hardworking brother.

12. In Edith Hamilton's classic telling, Charon is "an aged boatman [who] ferries the souls of the dead across the water to the farther bank, where stands the adamantine gate to Tartarus," the deepest level of the underworld (*Mythology: Timeless Tales of Gods and Heroes* [Boston: Little, Brown/Back Bay Books, 1998], 43). Five rivers separate the land of the living from that of the dead: Acheron, river of woe; Cocytus (lamentation), the aforementioned Phlegethon (see "The Other Gods," pp. 106–10, note 15, above), Styx (the gods' oath), and Lethe (forgetfulness).

Poe wrote of "the foul Charonian canal" bordering "those dim plains of Helusion," or Elysium, in "Shadow—A Parable" (1835); he is said to have found the word "Charonian" in Jacob Bryant's *A New System; or, an Analysis of Antient Mythology* (1806), where Bryant records that Strabo and Pliny used the term to describe caves and springs that were fetid, foul, or hot; hence "Charonian" in this context means "hellish." While no such mention has been found in Pliny's *Natural History*, the Horace Leonard Jones (1879–1954) translation of Strabo's seventeen-book *Geography* (Cambridge, MA: Harvard University Press/Loeb Classical Library, 1923) contains references to vaporous Plutonia and two Charonia (both are the plural forms of the words); Jones notes: "'Plutonia' were precincts where mephitic vapours arose, and they were so called because they were regarded as entrances to the nether world. The cave itself, within the 'Plutonium,' was called 'Charonium'" (book 5, chapter 4, note 317).

awoke to red madness and the mockery of diabolism, as farther and farther down inconceivable vistas that phobic and crystalline anguish retreated and reverberated. There was no light, but I knew from the empty space at my right that Tobey was gone, God alone knew whither. Across my chest still lay the heavy arm of the sleeper at my left.

Then came the devastating stroke of lightning which shook the whole mountain, lit the darkest crypts of the hoary grove, and splintered the patriarch of the twisted trees. In the daemon flash of a monstrous fireball the sleeper started up suddenly while the glare from beyond the window threw his shadow vividly upon the chimney above the fireplace from which my eyes had never strayed. That I am still alive and sane, is a marvel I cannot fathom. I cannot fathom it, for the shadow on that chimney was not that of George Bennett or of any other human creature, but a blasphemous abnormality from hell's nethermost craters; a nameless, shapeless abomination which no mind could fully grasp and no pen even partly describe. In another second I was alone in the accursed mansion, shivering and gibbering. George Bennett and William Tobey had left no trace, not even of a struggle. They were never heard of again.

II. A PASSER IN THE STORM

FOR DAYS AFTER that hideous experience in the forest-swathed mansion I lay nervously exhausted in my hotel room at Lefferts Corners. I do not remember exactly how I managed to reach the motor-car, start it, and slip unobserved back to the village; for I retain no distinct impression save of wild-armed titan trees, daemoniac mutterings of thunder, and Charonian[12] shadows athwart the low mounds that dotted and streaked the region.

As I shivered and brooded on the casting of that brain-blasting shadow, I knew that I had at last pried out one of earth's supreme horrors—one of those nameless blights of outer voids whose faint daemon scratchings we sometimes hear on the farthest rim of space, yet from which our own finite vision has given us a merciful immunity. The shadow I had seen, I hardly dared to analyse or identify. Something had lain between me and the window that night, but I shuddered whenever I could not cast off the instinct to classify it. If it had only snarled, or bayed, or laughed titteringly—even that would have relieved the abysmal hideousness. But it was so silent. It had rested a heavy arm or fore leg on my chest. . . . Obviously it was organic, or had once been organic. . . . Jan Martense, whose room I had invaded, was buried in the graveyard near the mansion. . . . I must find Bennett and Tobey, if they lived . . . why had it picked them, and left me for the last? . . . Drowsiness is so stifling, and dreams are so horrible. . . .

In a short time I realised that I must tell my story to someone or break down completely. I had already decided not to abandon the quest for the lurking fear, for in my rash ignorance it seemed to me that uncertainty was worse than enlightenment, however terrible the latter might prove to be. Accordingly I resolved in my mind the best course to pursue; whom to select for my confidences, and how to track down the thing which had obliterated two men and cast a nightmare shadow.

My chief acquaintances at Lefferts Corners had been the affable reporters, of whom several still remained to collect final echoes of the tragedy. It was from these that I determined to choose a colleague, and the more I reflected the more my preference inclined toward one Arthur Munroe, a dark, lean man of about thirty-five, whose education, taste, intelligence, and temperament all seemed to mark him as one not bound to conventional ideas and experiences.

On an afternoon in early September Arthur Munroe listened to my story. I saw from the beginning that he was both interested and sympathetic, and when I had finished he analysed and discussed the thing with the greatest shrewdness and judgment. His advice, moreover, was eminently practical; for he recommended a postponement of operations at the Martense mansion until we might become fortified with more detailed historical and geographical data. On his initiative we combed the countryside for information regarding the terrible Martense family, and discovered a man who possessed a marvellously illuminating ancestral diary. We also talked at length with such of the mountain mongrels as had not fled from the terror and confusion to remoter slopes, and arranged to precede our culminating task—the exhaustive and definitive examination of the mansion in the light of its detailed history—with an equally exhaustive and definitive examination of spots associated with the various tragedies of squatter legend.

The results of this examination were not at first very enlightening, though our tabulation of them seemed to reveal a fairly significant trend; namely, that the number of reported horrors was by far the greatest in areas either comparatively near the avoided house or connected with it by stretches of the morbidly overnourished forest. There were, it is true, exceptions; indeed, the horror which had caught the world's ear had happened in a treeless space remote alike from the mansion and from any connecting woods.

As to the nature and appearance of the lurking fear, nothing could be gained from the scared and witless shanty-dwellers. In the same breath they called it a snake and a giant, a thunder-devil and a bat, a vulture and a walking tree. We did, however, deem ourselves justified in assuming that it was a living organism highly susceptible to electrical storms; and although certain of the stories suggested wings, we believed that its aversion for open spaces made land locomotion a more probable theory. The only thing really incompatible with the latter view was the rapidity with which the creature must have travelled in order to perform all the deeds attributed to it.

When we came to know the squatters better, we found them curiously likeable in many ways. Simple animals they were, gently descending the evolutionary scale because of their unfortunate ancestry and stultifying isolation. They feared outsiders, but slowly grew accustomed to us; finally helping vastly when we beat down all the thickets and tore out all the partitions of the mansion in our search for the lurking fear. When we asked them to help us find Bennett and Tobey they were truly distressed; for they wanted to help us, yet knew that these victims had gone as wholly out of the world as their own missing people. That great numbers of them had actually been killed and removed, just as the wild animals had long been exterminated, we were of course thoroughly convinced; and we waited apprehensively for further tragedies to occur.

By the middle of October we were puzzled by our lack of progress. Owing to the clear nights no daemoniac aggressions had taken place, and the completeness of our vain searches of house and country almost drove us to regard the lurking fear as a non-material agency. We feared that the cold weather would come on and halt our explorations, for all agreed that the daemon was generally quiet in winter. Thus there was a kind of haste and desperation in our last daylight canvass of the horror-visited hamlet; a hamlet now deserted because of the squatters' fears.

The ill-fated squatter hamlet had borne no name, but had long stood in a sheltered though treeless cleft between two elevations called respectively Cone Mountain[13] and Maple Hill.[14] It was closer to Maple Hill than to Cone Mountain, some of the crude abodes indeed being dugouts on the side of the former eminence. Geographically it lay about two miles northwest of the base of Tempest Mountain, and three miles from the oak-girt mansion. Of the distance between the hamlet and the mansion, fully two miles and a quarter on the hamlet's side was entirely open country; the plain being of fairly level character save for some of the low snake-like mounds, and having as vegetation only grass and scattered weeds. Considering this topography, we had finally concluded that the daemon must have come by way of Cone Mountain, a wooded southern prolongation of which ran to within a short distance of the westernmost spur of Tempest Mountain. The upheaval of ground we traced conclusively to a landslide from Maple Hill, a tall lone splintered tree on whose side had been the striking point of the thunderbolt which summoned the fiend.

As for the twentieth time or more Arthur Munroe and I went minutely over every inch of the violated village, we were filled with a certain discouragement coupled with vague and novel fears. It was acutely uncanny, even when frightful and uncanny things were common, to encounter so blankly clueless a scene after such overwhelming occurrences; and we moved about beneath the leaden, darkening sky with that tragic directionless zeal which results from a combined sense of futility and necessity of action. Our care was gravely minute; every cottage was again entered, every hillside dugout again searched for bodies, every thorny foot of adjacent slope again scanned for dens and caves, but all without result. And yet, as I have said, vague new

13. There is a Cone Mountain in New Hampshire, several in Colorado, and one near Scottsdale, Arizona, but none in New York, although there is a Cone Mountain *Drive* in Queensbury, NY, south of Lake George—about 100 miles north of the town of Catskill.

14. According to the writer S. E. Dahlinger (in private correspondence with the editor), the hamlet of Maple Hill is in the village of Rosendale, northwest of the town of New Paltz, New York, on State Route 32, but has an elevation of only 200 feet.

15. See "The Nameless City," in the previous volume, pp. 80–93, note 26, for a discussion of the angel/demon Abaddon.

fears hovered menacingly over us; as if giant bat-winged gryphons squatted invisibly on the mountain-tops and leered with Abaddon-eyes[15] that had looked on trans-cosmic gulfs.

"Giant bat-winged gryphons."
Home Brew (February 1923) (artist: Clark Ashton Smith; reprinted with permission of CASiana Enterprises, the Literary Estate of Clark Ashton Smith)

"On Tempest Mountain."
Home Brew (January 1923) (artist: Clark Ashton Smith; reprinted with
permission of CASiana Enterprises, the Literary Estate of Clark Ashton Smith)

As the afternoon advanced, it became increasingly difficult
to see; and we heard the rumble of a thunderstorm gathering
over Tempest Mountain. This sound in such a locality naturally
stirred us, though less than it would have done at night. As it
was, we hoped desperately that the storm would last until well
after dark; and with that hope turned from our aimless hillside
searching toward the nearest inhabited hamlet to gather a body
of squatters as helpers in the investigation. Timid as they were, a
few of the younger men were sufficiently inspired by our protective leadership to promise such help.

We had hardly more than turned, however, when there
descended such a blinding sheet of torrential rain that shelter
became imperative. The extreme, almost nocturnal darkness of
the sky caused us to stumble sadly, but guided by the frequent
flashes of lightning and by our minute knowledge of the hamlet
we soon reached the least porous cabin of the lot; an heteroge-

neous combination of logs and boards whose still existing door and single tiny window both faced Maple Hill. Barring the door after us against the fury of the wind and rain, we put in place the crude window shutter which our frequent searches had taught us where to find. It was dismal sitting there on rickety boxes in the pitchy darkness, but we smoked pipes and occasionally flashed our pocket lamps about. Now and then we could see the lightning through the cracks in the wall; the afternoon was so incredibly dark that each flash was extremely vivid.

The stormy vigil reminded me shudderingly of my ghastly night on Tempest Mountain. My mind turned to that odd question which had kept recurring ever since the nightmare thing had happened; and again I wondered why the daemon, approaching the three watchers either from the window or the interior, had begun with the men on each side and left the middle man till the last, when the titan fireball had scared it away. Why had it not taken its victims in natural order, with myself second, from whichever direction it had approached? With what manner of far-reaching tentacles did it prey? Or did it know that I was the leader, and save me for a fate worse than that of my companions?

In the midst of these reflections, as if dramatically arranged to intensify them, there fell near by a terrific bolt of lightning followed by the sound of sliding earth. At the same time the wolfish wind rose to daemoniac crescendoes of ululation. We were sure that the lone tree on Maple Hill had been struck again, and Munroe rose from his box and went to the tiny window to ascertain the damage. When he took down the shutter the wind and rain howled deafeningly in, so that I could not hear what he said; but I waited while he leaned out and tried to fathom Nature's pandemonium.

Gradually a calming of the wind and dispersal of the unusual darkness told of the storm's passing. I had hoped it would last into the night to help our quest, but a furtive sunbeam from a knothole behind me removed the likelihood of such a thing. Suggesting to Munroe that we had better get some light even if more showers came, I unbarred and opened the crude door. The ground outside was a singular mass of mud and pools, with fresh heaps of earth from the slight landslide; but I saw nothing to justify the interest which kept my companion silently leaning out the window. Crossing to where he leaned, I touched his shoulder; but he did not move. Then, as I playfully shook him and turned him around, I felt the strangling tendrils of a cancerous horror whose roots reached into illimitable pasts and fathomless abysms of the night that broods beyond time.

For Arthur Munroe was dead. And on what remained of his chewed and gouged head there was no longer a face.

III. WHAT THE RED GLARE MEANT

ON THE TEMPEST-RACKED night of November 8, 1921, with a lantern which cast charnel shadows, I stood digging alone and idiotically in the grave of Jan Martense. I had begun to dig in the afternoon, because a thunderstorm was brewing, and now that it was dark and the storm had burst above the maniacally thick foliage I was glad.

I believe that my mind was partly unhinged by events since August 5th; the daemon shadow in the mansion, the general strain and disappointment, and the thing that occurred at the hamlet in an October storm. After that thing I had dug a grave for one whose death I could not understand. I knew that others could not understand either, so let them think Arthur Munroe had wandered

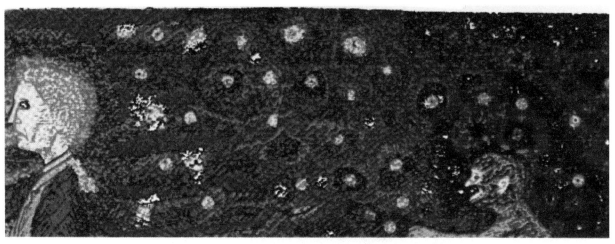

"Crossing to where he leaned, I playfully shook his shoulder."
Home Brew (Febuary 1923) (artist: Clark Ashton Smith; reprinted with permission of CASiana Enterprises, the Literary Estate of Clark Ashton Smith)

16. Present-day Manhattan; but until the mid-seventeenth century, the Dutch settlement of New Amsterdam, on Manhattan Island—itself acquired by the Dutch for sixty guilders, approximately a thousand dollars today. (Said for two centuries to have been purchased for the equivalent of twenty-four dollars, Manhattan Island was in fact "not 'sold' at all," argues University of Virginia legal historian G. Edward White, "at least not in the English sense of being transferred in fee simple"; see his *Law in American History: Vol. 1—From the Colonial Years Through the Civil War* (New York: Oxford University Press, 2012), 35.

Lovecraft is here using the old name: By September 1664, New Amsterdam had been renamed "New York" in honor of James, Duke of York (King James II of England), for whom it had been captured, by English forces, from the Dutch West India Company's then-director general Peter Stuyvesant. It was retained by the English through the Treaty of Breda, signed on July 31, 1667.

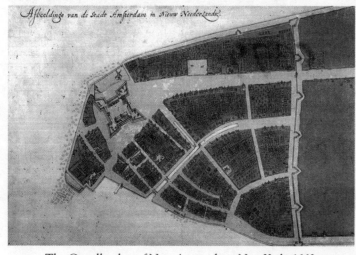

The Castello plan of New Amsterdam, New York, 1660.

away. They searched, but found nothing. The squatters might have understood, but I dared not frighten them more. I myself seemed strangely callous. That shock at the mansion had done something to my brain, and I could think only of the quest for a horror now grown to cataclysmic stature in my imagination; a quest which the fate of Arthur Munroe made me vow to keep silent and solitary.

The scene of my excavations would alone have been enough to unnerve any ordinary man. Baleful primal trees of unholy size, age, and grotesqueness leered above me like the pillars of some hellish Druidic temple; muffling the thunder, hushing the clawing wind, and admitting but little rain. Beyond the scarred trunks in the background, illumined by faint flashes of filtered lightning, rose the damp ivied stones of the deserted mansion, while somewhat nearer was the abandoned Dutch garden whose walks and beds were polluted by a white, fungous, foetid, over-nourished vegetation that never saw full daylight. And nearest of all was the graveyard, where deformed trees tossed insane branches as their roots displaced unhallowed slabs and sucked venom from what lay below. Now and then, beneath the brown pall of leaves that rotted and festered in the antediluvian forest darkness, I could trace the sinister outlines of some of those low mounds which characterised the lightning-pierced region.

History had led me to this archaic grave. History, indeed, was all I had after everything else ended in mocking Satanism. I now believed that the lurking fear was no material thing, but a wolf-fanged ghost that rode the midnight lightning. And I believed, because of the masses of local tradition I had unearthed in my search with Arthur Munroe, that the ghost was that of Jan Martense, who died in 1762. That is why I was digging idiotically in his grave.

The Martense mansion was built in 1670 by Gerrit Martense, a wealthy New-Amsterdam[16] merchant who disliked the changing order under British rule, and had constructed this magnificent domicile on a remote woodland summit whose untrodden solitude and unusual scenery pleased him.

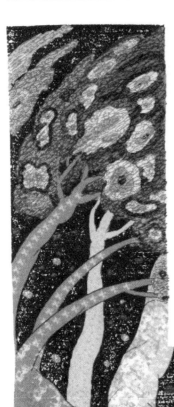

"Nearest of all was the grave-yard."
Home Brew (March 1923) (artist: Clark
Ashton Smith; reprinted with
permission of CASiana Enterprises, the
Literary Estate of Clark Ashton Smith)

The only substantial disappointment encountered in this site was that which concerned the prevalence of violent thunderstorms in summer. When selecting the hill and building his mansion, Mynheer Martense had laid these frequent natural outbursts to some peculiarity of the year; but in time he perceived that the locality was especially liable to such phenomena. At length, having found these storms injurious to his health, he fitted up a cellar into which he could retreat from their wildest pandemonium.

17. The Albany Convention was a civilian/military governing body whose members (drawn from the city of Albany and from Ulster County) were loyal to King William and Queen Mary of Holland and did not support the 1689–91 rebellion led by Jacob Leisler, a Protestant New Yorker and wealthy merchant who opposed the joint Dutch-British administration imposed by England after its capture of New Amsterdam. Leisler, who had appointed himself lieutenant governor of New York in December 1689, was hanged for treason in 1691. Leisler's Rebellion has been extensively studied for, among other reasons, the glimpse it provides of not only religious but political loyalties at the time—for instance, one stage of the rebellion found Long Island Puritans marching on the city. For a careful and fascinating treatment of this seventeenth-century battle for New York, including an analysis of the preceding "Glorious Revolution" (1688) that ousted King James II, see Steven Terry, "'[F]or King William and Queen Mary, for the Defence of the Protestant Religion and the Good of the Country,' Leisler's Rebellion: A Study of Colonial New York and the Formation of Political and Religious Coalitions on the Frontier, 1620–1691," master's thesis, City University of New York (CUNY), 2013.

By reference to the dates mentioned here (1754–1760), however, we can determine that the narrator meant another body, the Albany Congress—confusingly also known as the Albany Conference—a convocation (by the British Board of Trade) of seven of the nine northern British colonies in North America and the Six Nations of the Iroquois Confederacy (which withdrew early in the process), chiefly to discuss defense against the French. Benjamin Franklin was among the attendees (as the Pennsylvania delegate) and presented the Albany Plan of Union, principles of which were

Of Gerrit Martense's descendants less is known than of himself; since they were all reared in hatred of the English civilisation, and trained to shun such of the colonists as accepted it. Their life was exceedingly secluded, and people declared that their isolation had made them heavy of speech and comprehension. In appearance all were marked by a peculiar inherited dissimilarity of eyes; one generally being blue and the other brown. Their social contacts grew fewer and fewer, till at last they took to intermarrying with the numerous menial class about the estate. Many of the crowded family degenerated, moved across the valley, and merged with the mongrel population which was later to produce the pitiful squatters. The rest had stuck sullenly to their ancestral mansion, becoming more and more clannish and taciturn, yet developing a nervous responsiveness to the frequent thunderstorms.

Most of this information reached the outside world through young Jan Martense, who from some kind of restlessness joined the colonial army when news of the Albany Convention[17] reached Tempest Mountain. He was the first of Gerrit's descendants to see much of the world; and when he returned in 1760 after six years of campaigning,[18] he was hated as an outsider by his father, uncles, and brothers, in spite of his dissimilar Martense eyes. No longer could he share the peculiarities and prejudices of the Martenses, while the very mountain thunderstorms failed

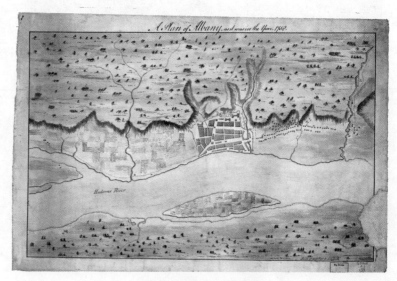

Plan of Albany in 1758.

to intoxicate him as they had before. Instead, his surroundings depressed him; and he frequently wrote to a friend in Albany of plans to leave the paternal roof.

In the spring of 1763 Jonathan Gifford, the Albany friend of Jan Martense, became worried by his correspondent's silence; especially in view of the conditions and quarrels at the Martense mansion. Determined to visit Jan in person, he went into the mountains on horseback. His diary states that he reached Tempest Mountain on September 20, finding the mansion in great decrepitude. The sullen, odd-eyed Martenses, whose unclean animal aspect shocked him, told him in broken gutturals that Jan was dead. He had, they insisted, been struck by lightning the autumn before; and now lay buried behind the neglected sunken gardens. They shewed the visitor the grave, barren and devoid of markers. Something in the Martenses' manner gave Gifford a feeling of repulsion and suspicion, and a week later he returned with spade and mattock to explore the sepulchral spot. He found what he expected—a skull crushed cruelly as if by savage blows— so returning to Albany he openly charged the Martenses with the murder of their kinsman.

Legal evidence was lacking, but the story spread rapidly round the countryside; and from that time the Martenses were ostracised by the world. No one would deal with them, and their distant manor was shunned as an accursed place. Somehow they managed to live on independently by the products of their estate, for occasional lights glimpsed from far-away hills attested their continued presence. These lights were seen as late as 1810, but toward the last they became very infrequent.

Meanwhile there grew up about the mansion and the mountain a body of diabolic legendry. The place was avoided with doubled assiduousness, and invested with every whispered myth tradition could supply. It remained unvisited till 1816, when the continued absence of lights was noticed by the squatters. At that time a party made investigations, finding the house deserted and partly in ruins.

There were no skeletons about, so that departure rather than death was inferred. The clan seemed to have left several years before, and improvised penthouses shewed how numerous it had grown prior to its migration. Its cultural level had fallen very low, as proved by decaying furniture and scattered silverware which

later reflected in the U.S. Constitution. The Albany Plan begins: "It is proposed that humble application be made for an act of Parliament of Great Britain, by virtue of which one general government may be formed in America, including all the said colonies." The Congress, held in Albany June 19–July 11, 1754, became a template for the later Stamp Act Congress (1765) and the First Continental Congress (1774), both of which figured prominently in Revolutionary American history.

18. Martense must have been campaigning in the French and Indian War, 1754–63, the North American phase of the global Seven Years' War principally waged, despite the name, between England and France (1756–63). The British North American colonies and Native American tribes loyal to them fought against New France (Canada, Acadia, Newfoundland, and Louisiana) and other Native American tribes loyal to the French.

must have been long abandoned when its owners left. But though the dreaded Martenses were gone, the fear of the haunted house continued; and grew very acute when new and strange stories arose among the mountain decadents. There it stood; deserted, feared, and linked with the vengeful ghost of Jan Martense. There it still stood on the night I dug in Jan Martense's grave.

I have described my protracted digging as idiotic, and such it indeed was in object and method. The coffin of Jan Martense had soon been unearthed—it now held only dust and nitre—but in my fury to exhume his ghost I delved irrationally and clumsily down beneath where he had lain. God knows what I expected to find—I only felt that I was digging in the grave of a man whose ghost stalked by night.

It is impossible to say what monstrous depth I had attained when my spade, and soon my feet, broke through the ground beneath. The event, under the circumstances, was tremendous; for in the existence of a subterranean space here, my mad theories had terrible confirmation. My slight fall had extinguished the lantern, but I produced an electric pocket lamp and viewed the small horizontal tunnel which led away indefinitely in both directions. It was amply large enough for a man to wriggle through; and though no sane person would have tried it at that time, I forgot danger, reason, and cleanliness in my single-minded fever to unearth the lurking fear. Choosing the direction toward the house, I scrambled recklessly into the narrow burrow; squirming ahead blindly and rapidly, and flashing but seldom the lamp I kept before me.

What language can describe the spectacle of a man lost in infinitely abysmal earth; pawing, twisting, wheezing; scrambling madly through sunken convolutions of immemorial blackness without an idea of time, safety, direction, or definite object? There is something hideous in it, but that is what I did. I did it for so long that life faded to a far memory, and I became one with the moles and grubs of nighted depths. Indeed, it was only by accident that after interminable writhings I jarred my forgotten electric lamp alight, so that it shone eerily along the burrow of caked loam that stretched and curved ahead.

I had been scrambling in this way for some time, so that my battery had burned very low, when the passage suddenly inclined sharply upward, altering my mode of progress. And as I raised my glance it was without preparation that I saw glistening in the distance two daemoniac reflections of my expiring lamp; two reflections glowing with a baneful and unmistakable effulgence, and provoking maddeningly nebulous memories. I stopped automatically, though lacking the brain to retreat. The eyes approached, yet of the thing that bore them I could distinguish only a claw. But what a claw! Then far overhead I heard a faint crashing which I recognised. It was the wild thunder of the mountain, raised to hysteric fury—I must have been crawling upward for some time, so that the surface was now quite near. And as the muffled thunder clattered, those eyes still stared with vacuous viciousness.

Thank God I did not then know what it was, else I should have died. But I was saved by the very thunder that had summoned it, for after a hideous wait there burst from the unseen

"The Eyes and the Claw."
Home Brew (March 1923) (artist: Clark Ashton Smith; reprinted with permission of CASiana Enterprises, the Literary Estate of Clark Ashton Smith)

19. In this context, "Cyclopean" refers to the towering rage of Polyphemus, the Cyclops blinded by Odysseus (as recounted in Homer's *Odyssey*). See also "Under the Pyramids," pp. 175–213, below, note 53.

20. See note 12, above. The Acheron is also mentioned in "The Dunwich Horror," in the previous volume, pp. 343–87.

outside sky one of those frequent mountainward bolts whose aftermath I had noticed here and there as gashes of disturbed earth and fulgurites of various sizes. With Cyclopean rage[19] it tore through the soil above that damnable pit, blinding and deafening me, yet not wholly reducing me to a coma.

In the chaos of sliding, shifting earth I clawed and floundered helplessly till the rain on my head steadied me and I saw that I had come to the surface in a familiar spot; a steep unforested place on the southwest slope of the mountain. Recurrent sheet lightnings illumed the tumbled ground and the remains of the curious low hummock which had stretched down from the wooded higher slope, but there was nothing in the chaos to shew my place of egress from the lethal catacomb. My brain was as great a chaos as the earth, and as a distant red glare burst on the landscape from the south I hardly realised the horror I had been through.

But when two days later the squatters told me what the red glare meant, I felt more horror than that which the mound-burrow and the claw and eyes had given; more horror because of the overwhelming implications. In a hamlet twenty miles away an orgy of fear had followed the bolt which brought me above ground, and a nameless thing had dropped from an overhanging tree into a weak-roofed cabin. It had done a deed, but the squatters had fired the cabin in frenzy before it could escape. It had been doing that deed at the very moment the earth caved in on the thing with the claw and eyes.

IV. THE HORROR IN THE EYES

THERE CAN BE nothing normal in the mind of one who, knowing what I knew of the horrors of Tempest Mountain, would seek alone for the fear that lurked there. That at least two of the fear's embodiments were destroyed, formed but a slight guarantee of mental and physical safety in this Acheron[20] of multiform diabolism; yet I continued my quest with even greater zeal as events and revelations became more monstrous.

When, two days after my frightful crawl through that crypt of the eyes and claw, I learned that a thing had malignly hovered twenty miles away at the same instant the eyes were glaring at me,

I experienced virtual convulsions of fright. But that fright was so mixed with wonder and alluring grotesqueness, that it was almost a pleasant sensation. Sometimes, in the throes of a nightmare when unseen powers whirl one over the roofs of strange dead cities toward the grinning chasm of Nis,[21] it is a relief and even a delight to shriek wildly and throw oneself voluntarily along with the hideous vortex of dream-doom into whatever bottomless gulf may yawn. And so it was with the waking nightmare of Tempest Mountain; the discovery that two monsters had haunted the spot gave me ultimately a mad craving to plunge into the very earth of the accursed region, and with bare hands dig out the death that leered from every inch of the poisonous soil.

As soon as possible I visited the grave of Jan Martense and dug vainly where I had dug before. Some extensive cave-in had obliterated all trace of the underground passage, while the rain had washed so much earth back into the excavation that I could not tell how deeply I had dug that other day. I likewise made a difficult trip to the distant hamlet where the death-creature had been burnt, and was little repaid for my trouble. In the ashes of the fateful cabin I found several bones, but apparently none of the monster's. The squatters said the thing had had only one victim; but in this I judged them inaccurate, since besides the complete skull of a human being, there was another bony fragment which seemed certainly to have belonged to a human skull at some time. Though the rapid drop of the monster had been seen, no one could say just what the creature was like; those who had glimpsed it called it simply a devil. Examining the great tree where it had lurked, I could discern no distinctive marks. I tried to find some trail into the black forest, but on this occasion could not stand the sight of those morbidly large boles, or of those vast serpent-like roots that twisted so malevolently before they sank into the earth.

My next step was to re-examine with microscopic care the deserted hamlet where death had come most abundantly, and where Arthur Munroe had seen something he never lived to describe. Though my vain previous searches had been exceedingly minute, I now had new data to test; for my horrible grave-crawl convinced me that at least one of the phases of the monstrosity had been an underground creature. This time, on the 14th of

21. This mysterious place never appears again in HPL's stories, nor does it appear in any gazetteer or mythological source (though HPL mentions "the valley of Nis" in the prose poem "Memory," written in 1919). It is perhaps drawn from Poe's 1831 poem "The Valley Nis," retitled "The Valley of Unrest." Scholars debate Poe's use of the name, one suggesting that it was a mishearing of the Gaelic word "*innis*," meaning "island," another positing that it was based on the Old English contraction "n'is," meaning "is not" (that is, unreality). In Scandinavian folklore, a *nis* is a friendly goblin or spirit. The great Poe scholar Thomas Mabbott notes, "Many readers notice that Nis is Sin backwards" (Edgar Allan Poe, *Complete Poems*, vol. 1 of *Complete Works*, ed. Thomas Ollive Mabbott [Cambridge, MA: Harvard University Press, 1978], 194).

22. In antiquity, Arcadia was a mountainous region of Greece. It has come to mean (or allude to) any pastoral paradise. In his *Eclogues* (37 BCE), Virgil writes of Arcadians "alone [having] skill to sing" (Eclogue X). *Arcadia* (1504), a story of unrequited love told in prose and verse by the Renaissance poet Jacopo Sannazaro, is said to have been reprinted at least one hundred times throughout the sixteenth century—a minimum of once each year; it was succeeded in popularity by Sir Philip Sidney's two versions of his *Arcadia* (1580 and after), the depth of whose female characters, C. S. Lewis said in 1954, remained unparalleled until the emergence shortly after of Shakespeare.

23. This reflects the theories of Alfred Watkins, the principal spokesperson for the theory of "ley lines." See "The Rats in the Walls," pp. 150–74, below, note 5. HPL's knowledge of Watkins's theories is explored in David Haden's "The Annotated 'The Lurking Fear'" (see note 3, above), 74–75, note 76.

November, my quest concerned itself mostly with the slopes of Cone Mountain and Maple Hill where they overlook the unfortunate hamlet, and I gave particular attention to the loose earth of the landslide region on the latter eminence.

The afternoon of my search brought nothing to light, and dusk came as I stood on Maple Hill looking down at the hamlet and across the valley to Tempest Mountain. There had been a gorgeous sunset, and now the moon came up, nearly full and shedding a silver flood over the plain, the distant mountainside, and the curious low mounds that rose here and there. It was a peaceful Arcadian[22] scene, but knowing what it hid I hated it. I hated the mocking moon, the hypocritical plain, the festering mountain, and those sinister mounds. Everything seemed to me tainted with a loathsome contagion, and inspired by a noxious alliance with distorted hidden powers.

Presently, as I gazed abstractedly at the moonlit panorama, my eye became attracted by something singular in the nature and arrangement of a certain topographical element. Without having any exact knowledge of geology, I had from the first been interested in the odd mounds and hummocks of the region. I had noticed that they were pretty widely distributed around Tempest Mountain, though less numerous on the plain than near the hill-top itself, where prehistoric glaciation had doubtless found feebler opposition to its striking and fantastic caprices. Now, in the light of that low moon which cast long weird shadows, it struck me forcibly that the various points and lines of the mound system had a peculiar relation to the summit of Tempest Mountain. That summit was undeniably a centre from which the lines or rows of points radiated indefinitely and irregularly, as if the unwholesome Martense mansion had thrown visible tentacles of terror.[23] The idea of such tentacles gave me an unexplained thrill, and I stopped to analyse my reason for believing these mounds glacial phenomena.

The more I analysed the less I believed, and against my newly opened mind there began to beat grotesque and horrible analogies based on superficial aspects and upon my experience beneath the earth. Before I knew it I was uttering frenzied and disjointed words to myself: "My God! . . . Molehills . . . the damned place must be honeycombed . . . how many . . . that night at the mansion . . . they took Bennett and Tobey first . . . on each side of us. . . ." Then I was digging frantically into the mound which had stretched nearest me; digging desperately, shiveringly, but almost jubilantly; digging and at last shrieking aloud with some unplaced emotion as I came upon a tunnel or burrow just like the one through which I had crawled on that other daemoniac night.

After that I recall running, spade in hand; a hideous run across moon-litten, mound-marked meadows and through diseased, precipitous abysses of haunted hillside forest; leaping, screaming, panting, bounding toward the terrible Martense mansion. I recall digging unreasoningly in all parts of the brier-choked cellar; digging to find the core and centre of that malignant universe of mounds. And then I recall how I laughed when I stumbled on the

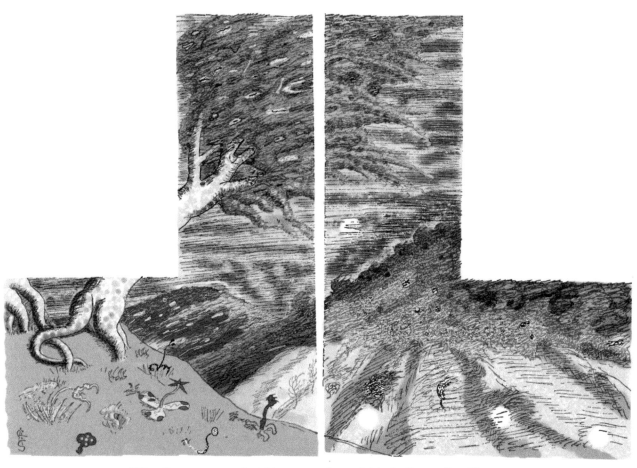

"That Summit was undeniably a center from which the lines radiated."
Home Brew (April 1923) (artist: Clark Ashton Smith; reprinted with permission of
CASiana Enterprises, the Literary Estate of Clark Ashton Smith)

passageway; the hole at the base of the old chimney, where the thick weeds grew and cast queer shadows in the light of the lone candle I had happened to have with me. What still remained down in that hell-hive, lurking and waiting for the thunder to arouse it, I did not know. Two had been killed; perhaps that had finished it. But still there remained that burning determination to reach the innermost secret of the fear, which I had once more come to deem definite, material, and organic.

My indecisive speculation whether to explore the passage alone and immediately with my pocket-light or to try to assemble a band of squatters for the quest, was interrupted after a time by a sudden rush of wind from outside which blew out the candle and left me in stark blackness. The moon no longer shone through the chinks and apertures above me, and with a sense of fateful alarm I heard the sinister and significant rumble of approaching thunder. A confusion of associated ideas possessed my brain, leading me to grope back toward the farthest corner of the cellar. My eyes, however, never turned away from the horrible opening at the base of the chimney; and I began to get glimpses of the crumbling bricks and unhealthy weeds as faint glows of lightning penetrated the woods outside and illumined the chinks in the upper wall. Every second I was consumed with a mixture of fear and curiosity. What would the storm call forth—or was there anything left for it to call? Guided by a lightning flash I settled myself down behind a dense clump of vegetation, through which I could see the opening without being seen.

If heaven is merciful, it will some day efface from my consciousness the sight that I saw, and let me live my last years in peace. I cannot sleep at night now, and have to take opiates when it thunders. The thing came abruptly and unannounced; a daemon, rat-like scurrying from pits remote and unimaginable, a hellish panting and stifled grunting, and then from that opening beneath the chimney a burst of multitudinous and leprous life—a loathsome night-spawned flood of organic corruption more devastatingly hideous than the blackest conjurations of mortal madness and morbidity. Seething, stewing, surging, bubbling like serpents' slime it rolled up and out of that yawning hole, spreading like a septic contagion and streaming from the cellar at every point of egress—streaming out to scatter through the accursed midnight forests and strew fear, madness, and death.

God knows how many there were—there must have been thousands. To see the stream of them in that faint, intermittent lightning was shocking. When they had thinned out enough to be glimpsed as separate organisms, I saw that they were dwarfed, deformed hairy devils or apes—monstrous and diabolic caricatures of the monkey tribe. They were so hideously silent; there was hardly a squeal when one of the last stragglers turned with the skill of long practice to make a meal in accustomed fashion on a weaker companion. Others snapped up what it left and ate with slavering relish. Then, in spite of my daze of fright and disgust, my morbid curiosity triumphed; and as the last of the monstrosities oozed up alone from that nether world of unknown nightmare, I drew my automatic pistol and shot it under cover of the thunder.

"Spreading Like a Septic Contagion."
Home Brew (April 1923) (artist: Clark Ashton Smith; reprinted with permission of CASiana Enterprises, the Literary Estate of Clark Ashton Smith)

24. Flashing or resembling lightning flashes. Charles Fort's *The Book of the Damned* (1919; New York: Cosimo Classics, 2004), with which HPL may have been familiar (Fort and his books are mentioned in "The Whisperer in Darkness," in the previous volume, pp. 388–456), quotes one Tallius, writing in 1649, describing "thunderstones"—stones that fall from the sky—as saying, "The naturalists say they are generated in the sky by fulgurous exhalation conglobed in a cloud by the circumfused humor" (39).

25. And so, for the third time, the narrator inexplicably escapes the horror. "Why should the Martenses, who kill for malice as well as for food, repeatedly spare the narrator," asks Michael Cisco, in "The Shadow over 'The Lurking Fear,'" *Lovecraft Annual* 6 (2012), 43–53, "and what cause could there be for the 'hideous wait' . . . or hesitancy of the Martense-being in the tunnel, unless perhaps it had recognized the narrator, by some subtle token, as a member of the family?" (44). Cisco concludes that HPL originally intended to make a family connection clear, but that the idea was abandoned as the story developed.

Shrieking, slithering, torrential shadows of red viscous madness chasing one another through endless, ensanguined corridors of purple fulgurous[24] sky . . . formless phantasms and kaleidoscopic mutations of a ghoulish, remembered scene; forests of monstrous overnourished oaks with serpent roots twisting and sucking unnamable juices from an earth verminous with millions of cannibal devils; mound-like tentacles groping from underground nuclei of polypous perversion . . . insane lightning over malignant ivied walls and daemon arcades choked with fungous vegetation. . . . Heaven be thanked for the instinct which led me unconscious to places where men dwell; to the peaceful village that slept under the calm stars of clearing skies.[25]

I had recovered enough in a week to send to Albany for a gang of men to blow up the Martense mansion and the entire top of Tempest Mountain with dynamite, stop up all the discoverable mound-burrows, and destroy certain overnourished trees whose very existence seemed an insult to sanity. I could sleep a little after they had done this, but true rest will never come as long as I remember that nameless secret of the lurking fear. The thing will

"They were slithering shadows of red madness."
Weird Tales (June 1928) (artist: Hugh Rankin)

haunt me, for who can say the extermination is complete, and that analogous phenomena do not exist all over the world? Who can, with my knowledge, think of the earth's unknown caverns without a nightmare dread of future possibilities? I cannot see a well or a subway entrance without shuddering . . . why cannot the doctors give me something to make me sleep, or truly calm my brain when it thunders?

What I saw in the glow of my flashlight after I shot the unspeakable straggling object was so simple that almost a minute elapsed before I understood and went delirious. The object was nauseous; a filthy whitish gorilla thing with sharp yellow fangs and matted fur. It was the ultimate product of mammalian degeneration; the frightful outcome of isolated spawning, multiplication, and cannibal nutrition above and below the ground; the embodiment of all the snarling chaos and grinning fear that lurk behind life. It had looked at me as it died, and its eyes had the same odd quality that marked those other eyes which had stared at me underground and excited cloudy recollections. One eye was blue, the other brown. They were the dissimilar Martense eyes of the old legends, and I knew in one inundating cataclysm of voiceless horror what had become of that vanished family; the terrible and thunder-crazed house of Martense.

The Rats in the Walls[1]

The arrogant narrator of "The Rats in the Walls" sets out to discover his family's heritage, only to find darkness where none was suspected. In this tale, HPL combined legends of England with his own ideas about degeneracy and atavism— the recurrence of hereditary traits. The narrator's casual recitals of his and his family's racism reveals Lovecraft's own attitudes. Psychoanalytic criticism has noted that the narrator's journey literally downward is a journey into his past and his own psyche, where he discovers madness waiting for him.[2] HPL himself admitted that the story was "too horrible for the tender sensibilities of a delicately nurtured publick."[3] Nonetheless, he persisted in his attempts to sell the tale, and ultimately he succeeded, publishing it in Weird Tales. Whether the story is viewed as a psychological case study or as a tale of objective manifestations of horrors, its disturbing conclusion will not soon fade from memory.

1. "The Rats in the Walls" was written in August or September 1923 and appeared in *Weird Tales* 3, no. 3 (March 1924), 25–31. Both Gavin Callaghan and Robert H. Waugh point out similarities between the tale and Conan Doyle's *The Hound of the Baskervilles* (written in 1901)—see Callaghan's "Elementary, My Dear Lovecraft: H. P. Lovecraft and Sherlock Holmes," *Lovecraft Annual* 6 (2012), 198–228, and Waugh's "Lovecraft's Rats and Doyle's Hound: A Study in Reason and Madness," *Lovecraft Annual* 7 (2013), 60–75. HPL himself called Poe his "God of Fiction" but Doyle his "model" (Letter to Reinhardt Kleiner, February 2, 1916, *Selected Letters*, I, 20–21).

2. See, for example, Dirk W. Mosig's "Toward a Greater Appreciation of H. P. Lovecraft: The Analytic Approach."

On July 16, 1923, I moved into Exham Priory[4] after the last workman had finished his labours. The restoration had been a stupendous task, for little had remained of the deserted pile but a shell-like ruin; yet because it had been the seat of my ancestors I let no expense deter me.[5] The place had not been inhabited since the reign of James the First,[6] when a tragedy of intensely hideous, though largely unexplained, nature had struck down the master, five of his children, and several servants; and driven forth under a cloud of suspicion and terror the third son, my lineal progenitor and the only survivor of the abhorred line. With this sole heir denounced as a murderer, the estate had reverted to the crown, nor had the accused man made any attempt to exculpate himself or regain his property. Shaken by some horror greater than that of conscience or the law, and expressing only a frantic wish to exclude the ancient edifice from his sight and memory, Walter de la Poer, eleventh Baron Exham,[7] fled to Virginia and there founded

Weird Tales (March 1924) (artist unknown)

the family which by the next century had become known as Delapore.[8]

Exham Priory had remained untenanted, though later allotted to the estates of the Norrys family[9] and much studied because of its peculiarly composite architecture; an architecture involving Gothic towers[10] resting on a Saxon or Romanesque substructure,[11] whose foundation in turn was of a still earlier order or blend of orders—Roman, and even Druidic or native Cymric,[12] if legends speak truly. This foundation was a very singular thing, being merged on one side with the solid limestone of the precipice from whose brink the priory overlooked a desolate valley three miles west of the village of Anchester.[13] Architects and antiquarians loved to examine this strange relic of forgotten centuries, but the country folk hated it. They had hated it hundreds of years before, when my ancestors lived there, and they hated it now, with the moss and mould of abandonment on it. I had not been a day in Anchester before I knew I came of an accursed house. And this week workmen have blown up Exham Priory, and are busy obliterating the traces of its foundations.

The bare statistics of my ancestry I had always known,

3. Letter to Frank Belknap Long, November 8, 1923, in *Selected Letters*, I, 259.

4. There is no Exham Priory in England. Hexham Priory School and Hexham Abbey are in the north of England, west of Newcastle upon Tyne, in the town of Hexham (southwest Northumberland). A detailed history of the area from early Saxon times may be found in James Raine, ed., *The Priory of Hexham: Title Deeds, Black Book, Etc.* (London: Durham, 1865), two volumes paginated entirely in Roman numerals and with many sections in Latin. Raine's heavily annotated annals of the priory, in vol. 1, range from disease (murrain) among the local cattle (xcix, lxiv *n.*) and the "wretched imbecility" (xc) of at least one English monarch to battles, land forms, castles, and waterways ("a little beck called Denises burn," xiii *n.*). Like Lovecraft, Raine favors the use of the verb form "shewn."

5. The idea that important and sacred structures have been built atop one another on the same site over time, at least in England, appears to originate with amateur archaeologist Alfred Watkins's 1922 *Early British Trackways: Moats, Mounds, Camps, and Sites* (Hereford: The Watkins Meter Co., and London: Simpkin, Marshall, Hamilton, Kent, & Co.). Watkins suggested that "sighting lines" or "leys" marking many important archaeological sites were ancient ceremonial or mercantile pathways: "The sighting line was called the ley or lay," a "fact . . . embedded in the rural mind" (12). See David Haden's "'The Rats in the Walls': Otherness and British Culture," in *Lovecraft in Historical Context: Essays*, 32–37 (self-published, 2010).

6. King of England (1603–1625) and Scotland (1567–1625).

7. Not surprisingly, the "Exham" title does not appear in *Peerage, Baronetage and Knightage of Great Britain and Ireland* (1886 edition). The *Peerage* was originally created by the Irish journalist Charles Dod in 1841 and appeared as an annual volume even after Dod's death in 1855.

8. There are no Delapores listed in any U.S. historical records prior to the end of the nineteenth century. One appeared in Boston in 1882, and some are reported in Manhattan in the 1905 New York census; one Jose Delapore, resided in Los Angeles in 1918. The name "De la Poer" seems to be an homage to both Edgar Allan Poe and Sarah Helen (Power) Whitman (see "The Shunned House," pp. 213–48, note 2, below). Caroline Ticknor's *Poe's Helen*, a book owned by HPL, includes a concise history of the Poe family and of his "Helen." Ticknor makes reference to Sarah's father, Nicholas Power, having "claimed descent from that Nicholas le Poer, whose castle Don Isle was one of

together with the fact that my first American forbear had come to the colonies under a strange cloud. Of details, however, I had been kept wholly ignorant through the policy of reticence always maintained by the Delapores. Unlike our planter neighbours, we seldom boasted of crusading ancestors or other mediaeval and Renaissance heroes; nor was any kind of tradition handed down except what may have been recorded in the sealed envelope left before the Civil War[14] by every squire to his eldest son for posthumous opening. The glories we cherished were those achieved since the migration; the glories of a proud and honourable, if somewhat reserved and unsocial Virginia line.

During the war our fortunes were extinguished and our whole existence changed by the burning of Carfax,[15] our home on the banks of the James.[16] My grandfather, advanced in years, had perished in that incendiary outrage, and with him the envelope that bound us all to the past. I can recall that fire today as I saw it then at the age of seven, with the Federal soldiers shouting, the women screaming, and the negroes howling and praying.[17] My father was in the army, defending Richmond,[18] and after many formalities my mother and I were passed through the lines to join him. When the war ended we all moved north, whence my mother had come; and I grew to manhood, middle age, and ultimate wealth as a stolid Yankee. Neither my father nor I ever knew what our hereditary envelope had contained, and as I merged into the greyness of Massachusetts business life I lost all interest in the mysteries which evidently lurked far back in my family tree. Had I suspected their nature, how gladly I would have left Exham Priory to its moss, bats, and cobwebs!

My father died in 1904, but without any message to leave me, or to my only child, Alfred, a motherless boy of ten.[19] It was this boy who reversed the order of family information; for although I could give him only jesting conjectures about the past, he wrote me of some very interesting ancestral legends when the late war took him to England in 1917 as an aviation officer. Apparently the Delapores had a colourful and perhaps sinister history, for a friend of my son's, Capt. Edward Norrys of the Royal Flying Corps,[20] dwelt near the family seat at Anchester and related some peasant superstitions which few novelists could equal for wildness and incredibility. Norrys himself, of course, did not take them seriously;

but they amused my son and made good material for his letters to me. It was this legendry which definitely turned my attention to my transatlantic heritage, and made me resolve to purchase and restore the family seat which Norrys shewed to Alfred in its picturesque desertion, and offered to get for him at a surprisingly reasonable figure, since his own uncle was the present owner.

I bought Exham Priory in 1918, but was almost immediately distracted from my plans of restoration by the return of my son as a maimed invalid. During the two years that he lived I thought of nothing but his care, having even placed my business under the direction of partners. In 1921, as I found myself bereaved and aimless, a retired manufacturer no longer young, I resolved to divert my remaining years with my new possession. Visiting Anchester in December, I was entertained by Capt. Norrys, a plump, amiable young man who had thought much of my son, and secured his assistance in gathering plans and anecdotes to guide in the coming restoration. Exham Priory itself I saw without emotion, a jumble of tottering mediaeval ruins covered with lichens and honeycombed with rooks' nests, perched perilously upon a precipice, and denuded of floors or other interior features save the stone walls of the separate towers.

As I gradually recovered the image of the edifice as it had been when my ancestor left it over three centuries before, I began to hire workmen for the reconstruction. In every case I was forced to go outside the immediate locality, for the Anchester villagers had an almost unbelievable fear and hatred of the place. This sentiment was so great that it was sometimes communicated to the outside labourers, causing numerous desertions; whilst its scope appeared to include both the priory and its ancient family.

My son had told me that he was somewhat avoided during his visits because he was a de la Poer, and I now found myself subtly ostracised for a like reason until I convinced the peasants how little I knew of my heritage. Even then they sullenly disliked me,[21] so that I had to collect most of the village traditions through the mediation of Norrys. What the people could not forgive, perhaps, was that I had come to restore a symbol so abhorrent to them; for, rationally or not, they viewed Exham Priory as nothing less than a haunt of fiends and werewolves.

Piecing together the tales which Norrys collected for me, and

the first to fall under Cromwell's hand" (286). Ticknor quotes Poe's reaction: "He looked suddenly up with an expression of surprise and pleasure on his face and said, 'Helen[,] you startle me! For among some papers of my grandfather's (David Poe, Sr.) there is one in which some reference is made to a certain Chevalier Le *Poer*, who was a friend of the Marquis de Grammont and a relative of our family'" (159). "In any case," concludes John Kipling Hitz, in "Lovecraft and the Whitman Memoir," *Lovecraft Studies* 37 (Fall 1997), 15–17, "it appears very likely that Lovecraft, intrigued by Ticknor's ambivalence, used the controversial le Poer family as a historical springboard for the atrocious activities of the de la Poers in 'The Rats in the Walls'" (16).

9. There were long-established Norrys families in Hampshire and Lincolnshire in the nineteenth century; there is no record of a Norrys family in the north of England. There are Norreys, Norris, Norie, Norrie, and Norran families listed in the *Peerage, Baronetage, and Knightage of Great Britain and Ireland* (1886) but none of these are in northern England, either. In any event, they received their titles only in the nineteenth century.

10. The Gothic style of architecture prevailed from the twelfth century to the sixteenth century and emphasized verticality and light. "Gothic towers" would be very tall and probably pointy, with filigreed window tracery (decorative ornamental lines). There are few nonecclesiastical examples remaining.

11. "Romanesque" refers to the architecture of the eleventh and twelfth centuries, which featured circular arches and preceded the Gothic style.

12. The early populations of the British Isles, according to most ethnologists,

Gothic tower at Cardiff Castle.
Shutterstock.com

Notre-Dame la Grande, Poitres, an
example of Romanesque architecture.
Shutterstock.com

were Celts. They arrived from western Europe in the first millennium BCE and up to the time of the assumption of control of the British Isles by the Roman Empire, around the first century CE.

supplementing them with the accounts of several savants who had studied the ruins, I deduced that Exham Priory stood on the site of a prehistoric temple; a Druidical or ante-Druidical thing which must have been contemporary with Stonehenge.[22] That indescribable rites had been celebrated there, few doubted; and there were unpleasant tales of the transference of these rites into the Cybele-worship[23] which the Romans had introduced. Inscriptions still visible in the sub-cellar bore such unmistakable letters as "DIV . . . OPS . . . MAGNA. MAT . . ."[24] sign of the Magna Mater whose dark worship was once vainly forbidden to Roman citizens. Anchester had been the camp of the third Augustan legion,[25] as many remains attest, and it was said that the temple of Cybele was splendid and thronged with worshippers who performed nameless ceremonies at the bidding of a Phrygian[26] priest. Tales added that the fall of the old religion did not end the orgies at the temple, but that the priests lived on in the new faith without real change. Likewise was it said that the rites did not vanish with the Roman power, and that certain among the Saxons[27] added to what remained of the temple, and gave it the essential outline it subsequently preserved, making it the centre of a cult feared through half the heptarchy.[28] About 1000 A.D. the place is mentioned in a chronicle[29] as being a substantial stone priory housing a strange and powerful monastic order and surrounded by extensive gardens which needed no walls to exclude a frightened populace. It was never destroyed by the Danes,[30] though after the Norman Conquest it must have declined tremendously; since there was no impediment when Henry the Third granted the site to my ancestor, Gilbert de la Poer, First Baron Exham, in 1261.[31]

Of my family before this date there is no evil report, but something strange must have happened then. In one chronicle there is a reference to a de la Poer as "cursed of God" in 1307, whilst village legendry had nothing but evil and frantic fear to tell of the castle that went up on the foundations of the old temple and priory. The fireside tales were of the most grisly description, all the ghastlier because of their frightened reticence and cloudy evasiveness. They represented my ancestors as a race of hereditary daemons beside whom Gilles de Retz[32] and the Marquis de Sade[33] would seem the veriest tyros, and hinted whisperingly at their responsibility for the occasional disappearances of villagers through several generations.

The worst characters, apparently, were the barons and their direct heirs; at least, most was whispered about these. If of healthier inclinations, it was said, an heir would early and mysteriously die to make way for another more typical scion. There seemed to be an inner cult in the family, presided over by the head of the house, and sometimes closed except to a few members. Temperament rather than ancestry was evidently the basis of this cult, for it was entered by several who married into the family. Lady Margaret Trevor from Cornwall, wife of Godfrey, the second son of the fifth baron, became a favourite bane of children all over the countryside, and the daemon heroine of a particularly horrible old ballad not yet extinct near the Welsh border. Preserved in balladry, too, though not illustrating the same point, is the hideous tale of Lady Mary de la Poer, who shortly after her marriage to the Earl of Shrewsfield was killed by him and his mother, both of the slayers being absolved and blessed by the priest to whom they confessed what they dared not repeat to the world.

These myths and ballads, typical as they were of crude superstition, repelled me greatly. Their persistence, and their application to so long a line of my ancestors, were especially annoying; whilst the imputations of monstrous habits proved unpleasantly reminiscent of the one known scandal of my immediate forbears—the case of my cousin, young Randolph Delapore of Carfax, who went among the negroes and became a voodoo[34] priest after he returned from the Mexican War.[35]

I was much less disturbed by the vaguer tales of wails and howlings in the barren, windswept valley beneath the limestone cliff; of the graveyard stenches after the spring rains; of the floundering, squealing white thing on which Sir John Clave's horse had trod one night in a lonely field;[36] and of the servant who had gone mad at what he saw in the priory in the full light of day. These things were hackneyed spectral lore, and I was at that time a pronounced sceptic. The accounts of vanished peasants were less to be dismissed, though not especially significant in view of mediaeval custom. Prying curiosity meant death, and more than one severed head had been publicly shewn on the bastions—now effaced—around Exham Priory.

After the withdrawal of the Romans from Britain in the fifth century CE, the indigenous Celtic population in the south were the Welsh, or Cymry (meaning "the people"), while the north was occupied by the Gaels. The Druids were the educated or priestly class of the Celts; the earliest references in historical documents date only to the second century BCE, though of course the culture may be much older.

13. Anchester does not appear in any English gazetteers. There is an Ancaster is the county of Lincolnshire, but it is almost two hundred miles from Hexham. David Haden identifies Ancaster with Corbridge, three miles east of Hexham Priory (see note 4, above), quite near the location of the ancient Roman city of Corstopitum, a military encampment. Haden argues that archaeological finds at Corstopitum support the belief that the city fostered a Cybele/Atys cult ("Of Rats and Legions: H. P. Lovecraft in Northumbria," in Haden's *Lovecraft in Historical Context: Fourth Collection* [self-published, 2013], 109–24). James Raine, in *The Priory of Hexham*, vol. 2 (see note 4, above), notes that Corbryg, Corebrig, and Choresbridge are alternate spellings, and that Gilbert de Corbridge was the given name of a carpenter in York (one hundred miles south).

14. The reference to "planter neighbours" (Virginia was of course the land of tobacco plantations owned by gentlemen planters) clarifies that the narrator means the American Civil War (1861–1865), not the English Civil War(s) (1642–1651).

15. Historically, the place name Carfax is derived from the Latin word "*quadrifurcus*," "four-forked"—in other words, where four roads meet: a crossroads. However, the whimsies of Southern gentlemen may have suggested the name for

fanciful reasons. For example, Carfax is the junction of four streets at the heart of Oxford, England, deemed to be the city center, and the ancient name may have sounded cosmopolitan to the Delapore family. Perhaps the most famous "Carfax" is the principal resting place of Dracula near London, inaccurately called "Carfax Abbey" in the 1931 film of *Dracula*. There is a Carfax Place in London's Clapham Common. According to the Sussex Archaeological Society's *Sussex Archaeological Collections Relating to the History and Antiquities of the County* (Lewes, UK: Farncombe & Co., 1904), Carfax in Horsham, Sussex, was, in the late nineteenth century, a residential street address (xxvi). Today it is a pedestrian roundabout, a bandstand/gazebo, and a town meeting place..

16. A 350-mile-long river entirely within the borders of the state of Virginia. With the capital of the Confederacy at Richmond (see note 17, below), much of the fighting in the eastern theater of the Civil War took place in Virginia. Richmond burned extensively in the final days of the war, but there was much burning in outlying areas as well, and so the fact that Carfax burned too does not pinpoint its location in Virginia.

17. Though the narrator seems to remember the day with horror, the "howling and praying" may well have been rejoicing on the part of the soon-to-be-emancipated slaves. Although early in the Civil War, enslaved individuals who were captured were returned to their "owners," by the time of the destruction of Richmond, they were treated as contraband to be confiscated by the Union army and subsequently freed, and slaves often sought refuge behind Union lines. The narrator's early pro-slavery upbringing is further made apparent by the insensitive naming of his cat.

A few of the tales were exceedingly picturesque, and made me wish I had learnt more of comparative mythology in my youth. There was, for instance, the belief that a legion of bat-winged devils kept Witches' Sabbath each night at the priory—a legion whose sustenance might explain the disproportionate abundance of coarse vegetables harvested in the vast gardens. And, most vivid of all, there was the dramatic epic of the rats—the scampering army of obscene vermin which had burst forth from the castle three months after the tragedy that doomed it to desertion—the lean, filthy, ravenous army which had swept all before it and devoured fowl, cats, dogs, hogs, sheep, and even two hapless human beings before its fury was spent. Around that unforgettable rodent army a whole separate cycle of myths revolves, for it scattered among the village homes and brought curses and horrors in its train.[37]

Such was the lore that assailed me as I pushed to completion, with an elderly obstinacy, the work of restoring my ancestral home. It must not be imagined for a moment that these tales formed my principal psychological environment. On the other hand, I was constantly praised and encouraged by Capt. Norrys and the antiquarians who surrounded and aided me. When the task was done, over two years after its commencement, I viewed the great rooms, wainscotted walls, vaulted ceilings, mullioned windows, and broad staircases with a pride which fully compensated for the prodigious expense of the restoration. Every attribute of the Middle Ages was cunningly reproduced, and the new parts blended perfectly with the original walls and foundations. The seat of my fathers was complete, and I looked forward to redeeming at last the local fame of the line which ended in me. I would reside here permanently, and prove that a de la Poer (for I had adopted again the original spelling of the name) need not be a fiend. My comfort was perhaps augmented by the fact that, although Exham Priory was mediaevally fitted, its interior was in truth wholly new and free from old vermin and old ghosts alike.

As I have said, I moved in on July 16, 1923. My household consisted of seven servants and nine cats, of which latter species I am particularly fond. My eldest cat, "Nigger-Man,"[38] was seven years old and had come with me from my home in Bolton, Massachusetts;[39] the others I had accumulated whilst living with Capt.

Richmond, Virginia, after the fire, 1865.

18. The capital of Virginia and, during the Civil War years, the capital of the Confederacy. Delapore may have served there at any time during the war. In 1862, Union general George McClellan waged what became known as the Seven Days Battle for the city but lost. After numerous Union victories in Virginia, however, Richmond became indefensible and was devastated by the Union army in April 1865. Over 25 percent of the city's structures were destroyed by fire, many set by retreating Confederate soldiers.

19. How old is the narrator? Robert H. Waugh has carefully computed his approximate age:

> Seven years old when the plantation was burned, apparently during the siege of Richmond in 1865, he was probably born in 1858. After the war the family came north, where he became over the years "a stolid Yankee" . . . so stolid a Yankee that he exhibits Republication sympathies at the death of Harding. When his son was ten years old in 1904, he was 46. He was 59 when his son went to war and 60 at the war's conclusion, when his son returned "a maimed invalid" . . . and he bought Exham Priory. He began the rebuilding of the Priory when he was 63 years old and 65 at its completion when he moved in and

Norrys' family during the restoration of the priory. For five days our routine proceeded with the utmost placidity, my time being spent mostly in the codification of old family data. I had now obtained some very circumstantial accounts of the final tragedy and flight of Walter de la Poer, which I conceived to be the probable contents of the hereditary paper lost in the fire at Carfax. It appeared that my ancestor was accused with much reason of having killed all the other members of his household, except four servant confederates, in their sleep, about two weeks after a shocking discovery which changed his whole demeanour,[40] but which, except by implication, he disclosed to no one save perhaps the servants who assisted him and afterward fled beyond reach.

This deliberate slaughter, which included a father, three brothers, and two sisters, was largely condoned by the villagers, and so slackly treated by the law that its perpetrator escaped honoured, unharmed, and undisguised to Virginia; the general whispered sentiment being that he had purged the land of an immemorial curse. What discovery had prompted an act so terrible, I could scarcely even conjecture. Walter de la Poer must have known for years the sinister tales about his family, so that this material could have given him no fresh impulse. Had he, then, witnessed some appalling ancient rite, or stumbled upon some frightful and revealing symbol in the priory or its vicinity? He was reputed to have been a shy, gentle youth in England. In Virignia he seemed

392 Main Street, home of the Bolton, Massachusetts Historical Society, built ca. 1750.

(John Phelan)

the events of the story overwhelmed him. Since it is possible that he was born earlier than we have supposed, we can be certain, considering the normal life spans of the time, that this is indeed the narration of on old man who shall soon die, believing himself the last of his line. (*A Monster of Voices: Speaking for H. P. Lovecraft* [New York: Hippocampus Press, 2011], 61–62)

20. The Royal Flying Corps, part of the British Army, merged with the Royal Naval Air Service on April 1, 1918, to become the Royal Air Force. It was quite small—one observation balloon squadron, for static observation of enemy defense, and four aircraft squadrons—but gained in importance during the Great War with the advent of aerial photography and wireless communication. At war's end there were nearly two hundred active squadrons and an equal number of training squadrons. RFC pilots did not carry parachutes; as retired RAF wing commander Ian Philpott notes, "British pilots had no option but to shoot themselves if their aircraft caught fire, since parachutes were not issued during the Great War" (*The Birth of the Royal Air Force: An Encyclopedia of British Air Power Before and During the Great War—1914–1918* [Barnsley, South Yorkshire, UK: Pen & Sword Military, 2013], 287).

21. Perhaps because he showed so little interest in his heritage and took no responsibility for the acts of his forebears?

22. One of the world's most readily recognized prehistoric ceremonial monuments. It is made of standing stones, or menhirs, topped by stone lintels, and is located in Wiltshire, England. Thousands of years old, it was built in stages from about 3100 or 3000 BCE (perhaps

not so much hard or bitter as harassed and apprehensive. He was spoken of in the diary of another gentleman-adventurer, Francis Harley of Bellview,[41] as a man of unexampled justice, honour, and delicacy.

On July 22 occurred the first incident which, though lightly dismissed at the time, takes on a preternatural significance in relation to later events. It was so simple as to be almost negligible, and could not possibly have been noticed under the circumstances; for it must be recalled that since I was in a building practically fresh and new except for the walls, and surrounded by a well-balanced staff of servitors, apprehension would have been absurd despite the locality. What I afterward remembered is merely this—that my old black cat, whose moods I know so well, was undoubtedly alert and anxious to an extent wholly out of keeping with his natural character. He roved from room to room, restless and disturbed, and sniffed constantly about the walls which formed part of the old Gothic structure. I realise how trite this sounds—like the inevitable dog in the ghost story, which always growls before his master sees the sheeted figure—yet I cannot consistently suppress it.

The following day a servant complained of restlessness among all the cats in the house. He came to me in my study, a lofty west room on the second story, with groined arches, black oak panel-

Stonehenge.

Statue of the goddess Cybele in Madrid.

Shutterstock.com

ling, and a triple Gothic window overlooking the limestone cliff and desolate valley; and even as he spoke I saw the jetty form of Nigger-Man creeping along the west wall and scratching at the new panels which overlaid the ancient stone. I told the man that there must be some singular odour or emanation from the old stonework, imperceptible to human senses, but affecting the delicate organs of cats even through the new woodwork. This I truly believed, and when the fellow suggested the presence of mice or rats, I mentioned that there had been no rats there for three hundred years, and that even the field mice of the surrounding country could hardly be found in these high walls, where they had never been known to stray. That afternoon I called on Capt. Norrys, and he assured me that it would be quite

before: 3700 BCE, according to some sources) to 1600 BCE.

23. The cult of Cybele, the Magna Mater (Great Mother), may have developed as early as the eighth century BCE—or, according to Mara Lynn Keller, in "The Eleusinian Mysteries of Demeter and Persephone: Fertility, Sexuality, and Rebirth," *Journal of Feminist Studies in Religion* 4, no. 1 (Spring 1988), 27–39, "the third millennium BCE or even earlier in the Neolithic, with links to religious practices in Crete, Egypt, Anatolia and Mesopotamia." Cybele can be identified with Ishtar, Isis, Ma, Ops, and other figures. The god Attis is her son or lover, depending on the myth. Robert Graves, in his seminal *The White Goddess: A Historical Grammar of Poetic Myth* (amended and enlarged ed. [New York: Farrar, Straus and Giroux, 1966]), describes this central figure:

> The Goddess is a lovely, slender woman with a hooked nose, deathly pale face, lips red as rowan-berries, startlingly blue eyes and long fair hair; she will suddenly transform herself into sow, mare, bitch, vixen, she-ass, weasel, serpent, owl, she-wolf, tigress, mermaid or loathsome hag. Her names and titles are innumerable. In ghost stories she often figures as "The White Lady," and in ancient religions, from the British Isles to the Caucasus, as the "White Goddess." . . . The reason why the hairs stand on end, the eyes water, the throat is constricted, the skin crawls and a shiver runs down the spine when one writes or reads a true poem is that a true poem is necessarily an invocation of the White Goddess, or Muse, the Mother of All Living, the ancient power of fright and lust—the female spider or the queen-bee whose embrace is death. (24)

Fred Blosser, in "The Sign of the Magna Mater," *Crypt of Cthulhu* 97 (Hallowmas 1997), 25–27, describes the cult as follows:

> A religion based on fertility rites, it originated in Asia Minor, spreading from there to Rome in the 3rd century BC. The creed was distinguished by a yearly orgiastic festival on the threshold of spring in which the priests of the sect, the Galli, drew their own blood to speed the resurrection of Atys or Attis, the Goddess's lover or son, who had died after castrating himself. The cult was also notorious for the fact that the Galli were eunuchs. As novices, they emulated Atys on the Day of Blood and presented their severed genitals as a further sacrifice to hasten the god's rebirth. (25)

Although it is tempting to see in the material here a glancing reference to Margaret Alice Murray's *The Witch-Cult in Western Europe* (see "The Horror at Red Hook," pp. 249–76, note 18, below), Robert H. Waugh concludes that HPL had not yet read the book when he wrote this tale. See "Dr. Margaret Murray and H. P. Lovecraft: The Witch-Cult in New England," *Lovecraft Studies* 31 (Fall 1994), 6.

24. DIV could be a Romanized "DIU," meaning "lasting for a long time" or "eternal." OPS is the Roman goddess of fertility, wealth, and plenty, the wife of Saturn, and allied with Cybele (some of the letters evidently eroded); thus, the inscription read "Eternal Ops Magna Mater." HPL could have read of Ops in J. G. Frazer's article on Saturn in the *Encyclopaedia Britannica* (9th ed.).

25. The third Augustan legion was not stationed in England; rather, the Second Augustan Legion was stationed in Isca Silurum (Caerleon-on-Usk) in Wales. These were units of the Roman army,

incredible for field mice to infest the priory in such a sudden and unprecedented fashion.

That night, dispensing as usual with a valet, I retired in the west tower chamber which I had chosen as my own, reached from the study by a stone staircase and short gallery—the former partly ancient, the latter entirely restored. This room was circular, very high, and without wainscotting, being hung with arras which I had myself chosen in London. Seeing that Nigger-Man was with me, I shut the heavy Gothic door and retired by the light of the electric bulbs which so cleverly counterfeited candles, finally switching off the light and sinking on the carved and canopied four-poster, with the venerable cat in his accustomed place across my feet. I did not draw the curtains, but gazed out at the narrow north window which I faced. There was a suspicion of aurora in the sky, and the delicate traceries of the window were pleasantly silhouetted.

At some time I must have fallen quietly asleep, for I recall a distinct sense of leaving strange dreams, when the cat started violently from his placid position. I saw him in the faint auroral glow, head strained forward, fore feet on my ankles, and hind feet stretched behind. He was looking intensely at a point on the wall somewhat west of the window, a point which to my eye had nothing to mark it, but toward which all my attention was now directed. And as I watched, I knew that Nigger-Man was not vainly excited. Whether the arras actually moved I cannot say. I think it did, very slightly. But what I can swear to is that behind it I heard a low, distinct scurrying as of rats or mice. In a moment the cat had jumped bodily on the screening tapestry, bringing the affected section to the floor with his weight, and exposing a damp, ancient wall of stone; patched here and there by the restorers, and devoid of any trace of rodent prowlers. Nigger-Man raced up and down the floor by this part of the wall, clawing the fallen arras and seemingly trying at times to insert a paw between the wall and the oaken floor. He found nothing, and after a time returned wearily to his place across my feet. I had not moved, but I did not sleep again that night.

In the morning I questioned all the servants, and found that none of them had noticed anything unusual, save that the cook remembered the actions of a cat which had rested on her windowsill. This cat had howled at some unknown hour of the night, awaking the cook in time for her to see him dart purposefully out of the open door down the stairs. I drowsed away the noontime, and in the afternoon called again on Capt. Norrys, who became exceedingly interested in what I told him. The odd incidents—so slight yet so curious—appealed to his sense of the picturesque, and elicited from him a number of reminiscences of local ghostly lore. We were genuinely perplexed at the presence of rats, and Norrys lent me some traps and Paris green,[42] which I had the servants place in strategic localities when I returned.

I retired early, being very sleepy, but was harassed by dreams of the most horrible sort. I seemed to be looking down from an immense height upon a twilit grotto, knee-deep with filth, where a white-bearded daemon swineherd drove about with his staff a flock of fungous,[43] flabby beasts whose appearance filled me with unutterable loathing. Then, as the swineherd paused and nodded

Phrygians
(from *Nouveau Larousse*).

founded during the reign of Augustus Caesar in 25 BCE.

26. The Phrygian kingdom thrived from 700 to 300 BCE in a region of Anatolia.

27. The Saxons and the Angles (and other Germanic tribes of Europe) invaded Britain in the fifth century CE and colonized the island when the Romans left.

28. The "heptarchy" was the rule of the seven kingdoms of Anglo-Saxon England, namely, Northumbria, Mercia, East Anglia, Wessex, Kent, Essex, and Sussex.

29. The principal "chronicles" for this period were histories of Anglo-Saxon England, the first of which is believed to have been written in the eighth and ninth centuries CE. They are collectively called *The Anglo-Saxon Chronicles*. The reference here is likely to a recension, or revision, of the Winchester Chronicle, covering the years 1–1070 and the oldest of the extant records. In the eleventh century, it was copied from the original Winchester Chronicle, with material being added from a tenth-century copy of an Old English translation of Bede's *Ecclesiastical History of the English People* and an annal for 1001. This updated copy, probably made in 1013, was badly damaged in a 1731 fire; a transcript had been made in the sixteenth century and was the basis for an edition of the Chronicle printed in 1643. The narrator refers later to another chronicle calling "a de la Poer . . . 'cursed of god' in 1307," but this should not be confused with the contents of *The Anglo-Saxon Chronicles*, which do not record any matters after 1154 CE.

30. The Danes and their Norwegian allies began landing raiding parties in England around 990 CE. Over the next twenty-five years, the influx became a full-scale invasion, and on St. Brice's Day, Novem-

ber 13, 1002, King Aethelred ordered "a most just extermination" of all Danes in England—one of a series of ill-advised actions taken by a monarch to whom history has assigned the unfortunate sobriquet "the Unready," both a play on his name (which means "good counsel") and a corruption of the word *"unraed"* ("lacking in counsel"). Having failed to achieve the desired banishment, and following more blunders that had the effect of inviting further Viking domination, Aethelred eventually sought exile in Normandy and then the Isle of Wight. In 1016, the son of Sweyn Forkbeard of Denmark, Canute (Cnut), was crowned king of England. (Two years earlier, the death of Sweyn, who had ruled England for a brief five weeks, occasioned a reappearance of Aethelred, plucked out of exile by the English authorities to fill the interregnum. For more on Aethelred, see Levi Roach, *Aethelred: The Unready* [New Haven: Yale University Press, 2016]. Roach generously concludes that his subject was "neither unready nor ill-counselled, but certainly ill-fated" [19].)

Canute's reign—recorded in another of the *Anglo-Saxon Chronicles* (see note 29, above), the Peterborough Chronicle—represented a formidable consolidation of power; he became, in 1018 and 1028, respectively, king of Denmark and Norway, ruling all three countries till 1035. It was not until 1066 that the throne was wrested from the Danes by William the Conqueror, establishing the line of Norman kings.

31. Henry III, son of King John and Isabel of Angoulême, took the throne at the age of nine and ruled England from 1216 to 1272. The Magna Carta signed by his father only a year before the accession recognized the power of the English barons and represented the first steps taken toward an English common law. Henry was in conflict with the

over his task, a mighty swarm of rats rained down on the stinking abyss and fell to devouring beasts and man alike.

From this terrific vision I was abruptly awaked by the motions of Nigger-Man, who had been sleeping as usual across my feet. This time I did not have to question the source of his snarls and hisses, and of the fear which made him sink his claws into my ankle, unconscious of their effect; for on every side of the chamber the walls were alive with nauseous sound—the verminous slithering of ravenous, gigantic rats. There was now no aurora to shew the state of the arras—the fallen section of which had been replaced—but I was not too frightened to switch on the light.

As the bulbs leapt into radiance I saw a hideous shaking all over the tapestry, causing the somewhat peculiar designs to execute a singular dance of death. This motion disappeared almost at once, and the sound with it. Springing out of bed, I poked at the arras with the long handle of a warming-pan that rested near, and lifted one section to see what lay beneath. There was nothing but the patched stone wall, and even the cat had lost his tense realisation of abnormal presences. When I examined the circular trap that had been placed in the room, I found all of the openings sprung, though no trace remained of what had been caught and had escaped.

Further sleep was out of the question, so, lighting a candle, I opened the door and went out in the gallery toward the stairs to my study, Nigger-Man following at my heels. Before we had reached the stone steps, however, the cat darted ahead of me and vanished down the ancient flight. As I descended the stairs myself, I became suddenly aware of sounds in the great room below; sounds of a nature which could not be mistaken. The oak-panelled walls were alive with rats, scampering and milling, whilst Nigger-Man was racing about with the fury of a baffled hunter. Reaching the bottom, I switched on the light, which did not this time cause the noise to subside. The rats continued their riot, stampeding with such force and distinctness that I could finally assign to their motions a definite direction. These creatures, in numbers apparently inexhaustible, were engaged in one stupendous migration from inconceivable heights to some depth conceivably, or inconceivably, below.

I now heard steps in the corridor, and in another moment

two servants pushed open the massive door. They were searching the house for some unknown source of disturbance which had thrown all the cats into a snarling panic and caused them to plunge precipitately down several flights of stairs and squat, yowling, before the closed door to the sub-cellar. I asked them if they had heard the rats, but they replied in the negative. And when I turned to call their attention to the sounds in the panels, I realised that the noise had ceased. With the two men, I went down to the door of the sub-cellar, but found the cats already dispersed. Later I resolved to explore the crypt below, but for the present I merely made a round of the traps. All were sprung, yet all were tenantless. Satisfying myself that no one had heard the rats save the felines and me, I sat in my study till morning; thinking profoundly, and recalling every scrap of legend I had unearthed concerning the building I inhabited.

I slept some in the forenoon, leaning back in the one comfortable library chair which my mediaeval plan of furnishing could not banish. Later I telephoned to Capt. Norrys, who came over and helped me explore the sub-cellar. Absolutely nothing untoward was found, although we could not repress a thrill at the knowledge that this vault was built by Roman hands. Every low arch and massive pillar was Roman—not the debased Romanesque of the bungling Saxons, but the severe and harmonious classicism of the age of the Caesars; indeed, the walls abounded with inscriptions familiar to the antiquarians who had repeatedly explored the place—things like "P.GETAE. PROP . . . TEMP . . . DONA . . ." and "L. PRAEC . . . VS . . . PONTIFI . . . ATYS . . ."[44]

The reference to Atys made me shiver, for I had read Catullus and knew something of the hideous rites of the Eastern god, whose worship was so mixed with that of Cybele.[45] Norrys and I, by the light of lanterns, tried to interpret the odd and nearly effaced designs on certain irregularly rectangular blocks of stone generally held to be altars, but could make nothing of them. We remembered that one pattern, a sort of rayed sun,[46] was held by students to imply a non-Roman origin, suggesting that these altars had merely been adopted by the Roman priests from some older and perhaps aboriginal temple on the same site. On one of these blocks were some brown stains which made me wonder.[47] The largest, in the centre of the room, had certain features on the

barons throughout his long reign, especially, beginning in 1258, with Simon de Montfort and his family—and with his own son Edward. After negotiations with various foreign powers—including the pope—to bolster his power, in 1261 Henry began appointing barons friendly to his rule. In making Gilbert de la Poer a baron, he would have been seeking a political ally. In 1263, de Montfort seized power, igniting, the following year, the second phase of the Barons' War, a civil conflict. Henry's rule weakened in his last years, and he slowly ceded power to Edward, who succeeded him on the throne as Edward I (known as Edward Longshanks).

32. Gilles de Rais (ca. 1405–1440), also known as the Maréchal de Retz, is described by John Fiske, in his *Myths and Myth-Makers: Old Tales and Superstitions Interpreted by Comparative Mythology* (Boston and New York: Houghton, Mifflin & Company, 1872/1896, 21st ed.), as follows: "A marshal of France, a scholarly man, a patriot and a man of holy life, he became suddenly possessed by an uncontrollable desire to murder children. During seven years he continued to inveigle little boys and girls into his castle, at the rate of about *two each week*, (?) and then put them to death in various ways, that he might witness their agonies and bathe in their blood; experiencing after each occasion the most dreadful remorse, but led on by an irresistible craving to repeat the crime. When this unparalleled iniquity was finally brought to light, the castle was found to contain bins full of children's bones. The horrible details of the trial are to be found in the histories of France by Michelet and Martin" (81).

33. Donatien Alphonse François, Marquis de Sade (1740–1814), is a byword for libertine eroticism. His novels, poetry, essays, and plays combined revolution-

ary philosophy (he was a delegate to the National Convention during the French Revolution), religious blasphemy, and sexual adventure, and he was an outspoken advocate of action without the restraint of law, religion, or morals. He spent more than thirty-two years incarcerated, ten of them in the Bastille and many others in lunatic asylums; he died in the asylum at Charenton.

34. Vodun, popularly known as voodoo, is a polytheistic religion that developed when West Africans from Kongo, Angola, Dahomey (now southern Benin), and elsewhere who had been sold into slavery syncretized their beliefs and practices with those of Christians in Haiti, Puerto Rico, Cuba, Brazil, and the Caribbean islands. Toyin Falola and Kevin D. Roberts, editors of *The Atlantic World, 1450–2000* (Bloomington: University of Indiana Press, 2008), note that "[i]n Abomey in the Republic of Benin, deities are called *vodun*," or "mysteries" (124).

35. Also known as the Mexican-American War, 1846–1848, under the presidency of James K. Polk, it was the then-largest annexation of land by the United States, ending with the Treaty of Guadalupe Hidalgo, in which Mexico ceded to the United States the territories of Texas, Arizona, New Mexico, California, Utah, Nevada, Oregon, and Washington, as well as land later incorporated into Oklahoma, Colorado, Kansas, Wyoming, and Montana.

36. Sir John Clavering (1672–1714) was the third baronet of Clavering of Axwell in Northumberland, in the same county as Hexham Priory, and is a likely candidate for the man mentioned here; the Clavering baronetcy was created in 1620 and was extinguished in 1893 with the death of Sir Henry Clavering.

upper surface which indicated its connexion with fire—probably burnt offerings.

Such were the sights in that crypt before whose door the cats had howled, and where Norrys and I now determined to pass the night. Couches were brought down by the servants, who were told not to mind any nocturnal actions of the cats, and Nigger-Man was admitted as much for help as for companionship. We decided to keep the great oak door—a modern reproduction with slits for ventilation—tightly closed; and, with this attended to, we retired with lanterns still burning to await whatever might occur.

The vault was very deep in the foundations of the priory, and undoubtedly far down on the face of the beetling limestone cliff overlooking the waste valley. That it had been the goal of the scuffling and unexplainable rats I could not doubt, though why, I could not tell. As we lay there expectantly, I found my vigil occasionally mixed with half-formed dreams from which the uneasy motions of the cat across my feet would rouse me. These dreams were not wholesome, but horribly like the one I had had the night before. I saw again the twilit grotto, and the swineherd with his unmentionable fungous beasts wallowing in filth, and as I looked at these things they seemed nearer and more distinct—so distinct that I could almost observe their features. Then I did observe the flabby features of one of them—and awaked with such a scream that Nigger-Man started up, whilst Capt. Norrys, who had not slept, laughed considerably. Norrys might have laughed more—or perhaps less—had he known what it was that made me scream. But I did not remember myself till later. Ultimate horror often paralyses memory in a merciful way.

Norrys waked me when the phenomena began. Out of the same frightful dream I was called by his gentle shaking and his urging to listen to the cats. Indeed, there was much to listen to, for beyond the closed door at the head of the stone steps was a veritable nightmare of feline yelling and clawing, whilst Nigger-Man, unmindful of his kindred outside, was running excitedly around the bare stone walls, in which I heard the same babel of scurrying rats that had troubled me the night before.

An acute terror now rose within me, for here were anomalies which nothing normal could well explain. These rats, if not the creatures of a madness which I shared with the cats alone, must be burrowing and sliding in Roman walls I had thought to be of solid limestone blocks . . . unless perhaps the action of water through more than seventeen centuries had eaten winding tunnels which rodent bodies had worn clear and ample. . . . But even so, the spectral horror was no less; for if these were living vermin why did not Norrys hear their disgusting commotion? Why did he urge me to watch Nigger-Man and listen to the cats outside, and why did he guess wildly and vaguely at what could have aroused them?

By the time I had managed to tell him, as rationally as I could, what I thought I was hearing, my ears gave me the last fading impression of the scurrying; which had retreated *still downward,* far underneath this deepest of sub-cellars till it seemed as if the whole cliff below were riddled with questing rats. Norrys was not as sceptical as I had anticipated, but instead seemed profoundly moved. He motioned to me to notice that the cats at the door had ceased their clamour, as if giving up the rats for lost; whilst Nigger-Man had a burst of renewed restlessness, and was clawing frantically around the bottom of the large stone altar in the centre of the room, which was nearer Norrys' couch than mine.

My fear of the unknown was at this point very great. Something astounding had occurred, and I saw that Capt. Norrys, a younger, stouter, and presumably more naturally materialistic man, was affected fully as much as myself—perhaps because of his lifelong and intimate familiarity with local legend. We could for the moment do nothing but watch the old black cat as he pawed with decreasing fervour at the base of the altar, occasionally looking up and mewing to me in that persuasive manner which he used when he wished me to perform some favour for him.

Norrys now took a lantern close to the altar and examined the place where Nigger-Man was pawing; silently kneeling and scraping away the lichens of centuries which joined the massive pre-Roman block to the tessellated floor. He did not find anything, and was about to abandon his efforts when I noticed a trivial circumstance which made me shudder, even though it implied nothing more than I had already imagined. I told him of it, and we both looked at its almost imperceptible manifestation with

37. Sabine Baring-Gould's *Curious Myths of the Middle Ages,* Second Series (London, Oxford and Cambridge: Rivingtons, 1868), first published in 1834, contains a long chapter on the legend of the German bishop Hatto. Hatto, it is told, invited to his castle poor parishioners who had complained bitterly of famine. Herding them into a barn, he burned them to death, exclaiming that he had rid the countryside of these "rats." Shortly thereafter, he was attacked by plagues of rats and mice. He fled to a tower but was overcome by an army of vermin (182–205).

Baring-Gould collects a number of similar stories from other countries and concludes that all of these myths (for none could be given any historical credibility) stemmed from ancient practices of human sacrifice, in which a priest or prince was given to the rats to appease the gods. Rats and mice, he points out, are often sacred animals, representing the souls of men or even deities. Baring-Gould's book was in HPL's library, according to S. T. Joshi; see *Lovecraft's Library, A Catalogue, Revised and Enlarged* (New York: Hippocampus Press, 2002).

38. It is well known that HPL had a childhood pet of the same name. The name shocks the modern reader, but it was unfortunately consistent with white, mainstream depictions of African American life in the nineteenth and early twentieth centuries. Donald R. Burleson (in his *H. P. Lovecraft: A Critical Study,* 93, note 19) is prepared to give HPL a free pass for sharing the dominant attitudes of his era, but we should not: Lovecraft knew well the impact of the word. His infamous 1912 poem "On the Creation of Niggers" reflects his attitude toward all people who were not white Anglo-Saxons:

When, long ago, the gods created Earth
In Jove's fair image Man was shaped
    at birth.
The beasts for lesser parts were next
    designed;
Yet were they too remote from
    humankind.
To fill the gap, and join the rest to
    Man,
Th' Olympian host conceiv'd a clever
    plan.
A beast they wrought, in semi-human
    figure,
Filled it with vice, and called the
    thing a Nigger.

The casual racism of de la Poer is not disagreeable to HPL; rather, as he tells the tale, de la Poer's ultimate downfall is not *who* he is but his failure to embrace that heritage. For further reading, see Bernard A. Drew's *Black Stereotypes in Popular Series Fiction, 1851–1944: Jim Crow Era Authors and Their Characters* (Jefferson, NC: McFarland, 2015).

39. See "Herbert West: Reanimator," in the previous volume, pp. 45–79, note 31.

40. Compare "Facts concerning the Late Arthur Jermyn," pp. 44–54, above, where similar events are described.

41. Daniel Harley was a well-regarded British explorer of the Arctic who died in 1878. This may well have been his son. Bellview was a well-known North Carolina plantation, sold in 1811; there was also a Bellview plantation near Franklin, Louisiana, owned by Bradish Johnson in 1878.

42. An insecticide made from arsenic trioxide and acetate of copper.

43. Like a fungus. What that means here is unclear, but it sounds bad.

the fixedness of fascinated discovery and acknowledgment. It was only this—that the flame of the lantern set down near the altar was slightly but certainly flickering from a draught of air which it had not before received, and which came indubitably from the crevices between floor and altar where Norrys was scraping away the lichens.

We spent the rest of the night in the brilliantly lighted study, nervously discussing what we should do next. The discovery that some vault deeper than the deepest known masonry of the Romans underlay this accursed pile—some vault unsuspected by the curious antiquarians of three centuries—would have been sufficient to excite us without any background of the sinister. As it was, the fascination became twofold; and we paused in doubt whether to abandon our search and quit the priory for ever in superstitious caution, or to gratify our sense of adventure and brave whatever horrors might await us in the unknown depths. By morning we had compromised, and decided to go to London to gather a group of archaeologists and scientific men fit to cope with the mystery. It should be mentioned that before leaving the sub-cellar we had vainly tried to move the central altar which we now recognised as the gate to a new pit of nameless fear. What secret would open the gate, wiser men than we would have to find.

During many days in London Capt. Norrys and I presented our facts, conjectures, and legendary anecdotes to five eminent authorities, all men who could be trusted to respect any family disclosures which future explorations might develop. We found most of them little disposed to scoff, but instead intensely interested and sincerely sympathetic. It is hardly necessary to name them all, but I may say that they included Sir William Brinton, whose excavations in the Troad[48] excited most of the world in their day. As we all took the train for Anchester I felt myself poised on the brink of frightful revelations, a sensation symbolised by the air of mourning among the many Americans at the unexpected death of the President on the other side of the world.[49]

On the evening of August 7th we reached Exham Priory, where the servants assured me that nothing unusual had occurred. The cats, even old Nigger-Man, had been perfectly placid; and not a trap in the house had been sprung. We were to begin exploring on the following day, awaiting which I assigned well-appointed rooms to all my guests. I myself retired in my own tower chamber, with Nigger-Man across my feet. Sleep came quickly, but hideous dreams assailed me. There was a vision of a Roman feast like that of Trimalchio,[50] with a horror in a covered platter. Then came that damnable, recurrent thing about the swineherd and his filthy drove in the twilit grotto. Yet when I awoke it was full daylight, with normal sounds in the house below. The rats, living or spectral, had not troubled me; and Nigger-Man was still quietly asleep. On going down, I found that the same tranquillity had prevailed elsewhere; a condition which one of the assembled savants—a fellow named Thornton, devoted to the psychic—rather absurdly laid to the fact that I had now been shewn the thing which certain forces had wished to shew me.

All was now ready, and at eleven a.m. our entire group of seven men, bearing powerful electric searchlights and implements of excavation, went down to the sub-cellar and bolted the door behind us. Nigger-Man was with us, for the investigators found no occasion to despise his excitability, and were indeed anxious that he be present in case of obscure rodent manifestations. We noted the Roman inscriptions and unknown altar designs only briefly, for three of the savants had already seen them, and all knew their characteristics. Prime attention was paid to the momentous central altar, and within an hour Sir William Brinton had caused it to tilt backward, balanced by some unknown species of counterweight.

There now lay revealed such a horror as would have overwhelmed us had we not been prepared. Through a nearly square opening in the tiled floor, sprawling on a flight of stone steps so prodigiously worn that it was little more than an inclined plane at the centre, was a ghastly array of human or semi-human bones. Those which retained their collocation as skeletons shewed attitudes of panic fear, and over all were the marks of rodent gnawing. The skulls denoted nothing short of utter idiocy, cretinism,[51] or primitive semi-apedom. Above the hellishly littered steps arched a descending passage seemingly chiselled from the solid rock, and conducting a current of air. This current was not a sudden and noxious rush as from a closed vault, but a cool breeze with something of freshness in it. We did not pause long, but shiveringly

44. The Getae, or Daci, were a Thracian tribe, eventually combined into the West Goths, or Tervingi or Thervingi, who were scattered in settlements from the Danube to the Dneister River. (The land of the East Goths, or Greutungi or Greuthungi, was between the Dneister and the Don Rivers.) See J. B. Calvert, "History of Central Europe," http://mysite.du.edu~etuttle/misc/europe.htm/#Goth, who further refers the reader to L. R. Johnson, *Central Europe* (New York: Oxford University Press, 1996). It is impossible to affix definite meanings to these fragments—there are so many possibilities. Are these room designations—for example, "*Liber Praeceptiones*" meaning the location of books of instruction? The "*templum*" (temple)? The "*pontificatus*" (perhaps the priests' quarters)? "Dona"—the place where gifts (*dona*) or offerings were kept?

45. Gaius Valerius Catullus, the Roman poet (ca. 84–54 BCE), wrote in poem 63 of the flight of Attis (spelled "Atys" in the *Encyclopaedia Britannica*, 9th ed.) from his lover-mother Cybele. In the poem, Attis castrates himself, and the lyric is as much about sexuality and its fluidity as it is about the myth. The poem is newly translated by S. T. Joshi in "Attis and Cybele."

46. The "rayed sun" shown here is known as the Vergina Sun and appeared in

An example of the Vergina sun.
Shutterstock.com

Greek art from the sixth to the second century BCE, associated with Macedonia. It was adopted in 1993 as an official Greek national symbol.

47. Wonder, that is, if these were blood-stains from offerings, human or otherwise.

48. The Biga peninsula, in northwestern Anatolia, Turkey, not far from the ruins of Troy, in which Greek settlements flourished in classical times. For Strabo (ca. 64 BCE–ca. 23 CE): *Strabo on the Troad*, Book XIII, Cap. I, ed. with translation and commentary by Walter Leaf (Cambridge: Cambridge University Press, 1923). S. T. Joshi observes that "[t]he very nature of the reference places these excavations well before 1923, the date of the tale's events, and Brinton's work must surely have occurred after Schliemann's spectacular discovery of the site of Troy in 1867" ("Topical References in Lovecraft," in *Primal Sources: Essays on H. P. Lovecraft* [New York: Hippocampus Press, 2003], 135).

49. President Warren G. Harding died unexpectedly, of a heart attack (although there was suspicion of foul play), while staying at the Palace Hotel in San Francisco on August 2, 1923. Harding was the sixth U.S. president to die in office.

50. The Roman courtier Gaius Petronius Arbiter (ca. 27–66 CE), or simply Petronius, invented a character named Trimalchio, a former slave who rises to wealth, for his novel *The Satyricon*. Trimalchio is known for his lavish banquets and, although he was probably intended as a satire of the then-emperor Nero, has come to symbolize the excesses of the newly wealthy (F. Scott Fitzgerald at first gave *The Great Gatsby* another name: *Trimalchio at West Egg*). Harding, whose numerous extramarital affairs became public after his death, was long rumored

Greek Colonization of western Asia Minor during the Greek Dark Age (or Geometric Age) eleventh–eighth centuries BCE, showing the Troad.
Library of Congress, Geography and Map Division

began to clear a passage down the steps. It was then that Sir William, examining the hewn walls, made the odd observation that the passage, according to the direction of the strokes, must have been chiselled *from beneath*.

I must be very deliberate now, and choose my words.

After ploughing down a few steps amidst the gnawed bones we saw that there was light ahead; not any mystic phosphorescence, but a filtered daylight which could not come except from unknown fissures in the cliff that overlooked the waste valley. That such fissures had escaped notice from outside was hardly remarkable, for not only is the valley wholly uninhabited, but the cliff is so high and beetling that only an aëronaut could study its face in detail. A few steps more, and our breaths were liter-

A cretin, painted by Leopold Müller, 1819.

ally snatched from us by what we saw; so literally that Thornton, the psychic investigator, actually fainted in the arms of the dazed man who stood behind him. Norrys, his plump face utterly white and flabby, simply cried out inarticulately; whilst I think that what I did was to gasp or hiss, and cover my eyes. The man behind me—the only one of the party older than I—croaked the hackneyed "My God!" in the most cracked voice I ever heard. Of seven cultivated men, only Sir William Brinton retained his composure; a thing more to his credit because he led the party and must have seen the sight first.

It was a twilit grotto of enormous height, stretching away farther than any eye could see; a subterraneous world of limitless mystery and horrible suggestion.[52] There were buildings and other architectural remains—in one terrified glance I saw a weird pattern of tumuli,[53] a savage circle of monoliths, a low-domed Roman ruin, a sprawling Saxon pile, and an early English edifice of wood—but all these were dwarfed by the ghoulish spectacle presented by the general surface of the ground. For yards about the steps extended an insane tangle of human bones, or bones at least as human as those on the steps. Like a foamy sea they stretched, some fallen apart, but others wholly or partly articulated as skeletons; these latter invariably in postures of daemoniac frenzy, either fighting off some menace or clutching other forms with cannibal intent.

to have an African American great-grandmother (though 2015 DNA testing of his descendants proved that to be very unlikely).

51. Cretinism, or congenital hypothyroidism, usually caused by an iodine deficiency. It was prevalent in parts of Europe and Asia where the soil was deficient in iodine.

52. Steven J. Mariconda, in "Curious Myths of the Middle Ages and 'The Rats in the Walls'" (in On the Emergence of "Cthulhu" & Other Observations, 53–56 [West Warwick, RI: Necronomicon Press, 1995]), points out the many similarities between the abyss at Exham Priory and the cave at St. Patrick's Purgatory, in Lough Derg, described in Sabine Baring-Gould's Curious Myths of the Middle Ages, First Series, 230–49, as being "two days' journey" from the (fictional) town of Valdric, Ireland. Upon entering, the hermit Patrick became aware of "piteous cries issuing from the depths of the cave, just such as would be the wailings of souls in purgatory." The Purgatory was closed by order of the pope at the end of the fifteenth century and eventually replaced by a church. Today, fifteen thousand pilgrims per year undertake a three-day fast at the site, which is on Station Island, reached by ferry. The nearest (actual) village is Pettigo, in County Donegal, and the nearest train station is in Sligo, with trains operated by Iarnród Éireann (Irish Rail).

53. Mounds of earth, barrows, or burial mounds over graves.

54. See "Dagon," in the previous volume, pp. 3–10, note 16.

55. Ernst Theodor Amadeus Hoffmann, born Ernst Theodor Wilhelm Hoffmann (1776–1822), who wrote as E. T. A. Hoffmann, is perhaps best known for his 1816 "Nutcracker and Mouse King" ("Der Nußknacker und der Mausekönig"), which became the basis for Tchaikovsky's ballet *The Nutcracker* (1892), and for his stories that feature in Offenbach's opera *The Tales of Hoffmann* (1881). In his essay "Supernatural Horror in Literature," Lovecraft called Hoffmann's "short tales and novels and short stories . . . a byword for mellowness of background and maturity of form, though they incline to levity and extravagance, and lack the exalted moments of stark, breathless terror which a less sophisticated writer might have achieved. Generally they convey the grotesque rather than the terrible" (in *Dagon and Other Macabre Tales*, 389–90). A polymath who studied law, was employed as a civil servant, painted, and was himself a composer and a conductor before he turned to fiction, Hoffmann became one of the most influential authors of the Romantic era. Many critics consider *The Life and Opinions of the Tomcat Murr* (*Die Lebensansichten des Katers Murr*), written in 1820–22, which splices the autobiography of a cat into the biography of a conductor, to be his greatest work.

56. Charles-Marie-Georges Huysmans (1848–1907), or simply J. K. Huysmans, is best remembered for his dark novel *À rebours* (1884, published in English as *Against the Grain* or *Against Nature*). HPL wrote of French supernatural horror literature, "Later on [after Victor Hugo, Théophile Gautier, and Gustave Flaubert] we see the stream divide, producing strange poets and fantaisistes of

When Dr. Trask, the anthropologist, stooped to classify the skulls, he found a degraded mixture which utterly baffled him. They were mostly lower than the Piltdown man[54] in the scale of evolution, but in every case definitely human. Many were of higher grade, and a very few were the skulls of supremely and sensitively developed types. All the bones were gnawed, mostly by rats, but somewhat by others of the half-human drove. Mixed with them were many tiny bones of rats—fallen members of the lethal army which closed the ancient epic.

I wonder that any man among us lived and kept his sanity through that hideous day of discovery. Not Hoffmann[55] or Huysmans[56] could conceive a scene more wildly incredible, more frenetically repellent, or more Gothically grotesque than the twilit grotto through which we seven staggered; each stumbling on revelation after revelation, and trying to keep for the nonce from thinking of the events which must have taken place there three hundred, or a thousand, or two thousand, or ten thousand years ago. It was the antechamber of hell, and poor Thornton fainted again when Trask told him that some of the skeleton things must have descended as quadrupeds through the last twenty or more generations.

Horror piled on horror as we began to interpret the architectural remains. The quadruped things—with their occasional recruits from the biped class—had been kept in stone pens, out of which they must have broken in their last delirium of hunger or rat-fear. There had been great herds of them, evidently fattened on the coarse vegetables whose remains could be found as a sort of poisonous ensilage[57] at the bottom of huge stone bins older than Rome. I knew now why my ancestors had had such excessive gardens—would to heaven I could forget! The purpose of the herds I did not have to ask.

Sir William, standing with his searchlight in the Roman ruin, translated aloud the most shocking ritual I have ever known; and told of the diet of the antediluvian cult which the priests of Cybele found and mingled with their own. Norrys, used as he was to the trenches, could not walk straight when he came out of the English building. It was a butcher shop and kitchen—he had expected that—but it was too much to see familiar English implements in such a place, and to read familiar English *graffiti* there, some as recent as 1610.[58] I could not go in that building—that building whose daemon activities were stopped only by the dagger of my ancestor Walter de la Poer.

What I did venture to enter was the low Saxon building, whose oaken door had fallen, and there I found a terrible row of ten stone cells with rusty bars. Three had tenants, all skeletons of high grade, and on the bony forefinger of one I found a seal ring with my own coat-of-arms. Sir William found a vault with far older cells below the Roman chapel, but these cells were empty. Below them was a low crypt with cases of formally arranged bones, some of them bearing terrible parallel inscriptions carved in Latin, Greek, and the tongue of Phrygia. Meanwhile, Dr. Trask had opened one of the prehistoric tumuli, and brought to light skulls which were slightly[59] more human than a gorilla's, and which bore indescribable ideographic carvings. Through all this horror my cat stalked unperturbed. Once I saw him monstrously perched atop a mountain of bones, and wondered at the secrets that might lie behind his yellow eyes.

Having grasped to some slight degree the frightful revelations of this twilit area—an area so hideously foreshadowed by my recurrent dream—we turned to that apparently boundless depth of midnight cavern where no ray of light from the cliff could penetrate. We shall never know what sightless Stygian worlds yawn beyond the little distance we went, for it was decided that such secrets are not good for mankind. But there was plenty to engross us close at hand, for we had not gone far before the searchlights shewed that accursed infinity of pits in which the rats had feasted, and whose sudden lack of replenishment had driven the ravenous rodent army first to turn on the living herds of starving things, and then to burst forth from the priory in that historic orgy of devastation which the peasants will never forget.

God! those carrion black pits of sawed, picked bones and opened skulls! Those nightmare chasms choked with the pithecanthropoid,[60] Celtic, Roman, and English bones of countless unhallowed centuries! Some of them were full, and none can say how deep they had once been. Others were still bottomless to our searchlights, and peopled by unnamable fancies. What, I thought, of the hapless rats that stumbled into such traps amidst the blackness of their quests in this grisly Tartarus?

the Symbolist and Decadent schools whose dark interests really centre more in abnormalities of human thought and instinct than in the actual supernatural, and subtle story-tellers whose thrills are quite directly derived from the night-black wells of cosmic unreality. Of the former class of 'artists in sin' the illustrious poet Baudelaire, influenced vastly by Poe, is the supreme type; whilst the psychological novelist Joris-Karl Huysmans, a true child of the eighteen-nineties, is at once the summation and finale" ("Supernatural Horror in Literature," in *Dagon and Other Macabre Tales*, 392).

57. Ensilage, or silage, is the process of harvesting plants (corn, grain, or other crops) and storing them in a silo.

58. Graffiti—writings or inscriptions illicitly or without authorization placed on walls, doors, and other public places—has a long and venerable past. Graffiti found in such places as the ruins of Pompeii, the Parthenon, and the Colosseum is of the predictable sort: "X was here," "X loves Y," "X fornicated with Y," "Z is a [bad person]," and "the [entertainment/food/service] here is [excellent/terrible]." See, for example, http://www.pompeiana.org/Resources/Ancient/Graffiti%20from%20Pompeii.htm.

59. Published editions have "slighty"—an error not noted in the *Variorum Edition* compiled by S. T. Joshi.

60. A pithecanthropoid is a member of the (former) species *Pithecanthropus erectus*. Bones found in 1891 by Dr. Eugène Dubois were thought to represent a species ("Java man") that was the "missing link" between humans and apes. The name *Pithecanthropus* is a Latinized combination of the Greek πίθηκος (pithekos), monkey or ape, and ἄνθρωπος

(anthrōpos), human being. "Much discussion followed the 'find,'" reported the *Encyclopaedia Britannica* (11th ed.) in 1910–11, "and many authorities have given an opinion adverse to Dr. Dubois's theory. The prevailing opinion is that the bones are human. They are not held to represent what has been called 'the missing link,' bridging over the gulf between man and the apes, but almost all authorities are agreed that they constitute a further link in the chain, bringing man nearer his Simian prototype" (vol. 21, 665). *Pithecanthropus* is now classified as part of the broader species of hominid (prehuman), *Homo erectus*, which now includes the so-called Peking man bones discovered in Zhoukoudian, China, in 1921 and *Homo erectus georgicus*, the subspecies name given to fossil remains found in Dmanisi, Georgia (southern Caucasus), in 1991.

61. The Egyptian goddess Isis was often depicted as winged, but Bast (Bastet), usually depicted as a cat or lioness, had no wings. Originally a warrior, she evolved into a protective deity.

62. In "Behind the Mask of Nyarlathotep," Will Murray points out that "[t]o 1924 readers of *Weird Tales*, where [this] story first appeared, the vaguely suggestive name of Nyarlathotep would have evoked only an eerie sensation, not recognition" (25). The prose poem "Nyarlathotep" had appeared in 1920 only in *The United Amateur*, an obscure journal. Murray suggests that Nyarlathotep is an homage to the scientist Nikola Tesla, but there is no real evidence supporting this linkage. See "Nyarlathotep," in the previous volume, pp. 30–34, note 6, and in particular, *The Dream-Quest of Unknown Kadath*, pp. 329–432, below.

63. "Would you use me this way?"

Once my foot slipped near a horribly yawning brink, and I had a moment of ecstatic fear. I must have been musing a long time, for I could not see any of the party but the plump Capt. Norrys. Then there came a sound from that inky, boundless, farther distance that I thought I knew; and I saw my old black cat dart past me like a winged Egyptian god,[61] straight into the illimitable gulf of the unknown. But I was not far behind, for there was no doubt after another second. It was the eldritch scurrying of those fiend-born rats, always questing for new horrors, and determined to lead me on even unto those grinning caverns of earth's centre where Nyarlathotep,[62] the mad faceless god, howls blindly in the darkness to the piping of two amorphous idiot flute-players.

My searchlight expired, but still I ran. I heard voices, and yowls, and echoes, but above all there gently rose that impious, insidious scurrying; gently rising, rising, as a stiff bloated corpse gently rises above an oily river that flows under endless onyx bridges to a black, putrid sea. Something bumped into me—something soft and plump. It must have been the rats; the viscous, gelatinous, ravenous army that feast on the dead and the living. . . . Why shouldn't rats eat a de la Poer as a de la Poer eats forbidden things? . . . The war ate my boy, damn them all . . . and the Yanks ate Carfax with flames and burnt Grandsire Delapore and the secret . . . No, no, I tell you, I am *not* that daemon swineherd in the twilit grotto! It was *not* Edward Norrys' fat face on that flabby, fungous thing! Who says I am a de la Poer? He lived, but my boy died! . . . Shall a Norrys hold the lands of a de la Poer? . . . It's voodoo, I tell you . . . that spotted snake . . . Curse you, Thornton, I'll teach you to faint at what my family do! . . . 'Sblood, thou stinkard, I'll learn ye how to gust . . . wolde ye swynke me thilke wys?[63] . . . *Magna Mater! Magna Mater!* . . . *Atys*[64] . . . *Dia ad aghaidh 's ad aodann . . . agus bas dunach ort! Dhonas 's dholas ort, agus leat-sa!*[65] . . . *Ungl . . . ungl . . . rrrlh . . . chchch . . .*[66]

That is what they say I said when they found me in the blackness after three hours; found me crouching in the blackness over the plump, half-eaten body of Capt. Norrys, with my own cat leaping and tearing at my throat. Now they have blown up Exham Priory, taken my Nigger-Man away from me, and shut me into this barred room at Hanwell[67] with fearful whispers about my heredity and experiences. Thornton is in the next room, but they prevent me from talking to him. They are trying, too, to suppress most of the facts concerning the priory. When I speak of poor Norrys they accuse me of a hideous thing, but they must know that I did not do it. They must know it was the rats; the slithering, scurrying rats whose scampering will never let me sleep; the daemon rats that race behind the padding in this room and beckon me down to greater horrors than I have ever known; the rats they can never hear; the rats, the rats in the walls.

64. Fred Blosser, note 23, above, sees these cries as evidence that Delapore's ancestors were high priests of the cult of the Magna Mater (25).

65. The phrase also appears in "The Sin-Eater" (1895), by Fiona Macleod (pseudonym of William Sharp, 1856–1905), who translates it as "God against thee and in thy face . . . and may a death of woe be yours . . . Evil and sorrow to thee and thine!"

66. Note that the narrator is speaking in retrogressive tongues: Archaic English, then Middle English, then Latin, Gaelic, and finally grunts. Conan creator Robert E. Howard wrote a letter to Farnsworth Wright, editor of *Weird Tales*, noting the use of the Gaelic instead of Cymric: "I note . . . that Mr. Lovecraft . . . holds to Lhuyd's theory as to the settling of Britain by the Celts." This led to a six-year correspondence between Howard and HPL.

Hanwell Insane Asylum, ca. 1890.

67. The Hanwell (1st Middlesex) County Asylum, popularly known as Hanwell Asylum or the Hanwell Insane Asylum, opened on May 16, 1831, eight miles west of central London. Its mandate (by Act of Parliament) was to house pauper lunatics, and its original superintendent and matron, a married couple, William Charles Ellis and Mildred Ellis, successfully used therapeutic employment in treating residents; on the property were, among other workplaces, a bakery, a firehouse, a farm, a gasworks, and a brewery—closed in 1888 when an 1879 Act of Parliament "to facilitate the control and care of Habitual Drunkards [later 'Inebriates']" was made permanent. John Conolly, Hanwell's third superintendent, banned the use of metal restraints that had been used to tie patients down. By 1880 there were two thousand under supervision, and in 1937, extra wings were added. The following year, the name was changed to St. Bernard's Hospital. The institution became part of Ealing Hospital in 1985, and today it is part of the West London Mental Health Trust (West London Healthcare NHS Trust).

Under the Pyramids[1]

It is uncertain whether the germ of the idea for this story came from its purported coauthor, Harry Houdini, or was wholly HPL's invention, but the themes are all Lovecraft: Set amid meticulously researched details of Egyptian history and geography, the tale suggests that modern Cairo is but a thin veneer over a dark abyss, peopled by creatures far beyond the understanding of humans. Houdini, in public a man of adventure with a well-established reputation for rationalism, and in private a figure of permanent mystery, is the perfect narrator for this tale.

I.

MYSTERY ATTRACTS MYSTERY. Ever since the wide appearance of my name as a performer of unexplained feats, I have encountered strange narratives and events which my calling has led people to link with my interests and activities.[2] Some of these have been trivial and irrelevant, some deeply dramatic and absorbing, some productive of weird and perilous experiences, and some involving me in extensive scientific and historical research. Many of these matters I have told and shall continue to tell freely;[3] but there is one of which I speak with great reluctance, and which I am now relating only after a session of grilling persuasion from the publishers of this magazine, who had heard vague rumours of it from other members of my family.

The hitherto guarded subject pertains to my non-professional visit to Egypt fourteen years ago, and has been avoided by me for several reasons. For one thing, I am averse to exploiting certain unmistakably actual facts and conditions obviously unknown to the myriad tourists who throng about the pyramids and apparently secreted with much diligence by the authorities at Cairo, who cannot be wholly ignorant of them. For another thing, I

1. Written at the behest of J. C. Henneberger, founder of *Weird Tales*, the story originally appeared under the byline of the famous magician and escape artist Harry Houdini, a regular columnist ("Ask Houdini") whose name had been attached to at least two previous stories in the journal. Henneberger paid Lovecraft one hundred dollars for the ghostwriting assignment, the greatest sum he had ever received for his work. Shortly before he was due to submit the story to *Weird Tales*, Lovecraft mislaid his only typescript in Providence's Union Station en route to Manhattan for his own wedding, to Sonia Greene. He and she then spent their Philadelphia honeymoon creating a fresh typescript, working from the original handwritten draft, which HPL had kept.

The story was published (as "Imprisoned with the Pharaohs") in *Weird Tales* 4, no. 2 (May–June–July 1924), 3–12; it was reprinted, under the same title, in *Weird Tales* 34, no. 1 (June–July 1939), 133–50, with Lovecraft's authorship only then cited, in an editor's note: "Harry

Houdini, escape artist and one of the greatest magicians of all time, dictated the facts of this exciting experience to a public stenographer in the dressing-room of the theatre where he was playing, one night fifteen years ago. But though the events were narrated by Houdini, and the printer's proofs were all O.K.'d by him, the actual writing was done by the late great master of weird fiction, H. P. Lovecraft" (133). That the original title of the work was intended to be "Under the Pyramids" is evidenced by an advertisement HPL took out in March 1924 seeking the return of a lost typescript of the story, but it was not published under that title until S. T. Joshi's collection *The Thing on the Doorstep and Other Weird Stories* (2001). See *I Am Providence*, 498–99, for the story of the lost typescript.

The handsome, heavily muscled Houdini was to die two years after publication, at the age of only fifty-two, following an incident in which a fan, testing his reputation for taking blows to the stomach, repeatedly punched him in his dressing room; over the next eight days Houdini collapsed onstage and was hospitalized for appendicitis, finally succumbing to peritonitis. The link between the dressing room incident and Houdini's death has never been definitively established.

2. Harry Houdini was the stage name of Erik Weisz, later Ehrich Weiss (1874–1926), the son of an émigré Hungarian rabbi, who achieved fame first at Coney Island and later on vaudeville stages around the world. Houdini was best known for his sensational escapes, first from handcuffs, straitjackets, and similar restraints and later from elaborate enclosures and prisons. He was also a highly popular stage magician and illusionist. He tried to turn his stage successes into a career in film, starring in five movies and creating his own pro-

"Imprisoned with the Pharaohs," as "Under the Pyramids" was titled. *Weird Tales* (May/June/July 1924) (artist unknown)

Houdini (Ehrich Weiss), his mother, Cecilia Steiner Weiss, and his wife, Bess, ca. 1907.

dislike to recount an incident in which my own fantastic imagination must have played so great a part. What I saw—or thought I saw—certainly did not take place; but is rather to be viewed as a result of my then recent readings in Egyptology, and of the speculations anent this theme which my environment naturally prompted. These imaginative stimuli, magnified by the excitement of an actual event terrible enough in itself, undoubtedly gave rise to the culminating horror of that grotesque night so long past.

In January, 1910, I had finished a professional engagement in England and signed a contract for a tour of Australian theatres. A liberal time being allowed for the trip, I determined to make the most of it in the sort of travel which chiefly interests me; so accompanied by my wife[4] I drifted pleasantly down the Continent and embarked at Marseilles on the P. & O. Steamer Malwa, bound for Port Said.[5] From that point I proposed to visit the principal historical localities of lower Egypt before leaving finally for Australia.

The voyage was an agreeable one, and enlivened by many of the amusing incidents which befall a magical performer apart from his work. I had intended, for the sake of quiet travel, to keep my name a secret; but was goaded into betraying myself by a fellow-magician whose anxiety to astound the passengers with ordinary tricks tempted me to duplicate and exceed his feats in a manner quite destructive of my incognito. I mention this because of its ultimate effect—an effect I should have forseen before unmasking to a shipload of tourists about to scatter throughout the Nile Valley. What it did was to herald my identity wherever I subsequently went, and deprive my wife and me of all the placid inconspicuousness we had sought. Travelling to seek curiosities, I was often forced to stand inspection as a sort of curiosity myself!

We had come to Egypt in search of the picturesque and the mystically impressive, but found little enough when the ship edged up to Port Said and discharged its passengers in small boats. Low dunes of sand, bobbing buoys in shallow water, and a drearily European small town with nothing of interest save the great De Lesseps statue, made us anxious to get on to something more worth our while. After some discussion we decided to proceed at

duction company. The films did poorly, and he returned to his reliable magic act. Since his untimely death, "Houdini" has become a synonym for a person who can escape from anything.

Houdini despised fraudulent psychic mediums and devoted energy to exposing them. In 1926, he engaged the services of HPL and his friend C. M. (Clifford Martin) Eddy Jr. to write a book, to be called *The Cancer of Superstition*, about religious miracles. According to August Derleth's introduction to HPL's detailed outline for the book, published in *The Dark Brotherhood and Other Pieces*, by H. P. Lovecraft & divers hands (Sauk City, WI: Arkham House, 1966), "Houdini outlined sketchily a book he thought ought to be done on the origins, growth and fallacy of superstition. He suggested that Eddy might prepare the book, and furnished him with voluminous notes and ideas that he wanted incorporated in the book; he suggested also that perhaps H. P. Lovecraft could put the notes into shape so that Eddy would work from the outline Lovecraft prepared. Lovecraft was not averse to the idea and duly prepared [an] outline." In 2016, a thirty-one-page manuscript of the first three chapters, all that is known to be extant of the book, was auctioned by Porter & Porter, purporting to be the product of Lovecraft. Without further study, it is not clear whether Lovecraft or Eddy—or both—wrote the draft.

3. Houdini wrote *The Adventurous Life of a Versatile Artist* (which he self-published ca. 1906 and which was reprinted in 1922 by Audubon Printers in a revised edition), a number of promotional pamphlets, and the article "The Thrills in the Life of a Magician" (*Strand Magazine*, January 5, 1919).

4. Wilhelmina Beatrice Rahner (1876–1943), known as Bess Houdini, born in

Brooklyn, raised as a Roman Catholic, married Houdini in 1894. Short and athletic, she performed as a singer and dancer before meeting him and worked as his stage assistant until his death, later devoting herself to preserving his legacy.

5. The SS *Malwa* sailed in the fleet of the Peninsular and Oriental Steam Navigation Company from 1908 to 1932, with two interruptions: in 1910, when she collided with a British steamer, and when she served as a World War I troopship. She carried 407 first-class passengers and 198 or 200 second-class, with a crew of 341, and sailed from the UK to Australia and from the UK to India. She would have stopped at Port Said, north of the Suez Canal, in the northeast corner of Egypt, en route through the canal and on to Australia.

Cairo railway station, 1920.

Port Said, Egypt.
Shutterstock.com

6. One of the greatest feats of engineering of the nineteenth century, the canal connects the Mediterranean and the Red Sea over a distance of about 120 miles. The project was led by the French diplomat-developer Ferdinand de Lesseps, who founded the Suez Canal Company; it employed over one and a half million workers and took more than ten years to complete, opening in 1869. A statue of de Lesseps was erected on the thirtieth anniversary of the opening of the canal in 1899.

Alexandria, 1924.

once to Cairo and the Pyramids, later going to Alexandria for the Australian boat and for whatever Graeco-Roman sights that ancient metropolis might present.

The railway journey was tolerable enough, and consumed only four hours and a half. We saw much of the Suez Canal,[6] whose route we followed as far as Ismailiya,[7] and later had a taste of

Old Egypt in our glimpse of the restored fresh-water canal of the Middle Empire. Then at last we saw Cairo glimmering through the growing dusk; a twinkling constellation which became a blaze as we halted at the great Gare Centrale.

But once more disappointment awaited us, for all that we beheld was European save the costumes and the crowds. A prosaic subway led to a square teeming with carriages, taxicabs, and trolley-cars, and gorgeous with electric lights shining on tall buildings; whilst the very theatre where I was vainly requested to play, and which I later attended as a spectator, had recently been renamed the "American Cosmograph."[8] We stopped at Shepherd's Hotel,[9] reached in a taxi that sped along broad, smartly built-up streets; and amidst the perfect service of its restaurant, elevators, and generally Anglo-American luxuries the mysterious East and immemorial past seemed very far away.

The next day, however, precipitated us delightfully into the heart of the Arabian Nights atmosphere; and in the winding ways and exotic skyline of Cairo, the Bagdad[10] of Haroun-al-Raschid[11] seemed to live again. Guided by our Baedeker,[12] we had struck east past the Ezbekiyeh Gardens[13] along the Mouski[14] in quest of the native quarter, and were soon in the hands of a clamorous cicerone[15] who—notwithstanding later developments—was assuredly a master at his trade. Not until afterward did I see that

7. Ismailia (الإسماعيلية) is a city about halfway along the canal, between Port Said and Suez, on the west bank.

Base of the statue of De Lesseps that formerly stood at the entrance to the Suez Canal, now in the Port Fouad shipyard.

Shutterstock.com

8. Then the largest theater in Cairo, on Emad-el-Dine Street, with a seating capacity of two thousand.

Passengers alighting at the Casino San Stefano, Alexandria, Egypt, ca. 1920.

Program from the American Cosmograph Theater, Cairo, Egypt, 1916.

9. Properly Shepheard's Hotel, which originally operated under the name Hotel des Anglais (the English Hotel) when it first opened in the 1840s. An opulent establishment, it was extensively renovated in 1909 just before Houdini's visit. The hotel burned down in 1952 and was reopened at a different location; it closed for renovation in 2014.

Shepheard's Hotel, Cairo, Egypt, 1880s.

Shepheard's Hotel, Cairo, Egypt, 1920s.

10. Historian Joseph McCabe describes the cultural and intellectual metropolis that was Baghdad:

> Schools were opened for the people, and there were colleges of translators to make the best works of ancient Greece available to Arabic readers. Libraries were founded, and an intense literary activity set in. An

I should have applied at the hotel for a licenced guide. This man, a shaven, peculiarly hollow-voiced, and relatively cleanly fellow who looked like a Pharaoh[16] and called himself "Abdul Reis el Drogman," appeared to have much power over others of his kind; though subsequently the police professed not to know him, and to suggest that reis is merely a name for any person in authority, whilst "Drogman" is obviously no more than a clumsy modification of the word for a leader of tourist parties—dragoman.

Abdul led us among such wonders as we had before only read and dreamed of. Old Cairo is itself a story-book and a dream—labyrinths of narrow alleys redolent of aromatic secrets; Arabesque balconies and oriels nearly meeting above the cobbled streets; maelstroms of Oriental traffic with strange cries, cracking whips, rattling carts, jingling money, and braying donkeys; kaleidoscopes of polychrome robes, veils, turbans, and tarbushes; water-carriers and dervishes, dogs and cats, soothsayers and barbers; and over all the whining of blind beggars crouched in alcoves, and the sonorous chanting of muezzins from minarets limned delicately against a sky of deep, unchanging blue.

The roofed, quieter bazaars were hardly less alluring. Spice, perfume, incense, beads, rugs, silks, and brass—old Mahmoud Suleiman squats cross-legged amidst his gummy bottles while chattering youths pulverise mustard in the hollowed-out capital of an ancient classic column—a Roman Corinthian, perhaps from neighbouring Heliopolis, where Augustus stationed one of his

Garden on the road to Heliopolis, Egypt, 1878.

three Egyptian legions.[17] Antiquity begins to mingle with exoticism. And then the mosques and the museum—we saw them all, and tried not to let our Arabian revel succumb to the darker charm of Pharaonic Egypt which the museum's priceless treasures offered. That was to be our climax, and for the present we concentrated on the mediaeval Saracenic glories of the Caliphs whose magnificent tomb-mosques form a glittering faery necropolis on the edge of the Arabian Desert.

At length Abdul took us along the Sharia Mohammed Ali[18] to the ancient mosque of Sultan Hassan,[19] and the tower-flanked Bab-el-Azab,[20] beyond which climbs the steep-walled pass to the mighty citadel that Saladin himself built with the stones of forgotten pyramids. It was sunset when we scaled that cliff, circled the modern mosque of Mohammed Ali, and looked down from the dizzying parapet over mystic Cairo—mystic Cairo all golden with its carven domes, its ethereal minarets, and its flaming gardens. Far over the city towered the great Roman dome of the new museum; and beyond it—across the cryptic yellow Nile that is the mother of aeons and dynasties—lurked the menacing sands of the Libyan Desert, undulant and iridescent and evil with older arcana. The red sun sank low, bringing the relentless chill of Egyptian dusk; and as it stood poised on the world's rim like that ancient god of Heliopolis—Re-Harakhte, the Horizon-Sun[21]—

Libyan Desert, Africa.
Shutterstock.com

excellent police-system was created . . . and hospitals and medical schools were founded. A Jewish traveler of a later date tells us that . . . he found "many large houses, streets, and hostelries for the sick poor" and "sixty medical warehouses" which were supported by the Caliph. Every poor man who fell ill was maintained out of royal funds until he recovered. There was also a large asylum for the insane, in which the patients were examined once a month. Inspectors of the markets were appointed, and the merchants and traders formed a guild for the suppression of fraud. And in the course of time these schools, libraries, hospitals and other institutions were expanded to the other cities of the kingdom." (*Morals in the Arab-Persian Civilization* [Big Blue Books B-488. *History of Human Morals*, vol. 6], ed. E. Haldeman-Julius [Girard, KS: Haldeman-Julius Company, 1930], 36)

11. Haroun al-Rasheed (spellings are all phonetic transliterations) (763–809 CE) became the caliph in September 786. He was the second son of al-Mahdi, the fourth caliph of the Abbasid dynasty, and al-Khayzuran bint Atta, a Yemeni slave turned state adviser. His older brother died mysteriously (some say by the hand of their mother) a year after the death of his father, whereupon al-Rasheed took the throne, ruling until his death twenty-three years later. In *The New Plutarch: Lives of Men and Women of Action* (London: Marcus Ward & Co., 1881), Arabic scholar Edward Henry Palmer wrote that his reign "was one of the most brilliant in the annals of the caliphate, and the limits of the empire were then more widely extended than at any other period; that the greater part of the Eastern world and a large portion of Western Africa submitted to his laws, and paid tribute into his treasury" (54).

According to the *Encyclopaedia Britannica* (9th ed.), "Egypt itself was only a province under his sway, and its ruler an officer appointed by himself. No caliph ever gathered round him so great a number of learned men, jurists, poets, grammarians, cadis and scribes, to say nothing of the wits and musicians who enjoyed his patronage. Haroun himself was an accomplished scholar and an excellent poet. He was well versed in history, tradition, and poetry, which he could always quote on appropriate occasions. He possessed exquisite taste and unerring discernment, and his dignified demeanour made him an object of profound respect to high and low." His reign is immortalized in the tales of Scheherazade and *One Thousand and One Nights* (also known as *The Arabian Nights*), and many scholars believe that the central figure of the stories, King Shahryar, is a thinly disguised portrait of al-Rasheed.

12. The most popular guidebook-publisher of the era, Baedeker (founded in 1830 by Karl Baedeker), published the 1908 *Egypt and the Sûdân: Handbook for Travellers*, the Sixth Remodelled Edition, which would have been the edition at hand. The Seventh Edition was not published until 1914 but may have been what HPL consulted when he wrote the tale—there are minor differences between it and the previous edition.

13. According to the 1908 *Baedeker*, "Ezbekîyeh Garden . . . or simply the *Ezbekîyeh*, on the site of the former Ezbekîyeh Lake and named after the heroic Emîr Ezbek, the general of Sultan Kâït Bey (1468–96), who brought the general and son-in-law of Bayazid I. as a captive to Cairo. A mosque, now vanished, was erected here in 1495 in honour of his victory; and though the building no longer exists, its name still attaches to the site. The fine gardens, which have

Photograph of the pyramids at Gizeh (Giza), Egypt, taken from a balloon, 1904.

Ezbekiah Gardens, aerial view taken from a balloon, 1904.

we saw silhouetted against its vermeil holocaust the black outlines of the Pyramids of Gizeh—the palaeogean tombs there were
hoary with a thousand years when Tut-Ankh-Amen mounted his
golden throne in distant Thebes.[22] Then we knew that we were
done with Saracen Cairo, and that we must taste the deeper mysteries of primal Egypt—the black Khem[23] of Re and Amen, Isis
and Osiris.[24] The next morning we visited the pyramids, riding
out in a Victoria[25] across the great Nile bridge with its bronze
lions,[26] the island of Ghizereh with its massive lebbakh trees,[27]
and the smaller English bridge to the western shore. Down the
shore road we drove, between great rows of lebbakhs and past
the vast Zoölogical Gardens to the suburb of Gizeh, where a new
bridge to Cairo proper has since been built. Then, turning inland
along the Sharia-el-Haram,[28] we crossed a region of glassy canals
and shabby native villages till before us loomed the objects of our
quest, cleaving the mists of dawn and forming inverted replicas
in the roadside pools. Forty centuries, as Napoleon had told his
campaigners there, indeed looked down upon us.

The road now rose abruptly, till we finally reached our place
of transfer between the trolley station and the Mena House
Hotel.[29] Abdul Reis, who capably purchased our pyramid tick-
ets, seemed to have an understanding with the crowding, yelling, and offensive Bedouins who inhabited a squalid mud village

Ghezireh Palace, Egypt, 1861.

several entrances . . ., were laid out in
1870 by M. Barillet, formerly chief gar-
dener to the city of Paris. They cover an
area of 20½ acres and contain a variety of
rare and beautiful trees and shrubs" (47).

14. The "Mouski" was one of three
entrances to the Jewish quarter of Cairo,
so named by reason of the musk dealers
who frequented the area.

The "Mouski," Cairo, Egypt, ca. 1920.

15. A guide.

16. Joel Lane sees this description as a clue
that Reis is to be identified with Nyarlathotep. See "The Master of Masks," Nyctalops 4, no. 1 (April 1991), 63.

17. Augustus (63 BCE to 19 CE) was the
first emperor of Rome, ruling from 27 BCE
until his death. According to Strabo's
Geographica (ca. 20 BCE, with the last
edition ca. 23 CE), "Three legions [of
about 5,000 soldiers each] are stationed
in Egypt, one in the city of Alexandria,
the rest in the country. Besides these,
there are also nine Roman cohorts [of

about 480 men each] quartered in the city, three on the borders of Ethiopia in Syene, as a guard to that tract, and three in other parts of the country. There are also three bodies of cavalry distributed at convenient posts."

18. A street in Cairo, near the Citadel, the home of Egypt's rulers for seven hundred years commencing in the twelfth century CE.

19. A Mamluk mosque, built in the fourteenth century CE. The 1908 *Baedeker* reports "the 'superb mosque,' and the finest existing monument of Egypto-Arabian architecture. It was built in 1366–59 for Sultan Hasan . . . perhaps by a Syrian architect, and has been restored by Herz-Pasha. The huge proportions of the building, which occupies a shelving rock below the citadel, taken in conjunction with the masterly execution of its details, produce an effect of great majesty" (66).

20. The gate protecting the entry to the Citadel.

Zoological Gardens, Cairo, ca. 1930.

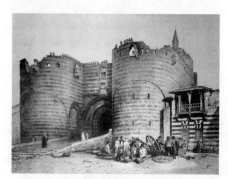

The Bab-el-Azab gate, Cairo, Egypt, nineteenth century.

21. The merger of the sun-god Ra or Re and Horus; he was the ruler of the world: the sky, the earth, and the underworld.

22. Tutankhamen ruled Egypt from 1332 to 1323 BCE, relocating the capital from

Sharia Mohammed Ali, Cairo.
Shutterstock.com

The mosque of Sultan Hassan, Cairo, Egypt.

some distance away and pestiferously assailed every traveller; for he kept them very decently at bay and secured an excellent pair of camels for us, himself mounting a donkey and assigning the leadership of our animals to a group of men and boys more expensive than useful. The area to be traversed was so small that camels were hardly needed, but we did not regret adding to our experience this troublesome form of desert navigation.

The pyramids stand on a high rock plateau, this group forming next to the northernmost of the series of regal and aristocratic cemeteries built in the neighbourhood of the extinct capital Memphis, which lay on the same side of the Nile, somewhat south of Gizeh, and which flourished between 3400 and 2000 B. C. The

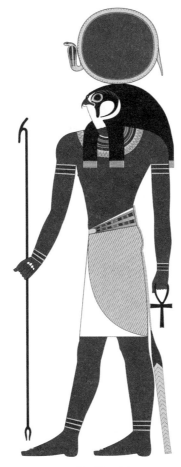

Re-Harahkte.

Akhetaten, or Amarna, to Thebes. (It had previously been moved by Amenhotep IV in the opposite direction: from Thebes to Akhetaten.) The tomb of King Tut, as he was popularly known in the twentieth century, was discovered and explored by Howard Carter—whose name was possibly the inspiration for that of HPL's character Randolph Carter—in 1922. The news coverage of the event included two *New York Times* stories, headlined "Gem Studded Relics in Tomb Amaze Explorers" and "Tutankhamen's Tomb Is Revising History," on December 4 and December 27. Such press led to a wave of interest in all things Egyptian.

23. "Khem" merely means black, as in the black soil of the Nile delta (as contrasted with the red soil of the desert), but it was the ancient name of the country.

24. The ancient gods of Egypt. Re (or Ra), a sun god, merged at night with Osiris, a god of darkness and the afterlife. Isis, the sister of Osiris, was usually depicted as the mother goddess. As the most unknown and unknowable of the gods, Amen or Amun was supremely holy. He fused at some point with Re (Amun-Ra), which, in his new association with the sun (Re), made him less inscrutable. In different eras, different gods, including Re and Isis (and of course the mysterious Amen), were viewed as the supreme deity, credited with creating the world.

25. A carriage for two passengers, with an elevated seat for the driver.

A Riker Victoria horseless cab, 1900.

26. The Kobri el Gezira Bridge, made of iron, was built in 1871–72, upgraded in 1913, and torn down in 1931, replaced in 1933 by the 3,701-ton steel Qasr al-Nil Bridge. It connected downtown Cairo to Gezira Island and the Zamalek district (all of which was then the south end of uninhabited Boulac), spanning the Nile River. Henri Alfred Marie Jacquemart (1824–1896) sculpted the bronze lions at each of the four corners of the bridge, which in 1931 were removed and placed in the Giza Zoological Garden.

The Kobri el Gezira Bridge, Cairo, 1872.

27. The 1908 *Baedeker* describes the lebbakh tree: "The finest of the shade-trees, both on account of its umbrageousness and the excellence of its wood, and one which thrives admirably, is the *lebbakh* (Albizzia Lebbek), which has long been erroneously called by travellers the acacia of the Nile (the latter being properly the *sunt* tree). Within forty years the lebbakh attains a height of 80 ft. and a great thickness, while the branches project to a long distance over the roads, covering them with a dense leafy canopy within a remarkably short time" (lvii).

28. Literally, the "Street of the Pyramids."

29. The 1908 *Baedeker* reports, "Mena House Hotel (Nungovich Co., manager,

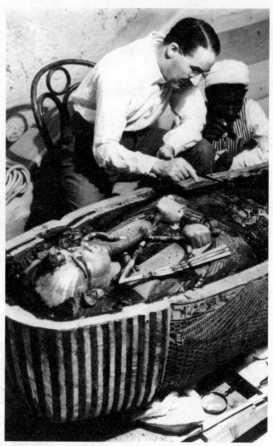

Howard Carter examining King Tutankhamen's sarcophagus, 1923.

greatest pyramid, which lies nearest the modern road, was built by King Cheops or Khufu about 2800 B. C.,[30] and stands more than 450 feet in perpendicular height. In a line southwest from this are successively the Second Pyramid, built a generation later by King Khephren,[31] and though slightly smaller, looking even larger because set on higher ground, and the radically smaller Third Pyramid of King Mycerinus, built about 2700 B. C. Near the edge of the plateau and due east of the Second Pyramid, with a face probably altered to form a colossal portrait of Khephren, its royal restorer, stands the monstrous Sphinx—mute, sardonic, and wise beyond mankind and memory.

Minor pyramids and the traces of ruined minor pyramids are found in several places, and the whole plateau is pitted with the tombs of dignitaries of less than royal rank. These latter were originally marked by mastabas, or stone bench-like structures about the deep burial shafts, as found in other Memphian cemeteries and exemplified by Perneb's Tomb in the Metropolitan Museum of New York.[32] At Gizeh, however, all such visible things have been swept away by time and pillage; and only the rock-hewn shafts, either sand-filled or cleared out by archaeologists, remain to attest their former existence. Connected with each tomb was a chapel in which priests and relatives offered food and prayer to the hovering ka or vital principle of the deceased. The small tombs have their chapels contained in their stone mastabas or superstructures, but the mortuary chapels of the pyramids, where regal Pharaohs lay, were separate temples, each to the east of its corresponding pyramid, and connected by a causeway to a massive gate-chapel or propylon at the edge of the rock plateau.

The gate-chapel leading to the Second Pyramid, nearly buried in the drifting sands, yawns subterraneously southeast of the Sphinx. Persistent tradition dubs it the "Temple of the Sphinx"; and it may perhaps be rightly called such if the Sphinx indeed represents the Second Pyramid's builder Khephren. There are unpleasant tales of the Sphinx before Khephren—but whatever its elder features were, the monarch replaced them with his own

Herr Klingler[!], an extensive establishment, with 180 rooms, swimming and other baths, stables, riding-track, carriages, sand-carts, dog-carts, and cycles for hire, lawn-tennis courts, library of 600 English books, etc." (31).

Mena House Hotel, Gizeh, Egypt (now Marriott Mena House).
Shutterstock.com

30. Current thinking is that Cheops, the second king of the Fourth Dynasty, reigned from 2589 to 2566 BCE (see Ian Shaw's *The Oxford History of Ancient Egypt* [Oxford: Oxford University Press, 2000], 482), and that the Great Pyramid was built then. Kephren reigned 2558–2532 BCE and Mycerinus from 2421 to 2414 BCE. The dates used in the story may be found in both the 1908 and the 1914 *Baedekers*, which place the reigns of Cheops, Chephren, and Mycerinus in the period 2850–2700 BCE. (See note 31.) Egyptologists have argued about the dates of the various dynasties and the construction associated with them for as long as the field of study has existed. Some have dated the reign of Cheops as early as 3700 BCE. As recently as the 1980s, many scholars still used the dates HPL assigned in this paragraph. Modern carbon dating of the pyramids has proven inconclusive, though the later dates are now widely accepted.

The "Cairo Museum," properly, the Egyptian Museum, Cairo, Egypt.

31. Also called Khafre or Khafra (or Chephren, see note 30), this was the son of Khufu. Mycerinus, also known as Menkauhor or Menkauré, was Khafre's son. Most Egyptologists agree that Chephren built the Sphinx, but some speculate—without any tangible evidence—that it and some of the pyramids are as much as eight thousand years older.

32. The Egyptian dignitary Perneb's tomb was built ca. 2381–2323 BCE at Saqqara, twenty-five miles (forty kilometers) south of Cairo, and is of the mastaba variety, with terraced sides and a flat roof. Much of the original structure, purchased from the Egyptian government in 1913, is at New York's Metropolitan Museum of Art and was described at the time of its acquisition as "less pretentious and elaborate than the adjoining tomb of Shepsesre" (Metropolitan Museum of Art, *The Tomb of Perneb* [New York: The Metropolitan Museum of Art, 1916], 10). Once presumed to have been Perneb's son, Shepsesre is now thought to have been his father (ibid.). The Met exhibit of Perneb's tomb includes a partial reconstruction of the west wall of the Shepsesre mastaba.

Tomb of Perneb.

that men might look at the colossus without fear. It was in the great gateway-temple that the life-size diorite statue of Khephren now in the Cairo Museum was found; a statue before which I stood in awe when I beheld it. Whether the whole edifice is now excavated I am not certain, but in 1910 most of it was below ground, with the entrance heavily barred at night. Germans were in charge of the work, and the war or other things may have stopped them. I would give much, in view of my experience and of certain Bedouin whisperings discredited or unknown in Cairo, to know what has developed in connexion with a certain well in a transverse gallery where statues of the Pharaoh were found in curious juxtaposition to the statues of baboons.

The road, as we traversed it on our camels that morning, curved sharply past the wooden police quarters, post-office, drugstore, and shops on the left, and plunged south and east in a complete bend that scaled the rock plateau and brought us face to face with the desert under the lee of the Great Pyramid. Past Cyclopean masonry we rode, rounding the eastern face and looking down ahead into a valley of minor pyramids beyond which the eternal Nile glistened to the east, and the eternal desert shimmered to the west. Very close loomed the three major pyramids, the greatest devoid of outer casing and shewing its bulk of great stones, but the others retaining here and there the neatly fitted covering which had made them smooth and finished in their day.

Presently we descended toward the Sphinx, and sat silent beneath the spell of those terrible unseeing eyes. On the vast stone breast we faintly discerned the emblem of Re-Harakhte, for whose image the Sphinx was mistaken in a late dynasty; and though sand covered the tablet between the great paws, we recalled what Thutmosis IV inscribed thereon, and the dream he had when a prince.[33] It was then that the smile of the Sphinx vaguely displeased us, and made us wonder about the legends of subterranean passages beneath the monstrous creature, leading down, down, to depths none might dare hint at—depths connected with mysteries older than the dynastic Egypt we excavate, and having a sinister relation to the persistence of abnormal, animal-headed gods in the ancient Nilotic pantheon. Then, too, it was I asked myself an idle question whose hideous significance was not to appear for many an hour.

Other tourists now began to overtake us, and we moved on to the sand-choked Temple of the Sphinx, fifty yards to the southeast, which I have previously mentioned as the great gate of the causeway to the Second Pyramid's mortuary chapel on the plateau. Most of it was still underground, and although we dismounted and descended through a modern passageway to its alabaster corridor and pillared hall, I felt that Abdul and the local

The "Dream Stele."
Shutterstock.com

33. Thutmose IV, in his quest to become pharaoh of Egypt (in which he succeeded, ruling in the fourteenth century BCE), claimed that he had a dream while sleeping between the paws of the Sphinx, most of which was buried in sand. To commemorate his dream, he cleared the sand away and erected a tablet (the "Dream Stele") there. The stele is translated as follows:

> Now the statue of the very great Khepri . . . rested in this place, great of fame, sacred of respect, the shade of Ra resting on him. Memphis and every city on its two sides came to him, their arms in adoration to his face, bearing great offerings for his *ka*. One of these days it happened that prince Thutmose came travelling at the time of midday. He rested in the shadow of this great god. [Sleep and] dream [took possession of him] at the moment the sun was at zenith. Then he found the majesty of this noble god speaking from his own mouth like a father speaks to his son, and saying: "Look at me, observe me, my son Thutmose. I am your father Horemakhet-Khepri-Ra-Atum. I shall give to you the kingship [upon the land before the living]. . . . [Behold, my condition is like one in illness], all [my limbs being ruined]. The sand of the desert, upon which I used to be, (now) confronts me; and it is in order to cause that you do what is in my heart that I have waited." (Shaw, *The Oxford History of Ancient Egypt*, 254)

34. The 1908 *Baedeker* describes this as a family tomb of the Twenty-sixth Dynasty,

> discovered by Col. Vyse in 1837 and named by him after Col. Campbell, the British consul-general in Egypt at that period. The upper part, the mastaba proper, has been entirely destroyed, and the shaft (53 ft. deep), at the bottom of which is a tomb-chamber vaulted with an arch having a span of 11 ft., is now uncovered. The sides of the shaft are separated from the surrounding rock by a trench, which is spanned by bridges of stone at only a few points. The sarcophagus which stands in the tomb-chamber contained the remains of the royal scribe *Pe-kop Wah-eb-rē-em-yekhet*, a contemporary of King Apries. Beside the sarcophagus lies a stone lid shaped like a mummy. In niches in the S. and W. sides of the shaft are two other sarcophagi; a fourth sarcophagus found here is now in the British Museum. All these sarcophagi had been opened and plundered. (135)

35. According to *Baedeker*, "The Pyramids of Dahshûr were examined in 1894–95 by De Morgans; those of Lisht in 1895 by Gautier and Jéquier; and those of Abu Roash by the Institut Français in 1900–2" (127).

German attendant had not shewn us all there was to see. After this we made the conventional circuit of the pyramid plateau, examining the Second Pyramid and the peculiar ruins of its mortuary chapel to the east, the Third Pyramid and its miniature southern satellites and ruined eastern chapel, the rock tombs and the honeycombings of the Fourth and Fifth Dynasties, and the famous Campbell's Tomb[34] whose shadowy shaft sinks precipitously for 53 feet to a sinister sarcophagus which one of our camel-drivers divested of the cumbering sand after a vertiginous descent by rope.

Cries now assailed us from the Great Pyramid, where Bedouins were besieging a party of tourists with offers of guidance to the top, or of displays of speed in the performance of solitary trips up and down. Seven minutes is said to be the record for such an ascent and descent, but many lusty sheiks and sons of sheiks assured us they could cut it to five if given the requisite impetus of liberal baksheesh. They did not get this impetus, though we did let Abdul take us up, thus obtaining a view of unprecedented magnificence which included not only remote and glittering Cairo with its crowned citadel and background of gold-violet hills, but all the pyramids of the Memphian district as well, from Abu Roash on the north to the Dashur on the south.[35]

Entrance to Abu Roash pyramid.
Shutterstock.com

The Sakkara step-pyramid,[36] which marks the evolution of the low mastaba into the true pyramid, shewed clearly and alluringly in the sandy distance. It is close to this transition-monument that the famed Tomb of Perneb was found—more than 400 miles north of the Theban rock valley where Tut-Ankh-Amen sleeps.[37] Again I was forced to silence through sheer awe. The prospect of such antiquity, and the secrets each hoary monument seemed to hold and brood over, filled me with a reverence and sense of immensity nothing else ever gave me.

Fatigued by our climb, and disgusted with the importunate Bedouins whose actions seemed to defy every rule of taste, we omitted the arduous detail of entering the cramped interior passages of any of the pyramids, though we saw several of the hardiest tourists preparing for the suffocating crawl through Cheops' mightiest memorial. As we dismissed and overpaid our local bodyguard and drove back to Cairo with Abdul Reis under the afternoon sun, we half regretted the omission we had made. Such fascinating things were whispered about lower pyramid passages not in the guide-books; passages whose entrances had been hastily blocked up and concealed by certain uncommunicative archaeologists who had found and begun to explore them. Of course, this whispering was largely baseless on the face of it; but it was curious to reflect how persistently visitors were forbidden to enter the pyramids at night, or to visit the lowest burrows and crypt of the Great Pyramid. Perhaps in the latter case it was the psychological effect which was feared—the effect on the visitor of feeling himself huddled down beneath a gigantic world of solid masonry; joined to the life he has known by the merest tube, in which he may only crawl, and which any accident or evil design might block. The whole subject seemed so weird and alluring that we resolved to pay the pyramid plateau another visit at the earliest possible opportunity. For me this opportunity came much earlier than I expected.

That evening, the members of our party feeling somewhat tired after the strenuous programme of the day, I went alone with Abdul Reis for a walk through the picturesque Arab quarter. Though I had seen it by day, I wished to study the alleys and bazaars in the dusk, when rich shadows and mellow gleams of light would add to their glamour and fantastic illusion. The

36. The 1908 *Baedeker* describes the site: "The Step Pyramid of Sakkara (Arab. El-Haram el-Mudarrag, i.e. 'the pyramid provided with steps' . . .), a very conspicuous feature in the landscape, may be regarded as the 'Cognizance of Sakkara.' It was the tomb of the ancient king *Zoser* (3rd Dyn.) and is one of the oldest stone buildings in Egypt that have come down to our days. The pyramid consists of six stages, the lowest of which is about 37¾ ft. in height, the next 36 ft., the third 34½ ft., the fourth 32¾ ft., the fifth 30¾ ft., and the sixth 29⅓ ft., while each stage recedes about 6½ ft. as compared with the one below. The perpendicular height is 196 ft." (142).

37. Duncan Norris, in "Lovecraft and Egypt: A Closer Examination," 31, points out that Howard Carter's excavation of Tutankhamen's tomb would not occur until February 12, 1924, and thus Houdini's description of Tut as "sleeping" was still accurate, though of course Houdini could not have known in 1910 of the location of Tut's actual tomb, then still commonly believed to be in KV54 in the Valley of the Kings.

38. A tarbush or tarboush is a flat-topped, brimless hat, usually felt, worn frequently by Muslim men. Often synonymous with "fez."

Fez.
(Edouard Hue)

native crowds were thinning, but were still very noisy and numerous when we came upon a knot of revelling Bedouins in the Suken-Nahhasin, or bazaar of the coppersmiths. Their apparent leader, an insolent youth with heavy features and saucily cocked tarbush,[38] took some notice of us; and evidently recognised with no great friendliness my competent but admittedly supercilious and sneeringly disposed guide. Perhaps, I thought, he resented the odd reproduction of the Sphinx's half-smile which I had often remarked with amused irritation; or perhaps he did not like the hollow and sepulchral resonance of Abdul's voice. At any rate, the exchange of ancestrally opprobrious language became very brisk; and before long Ali Ziz, as I heard the stranger called when called by no worse name, began to pull violently at Abdul's robe, an action quickly reciprocated, and leading to a spirited scuffle in which both combatants lost their sacredly cherished headgear and would have reached an even direr condition had I not intervened and separated them by main force.

My interference, at first seemingly unwelcome on both sides, succeeded at last in effecting a truce. Sullenly each belligerent composed his wrath and his attire; and with an assumption of dignity as profound as it was sudden, the two formed a curious pact of honour which I soon learned is a custom of great antiquity in Cairo—a pact for the settlement of their difference by means of a nocturnal fist fight atop the Great Pyramid, long after the departure of the last moonlight sightseer. Each duellist was to assemble a party of seconds, and the affair was to begin at midnight, proceeding by rounds in the most civilised possible fashion. In all this planning there was much which excited my interest. The fight itself promised to be unique and spectacular, while the thought of the scene on that hoary pile overlooking the antediluvian plateau of Gizeh under the wan moon of the pallid small hours appealed to every fibre of imagination in me. A request found Abdul exceedingly willing to admit me to his party of seconds; so that all the rest of the early evening I accompanied him to various dens in the most lawless regions of the town—mostly northeast of the Ezbekiyeh—where he gathered one by one a select and formidable band of congenial cutthroats as his pugilistic background.

Shortly after nine our party, mounted on donkeys bearing

such royal or tourist-reminiscent names as "Rameses," "Mark Twain," "J. P. Morgan," and "Minnehaha," edged through street labyrinths both Oriental and Occidental, crossed the muddy and mast-forested Nile by the bridge of the bronze lions, and cantered philosophically between the lebbakhs on the road to Gizeh. Slightly over two hours were consumed by the trip, toward the end of which we passed the last of the returning tourists, saluted the last in-bound trolley-car, and were alone with the night and the past and the spectral moon.

Then we saw the vast pyramids at the end of the avenue, ghoulish with a dim atavistical menace which I had not seemed to notice in the daytime. Even the smallest of them held a hint of the ghastly—for was it not in this that they had buried Queen Nitokris alive in the Sixth Dynasty; subtle Queen Nitokris, who once invited all her enemies to a feast in a temple below the Nile, and drowned them by opening the water-gates?[39] I recalled that the Arabs whisper things about Nitokris, and shun the Third Pyramid at certain phases of the moon. It must have been over her that Thomas Moore was brooding when he wrote a thing muttered about by Memphian boatmen—

> *"The subterranean nymph that dwells*
> *'Mid sunless gems and glories hid—*
> *The lady of the Pyramid!"*[40]

Early as we were, Ali Ziz and his party were ahead of us; for we saw their donkeys outlined against the desert plateau at Kafr-el-Haram;[41] toward which squalid Arab settlement, close to the Sphinx, we had diverged instead of following the regular road to the Mena House, where some of the sleepy, inefficient police might have observed and halted us. Here, where filthy Bedouins stabled camels and donkeys in the rock tombs of Khephren's courtiers, we were led up the rocks and over the sand to the Great Pyramid, up whose time-worn sides the Arabs swarmed eagerly, Abdul Reis offering me the assistance I did not need.

As most travellers know, the actual apex of this structure has long been worn away, leaving a reasonably flat platform twelve yards square. On this eerie pinnacle a squared circle was formed, and in a few moments the sardonic desert moon leered down

39. See "The Outsider," pp. 97–105, note 13, above.

40. From Letter IV of the long poem *Alciphron*, by Thomas Moore, first published with his novel *The Epicurean* (1839), about the life of the third-century historical figure of the title. Greatly admired by Edgar Allan Poe, the work represented, for Moore, a failure of sorts, by his own reckoning: "My original plan, in commencing the story of the Epicurean, was to write it all in verse. . . . But the great difficulty of managing, in rhyme, the minor details of a story, so as to be clear without becoming prosaic, and, still more, the diffuse length to which I saw narration in verse would be likely to run, deterred me from pursuing this plan any further" (*The Epicurean, a Tale, and Alciphron, A Poem* [London: Chatto & Windus, 1890], v).

In Moore's poem, addressed "from Alciphron at Alexandria to Cleon at Athens," Alciphron wanders beneath ancient temples in Memphis, Egypt, having been called there by a dream. The temples' "great shadows, stretching from the light, / Look like the first colossal steps of Night, / Stretching across the valley, to invade / The distant hills of porphyry with their shade" (Letter II, 256). The real-life Alciphron was famous for having engaged in such literary gamesmanship as the popular comic art of penning fictional letters—writing in the putative voice of, for example, a pig farmer, an abandoned courtesan, and various "parasites," or stock characters in Greek comedy. See Patricia A. Rosenmeyer, *Ancient Epistolary Fictions: The Letter in Greek Literature* (Cambridge: Cambridge University Press, 2004).

41. An Arab village mentioned in *Baedeker* (138); said by an early twentieth-century Egyptologist and assistant professor of Semitic languages at Harvard to have been

regularly looted for antiquities (George A. Reisner, "Recent Explorations in Egypt," *The Independent*, February 10, 1910).

42. The peasants or agricultural workers of Egypt and the Middle East.

upon a battle which, but for the quality of the ringside cries, might well have occurred at some minor athletic club in America. As I watched it, I felt that some of our less desirable institutions were not lacking; for every blow, feint, and defence bespoke "stalling" to my not inexperienced eye. It was quickly over, and despite my misgivings as to methods I felt a sort of proprietary pride when Abdul Reis was adjudged the winner.

Reconciliation was phenomenally rapid, and amidst the singing, fraternising, and drinking which followed, I found it difficult to realise that a quarrel had ever occurred. Oddly enough, I myself seemed to be more of a centre of notice than the antagonists; and from my smattering of Arabic I judged that they were discussing my professional performances and escapes from every sort of manacle and confinement, in a manner which indicated not only a surprising knowledge of me, but a distinct hostility and scepticism concerning my feats of escape. It gradually dawned on me that the elder magic of Egypt did not depart without leaving traces, and that fragments of a strange secret lore and priestly cult-practices have survived surreptitiously amongst the fellaheen[42] to such an extent that the prowess of a strange "hahwi" or magician is resented and disputed. I thought of how much my hollow-voiced guide Abdul Reis looked like an old Egyptian priest or Pharaoh or smiling Sphinx . . . and wondered.

Suddenly something happened which in a flash proved the correctness of my reflections and made me curse the denseness whereby I had accepted this night's events as other than the empty and malicious "frameup" they now shewed themselves to be. Without warning, and doubtless in answer to some subtle sign from Abdul, the entire band of Bedouins precipitated itself upon me; and having produced heavy ropes, soon had me bound as securely as I was ever bound in the course of my life, either on the stage or off. I struggled at first, but soon saw that one man could make no headway against a band of over twenty sinewy barbarians. My hands were tied behind my back, my knees bent to their fullest extent, and my wrists and ankles stoutly linked together with unyielding cords. A stifling gag was forced into my mouth, and a blindfold fastened tightly over my eyes. Then, as the Arabs bore me aloft on their shoulders and began a jouncing descent of the pyramid, I heard the taunts of my late guide Abdul, who mocked and jeered delightedly in his hollow voice, and assured me that I was soon to have my "magic powers" put to a supreme test which would quickly remove any egotism I might have gained through triumphing over all the tests offered by America and Europe. Egypt, he reminded me, is very old; and full of inner mysteries and antique powers not even conceivable to the experts of today, whose devices had so uniformly failed to entrap me.

How far or in what direction I was carried, I cannot tell; for the circumstances were all against the formation of any accurate judgment. I know, however, that it could not have been a great distance; since my bearers at no point hastened beyond a walk, yet kept me aloft a surprisingly short time. It is this perplexing brevity which makes me feel almost like shuddering whenever I think of Gizeh and its plateau—for one is oppressed by hints of the closeness to every-day tourist routes of what existed then and must exist still.

The evil abnormality I speak of did not become manifest at first. Setting me down on a surface which I recognised as sand rather than rock, my captors passed a rope around my chest and dragged me a few feet to a ragged opening in the ground, into which they presently lowered me with much rough handling. For apparent aeons I bumped against the stony irregular sides of a narrow hewn well which I took to be one of the numerous burial shafts of the plateau until the prodigious, almost incredible depth of it robbed me of all bases of conjecture.

The horror of the experience deepened with every dragging second. That any descent through the sheer solid rock could be so vast without reaching the core of the planet itself, or that any rope made by man could be so long as to dangle me in these unholy and seemingly fathomless profundities of nether earth, were beliefs of such grotesqueness that it was easier to doubt my agitated senses than to accept them. Even now I am uncertain, for I know how deceitful the sense of time becomes when one or more of the usual perceptions or conditions of life is removed or distorted. But I am quite sure that I preserved a logical consciousness that far; that at least I did not add any full-grown phantoms of imagination to a picture hideous enough in its reality, and explicable by a type of cerebral illusion vastly short of actual hallucination.

All this was not the cause of my first bit of fainting. The shocking ordeal was cumulative, and the beginning of the later terrors was a very perceptible increase in my rate of descent. They were paying out that infinitely long rope very swiftly now, and I scraped cruelly against the rough and constricted sides of the shaft as I shot madly downward. My clothing was in tatters, and I felt the trickle of blood all over, even above the mounting and excruciating pain. My nostrils, too, were assailed by a scarcely definable menace; a creeping odour of damp and staleness curiously unlike anything I had ever smelt before, and having faint overtones of spice and incense that lent an element of mockery.

Then the mental cataclysm came. It was horrible—hideous beyond all articulate description because it was all of the soul, with nothing of detail to describe. It was the ecstasy of nightmare and the summation of the fiendish. The suddenness of it was apocalyptic and daemoniac—one moment I was plunging agonisingly down that narrow well of million-toothed torture, yet the next moment I was soaring on bat-wings in the gulfs of hell; swinging free and swoopingly through illimitable miles of boundless, musty space; rising dizzily to measureless pinnacles of chilling ether, then diving gaspingly to sucking nadirs of ravenous, nauseous lower vacua. . . . Thank God for the mercy that shut out in oblivion those clawing Furies of consciousness which half unhinged my faculties, and tore Harpy-like at my spirit! That one respite, short as it was, gave me the strength and sanity to endure those still greater sublimations of cosmic panic that lurked and gibbered on the road ahead.

II.

IT WAS VERY gradually that I regained my senses after that eldritch flight through Stygian space. The process was infinitely painful, and coloured by fantastic dreams in which my bound and gagged condition found singular embodiment. The precise nature of these dreams was very clear while I was experiencing them, but became blurred in my recollection almost immediately afterward, and was soon reduced to the merest outline by the terrible events—real or imaginary—which followed. I dreamed that I was in the grasp of a great and horrible paw; a yellow, hairy, five-clawed paw which had reached out of the earth to crush and engulf me. And when I stopped to reflect what the paw was, it seemed to me that it was Egypt. In the dream I looked back at the events of the preceding weeks, and saw myself lured and enmeshed little by little, subtly and insidiously, by some hellish ghoul-spirit of the elder Nile sorcery; some spirit that was in Egypt before ever man was, and that will be when man is no more.

I saw the horror and unwholesome antiquity of Egypt, and the grisly alliance it has always had with the tombs and temples of the dead. I saw phantom processions of priests with the heads of bulls, falcons, cats, and ibises; phantom processions marching interminably through subterranean labyrinths and avenues of titanic propylaea[43] beside which a man is as a fly, and offering unnamable sacrifices to indescribable gods. Stone colossi marched in endless night and drove herds of grinning androsphinxes[44] down to the shores of illimitable stagnant rivers of pitch. And behind it all I saw the ineffable malignity of primordial necromancy, black and amorphous, and fumbling greedily after me in the darkness to choke out the spirit that had dared to mock it by emulation. In my sleeping brain there took shape a melodrama of sinister hatred and pursuit, and I saw the black soul of Egypt singling me out and calling me in inaudible whispers; calling and luring me, leading me on with the glitter and glamour of a Saracenic surface, but ever pulling me down to the age-mad catacombs and horrors of its dead and abysmal pharaonic heart.

Then the dream-faces took on human resemblances, and I saw my guide Abdul Reis in the robes of a king, with the sneer of the Sphinx on his features. And I knew that those features were the features of Khephren the Great, who raised the Second Pyramid, carved over the Sphinx's face in the likeness of his own, and built that titanic gateway temple whose myriad corridors the archaeologists think they have dug out of the cryptical sand and the uninformative rock. And I looked at the long, lean, rigid hand of Khephren; the long, lean, rigid hand as I had seen it on the diorite statue in the Cairo Museum—the statue they had found in the terrible gateway temple—and wondered that I had not shrieked when I saw it on Abdul Reis. . . . That hand! It was hideously cold, and it was crushing me; it was the cold and

43. Entryway that is itself of architectural significance. The singular is "propylaeum," but the word is most often used in the plural.

44. A sphinx is the amalgam of the head of a creature (animal or human) and the body of a lion; an androsphinx is a sphinx with a human head.

cramping of the sarcophagus . . . the chill and constriction of unrememberable Egypt. . . . It was nighted, necropolitan Egypt itself . . . that yellow paw . . . and they whisper such things of Khephren. . . .

But at this juncture I began to awake—or at least, to assume a condition less completely that of sleep than the one just preceding. I recalled the fight atop the pyramid, the treacherous Bedouins and their attack, my frightful descent by rope through endless rock depths, and my mad swinging and plunging in a chill void redolent of aromatic putrescence. I perceived that I now lay on a damp rock floor, and that my bonds were still biting into me with unloosened force. It was very cold, and I seemed to detect a faint current of noisome air sweeping across me. The cuts and bruises I had received from the jagged sides of the rock shaft were paining me woefully, their soreness enhanced to a stinging or burning acuteness by some pungent quality in the faint draught, and the mere act of rolling over was enough to set my whole frame throbbing with untold agony. As I turned I felt a tug from above, and concluded that the rope whereby I was lowered still reached to the surface. Whether or not the Arabs still held it, I had no idea; nor had I any idea how far within the earth I was. I knew that the darkness around me was wholly or nearly total, since no ray of moonlight penetrated my blindfold; but I did not trust my senses enough to accept as evidence of extreme depth the sensation of vast duration which had characterised my descent.

Knowing at least that I was in a space of considerable extent reached from the surface directly above by an opening in the rock, I doubtfully conjectured that my prison was perhaps the buried gateway chapel of old Khephren—the Temple of the Sphinx—perhaps some inner corridor which the guides had not shewn me during my morning visit, and from which I might easily escape if I could find my way to the barred entrance. It would be a labyrinthine wandering, but no worse than others out of which I had in the past found my way. The first step was to get free of my bonds, gag, and blindfold; and this I knew would be no great task, since subtler experts than these Arabs had tried every known species of fetter upon me during my long and varied career as an exponent of escape, yet had never succeeded in defeating my methods.

Then it occurred to me that the Arabs might be ready to meet and attack me at the entrance upon any evidence of my probable escape from the binding cords, as would be furnished by any decided agitation of the rope which they probably held. This, of course, was taking for granted that my place of confinement was indeed Khephren's Temple of the Sphinx. The direct opening in the roof, wherever it might lurk, could not be beyond easy reach of the ordinary modern entrance near the Sphinx; if in truth it were any great distance at all on the surface, since the total area known to visitors is not at all enormous. I had not noticed any such opening during my daytime pilgrimage, but knew that these things are easily overlooked amidst the drifting sands. Thinking these matters over as I lay bent and bound on the rock floor, I nearly forgot the horrors of the abysmal descent and cavernous swinging which had so lately reduced me to a coma. My present thought was only to outwit the Arabs, and I accordingly determined to work myself free as quickly as possible, avoiding any tug on the descending line which might betray an effective or even problematical attempt at freedom.

This, however, was more easily determined than effected. A few preliminary trials made it clear that little could be accomplished without considerable motion; and it did not surprise me when, after one especially energetic struggle, I began to feel the coils of falling rope as they piled up about me and upon me. Obviously, I thought, the Bedouins had felt my movements and released their end of the rope; hastening no doubt to the temple's true entrance to lie murderously in wait for me. The prospect was not pleasing—but I had faced worse in my time without flinching, and would not flinch now. At present I must first of all free myself of bonds, then trust to ingenuity to escape from the temple unharmed. It is curious how implicitly I had come to believe myself in the old temple of Khephren beside the Sphinx, only a short distance below the ground.

That belief was shattered, and every pristine apprehension of preternatural depth and daemoniac mystery revived, by a circumstance which grew in horror and significance even as I formulated my philosophical plan. I have said that the falling rope was piling up about and upon me. Now I saw that it was continuing to pile, as no rope of normal length could possibly do. It gained in momentum and became an avalanche of hemp, accumulating mountainously on the floor, and half burying me beneath its swiftly multiplying coils. Soon I was completely engulfed and gasping for breath as the increasing convolutions submerged and stifled me. My senses tottered again, and I vainly tried to fight off a menace desperate and ineluctable. It was not merely that I was tortured beyond human endurance—not merely that life and breath seemed to be crushed slowly out of me—it was the knowledge of what those unnatural lengths of rope implied, and the consciousness of what unknown and incalculable gulfs of inner earth must at this moment be surrounding me. My endless descent and swinging flight through goblin space, then, must have been real; and even now I must be lying helpless in some nameless cavern world toward the core of the planet. Such a sudden confirmation of ultimate horror was insupportable, and a second time I lapsed into merciful oblivion.

When I say oblivion, I do not imply that I was free from dreams. On the contrary, my absence from the conscious world was marked by visions of the most unutterable hideousness. God! . . . If only I had not read so much Egyptology before coming to this land which is the fountain of all darkness and terror! This second spell of fainting filled my sleeping mind anew with shivering realisation of the country and its archaic secrets, and through some damnable chance my dreams turned to the ancient notions of the dead and their sojournings in soul and body beyond those mysterious tombs which were more houses than graves. I recalled, in dream-shapes which it is well that I do not remember, the peculiar and elaborate construction of Egyptian sepulchres; and the exceedingly singular and terrific doctrines which determined this construction.

All these people thought of was death and the dead. They conceived of a literal resurrection of the body which made them mummify it with desperate care, and preserve all the vital organs in canopic jars near the corpse; whilst besides the body they believed in two other elements, the soul, which after its weighing and approval by Osiris dwelt in the land of the blest, and the obscure and portentous ka or life-principle which wandered about the upper and lower worlds in a horrible way, demanding occasional access to the preserved body, consuming the food offerings brought by priests and pious relatives to the mortuary chapel, and sometimes—as men whispered—taking its body or the wooden double always buried beside it and stalking noxiously abroad on errands peculiarly repellent.

For thousands of years those bodies rested gorgeously encased and staring glassily upward when not visited by the ka, awaiting the day when Osiris should restore both ka and soul, and lead forth the stiff legions of the dead from the sunken houses of sleep.[45] It was to have been a glorious rebirth—but not all souls were approved, nor were all tombs inviolate, so that certain grotesque mistakes and fiendish abnormalities were to be looked for. Even today the Arabs murmur of unsanctified convocations and unwholesome worship in forgotten nether abysses, which only winged invisible kas and soulless mummies may visit and return unscathed.

Perhaps the most leeringly blood-congealing legends are those which relate to certain perverse products of decadent priestcraft—composite mummies made by the artificial union of human trunks and limbs with the heads of animals in imitation of the elder gods. At all stages of history the sacred animals were mummified, so that consecrated bulls, cats, ibises, crocodiles, and the like might return some day to greater glory. But only in the decadence did they mix the human and animal in the same mummy—only in the decadence, when they did not understand the rights and prerogatives of the ka and the soul. What happened to those composite mummies is not told of—at least publicly—and it is certain that no Egyptologist ever found one. The whispers of Arabs are very wild, and cannot be relied upon. They even hint that old Khephren—he of the Sphinx, the Second Pyramid, and the yawning gateway temple—lives far underground wedded to the ghoul-queen Nitokris and ruling over the mummies that are neither of man nor of beast.

It was of these—of Khephren and his consort and his strange armies of the hybrid dead—that I dreamed, and that is why I am glad the exact dream-shapes have faded from my memory. My most horrible vision was connected with an idle question I had asked myself the day before when looking at the great carven riddle of the desert and wondering with what unknown depths the temple so close to it might be secretly connected. That question, so innocent and whimsical then, assumed in my dream a

45. Duncan Norris, in "Lovecraft and Egypt: A Closer Examination," writes that HPL does Osiris "a grave disservice. Whilst modern conceptions of gods of the dead tend to be negative, Osiris was the lord of the afterlife and resurrection, a decidedly positive deity in the eyes of ancient Egyptians" (33).

meaning of frenetic and hysterical madness . . . what huge and loathsome abnormality was the Sphinx originally carven to represent?

My second awakening—if awakening it was—is a memory of stark hideousness which nothing else in my life—save one thing which came after—can parallel; and that life has been full and adventurous beyond most men's. Remember that I had lost consciousness whilst buried beneath a cascade of falling rope whose immensity revealed the cataclysmic depth of my present position. Now, as perception returned, I felt the entire weight gone; and realised upon rolling over that although I was still tied, gagged, and blindfolded, some agency had removed completely the suffocating hempen landslide which had overwhelmed me. The significance of this condition, of course, came to me only gradually; but even so I think it would have brought unconsciousness again had I not by this time reached such a state of emotional exhaustion that no new horror could make much difference. I was alone . . . with what?

Before I could torture myself with any new reflection, or make any fresh effort to escape from my bonds, an additional circumstance became manifest. Pains not formerly felt were racking my arms and legs, and I seemed coated with a profusion of dried blood beyond anything my former cuts and abrasions could furnish. My chest, too, seemed pierced by an hundred wounds, as though some malign, titanic ibis had been pecking at it. Assuredly the agency which had removed the rope was a hostile one, and had begun to wreak terrible injuries upon me when somehow impelled to desist. Yet at the time my sensations were distinctly the reverse of what one might expect. Instead of sinking into a bottomless pit of despair, I was stirred to a new courage and action; for now I felt that the evil forces were physical things which a fearless man might encounter on an even basis.

On the strength of this thought I tugged again at my bonds, and used all the art of a lifetime to free myself as I had so often done amidst the glare of lights and the applause of vast crowds. The familiar details of my escaping process commenced to engross me, and now that the long rope was gone I half regained my belief that the supreme horrors were hallucinations after all, and that there had never been any terrible shaft, measureless abyss, or interminable rope. Was I after all in the gateway temple of Khephren beside the Sphinx, and had the sneaking Arabs stolen in to torture me as I lay helpless there? At any rate, I must be free. Let me stand up unbound, ungagged, and with eyes open to catch any glimmer of light which might come trickling from any source, and I could actually delight in the combat against evil and treacherous foes!

How long I took in shaking off my encumbrances I cannot tell. It must have been longer than in my exhibition performances, because I was wounded, exhausted, and enervated by the experiences I had passed through. When I was finally free, and taking deep breaths of a chill, damp, evilly spiced air all the more horrible when encountered without the screen of gag and blindfold edges, I found that I was too cramped and fatigued to move at once. There I lay, trying to stretch a frame bent and mangled, for an indefinite period, and straining my eyes to catch a glimpse of some ray of light which would give a hint as to my position.

By degrees my strength and flexibility returned, but my eyes beheld nothing. As I staggered to my feet I peered diligently in every direction, yet met only an ebony blackness as great as that I had known when blindfolded. I tried my legs, blood-encrusted beneath my shredded trousers, and found that I could walk; yet could not decide in what direction to go. Obviously I ought not to walk at random, and perhaps retreat directly from the entrance I sought; so I paused to note the direction of the cold, foetid, natron-scented[46] air-current which I had never ceased to feel. Accepting the point of its source as the possible entrance to the abyss, I strove to keep track of this landmark and to walk consistently toward it.

I had had a match box with me, and even a small electric flashlight; but of course the pockets of my tossed and tattered clothing were long since emptied of all heavy articles. As I walked cautiously in the blackness, the draught grew stronger and more offensive, till at length I could regard it as nothing less than a tangible stream of detestable vapour pouring out of some aperture like the smoke of the genie from the fisherman's jar in

46. A salt mixture found in lakebeds in ancient Egypt, used for embalming, in the creation of ceramics, and as a cleanser in the home or for teeth or, in liquid, as a mouthwash.

47. The narrator refers to "The Fisherman and the Djinn," the second story related directly by Scheherazade in *One Thousand and One Nights*.

the Eastern tale.[47] The East . . . Egypt . . . truly, this dark cradle of civilisation was ever the well-spring of horrors and marvels unspeakable! The more I reflected on the nature of this cavern wind, the greater my sense of disquiet became; for although despite its odour I had sought its source as at least an indirect clue to the outer world, I now saw plainly that this foul emanation could have no admixture or connexion whatsoever with the clean air of the Libyan Desert, but must be essentially a thing vomited from sinister gulfs still lower down. I had, then, been walking in the wrong direction!

After a moment's reflection I decided not to retrace my steps. Away from the draught I would have no landmarks, for the roughly level rock floor was devoid of distinctive configurations. If, however, I followed up the strange current, I would undoubtedly arrive at an aperture of some sort, from whose gate I could perhaps work round the walls to the opposite side of this Cyclopean and otherwise unnavigable hall. That I might fail, I well realised. I saw that this was no part of Khephren's gateway temple which tourists know, and it struck me that this particular hall might be unknown even to archaeologists, and merely stumbled upon by the inquisitive and malignant Arabs who had imprisoned me. If so, was there any present gate of escape to the known parts or to the outer air?

What evidence, indeed, did I now possess that this was the gateway temple at all? For a moment all my wildest speculations rushed back upon me, and I thought of that vivid mélange of impressions—descent, suspension in space, the rope, my wounds, and the dreams that were frankly dreams. Was this the end of life for me? Or indeed, would it be merciful if this moment were the end? I could answer none of my own questions, but merely kept on till Fate for a third time reduced me to oblivion. This time there were no dreams, for the suddenness of the incident shocked me out of all thought either conscious or subconscious. Tripping on an unexpected descending step at a point where the offensive draught became strong enough to offer an actual physical resistance, I was precipitated headlong down a black flight of huge stone stairs into a gulf of hideousness unrelieved.

That I ever breathed again is a tribute to the inherent vitality of the healthy human organism. Often I look back to that night and feel a touch of actual humour in those repeated lapses of consciousness; lapses whose succession reminded me at the time of nothing more than the crude cinema melodramas of that period. Of course, it is possible that the repeated lapses never occurred; and that all the features of that underground nightmare were merely the dreams of one long coma which began with the shock of my descent into that abyss and ended with the healing balm of the outer air and of the rising sun which found me stretched on the sands of Gizeh before the sardonic and dawn-flushed face of the Great Sphinx.

I prefer to believe this latter explanation as much as I can, hence was glad when the police told me that the barrier to Khephren's gateway temple had been found unfastened, and that a sizeable rift to the surface did actually exist in one corner of the still buried part. I was glad, too, when the doctors pronounced my wounds only those to be expected from my seizure, blindfolding, lowering, struggling with bonds, falling some distance—perhaps into a depression in the temple's inner gallery—dragging myself to the outer barrier and escaping from it, and experiences like that . . . a very soothing diagnosis. And yet I know that there must be more than appears on the surface. That extreme descent is too vivid a memory to be dismissed—and it is odd that no one has ever been able to find a man answering the description of my guide Abdul Reis el Drogman—the tomb-throated guide who looked and smiled like King Khephren.

I have digressed from my connected narrative—perhaps in the vain hope of evading the telling of that final incident; that incident which of all is most certainly an hallucination. But I promised to relate it, and do not break promises. When I recovered—or seemed to recover—my senses after that fall down the black stone stairs, I was quite as alone and in darkness as before. The windy stench, bad enough before, was now fiendish; yet I had acquired enough familiarity by this time to bear it stoically. Dazedly I began to crawl away from the place whence the putrid wind came, and with my bleeding hands felt the colossal blocks of a mighty pavement. Once my head struck against a hard object, and when I felt of it I learned that it was the base

48. An ancient string instrument, probably a triangular harp. In an entry for "sambuca," Iain Fenlon, referencing the twenty-volume seventh-century encyclopedia *Etymologies*, quotes its author: "Isidore [of Seville] mentions this amongst the wind instruments, but it is hard to know what he is talking about. Properly, *sambuca* in Latin means a harp, but it is unlikely that Isidore was thinking of a string instrument. He describes the *sambuca* as a 'symphonia,' which may mean one of two things: a polyphonic instrument, or more specifically a double-skinned drum." Referencing a second scholar, the sixteenth-century musicologist Pietro Aaron, Fenlon adds: "*sambuca* may have had another meaning: in Italian, *sambuca* encompasses various wind instruments (bagpipe, sackbut), but also string instruments (harp, hurdy-gurdy)": see Fenlon, ed., *Studies in Medieval and Modern Music* (Cambridge: Cambridge University Press, 2002), 17.

49. A percussion instrument of metal rings on a handle; Fenlon, quoting Aaron, offers two more possibilities: "the ancestor of the triangle . . . with metal roundels that clash when the instrument is shaken" or "the *cymbalo* used by Florentine girls in their dances" (Fenlon, *Studies in Medieval and Modern Music*, 18).

50. A Greek hand-drum, like a tambourine.

of a —a column of unbelievable immensity—whose surface was covered with gigantic chiselled hieroglyphics very perceptible to my touch. Crawling on, I encountered other titan columns at incomprehensible distances apart; when suddenly my attention was captured by the realisation of something which must have been impinging on my subconscious hearing long before the conscious sense was aware of it.

From some still lower chasm in earth's bowels were proceeding certain sounds, measured and definite, and like nothing I had ever heard before. That they were very ancient and distinctly ceremonial, I felt almost intuitively; and much reading in Egyptology led me to associate them with the flute, the sambuke,[48] the sistrum,[49] and the tympanum.[50] In their rhythmic piping, droning, rattling, and beating I felt an element of terror beyond all the known terrors of earth—a terror peculiarly dissociated from personal fear, and taking the form of a sort of objective pity for our planet, that it should hold within its depths such horrors as must lie beyond these aegipanic cacophonies. The sounds increased in volume, and I felt that they were approaching. Then—and may all the gods of all pantheons unite to keep the like from my ears again—I began to hear, faintly and afar off, the morbid and millennial tramping of the marching things.

It was hideous that footfalls so dissimilar should move in such perfect rhythm. The training of unhallowed thousands of years must lie behind that march of earth's inmost monstrosities . . . padding, clicking, walking, stalking, rumbling, lumbering, crawling . . . and all to the abhorrent discords of those mocking instruments. And then . . . God keep the memory of those Arab legends out of my head! The mummies without souls . . . the meeting-place of the wandering kas . . . the hordes of the devil-cursed pharaonic dead of forty centuries . . . the composite mummies led through the uttermost onyx voids by King Khephren and his ghoul-queen Nitokris. . . .

The tramping drew nearer—heaven save me from the sound of those feet and paws and hooves and pads and talons as it commenced to acquire detail! Down limitless reaches of sunless pavement a spark of light flickered in the malodorous wind, and I drew behind the enormous circumference of a Cyclopic column that I might escape for a while the horror that was stalking million-footed toward me through gigantic hypostyles[51] of inhuman dread and phobic antiquity. The flickers increased, and the tramping and dissonant rhythm grew sickeningly loud. In the quivering orange light there stood faintly forth a scene of such stony awe that I gasped from a sheer wonder that conquered even fear and repulsion. Bases of columns whose middles were higher than human sight . . . mere bases of things that must each dwarf the Eiffel Tower to insignificance . . . hieroglyphics carved by unthinkable hands in caverns where daylight can be only a remote legend. . . .

I would not look at the marching things. That I desperately resolved as I heard their creaking joints and nitrous wheezing above the dead music and the dead tramping. It was merciful that they did not speak . . . but God! their crazy torches began to cast shadows on the surface of those stupendous columns. Heaven take it away! Hippopotami should not have human hands and carry torches . . . men should not have the heads of crocodiles. . . .

I tried to turn away, but the shadows and the sounds and the stench were everywhere. Then I remembered something I used to do in half-conscious nightmares as a boy, and began to repeat to myself, "This is a dream! This is a dream!" But it was of no use, and I could only shut my eyes and pray . . . at least, that is what I think I

51. Columns.

Eiffel Tower, at the heart of the Paris Exposition in 1900.

52. A thaumatrope was a nineteenth-century device, a scientific toy, consisting of a card or a disk on a string or a piece of silk, with two different images, one on each side. One twirls the excess string dangling from each side of the card/disk, and soon the two images, rotating, create an illusion that they are one. The effect demonstrates the fact that images stay on the retina. One of the most popular sets of images was of a bird on one side, a cage on the other; when the thaumatrope was spun, the bird appeared to be in the cage. The name "thaumatrope" was also applied to a rotating disk or cylinder with images viewed through a slit, producing the illusion of motion (an early animation device). This form was also known as a "zoetrope" or "phenakistoscope" (following the continuum, we arrive at the flip book). "Thaumatropically" therefore means "creating an illusion." The word also eventually came to be used metaphorically: Seeing incarceration in a penal colony as a positive good might be considered an intellectual thaumatrope, for instance: "The prosperity of the Colony, and the repression of crime, are, by a sort of rapid whirl, presented to the mind as combined in one picture. A very moderate degree of calm and fixed attention soon shows that the two objects are painted on opposite sides of the card" (Richard Whately, *Elements of Logic* [Boston and Cambridge, MA: James Munroe and Company, 1855], 217). The thaumatrope, then, became a metaphor for the ability to simultaneously contemplate contradictory thoughts— for example, the horrors of imprisonment and the benefits to a society.

did, for one is never sure in visions—and I know this can have been nothing more. I wondered whether I should ever reach the world again, and at times would furtively open my eyes to see if I could discern any feature of the place other than the wind of spiced putrefaction, the topless columns, and the thaumatropically[52] grotesque

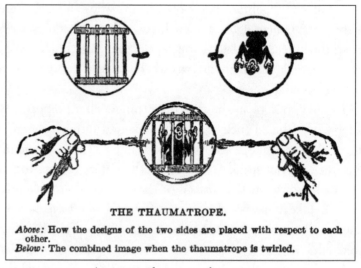

A nineteenth-century thaumatrope.

Advertisement for a "zoetrope."

shadows of abnormal horror. The sputtering glare of multiplying torches now shone, and unless this hellish place were wholly without walls, I could not fail to see some boundary or fixed landmark soon. But I had to shut my eyes again when I realised how many of the things were assembling—and when I glimpsed a certain object walking solemnly and steadily without any body above the waist.

A fiendish and ululant corpse-gurgle or death-rattle now split the very atmosphere—the charnel atmosphere poisonous with naphtha and bitumen blasts—in one concerted chorus from the ghoulish legion of hybrid blasphemies. My eyes, perversely shaken open, gazed for an instant upon a sight which no human creature could even imagine without panic fear and physical exhaustion. The things had filed ceremonially in one direction, the direction of the noisome wind, where the light of their torches shewed their bended heads . . . or the bended heads of such as had heads. . . . They were worshipping before a great black foetor-belching aperture which reached up almost out of sight, and which I could see was flanked at right angles by two giant staircases whose ends were far away in shadow. One of these was indubitably the staircase I had fallen down.

The dimensions of the hole were fully in proportion with those of the columns—an ordinary house would have been lost in it, and any average public building could easily have been moved in and out. It was so vast a surface that only by moving the eye could one trace its boundaries . . . so vast, so hideously black, and so aromatically stinking. . . . Directly in front of this yawning Polyphemus-door[53] the things were throwing objects—evidently sacrifices or religious offerings, to judge by their gestures. Khephren was their leader; sneering King Khephren or the guide Abdul Reis, crowned with a golden pshent[54] and intoning endless formulae with the hollow voice of the dead. By his side knelt beautiful Queen Nitokris, whom I saw in profile for a moment, noting that the right half of her face was eaten away by rats or other ghouls. And I shut my eyes again when I saw what objects were being thrown as offerings to the foetid aperture or its possible local deity.

It occurred to me that judging from the elaborateness of this worship, the concealed deity must be one of considerable importance. Was it Osiris or Isis, Horus or Anubis, or some

53. See "The Lurking Fear," pp. 121–49, note 19, above. Polyphemus closed off his cave with an enormous boulder, so large that, according to Odysseus, twenty teams of horses could not budge it.

54. Usually spelled "pschent" (from the Greek ψχεντ), the double crown worn by the ancient kings of Egypt.

A pschent.

vast unknown God of the Dead still more central and supreme? There is a legend that terrible altars and colossi were reared to an Unknown One before ever the known gods were worshipped. . . .

And now, as I steeled myself to watch the rapt and sepulchral adorations of those nameless things, a thought of escape flashed upon me. The hall was dim, and the columns heavy with shadow. With every creature of that nightmare throng absorbed in shocking raptures, it might be barely possible for me to creep past to the faraway end of one of the staircases and ascend unseen; trusting to Fate and skill to deliver me from the upper reaches. Where I was, I neither knew nor seriously reflected upon—and for a moment it struck me as amusing to plan a serious escape from that which I knew to be a dream. Was I in some hidden and unsuspected lower realm of Khephren's gateway temple—that temple which generations have persistently called the Temple of the Sphinx? I could not conjecture, but I resolved to ascend to life and consciousness if wit and muscle could carry me.

Wriggling flat on my stomach, I began the anxious journey toward the foot of the left-hand staircase, which seemed the more accessible of the two. I cannot describe the incidents and sensations of that crawl, but they may be guessed when one reflects on what I had to watch steadily in that malign, wind-blown torchlight in order to avoid detection. The bottom of the staircase was, as I have said, far away in shadow; as it had to be to rise without a bend to the dizzy parapeted landing above the titanic aperture. This placed the last stages of my crawl at some distance from the noisome herd, though the spectacle chilled me even when quite remote at my right.

At length I succeeded in reaching the steps and began to climb; keeping close to the wall, on which I observed decorations of the most hideous sort, and relying for safety on the absorbed, ecstatic interest with which the monstrosities watched the foul-breezed aperture and the impious objects of nourishment they had flung on the pavement before it. Though the staircase was huge and steep, fashioned of vast porphyry blocks as if for the feet of a giant, the ascent seemed virtually interminable. Dread of discovery and the pain which renewed exercise had brought to my wounds combined to make that upward crawl a thing of agonising memory. I had intended, on reaching the landing, to climb immediately onward along whatever upper staircase might mount from there; stopping for no last look at the carrion abominations that pawed and genuflected some seventy or eighty feet below—yet a sudden repetition of that thunderous corpse-gurgle and death-rattle chorus, coming as I had nearly gained the top of the flight and shewing by its ceremonial rhythm that it was not an alarm of my discovery, caused me to pause and peer cautiously over the parapet.

The monstrosities were hailing something which had poked itself out of the nauseous aperture to seize the hellish fare proffered it. It was something quite ponderous, even as seen from my height; something yellowish and hairy, and endowed with a sort of nervous motion. It was as large, perhaps, as a good-sized hippopotamus, but very curiously shaped. It seemed to have no neck, but five separate shaggy heads springing in a row from a roughly cylindrical trunk; the first very small, the second good-sized, the third and fourth equal and largest of all, and the fifth rather small, though not so small as the first. Out of these heads darted curious rigid tentacles which seized ravenously on the excessively great quantities of unmentionable food placed before the aperture. Once in a while the thing would leap up, and occasionally it would retreat into its den in a very odd manner. Its locomotion was so inexplicable that I stared in fascination, wishing it would emerge further from the cavernous lair beneath me.

Then it did emerge . . . it did emerge, and at the sight I turned and fled into the darkness up the higher staircase that rose behind me; fled unknowingly up incredible steps and ladders and inclined planes to which no human sight or logic guided me, and which I must ever relegate to the world of dreams for want of any confirmation. It must have been dream, or the dawn would never have found me breathing on the sands of Gizeh before the sardonic dawn-flushed face of the Great Sphinx.

The Great Sphinx! God!—that idle question I asked myself on that sun-blest morning before . . . what huge and loathsome abnormality was the Sphinx originally carven to represent? Accursed is the sight, be it in dream or not, that revealed to

55. Some critics have been harsh regarding this disclaimer: Donald R. Burleson, for example, writes, "Astonishingly, though, after providing a work that deftly adapts Egyptian lore to horrific purposes, and does so with unforgettably powerful descriptive passages well prepared by careful buildup of realism, Lovecraft rather spoils the tale with the closing sentence" (*H. P. Lovecraft: A Critical Study*, 112). But it can also be read as the very plausible self-denial by a man (Houdini) who scoffed at the supernatural and prided himself on exposing fraudulent psychic phenomena.

me the supreme horror—the Unknown God of the Dead, which licks its colossal chops in the unsuspected abyss, fed hideous morsels by soulless absurdities that should not exist. The five-headed monster that emerged . . . that five-headed monster as large as a hippopotamus . . . the five-headed monster—and that of which it is the merest fore paw. . . .

But I survived, and I know it was only a dream.[55]

The Shunned House[1]

On the surface a traditional tale of a haunted house, drawing on local vampire legends and set in an actual Providence residence, "The Shunned House" finds Lovecraft essentially inventing his own form. As in "The Dunwich Horror," "The Call of Cthulhu," and At the Mountains of Madness, *science confronts the supernatural. Meticulous detail builds to a horrifyingly believable climax. Rejected initially by* Weird Tales, *it finally appeared there several years after Lovecraft's death.*

1. "The Shunned House" was written in October 1924 and first published in 1928 as a booklet. It was eventually published in *Weird Tales* 30, no. 4 (October 1937), 418–36.

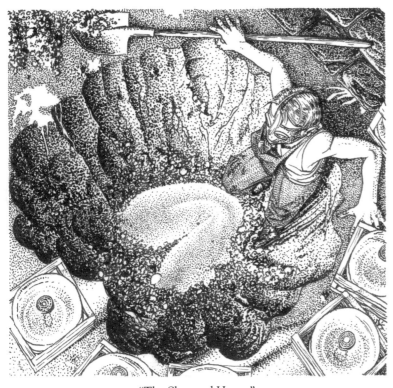

"The Shunned House."
Cover of *Lovecraft Studies*, no.35 (Fall 1996) (artist: Jason Eckhardt;
reproduced with permission)

88 Benefit Street, Providence, 2010, occupied by Sarah Helen Whitman at the time of the visit of Edgar Allan Poe. Photograph courtesy of Donovan K. Loucks

2. Poe courted the writer Sarah Helen (Power) Whitman, whom he first met at her home in Providence, during a three-month period in late 1848. In December, she consented to an "immediate marriage," but two days later, the engagement was broken off, and Poe returned to New York, never to see Whitman again.

A portrait of Sarah Helen Whitman, by John Nelson Arnold (1869), after an original by Cephas Giovanni Thompson in 1838.

I.

FROM EVEN THE greatest of horrors irony is seldom absent. Sometimes it enters directly into the composition of the events, while sometimes it relates only to their fortuitous position among persons and places. The latter sort is splendidly exemplified by a case in the ancient city of Providence, where in the late forties Edgar Allan Poe used to sojourn often during his unsuccessful wooing of the gifted poetess, Mrs. Whitman.[2] Poe generally stopped at the Mansion House[3] in Benefit Street—the renamed Golden Ball Inn whose roof has sheltered Washington, Jefferson, and Lafayette—and his favourite walk led northward along the same street to Mrs. Whitman's home and the neighbouring hillside churchyard of St. John's,[4] whose hidden expanse of eighteenth-century gravestones had for him a peculiar fascination.[5]

Now the irony is this. In this walk, so many times repeated, the world's greatest master of the terrible and the bizarre was obliged to pass a particular house on the eastern side of the street; a dingy, antiquated structure perched on the abruptly rising side-hill, with a great unkempt yard dating from a time when the region was partly open country.[6] It does not appear that he ever wrote or spoke of it, nor is there any evidence that he even noticed it. And yet that house, to the two persons in possession of certain information, equals or outranks in horror the wildest phantasy of the genius who so often passed it unknowingly, and stands starkly leering as a symbol of all that is unutterably hideous.

The house was—and for that matter still is—of a kind to attract the attention of the curious. Originally a farm or semi-farm building, it followed the average New England colonial lines of the middle eighteenth century—the prosperous peaked-roof sort, with two stories and dormerless attic, and with the Georgian doorway and interior panelling dictated by the progress of taste at that time. It faced south, with one gable end buried to the lower windows in the eastward rising hill, and the other exposed to the foundations toward the street. Its construction, over a century and a half ago, had followed the grading and straightening of the road in that especial vicinity; for Benefit Street—at first called Back Street—was laid out as a lane winding amongst the graveyards of the first settlers, and straightened only when the removal of the bodies to the North Burial Ground[7] made it decently possible to cut through the old family plots.

At the start, the western wall had lain some twenty feet up a precipitous lawn from the roadway; but a widening of the street at about the time of the Revolution sheared off most of the intervening space, exposing the foundations so that a brick basement wall had to be made, giving the deep cellar a street frontage with door and two windows above ground, close to the new line of public travel. When the sidewalk was laid out a century ago the last of the intervening space was removed; and Poe in his walks must have seen only a sheer ascent of dull grey brick flush with the sidewalk and surmounted at a height of ten feet by the antique shingled bulk of the house proper.

The farm-like grounds extended back very deeply up the hill, almost to Wheaton Street.[8] The space south of the house, abutting on Benefit Street, was of course greatly above the existing sidewalk level, forming a terrace bounded by a high bank wall of damp, mossy stone pierced by a steep flight of narrow steps which led inward between canyon-like surfaces to the upper region of mangy lawn, rheumy brick walls, and neglected gardens whose dismantled cement urns, rusted kettles fallen from tripods of knotty sticks, and similar paraphernalia set off the weather-

Cathedral of St. John, Episcopal, 271 North Main Street, Providence, 2012.
Photograph courtesy of Donovan K. Loucks

3. This was at 159 Benefit Street, since demolished.

Mansion House, Providence, in the 1940s.

4. See *The Case of Charles Dexter Ward*, in the previous volume, pp. 171–309, note 17; much of the action of that story, written in January–March 1927, also takes place in Providence. The church and the Golden Ball Inn are both mentioned.

5. These are not "eighteenth-century gravestones." According to Gertrude S. Kimball's *Providence in Colonial Times* (Boston and New York: Houghton Mifflin Company, 1912; hereafter Kimball), a source often consulted by HPL, "When the new church [replacing King's Church on Towne Street]—the present St. John's—was built in 1810, all the graves and gravestones in front of the church disappeared. Their disposition is not known. Many of the old gravestones were destroyed or carted away" (180).

6. The "Babbitt house," as HPL referred to this structure, is located at 135 Benefit Street and is today called the John Mawney House or the Stephen Harris House. In the 1920s, it was co-owned by Sophia C. H. Babbitt; following her death, a succession of Babbitts lived

there (as had Lovecraft's aunt Lillian D. Clark, in 1919–20, serving as a "caretaker," according to Providence town records). But HPL offered his aunt an additional possible source of inspiration: He had seen a house in Elizabeth, New Jersey, that "reminded [him] of the Babbitt house. . . . Later its image came up again with renewed vividness, finally causing me to write a new horror story with its scene in Providence and with the Babbitt house as its basis." The Elizabeth house, he said, stood "on the northeast corner of Bridge St. and Elizabeth Ave. . . . a terrible old house—a hellish place where night-black deeds must have been done in the early seventeen-hundreds— with a blackish unpainted surface, unnaturally steep roof, and an outside flight of steps leading to the second story, suffocatingly embowered in a tangle of ivy so dense that one cannot but imagine it accursed or corpse-fed" (Letter to Lillian D. Clark, November 4–6, 1924, *Selected Letters*, I, 357).

7. A large cemetery at North Main Street and Branch Avenue in Providence. The Burial Ground is the site of exhumations in *The Case of Charles Dexter Ward*.

8. This is off Prospect Terrace Park, near the Old State House and only a few blocks from the newly minted H. P. Lovecraft Square (Angell and Prospect Streets).

Wheaton Street map, 1908.
Geo. H. Walker & Co.

135 Benefit Street, Providence, 2010—the "Shunned House" itself?
Photograph courtesy of Donovan K. Loucks

beaten front door with its broken fanlight, rotting Ionic pilasters, and wormy triangular pediment.

What I heard in my youth about the shunned house was merely that people died there in alarmingly great numbers. That, I was told, was why the original owners had moved out some twenty years after building the place. It was plainly unhealthy, perhaps because of the dampness and fungous growth in the cellar, the general sickish smell, the draughts of the hallways, or the quality of the well and pump water. These things were bad enough, and these were all that gained belief among the persons whom I knew. Only the notebooks of my antiquarian uncle, Dr. Elihu Whipple,[9] revealed to me at length the darker, vaguer surmises which formed an undercurrent of folklore among old-time servants and humble folk; surmises which never travelled far, and which were largely forgotten when Providence grew to be a metropolis with a shifting modern population.

The general fact is, that the house was never regarded by the solid part of the community as in any real sense "haunted." There were no widespread tales of rattling chains, cold currents of air, extinguished lights, or faces at the window. Extremists sometimes said the house was "unlucky," but that is as far as even they went. What was really beyond dispute is that a frightful proportion of persons died there; or more accurately, *had* died there, since after some peculiar happenings over sixty years ago the building had become deserted through the sheer impossibility of renting it. These persons were not all cut off suddenly by any one cause; rather did it seem that their vitality was insidiously sapped, so that each one died the sooner from whatever tendency to weakness he may have naturally had. And those who did not die displayed in varying degree a type of anaemia or consumption, and sometimes a decline of the mental faculties, which spoke ill for

9. It is surely coincidental that Whipple was also the family name of HPL's great-great-grandmother, and the family name was preserved as the first name of HPL's grandfather as well as his great-uncle. Dr. Whipple may have been the descendant of Captain Abraham Whipple, who commanded one of the ships in the *Gaspée* incident. See *The Case of Charles Dexter Ward*, in the previous volume, pp. 171–309, notes 64 and 104.

In his *Lovecraft's Providence & Adjacent Parts*, Henry L. P. Beckwith suggests this as the home of Dr. Elihu Whipple, despite the fact that it is an Italianate building situated at 144 Benefit Street rather than a Georgian home on adjacent North Court Street.
Photograph courtesy of Donovan K. Loucks, 2001

The North Burial Ground, Providence, 2010.
Photograph courtesy of Donovan K. Loucks

38 North Court Street, 2014, the third oldest house on College Hill, built in 1737, the choice of Donovan K. Loucks for the home of Dr. Elihu Whipple.
Photograph courtesy of Donovan K. Loucks

The Old State House, 150 Benefit Street, Providence, 2016.

Photograph courtesy of Donovan K. Loucks

10. *Monotropa uniflora* (family Monotropoideae), also known (appropriately) as the "ghost plant" or "corpse plant," contains no chlorophyll. It is a parasite—that is, it does not photosynthesize—and can grow readily in areas with no sunlight.

Monotropa uniflora, "Indian pipes."

Shutterstock.com

the salubriousness of the building. Neighbouring houses, it must be added, seemed entirely free from the noxious quality.

This much I knew before my insistent questioning led my uncle to shew me the notes which finally embarked us both on our hideous investigation. In my childhood the shunned house was vacant, with barren, gnarled, and terrible old trees, long, queerly pale grass, and nightmarishly misshapen weeds in the high terraced yard where birds never lingered. We boys used to overrun the place, and I can still recall my youthful terror not only at the morbid strangeness of this sinister vegetation, but at the eldritch atmosphere and odour of the dilapidated house, whose unlocked front door was often entered in quest of shudders. The small-paned windows were largely broken, and a nameless air of desolation hung round the precarious panelling, shaky interior shutters, peeling wall-paper, falling plaster, rickety staircases, and such fragments of battered furniture as still remained. The dust and cobwebs added their touch of the fearful; and brave indeed was the boy who would voluntarily ascend the ladder to the attic, a vast raftered length lighted only by small blinking windows in the gable ends, and filled with a massed wreckage of chests, chairs, and spinning-wheels which infinite years of deposit had shrouded and festooned into monstrous and hellish shapes.

But after all, the attic was not the most terrible part of the house. It was the dank, humid cellar which somehow exerted the strongest repulsion on us, even though it was wholly above ground on the street side, with only a thin door and window-pierced brick wall to separate it from the busy sidewalk. We scarcely knew whether to haunt it in spectral fascination, or to shun it for the sake of our souls and our sanity. For one thing, the bad odour of the house was strongest there; and for another thing, we did not like the white fungous growths which occasionally sprang up in rainy summer weather from the hard earth floor. Those fungi, grotesquely like the vegetation in the yard outside, were truly horrible in their outlines; detestable parodies of toadstools and Indian pipes,[10] whose like we had never seen in any other situation. They rotted quickly, and at one stage became slightly phosphorescent; so that nocturnal passers-by sometimes spoke of witch-fires glowing behind the broken panes of the foetor-spreading windows.

We never—even in our wildest Hallowe'en moods—visited this cellar by night, but in some of our daytime visits could detect the phosphorescence, especially when the day was dark and wet. There was also a subtler thing we often thought we detected—a very strange thing which was, however, merely suggestive at most. I refer to a sort of cloudy whitish pattern on the dirt floor—a vague, shifting deposit of mould or nitre which we sometimes thought we could trace amidst the sparse fungous growths near the huge fireplace of the basement kitchen. Once in a while it struck us that this patch bore an uncanny resemblance to a doubled-up human figure, though generally no such kinship existed, and often there was no whitish deposit whatever. On a certain rainy afternoon when this illusion seemed phenomenally strong, and when, in addition, I had fancied I glimpsed a kind of thin, yellowish, shimmering exhalation rising from the nitrous pattern toward the yawning fireplace, I spoke to my uncle about the matter. He smiled at this odd conceit, but it seemed that his smile was tinged with reminiscence. Later I heard that a similar notion entered into some of the wild ancient tales of the common folk—a notion likewise alluding to ghoulish, wolfish shapes taken by smoke from the great chimney, and queer contours assumed by certain of the sinuous tree-roots that thrust their way into the cellar through the loose foundation-stones.

II.

NOT TILL MY adult years did my uncle set before me the notes and data which he had collected concerning the shunned house. Dr. Whipple was a sane, conservative physician of the old school, and for all his interest in the place was not eager to encourage young thoughts toward the abnormal. His own view, postulating simply a building and location of markedly unsanitary qualities, had nothing to do with abnormality; but he realised that the very picturesqueness which aroused his own interest would in a boy's fanciful mind take on all manner of gruesome imaginative associations.

The doctor was a bachelor; a white-haired, clean-shaven, old-fashioned gentleman, and a local historian of note, who had often

11. Sidney S. Rider (1833–1917) was a popular historian of Rhode Island. The Rhode Island Heritage Hall of Fame wrote, in its entry for Rider in 2007, on the occasion of his induction, "Coming to Providence as a boy, he went into the book business, eventually taking over the store of Charles Burnett. After the Civil War, Rider began publishing pamphlets on Rhode Island history. In 1883, he started a twice-monthly magazine, called *Book Notes*, a publication he continued for thirty-three years. It was jammed full of reviews, lively—sometimes cantankerous—criticism, and opinionated essays that challenged then current interpretations of Rhode Island history. In today's bibliography of the New England states, edited by Roger Parks, there are more than 100 citations for Sidney Rider" (http://www.riheritagehalloffame .org/inductees_detail.cfm?iid=578). In 1888, he wrote an essay on "The Belief in Vampires in Rhode Island" (*Book Notes* 5, no. 7, 37–39).

12. Thomas W. Bicknell (1834–1925) was a well-regarded historian of Rhode Island. In 1920 he published the three-volume *History of the State of Rhode Island and Providence Plantations*, supplemented by three biographical volumes.

13. See note 8, above, and the map there.

14. See *The Case of Charles Dexter Ward*, in the previous volume, pp. 171–309, and note 9, above.

15. Congress advised all of the original thirteen colonies to adopt self-government. On May 4, 1776, Rhode Island became the first of the colonies to renounce its allegiance to the Crown; however, delegates boycotted the 1787 Constitutional Convention, and Rhode Island was the last of the thirteen colonies to ratify the Constitution and become a state, on May 29, 1790.

broken a lance with such controversial guardians of tradition as Sidney S. Rider[11] and Thomas W. Bicknell.[12] He lived with one manservant in a Georgian homestead with knocker and iron-railed steps, balanced eerily on a steep ascent of North Court Street[13] beside the ancient brick court and colony house where his grandfather—a cousin of that celebrated privateersman, Capt. Whipple, who burnt His Majesty's armed schooner *Gaspee* in 1772[14]—had voted in the legislature on May 4, 1776, for the independence of the Rhode-Island Colony.[15] Around him in the damp, low-ceiled library with the musty white panelling, heavy carved overmantel, and small-paned, vine-shaded windows, were the relics and records of his ancient family, among which were many dubious allusions to the shunned house in Benefit Street. That pest spot lies not far distant—for Benefit runs ledgewise just above the court-house along the precipitous hill up which the first settlement climbed.

When, in the end, my insistent pestering and maturing years evoked from my uncle the hoarded lore I sought, there lay before me a strange enough chronicle. Long-winded, statistical, and drearily genealogical as some of the matter was, there ran through it a continuous thread of brooding, tenacious horror and preternatural malevolence which impressed me even more than it had impressed the good doctor. Separate events fitted together uncannily, and seemingly irrelevant details held mines of hideous possibilities. A new and burning curiosity grew in me, compared to which my boyish curiosity was feeble and inchoate. The first revelation led to an exhaustive research, and finally to that shuddering quest which proved so disastrous to myself and mine. For at last my uncle insisted on joining the search I had commenced, and after a certain night in that house he did not come away with me. I am lonely without that gentle soul whose long years were filled only with honour, virtue, good taste, benevolence, and learning. I have reared a marble urn to his memory in St. John's churchyard—the place that Poe loved—the hidden grove of giant willows on the hill, where tombs and headstones huddle quietly between the hoary bulk of the church and the houses and bank walls of Benefit Street.

The history of the house, opening amidst a maze of dates, revealed no trace of the sinister either about its construction or about the prosperous and honourable family who built it. Yet from the first a taint of calamity, soon increased to boding significance, was apparent. My uncle's carefully compiled record began with the building of the structure in 1763, and followed the theme with an unusual amount of detail. The shunned house, it seems, was first inhabited by William Harris[16] and his wife Rhoby Dexter, with their children, Elkanah, born in 1755, Abigail, born in 1757, William, Jr., born in 1759, and Ruth, born in 1761. Harris was a substantial merchant and seaman in the West India trade, connected with the firm of Obadiah Brown and his nephews.[17] After Brown's death in 1761, the new firm of Nicholas Brown & Co. made him master of the brig *Prudence*, Providence-built, of 120 tons, thus enabling him to erect the new homestead he had desired ever since his marriage.

The site he had chosen—a recently straightened part of the new and fashionable Back Street, which ran along the side of the hill above crowded Cheapside[18]—was all that could be wished, and the building did justice to the location. It was the best that moderate means could afford, and Harris hastened to move in before the birth of a fifth child which the family expected. That child, a boy, came in December; but was still-born. Nor was any child to be born alive in that house for a century and a half.

Cheapside, Providence, ca. 1903.

16. A man named William Harris was one of the original settlers of Providence, in 1636; however, the son of the William Harris who owned the shunned house is a "Junior," and therefore neither was a direct descendant of the founding father.

Philip A. Shreffler, in *The H. P. Lovecraft Companion*, writes:

The sources and inspiration for this story represent another of Lovecraft's combinations of historical fact and legend. The shunned house of the tale, which may still be seen today in Providence, Rhode Island, is the Stephen Harris house, built in 1764. [See note 6, above.] Thinly disguised as 'the William Harris house' in the story, the Stephen Harris house stands at 135 Benefit Street on the eastern or uphill side of the street. . . . Lovecraft accurately described the house in his story, and it is because College Hill, which Benefit Street traverses, is so steep that most of the dwellings on the eastern side are constructed with their basements at sidewalk level (and going back into the hill), while the upper floors of the houses soar high into the trees. . . . According to a story about the original owners of the Harris house, this building was reared upon the site of an old burying ground from which all the remains save two were removed. Apparently the graves of a French husband and wife were overlooked and still remain beneath the house. Supposedly, when the two children of Mrs. Stephen Harris died, the woman, crazed with grief, was often heard to cry out in French from one of the second-story windows. (94)

17. Brothers Obadiah Brown (1712–1762) and James Brown II (1698–1739) were the first Providence merchants to

enter into the West Indian slave trade. With Obadiah initially acting as master of James's vessels, their initial involvement was said to have been brief and unprofitable. Twenty-seven when his older brother died, and having extricated himself from human trafficking and married his cousin Mary Harris (a descendant of the settler William Harris—see note 16) two years earlier, he assumed responsibility for his nephews, Joseph, John, Nicholas Jr., and Moses, teaching them the family trade in rum, cocoa, and molasses. The family briefly reentered the slave trade in 1759 and then left it finally when privateers seized one of their ships. Also see *The Case of Charles Dexter Ward*, in the previous volume, pp. 171–309, notes 84, 100, and 114.

18. An early business center in Providence; by 1820, according to Kimball, it was "the fashionable shopping-district,"

The Cheapside Block, 2011,
one of the few period buildings
remaining in the area.
Photograph courtesy of Donovan K. Loucks

The next April sickness occurred among the children, and Abigail and Ruth died before the month was over. Dr. Job Ives diagnosed the trouble as some infantile fever, though others declared it was more of a mere wasting-away or decline. It seemed, in any event, to be contagious; for Hannah Bowen, one of the two servants, died of it in the following June. Eli Liddeason, the other servant, constantly complained of weakness; and would have returned to his father's farm in Rehoboth[19] but for a sudden attachment for Mehitabel Pierce, who was hired to succeed Hannah. He died the next year—a sad year indeed, since it marked the death of William Harris himself, enfeebled as he was by the climate of Martinique,[20] where his occupation had kept him for considerable periods during the preceding decade.

The widowed Rhoby Harris never recovered from the shock of her husband's death, and the passing of her first-born Elkanah two years later was the final blow to her reason. In 1768 she fell victim to a mild form of insanity, and was thereafter confined to the upper part of the house;[21] her elder maiden sister, Mercy Dexter, having moved in to take charge of the family. Mercy was a plain, raw-boned woman of great strength; but her health visibly declined from the time of her advent. She was greatly devoted to her unfortunate sister, and had an especial affection for her only surviving nephew William, who from a sturdy infant had become a sickly, spindling lad. In this year the servant Mehitabel died, and the other servant, Preserved Smith, left without coherent explanation—or at least, with only some wild tales and a complaint that he disliked the smell of the place. For a time Mercy could secure no more help, since the seven deaths and case of madness, all occurring within five years' space, had begun to set in motion the body of fireside rumour which later became so bizarre. Ultimately, however, she obtained new servants from out of town; Ann White, a morose woman from that part of North Kingstown now set off as the township of Exeter,[22] and a capable Boston man named Zenas Low.

It was Ann White who first gave definite shape to the sinister idle talk. Mercy should have known better than to hire anyone from the Nooseneck Hill country,[23] for that remote bit of backwoods was then, as now, a seat of the most uncomfortable superstitions. As lately as 1892 an Exeter community exhumed a dead body and ceremoniously burnt its heart in order to prevent certain alleged visitations injurious to the public health and peace,[24] and one may imagine the point of view of the same section in 1768. Ann's tongue was perniciously active, and within a few months Mercy discharged her, filling her place with a faithful and amiable Amazon from Newport, Maria Robbins.

Meanwhile poor Rhoby Harris, in her madness, gave voice to dreams and imaginings of the most hideous sort. At times her screams became insupportable, and for long periods she would utter shrieking horrors which necessitated her son's temporary residence with his cousin, Peleg Harris, in Presbyterian Lane[25] near the new college building. The boy would seem to improve after these visits, and had Mercy been as wise as she was well-meaning, she would have let him live permanently with Peleg. Just what Mrs. Harris cried out in her fits of violence, tradition hesitates to say; or rather, presents such extravagant accounts that they nullify themselves through sheer absurdity. Certainly

North Kingstown, Rhode Island, ca. 1925–30.

Cheapside being "a name given to the west side of North Main Street from Market Square northward for perhaps four or five blocks" (373).

19. A small rural village in Bristol County, Massachusetts, only eleven miles east of Providence.

The Thomas Carpenter cottage and farm in Rehoboth, Massachussetts, built around 1789—could this be the Liddeason farm?

20. A tropical island in the eastern Caribbean, active in the sugar trade; it was controlled by England occasionally during the Seven Years' War and continuously from 1794 to 1815; at other times, it was controlled by France. It remains a French administrative *région*.

21. Cf. "The Yellow Wallpaper," by Charlotte Perkins Gilman (1860–1935), who also published as Charlotte Anna Perkins and Charlotte Perkins Stetson. A prolific author of novels, short stories, and nonfiction and a prominent feminist, after suffering postpartum depression she wrote the timeless tale of a young woman confined to an upper bedroom decorated with hideous yellow wallpaper and driven to madness. Today a mainstay of high school English curriculums, it first appeared in the *New England Magazine* in 1892. The story receives favorable treatment in HPL's "Supernatural Horror in Literature."

22. Originally part of North Kingstown but later incorporated in 1743.

23. The Nooseneck Hill agricultural region, situated above the Nooseneck River, prospered in the nineteenth century. Beginning in 1800, a succession of mills sprang up for the manufacture of cotton yarn, wool, and later braided sash cord, warp, and twine. Nooseneck reached the size of a village by the mid-1830s and grew until the 1860s, when post–Civil War changes in industry forced the closing of the mills. The railways then bypassed the area, and those who remained had few choices other than a land-poor agricultural lifestyle crippled by poor soil conditions and lack of mechanization. By the time "The Shunned House" was written, many of the farmsteads had been deserted, and the population of the entire West Greenwich area dropped precipitously.

The source of the area's name is in dispute. According to "Historic and Architectural Resources of West Greenwich, Rhode Island: A Preliminary Report" (1978): "Local lore has it that it originated from the fact that a running noose was used [by the Narragansett Indians] to trap deer here. The theory proposed by [J. R.] Cole in his *History of Washington and Kent Counties* (1889) is that the tract of land designated by the name 'Nooseneck,' as early as 1819, on Benoni Lockwood's *Map of the State of Rhode Island*, is a narrow neck lying between two streams which unite and become a tributary to the Pawtuxet River."

24. This was a well-known precaution relating to vampires, recorded by the *Encyclopaedia Britannica* (9th ed.). HPL likely found the 1892 Exeter incident in Charles M. Skinner's *Myths and Legends of Our Own Land,* 4th ed. (New York and Philadelphia: J. B. Lippincott & Co., 1896). Skinner wrote, "As late

Looking east from College Hill into East Providence, 1990.
Photograph courtesy of Will Hart

it sounds absurd to hear that a woman educated only in the rudiments of French often shouted for hours in a coarse and idiomatic form of that language, or that the same person, alone and guarded, complained wildly of a staring thing which bit and chewed at her. In 1772 the servant Zenas died, and when Mrs. Harris heard of it she laughed with a shocking delight utterly foreign to her. The next year she herself died, and was laid to rest in the North Burial Ground beside her husband.

Upon the outbreak of trouble with Great Britain in 1775, William Harris, despite his scant sixteen years and feeble constitution, managed to enlist in the Army of Observation under General Greene;[26] and from that time on enjoyed a steady rise in health and prestige. In 1780, as a Captain in Rhode Island forces in New Jersey under Colonel Angell,[27] he met and married Phebe Hetfield of Elizabethtown,[28] whom he brought to Providence upon his honourable discharge in the following year.

The young soldier's return was not a thing of unmitigated happiness. The house, it is true, was still in good condition; and the street had been widened and changed in name from Back

Street to Benefit Street. But Mercy Dexter's once robust frame had undergone a sad and curious decay, so that she was now a stooped and pathetic figure with hollow voice and disconcerting pallor—qualities shared to a singular degree by the one remaining servant Maria. In the autumn of 1782 Phebe Harris gave birth to a still-born daughter, and on the fifteenth of the next May Mercy Dexter took leave of a useful, austere, and virtuous life.

William Harris, at last thoroughly convinced of the radically unhealthful nature of his abode, now took steps toward quitting it and closing it for ever. Securing temporary quarters for himself and his wife at the newly opened Golden Ball Inn, he arranged for the building of a new and finer house in Westminster Street, in the growing part of the town across the Great Bridge.[29] There, in 1785, his son Dutee was born; and there the family dwelt till the encroachments of commerce drove them back across the river and over the hill to Angell Street,[30] in the newer East Side residence district, where the late Archer Harris built his sumptuous but hideous French-roofed mansion

276 Angell Street, Providence, 2014, identified by Philip A. Shreffler in his *The H. P. Lovecraft Companion* as the "sumptuous but hideous French-roofed mansion."

Photograph courtesy of Donovan K. Loucks

as 1892 the ceremony of heart-burning was performed at Exeter, Rhode Island, to save the family of a dead woman that was threatened with the same disease that removed her, namely, consumption" (vol. 1, 76). George R. Stetson, in "The Animistic Vampire in New England," echoed this: "In New England the vampire superstition is unknown by its proper name. It is there believed that consumption is not a physical but a spiritual disease, obsession, or visitation; that as long of the body of a dead consumptive relative has blood in its heart, it is proof that an occult influence steals from it for death and is at work draining the blood of living into the heart of the dead and causing its rapid decline" (xx). Bram Stoker also used New England lore in the course of writing *Dracula* (1897). He pasted a February 2, 1896, *New York World* article headlined "Vampires in New England" into his notes for the novel (now at the Rosenbach Museum and Library in Philadelphia). Faye Ringel Hazel explores Lovecraft's use of the New England vampire legends in "Some Strange New England Mortuary Practices: Lovecraft Was Right," *Lovecraft Studies* 29 (Fall 1993), 13–18.

25. According to Kimball, "The thoroughfare now known as College Street first came into existence in 1720, under the name of Rosemary Lane. When, however, the atmosphere became charged with theology, this dainty cognomen was discarded in favor of the more distinctive Presbyterian Lane, and a strait and narrow path to salvation it must have proved, its recorded width being but twenty feet" (194).

26. Nathanael Greene (1742–1786) began his military career as a private in the Rhode Island militia known as the Kentish Guards. Eventually brigadier general in the "army of observation"

raised in response to the July 1775 siege of Boston, by August of the following year he had attained the rank of major general in the Continental army. At the end of the Revolutionary War, he was widely regarded as one of the most able of Washington's officers.

27. Israel Angell (1740–1832) was first commissioned as a major of Rhode Island troops in the Eleventh Continental Infantry. He was promoted to lieutenant colonel of the Second Rhode Island Regiment, then to colonel. He led troops at the Battle of Monmouth, or the Battle of Monmouth Court House, on June 28, 1778, in New Jersey, when American troops attacked the rear of the British columns, which were protected by Cornwallis. It was the war's longest engagement. Though British losses were higher, the battle was inconclusive, with both sides claiming victory—a tactical draw whose chief features on the American side included General Anthony Wayne's lead in the attack; General Charles Lee's retreat and later court-martial; and the role of "Molly Pitcher" (assumed to have been Mary Ludwig Hays McCauley, then twenty-four years old) in providing water to soldiers and later loading and reloading a cannon when her husband, a gunner, was wounded. She later worked as a domestic in the Carlisle State House, eventually receiving a soldier's pension from the Pennsylvania State legislature.

28. Now Elizabeth. (See note 6, above.) The first capital of New Jersey, it was founded in 1664 and named after the wife of Sir George Carteret, one of the two original founders of the colony.

29. Also known as the Weybosset Bridge, this connects Market Square with Westminster Street. Kimball reports that in 1770, "The number of inhabitants is estimated at twelve hundred, 'among whom

in 1876. William and Phebe both succumbed to the yellow fever epidemic of 1797, but Dutee was brought up by his cousin Rathbone Harris, Peleg's son.

Rathbone was a practical man, and rented the Benefit Street house despite William's wish to keep it vacant. He considered it an obligation to his ward to make the most of all the boy's property, nor did he concern himself with the deaths and illnesses which caused so many changes of tenants, or the steadily growing aversion with which the house was generally regarded. It is likely that he felt only vexation when, in 1804, the town council ordered him to fumigate the place with sulphur, tar, and gum camphor on account of the much-discussed deaths of four persons, presumably caused by the then diminishing fever epidemic. They said the place had a febrile smell.

Dutee himself thought little of the house, for he grew up to be a privateersman, and served with distinction on the *Vigilant* under Capt. Cahoone[31] in the War of 1812.[32] He returned unharmed, married in 1814, and became a father on that memorable night of September 23, 1815, when a great gale[33] drove the waters of the bay over half the town, and floated a tall sloop well up Westminster Street so that its masts almost tapped the Harris windows in symbolic affirmation that the new boy, Welcome, was a seaman's son.

View Near Elizabethtown, N. J., oil painting by Régis François Gignoux, 1847.

The Crawford Street Bridge, aka the "Great Bridge," Providence, 1906, removed in the 1990s.

Welcome did not survive his father, but lived to perish gloriously at Fredericksburg in 1862.[34] Neither he nor his son Archer knew of the shunned house as other than a nuisance almost impossible to rent—perhaps on account of the mustiness and sickly odour of unkempt old age. Indeed, it never was rented after a series of deaths culminating in 1861, which the excitement of the war tended to throw into obscurity. Carrington Harris, last of the male line, knew it only as a deserted and somewhat

The storm of 1815, from *The Providence Plantations for 250 Years* (1886).

are at least one Hundred Freemen,—altho it is but a few Years since building Houses took Place there.' The people are described as 'Tradesmen chiefly . . . [who] by Diligence and Industry . . . surmounted many Difficulties to effect a Settlement'" (289).

30. Named after Thomas Angell, an associate of Roger Williams; Lovecraft was born at 194 Angell Street (later renumbered 454).

31. John Cahoone was in fact the master of the *Vigilant*, a 60-foot cutter, and remained in command until 1830. During the War of 1812 (see note 32), the *Vigilant* attacked the British privateer *Dart*, which had preyed on American ships. The attack occurred as the *Dart* was approaching Block Island, Rhode Island.

32. A war of the fledgling American nation against the British Empire, including its North American colonies, declared in an effort to stop trade restrictions, the impressment of American citizens by the Royal Navy, and British support of Native Americans. It was resolved by the Treaty of Ghent in 1814, and although the Americans obtained few rights, with the suppression of Napoleonic aggression, the government had no practical issues remaining.

33. On September 23, 1815, a major hurricane struck New England, sending massive quantities of water and not a few ships into Providence. Damage estimates were as high as one-quarter of the entire value of the city. William R. Staples, in *Annals of the Town of Providence, from Its First Settlement, to the Organization of the City Government, in June, 1832* (Providence: Knowles & Vose, 1843), reports: "A sloop of about sixty tons floated across Weybosset-street and lodged in Pleasant-

street, her mast standing above and she by the side of a three story brick house" (379–80).

34. Nearly two hundred thousand men fought in the Battle of Fredericksburg (December 11–15, 1862), more than in any previous Civil War battle. Though Union forces outnumbered Confederate troops (under the command of Robert E. Lee) by more than 50 percent, the Southern defenders turned back the Northerners' assault, albeit with heavy casualties. Union morale sank after the battle, and the Confederates, who had been demoralized by the failure of Lee's Antietam invasion three months earlier, were reinvigorated.

Fredericksburg, Virginia, 1863.

picturesque centre of legend until I told him my experience. He had meant to tear it down and build an apartment house on the site, but after my account decided to let it stand, install plumbing, and rent it. Nor has he yet had any difficulty in obtaining tenants. The horror has gone.

III.

IT MAY WELL be imagined how powerfully I was affected by the annals of the Harrises. In this continuous record there seemed to me to brood a persistent evil beyond anything in Nature as I had known it; an evil clearly connected with the house and not with the family. This impression was confirmed by my uncle's less systematic array of miscellaneous data—legends transcribed from servant gossip, cuttings from the papers, copies of death-certificates by fellow-physicians, and the like. All of this material I cannot hope to give, for my uncle was a tireless antiquarian and very deeply interested in the shunned house; but I may refer to several dominant points which earn notice by their recurrence through many reports from diverse sources. For example, the servant gossip was practically unanimous in attributing to the fungous and malodorous *cellar* of the house a vast supremacy in evil influence. There had been servants—Ann White especially—who would not use the cellar kitchen, and at least three well-defined legends bore upon the queer quasi-human or diabolic outlines assumed by tree-roots and patches of mould in that region. These latter narratives interested me profoundly, on account of what I had seen in my boyhood, but I felt that most of the significance had in each case been largely obscured by additions from the common stock of local ghost lore.

Ann White, with her Exeter superstition, had promulgated the most extravagant and at the same time most consistent tale; alleging that there must lie buried beneath the house one of those vampires—the dead who retain their bodily form and live on the blood or breath of the living—whose hideous legions send their preying shapes or spirits abroad by night. To destroy a vampire one must, the grandmothers say, exhume it and burn its heart, or at least drive a stake through that organ; and Ann's dogged insistence on a search under the cellar had been prominent in bringing about her discharge.

Her tales, however, commanded a wide audience, and were the more readily accepted because the house indeed stood on land once used for burial purposes. To me their interest depended less on this circumstance than on the peculiarly appropriate way in which they dovetailed with certain other things—the complaint of the departing servant Preserved Smith, who had preceded Ann and never heard of her, that something "sucked his breath" at night; the death-certificates of fever victims of 1804, issued by Dr. Chad Hopkins, and shewing the four deceased persons all unaccountably lacking in blood; and the obscure passages of poor Rhoby Harris's ravings, where she complained of the sharp teeth of a glassy-eyed, half-visible presence.

Free from unwarranted superstition though I am, these things produced in me an odd sensation, which was intensified by a pair of widely separated newspaper cuttings relating to deaths in the shunned house—one from the *Providence Gazette and Country-Journal*[35] of April 12, 1815, and the other from the *Daily Transcript and Chronicle*[36] of October 27, 1845—each of which detailed an appallingly grisly circumstance whose duplication was remarkable. It seems that in both instances the dying person, in 1815 a gentle old lady named Stafford and in 1845 a school-teacher of middle age named Eleazar Durfee, became transfigured in a horrible way; glaring glassily and attempting to bite the throat of the attending physician. Even more puzzling, though, was the final case which put an end to the renting of the house—a series of anaemia deaths preceded by progressive madnesses wherein the patient would craftily attempt the lives of his relatives by incisions in the neck or wrist.

This was in 1860 and 1861, when my uncle had just begun his medical practice; and before leaving for the front he heard much of it from his elder professional colleagues. The really inexplicable thing was the way in which the victims—ignorant people, for the ill-smelling and widely shunned house could now be rented to no others—would babble maledictions in French, a language they could not possibly have studied to any extent. It made one think of poor Rhoby Harris nearly a century before, and so moved my uncle that he commenced collecting historical data on the house

35. First published in 1762 by William Goddard. In 1825, it was consolidated with the *Rhode Island American*.

36. The *Daily Transcript and Chronicle* (established in 1844) changed its name to the *Daily Transcript* in 1847 and ceased publication in 1855.

after listening, some time subsequent to his return from the war, to the first-hand account of Drs. Chase and Whitmarsh. Indeed, I could see that my uncle had thought deeply on the subject, and that he was glad of my own interest—an open-minded and sympathetic interest which enabled him to discuss with me matters at which others would merely have laughed. His fancy had not gone so far as mine, but he felt that the place was rare in its imaginative potentialities, and worthy of note as an inspiration in the field of the grotesque and macabre.

For my part, I was disposed to take the whole subject with profound seriousness, and began at once not only to review the evidence, but to accumulate as much more as I could. I talked with the elderly Archer Harris, then owner of the house, many times before his death in 1916; and obtained from him and his still surviving maiden sister Alice an authentic corroboration of all the family data my uncle had collected. When, however, I asked them what connexion with France or its language the house could have, they confessed themselves as frankly baffled and ignorant as I. Archer knew nothing, and all that Miss Harris could say was that an old allusion her grandfather, Dutee Harris, had heard of might have shed a little light. The old seaman, who had survived his son Welcome's death in battle by two years, had not himself known the legend; but recalled that his earliest nurse, the ancient Maria Robbins, seemed darkly aware of something that might have lent a weird significance to the French ravings of Rhoby Harris, which she had so often heard during the last days of that hapless woman. Maria had been at the shunned house from 1769 till the removal of the family in 1783, and had seen Mercy Dexter die. Once she hinted to the child Dutee of a somewhat peculiar circumstance in Mercy's last moments, but he had soon forgotten all about it save that it was something peculiar. The granddaughter, moreover, recalled even this much with difficulty. She and her brother were not so much interested in the house as was Archer's son Carrington, the present owner, with whom I talked after my experience.

Having exhausted the Harris family of all the information it could furnish, I turned my attention to early town records and deeds with a zeal more penetrating than that which my uncle had occasionally shewn in the same work. What I wished was a comprehensive history of the site from its very settlement in 1636—or even before, if any Narragansett Indian[37] legend could be unearthed to supply the data. I found, at the start, that the land had been part of the long strip of home lot granted originally to John Throckmorton;[38] one of many similar strips beginning at the Town Street beside the river and extending up over the hill to a line roughly corresponding with the modern Hope Street. The Throckmorton lot had later, of course, been much subdivided; and I became very assiduous in tracing that section through which Back or Benefit Street was later run. It had, a rumour indeed said, been the Throckmorton graveyard; but as I examined the records more carefully, I found that the graves had all been transferred at an early date to the North Burial Ground on the Pawtucket West Road.

Then suddenly I came—by a rare piece of chance, since it was not in the main body of records and might easily have been missed—upon something which aroused my keenest eagerness, fitting in as it did with several of the queerest phases of the affair. It was the record of a lease, in 1697, of a small tract of ground to an Etienne Roulet and wife. At last the French element had appeared—that, and another deeper element of horror which the name conjured up from the darkest recesses of my weird and heterogeneous reading—and I feverishly studied the platting of

37. Their inhabitancy of Rhode Island probably preceded that of Roger Williams and the colonists by thirty thousand years.

38. A compatriot of Roger Williams and one of the original Providence settlers in 1636.

The Lippitt Mansion on Hope Street, Providence, from *The Providence Plantations for 250 Years* (1886), by Welcome Arnold Greene.

39. See *The Case of Charles Dexter Ward*, in the previous volume, 171–309, note 11. Founded in 1822, its website is http://www.rihs.org.

Former Cabinet of the Rhode Island Historical Society, 68 Waterman Street, Providence, 2014.

Photograph courtesy of Donovan K. Loucks

40. See *The Case of Charles Dexter Ward*, in the previous volume, pp. 171–309, note 13.

Shepley Library, Providence, ca. 1920

41. About eighteen miles south-southwest of Providence, East Greenwich has a

the locality as it had been before the cutting through and partial straightening of Back Street between 1747 and 1758. I found what I had half expected, that where the shunned house now stood the Roulets had laid out their graveyard behind a one-story and attic cottage, and that no record of any transfer of graves existed. The document, indeed, ended in much confusion; and I was forced to ransack both the Rhode Island Historical Society[39] and Shepley Library[40] before I could find a local door which the name Etienne Roulet would unlock. In the end I did find something; something of such vague but monstrous import that I set about at once to examine the cellar of the shunned house itself with a new and excited minuteness.

The Roulets, it seemed, had come in 1696 from East Greenwich,[41] down the west shore of Narragansett Bay. They were Huguenots from Caude,[42] and had encountered much opposition before the Providence selectmen allowed them to settle in the town. Unpopularity had dogged them in East Greenwich, whither they had come in 1686, after the revocation of the Edict of Nantes, and rumour said that the cause of dislike extended beyond mere racial and national prejudice, or the land disputes which involved other French settlers with the English in rivalries which not even Governor Andros[43] could quell. But their ardent Protestantism—too ardent, some whispered—and their evident distress when virtually driven from the village down the bay, had moved the sympathy of the town fathers. Here the strangers had been granted a haven; and the swarthy Etienne Roulet, less apt at agriculture than at reading queer books and drawing queer diagrams, was given a clerical post in the warehouse at Pardon Tillinghast's wharf,[44] far south in Town Street. There had, however, been a riot of some sort later on—perhaps forty years later, after old Roulet's death—and no one seemed to hear of the family after that.

For a century and more, it appeared, the Roulets had been well remembered and frequently discussed as vivid incidents in the quiet life of a New England seaport. Etienne's son Paul, a surly fellow whose erratic conduct had probably provoked the riot which wiped out the family, was particularly a source of speculation; and though Providence never shared the witchcraft panics of her Puritan neighbours, it was freely intimated by old wives that

Narragansett Bay, map by Charles Blaskowitz (1777).

his prayers were neither uttered at the proper time nor directed toward the proper object. All this had undoubtedly formed the basis of the legend known by old Maria Robbins. What relation it had to the French ravings of Rhoby Harris and other inhabitants of the shunned house, imagination or future discovery alone could determine. I wondered how many of those who had known the legends realised that additional link with the terrible which my wider reading had given me; that ominous item in the annals of morbid horror which tells of the creature *Jacques Roulet, of Caude*, who in 1598 was condemned to death as a daemoniac but afterward saved from the stake by the Paris parliament and shut in a madhouse. He had been found covered with blood and shreds of flesh in a wood, shortly after the killing and rending of a boy by a pair of wolves.[45] One wolf was seen to lope away unhurt. Surely a pretty hearthside tale, with a queer significance as to name and place; but I decided that the Providence gossips could

population today of about thirteen thousand and is the wealthiest municipality in Rhode Island. For neighboring West Greenwich, see note 23, above.

42. There is no contemporary village in France named Caude, though there is a Caudecoste and a Gaude. Sabine Baring-Gould traces a Jean Roulet (see note 45, below) to Caude, but he cites no source for the village name.

The Huguenots were the French Protestants of the sixteenth century; with the Edict of Nantes, issued in 1598 by King Henry IV, they achieved relative autonomy. However, the wars of religion began again in the seventeenth century, and the Huguenots were increasingly persecuted. In 1685, following the *dragonnades* (a policy of forced conversion) put in place four years earlier, the Edict of Nantes was revoked by Louis XIV and replaced by the entirely unfavorable Edict of Fontainebleau, which amounted to utter religious intolerance, and by the early eighteenth century, hundreds of thousands of Huguenots had fled France.

43. Sir Edmund Andros (1637–1714) was the royal governor of the Dominion of New England from 1686 to 1689, when he was captured by rebels and effectively deposed.

44. Kimball notes: "In the records of 1680 there appears another unmistakable symptom of progress [of seaport life in Providence]. Pardon Tillinghast asked for, and obtained, 'a little Spott of Land against [that is, opposite] his dwelling place (above high-water mark) of Twenty Foott Square, for building himselfe A store house with the prieveladge of A whorfe Alsoe'" (128–29).

45. See Fiske's account of Roulet in *Myths and Myth-Makers*, which names Sabine Baring-Gould's *Book of Were-*

wolves, *Being an Account of a Terrible Superstition* (1865) as its source. Fiske repeats the "Caude" error of Baring-Gould, but Roulet, Fiske concludes, was a victim of atavism rather than a werewolf: "Whether there were any wolves in the case, except what the excited imaginations of the men may have conjured up, I will not presume to determine; but it is certain that Roulet supposed himself to be a wolf, and killed and ate several persons under the influence of the delusion" (115).

46. The description is quite similar to that found in Skinner's *Myths and Legends of Our Own Land*:

In a cellar in Green Street, Schenectady, there appeared, some years ago, the silhouette of a human form, painted on the floor in mould. It was swept and scrubbed away, but presently it was there again, and month by month, after each removal, it returned: a mass of fluffy mould, always in the shape of a recumbent man. When it was found that the house stood on the site of the old Dutch burial ground, the gossips fitted this and that together and concluded that the mould was planted by a spirit whose mortal part was put to rest a century and more ago, on the spot covered by the house, and that the spirit took this way of apprising people that they were trespassing on its grave ... But a darker meaning was that it was the outline of a vampire that vainly strove to leave its grave, and could not because a virtuous spell had been worked about the place. (See note 24, above)

not have generally known of it. Had they known, the coincidence of names would have brought some drastic and frightened action—indeed, might not its limited whispering have precipitated the final riot which erased the Roulets from the town?

I now visited the accursed place with increased frequency; studying the unwholesome vegetation of the garden, examining all the walls of the building, and poring over every inch of the earthen cellar floor. Finally, with Carrington Harris's permission, I fitted a key to the disused door opening from the cellar directly upon Benefit Street, preferring to have a more immediate access to the outside world than the dark stairs, ground floor hall, and front door could give. There, where morbidity lurked most thickly, I searched and poked during long afternoons when the sunlight filtered in through the cobwebbed above-ground windows, and a sense of security glowed from the unlocked door which placed me only a few feet from the placid sidewalk outside. Nothing new rewarded my efforts—only the same depressing mustiness and faint suggestions of noxious odours and nitrous outlines on the floor—and I fancy that many pedestrians must have watched me curiously through the broken panes.

At length, upon a suggestion of my uncle's, I decided to try the spot nocturnally; and one stormy midnight ran the beams of an electric torch over the mouldy floor with its uncanny shapes and distorted, half-phosphorescent fungi. The place had dispirited me curiously that evening, and I was almost prepared when I saw—or thought I saw—amidst the whitish deposits a particularly sharp definition of the "huddled form" I had suspected from boyhood. Its clearness was astonishing and unprecedented—and as I watched I seemed to see again the thin, yellowish, shimmering exhalation which had startled me on that rainy afternoon so many years before.

Above the anthropomorphic patch of mould by the fireplace it rose; a subtle, sickish, almost luminous vapour which as it hung trembling in the dampness seemed to develop vague and shocking suggestions of form, gradually trailing off into nebulous decay and passing up into the blackness of the great chimney with a foetor in its wake.[46] It was truly horrible, and the more so to me because of what I knew of the spot. Refusing to flee, I watched it fade—and as I watched I felt that it was in turn watching me greedily with eyes more imaginable than visible. When I told my uncle about it he was greatly aroused; and after a tense hour of reflection, arrived at a definite and drastic decision. Weighing in his mind the importance of the matter, and the significance of our relation to it, he insisted that we both test—and if possible destroy—the horror of the house by a joint night or nights of aggressive vigil in that musty and fungus-cursed cellar.

IV.

ON WEDNESDAY, June 25, 1919, after a proper notification of Carrington Harris which did not include surmises as to what we expected to find, my uncle and I conveyed to the shunned house two camp chairs and a folding camp cot, together with some scientific mechanism of greater weight and intricacy. These we placed in the cellar during the day, screening the windows with paper and planning to return in the evening for our first vigil. We had locked the door from the cellar to the ground floor; and having a key to the outside cellar door, we were prepared to leave our expensive and delicate apparatus—which we had obtained secretly and at great cost—as many days as our vigils might need to be protracted. It was our design to sit up together till very late, and then watch singly till dawn in two-hour stretches, myself first and then my companion; the inactive member resting on the cot.

The natural leadership with which my uncle procured the instruments from the laboratories of Brown University[47] and the Cranston Street Armoury,[48] and instinctively assumed direction of our venture, was a marvellous commentary on the potential vitality and resilience of a man of eighty-one. Elihu Whipple had lived according to the hygienic laws he had preached as a physician, and but for what happened later would be here in full vigour today. Only two persons suspect what did happen—Carrington Harris and myself. I had to tell Harris because he owned the house and deserved to know what had gone out of it. Then too, we had spoken to him in advance of our quest; and I felt after my uncle's going that he would understand and assist me in some vitally necessary public explanations. He turned very pale,

47. Founded in 1764 as The College in the English Colony of Rhode Island and Providence Plantations, Brown University was the first college to accept students of varied religious affiliations.

Which Brown laboratories contributed equipment is unclear in light of the eclectic nature of the instruments obtained. The School of Engineering was founded in 1847, and while it is tempting to suspect that the Marine Biological Laboratory, founded in 1888, was an important source, its partnership with Brown University spanned only the period from 2003 to 2013 (before that time it was wholly independent, and it is now affiliated with the University of Chicago).

48. Built in 1907, it was the home of the Rhode Island National Guard until 1996. By 1981, its condition had deteriorated so badly that it could no longer be used for public functions. Its final tenant was the State of Rhode Island Fire Marshal and Bomb Squad. In March 2016, state

Cranston Street Armoury,
Providence, 2017.
Photograph courtesy of Donovan K. Loucks

officials announced three equally unpalatable options, saying that it would take $100 million to rehabilitate the historic structure, $5.5 million to raze it, and $1.2 to make it safe for continued passive use (as storage).

Brown University campus.
Shutterstock.com

but agreed to help me, and decided that it would now be safe to rent the house.

To declare that we were not nervous on that rainy night of watching would be an exaggeration both gross and ridiculous. We were not, as I have said, in any sense childishly superstitious, but scientific study and reflection had taught us that the known universe of three dimensions embraces the merest fraction of the whole cosmos of substance and energy. In this case an overwhelming preponderance of evidence from numerous authentic sources pointed to the tenacious existence of certain forces of great power and, so far as the human point of view is concerned, exceptional malignancy. To say that we actually believed in vampires or werewolves would be a carelessly inclusive statement. Rather must it be said that we were not prepared to deny the possibility of certain unfamiliar and unclassified modifications of vital force and attenuated matter; existing very infrequently in three-dimensional space because of its more intimate connexion with other spatial units, yet close enough to the boundary of our own to furnish us occasional manifestations which we, for lack of a proper vantage-point, may never hope to understand.

In short, it seemed to my uncle and me that an incontrovertible array of facts pointed to some lingering influence in the shunned house; traceable to one or another of the ill-favoured French settlers of two centuries before, and still operative through rare and unknown laws of atomic and electronic motion.[49] That the family of Roulet had possessed an abnormal affinity for outer circles of entity—dark spheres which for normal folk hold only repulsion and terror—their recorded history seemed to prove. Had not, then, the riots of those bygone seventeen-thirties set moving certain kinetic patterns in the morbid brain of one or more of them—notably the sinister Paul Roulet—which obscurely survived the bodies murdered and buried by the mob, and continued to function in some multiple-dimensioned space along the original lines of force determined by a frantic hatred of the encroaching community?

Such a thing was surely not a physical or biochemical impossibility in the light of a newer science which includes the theories of relativity and intra-atomic action. One might easily imagine an alien nucleus of substance or energy, formless or otherwise, kept alive by imperceptible or immaterial subtractions from the life-force or bodily tissues and fluids of other and more palpably living things into which it penetrates and with whose fabric it sometimes completely merges itself. It might be actively hostile, or it might be dictated merely by blind motives of self-preservation. In any case such a monster must of necessity be in our scheme of things an anomaly and an intruder, whose extirpation forms a primary duty with every man not an enemy to the world's life, health, and sanity.

What baffled us was our utter ignorance of the aspect in which we might encounter the thing. No sane person had even seen it, and few had ever felt it definitely. It might be pure energy—a form ethereal and outside the realm of substance—or it might be partly material; some unknown and equivocal mass of plasticity, capable of changing at will to nebulous approximations of the solid, liquid, gaseous, or tenuously unparticled states. The anthropomorphic patch of mould on the floor, the form of the yellowish vapour, and the curvature of the tree-roots in some of the old tales, all argued at least a remote and reminiscent connexion with the human shape; but how representative or perma-

49. That is, the narrator suggests, with further study, the existence of vampires and werewolves would be explained by the laws of physics. Einstein's general theory of relativity was completed in 1915, nine years before Lovecraft wrote the story.

50. Developed in 1869–75 by British physicist William Crookes and others, the tubes were generally used in investigations into the properties of cathode rays (streams of electrons). It was discovered that the tubes also emitted X-rays. The next generation, primarily used for the generation of X-rays, were also styled "Crookes tubes." Here, apparently it was hoped that a stream of X-rays might prove to be a weapon against whatever occupied the cellar. It is ironic that HPL, who despised the pulp magazine science fiction of the day and railed against "Armageddons with ray-guns and spaceships" (in his essay "Some Notes on Interplanetary Fiction," *Californian* 3, no. 3 [Winter 1935], 39–42), should arm the duo here with a weapon that is essentially a large stationary ray-gun! For a considered view of why HPL may have thought that X-rays could harm a vampire, see T. R. Livesey's "Lovecraft and the Ray-Gun," *Lovecraft Annual* (2009), 3–9.

51. Flamethrowers date back to the Greeks of the first century CE and were used by both sides in the Great War. The basic operation has remained the same: an ignited flammable fluid or gas flame is projected. Why did the narrator not use the flamethrower, wonders T. R. Livesey (see note 50, above).

Flamethrowers in the Great War.

52. The narrator undoubtedly felt the need to point this out because daylight

nent that similarity might be, none could say with any kind of certainty.

We had devised two weapons to fight it; a large and specially fitted Crookes tube[50] operated by powerful storage batteries and provided with peculiar screens and reflectors, in case it proved intangible and opposable only by vigorously destructive ether radiations, and a pair of military flame-throwers of the sort used in the world-war,[51] in case it proved partly material and susceptible of mechanical destruction—for like the superstitious Exeter rustics, we were prepared to burn the thing's heart out if heart existed to burn. All this aggressive mechanism we set in the cellar in positions carefully arranged with reference to the cot and chairs, and to the spot before the fireplace where the mould had taken strange shapes. That suggestive patch, by the way, was only faintly visible when we placed our furniture and instruments, and when we returned that evening for the actual vigil. For a moment I half doubted that I had ever seen it in the more definitely limned form—but then I thought of the legends.

Our cellar vigil began at 10 p.m., daylight saving time,[52] and as it continued we found no promise of pertinent developments. A weak, filtered glow from the rain-harassed street-lamps outside, and a feeble phosphorescence from the detestable fungi within, shewed the dripping stone of the walls, from which all traces of whitewash had vanished; the dank, foetid, and mildew-tainted hard earth floor with its obscene fungi; the rotting remains of what had been stools, chairs, and tables, and other more shapeless furniture; the heavy planks and massive beams of the ground floor overhead; the decrepit plank door leading to bins and chambers beneath other parts of the house; the crumbling stone staircase with ruined wooden hand-rail; and the crude and cavernous fireplace of blackened brick where rusted iron fragments revealed the past presence of hooks, andirons, spit, crane, and a door to the Dutch oven—these things, and our austere cot and camp chairs, and the heavy and intricate destructive machinery we had brought.

We had, as in my own former explorations, left the door to the street unlocked; so that a direct and practical path of escape might lie open in case of manifestations beyond our power to deal with. It was our idea that our continued nocturnal presence would call forth whatever malign entity lurked there; and that being prepared, we could dispose of the thing with one or the other of our provided means as soon as we had recognised and observed it sufficiently. How long it might require to evoke and extinguish the thing, we had no notion. It occurred to us, too, that our venture was far from safe; for in what strength the thing might appear no one could tell. But we deemed the game worth the hazard, and embarked on it alone and unhesitatingly; conscious that the seeking of outside aid would only expose us to ridicule and perhaps defeat our entire purpose. Such was our frame of mind as we talked—far into the night, till my uncle's growing drowsiness made me remind him to lie down for his two-hour sleep.

Something like fear chilled me as I sat there in the small hours alone—I say alone, for one who sits by a sleeper is indeed alone; perhaps more alone than he can realise. My uncle breathed heavily, his deep inhalations and exhalations accompanied by the rain outside, and punctuated by another nerve-racking sound of distant dripping water within—for the house was repulsively damp even in dry weather, and in this storm positively swamp-like. I studied the loose, antique masonry of the walls in the fungus-light and the feeble rays which stole in from the street through the screened windows; and once, when the noisome atmosphere of the place seemed about to sicken me, I opened the door and looked up and down the street, feasting my eyes on familiar sights and my nostrils on the wholesome air. Still nothing occurred to reward my watching; and I yawned repeatedly, fatigue getting the better of apprehension.

Then the stirring of my uncle in his sleep attracted my notice. He had turned restlessly on the cot several times during the latter half of the first hour, but now he was breathing with unusual irregularity, occasionally heaving a sigh which held more than a few of the qualities of a choking moan. I turned my electric flashlight on him and found his face averted, so rising and crossing to the other side of the cot, I again flashed the light to see if he seemed in any pain. What I saw unnerved me most surprisingly, considering its relative triviality. It must have been merely the association of any odd circumstance with the sinister nature of our location and mission, for surely the circumstance was not in

saving time (DST) was not yet a universal standard. It was only officially adopted by the U.S. government in 1918, as part of the war effort, and it was repealed in 1919.

DST was surprisingly controversial. The repeal was enacted by Congress as part of an agricultural bill, but in July 1919, President Woodrow Wilson, opposing the repeal, refused to sign the legislation. A coalition of farmers and others lobbied Congress to override the repeal, and the repeal bill was again vetoed by President Wilson. Finally, on August 19, the House voted to override the second veto, and on August 20 the Senate concurred. Therefore, at the time of the events of "The Shunned House," the use of DST was a federal mandate for only another month.

After repeal, various states and cities (including Providence, on April 14, 1920) enacted their own DST laws, but opposition in the agricultural parts of the Northeast was fierce. National DST was not reinstituted until "war time" was put in place in 1942.

53. A French magazine covering literary, political, and cultural affairs continuously since 1829.

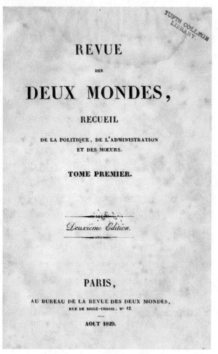

The *Revue des Deux Mondes.*

itself frightful or unnatural. It was merely that my uncle's facial expression, disturbed no doubt by the strange dreams which our situation prompted, betrayed considerable agitation, and seemed not at all characteristic of him. His habitual expression was one of kindly and well-bred calm, whereas now a variety of emotions seemed struggling within him. I think, on the whole, that it was this *variety* which chiefly disturbed me. My uncle, as he gasped and tossed in increasing perturbation and with eyes that had now started open, seemed not one but many men, and suggested a curious quality of alienage from himself.

All at once he commenced to mutter, and I did not like the look of his mouth and teeth as he spoke. The words were at first indistinguishable, and then—with a tremendous start—I recognised something about them which filled me with icy fear till I recalled the breadth of my uncle's education and the interminable translations he had made from anthropological and antiquarian articles in the *Revue des Deux Mondes.*[53] For the venerable Elihu Whipple was muttering *in French,* and the few phrases I could distinguish seemed connected with the darkest myths he had ever adapted from the famous Paris magazine.

Suddenly a perspiration broke out on the sleeper's forehead, and he leaped abruptly up, half awake. The jumble of French changed to a cry in English, and the hoarse voice shouted excitedly, "My breath, my breath!" Then the awakening became complete, and with a subsidence of facial expression to the normal state my uncle seized my hand and began to relate a dream whose nucleus of significance I could only surmise with a kind of awe.

He had, he said, floated off from a very ordinary series of dream-pictures into a scene whose strangeness was related to nothing he had ever read. It was of this world, and yet not of it—a shadowy geometrical confusion in which could be seen elements of familiar things in most unfamiliar and perturbing combinations. There was a suggestion of queerly disordered pictures superimposed one upon another; an arrangement in which the essentials of time as well as of space seemed dissolved and mixed in the most illogical fashion. In this kaleidoscopic vortex of phantasmal images were occasional snapshots, if one might use the term, of singular clearness but unaccountable heterogeneity.

Once my uncle thought he lay in a carelessly dug open pit,

with a crowd of angry faces framed by straggling locks and three-cornered hats frowning down on him. Again he seemed to be in the interior of a house—an old house, apparently—but the details and inhabitants were constantly changing, and he could never be certain of the faces or the furniture, or even of the room itself, since doors and windows seemed in just as great a state of flux as the more presumably mobile objects. It was queer—damnably queer—and my uncle spoke almost sheepishly, as if half expecting not to be believed, when he declared that of the strange faces many had unmistakably borne the features of the Harris family. And all the while there was a personal sensation of choking, as if some pervasive presence had spread itself through his body and sought to possess itself of his vital processes. I shuddered at the thought of those vital processes, worn as they were by eighty-one years of continuous functioning, in conflict with unknown forces of which the youngest and strongest system might well be afraid; but in another moment reflected that dreams are only dreams, and that these uncomfortable visions could be, at most, no more than my uncle's reaction to the investigations and expectations which had lately filled our minds to the exclusion of all else.

Conversation, also, soon tended to dispel my sense of strangeness; and in time I yielded to my yawns and took my turn at slumber. My uncle seemed now very wakeful, and welcomed his period of watching even though the nightmare had aroused him far ahead of his allotted two hours. Sleep seized me quickly, and I was at once haunted with dreams of the most disturbing kind. I felt, in my visions, a cosmic and abysmal loneness; with hostility surging from all sides upon some prison where I lay confined. I seemed bound and gagged, and taunted by the echoing yells of distant multitudes who thirsted for my blood. My uncle's face came to me with less pleasant associations than in waking hours, and I recall many futile struggles and attempts to scream. It was not a pleasant sleep, and for a second I was not sorry for the echoing shriek which clove through the barriers of dream and flung me to a sharp and startled awakeness in which every actual object before my eyes stood out with more than natural clearness and reality.

54. Wrinkled or corrugated.

V.

I HAD BEEN lying with my face away from my uncle's chair, so that in this sudden flash of awakening I saw only the door to the street, the more northerly window, and the wall and floor and ceiling toward the north of the room, all photographed with morbid vividness on my brain in a light brighter than the glow of the fungi or the rays from the street outside. It was not a strong or even a fairly strong light; certainly not nearly strong enough to read an average book by. But it cast a shadow of myself and the cot on the floor, and had a yellowish, penetrating force that hinted at things more potent than luminosity. This I perceived with unhealthy sharpness despite the fact that two of my other senses were violently assailed. For on my ears rang the reverberations of that shocking scream, while my nostrils revolted at the stench which filled the place. My mind, as alert as my senses, recognised the gravely unusual; and almost automatically I leaped up and turned about to grasp the destructive instruments which we had left trained on the mouldy spot before the fireplace. As I turned, I dreaded what I was to see; for the scream had been in my uncle's voice, and I knew not against what menace I should have to defend him and myself.

Yet after all, the sight was worse than I had dreaded. There are horrors beyond horrors, and this was one of those nuclei of all dreamable hideousness which the cosmos saves to blast an accursed and unhappy few. Out of the fungus-ridden earth steamed up a vaporous corpse-light, yellow and diseased, which bubbled and lapped to a gigantic height in vague outlines half human and half monstrous, through which I could see the chimney and fireplace beyond. It was all eyes—wolfish and mocking—and the rugose[54] insect-like head dissolved at the top to a thin stream of mist which curled putridly about and finally vanished up the chimney. I say that I saw this thing, but it is only in conscious retrospection that I ever definitely traced its damnable approach to form. At the time it was to me only a seething, dimly phosphorescent cloud of fungous loathsomeness, enveloping and dissolving to an abhorrent plasticity the one object to which all my attention was focussed. That object was my uncle—the venerable Elihu Whipple—who with blackening and decaying features leered and gibbered at me, and reached out dripping claws to rend me in the fury which this horror had brought.

It was a sense of routine which kept me from going mad. I had drilled myself in preparation for the crucial moment, and blind training saved me. Recognising the bubbling evil as no substance reachable by matter or material chemistry, and therefore ignoring the flame-thrower which loomed on my left, I threw on the current of the Crookes tube apparatus, and focussed toward that scene of immortal blasphemousness the strongest ether radiations which man's art can arouse from the spaces and fluids of Nature. There was a bluish haze and a frenzied sputtering, and the yellowish phosphorescence grew dimmer to my eyes. But I saw the dimness was only that of contrast, and that the waves from the machine had no effect whatever.

Then, in the midst of that daemoniac spectacle, I saw a fresh horror which brought cries to my lips and sent me fumbling and staggering toward that unlocked door to the quiet street, careless of what abnormal terrors I loosed upon the world, or what thoughts or judgments of men I brought down upon my head. In that dim blend of blue and yellow the form of my uncle had commenced a nauseous liquefaction whose essence eludes all description, and in which there played across his vanishing face such changes of identity as only madness can conceive. He was at once a devil and a multitude, a charnel-house and a pageant. Lit by the mixed and uncertain beams, that gelatinous face assumed a dozen—a score—a hundred—aspects; grinning, as it sank to the ground on a body that melted like tallow, in the caricatured likeness of legions strange and yet not strange.

I saw the features of the Harris line, masculine and feminine, adult and infantile, and other features old and young, coarse and refined, familiar and unfamiliar. For a second there flashed a degraded counterfeit of a miniature of poor mad Rhoby Harris that I had seen in the School of Design Museum,[55] and another time I thought I caught the raw-boned image of Mercy Dexter as I recalled her from a painting in Carrington Harris's house. It was frightful beyond conception; toward the last, when a curious blend of servant and baby visages flickered close to the fungous floor where a pool of greenish grease was spreading, it seemed as though the shifting features fought against themselves, and

55. See "The Call of Cthulhu," in the previous volume, pp. 123–57, note 19.

Panorama, downtown Providence to College Hill, 1990.
Photograph courtesy of Will Hart

56. On the east side of Providence, across the river, it is the epicenter of the action in "The Call of Cthulhu."

57. See *The Case of Charles Dexter Ward*, in the previous volume, pp. 171–309, note 10.

The Athenaeum, 251 Benefit Street, Providence, 2010.
Photograph courtesy of Donovan K. Loucks

Stephen Hopkins House at 15 Hopkins Street, Providence, 2010.
Photograph courtesy of Donovan K. Loucks

strove to form contours like those of my uncle's kindly face. I like to think that he existed at that moment, and that he tried to bid me farewell. It seems to me I hiccoughed a farewell from my own parched throat as I lurched out into the street; a thin stream of grease following me through the door to the rain-drenched sidewalk.

The rest is shadowy and monstrous. There was no one in the soaking street, and in all the world there was no one I dared tell. I walked aimlessly south past College Hill[56] and the Athenaeum,[57] down Hopkins Street, and over the bridge to the business section where tall buildings seemed to guard me as modern material things guard the world from ancient and unwholesome wonder. Then grey dawn unfolded wetly from the east, silhouetting the archaic hill and its venerable steeples, and beckoning me to the place where my terrible work was still unfinished. And in the end I went, wet, hatless, and dazed in the morning light, and entered that awful door in Benefit Street which I had left ajar, and which still swung cryptically in full sight of the early householders to whom I dared not speak.

The grease was gone, for the mouldy floor was porous. And in front of the fireplace was no vestige of the giant doubled-up form in nitre. I looked at the cot, the chairs, the instruments, my neglected hat, and the yellowed straw hat of my uncle. Dazedness was uppermost, and I could scarcely recall what was dream and what was reality. Then thought trickled back, and I knew that I had witnessed things more horrible than I had dreamed. Sitting down, I tried to conjecture as nearly as sanity would let me just what had happened, and how I might end the horror, if

"That awful door in Benefit Street which I had left ajar."
Weird Tales (October 1937) (artist: Virgil Finlay)

indeed it had been real. Matter it seemed not to be, nor ether, nor anything else conceivable by mortal mind. What, then, but some exotic *emanation;* some vampirish vapour such as Exeter rustics tell of as lurking over certain churchyards? This I felt was

58. A large container for transporting liquids, of no standard size but generally from five to fifteen gallons. Whom did the narrator call to place this eccentric order?

59. Jacqueline C. Schafer, in "H. P. Lovecraft: Aspiring Materialist," *Nyctalops* 4, no. 1 (April 1991), points out, "The use of sulphuric acid as a crucial agent of reaction has undeniable alchemical overtones, for Sulphur, in alchemical epistemology, represents the essential principle of combustion, or transformation" (56).

the clue, and again I looked at the floor before the fireplace where the mould and nitre had taken strange forms. In ten minutes my mind was made up, and taking my hat I set out for home, where I bathed, ate, and gave by telephone an order for a pickaxe, a spade, a military gas-mask, and six carboys[58] of sulphuric acid,[59] all to be delivered the next morning at the cellar door of the shunned house in Benefit Street. After that I tried to sleep; and failing, passed the hours in reading and in the composition of inane verses to counteract my mood.

At 11 a.m. the next day I commenced digging. It was sunny weather, and I was glad of that. I was still alone, for as much as I feared the unknown horror I sought, there was more fear in the thought of telling anybody. Later I told Harris only through sheer necessity, and because he had heard odd tales from old people which disposed him ever so little toward belief. As I turned up the stinking black earth in front of the fireplace, my spade causing a viscous yellow ichor to ooze from the white fungi which it severed, I trembled at the dubious thoughts of what I might uncover. Some secrets of inner earth are not good for mankind, and this seemed to me one of them.

My hand shook perceptibly, but still I delved; after a while standing in the large hole I had made. With the deepening of the hole, which was about six feet square, the evil smell increased; and I lost all doubt of my imminent contact with the hellish thing whose emanations had cursed the house for over a century and a half. I wondered what it would look like—what its form and substance would be, and how big it might have waxed through long ages of life-sucking. At length I climbed out of the hole and dispersed the heaped-up dirt, then arranging the great carboys of acid around and near two sides, so that when necessary I might empty them all down the aperture in quick succession. After that I dumped earth only along the other two sides; working more slowly and donning my gas-mask as the smell grew. I was nearly unnerved at my proximity to a nameless thing at the bottom of a pit.

Suddenly my spade struck something softer than earth. I shuddered, and made a motion as if to climb out of the hole, which was now as deep as my neck. Then courage returned, and I scraped away more dirt in the light of the electric torch I had provided. The surface I uncovered was fishy and glassy—a kind of semi-putrid congealed jelly with suggestions of translucency. I scraped further, and saw that it had form. There was a rift where a part of the substance was folded over. The exposed area was huge and roughly cylindrical; like a mammoth soft blue-white stove-pipe doubled in two, its largest part some two feet in diameter. Still more I scraped, and then abruptly I leaped out of the hole and away from the filthy thing; frantically unstopping and tilting the heavy carboys, and precipitating their corrosive contents one after another down that charnel gulf and upon the unthinkable abnormality whose titan *elbow* I had seen.

The blinding maelstrom of greenish-yellow vapour which surged tempestuously up from that hole as the floods of acid descended, will never leave my memory. All along the hill people tell of the yellow day, when virulent and horrible fumes arose from the factory waste dumped in the Providence River, but I know how mistaken they are as to the source. They tell, too, of the hideous roar which at the same time came from some disordered water-pipe or gas main underground—but again I could correct them if I dared. It was unspeakably shocking, and I do not see how I lived through it. I did faint after emptying the fourth carboy, which I had to handle after the fumes had begun

Providence River, 2013. The Industrial Trust building
may be seen at the left.
Photograph courtesy of Donovan K. Loucks

to penetrate my mask; but when I recovered I saw that the hole was emitting no fresh vapours.

The two remaining carboys I emptied down without particular result, and after a time I felt it safe to shovel the earth back into the pit. It was twilight before I was done, but fear had gone out of the place. The dampness was less foetid, and all the strange fungi had withered to a kind of harmless greyish powder which blew ash-like along the floor. One of earth's nethermost terrors had perished forever; and if there be a hell, it had received at last the daemon soul of an unhallowed thing. And as I patted down the last spadeful of mould, I shed the first of the many tears with which I have paid unaffected tribute to my beloved uncle's memory.

The next spring no more pale grass and strange weeds came up in the shunned house's terraced garden, and shortly afterward Carrington Harris rented the place. It is still spectral, but its strangeness fascinates me, and I shall find mixed with my relief a queer regret when it is torn down to make way for a tawdry shop or vulgar apartment building. The barren old trees in the yard have begun to bear small, sweet apples, and last year the birds nested in their gnarled boughs.

The Horror at Red Hook[1]

Lovecraft's antipathy to New York and its inhabitants is well documented. This story, written in the white heat of his flaming xenophobia and rage at his own failure to achieve success in the city, depicts a neighborhood—on the verge of the very neighborhood in which he lived—that has become a sinkhole of depravity and madness. Even in his anger, HPL's careful attention to detail is displayed in his inclusion of the history of the city's Dutch population. Lovecraft thought the story "long and rambling" and not very good, but he did attempt to extract horror from a location that he found devoid of merit "save vulgar commonplace." His narrator, Tom Malone, is a precursor to later detective protagonists such as Raymond Chandler's Philip Marlowe, who similarly venture out onto "mean streets," albeit with more success.

> There are sacraments of evil as well as of good about us, and we live and move to my belief in an unknown world, a place where there are caves and shadows and dwellers in twilight. It is possible that man may sometimes return on the track of evolution, and it is my belief that an awful lore is not yet dead.
>
> —ARTHUR MACHEN[2]

I.

NOT MANY WEEKS ago, on a street corner in the village of Pascoag, Rhode Island,[3] a tall, heavily built, and wholesome-looking pedestrian furnished much speculation by a singular lapse of behaviour. He had, it appears, been descending the hill by the road from Chepachet;[4] and encountering the compact section, had turned to his left into the main thoroughfare where several modest business blocks convey a touch of the urban. At this point, without visible provocation, he committed his astonishing lapse; staring queerly for a second at the tallest of the buildings before him, and then, with a

1. The story was written in August 1925 and first published in *Weird Tales* 9, no. 1 (January 1927), 59–73. According to the manuscript, the original title was "The Case of Robert Suydam," suggesting that Lovecraft may well have been aware of the similarities of Malone to the characters created by writers such as Dashiell Hammett; Hammett's work was appearing in the 1920s in magazines such as *Black Mask*. HPL changed his mind, however, and saved that for-

mulation for *The Case of Charles Dexter Ward*, written two years later.

2. From *The Red Hand*, chapter 2, "Incident of the Letter," first published in *Chapman's Magazine* 2, no. 4 (December 1895), 396–400. The influence of Machen (1864–1947), a Welsh writer whose stories HPL praised for their "elements of hidden horror and brooding fright" ("Supernatural Horror in Literature," 421), may be seen in contemporary writers such as Stephen King, argues Damien G. Walter, in "Machen Is the Forgotten Father of Weird Fiction," *Guardian*, September 29, 2009.

3. A small village in the northwesternmost Rhode Island town of Burrillville, Rhode Island, principally known at the time for textile manufacturing.

Pascoag, Rhode Island, ca. 1906.

4. An even smaller village nearby, in the town of Glocester, Rhode Island. Since 1926, the town has hosted the Ancients & Horribles Parade, an annual Fourth of July event, notable for its political statements and ribald humor. In 1927, HPL and C. M. Eddy Jr. (for whom HPL did several "revisions") ventured to Chepachet in search of a place known as "Dark Swamp," of which they had heard rumors. They never located it, but the region may have inspired at least the opening of Lovecraft's story "The Colour Out of Space" (see "The Colour Out of Space," in the previous volume, pp. 310–42, note 2) and the setting contributed to Eddy's unfinished story "Black Noon." In the

series of terrified, hysterical shrieks, breaking into a frantic run which ended in a stumble and fall at the next crossing. Picked up and dusted off by ready hands, he was found to be conscious, organically unhurt, and evidently cured of his sudden nervous attack. He muttered some shamefaced explanations involving a strain he had undergone, and with downcast glance turned back up the Chepachet road, trudging out of sight without once looking behind him. It was a strange incident to befall so large, robust, normal-featured, and capable-looking a man, and the strangeness was not lessened by the remarks of a bystander who had recognised him as the boarder of a well-known dairyman on the outskirts of Chepachet.

He was, it developed, a New York police detective[5] named Thomas F. Malone, now on a long leave of absence under medical treatment after some disproportionately arduous work on a gruesome local case which accident had made dramatic. There had been a collapse of several old brick buildings during a raid in which he had shared, and something about the wholesale loss of life, both of prisoners and of his companions, had peculiarly appalled him. As a result, he had acquired an acute and anomalous horror of any buildings even remotely suggesting the ones which had fallen in, so that in the end mental specialists forbade him the sight of such things for an indefinite period. A police surgeon with relatives in Chepachet had put forward that quaint hamlet of wooden colonial houses as an ideal spot for the psychological convalescence; and thither the sufferer had gone, promising never to venture among the brick-lined streets of larger villages till duly advised by the Woonsocket[6] specialist with whom he was put in touch. This walk to Pascoag for magazines had been a mistake, and the patient had paid in fright, bruises, and humiliation for his disobedience.

So much the gossips of Chepachet and Pascoag knew; and so much, also, the most learned specialists believed. But Malone had at first told the specialists much more, ceasing only when he saw that utter incredulity was his portion. Thereafter he held his peace, protesting not at all when it was generally agreed that the collapse of certain squalid brick houses in the Red Hook section of Brooklyn, and the consequent death of many brave officers, had unseated his nervous equilibrium. He had worked too hard,

Postcard of Chepachet, Rhode Island, ca. 1920.

all said, in trying to clean up those nests of disorder and violence; certain features were shocking enough, in all conscience, and the unexpected tragedy was the last straw. This was a simple explanation which everyone could understand, and because Malone was not a simple person he perceived that he had better let it suffice. To hint to unimaginative people of a horror beyond all human conception—a horror of houses and blocks and cities leprous and cancerous with evil dragged from elder worlds—would be merely to invite a padded cell instead of restful rustication, and Malone

Red Hook, Brooklyn, ca. 1875.

1990s Chepachet gained brief national attention in episodes of the popular television show *The X-Files* as the fictional location of the youth summer home of main character Fox Mulder (David Duchovny), who says that Chepachet is "twenty miles on RI Route 8." No Route 8 exists in Chepachet or, for that matter, in the state.

5. In the 1918 reorganization of the NYPD, detectives were moved from nine bureaus and spread out among the eighty-three precincts. There were 610 second-grade detectives (the lowest designation), all paid as patrolmen. The commissioner of police recommended that 150 of the 610 be upgraded to sergeant's pay; this group, designated first-grade, received a salary "exceeding by about 50 percent that which is provided for the highest-paid patrolman" (Annual Report for 1919, City of New York, Police Department, 1920).

6. On the northern edge of Rhode Island. In 1937, Woonsocket had a population of 49,376. About three-quarters were French Canadian immigrants, up from 60 percent in 1900, and there was a sizable contingent of Belgians.

Woonsocket, Rhode Island, train station, 1923.

7. That is, Trinity College, University of Dublin.

Dublin University, Dublin, Ireland, ca. 1830.

8. A large, beautiful park in the west of Dublin.

Phoenix Park, Dublin, Ireland.
Shutterstock.com

9. Published in London from 1836 to 1906.

10. From Edgar Allan Poe's "The Man of the Crowd," first published in both *Burton's Gentlemen's Magazine* and *The Casket* (December 1840). According to *Collected Works of Edgar Allan Poe: Tales and Sketches, 1831–1842*, ed. Thomas Ollive Mabbot (Cambridge, MA: Belknap Press of Harvard University Press): "The German quotation appears also (applied to a book by 'Mr. Mathews') in the forty-sixth of Poe's 'Fifty Suggestions.' . . . although *Buch* is neuter (calling for *es*), the word "*hortulus*" is masculine. . . . Poe translated the German literally, 'It does not permit itself to be read.' Here he took this to

was a man of sense despite his mysticism. He had the Celt's far vision of weird and hidden things, but the logician's quick eye for the outwardly unconvincing; an amalgam which had led him far afield in the forty-two years of his life, and set him in strange places for a Dublin University[7] man born in a Georgian villa near Phoenix Park.[8]

And now, as he reviewed the things he had seen and felt and apprehended, Malone was content to keep unshared the secret of what could reduce a dauntless fighter to a quivering neurotic; what could make old brick slums and seas of dark, subtle faces a thing of nightmare and eldritch portent. It would not be the first time his sensations had been forced to bide uninterpreted—for was not his very act of plunging into the polyglot abyss of New York's underworld a freak beyond sensible explanation? What could he tell the prosaic of the antique witcheries and grotesque marvels discernible to sensitive eyes amidst the poison cauldron where all the varied dregs of unwholesome ages mix their venom and perpetuate their obscene terrors? He had seen the hellish green flame of secret wonder in this blatant, evasive welter of outward greed and inward blasphemy, and had smiled gently when all the New-Yorkers he knew scoffed at his experiment in police work. They had been very witty and cynical, deriding his fantastic pursuit of unknowable mysteries and assuring him that in these days New York held nothing but cheapness and vulgarity. One of them had wagered him a heavy sum that he could not—despite many poignant things to his credit in the *Dublin Review*[9]—even write a truly interesting story of New York low life; and now, looking back, he perceived that cosmic irony had justified the prophet's words while secretly confuting their flippant meaning. The horror, as glimpsed at last, could not make a story—for like the book cited by Poe's German authority, "*er lasst sich nicht lesen—it does not permit itself to be read.*"[10]

II.

TO MALONE THE sense of latent mystery in existence was always present. In youth he had felt the hidden beauty and ecstasy of things, and had been a poet; but poverty and sorrow and exile had turned his gaze in darker directions, and he had thrilled at the imputations of evil in the world around. Daily life had for him come to be a phantasmagoria of macabre shadow-studies; now glittering and leering with concealed rottenness as in Beardsley's best manner,[11] now hinting terrors behind the commonest shapes and objects as in the subtler and less obvious work of Gustave Doré.[12] He would often regard it as merciful that most persons of high intelligence jeer at the inmost mysteries; for, he argued, if superior minds were ever placed in fullest contact with the secrets preserved by ancient and lowly cults, the resultant abnormalities would soon not only wreck the world, but threaten the very integrity of the universe. All this reflection was no doubt morbid, but keen logic and a deep sense of humour ably offset it. Malone was satisfied to let his notions remain as half-spied and forbidden visions to be lightly played with; and hysteria came only when duty flung him into a hell of revelation too sudden and insidious to escape.

He had for some time been detailed to the Butler Street station[13] in Brooklyn when the Red Hook matter came to his notice.

Former NYPD 18th Precinct building in Brooklyn, probably similar to the Butler Street station (including a stable).

mean that the book was too shocking for a reader to peruse it completely; but the meaning of his source may have been that the book referred to was execrably printed, or that no copy was available" (518, note 19).

11. Aubrey Beardsley (1872–1898) was a prominent English illustrator remembered for his morbidly erotic and decadent drawings. His illustrations for Oscar Wilde's *Salomé* (1894) are probably his best-known print work. Prior to *Salomé*, a commission he received from the London publisher J. Dent at the age of only twenty, to illustrate Sir Thomas Malory's *Le Morte d'Arthur*, gave him his start as a practicing artist; after he completed the drawings, which were enormously well received, he never had to return to the office clerkships to which he had very briefly been tied and for which, as a young man who suffered tubercular hemorrhages, he was ill-suited. See Linda Gertner Zatlin's impeccably researched *Aubrey Beardsley: A Catalogue Raisonné* (New Haven: Yale University Press, 2016).

12. Gustave Doré (1832–1883) was a French illustrator and painter celebrated for, among other work, his woodcut engravings for Coleridge's *Rime of the Ancient Mariner* (1876) and the stunning original work *London: A Pilgrimage* (1872), a collaboration with the journalist Blanchard Jerrold that highlighted both the elegance and the privations of mid-Victorian city dwellers pressed together on third-class railway platforms, hoisting loads at a warehouse, selling fish at Billingsgate Market. HPL knew his work, especially his illustrated *Paradise Lost* (1866), and mentions him specifically in "Pickman's Model," pp. 311–28, below.

13. The 90th Precinct Station House, then located at 17 and 19 Butler Street in

Brooklyn, closed for substantial remodeling in 1920. At that time, the complement was a captain, four lieutenants, six sergeants, and sixty patrolmen.

14. Rehabilitated in 2016 as a public park and concert venue, Governors Island (the apostrophe has been dropped) is a 172-acre island just off (by only 800 yards) the southern tip of Manhattan and closer still to Pier 6 in Brooklyn Bridge Park (a 400-yard ferry ride). Almost every vantage point affords spectacular views of the Statue of Liberty, which is just 1.5 miles away. From 1783 to 1966, Governors Island was a U.S. Army base.

15. HPL lived at 169 Clinton Street in Brooklyn Heights from 1925 to 1926. The street took its name from George Clinton, royal governor of the Province of New York (appointed in 1741).

Corner of Court Street and Atlantic Avenue, Brooklyn, 1919.

Red Hook is a maze of hybrid squalor near the ancient waterfront opposite Governor's Island,[14] with dirty highways climbing the hill from the wharves to that higher ground where the decayed lengths of Clinton[15] and Court Streets lead off toward the Borough Hall.[16] Its houses are mostly of brick, dating from the first quarter to the middle of the nineteenth century, and some of the obscurer alleys and byways have that alluring antique flavour which conventional reading leads us to call "Dickensian." The population is a hopeless tangle and enigma; Syrian, Spanish, Italian, and negro elements impinging upon one another, and fragments of Scandinavian and American belts lying not far

Governor's Island, New York, 1911, as seen from Battery Park (Red Hook is on the other side of the island).

Clinton Street, Brooklyn, ca. 1935.

Brooklyn Borough Hall, present day.

distant.[17] It is a babel of sound and filth, and sends out strange cries to answer the lapping of oily waves at its grimy piers and the monstrous organ litanies of the harbour whistles. Here long ago a brighter picture dwelt, with clear-eyed mariners on the lower streets and homes of taste and substance where the larger houses line the hill. One can trace the relics of this former happiness in the trim shapes of the buildings, the occasional graceful churches, and the evidences of original art and background in bits of detail here and there—a worn flight of steps, a battered doorway, a wormy pair of decorative columns or pilasters, or a fragment of once green space with bent and rusted iron railing. The houses are generally in solid blocks, and now and then a many-windowed cupola arises to tell of days when the households of captains and ship-owners watched the sea.

From this tangle of material and spiritual putrescence the blasphemies of an hundred dialects assail the sky. Hordes of prowlers reel shouting and singing along the lanes and thoroughfares, occasional furtive hands suddenly extinguish lights and pull down curtains, and swarthy, sin-pitted faces disappear from windows when visitors pick their way through. Policemen despair of order or reform, and seek rather to erect barriers protecting the outside world from the contagion. The clang of the patrol is answered by a kind of spectral silence, and such prisoners as are taken are never communicative. Visible offences are as varied as the local dialects, and run the gamut from the smuggling of rum and prohibited aliens through diverse stages of lawlessness and obscure vice to murder and mutilation in their most abhorrent guises. That these visible affairs are not more frequent is not to the neighbourhood's credit, unless the power of concealment be an art demanding credit. More people enter Red Hook than leave it—or at least, than leave it by the landward side—and those who are not loquacious are the likeliest to leave.

Malone found in this state of things a faint stench of secrets more terrible than any of the sins denounced by citizens and bemoaned by priests and philanthropists. He was conscious, as one who united imagination with scientific knowledge, that modern people under lawless conditions tend uncannily to repeat the darkest instinctive patterns of primitive half-ape savagery in their daily life and ritual observances; and he had often viewed

16. The building, at 209 Joralemon Street, created by a grocer and contractor who won a design competition and had never practiced architecture, was built in 1848 to serve as Brooklyn City Hall. When Brooklyn merged with Manhattan in 1898, it became Brooklyn Borough Hall.

Brooklyn Borough Hall, 1888.

17. "The Horror at Red Hook" is HPL's most racist story, and characteristically, he never particularizes any of the immigrants he so despised. Andrew Lenoir, in "Dead Lies Dreaming: Lovecraft and the Other Side of Modernity," *Lovecraftian Proceedings: Papers from NecronomiCon Providence: 2013*, no. 1, suggests that the story was fueled by the passage in May 1924 of a sweeping federal immigration law establishing racial homogeneity as national policy. The act (known as the Johnson-Reed Act) not only sharply limited the annual number of immigrants from any one country, it banned outright immigration from Japan, China, the Philippines, Thailand, Vietnam, Laos, Singapore, Indonesia, India, Malaysia, Burma, and Korea. It also loosened the restrictions on German, English, and Irish immigration (the races Lovecraft most admired), while tightening those on East European and Italian immigration.

While the law was being debated, Lovecraft wrote:

I find it hard to conceive of anything more utterly and ultimately loathsome than certain streets of the *lower* East Side where [Rheinhart] Kleiner took [HPL's Jewish friend Samuel] Loveman and me in April 1922. The organic things—Italo-Semitico-Mongoloid—inhabiting that awful cesspool could not by any stretch of the imagination be call'd human. . . . From that nightmare of perverse infection I could not carry away the memory of any living face. The individually grotesque was lost in the collectively devastating; which left on the eye only the broad, phantasmal lineaments of the morbid soul of disintegration and decay. (Letter to Frank Belknap Long, March 21, 1924, *Selected Letters*, I, 333–34)

Lovecraft extolled the xenophobic policy of the new law as "discourag[ing] the immigration of racial elements radically alien to the original American people" and, in a bit of wishful thinking nine years later, crowed, "I do not believe this sound policy will ever be rescinded" (Letter to J. Vernon Shea, September 25, 1933, *Selected Letters, 1932–1934*, ed. August Derleth and James Turner [Sauk City, WI: Arkham House, 1971], 250; hereinafter *Selected Letters*, IV).

18. Murray's controversial *The Witch-Cult in Western Europe* (see "The Rats in the Walls," pp. 150–74, note 23, above) is also mentioned in "The Call of Cthulhu," in the previous volume, pp. 123–57, note 18.

19. This referred to languages (the so-called Ural-Altaic group), now discarded, that united the peoples of Eurasia.

20. The name Suydam is a venerable one in Brooklyn; the Dutch family and other early colonists are well represented

with an anthropologist's shudder the chanting, cursing processions of blear-eyed and pockmarked young men which wound their way along in the dark small hours of morning. One saw groups of these youths incessantly; sometimes in leering vigils on street corners, sometimes in doorways playing eerily on cheap instruments of music, sometimes in stupefied dozes or indecent dialogues around cafeteria tables near Borough Hall, and sometimes in whispering converse around dingy taxicabs drawn up at the high stoops of crumbling and closely shuttered old houses. They chilled and fascinated him more than he dared confess to his associates on the force, for he seemed to see in them some monstrous thread of secret continuity; some fiendish, cryptical, and ancient pattern utterly beyond and below the sordid mass of facts and habits and haunts listed with such conscientious technical care by the police. They must be, he felt inwardly, the heirs of some shocking and primordial tradition; the sharers of debased and broken scraps from cults and ceremonies older than mankind. Their coherence and definiteness suggested it, and it shewed in the singular suspicion of order which lurked beneath their squalid disorder. He had not read in vain such treatises as Miss Murray's "Witch-Cult in Western Europe";[18] and knew that up to recent years there had certainly survived among peasants and furtive folk a frightful and clandestine system of assemblies and orgies descended from dark religions antedating the Aryan world, and appearing in popular legends as Black Masses and Witches' Sabbaths. That these hellish vestiges of old Turanian-Asiatic[19] magic and fertility-cults were even now wholly dead he could not for a moment suppose, and he frequently wondered how much older and how much blacker than the very worst of the muttered tales some of them might really be.

III.

IT WAS THE case of Robert Suydam[20] which took Malone to the heart of things in Red Hook. Suydam was a lettered recluse of ancient Dutch family, possessed originally of barely independent means, and inhabiting the spacious but ill-preserved mansion which his grandfather had built in Flatbush[21] when that village was little more than a pleasant group of colonial cottages surrounding the steepled and ivy-clad Reformed Church with its iron-railed yard of Netherlandish gravestones. In his lonely house, set back from Martense Street[22] amidst a yard of venerable trees, Suydam had read and brooded for some six decades except for a period a generation before, when he had sailed for the Old World and remained there out of sight for eight years. He could afford no servants, and would admit but few visitors to his absolute solitude; eschewing close friendships and receiving his rare acquaintances in one of the three ground-floor rooms which he kept in order—a vast, high-ceiled library whose walls were solidly packed with tattered books of ponderous, archaic, and vaguely repellent aspect. The growth of the town and its final absorption in the Brooklyn district had meant nothing to Suydam, and he had come to mean less and less to the town. Elderly people still pointed him out on the streets, but to most of the recent population he was merely a queer, corpulent old fellow whose unkempt white hair, stubbly beard, shiny black clothes, and gold-headed cane earned him an amused glance and nothing more. Malone did not know him by sight till duty called him to the case, but had heard of him indirectly as a really profound authority on mediaeval superstition, and had once idly meant to look up an

in the graveyard of the Flatbush Dutch Reformed Church, at 890 Flatbush Avenue, and Suydam Place and Suydam Street are located in two different neighborhoods north of the church. The 1920 census listed 175 Suydams in New York. See the Rev. J. Howard Suydam's *Hendrick Rycken, the Progenitor of the Suydam Family in America*, https://archive.org/stream/hendrickryckenpr00suyd/hendrickryckenpr00suyd_djvu.txt.

21. An area of Brooklyn originally built by the Dutch colonists, but by the early twentieth century, it had become predominately occupied by Irish, Italian, and Jewish immigrants.

22. Named after Joris Martense, a Revolutionary War–era Dutch colonist and one of twelve founders of Erasmus Hall Academy (1786). His grandfather, Martin Adriance (1668–1754), owned the largest farm in Flatbush, stretching "from Caton Avenue to the northerly line of Mrs. WILBUR'S present holdings along Flatbush Avenue, back to the boundary line between New Utrecht and Flatbush, south for some distance along the said boundary and across it into New Utrecht" (http://bklyn-genealogy -info.stevemorse.org/Town/Homesteads/ MartenseStory.html).

Reformed Church, Flatbush, ca. 1899–1909.

The Reformed Church, 2010. Photograph courtesy of Donovan K. Loucks

23. Kabbalah, from the Hebrew word for "receive," is a mystical tradition and discipline originating in Jewish thought and study—specifically, with Moses on Mount Sinai, argues Hebrew University of Jerusalem professor Joseph Dan, in *Kaballah: A Very Short Introduction* (New York: Oxford University Press, 2005). During the Renaissance, Jewish kabbalistic texts, drawn from two sections of the Torah that the Talmud forbids discussion of—the world's creation (Genesis) and Ezekiel's chariot vision (Ezekiel 10:8–22)—were studied by many Christians, and they became part of the alchemical studies of hermeticism.

24. The German legend tells of a scholar who trades his soul to the devil for knowledge. It has been dramatized and used as a theme by writers throughout history. Two of the most notable treatments are Christopher Marlowe's play *The Tragi-*

lave you not led this
fe quite long enough?

Dr. Faustus, from 1925 illustration by Harry Clarke of Bayard Taylor's 1870–71 translation of Goethe's play.

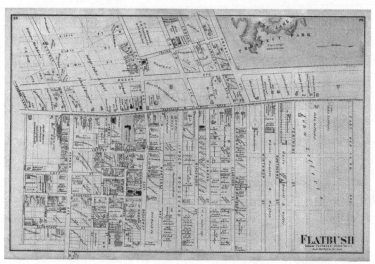

Map of Brooklyn showing Martense Street, Flatbush, 1873.

out-of-print pamphlet of his on the Kabbalah[23] and the Faustus legend,[24] which a friend had quoted from memory.

Suydam became a "case" when his distant and only relatives sought court pronouncements on his sanity. Their action seemed sudden to the outside world, but was really undertaken only after prolonged observation and sorrowful debate. It was based on certain odd changes in his speech and habits; wild references to impending wonders, and unaccountable hauntings of disreputable Brooklyn neighbourhoods. He had been growing shabbier and shabbier with the years, and now prowled about like a veritable mendicant; seen occasionally by humiliated friends in subway stations, or loitering on the benches around Borough Hall in conversation with groups of swarthy, evil-looking strangers. When he spoke it was to babble of unlimited powers almost within his grasp, and to repeat with knowing leers such mystical words or names as "Sephiroth," "Ashmodai," and "Samaël."[25] The court action revealed that he was using up his income and wasting his principal in the purchase of curious tomes imported from London and Paris, and in the maintenance of a squalid basement flat in the Red Hook district where he spent nearly every night, receiving odd delegations of mixed rowdies and foreigners, and apparently conducting some kind of ceremonial service behind the green blinds of secretive windows. Detectives assigned to follow him reported strange cries and chants and prancing of feet filtering out from these nocturnal rites, and shuddered at their peculiar ecstasy and abandon despite the commonness of weird orgies in that sodden section. When, however, the matter came to a hearing, Suydam managed to preserve his liberty. Before the judge his manner grew urbane and reasonable, and he freely admitted the queerness of demeanour and extravagant cast of language into which he had fallen through excessive devotion to study and research. He was, he said, engaged in the investigation of certain details of European tradition which required the closest contact with foreign groups and their songs and folk dances. The notion that any low secret society was preying upon him, as hinted by his relatives, was obviously absurd; and shewed how sadly limited was their understanding of him and his work. Triumphing with his calm explanations, he was suffered to depart unhindered; and the paid detectives of the Suydams, Corlears,[26] and Van Brunts[27] were withdrawn in resigned disgust.

It was here that an alliance of Federal inspectors and police, Malone with them, entered the case. The law had watched the Suydam action with interest, and had in many instances been called upon to aid the private detectives. In this work it developed that Suydam's new associates were among the blackest and most vicious criminals of Red Hook's devious lanes, and that at least a third of them were known and repeated offenders in the matter of thievery, disorder, and the importation of illegal

Asmodeus.

cal *History of Doctor Faustus*, usually published as *Doctor Faustus* (1604), and Johann Wolfgang von Goethe's play *Faust* (1808), the theme of which preoccupied the author even as a young child, writes Rüdiger Safranski, in *Goethe: Life as a Work of Art*, trans. David Dollenmayer (New York Liveright, 2017), 522. A third is, of course, Thomas Mann's 1947 novel *Doctor Faustus*, an allegory of the rise of Nazism.

25. The Sephiroth (ספירות) are the ten emanations of God in the kabbalistic tradition. According to *A Dictionary of Angels: Including the Fallen Angels*, by Gustav Davidson (New York: Free Press, 1967), Sephiroth is also "a power angel . . . invoked in cabalistic conjuring rites" (266). Ashmedai (אשמדאי), or Asmodeus, is a king of demons, according to the deuterocanonical Book of Tobit (accepted as canonical by the Roman Catholic and Eastern Orthodox churches); according to kabbalah, however, Ashmedai is a cambion, the mythical offspring of a succubus and a human, in this case Agrat bat Mahlat (מחלת בת אגרת—Agrat, daughter of Mahlat), a demon, and King David. Samael (סמאל), meaning poison (or venom) of God, is identified in the Talmud as the principal archangel of death and, according to Davidson, is "chief of the Satans. . . one of the greatest and . . . one of the foulest spirits operating in Heaven, on earth, and in Hell" (255).

26. In the seventeenth century, Jacobus Van Corlaer owned the farmland leading up to the beach at what was then known as Corlaer's Hook, on the southern tip of Manhattan, and sold it to William Beekman. During the British occupation of New York, it became known as Crown Point, but by the nineteenth century it had reverted to a misspelled version of its earlier name, Corlear's (with or with-

Anthony Van Corlaer, trumpeter for the garrison at New Amsterdam.

out the apostrophe) Hook (probably the basis for Lovecraft's mistaken spelling). The area was filled with docks and shipyards, and unsurprisingly it became well populated with streetwalkers. John Russell Bartlett's 1859 *Dictionary of Americanisms* defines "hooker" as follows: "A resident of the Hook, i.e., a strumpet, a sailor's trull. So called from the number of houses of ill-fame frequented by sailors at the Hook (i.e., Corlear's Hook) in the city of New York." Irving Lewis Allen covers some of the same ground in *The City in Slang: New York Life and Popular Speech* (New York: Oxford University Press, 1993), 184–86. See also Luc Sante, *Low Life* (New York: Farrar, Straus and Giroux, 2003), 16, 29, 204–7.

27. The Van Brunt family was well represented in New York in the 1920 census, and there is a Van Brunt Stillhouse, an artisanal distillery, now in Red Hook. Ichabod Crane's foil in Washington Irving's 1820 story "The Legend of Sleepy Hollow," set in late eighteenth-century "Tarry Town" (Tarrytown), New York, is Abraham Van Brunt (Brom Bones).

immigrants. Indeed, it would not have been too much to say that the old scholar's particular circle coincided almost perfectly with the worst of the organised cliques which smuggled ashore certain nameless and unclassified Asian dregs wisely turned back by Ellis Island. In the teeming rookeries of Parker Place[28]—since renamed—where Suydam had his basement flat, there had grown up a very unusual colony of unclassified slant-eyed folk who used the Arabic alphabet but were eloquently repudiated by the great mass of Syrians in and around Atlantic Avenue. They could all have been deported for lack of credentials, but legalism is slow-moving, and one does not disturb Red Hook unless publicity forces one to.

These creatures attended a tumbledown stone church, used Wednesdays as a dance-hall, which reared its Gothic buttresses near the vilest part of the waterfront. It was nominally Catholic; but priests throughout Brooklyn denied the place all standing and authenticity, and policemen agreed with them when they listened to the noises it emitted at night. Malone used to fancy he heard terrible cracked bass notes from a hidden organ far underground when the church stood empty and unlighted, whilst all observers dreaded the shrieking and drumming which accompanied the visible services. Suydam, when questioned, said he thought the ritual was some remnant of Nestorian Christianity[29]

Long Island R.R. station, Atlantic Avenue, Brooklyn, ca. 1910.

tinctured with the Shamanism of Thibet.[30] Most of the people, he conjectured, were of Mongoloid stock, originating somewhere in or near Kurdistan[31]—and Malone could not help recalling that Kurdistan is the land of the Yezidis,[32] last survivors of the Persian devil-worshippers. However this may have been, the stir of the Suydam investigation made it certain that these unauthorised newcomers were flooding Red Hook in increasing numbers; entering through some marine conspiracy unreached by revenue officers and harbour police, overrunning Parker Place and rapidly spreading up the hill, and welcomed with curious fraternalism by the other assorted denizens of the region. Their squat figures and characteristic squinting physiognomies, grotesquely combined with flashy American clothing, appeared more and more numerously among the loafers and nomad gangsters of the Borough Hall section; till at length it was deemed necessary to compute their numbers, ascertain their sources and occupations, and find if possible a way to round them up and deliver them to the proper immigration authorities. To this task Malone was assigned by agreement of Federal and city forces, and as he commenced his canvass of Red Hook he felt poised upon the brink of nameless terrors, with the shabby, unkempt figure of Robert Suydam as arch-fiend and adversary.

IV.

POLICE METHODS ARE varied and ingenious. Malone, through unostentatious rambles, carefully casual conversations, well-timed offers of hip-pocket liquor, and judicious dialogues with frightened prisoners, learned many isolated facts about the movement whose aspect had become so menacing. The newcomers were indeed Kurds, but of a dialect obscure and puzzling to exact philology. Such of them as worked lived mostly as dock-hands and unlicenced pedlars, though frequently serving in Greek restaurants and tending corner news stands. Most of them, however, had no visible means of support; and were obviously connected with underworld pursuits, of which smuggling and "bootlegging"[33] were the least indescribable. They had come in steamships, apparently tramp freighters, and had been unloaded

28. The 1908 *Street Directory of the Principal Cities of the United States* issued by the U.S. Post Office does not list a Parker or Parker's Place in any of the boroughs, although entries in *The City Record: Official Journal of the City of New York*, Vol. 33, Part 5, 1905, list Parker *Street*, in the Bronx, and Parker *Place*, in Yonkers. (And, of course, there is a *Park* Place in Brooklyn.) There was a Parker Place in Providence, and HPL may have used that name to conceal the location of Suydam's flat.

29. Nestorianism treats the disunion between the human and the divine aspects of Jesus. The principal teachings were enunciated by Nestorius (386–450 CE), Patriarch of Constantinople, and are carried on by the Church of the East, also known as the Assyrian or Nestorian Church.

30. John Myrdhin Reynolds, in "The Soul, Nature Spirits, and Developing a Personal Relationship with Nature and the Natural Environment in the Light of Tibetan Shamanism," writes, "For centuries in Tibet, shamanist practitioners have been either Nyingmapa [ancient ones] or Bonpo [practitioners of Bon]" (62). He dates Bon as pre-Buddhist—that is, as having predated the arrival of Indian Buddhism in central Tibet in the seventh century—and he makes a distinction between what he calls "the high literary culture of Buddhism and Bon, on the one hand, and Tibetan folk culture and practice, especially shamanism and shamanic healing, on the other" (58), noting that Bonpo texts and rituals have been incorporated into Buddhist practice. The term "Bon," he says, may derive from an old Tibetan verb, 'bond pa, "meaning 'to invoke the gods and spirits'" (61).

 A central tenet of Bon is restoration of primordial harmony, and a key practice is communication with other species through ritual magic and clairvoyance, performed by the shaman or priest. For shamanic and Buddhist ritual texts, principles, and models of consciousness, see Reynolds, 63–64, 75–77, and elsewhere. Reynolds also refers the reader to Mircea Eliade's classic *Shamanism: Archaic Techniques of Ecstasy* (New York: Pantheon, 1964), based on fieldwork carried out not in Tibet but Siberia.

31. To define Kurdistan, one must specify a period, as borders have shifted over time. In ancient times, the "land of the Kurds" was situated between Mesopotamia and Persia; by the Middle Ages, it consisted of a number of emirates in the Middle East. Some parts were later in the Ottoman Empire, other parts in the Safavid (Persian) Empire (1501–1722)—present-day Iran.

In 1920, after the dissolution of the Ottoman Empire, the Treaty of Sèvres failed to provide agreement on a Kurdish state. The BBC estimates that today 25 to 35 million Kurds—"the fourth-largest ethnic group in the Middle East"—"inhabit a mountainous region straddling the borders of Turkey, Iraq, Syria, Iran, and Armenia" ("Who Are the Kurds?," BBC News, March 14, 2016). In *"Zare and Kurds-Yezids,"* Cinergie, March 7, 2015, the Armenian film critic Artsvi Bakhchinyan looks at Kurdish-Armenian cultural relations through the lens of Soviet film history: the lost movie *Under the Kurdish Yoke* (*Pod vlasyu kurdov*), or *The Tragedy of Turkish Armenia*, directed by A. I. Minervin (1915); the World War I love story *Zare* (1926), directed by Amo Bek-Nazaryan; and *Kurds-Yezids* (1932), directed by Amasi Martirosyan, about the Soviet imposition of collective farming in a Kurdish village.

In 2016–17, the Kurdish militia YPG famously battled the Islamic State for control of Rojava, Syria, its female guer-

by stealth on moonless nights in rowboats which stole under a certain wharf and followed a hidden canal to a secret subterranean pool beneath a house. This wharf, canal, and house Malone could not locate, for the memories of his informants were exceedingly confused, while their speech was to a great extent beyond even the ablest interpreters; nor could he gain any real data on the reasons for their systematic importation. They were reticent about the exact spot from which they had come, and were never sufficiently off guard to reveal the agencies which had sought them out and directed their course. Indeed, they developed something like acute fright when asked the reasons for their presence. Gangsters of other breeds were equally taciturn, and the most that could be gathered was that some god or great priesthood had promised them unheard-of powers and supernatural glories and rulerships in a strange land.

The attendance of both newcomers and old gangsters at Suydam's closely guarded nocturnal meetings was very regular, and the police soon learned that the erstwhile recluse had leased additional flats to accommodate such guests as knew his password; at last occupying three entire houses and permanently harbouring many of his queer companions. He spent but little time now at his Flatbush home, apparently going and coming only to obtain and return books; and his face and manner had attained an appalling pitch of wildness. Malone twice interviewed him,

Kurdistan landscape.
Shutterstock.com

but was each time brusquely repulsed. He knew nothing, he said, of any mysterious plots or movements; and had no idea how the Kurds could have entered or what they wanted. His business was to study undisturbed the folklore of all the immigrants of the district; a business with which policemen had no legitimate concern. Malone mentioned his admiration for Suydam's old brochure on the Kabbalah and other myths, but the old man's softening was only momentary. He sensed an intrusion, and rebuffed his visitor in no uncertain way; till Malone withdrew disgusted, and turned to other channels of information.

What Malone would have unearthed could he have worked continuously on the case, we shall never know. As it was, a stupid conflict between city and Federal authority suspended the investigations for several months, during which the detective was busy with other assignments. But at no time did he lose interest, or fail to stand amazed at what began to happen to Robert Suydam. Just at the time when a wave of kidnappings and disappearances spread its excitement over New York, the unkempt scholar embarked upon a metamorphosis as startling as it was absurd. One day he was seen near Borough Hall with clean-shaved face, well-trimmed hair, and tastefully immaculate attire, and on every day thereafter some obscure improvement was noticed in him. He maintained his new fastidiousness without interruption, added to it an unwonted sparkle of eye and crispness of speech, and began little by little to shed the corpulence which had so long deformed him. Now frequently taken for less than his age, he acquired an elasticity of step and buoyancy of demeanour to match the new tradition, and shewed a curious darkening of the hair which somehow did not suggest dye. As the months passed, he commenced to dress less and less conservatively, and finally astonished his new friends by renovating and redecorating his Flatbush mansion, which he threw open in a series of receptions, summoning all the acquaintances he could remember, and extending a special welcome to the fully forgiven relatives who had so lately sought his restraint. Some attended through curiosity, others through duty; but all were suddenly charmed by the dawning grace and urbanity of the former hermit. He had, he asserted, accomplished most of his allotted work; and having just inherited some property from a half-forgotten European friend,

rillas commanding international attention and spawning militias such as the Women's Protection Unit-Sinjar (or Shengal).

32. A Kurdish minority whose faith, with links to ancient Mesopotamian religions, is said to be older than Islam and Christianity. At least 40,000 Yazidis live in Iraq's Sinjar Mountains today, according to the United Nations; the population worldwide is estimated at 400,000 to 800,000. Yazidis' veneration of Melek Taus, the "Peacock Angel"—whose parallel story in Islam, of a fall from grace with God, provoked a fatwa against all practitioners in 2007—has led to years of persecution, and is a reprisal of historic baseless charges of Yazidis as "infidels."

33. Although the term itself dates back to the 1880s, when Americans would smuggle liquor to Native Americans in their boot tops, it entered the national vernacular when the Eighteenth Amendment to the U.S. Constitution prohibited the sale (and the making and shipping) of alcoholic beverages in the United States ("Prohibition") from 1920 to 1933. Bootleggers were originally importers of foreign-produced alcoholic beverages but eventually encompassed all illegal producers of alcoholic beverages sold in the United States.

34. The *Brooklyn Eagle* was a daily afternoon newspaper from 1844 to 1955. According to the paper's website, "By the Civil War, the *Eagle* had the largest circulation of any evening paper in the United States, a fact the paper made a point of printing in the top left corner of page 2 every day, followed by, 'Its value as an advertising medium is therefore apparent'"(http://www.brooklyneagle.com/aboutus). Walt Whitman served as its editor from 1846 to 1848.

35. Bayside is the far northwestern portion of Queens, about twenty miles from Flatbush. Members of the Gerritsens, another Dutch family, may be found, in the 1910 census, living in Brooklyn but not Queens.

36. This incantation is lifted directly from the *Encyclopaedia Britannica* (9th ed.), vol. XV, 202, from the article on "Magic" by Edward Burnett Tylor, LLD, DCL, FRS, keeper of the University Museum, Oxford, as an example of the rites used to evoke Hecate, the moon, "sender of midnight phantasms." According to Dirk Mosig, his friend Robert C. Culp traced the *Britannica* quotation to its source in the third-century CE work *Philosophumena* (known in English as *The Refutation of All Heresies*), attributed to Hippolytus of Rome, who quoted Porphyry of Tyre as follows: "Come, infernal, terrestrial, and heavenly Bombo, goddess of the broad roadways, of the cross-road, thou who goest to and fro at night, torch in hand, enemy of the day, friend and lover of darkness, thou who dost rejoice when bitches are howling and warm blood is spilled, thou who art walking amid the phantom and in the place of tombs, thou whose thirst is blood, thou who dost strike fear into mortal heart, Gorgo, Mormo, Moon of a thousand forms, cast a propitious eye upon our sacrifice." (Dirk W. Mosig, "A Note on *The*

was about to spend his remaining years in a brighter second youth which ease, care, and diet had made possible to him. Less and less was he seen at Red Hook, and more and more did he move in the society to which he was born. Policemen noted a tendency of the gangsters to congregate at the old stone church and dance-hall instead of at the basement flat in Parker Place, though the latter and its recent annexes still overflowed with noxious life.

Then two incidents occurred—wide enough apart, but both of intense interest in the case as Malone envisaged it. One was a quiet announcement in the *Eagle*[34] of Robert Suydam's engagement to Miss Cornelia Gerritsen of Bayside,[35] a young woman of excellent position, and distantly related to the elderly bridegroom-elect; whilst the other was a raid on the dance-hall church by city police, after a report that the face of a kidnapped child had been seen for a second at one of the basement windows. Malone had participated in this raid, and studied the place with much care when inside. Nothing was found—in fact, the building was entirely deserted when visited—but the sensitive Celt was vaguely disturbed by many things about the interior. There were crudely painted panels he did not like—panels which depicted sacred faces with peculiarly worldly and sardonic expressions, and which occasionally took liberties that even a layman's sense of decorum could scarcely countenance. Then, too, he did not relish the Greek inscription on the wall above the pulpit; an ancient incantation which he had once stumbled upon in Dublin college days, and which read, literally translated,

"O friend and companion of night, thou who rejoicest in the baying of dogs and spilt blood, who wanderest in the midst of shades among the tombs, who longest for blood and bringest terror to mortals, Gorgo, Mormo, thousand-faced moon, look favourably on our sacrifices!"[36]

When he read this he shuddered, and thought vaguely of the cracked bass organ notes he fancied he had heard beneath the church on certain nights. He shuddered again at the rust around the rim of a metal basin which stood on the altar, and paused nervously when his nostrils seemed to detect a curious and ghastly stench from somewhere in the neighbourhood. That organ memory haunted him, and he explored the basement with particular assiduity before he left. The place was very hateful to him; yet after all, were the blasphemous panels and inscriptions more than mere crudities perpetrated by the ignorant?

By the time of Suydam's wedding the kidnapping epidemic had become a popular newspaper scandal. Most of the victims were young children of the lowest classes, but the increasing number of disappearances had worked up a sentiment of the strongest fury. Journals clamoured for action from the police, and once more the Butler Street station sent its men over Red Hook for clues, discoveries, and criminals. Malone was glad to be on the trail again, and took pride in a raid on one of Suydam's Parker Place houses. There, indeed, no stolen child was found, despite the tales of screams and the red sash picked up in the areaway; but the paintings and rough inscriptions on the peeling walls of most of the rooms, and the primitive chemical laboratory in the attic, all helped to convince the detective that he was on the track of something tremendous. The paintings were appalling—hideous monsters of every shape and size, and parodies on human outlines which cannot be described. The writing was in red, and varied from Arabic to Greek, Roman, and Hebrew letters. Malone could not read much of it, but what he did decipher was portentous and cabbalistic enough. One frequently repeated motto was in a sort of Hebraised Hellenistic Greek, and suggested the most terrible daemon-evocations of the Alexandrian decadence:

"HEL . HELOYM . SOTHER . EMMANUEL . SABAOTH . AGLA . TETRAGRAMMATON . AGYROS . OTHEOS . ISCHYROS . ATHANATOS . JEHOVA . VA . ADONAI . SADAY . HOMOVSION . MESSIAS . ESCHEREHEYE."[37]

Circles and pentagrams loomed on every hand, and told indubitably of the strange beliefs and aspirations of those who dwelt so squalidly here. In the cellar, however, the strangest thing was found—a pile of genuine gold ingots covered carelessly with a piece of burlap, and bearing upon their shining surfaces the same weird hieroglyphics which also adorned the walls. During the raid the police encountered only a passive resistance from the squinting Orientals that swarmed from every door. Finding

Occult Lovecraft," The Miskatonic, EOD 11 (August 1975), reprinted in *The Miskatonic: The Lovecraft Centenary Edition* (Glenview, Il: The Moshassuck Press, 1991), 210–11.

37. He copied the incantation from Tylor's "Magic" (see note 36). Tylor in turn notes that it was "copied [by him] with its mistakes as an illustration of magical scholarship in its lowest stage"— that is, Tylor intentionally did not correct the words or grammar of this jumbled expression (explained in some detail in Appendix 3, below), because he wished to demonstrate the low state of previous magical scholarship, which had treated the incantation as a coherent exhortation. HPL miscopied the incantation from Tylor, changing "Homousion" to "Homovsion."

38. The Cunard Line during this period departed from Pier 51, on the "North River" (the Hudson River); later, its ocean liners, having become exponentially bigger, left from the longer (1,000-foot) Piers 84–92 After 1910, Pier 51 was part of the newly constructed Chelsea Piers. The White Star Line and the Cunard Line piers were the principal waypoints for travelers to Europe. In 1994, reconstruction of the four remaining Chelsea Piers began, and today they are home to sports facilities and retail outlets (Chelsea Piers Sports and Entertainment Complex).

Cunard Pier, Manhattan, 1920.

39. The *Social Register* was a book purporting to be a directory of the perceived "upper class"—an American counterpart to England's *Burke's Peerage*. By 1924, when the Suydam wedding likely occurred, the Social Register Association published annually eighteen different books for twenty-six cities, and in addition to names and addresses, the *Social Register* also identified the clubs to which the listed individuals belonged, as well as "the marriage, death and European arrival and departure of each person as it may occur" (*Social Register, New York 1917* XXXI, no. 1, November 1916). There are seven listings for Suydams in the 1917 *Social Register*, but Robert was not among them.

Chelsea Piers, ca. 1910.

nothing relevant, they had to leave all as it was; but the precinct captain wrote Suydam a note advising him to look closely to the character of his tenants and protégés in view of the growing public clamour.

V.

THEN CAME THE June wedding and the great sensation. Flatbush was gay for the hour about high noon, and pennanted motors thronged the streets near the old Dutch church where an awning stretched from door to highway. No local event ever surpassed the Suydam-Gerritsen nuptials in tone and scale, and the party which escorted bride and groom to the Cunard Pier[38] was, if not exactly the smartest, at least a solid page from the Social Register.[39] At five o'clock adieux were waved, and the ponderous liner edged away from the long pier, slowly turned its nose seaward, discarded its tug, and headed for the widening water spaces that led to Old World wonders. By night the outer harbour was cleared, and late passengers watched the stars twinkling above an unpolluted ocean.

Whether the tramp steamer or the scream was first to gain

attention, no one can say. Probably they were simultaneous, but it is of no use to calculate. The scream came from the Suydam stateroom, and the sailor who broke down the door could perhaps have told frightful things if he had not forthwith gone completely mad—as it is, he shrieked more loudly than the first victims, and thereafter ran simpering about the vessel till caught and put in irons. The ship's doctor who entered the stateroom and turned on the lights a moment later did not go mad, but told nobody what he saw till afterward, when he corresponded with Malone in Chepachet. It was murder—strangulation—but one need not say that the claw-mark on Mrs. Suydam's throat could not have come from her husband's or any other human hand, or that upon the white wall there flickered for an instant in hateful red a legend which, later copied from memory, seems to have been nothing less than the fearsome Chaldee[40] letters of the word "LILITH."[41] One need not mention these things because they vanished so quickly—as for Suydam, one could at least bar others from the room until one knew what to think oneself. The doctor has distinctly assured Malone that he did not see IT. The open porthole, just before he turned on the lights, was clouded for a second with a certain phosphorescence, and for a moment there seemed to echo in the night outside the suggestion of a faint and hellish tittering; but no real outline met the eye. As proof, the doctor points to his continued sanity.

Then the tramp steamer claimed all attention. A boat put off, and a horde of swart, insolent ruffians in officers' dress swarmed aboard the temporarily halted Cunarder.[42] They wanted Suydam or his body—they had known of his trip, and for certain reasons were sure he would die. The captain's deck was almost a pandemonium; for at the instant, between the doctor's report from the stateroom and the demands of the men from the tramp, not even the wisest and gravest seaman could think what to do. Suddenly the leader of the visiting mariners, an Arab with a hatefully negroid mouth, pulled forth a dirty, crumpled paper and handed it to the captain. It was signed by Robert Suydam, and bore the following odd message:

"In case of sudden or unexplained accident or death on my part, please deliver me or my body unquestioningly into the hands of the

40. A dialect of the Aramaic language (although the Chaldean nation existed for about four centuries between the tenth and the sixth centuries BCE and presumably had a distinctive but unrecorded language). See David McCalman Turpie's *A Manual of the Chaldee Language* (London: Williams and Norgate, 1870).

41. Lilith has a long and complicated history, and her evolution across cultures says much about persistent anxieties around femininity and women and power. Originally the "maid of desolation" (*ardat lili*) of Babylonian tradition, a demon of waste places, and, in Assyrian tradition, a winged wind spirit, hair "tossed wildly like a dragon's" (according to King Solomon), she evolved into the first wife of Adam, preceding Eve. Lilith played a key part in harmonizing the Creation stories of Genesis 1 and Genesis 2: In the former, humans were created from dust (unnamed "male and female" at the same time), while in the latter, God made Eve from Adam's rib. Talmudic scholars suggested that Lilith was thrown out of paradise because of her refusal to admit that Adam was her superior. Three angels went to her to offer a chance to return, but when she refused, God created Eve. In the Middle Ages, Lilith was depicted as a lamia (akin to a vampire) or succubus (a demon that has intercourse with men as they sleep), and her offspring, the *lilim* (or *lilin*), were monstrous part-human winged creatures. In kabbalistic tradition, she is a wife of Samael (see note 25, above). She now symbolizes the seductive and evil or treacherous woman, the femme fatale.

42. That is, the ocean liner on which the Suydams were passengers. Although the vessel is unnamed, it was likely the RMS *Berengaria*, helmed by Captain W. R. D. Irvine, RD, RNR, the greatest and most

luxurious of the Cunard liners and the ship of choice for the rich and famous, sailing for Southampton via Cherbourg in late June 1924.

43. In what was then called South Brooklyn, the first Dutch agricultural settlement in 1636. Over two hundred years later, the Gowanus Canal (built over a twenty-year period, from 1853 to 1874) drew manufacturing plants, shipyards, and foundries. "[I]t was difficult to overlook one of the canal's most distinguishing features: it was an open sewer," writes Joseph Alexiou, who moved to the neighborhood in 2006, in *Gowanus: Brooklyn's Curious Canal* (New York: NYU Press, 2015), 11. Alexiou covers the Gowanus's fifty years as a thriving if fetid and disease-conferring transportation hub—including accounts of teenage stabbings, drowned kittens, and the Mafia—and takes in the neighborhood's twenty-first-century renaissance.

Gowanus Canal, Brooklyn, ca. 1910.

bearer and his associates. Everything, for me, and perhaps for you, depends on absolute compliance. Explanations can come later— do not fail me now.

ROBERT SUYDAM."

Captain and doctor looked at each other, and the latter whispered something to the former. Finally they nodded rather helplessly and led the way to the Suydam stateroom. The doctor directed the captain's glance away as he unlocked the door and admitted the strange seamen, nor did he breathe easily till they filed out with their burden after an unaccountably long period of preparation. It was wrapped in bedding from the berths, and the doctor was glad that the outlines were not very revealing. Somehow the men got the thing over the side and away to their tramp steamer without uncovering it. The Cunarder started again, and the doctor and a ship's undertaker sought out the Suydam stateroom to perform what last services they could. Once more the physician was forced to reticence and even to mendacity, for a hellish thing had happened. When the undertaker asked him why he had drained off all of Mrs. Suydam's blood, he neglected to affirm that he had not done so; nor did he point to the vacant bottle-spaces on the rack, or to the odour in the sink which shewed the hasty disposition of the bottles' original contents. The pockets of those men—if men they were—had bulged damnably when they left the ship. Two hours later, and the world knew by radio all that it ought to know of the horrible affair.

VI.

THAT SAME JUNE evening, without having heard a word from the sea, Malone was desperately busy among the alleys of Red Hook. A sudden stir seemed to permeate the place, and as if apprised by "grapevine telegraph" of something singular, the denizens clustered expectantly around the dance-hall church and the houses in Parker Place. Three children had just disappeared— blue-eyed Norwegians from the streets toward Gowanus[43]—and there were rumours of a mob forming among the sturdy Vikings of that section. Malone had for weeks been urging his colleagues to attempt a general cleanup; and at last, moved by conditions more obvious to their common sense than the conjectures of a Dublin dreamer, they had agreed upon a final stroke. The unrest and menace of this evening had been the deciding factor, and just about midnight a raiding party recruited from three stations descended upon Parker Place and its environs. Doors were battered in, stragglers arrested, and candlelighted rooms forced to disgorge unbelievable throngs of mixed foreigners in figured robes, mitres, and other inexplicable devices. Much was lost in the melee, for objects were thrown hastily down unexpected shafts, and betraying odours deadened by the sudden kindling of pungent incense. But spattered blood was everywhere, and Malone shuddered whenever he saw a brazier or altar from which the smoke was still rising.

He wanted to be in several places at once, and decided on Suydam's basement flat only after a messenger had reported the complete emptiness of the dilapidated dance-hall church. The flat, he thought, must hold some clue to a cult of which the occult scholar had so obviously become the centre and leader; and it was with real expectancy that he ransacked the musty rooms, noted their vaguely charnel odour, and examined the curious books, instruments, gold ingots, and glass-stoppered bottles scattered carelessly here and there. Once, a lean, black-and-white cat edged between his feet and tripped him, overturning at the same time a beaker half full of a red liquid. The shock was severe, and to this day Malone is not certain of what he saw; but in dreams he still pictures that cat as it scuttled away with certain monstrous alterations and peculiarities. Then came the locked cellar door, and the search for something to break it down. A heavy stool stood near, and its tough seat was more than enough for the antique panels. A crack formed and enlarged, and the whole door gave way—but from the *other* side; whence poured a howling tumult of ice-cold wind with all the stenches of the bottomless pit, and whence reached a sucking force not of earth or heaven, which, coiling sentiently about the paralysed detective, dragged him through the aperture and down unmeasured spaces filled with whispers and wails, and gusts of mocking laughter.

Of course it was a dream. All the specialists have told him

44. Worship of these fertility goddesses is discussed thoroughly in Murray's *Witch-Cult* (see note 18, above).

45. Aegipan is Pan in goat form, hence aegipans are satyrs.

46. See *The Case of Charles Dexter Ward*, in the previous volume, pp. 171–309, note 138, for a discussion of Walpurgisnacht (the night before May Day—that is, the night of April 30). In China, North Korea, Cuba, and the former Soviet Union, May Day (also called Labor Day) celebrates workers. In England it has long been "International Workers' Day."

so, and he has nothing to prove the contrary. Indeed, he would rather have it thus; for then the sight of old brick slums and dark foreign faces would not eat so deeply into his soul. But at the time it was all horribly real, and nothing can ever efface the memory of those nighted crypts, those titan arcades, and those half-formed shapes of hell that strode gigantically in silence holding half-eaten things whose still surviving portions screamed for mercy or laughed with madness. Odours of incense and corruption joined in sickening concert, and the black air was alive with the cloudy, semi-visible bulk of shapeless elemental things with eyes. Somewhere dark sticky water was lapping at onyx piers, and once the shivery tinkle of raucous little bells pealed out to greet the insane titter of a naked phosphorescent thing which swam into sight, scrambled ashore, and climbed up to squat leeringly on a carved golden pedestal in the background.

Avenues of limitless night seemed to radiate in every direction, till one might fancy that here lay the root of a contagion destined to sicken and swallow cities, and engulf nations in the foetor of hybrid pestilence. Here cosmic sin had entered, and festered by unhallowed rites had commenced the grinning march of death that was to rot us all to fungous abnormalities too hideous for the grave's holding. Satan here held his Babylonish court, and in the blood of stainless childhood the leprous limbs of phosphorescent Lilith were laved. Incubi and succubae howled praise to Hecate, and headless moon-calves bleated to the Magna Mater.[44] Goats leaped to the sound of thin accursed flutes, and Aegipans[45] chased endlessly after misshapen fauns over rocks twisted like swollen toads. Moloch and Ashtaroth were not absent; for in this quintessence of all damnation the bounds of consciousness were let down, and man's fancy lay open to vistas of every realm of horror and every forbidden dimension that evil had power to mould. The world and Nature were helpless against such assaults from unsealed wells of night, nor could any sign or prayer check the Walpurgis-riot[46] of horror which had come when a sage with the hateful key had stumbled on a horde with the locked and brimming coffer of transmitted daemon-lore.

Suddenly a ray of physical light shot through these phantasms, and Malone heard the sound of oars amidst the blasphemies of things that should be dead. A boat with a lantern in its prow darted into sight, made fast to an iron ring in the slimy stone pier, and vomited forth several dark men bearing a long burden swathed in bedding. They took it to the naked phosphorescent thing on the carved golden pedestal, and the thing tittered and pawed at the bedding. Then they unswathed it, and propped upright before the pedestal the gangrenous corpse[47] of a corpulent old man with stubbly beard and unkempt white hair. The phosphorescent thing tittered again, and the men produced bottles from their pockets and anointed its feet with red, whilst they afterward gave the bottles to the thing to drink from.

All at once, from an arcaded avenue leading endlessly away, there came the daemoniac rattle and wheeze of a blasphemous organ, choking and rumbling out the mockeries of hell in a cracked, sardonic bass. In an instant every moving entity was electrified; and forming at once into a ceremonial procession, the nightmare horde slithered away in quest of the sound—goat, satyr, and aegipan, incubus, succuba, and lemur,[48] twisted toad and shapeless elemental, dog-faced howler and silent strutter in darkness—all led by the abominable naked phosphorescent thing that had squatted on the carved golden throne, and that now strode insolently bearing in its arms the glassy-eyed corpse of the corpulent old man. The strange dark men danced in the rear, and the whole column skipped and leaped with Dionysiac fury. Malone staggered after them a few steps, delirious and hazy, and doubtful of his place in this or in any world. Then he turned, faltered, and sank down on the cold damp stone, gasping and shivering as the daemon organ croaked on, and the howling and drumming and tinkling of the mad procession grew fainter and fainter.

Vaguely he was conscious of chanted horrors and shocking croakings afar off. Now and then a wail or whine of ceremonial devotion would float to him through the black arcade, whilst eventually there rose the dreadful Greek incantation whose text he had read above the pulpit of that dance-hall church.

"O friend and companion of night, thou who rejoicest in the baying of dogs (*here a hideous howl burst forth*) and spilt blood (*here nameless sounds vied with morbid shriekings*), who wanderest in the midst of shades among the tombs (*here a whistling sigh occurred*), who longest for blood and bringest terror to mortals (*short, sharp*

47. If this description is meant literally, it is inaccurate, for Suydam died only hours before. But compare HPL's metaphorical description of the denizens of the Lower East Side, in note 17, above.

48. In Roman mythology, *lemures* are vengeful ghosts or spirits of the dead. Linnaeus gave the name "lemur" to the Madagascar primates because of their nocturnal activities.

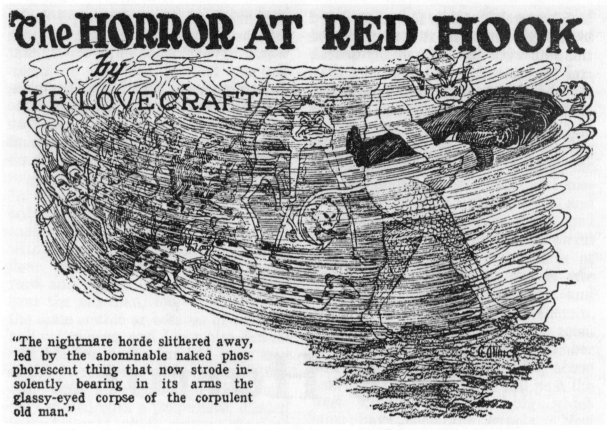

"The nightmare horde slithered away, led by the abominable naked phosphorescent thing that now strode insolently bearing in its arms the glassy-eyed corpse of the corpulent old man."

"The nightmare horde slithered away, led by the abominable naked phosphorescent thing that now strode insolently bearing in its arms the glassy-eyed corpse of the corpulent old man."
Weird Tales (January 1927) (artist: George Ochterlony Olinick)

cries *from myriad throats*), Gorgo (*repeated as response*), Mormo (*repeated with ecstasy*), thousand-faced moon (*sighs and flute notes*), look favourably on our sacrifices!"

As the chant closed, a general shout went up, and hissing sounds nearly drowned the croaking of the cracked bass organ. Then a gasp as from many throats, and a babel of barked and bleated words—"Lilith, Great Lilith, behold the Bridegroom!" More cries, a clamour of rioting, and the sharp, clicking footfalls of a running figure. The footfalls approached, and Malone raised himself to his elbow to look.

The luminosity of the crypt, lately diminished, had now slightly increased; and in that devil-light there appeared the fleeing form of that which should not flee or feel or breathe—the glassy-eyed, gangrenous corpse of the corpulent old man, now needing no support, but animated by some infernal sorcery of the rite just closed. After it raced the naked, tittering, phosphorescent thing that belonged on the carven pedestal, and still farther behind panted the dark men, and all the dread crew of sentient loathsomenesses. The corpse was gaining on its pursuers, and seemed bent on a definite object, straining with every rotting muscle toward the carved golden pedestal, whose necromantic importance was evidently so great. Another moment and it had reached its goal, whilst the trailing throng laboured on with more frantic speed. But they were too late, for in one final spurt of strength which ripped tendon from tendon and sent its noisome bulk floundering to the floor in a state of jellyish dissolution, the staring corpse which had been Robert Suydam achieved its object and its triumph. The push had been tremendous, but the force had held out; and as the pusher collapsed to a muddy blotch of corruption the pedestal he had pushed tottered, tipped, and finally careened from its onyx base into the thick waters below, sending up a parting gleam of carven gold as it sank heavily to undreamable gulfs of lower Tartarus. In that instant, too, the whole scene of horror faded to nothingness before Malone's eyes; and he fainted amidst a thunderous crash which seemed to blot out all the evil universe.

VII.

MALONE'S DREAM, EXPERIENCED in full before he knew of Suydam's death and transfer at sea, was curiously supplemented by some odd realities of the case; though that is no reason why anyone should believe it. The three old houses in Parker Place, doubtless long rotten with decay in its most insidious form, collapsed without visible cause while half the raiders and most of the prisoners were inside; and of both the greater number were instantly killed. Only in the basements and cellars was there much saving of life, and Malone was lucky to have been deep below the house of Robert Suydam. For he really was there, as no one is disposed to deny. They found him unconscious by the edge of a night-black pool, with a grotesquely horrible jumble of decay and bone, identifiable through dental work as the body of

THE NEW ANNOTATED H.P. LOVECRAFT

49. "Have there ever been demons, incubi, and succubæ, and from such a union [between an incubus or succubus and a human] can offspring be born?" The question appears in Martin Delrio's *Disquisitionum Magicarum Libri Sex* [Six Books of Disquisitions on Magic] (1603) and is included in the article on "Demonology" that appears in the *Encyclopaedia Britannica* (9th ed.), vol. VII, 62, by E. B. Tylor.

Suydam, a few feet away. The case was plain, for it was hither that the smugglers' underground canal led; and the men who took Suydam from the ship had brought him home. They themselves were never found, or at least never identified; and the ship's doctor is not yet satisfied with the simple certitudes of the police.

Suydam was evidently a leader in extensive man-smuggling operations, for the canal to his house was but one of several subterranean channels and tunnels in the neighbourhood. There was a tunnel from this house to a crypt beneath the dance-hall church; a crypt accessible from the church only through a narrow secret passage in the north wall, and in whose chambers some singular and terrible things were discovered. The croaking organ was there, as well as a vast arched chapel with wooden benches and a strangely figured altar. The walls were lined with small cells, in seventeen of which—hideous to relate—solitary prisoners in a state of complete idiocy were found chained, including four mothers with infants of disturbingly strange appearance. These infants died soon after exposure to the light; a circumstance which the doctors thought rather merciful. Nobody but Malone, among those who inspected them, remembered the sombre question of old Delrio: "*An sint unquam daemones incubi et succubae, et an ex tali congressu proles nasci queat?*"[49]

Before the canals were filled up they were thoroughly dredged, and yielded forth a sensational array of sawed and split bones of all sizes. The kidnapping epidemic, very clearly, had been traced home; though only two of the surviving prisoners could by any legal thread be connected with it. These men are now in prison, since they failed of conviction as accessories in the actual murders. The carved golden pedestal or throne so often mentioned by Malone as of primary occult importance was never brought to light, though at one place under the Suydam house the canal was observed to sink into a well too deep for dredging. It was choked up at the mouth and cemented over when the cellars of the new houses were made, but Malone often speculates on what lies beneath. The police, satisfied that they had shattered a dangerous gang of maniacs and man-smugglers, turned over to the Federal authorities the unconvicted Kurds, who before their deportation were conclusively found to belong to the Yezidi clan of devil-worshippers. The tramp ship and its crew remain an elusive mystery, though cynical detectives are once more ready to combat its smuggling and rum-running ventures. Malone thinks these detectives shew a sadly limited perspective in their lack of wonder at the myriad unexplainable details, and the suggestive obscurity of the whole case; though he is just as critical of the newspapers, which saw only a morbid sensation and gloated over a minor sadist cult when they might have proclaimed a horror from the universe's very heart. But he is content to rest silent in Chepachet, calming his nervous system and praying that time may gradually transfer his terrible experience from the realm of present reality to that of picturesque and semi-mythical remoteness.

Robert Suydam sleeps beside his bride in Greenwood Cemetery.[50] No funeral was held over the strangely released bones, and relatives are grateful for the swift oblivion which overtook the case as a whole. The scholar's connexion with the Red Hook horrors, indeed, was never emblazoned by legal proof; since his death forestalled the inquiry he would otherwise have faced. His own end is not much mentioned, and the Suydams hope that posterity may recall him only as a gentle recluse who dabbled in harmless magic and folklore.

As for Red Hook—it is always the same. Suydam came and went; a terror gathered and faded; but the evil spirit of darkness and squalor broods on amongst the mongrels in the old brick houses, and prowling bands still parade on unknown errands past windows where lights and twisted faces unaccountably appear and disappear. Age-old horror is a hydra with a thousand heads, and the cults of darkness are rooted in blasphemies deeper than the well of Democritus.[51] The soul of the beast is omnipresent and triumphant, and Red Hook's legions of blear-eyed, pockmarked youths still chant and curse and howl as they file from abyss to abyss, none knows whence or whither, pushed on by blind laws of biology which they may never understand. As of old, more people enter Red Hook than leave it on the landward side; and there are already rumours of new canals running underground to certain centres of traffic in liquor and less mentionable things.

The dance-hall church is now mostly a dance hall, and queer faces have appeared at night at the windows. Lately a policeman expressed the belief that the filled-up crypt has been dug out again, and for no simply explainable purpose. Who are we to

50. Properly, Green-Wood Cemetery, near Prospect Park in Brooklyn.

51. See "The Transition of Juan Romero," pp. 20–28, note 17, above.

combat poisons older than history and mankind? Apes danced in Asia to those horrors, and the cancer lurks secure and spreading where furtiveness hides in rows of decaying brick.

Malone does not shudder without cause—for only the other day an officer overheard a swarthy squinting hag teaching a small child some whispered patois in the shadow of an areaway. He listened, and thought it very strange when he heard her repeat over and over again,

"O friend and companion of night, thou who rejoicest in the baying of dogs and spilt blood, who wanderest in the midst of shades among the tombs, who longest for blood and bringest terror to mortals, Gorgo, Mormo, thousand-faced moon, look favourably on our sacrifices!"

He[1]

Written nine months before HPL fled New York City to return to the safe haven of Providence, and based on an actual expedition he made to "a little black court off [93] Perry Street" in Greenwich Village, the opening paragraph could not more closely mirror HPL's own sentiments about New York, expressed at length in correspondence. The story itself is an interesting mixture of genuine New York history and a typically dark vision of the future, and the image of ultimate destruction with which it ends brings the adventure to a surprising conclusion.

"A little black court off Perry Street"
(93 Perry Street, Manhattan, 2010).
Photograph courtesy of Donovan K. Loucks

I saw him on a sleepless night when I was walking desperately to save my soul and my vision. My coming to New York had been a mistake; for whereas I had looked for poignant wonder and inspiration in the teeming labyrinths of ancient streets that twist endlessly from forgotten courts and squares and waterfronts to courts and squares and waterfronts equally forgotten, and in the Cyclopean modern towers and pinnacles that rise blackly Babylonian under waning moons, I had found instead only a sense of horror and oppression which threatened to master, paralyse, and annihilate me.[2]

The disillusion had been gradual. Coming for the first time upon the town, I had seen it in the sunset from a bridge, majestic above its waters, its incredible peaks and pyramids rising flower-like and delicate from pools of violet mist to play with the flaming golden clouds and the first stars of evening. Then it had lighted up window by window above the shimmering tides where

1. This piece was written on August 11, 1925, and first published in *Weird Tales* 8, no. 3 (September 1926), 373–80.

2. A sentiment clearly shared by HPL. See the foreword to the previous volume, pp. xv–lxvii, note 39 and text accompanying, for a discussion of his hatred for the city.

Carcassonne.
Shutterstock.com

3. A fortified town in the Languedoc-Roussillon region of France. It is no doubt mentioned here because of the Cité de Carcassonne (La Cité), a medieval fortress located in the town that was restored in 1853 by Eugène-Emmanuel Viollet-le-Duc (who also restored the Cathedral of Notre-Dame) and became a popular tourist attraction.

4. Now in Uzbekistan, near Bukhara, the city of Samarkand is probably almost three thousand years old, and because of its central location on the Silk Road, it was a focal point of many civilizations.

Samarkand.
Shutterstock.com

5. A legendary city of gold, now largely dismissed as myth.

lanterns nodded and glided and deep horns bayed weird harmonies, and itself become a starry firmament of dream, redolent of faery music, and one with the marvels of Carcassonne[3] and Samarcand[4] and El Dorado[5] and all glorious and half-fabulous cities. Shortly afterward I was taken through those antique ways so dear to my fancy—narrow, curving alleys and passages where rows of red Georgian brick blinked with small-paned dormers above pillared doorways that had looked on gilded sedans and panelled coaches—and in the first flush of realisation of these long-wished things I thought I had indeed achieved such treasures as would make me in time a poet.

But success and happiness were not to be. Garish daylight shewed only squalor and alienage and the noxious elephantiasis of climbing, spreading stone where the moon had hinted of loveliness and elder magic; and the throngs of people that seethed through the flume-like streets were squat, swarthy strangers with hardened faces and narrow eyes, shrewd strangers without dreams and without kinship to the scenes about them, who could never mean aught to a blue-eyed man of the old folk, with the love of fair green lanes and white New England village steeples in his heart.

So instead of the poems I had hoped for, there came only a shuddering blankness and ineffable loneliness; and I saw at last a fearful truth which no one had ever dared to breathe before—the unwhisperable secret of secrets—the fact that this city of stone and stridor[6] is not a sentient perpetuation of Old New York as London is of Old London and Paris of Old Paris, but that it is in fact quite dead, its sprawling body imperfectly embalmed and infested with queer animate things which have nothing to do with it as it was in life. Upon making this discovery I ceased to sleep comfortably; though something of resigned tranquillity came back as I gradually formed the habit of keeping off the streets by day and venturing abroad only at night, when darkness calls forth what little of the past still hovers wraith-like about, and old white doorways remember the stalwart forms that once passed through them. With this mode of relief I even wrote a few poems, and still refrained from going home to my people lest I seem to crawl back ignobly in defeat.

Then, on a sleepless night's walk, I met the man. It was in a grotesque hidden courtyard of the Greenwich section, for there in my ignorance I had settled, having heard of the place as the natural home of poets and artists. The archaic lanes and houses and unexpected bits of square and court had indeed delighted me, and when I found the poets and artists to be loud-voiced pretenders whose quaintness is tinsel and whose lives are a denial of all that pure beauty which is poetry and art, I stayed on for love of these venerable things. I fancied them as they were in their prime, when Greenwich was a placid village not yet engulfed by the town; and in the hours before dawn, when all the revellers had slunk away, I used to wander alone among their cryptical windings and brood upon the curious arcana which generations must have deposited there. This kept my soul alive, and gave me a few of those dreams and visions for which the poet far within me cried out.

The man came upon me at about two one cloudy August morning, as I was threading a series of detached courtyards; now accessible only through the unlighted hallways of intervening buildings, but once forming parts of a continuous network of picturesque alleys. I had heard of them by vague rumour, and realised that they could not be upon any map of today; but the fact that they were forgotten only endeared them to me, so that I had sought them with twice my usual eagerness. Now that I had found them, my eagerness was again redoubled; for something in their arrangement dimly hinted that they might be only a few

6. A harsh, creaking sound; the term is now used in medicine to describe noisy breathing that sounds like the cawing of a crow.

of many such, with dark, dumb counterparts wedged obscurely betwixt high blank walls and deserted rear tenements, or lurking lamplessly behind archways, unbetrayed by hordes of the foreign-speaking or guarded by furtive and uncommunicative artists whose practices do not invite publicity or the light of day.

He spoke to me without invitation, noting my mood and glances as I studied certain knockered doorways above iron-railed steps, the pallid glow of traceried transoms feebly lighting my face. His own face was in shadow, and he wore a wide-brimmed hat which somehow blended perfectly with the out-of-date cloak he affected; but I was subtly disquieted even before he addressed me. His form was very slight, thin almost to cadaverousness; and his voice proved phenomenally soft and hollow, though not particularly deep. He had, he said, noticed me several times at my wanderings; and inferred that I resembled him in loving the vestiges of former years. Would I not like the guidance of one long practiced in these explorations, and possessed of local information profoundly deeper than any which an obvious newcomer could possibly have gained?

As he spoke, I caught a glimpse of his face in the yellow beam from a solitary attic window. It was a noble, even a handsome, elderly countenance; and bore the marks of a lineage and refinement unusual for the age and place. Yet some quality about it disturbed me almost as much as its features pleased me—perhaps it was too white, or too expressionless, or too much out of keeping with the locality, to make me feel easy or comfortable. Nevertheless I followed him; for in those dreary days my quest for antique beauty and mystery was all that I had to keep my soul alive, and I reckoned it a rare favour of Fate to fall in with one whose kindred seekings seemed to have penetrated so much farther than mine.

Something in the night constrained the cloaked man to silence, and for a long hour he led me forward without needless words; making only the briefest of comments concerning ancient names and dates and changes, and directing my progress very largely by gestures as we squeezed through interstices, tiptoed through corridors, clambered over brick walls, and once crawled on hands and knees through a low, arched passage of stone whose immense length and tortuous twistings effaced at last every hint of geographical location I had managed to preserve. The things we saw were very old and marvellous, or at least they seemed so in the few straggling rays of light by which I viewed them, and I shall never forget the tottering Ionic columns and fluted pilasters and urn-headed iron fence-posts and flaring-lintelled windows and decorative fanlights that appeared to grow quainter and stranger the deeper we advanced into this inexhaustible maze of unknown antiquity.

We met no person, and as time passed the lighted windows became fewer and fewer. The street-lights we first encountered had been of oil, and of the ancient lozenge pattern. Later I noticed some with candles; and at last, after traversing a horrible unlighted court where my guide had to lead with his gloved hand through total blackness to a narrow wooden gate in a high wall, we came upon a fragment of alley lit only by lanterns in front of every seventh house—unbelievably colonial tin lanterns with conical tops and holes punched in the sides. This alley led steeply uphill—more steeply than I thought possible in this part of New York—and the upper end was blocked squarely by the ivy-clad wall of a private estate, beyond which I could see a pale cupola, and the tops of trees waving against a vague lightness in the sky. In this wall was a small, low-arched gate of nail-studded black oak, which the man proceeded to unlock with a ponderous key. Leading me within, he steered a course in utter blackness over what seemed to be a gravel path, and finally up a flight of stone steps to the door of the house, which he unlocked and opened for me.

We entered, and as we did so I grew faint from a reek of infinite mustiness which welled out to meet us, and which must have been the fruit of unwholesome centuries of decay. My host appeared not to notice this, and in courtesy I kept silent as he piloted me up a curving stairway, across a hall, and into a room whose door I heard him lock behind us. Then I saw him pull the curtains of the three small-paned windows that barely shewed themselves against the lightening sky; after which he crossed to the mantel, struck flint and steel, lighted two candles of a candelabrum of twelve sconces, and made a gesture enjoining soft-toned speech.

In this feeble radiance I saw that we were in a spacious, well-furnished, and panelled library dating from the first quarter of the eighteenth century, with splendid doorway pediments, a delight-

7. Thomas Chippendale was a noted cabinetmaker in the eighteenth century; his name was applied to later furniture designs that bore little resemblance to his work—for example, "Chinese Chippendale," a descriptor for the railings at Monticello for which Thomas Jefferson drew up plans.

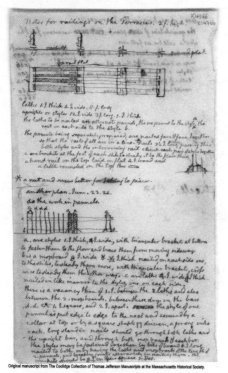

Original manuscript from The Coolidge Collection of Thomas Jefferson Manuscripts at the Massachusetts Historical Society.

Thomas Jefferson's plans for
"Chippendale" railings.

8. "Mid-Georgian" means around 1750. Styles were largely dictated by the French; men wore powdered wigs, greatcoats, and breeches.

9. Timo Airaksinen, in *The Philosophy of H. P. Lovecraft: The Route to Horror* (New York: Peter Lang Publishing, Inc., 1999), points out that "He" speaks as if he knows the narrator and suggests that the narrator and "He" are "counterparts in time" (68).

ful Doric cornice, and a magnificently carved overmantel with scroll-and-urn top. Above the crowded bookshelves at intervals along the walls were well-wrought family portraits; all tarnished to an enigmatical dimness, and bearing an unmistakable likeness to the man who now motioned me to a chair beside the graceful Chippendale[7] table. Before seating himself across the table from me, my host paused for a moment as if in embarrassment; then, tardily removing his gloves, wide-brimmed hat, and cloak, stood theatrically revealed in full mid-Georgian costume from queued hair and neck ruffles to knee-breeches, silk hose, and the buckled shoes I had not previously noticed.[8] Now slowly sinking into a lyre-back chair, he commenced to eye me intently.

Without his hat he took on an aspect of extreme age which was scarcely visible before, and I wondered if this unperceived mark of singular longevity were not one of the sources of my original disquiet. When he spoke at length, his soft, hollow, and carefully muffled voice not infrequently quavered; and now and then I had great difficulty in following him as I listened with a thrill of amazement and half-disavowed alarm which grew each instant.

"You behold, Sir," my host began, "a man of very eccentric habits, for whose costume no apology need be offered to one with your wit and inclinations.[9] Reflecting upon better times, I have not scrupled to ascertain their ways and adopt their dress and manners; an indulgence which offends none if practiced without ostentation. It hath been my good-fortune to retain the rural seat of my ancestors, swallowed though it was by two towns, first Greenwich, which built up hither after 1800, then New-York, which joined on near 1830. There were many reasons for the close keeping of this place in my family, and I have not been remiss in discharging such obligations. The squire who succeeded to it in 1768 studied sartain arts and made sartain discoveries, all connected with influences residing in this particular plot of ground, and eminently desarving of the strongest guarding. Some curious effects of these arts and discoveries I now purpose to shew you, under the strictest secrecy; and I believe I may rely on my judgment of men enough to have no distrust of either your interest or your fidelity."

He paused, but I could only nod my head. I have said that

I was alarmed, yet to my soul nothing was more deadly than the material daylight world of New York, and whether this man were a harmless eccentric or a wielder of dangerous arts I had no choice save to follow him and slake my sense of wonder on whatever he might have to offer. So I listened.

"To—my ancestor—" he softly continued, "there appeared to reside some very remarkable qualities in the will of mankind; qualities having a little-suspected dominance not only over the acts of one's self and of others, but over every variety of force and substance in Nature, and over many elements and dimensions deemed more univarsal than Nature herself. May I say that he flouted the sanctity of things as great as space and time, and that he put to strange uses the rites of sartain half-breed red Indians once encamped upon this hill? These Indians shewed choler when the place was built, and were plaguy pestilent in asking to visit the grounds at the full of the moon. For years they stole over the wall each month when they could, and by stealth performed sartain acts. Then, in '68, the new squire catched them at their doings, and stood still at what he saw. Thereafter he bargained with them and exchanged the free access of his grounds for the exact inwardness of what they did; larning that their grandfathers got part of their custom from red ancestors and part from an old Dutchman in the time of the States-General.[10] And pox on him, I'm afeared the squire must have sarved them monstrous bad rum—whether or not by intent—for a week after he larnt the secret he was the only man living that knew it. You, Sir, are the first outsider to be told there is a secret, and split me if I'd have risked tampering that much with—the powers—had ye not been so hot after bygone things."

I shuddered as the man grew colloquial—and with familiar speech of another day. He went on.

"But you must know, Sir, that what—the squire—got from those mongrel salvages was but a small part of the larning he came to have. He had not been at Oxford for nothing, nor talked to no account with an ancient chymist[11] and astrologer in Paris. He was, in fine, made sensible that all the world is but the smoke of our intellects; past the bidding of the vulgar, but by the wise to be puffed out and drawn in like any cloud of prime Virginia tobacco. What we want, we may make about us; and what we

10. The parliament of Holland.

11. An alchemist, that is.

12. The Brick Presbyterian Church opened in 1768 and was originally located on the corner of Beekman and Nassau Streets. It moved to the Murray Hill area, at Thirty-Seventh Street and Fifth Avenue, in 1858. It subsequently moved farther uptown, to Park Avenue and Ninety-First Street, in 1938. This view is presumably of the original church, prior to 1858. Trinity Church is an Episcopal church at 75 Broadway, near the intersection of Broadway and Wall Streets in lower Manhattan. The steeple visible would have been that of the structure built in 1790, the second reincarnation of the church building. (The first, built in 1698 or so, burned down prior to construction of the Brick Presbyterian Church.) "St. Paul's" refers to St. Paul's Chapel, part of Trinity Church, located on Vesey Street in lower Manhattan, and built in 1766. George Washington attended St. Paul's after his inauguration as president, and HPL and Sonia Greene were married there.

St. Paul's Chapel, 209 Broadway, Manhattan, 2010.

Photograph courtesy of Donovan K. Loucks

don't want, we may sweep away. I won't say that all this is wholly true in body, but 'tis sufficient true to furnish a very pretty spectacle now and then. You, I conceive, would be tickled by a better sight of sartain other years than your fancy affords you; so be pleased to hold back any fright at what I design to shew. Come to the window and be quiet."

My host now took my hand to draw me to one of the two windows on the long side of the malodorous room, and at the first touch of his ungloved fingers I turned cold. His flesh, though dry and firm, was of the quality of ice; and I almost shrank away from his pulling. But again I thought of the emptiness and horror of reality, and boldly prepared to follow whithersoever I might be led. Once at the window, the man drew apart the yellow silk curtains and directed my stare into the blackness outside. For a moment I saw nothing save a myriad of tiny dancing lights, far, far before me. Then, as if in response to an insidious motion of my host's hand, a flash of heat-lightning played over the scene, and I looked out upon a sea of luxuriant foliage—foliage unpolluted, and not the sea of roofs to be expected by any normal mind. On my right the Hudson glittered wickedly, and in the distance ahead I saw the unhealthy shimmer of a vast salt marsh constellated with nervous fireflies. The flash died, and an evil smile illumined the waxy face of the aged necromancer.

"That was before my time—before the new squire's time. Pray let us try again."

I was faint, even fainter than the hateful modernity of that accursed city had made me.

"Good God!" I whispered, "can you do that for *any time*?" And as he nodded, and bared the black stumps of what had once been yellow fangs, I clutched at the curtains to prevent myself from falling. But he steadied me with that terrible, ice-cold claw, and once more made his insidious gesture.

Again the lightning flashed—but this time upon a scene not wholly strange. It was Greenwich, the Greenwich that used to be, with here and there a roof or row of houses as we see it now, yet with lovely green lanes and fields and bits of grassy common. The marsh still glittered beyond, but in the farther distance I saw the steeples of what was then all of New York; Trinity and St. Paul's and the Brick Church[12] dominating their sisters, and a faint haze

Steeple of Trinity Church, New York.
Shutterstock.com

of wood smoke hovering over the whole. I breathed hard, but not so much from the sight itself as from the possibilities my imagination terrifiedly conjured up.

"Can you—dare you—go *far?*" I spoke with awe, and I think he shared it for a second, but the evil grin returned.

"*Far?* What I have seen would blast ye to a mad statue of stone! Back, back—forward, *forward*—look, ye puling lack-wit!"

And as he snarled the phrase under his breath he gestured anew; bringing to the sky a flash more blinding than either which had come before. For full three seconds I could glimpse that pandaemoniac sight, and in those seconds I saw a vista which will

13. This vision echoes HPL's frequent expressions of fear of and anxiety over the "yellow hordes" overwhelming the city. See also "Polaris," pp. 15–19, note 14, above, and "Nyarlathotep," in the previous volume, pp. 30–34, note 9.

14. The word has several related derivations. *MacBain's Dictionary* offers multiple meanings, from lichen, to the Middle Irish word for cymbal, to a "pear-shaped bell or rattle." In ancient Greece and Rome, the word referred to castanet-like instruments; in French, a "*crotale*" is also defined as a castanet or cymbal, said to have been used in the cult of Cybele, whose priests were eunuchs.

15. A hellish or infernal place. The term means "house of Daniel" and, according to Dan Clore, was "coined by Jacques Cazotte and Dom Denis Chavis in their *Continuation des mille et une nuits* (1788–93, trans. as *Arabian Tales*)," referring to "[a] fabled undersea cavern wherein a school of sorcerers held its meetings, which Cazotte places 'under the sea near Tunis,' and Southey places 'under the roots of the ocean'" (*Weird Words: A Lovecraftian Lexicon* [New York: Hippocampus Press, 2009], 196–97).

ever afterward torment me in dreams. I saw the heavens verminous with strange flying things, and beneath them a hellish black city of giant stone terraces with impious pyramids flung savagely to the moon, and devil-lights burning from unnumbered windows. And swarming loathsomely on aërial galleries I saw the yellow, squint-eyed people of that city,[13] robed horribly in orange and red, and dancing insanely to the pounding of fevered kettle-drums, the clatter of obscene crotala,[14] and the maniacal moaning of muted horns whose ceaseless dirges rose and fell undulantly like the waves of an unhallowed ocean of bitumen.

I saw this vista, I say, and heard as with the mind's ear the blasphemous domdaniel[15] of cacophony which companioned it. It was the shrieking fulfilment of all the horror which that corpse-city had ever stirred in my soul, and forgetting every injunction to silence I screamed and screamed and screamed as my nerves gave way and the walls quivered about me.

Then, as the flash subsided, I saw that my host was trembling too; a look of shocking fear half blotting from his face the serpent distortion of rage which my screams had excited. He tottered, clutched at the curtains as I had done before, and wriggled his head wildly, like a hunted animal. God knows he had cause, for as the echoes of my screaming died away there came another sound so hellishly suggestive that only numbed emotion kept me sane and conscious. It was the steady, stealthy creaking of the stairs beyond the locked door, as with the ascent of a barefoot or skin-shod horde; and at last the cautious, purposeful rattling of the brass latch that glowed in the feeble candlelight. The old man clawed and spat at me through the mouldy air, and barked things in his throat as he swayed with the yellow curtain he clutched.

"The full moon—damn ye—ye . . . ye yelping dog—ye called 'em, and they've come for me! Moccasined feet—dead men—Gad sink ye, ye red devils, but I poisoned no rum o' yours—han't I kept your pox-rotted magic safe?—ye swilled yourselves sick, curse ye, and ye must needs blame the squire—let go, you! Unhand that latch—I've naught for ye here—"

At this point three slow and very deliberate raps shook the panels of the door, and a white foam gathered at the mouth of the frantic magician. His fright, turning to steely despair, left room for a resurgence of his rage against me; and he staggered a step toward

"The old man clawed and spat at me through the moldy air, and barked things in his throat as he swayed with the yellow curtain he clutched."
Weird Tales (September 1926) (artist: George Ochterlony Olinick)

the table on whose edge I was steadying myself. The curtains, still clutched in his right hand as his left clawed out at me, grew taut and finally crashed down from their lofty fastenings; admitting to the room a flood of that full moonlight which the brightening of the sky had presaged. In those greenish beams the candles paled, and a new semblance of decay spread over the musk-reeking room with its wormy panelling, sagging floor, battered mantel, rickety furniture, and ragged draperies. It spread over the old man, too, whether from the same source or because of his fear and vehemence, and I saw him shrivel and blacken as he lurched near and strove to rend me with vulturine talons. Only his eyes stayed whole, and they glared with a propulsive, dilated incandescence which grew as the face around them charred and dwindled.

The rapping was now repeated with greater insistence, and this time bore a hint of metal. The black thing facing me had become only a head with eyes, impotently trying to wriggle across the sinking floor in my direction, and occasionally emitting feeble little spits of immortal malice. Now swift and splintering blows assailed the sickly panels, and I saw the gleam of a tomahawk as it cleft the rending wood. I did not move, for I could not; but watched dazedly as the door fell in pieces to admit a colossal, shapeless influx of inky substance starred with shining, malevolent eyes. It poured thickly, like a flood of oil bursting a rotten bulkhead, overturned a chair as it spread, and finally flowed under the table and across the room to where the blackened head with the eyes still glared at me. Around that head it closed, totally swallowing it up, and in another moment it had begun to recede; bearing away its invisible burden without touching me, and flowing again out of that black doorway and down the unseen stairs, which creaked as before, though in reverse order.

Then the floor gave way at last, and I slid gaspingly down into the nighted chamber below, choking with cobwebs and half swooning with terror. The green moon, shining through broken windows, shewed me the hall door half open; and as I rose from the plaster-strown floor and twisted myself free from the sagged ceilings, I saw sweep past it an awful torrent of blackness, with scores of baleful eyes glowing in it. It was seeking the door to the cellar, and when it found it, it vanished therein. I now felt the floor of this lower room giving as that of the upper chamber had done, and once a crashing above had been followed by the fall past the west window of something which must have been the cupola. Now liberated for the instant from the wreckage, I rushed through the hall to the front door; and finding myself unable to open it, seized a chair and broke a window, climbing frenziedly out upon the unkempt lawn where moonlight danced over yard-high grass and weeds. The wall was high, and all the gates were locked; but moving a pile of boxes in a corner I managed to gain the top and cling to the great stone urn set there.

About me in my exhaustion I could see only strange walls and windows and old gambrel roofs. The steep street of my approach was nowhere visible, and the little I did see succumbed rapidly to a mist that rolled in from the river despite the glaring moonlight.

Suddenly the urn to which I clung began to tremble, as if sharing my own lethal dizziness; and in another instant my body was plunging downward to I knew not what fate.

The man who found me said that I must have crawled a long way despite my broken bones, for a trail of blood stretched off as far as he dared look. The gathering rain soon effaced this link with the scene of my ordeal, and reports could state no more than that I had appeared from a place unknown, at the entrance of a little black court off Perry Street.[16]

I never sought to return to those tenebrous labyrinths, nor would I direct any sane man thither if I could. Of who or what that ancient creature was, I have no idea; but I repeat that the city is dead and full of unsuspected horrors. Whither *he* has gone, I do not know; but I have gone home to the pure New England lanes up which fragrant sea-winds sweep at evening.

16. Now in the West Village, in lower Manhattan; previously known as Henry Street, in 1813 it was renamed after Oliver Hazard Perry, an American admiral who gained fame in the War of 1812. See photograph on p. 277.

Cool Air[1]

This chilling tale (apologies) is a favorite of comic book artists and writers and resembles many horror stories of the 1950s. The last of HPL's stories set in New York, it has no real supernatural elements—rather, it is a dark tale of science gone wrong. There are also suggestions that Dr. Muñoz is in contact with like-minded scientists, as in the community of Joseph Curwen (in The Case of Charles Dexter Ward*) and his correspondents. Inspired by Poe's "Facts in the Case of M. Valdemar" and Machen's "The Novel of the White Powder," the story reflects HPL's feelings about the horrors of the masses of New York City.*

1. "Cool Air" was written in February 1926. Rejected by *Weird Tales* in March 1926, it first appeared in *Tales of Magic and Mystery* 1, no. 4 (March 1928), 29–34. It later appeared in *Weird Tales* 34, no. 3 (September 1939), 95–101.

You ask me to explain why I am afraid of a draught of cool air; why I shiver more than others upon entering a cold room, and seem nauseated and repelled when the chill of evening creeps through the heat of a mild autumn day. There are those who say I respond to cold as others do to a bad odour, and I am the last to deny the impression. What I will do is to relate the most horrible circumstance I ever encountered, and leave it to you to judge whether or not this forms a suitable explanation of my peculiarity.

It is a mistake to fancy that horror is associated inextricably with darkness, silence, and solitude. I found it in the glare of mid-afternoon, in the clangour of a metropolis, and in the teeming midst of a shabby and commonplace rooming-house with a prosaic landlady and two stalwart men by my side. In the spring of 1923 I had secured some dreary and unprofitable magazine work in the city of New York; and being unable to pay any substantial rent, began drifting from one cheap boarding establishment to another in search of a room which might combine the qualities of decent cleanliness, endurable furnishings, and very reasonable price. It soon developed that I had only a choice between different evils, but after a time I came upon a house in West

317 West Fourteenth Street, Manhattan, 2010. Photograph
courtesy of Donovan K. Loucks

2. HPL's close friend was George Kirk,
who lived at 317 West Fourteenth Street,
in a brownstone that, according to HPL's
biographer S. T. Joshi, is identical to the
one described here (*I Am Providence*,
390–91). The building is now the Chelsea Pines Inn, a few hundred yards from
tiny Jackson Square, which is bounded
by Horatio Street, Eighth Avenue, and
Greenwich Avenue.

"Baby . . . It's Cold Inside!" in
EC Comics' *Vault of Horror*, no. 17 (1951).

Fourteenth Street[2] which disgusted me much less than the others
I had sampled.

The place was a four-story mansion of brownstone, dating
apparently from the late 'forties, and fitted with woodwork and
marble whose stained and sullied splendour argued a descent
from high levels of tasteful opulence. In the rooms, large and
lofty, and decorated with impossible paper and ridiculously ornate
stucco cornices, there lingered a depressing mustiness and hint
of obscure cookery; but the floors were clean, the linen tolerably

3. As long ago as the early nineteenth century, frigorific solutions with temperatures colder than ice, primarily used for cooling food and wine, were made by adding ammoniac (ammonium chloride), combined with saltpeter, to water. The ancient Romans found large deposits of sal ammoniac near a Temple of Amun, and so they called it "salt of Amun." Glauber's salt (sodium sulfate), far less expensive than sal ammoniac (which was largely imported from Egypt), was often substituted.

regular, and the hot water not too often cold or turned off, so that I came to regard it as at least a bearable place to hibernate till one might really live again. The landlady, a slatternly, almost bearded Spanish woman named Herrero, did not annoy me with gossip or with criticisms of the late-burning electric light in my third-floor front hall room; and my fellow-lodgers were as quiet and uncommunicative as one might desire, being mostly Spaniards a little above the coarsest and crudest grade. Only the din of street cars in the thoroughfare below proved a serious annoyance.

I had been there about three weeks when the first odd incident occurred. One evening at about eight I heard a spattering on the floor and became suddenly aware that I had been smelling the pungent odour of ammonia for some time. Looking about, I saw that the ceiling was wet and dripping; the soaking apparently proceeding from a corner on the side toward the street. Anxious to stop the matter at its source, I hastened to the basement to tell the landlady; and was assured by her that the trouble would quickly be set right.

"Doctair Muñoz," she cried as she rushed upstairs ahead of me, "he have speel hees chemicals. He ees too seeck for doctair heemself—seecker and seecker all the time—but he weel not have no othair for help. He ees vairy queer in hees seeckness—all day he take funnee-smelling baths, and he cannot get excite or warm. All hees own housework he do—hees leetle room are full of bottles and machines, and he do not work as doctair. But he was great once—my fathair in Barcelona have hear of heem—and only joost now he feex a arm of the plumber that get hurt of sudden. He nevair go out, only on roof, and my boy Esteban he breeng heem hees food and laundry and mediceens and chemicals. My Gawd, the sal-ammoniac[3] that man use for keep heem cool!"

Mrs. Herrero disappeared up the staircase to the fourth floor, and I returned to my room. The ammonia ceased to drip, and as I cleaned up what had spilled and opened the window for air, I heard the landlady's heavy footsteps above me. Dr. Muñoz I had never heard, save for certain sounds as of some gasoline-driven mechanism; since his step was soft and gentle. I wondered for a moment what the strange affliction of this man might be, and whether his obstinate refusal of outside aid were not the result of a rather baseless eccentricity. There is, I reflected tritely, an infinite deal of pathos in the state of an eminent person who has come down in the world.

I might never have known Dr. Muñoz had it not been for the heart attack that suddenly seized me one forenoon as I sat writing in my room. Physicians had told me of the danger of those spells, and I knew there was no time to be lost; so remembering what the landlady had said about the invalid's help of the injured workman, I dragged myself upstairs and knocked feebly at the door above mine. My knock was answered in good English by a curious voice some distance to the right, asking my name and business; and these things being stated, there came an opening of the door next to the one I had sought.

A rush of cool air greeted me; and though the day was one of the hottest of late June, I shivered as I crossed the threshold into a large apartment whose rich and tasteful decoration surprised me in this nest of squalor and seediness. A folding couch now filled its diurnal role of sofa, and the mahogany furniture, sumptuous hangings, old paintings, and mellow bookshelves all bespoke a gentleman's study rather than a boarding-house bedroom. I now saw that the hall room above mine—the "leetle room" of bottles and machines which Mrs. Herrero had mentioned—was merely the laboratory of the doctor; and that his main living quarters lay in the spacious adjoining room whose convenient alcoves and large contiguous bathroom permitted him to hide all dressers and obtrusive utilitarian devices. Dr. Muñoz, most certainly, was a man of birth, cultivation, and discrimination.

The figure before me was short but exquisitely proportioned, and clad in somewhat formal dress of perfect cut and fit. A high-bred face of masterful though not arrogant expression was adorned by a short iron-grey full beard, and an old-fashioned pince-nez[4] shielded the full, dark eyes and surmounted an aquiline nose which gave a Moorish touch to a physiognomy otherwise dominantly Celtiberian.[5] Thick, well-trimmed hair that argued the punctual calls of a barber was parted gracefully above a high forehead; and the whole picture was one of striking intelligence and superior blood and breeding.

Nevertheless, as I saw Dr. Muñoz in that blast of cool air, I felt a repugnance which nothing in his aspect could justify. Only

4. "Pinch-nose" eyeglasses that use a nose clip instead of earpieces. Sherlock Holmes found them to be an important clue in "The Adventure of the Golden Pince-Nez" (1904), in which a woman's glasses are found clenched in the hand of a murder victim. HPL would have been very familiar with the story, first published when Lovecraft was fourteen years old and an avid reader of the Holmes canon.

5. The Celtic-speaking inhabitants of the Iberian peninsula before the Common Era. Their fierce warriors made a cult of physical fitness.

his lividly inclined complexion and coldness of touch could have afforded a physical basis for this feeling, and even these things should have been excusable considering the man's known invalidism. It might, too, have been the singular cold that alienated me; for such chilliness was abnormal on so hot a day, and the abnormal always excites aversion, distrust, and fear.

But repugnance was soon forgotten in admiration, for the strange physician's extreme skill at once became manifest despite the ice-coldness and shakiness of his bloodless-looking hands. He clearly understood my needs at a glance, and ministered to them with a master's deftness; the while reassuring me in a finely modulated though oddly hollow and timbreless voice that he was the bitterest of sworn enemies to death, and had sunk his fortune and lost all his friends in a lifetime of bizarre experiment devoted to its bafflement and extirpation. Something of the benevolent fanatic seemed to reside in him, and he rambled on almost garrulously as he sounded my chest and mixed a suitable draught of drugs fetched from the smaller laboratory room. Evidently he found the society of a well-born man a rare novelty in this dingy environment, and was moved to unaccustomed speech as memories of better days surged over him.

His voice, if queer, was at least soothing; and I could not even perceive that he breathed as the fluent sentences rolled urbanely out. He sought to distract my mind from my own seizure by speaking of his theories and experiments; and I remember his tactfully consoling me about my weak heart by insisting that will and consciousness are stronger than organic life itself, so that if a bodily frame be but originally healthy and carefully preserved, it may through a scientific enhancement of these qualities retain a kind of nervous animation despite the most serious impairments, defects, or even absences in the battery of specific organs. He might, he half jestingly said, some day teach me to live—or at least to possess some kind of conscious existence—without any heart at all! For his part, he was afflicted with a complication of maladies requiring a very exact regimen which included constant cold. Any marked rise in temperature might, if prolonged, affect him fatally; and the frigidity of his habitation—some 55 or 56 degrees Fahrenheit—was maintained by an absorption system of ammonia cooling,[6] the gasoline engine of whose pumps I had often heard in my own room below.

Relieved of my seizure in a marvellously short while, I left the shivery place a disciple and devotee of the gifted recluse. After that I paid him frequent overcoated calls; listening while he told of secret researches and almost ghastly results, and trembling a bit when I examined the unconventional and astonishingly ancient volumes on his shelves. I was eventually, I may add, almost cured of my disease for all time by his skilful ministrations. It seems that he did not scorn the incantations of the mediaevalists, since he believed these cryptic formulae to contain rare psychological stimuli which might conceivably have singular effects on the substance of a nervous system from which organic pulsations had fled. I was touched by his account of the aged Dr. Torres of Valencia, who had shared his earlier experiments with him through the great illness of eighteen years before, whence his present disorders proceeded. No sooner had the venerable practitioner saved his colleague than he himself succumbed to the grim enemy he had fought. Perhaps the strain had been too great; for Dr. Muñoz made it whisperingly clear—though not in detail—that the methods of healing had been most extraordinary, involving scenes and processes not welcomed by elderly and conservative Galens.[7]

As the weeks passed, I observed with regret that my new friend was indeed slowly but unmistakably losing ground physically, as Mrs. Herrero had suggested. The livid aspect of his countenance was intensified, his voice became more hollow and indistinct, his muscular motions were less perfectly coordinated, and his mind and will displayed less resilience and initiative. Of this sad change he seemed by no means unaware, and little by little his expression and conversation both took on a gruesome irony which restored in me something of the subtle repulsion I had originally felt.

He developed strange caprices, acquiring a fondness for exotic spices and Egyptian incense till his room smelled like the vault of a sepulchred Pharaoh in the Valley of Kings.[8] At the same time his demands for cold air increased, and with my aid he amplified the ammonia piping of his room and modified the pumps and

6. Ammonia-based cooling systems were invented in the nineteenth century, and although household refrigerators now use either tetrafluoroethane (new models) or Freon (older models), compounds of ammonia are still a common coolant in industrial refrigeration plants. In simple terms, the refrigerant (ammonia) absorbs the heat from the air; a mechanical engine (here powered by gasoline) operates a compressor, which compresses the coolant, releasing the absorbed heat as the coolant condenses.

7. Galen (129–ca. 200) was a prominent Roman physician and surgeon— "Galens" here is a collective term for doctors.

8. A valley in Luxor, Egypt, where for five hundred years, from the eleventh century BCE forward, most kings, or pharaohs, were entombed.

Valley of Kings, Luxor.

9. Bert Atsma, in "Living on Borrowed Time (A Biologist Looks at 'M. Valdemar' and 'Cool Air')," *Crypt of Cthulhu* 4 (Eastertide 1982), scoffs at the scientific-sounding explanation offered here, as if willpower could prevent the death of brain cells. Furthermore, he points out, at very low temperatures, DNA loses its functionality, and cells cannot reproduce. While cold might produce suspended animation, Dr. Muñoz is clearly not in that state (11–12).

feed of his refrigerating machine till he could keep the temperature as low as 34° or 40°, and finally even 28°; the bathroom and laboratory, of course, being less chilled, in order that water might not freeze, and that chemical processes might not be impeded. The tenant adjoining him complained of the icy air from around the connecting door, so I helped him fit heavy hangings to obviate the difficulty. A kind of growing horror, of outré and morbid cast, seemed to possess him. He talked of death incessantly, but laughed hollowly when such things as burial or funeral arrangements were gently suggested.

All in all, he became a disconcerting and even gruesome companion; yet in my gratitude for his healing I could not well abandon him to the strangers around him, and was careful to dust his room and attend to his needs each day, muffled in a heavy ulster which I bought especially for the purpose. I likewise did much of his shopping, and gasped in bafflement at some of the chemicals he ordered from druggists and laboratory supply houses.

An increasing and unexplained atmosphere of panic seemed to rise around his apartment. The whole house, as I have said, had a musty odour; but the smell in his room was worse—and in spite of all the spices and incense, and the pungent chemicals of the now incessant baths which he insisted on taking unaided. I perceived that it must be connected with his ailment, and shuddered when I reflected on what that ailment might be. Mrs. Herrero crossed herself when she looked at him, and gave him up unreservedly to me; not even letting her son Esteban continue to run errands for him. When I suggested other physicians, the sufferer would fly into as much of a rage as he seemed to dare to entertain. He evidently feared the physical effect of violent emotion, yet his will and driving force waxed rather than waned, and he refused to be confined to his bed. The lassitude of his earlier ill days gave place to a return of his fiery purpose, so that he seemed about to hurl defiance at the death-daemon even as that ancient enemy seized him. The pretence of eating, always curiously like a formality with him, he virtually abandoned; and mental power alone appeared to keep him from total collapse.[9]

He acquired a habit of writing long documents of some sort, which he carefully sealed and filled with injunctions that I transmit them after his death to certain persons whom he named—for the most part lettered East Indians, but including a once celebrated French physician now generally thought dead, and about whom the most inconceivable things had been whispered. As it happened, I burned all these papers undelivered and unopened. His aspect and voice became utterly frightful, and his presence almost unbearable. One September day an unexpected glimpse of him induced an epileptic fit in a man who had come to repair his electric desk lamp; a fit for which he prescribed effectively whilst keeping himself well out of sight. That man, oddly enough, had been through the terrors of the Great War without having incurred any fright so thorough.

Then, in the middle of October, the horror of horrors came with stupefying suddenness. One night about eleven the pump of the refrigerating machine broke down, so that within three hours the process of ammonia cooling became impossible. Dr. Muñoz summoned me by thumping on the floor, and I worked desperately to repair the injury while my host cursed in a tone whose lifeless, rattling hollowness surpassed description. My amateur efforts, however, proved of no use; and when I had brought in a mechanic from a neighbouring all-night garage we learned that nothing could be done till morning, when a new piston would have to be obtained. The moribund hermit's rage and fear, swelling to grotesque proportions, seemed likely to shatter what remained of his failing physique; and once a spasm caused him to clap his hands to his eyes and rush into the bathroom. He groped his way out with face tightly bandaged, and I never saw his eyes again.

The frigidity of the apartment was now sensibly diminishing, and at about 5 a.m. the doctor retired to the bathroom, commanding me to keep him supplied with all the ice I could obtain at all-night drug stores and cafeterias. As I would return from my sometimes discouraging trips and lay my spoils before the closed bathroom door, I could hear a restless splashing within, and a thick voice croaking out the order for "More—more!" At length a warm day broke, and the shops opened one by one. I asked Esteban either to help with the ice-fetching whilst I obtained the pump piston, or to order the piston while I continued with the ice; but instructed by his mother, he absolutely refused.

10. According to the *Encyclopaedia Britannica* (vol. 31 of the 12th edition, 1922), "In New York City, for instance, a very large proportion of the street traffic in 1920 was by motor, and in the main thoroughfares horse vehicles were almost a rarity" (995). Yet according to David Haden, "While it is certainly true that . . . [t]he sales of passenger cars alone in Brooklyn in 1926 was over 32,000 (*A Study of All American Markets*, [by Leslie M. Barton, Chicago, 1927]), . . . it appears that many cars were only used for special trips, or were purchased as 'prestige-only' Sunday roadsters as the economy started to take off into what was later called the Roaring Twenties, rather than being used as everyday commuting-and-school wagons as they are today. This can be evidenced by the apparent lack of the need for city-centre car parks (parking lots) at that time" ("The Nature of the New York Streets," in *Walking with Cthulhu: H. P. Lovecraft as Psychogeographer, New York City 1924–26*, 52–71 [self-published, 2011], 56). Instead, New

"He groped his way out with face tightly bandaged, and I never saw his eyes again."
Weird Tales (September 1939) (artist: Harry Ferman)

Finally I hired a seedy-looking loafer whom I encountered on the corner of Eighth Avenue to keep the patient supplied with ice from a little shop where I introduced him, and applied myself diligently to the task of finding a pump piston and engaging workmen competent to install it. The task seemed interminable, and I raged almost as violently as the hermit when I saw the hours slipping by in a breathless, foodless round of vain telephoning, and a hectic quest from place to place, hither and thither by subway and surface car.[10] About noon I encountered a suitable supply house far downtown, and at approximately 1:30 p.m. arrived at my boarding-place with the necessary paraphernalia and two sturdy and intelligent mechanics. I had done all I could, and hoped I was in time.

Black terror, however, had preceded me. The house was in utter turmoil, and above the chatter of awed voices I heard a man praying in a deep basso. Fiendish things were in the air, and lodg-

Manhattan motor traffic in 1923.

ers told over the beads of their rosaries as they caught the odour from beneath the doctor's closed door. The lounger I had hired, it seems, had fled screaming and mad-eyed not long after his second delivery of ice; perhaps as a result of excessive curiosity. He could not, of course, have locked the door behind him; yet it was now fastened, presumably from the inside. There was no sound within save a nameless sort of slow, thick dripping.

Briefly consulting with Mrs. Herrero and the workmen despite a fear that gnawed my inmost soul, I advised the breaking down of the door; but the landlady found a way to turn the key from the outside with some wire device. We had previously opened the doors of all the other rooms on that hall, and flung all the windows to the very top. Now, noses protected by handkerchiefs, we tremblingly invaded the accursed south room which blazed with the warm sun of early afternoon.

A kind of dark, slimy trail led from the open bathroom door to the hall door, and thence to the desk, where a terrible little pool had accumulated. Something was scrawled there in pencil in an awful, blind hand on a piece of paper hideously smeared as though by the very claws that traced the hurried last words. Then the trail led to the couch and ended unutterably.

What was, or had been, on the couch I cannot and dare not say here.[11] But this is what I shiveringly puzzled out on the stickily smeared paper before I drew a match and burned it to a crisp; what I puzzled out in terror as the landlady and two mechanics rushed frantically from that hellish place to babble their incoherent stories at the nearest police station. The nauseous words seemed well-nigh incredible in that yellow sunlight, with the clatter of cars and motor trucks ascending clamorously from crowded Fourteenth Street, yet I confess that I believed them then. Whether I believe them now I honestly do not know. There are things about which it is better not to speculate, and all that I can say is that I hate the smell of ammonia, and grow faint at a draught of unusually cool air.

"The end," ran that noisome scrawl, "is here. No more ice—the man looked and ran away. Warmer every minute, and the tissues can't last. I fancy you know—what I said about the will and the nerves and the preserved body after the organs ceased

York boasted capacious modes of public transport, including streetcars, buses, taxicabs, and the municipal railways. In 1920, for example, when the population of the New York metropolitan area stood at about 7.5 million, the steam railways alone carried an estimated 298,000 passengers per weekday, or almost 75 million passengers per year ("Transportation for Greater New York," *Electric Railway Journal* 56, no. 22 [November 27, 1920], 1095–106).

11. Darrell Schweitzer points out, in *The Dream Quest of H. P. Lovecraft* (San Bernardino, CA: Borgo Press, 1978), that "a frozen corpse quickly thawed should do nothing more than rot normally" (33).

to work. It was good theory, but couldn't keep up indefinitely. There was a gradual deterioration I had not foreseen. Dr. Torres knew, but the shock killed him. He couldn't stand what he had to do—he had to get me in a strange, dark place when he minded my letter and nursed me back. And the organs never would work again. It had to be done my way—artificial preservation—*for you see I died that time eighteen years ago.*"

The Strange High House in the Mist[1]

Although "The Strange High House in the Mist" is firmly set in Arkham country, in HPL's mythical city of Kingsport, Lovecraft's inspirations were "the titan cliffs of Magnolia" (on the east coast of Massachusetts) and the headlands near Gloucester, Massachusetts. The tone of the story resembles that of Lovecraft's Dunsanian tales, evoking gods of legend. Unlike the narrator of earlier such tales, however, Thomas Olney is moved by his experience with the supernatural to a place of contentment. Perhaps this reflects a growing maturity in Lovecraft himself.

I n the morning mist comes up from the sea by the cliffs beyond Kingsport.[2] White and feathery it comes from the deep to its brothers the clouds, full of dreams and dank pastures and caves of leviathan. And later, in still summer rains on the steep roofs of poets, the clouds scatter bits of those dreams, that men shall not live without rumour of old, strange secrets, and wonders that planets tell planets alone in the night. When tales fly thick in the grottoes of tritons, and conches in seaweed cities blow wild tunes learned from the Elder Ones, then great eager mists flock to heaven laden with lore, and oceanward eyes on the rocks see only a mystic whiteness, as if the cliff's rim were the rim of all earth, and the solemn bells of buoys tolled free in the aether of faery.

Now north of archaic Kingsport the crags climb lofty and curious, terrace on terrace, till the northernmost hangs in the sky like a grey frozen wind-cloud. Alone it is, a bleak point jutting in limitless space, for there the coast turns sharp where the great Miskatonic[3] pours out of the plains past Arkham, bringing woodland legends and little quaint memories of New England's hills. The sea-folk in Kingsport look up at that cliff as other sea-folk look up at the pole-star, and time the night's watches by

1. The story was written in November 1926 and was published five years later, in *Weird Tales* 18, no. 3 (October 1931), 394–400.

2. See "The Terrible Old Man," pp. 36–39, note 4, above, for a discussion of the location of Kingsport.

3. The valley of the Miskatonic is first mentioned in "The Picture in the House" (1920), vol. 1, 35–44. Arkham is also first mentioned in that story.

4. Ursa Major and Cassiopeia are discussed in notes 4 and 5 of "Polaris," pp. 15–19, above. "The Dragon," also known as the Great Snake, is the constellation Draco, in the far northern sky. As many as 220 of its stars are visible to the naked eye. The stars are circumpolar—that is, they do not set below the horizon and, as such, are visible in the Northern, but not the Southern, Hemisphere. Thuban, once its polestar, is now one of the more insignificant of the 220.

5. See "The Terrible Old Man," pp. 36–39, above.

6. Jonathan Belcher was royal governor of colonial Massachusetts from 1730 to 1741; William Shirley, from 1741 to 1749; Thomas Pownall, from 1757 to 1760; and Francis Bernard, from 1760 to 1769.

7. Thomas Olney (1605?–1682) was the first treasurer of Providence and later a councilman and clerk, and this may be a descendant.

the way it hides or shews the Great Bear, Cassiopeia, and the Dragon.[4] Among them it is one with the firmament, and truly, it is hidden from them when the mist hides the stars or the sun. Some of the cliffs they love, as that whose grotesque profile they call Father Neptune, or that whose pillared steps they term The Causeway; but this one they fear because it is so near the sky. The Portuguese sailors coming in from a voyage cross themselves when they first see it, and the old Yankees believe it would be much graver matter than death to climb it, if indeed that were possible. Nevertheless there is an ancient house on that cliff, and at evening men see lights in the small-paned windows.

The ancient house has always been there, and people say, One dwells therein who talks with the morning mists that come up from the deep, and perhaps sees singular things oceanward at those times when the cliff's rim becomes the rim of all earth, and solemn buoys toll free in the white aether of faery. This they tell from hearsay, for that forbidding crag is always unvisited, and natives dislike to train telescopes on it. Summer boarders have indeed scanned it with jaunty binoculars, but have never seen more than the grey primeval roof, peaked and shingled, whose eaves come nearly to the grey foundations, and the dim yellow light of the little windows peeping out from under those eaves in the dusk. These summer people do not believe that the same One has lived in the ancient house for hundreds of years, but cannot prove their heresy to any real Kingsporter. Even the Terrible Old Man[5] who talks to leaden pendulums in bottles, buys groceries with centuried Spanish gold, and keeps stone idols in the yard of his antediluvian cottage in Water Street can only say these things were the same when his grandfather was a boy, and that must have been inconceivable ages ago, when Belcher or Shirley or Pownall or Bernard was Governor of His Majesty's Province of the Massachusetts-Bay.[6]

Then one summer there came a philosopher into Kingsport. His name was Thomas Olney,[7] and he taught ponderous things in a college by Narragansett Bay. With stout wife and romping children he came, and his eyes were weary with seeing the same things for many years, and thinking the same well-disciplined thoughts. He looked at the mists from the diadem of Father Neptune, and tried to walk into their white world of mystery along the

"Nevertheless there is an ancient house on that cliff, and at
evening men see lights in the small-paned windows."
Weird Tales (October 1931) (artist: Joseph Doolin)

titan steps of The Causeway. Morning after morning he would lie
on the cliffs and look over the world's rim at the cryptical aether
beyond, listening to spectral bells and the wild cries of what might
have been gulls. Then, when the mist would lift and the sea stand
out prosy with the smoke of steamers, he would sigh and descend
to the town, where he loved to thread the narrow olden lanes up
and down hill, and study the crazy tottering gables and odd pillared doorways which had sheltered so many generations of sturdy
sea-folk. And he even talked with the Terrible Old Man, who was
not fond of strangers, and was invited into his fearsomely archaic
cottage where low ceilings and wormy panelling hear the echoes
of disquieting soliloquies in the dark small hours.

Of course it was inevitable that Olney should mark the grey
unvisited cottage in the sky, on that sinister northward crag which
is one with the mists and the firmament. Always over Kingsport
it hung, and always its mystery sounded in whispers through

8. The Orne family are mentioned as prominent residents of Innsmouth in "The Shadow over Innsmouth," in the previous volume, pp. 573–642, and Simon Orne appears in *The Case of Charles Dexter Ward*, also in that volume, pp. 171–309, though whether "Granny Orne" is descended from one or the other is unknown.

Kingsport's crooked alleys. The Terrible Old Man wheezed a tale that his father had told him, of lightning that shot one night *up from* that peaked cottage to the clouds of higher heaven; and Granny Orne,[8] whose tiny gambrel-roofed abode in Ship Street is all covered with moss and ivy, croaked over something her grandmother had heard at second-hand, about shapes that flapped out of the eastern mists straight into the narrow single door of that unreachable place—for the door is set close to the edge of the crag toward the ocean, and glimpsed only from ships at sea.

At length, being avid for new strange things and held back by neither the Kingsporter's fear nor the summer boarder's usual indolence, Olney made a very terrible resolve. Despite a conservative training—or because of it, for humdrum lives breed wistful longings of the unknown—he swore a great oath to scale that avoided northern cliff and visit the abnormally antique grey cottage in the sky. Very plausibly his saner self argued that the place must be tenanted by people who reached it from inland along the easier ridge beside the Miskatonic's estuary. Probably they traded in Arkham, knowing how little Kingsport liked their habitation, or perhaps being unable to climb down the cliff on the Kingsport side. Olney walked out along the lesser cliffs to where the great crag leaped insolently up to consort with celestial things, and became very sure that no human feet could mount it or descend it on that beetling southern slope. East and north it rose thousands of feet vertically from the water, so only the western side, inland and toward Arkham, remained.

One early morning in August Olney set out to find a path to the inaccessible pinnacle. He worked northwest along pleasant back roads, past Hooper's Pond and the old brick powder-house to where the pastures slope up to the ridge above the Miskatonic and give a lovely vista of Arkham's white Georgian steeples across leagues of river and meadow. Here he found a shady road to Arkham, but no trail at all in the seaward direction he wished. Woods and fields crowded up to the high bank of the river's mouth, and bore not a sign of man's presence; not even a stone wall or a straying cow, but only the tall grass and giant trees and tangles of briers that the first Indian might have seen. As he climbed slowly east, higher and higher above the estuary on his left and nearer and nearer the sea, he found the way growing in difficulty; till he wondered how ever the dwellers in that disliked place managed to reach the world outside, and whether they came often to market in Arkham.

Then the trees thinned, and far below him on his right he saw the hills and antique roofs and spires of Kingsport. Even Central Hill[9] was a dwarf from this height, and he could just make out the ancient graveyard by the Congregational Hospital,[10] beneath which rumour said some terrible caves or burrows lurked. Ahead lay sparse grass and scrub blueberry bushes, and beyond them the naked rock of the crag and the thin peak of the dreaded grey cottage. Now the ridge narrowed, and Olney grew dizzy at his loneness in the sky. South of him the frightful precipice above Kingsport, north of him the vertical drop of nearly a mile to the river's mouth. Suddenly a great chasm opened before him, ten feet deep, so that he had to let himself down by his hands and drop to a slanting floor, and then crawl perilously up a natural defile in the opposite wall. So this was the way the folk of the uncanny house journeyed betwixt earth and sky!

When he climbed out of the chasm a morning mist was gathering, but he clearly saw the lofty and unhallowed cottage ahead; walls as grey as the rock, and high peak standing bold against the milky white of the seaward vapours. And he perceived that there was no door on this landward end, but only a couple of small lattice windows with dingy bull's-eye panes leaded in seventeenth-century fashion. All around him was cloud and chaos, and he could see nothing below but the whiteness of illimitable space. He was alone in the sky with this queer and very disturbing house; and when he sidled around to the front and saw that the wall stood flush with the cliff's edge, so that the single narrow door was not to be reached save from the empty aether, he felt a distinct terror that altitude could not wholly explain. And it was very odd that shingles so worm-eaten could survive, or bricks so crumbled still form a standing chimney.

As the mist thickened, Olney crept around to the windows on the north and west and south sides, trying them but finding them all locked. He was vaguely glad they were locked, because the more he saw of that house the less he wished to get in. Then a sound halted him. He heard a lock rattle and bolt shoot, and a long creaking follow as if a heavy door were slowly and cautiously

9. Central Hill is also mentioned in "The Festival," in the previous volume, pp. 103–13, and in "The Silver Key," also in that volume, pp. 158–70. In the latter, Randolph Carter has a childhood memory of a steeple on the hill but then recalls that the church was torn down to build the Congregational Hospital.

10. The Congregational Hospital is mentioned in "The Silver Key" and in "The Festival" as a hospital that stood near the old churchyard on Central Hill.

opened. This was on the oceanward side that he could not see, where the narrow portal opened on blank space thousands of feet in the misty sky above the waves.

Then there was heavy, deliberate tramping in the cottage, and Olney heard the windows opening, first on the north side opposite him, and then on the west just around the corner. Next would come the south windows, under the great low eaves on the side where he stood; and it must be said that he was more than uncomfortable as he thought of the detestable house on one side and the vacancy of upper air on the other. When a fumbling came in the nearer casements he crept around to the west again, flattening himself against the wall beside the now opened windows. It was plain that the owner had come home; but he had not come from the land, nor from any balloon or airship that could be imagined. Steps sounded again, and Olney edged round to the north; but before he could find a haven a voice called softly, and he knew he must confront his host.

Stuck out of a west window was a great black-bearded face whose eyes shone phosphorescently with the imprint of unheard-of sights. But the voice was gentle, and of a quaint olden kind, so that Olney did not shudder when a brown hand reached out to help him over the sill and into that low room of black oak wainscots and carved Tudor furnishings. The man was clad in very ancient garments, and had about him an unplaceable nimbus of sea-lore and dreams of tall galleons. Olney does not recall many of the wonders he told, or even who he was; but says that he was strange and kindly, and filled with the magic of unfathomed voids of time and space. The small room seemed green with a dim aqueous light, and Olney saw that the far windows to the east were not open, but shut against the misty aether with dull thick panes like the bottoms of old bottles.

That bearded host seemed young, yet looked out of eyes steeped in the elder mysteries; and from the tales of marvellous ancient things he related, it must be guessed that the village folk were right in saying he had communed with the mists of the sea and the clouds of the sky ever since there was any village to watch his taciturn dwelling from the plain below. And the day wore on, and still Olney listened to rumours of old times and far places, and heard how the Kings of Atlantis fought with the slippery blasphemies that wriggled out of rifts in ocean's floor, and how the pillared and weedy temple of Poseidonis[11] is still glimpsed at midnight by lost ships, who know by its sight that they are lost. Years of the Titans were recalled, but the host grew timid when he spoke of the dim first age of chaos before the gods or even the Elder Ones were born, and when only *the other gods* came to dance on the peak of Hatheg-Kla in the stony desert near Ulthar, beyond the river Skai.[12]

It was at this point that there came a knocking on the door; that ancient door of nail-studded oak beyond which lay only the abyss of white cloud. Olney started in fright, but the bearded man motioned him to be still, and tiptoed to the door to look out through a very small peep-hole. What he saw he did not like, so pressed his fingers to his lips and tiptoed around to shut and lock all the windows before returning to the ancient settle beside his guest. Then Olney saw lingering against the translucent squares of each of the little dim windows in succession a queer black outline as the caller moved inquisitively about before leaving; and he was glad his host had not answered the knocking. For there are strange objects in the great abyss, and the seeker of dreams must take care not to stir up or meet the wrong ones.

Then the shadows began to gather; first little furtive ones under the table, and then bolder ones in the dark panelled corners. And the bearded man made enigmatical gestures of prayer, and lit tall candles in curiously wrought brass candlesticks. Frequently he would glance at the door as if he expected someone, and at length his glance seemed answered by a singular rapping which must have followed some very ancient and secret code. This time he did not even glance through the peep-hole, but swung the great oak bar and shot the bolt, unlatching the heavy door and flinging it wide to the stars and the mist.

And then to the sound of obscure harmonies there floated into that room from the deep all the dreams and memories of earth's sunken Mighty Ones. And golden flames played about weedy locks, so that Olney was dazzled as he did them homage. Trident-bearing Neptune was there, and sportive tritons and fantastic nereids, and upon dolphins' backs was balanced a vast crenulate shell wherein rode the grey and awful form of primal Nodens, Lord of the Great Abyss.[13] And the conches of the tri-

11. Poseidonis is discussed in detail in W. Scott-Elliot's *The Story of Atlantis and the Lost Lemuria* (1925), a book mentioned in "The Call of Cthulhu," in the previous volume, pp. 123–57 (see note 16 in that story). According to Scott-Elliot, it was an island due west of the present coast of Spain and was the nucleus of the great continents of Atlantis and Lemuria. After three prior cataclysms over eons, it was the last remnant of the continent of Atlantis and submerged in 9564 BCE (24).

12. See "The Other Gods," pp. 106–10, above.

13. A Celtic deity connected with hunting, dogs, the sea, and healing. Marco Frenschkowski, in "Nodens—Metamorphosis of a Deity," *Crypt of Cthulhu* 87 (Lammas 1994), 3–8, points out that Nodens becomes a symbol of "the enrichment and transformation prepared for him who seeks the depths of vision" (3). In *The Dream-Quest of Unknown Kadath,* Nodens provides guidance to the fleeing Randolph Carter (see *The Dream-Quest of Unknown Kadath,* pp. 329–432, text accompanying note 37, below). HPL may have seen mention of Nodens in Arthur Machen's novella *The Great God Pan,* published in 1894. Nodens does not appear in any Greek or Roman text (nor is he mentioned in Celtic legend); rather, his name is found in curious inscriptions at the ruins of a temple in Lydney Park, Gloucestershire County, England, seemingly dating from the fourth century CE. The inscriptions are discussed in detail by Frenschkowski. The most complete etymological study of the name "Nodens" is by J. R. R. Tolkien. See *Report on the Excavation of the Prehistoric, Roman and Post-Roman Site in Lydney Park, Gloucestershire,* by the archaeologists R. E. M. Wheeler and T. V. Wheeler (Reports of the Research Committee of the Society

of Antiquaries of London IX, Oxford, 1932), which includes Tolkien's essay.

tons gave weird blasts, and the nereids made strange sounds by striking on the grotesque resonant shells of unknown lurkers in black sea-caves. Then hoary Nodens reached forth a wizened hand and helped Olney and his host into the vast shell, whereat the conches and the gongs set up a wild and awesome clamour. And out into the limitless aether reeled that fabulous train, the noise of whose shouting was lost in the echoes of thunder.

All night in Kingsport they watched that lofty cliff when the storm and the mists gave them glimpses of it, and when toward the small hours the little dim windows went dark they whispered of dread and disaster. And Olney's children and stout wife prayed to the bland proper god of Baptists, and hoped that the traveller would borrow an umbrella and rubbers unless the rain stopped by morning. Then dawn swam dripping and mist-wreathed out of the sea, and the buoys tolled solemn in vortices of white aether. And at noon elfin horns rang over the ocean as Olney, dry and light-footed, climbed down from the cliffs to antique Kingsport with the look of far places in his eyes. He could not recall what he had dreamed in the sky-perched hut of that still nameless hermit, or say how he had crept down that crag untraversed by other feet. Nor could he talk of these matters at all save with the Terrible Old Man, who afterward mumbled queer things in his long white beard; vowing that the man who came down from that crag was not wholly the man who went up, and that somewhere under that grey peaked roof, or amidst inconceivable reaches of that sinister white mist, there lingered still the lost spirit of him who was Thomas Olney.

And ever since that hour, through dull dragging years of greyness and weariness, the philosopher has laboured and eaten and slept and done uncomplaining the suitable deeds of a citizen. Not any more does he long for the magic of farther hills, or sigh for secrets that peer like green reefs from a bottomless sea. The sameness of his days no longer gives him sorrow, and well-disciplined thoughts have grown enough for his imagination. His good wife waxes stouter and his children older and prosier and more useful, and he never fails to smile correctly with pride when the occasion calls for it. In his glance there is not any restless light, and if he ever listens for solemn bells or far elfin horns it is only at night when old dreams are wandering. He has never seen

Kingsport again, for his family disliked the funny old houses, and complained that the drains were impossibly bad. They have a trim bungalow now at Bristol Highlands,[14] where no tall crags tower, and the neighbours are urban and modern.

But in Kingsport strange tales are abroad, and even the Terrible Old Man admits a thing untold by his grandfather. For now, when the wind sweeps boisterous out of the north past the high ancient house that is one with the firmament, there is broken at last that ominous brooding silence ever before the bane of Kingsport's maritime cotters. And old folk tell of pleasing voices heard singing there, and of laughter that swells with joys beyond earth's joys; and say that at evening the little low windows are brighter than formerly. They say, too, that the fierce aurora comes oftener to that spot, shining blue in the north with visions of frozen worlds while the crag and the cottage hang black and fantastic against wild coruscations. And the mists of the dawn are thicker, and sailors are not quite so sure that all the muffled seaward ringing is that of the solemn buoys.

Worst of all, though, is the shrivelling of old fears in the hearts of Kingsport's young men, who grow prone to listen at night to the north wind's faint distant sounds. They swear no harm or pain can inhabit that high peaked cottage, for in the new voices gladness beats, and with them the tinkle of laughter and music. What tales the sea-mists may bring to that haunted and northernmost pinnacle they do not know, but they long to extract some hint of the wonders that knock at the cliff-yawning door when clouds are thickest. And patriarchs dread lest some day one by one they seek out that inaccessible peak in the sky, and learn what centuried secrets hide beneath the steep shingled roof which is part of the rocks and the stars and the ancient fears of Kingsport. That those venturesome youths will come back they do not doubt, but they think a light may be gone from their eyes, and a will from their hearts. And they do not wish quaint Kingsport with its climbing lanes and archaic gables to drag listless down the years while voice by voice the laughing chorus grows stronger and wilder in that unknown and terrible eyrie where mists and the dreams of mists stop to rest on their way from the sea to the skies.

They do not wish the souls of their young men to leave the

14. A region near Bristol, Rhode Island. If Kingsport is Marblehead, Massachusetts, Bristol is about eighty miles away.

U.S. Custom House, Bristol, Rhode Island, 1901. The Bristol Highlands are adjacent to Bristol.

15. Kadath is first mentioned in "The Other Gods," pp. 106–10, above.

pleasant hearths and gambrel-roofed taverns of old Kingsport, nor do they wish the laughter and song in that high rocky place to grow louder. For as the voice which has come has brought fresh mists from the sea and from the north fresh lights, so do they say that still other voices will bring more mists and more lights, till perhaps the olden gods (whose existence they hint only in whispers for fear the Congregational parson shall hear) may come out of the deep and from unknown Kadath in the cold waste[15] and make their dwelling on that evilly appropriate crag so close to the gentle hills and valleys of quiet simple fisherfolk. This they do not wish, for to plain people things not of earth are unwelcome; and besides, the Terrible Old Man often recalls what Olney said about a knock that the lone dweller feared, and a shape seen black and inquisitive against the mist through those queer translucent windows of leaded bull's-eyes.

All these things, however, the Elder Ones only may decide; and meanwhile the morning mist still comes up by that lonely vertiginous peak with the steep ancient house, that grey low-eaved house where none is seen but where evening brings furtive lights while the north wind tells of strange revels. White and feathery it comes from the deep to its brothers the clouds, full of dreams of dank pastures and caves of leviathan. And when tales fly thick in the grottoes of tritons, and conches in seaweed cities blow wild tunes learned from the Elder Ones, then great eager vapours flock to heaven laden with lore; and Kingsport, nestling uneasy on its lesser cliffs below that awesome hanging sentinel of rock, sees oceanward only a mystic whiteness, as if the cliff's rim were the rim of all earth, and the solemn bells of the buoys tolled free in the aether of faery.

Pickman's Model[1]

Like many a Lovecraftian protagonist, the narrator of this tale receives a life-changing shock when he glimpses a hitherto unknown reality. Here, a casual friendship with an artist, Richard Upton Pickman, leads to a perception of the underworld. Pickman is in many ways the perfect avatar for Lovecraft: the artist who brilliantly combines realism and a vision of cosmic horror. Pickman's paintings result in his ostracism from the "normal" world of art, much as Lovecraft felt that his own writing set him apart from the mainstream of literature. The story is set in a carefully researched location in north Boston, an area that Lovecraft explored personally. A year after publication, the area had been substantially demolished.

You needn't think I'm crazy, Eliot[2]—plenty of others have queerer prejudices than this. Why don't you laugh at Oliver's grandfather, who won't ride in a motor? If I don't like that damned subway, it's my own business; and we got here more quickly anyhow in the taxi. We'd have had to walk up the hill from Park Street[3] if we'd taken the car.

I know I'm more nervous than I was when you saw me last year, but you don't need to hold a clinic over it. There's plenty of reason, God knows, and I fancy I'm lucky to be sane at all. Why the third degree? You didn't use to be so inquisitive.

Well, if you must hear it, I don't know why you shouldn't. Maybe you ought to, anyhow, for you kept writing me like a grieved parent when you heard I'd begun to cut the Art Club[4] and keep away from Pickman.[5] Now that he's disappeared I go around to the club once in a while, but my nerves aren't what they were.

No, I don't know what's become of Pickman, and I don't like to guess. You might have surmised I had some inside information when I dropped him—and that's why I don't want to think where

1. "Pickman's Model" was probably written in September 1926; it first appeared in *Weird Tales* 10, no. 4 (October 1927), 505–14. Robert M. Price, in "Erich Zann and the Rue d'Auseil" (see "The Music of Erich Zann," pp. 111–20, note 2, above), concludes that "Pickman's Model" "is a treatment of the very same themes and even employs some of the same key images. . . . Lovecraft makes more nearly explicit in 'Pickman's Model' what he was driving at in 'Erich Zann.' One might say that in the two tales Lovecraft has simply treated the same subject in different media, music in one and painting in the other" (13).

2. "Elliot" is the audience of the tale, which is told, we later learn, by "Thurber," who is addressed thus by Pickman.

3. A downtown Boston hub of numerous subway (streetcars, as they were known—

hence the narrator's reference to a "car") and train lines, Park Street opened in 1897 and was substantially renovated in 1914–15. By the time of the story, it serviced only subway lines, the elevated trains having been relocated in 1908.

4. The Boston Art Club was founded in 1854, according to its website (although the first official meeting was in 1855), by a group of local artists. In 1882, a splendid clubhouse was built in the Back Bay; declining membership forced the members to sell the building at public auction in 1950.

Boston Art Club, Boston, 2003.
Photograph courtesy of Donovan K. Loucks

5. The Nathaniel Derby Pickman Foundation is mentioned in *At the Mountains of Madness,* in the previous volume, pp. 457–572, text accompanying note 11, as a sponsor of the Miskatonic University expedition to the Antarctic. The relation of Nathaniel Derby Pickman to Richard Pickman is unknown. Note that "Derby" is an Arkham family name of some prominence (see "The Thing on the Doorstep," also in the previous volume, pp. 681–710).

Robert H. Waugh, in *The Monster in the Mirror: Looking for H. P. Lovecraft* (New York: Hippocampus Press, 2006), 20, points out that "Pickman" means one who picks or one who seizes; in Arabic, غول (*ghūl*), an evil spirit that robs graves

Boston Art Club, Boston, ca. 1881–84.

he's gone. Let the police find what they can—it won't be much, judging from the fact that they don't know yet of the old North End[6] place he hired under the name of Peters. I'm not sure that I could find it again myself—not that I'd ever try, even in broad daylight! Yes, I do know, or am afraid I know, why he maintained it. I'm coming to that. And I think you'll understand before I'm through why I don't tell the police. They would ask me to guide them, but I couldn't go back there even if I knew the way. There was something there—and now I can't use the subway or (and you may as well have your laugh at this, too) go down into cellars any more.

I should think you'd have known I didn't drop Pickman for the same silly reasons that fussy old women like Dr. Reid or Joe Minot or Bosworth did. Morbid art doesn't shock me, and when a man has the genius Pickman had I feel it an honour to know him, no matter what direction his work takes. Boston never had a greater painter than Richard Upton Pickman. I said it at first and I say it still, and I never swerved an inch, either, when he shewed that "Ghoul Feeding."[7] That, you remember, was when Minot cut him.

You know, it takes profound art and profound insight into Nature[8] to turn out stuff like Pickman's. Any magazine-cover hack[9] can splash paint around wildly and call it a nightmare or a Witches' Sabbath or a portrait of the devil, but only a great

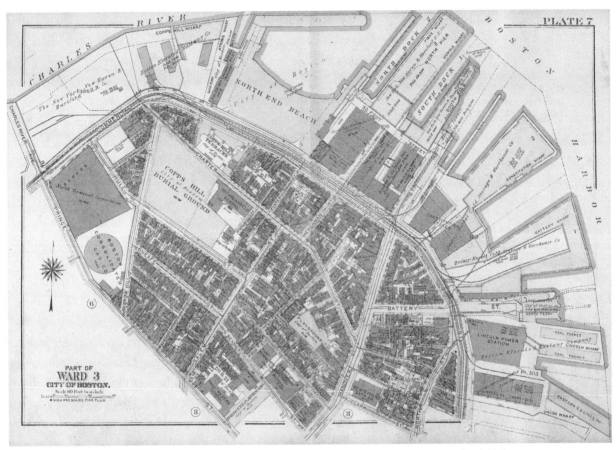

Map of North End of Boston, *Atlas of the City of Boston* by G. W. Bromley (1928).

painter can make such a thing really scare or ring true. That's because only a real artist knows the actual anatomy of the terrible or the physiology of fear—the exact sort of lines and proportions that connect up with latent instincts or hereditary memories of fright, and the proper colour contrasts and lighting effects to stir the dormant sense of strangeness. I don't have to tell you why a Fuseli[10] really brings a shiver while a cheap ghost-story frontispiece merely makes us laugh. There's something those fellows catch—beyond life—that they're able to make us catch for a second. Doré[11] had it. Sime[12] has it. Angarola of Chicago[13] has it. And Pickman had it as no man ever had it before or—I hope to heaven—ever will again.

Don't ask me what it is they see. You know, in ordinary art, there's all the difference in the world between the vital, breathing things drawn from Nature or models and the artificial truck

and feeds on corpses, derives from اغْتنام على (ghāla), "to seize." ("Gh" is a transliteration of the nineteenth letter of the Arabic alphabet, "ghayn," غ.) "Ghoul" first appeared in English in William Beckford's *Vathek, An Arabian Tale* (1786), with which HPL was quite familiar—see *The Dream-Quest of Unknown Kadath*, pp. 329–42, note 40, below.

See also Ahmed Al-Rawi, "The Mythical Ghoul in Arabic Culture," and Amira El-Zein's response, "Doctrinal Islam and Folk Islam," both in the University of California, Berkeley's *Cultural Analysis* 8 (2009), 45–69.

6. The North End is the oldest part of Boston, dating from colonial times;

facing Boston Harbor and the Charles River, by the 1920s it had become a slum, largely inhabited by Italian immigrants.

7. Pickman himself has become a ghoul by the time of the events of *The Dream-Quest of Unknown Kadath*, pp. 329–432, below.

8. The point here is that creatures, to be truly fearsome, must be a possible product of Darwinian evolution—that is, they could really exist. HPL contended, "Serious weird stories are . . . made realistically intense by close consistency and perfect fidelity to Nature except in the one supernatural direction which the author allows himself" ("Supernatural Horror in Literature," 421).

9. HPL deprecates a class of artists whose ranks include such recognized masters as Margaret Brundage, Hannes Bok, Virgil Finlay (all of whom created covers for *Weird Tales*), Ed Emshwiller, Frank Kelly Freas, and Norman Rockwell.

10. See "The Colour Out of Space," in the previous volume, pp. 310–42, note 26.

11. See "Dagon," in the previous volume, 3–10, note 14.

12. See "The Call of Cthulhu," in the previous volume, pp. 123–57, note 45.

13. See "The Call of Cthulhu," in the previous volume, note 46.

14. That Pickman is not a man seems to be the consensus of many critics; rather, he is a ghoul-changeling (and ultimately becomes a ghoul in *The Dream-Quest of Unknown Kadath*). See, for example, Robert M. Price's "Erich Zann and the Rue d'Auseil," 14.

that commercial small fry reel off in a bare studio by rule. Well, I should say that the really weird artist has a kind of vision which makes models, or summons up what amounts to actual scenes from the spectral world he lives in. Anyhow, he manages to turn out results that differ from the pretender's mince-pie dreams in just about the same way that the life painter's results differ from the concoctions of a correspondence-school cartoonist. If I had ever seen what Pickman saw—but no! Here, let's have a drink before we get any deeper. Gad, I wouldn't be alive if I'd ever seen what that man—if he was a man[14]—saw!

You recall that Pickman's forte was faces. I don't believe anybody since Goya[15] could put so much of sheer hell into a set of features or a twist of expression. And before Goya you have to go back to the mediaeval chaps who did the gargoyles and chimaeras on Notre Dame and Mont Saint-Michel. They believed all sorts of things—and maybe they saw all sorts of things, too, for the Middle Ages had some curious phases. I remember your asking Pickman yourself once, the year before you went away, wherever in thunder he got such ideas and visions. Wasn't that a nasty laugh he gave you? It was partly because of that laugh that Reid dropped him. Reid, you know, had just taken up comparative pathology, and was full of pompous "inside stuff" about the biological or evolutionary significance of this or that mental or

Notre-Dame Cathedral gargoyles.
Shutterstock.com

Mont-Saint-Michel, France.
Shutterstock.com

physical symptom. He said Pickman repelled him more and more every day, and almost frightened him toward the last—that the fellow's features and expression were slowly developing in a way he didn't like; in a way that wasn't human. He had a lot of talk about diet, and said Pickman must be abnormal and eccentric to the last degree. I suppose you told Reid, if you and he had any correspondence over it, that he'd let Pickman's paintings get on his nerves or harrow up his imagination. I know I told him that myself—then.

But keep in mind that I didn't drop Pickman for anything like this. On the contrary, my admiration for him kept growing; for that "Ghoul Feeding" was a tremendous achievement. As you know, the club wouldn't exhibit it, and the Museum of Fine Arts[16] wouldn't accept it as a gift; and I can add that nobody would buy it, so Pickman had it right in his house till he went. Now his father has it in Salem—you know Pickman comes of old Salem stock, and had a witch ancestor hanged in 1692.[17]

I got into the habit of calling on Pickman quite often, especially after I began making notes for a monograph on weird art. Probably it was his work which put the idea into my head, and anyhow, I found him a mine of data and suggestions when I came to develop it. He shewed me all the paintings and drawings he had about; including some pen-and-ink sketches that would, I verily believe, have got him kicked out of the club if many of the

15. See "The Hound," in the previous volume, pp. 94–102, note 7.

16. The Boston Museum of Fine Arts, founded on July 4, 1876, in Copley Square, moved to Huntington Avenue in the Fenway neighborhood in 1909.

Boston Museum of Fine Arts, Boston, 2017.
Photograph courtesy of Donovan K. Loucks

17. See generally "The Festival," in the previous volume, pp. 103–13, note 11, and in various places in *The Case of Charles Dexter Ward*, also in that volume, pp. 171–309, for a discussion of the Salem witch trials.

There are reports that Pickman owned a copy of the *Necronomicon*. In HPL's *History of the Necronomicon*, written in 1927 but not published until 1938 (as a pamphlet, by Rebel Press [Oakman, AL]), he recorded: "A still vaguer rumour credits the preservation of a sixteenth-century Greek text in the Salem family of Pickman; but if it was so preserved, it vanished with the artist R. U. Pickman, who disappeared early in 1926."

Procter's Ledge Memorial, 2017, commemorating the victims of the Salem witch trials.
Photograph courtesy of Donovan K. Loucks

18. See "The Shadow over Innsmouth," in the previous volume, pp. 573–642, note 14.

Danvers State Hospital, Danvers, Massachussetts, 2015.
Photograph courtesy of Donovan K. Loucks

19. A fashionable street in the Back Bay.

20. Copp's Hill Burying Ground, in the North End, is one of the oldest cemeteries in Boston. The first burials may have been as early as 1639, although the cemetery was not laid out until twenty years later.

Copp's Hill Burying Ground, Boston, 1990.
Photograph courtesy of Will Hart

members had seen them. Before long I was pretty nearly a devotee, and would listen for hours like a schoolboy to art theories and philosophic speculations wild enough to qualify him for the Danvers asylum.[18] My hero-worship, coupled with the fact that people generally were commencing to have less and less to do with him, made him get very confidential with me; and one evening he hinted that if I were fairly close-mouthed and none too squeamish, he might shew me something rather unusual—something a bit stronger than anything he had in the house.

"You know," he said, "there are things that won't do for Newbury Street[19]—things that are out of place here, and that can't be conceived here, anyhow. It's my business to catch the overtones of the soul, and you won't find those in a parvenu set of artificial streets on made land. Back Bay isn't Boston—it isn't anything yet, because it's had no time to pick up memories and attract local spirits. If there are any ghosts here, they're the tame ghosts of a salt marsh and a shallow cove; and I want human ghosts—the ghosts of beings highly organised enough to have looked on hell and known the meaning of what they saw.

"The place for an artist to live is the North End. If any aesthete were sincere, he'd put up with the slums for the sake of the massed traditions. God, man! Don't you realise that places like that weren't merely *made*, but actually *grew*? Generation after generation lived and felt and died there, and in days when people weren't afraid to live and feel and die. Don't you know there was a mill on Copp's Hill in 1632,[20] and that half the present streets

Newbury Street at Massachusetts Avenue, Back Bay, Boston, 1919.

Gallows Hill, the area known as Proctor's Ledge, in Salem,
Massachusetts, identified by historian Sidney Perley (1861 image).

Copp's Hill Burying Ground, Boston, 2017.
Photograph courtesy of Donovan K. Loucks

were laid out by 1650? I can shew you houses that have stood two centuries and a half and more; houses that have witnessed what would make a modern house crumble into powder. What do moderns know of life and the forces behind it? You call the Salem witchcraft a delusion, but I'll wage my four-times-great-grandmother could have told you things. They hanged her on Gallows Hill, with Cotton Mather[21] looking sanctimoniously on. Mather, damn him, was afraid somebody might succeed in kicking free of this accursed cage of monotony—I wish someone had laid a spell on him or sucked his blood in the night!

"I can shew you a house he lived in, and I can shew you another one he was afraid to enter in spite of all his fine bold talk. He knew things he didn't dare put into that stupid "Magnalia" or that puerile "Wonders of the Invisible World."[22] Look here, do you know the whole North End once had a set of tunnels that kept certain people in touch with each other's houses, and the burying-ground, and the sea? Let them prosecute and persecute above ground—things went on every day that they couldn't reach, and voices laughed at night that they couldn't place!"[23]

"Why, man, out of ten surviving houses built before 1700 and not moved since, I'll wager that in eight I can shew you something queer in the cellar. There's hardly a month that you don't read of workmen finding bricked-up arches and wells leading nowhere

21. See "The Picture in the House," in the previous volume, pp. 35–44, note 12.

22. *The Wonders of the Invisible World*, Mather's version of the Salem witch trials, was published in 1693, one year after they ended.

23. George T. Wetzel writes, "In 1840 excavators in Boston's old North End, when digging foundations for houses on the east side of Henchman Street, found part of a subsurface arch which, up to at least 1900, could still be seen in part of the cellar of one house there. Subsequent researchers traced a tunnel to the house of Sir William Phipps abutting the Copps Hill Burying Ground in the same neighbourhood. Some antiquarians said this tunnel was built by a Captain Grouchy, a later owner of the Phipps house, during the French Wars for smuggling purposes. Another such tunnel was found extending from the William Hitchinson house on North Street opposite the old Hancock Wharf near Fleet Street" ("The Cthulhu Mythos: A Study," 89).

Beacon Street, Boston, ca. 1920.

24. Another fashionable street in the Back Bay.

25. A main thoroughfare in the North End, with many banks, shops, and markets.

Henchman Street, ca. 1895–1905.

in this or that old place as it comes down—you could see one near Henchman Street from the elevated last year. There were witches and what their spells summoned; pirates and what they brought in from the sea; smugglers; privateers—and I tell you, people knew how to live, and how to enlarge the bounds of life, in the old times! This wasn't the only world a bold and wise man could know—faugh! And to think of today in contrast, with such pale-pink brains that even a club of supposed artists gets shudders and convulsions if a picture goes beyond the feelings of a Beacon Street[24] tea-table!

"The only saving grace of the present is that it's too damned stupid to question the past very closely. What do maps and records and guide-books really tell of the North End? Bah! At a guess I'll guarantee to lead you to thirty or forty alleys and networks of alleys north of Prince Street[25] that aren't suspected by ten living beings outside of the foreigners that swarm them. And what do those Dagoes know of their meaning? No, Thurber, these ancient places are dreaming gorgeously and overflowing with wonder and terror and escape from the commonplace, and yet there's not a living soul to understand or profit by them. Or rather, there's only one living soul—for I haven't been digging around in the past for nothing!

"See here, you're interested in this sort of thing. What if I told you that I've got another studio up there, where I can catch the night-spirit of antique horror and paint things that I couldn't even think of in Newbury Street? Naturally I don't tell those cursed old maids at the club—with Reid, damn him, whispering even as it is that I'm a sort of monster bound down the toboggan of reverse evolution. Yes, Thurber, I decided long ago that one must paint terror as well as beauty from life, so I did some exploring in places where I had reason to know terror lives.

"I've got a place that I don't believe three living Nordic men besides myself have ever seen. It isn't so very far from the elevated as distance goes, but it's centuries away as the soul goes. I took it because of the queer old brick well in the cellar—one of the sort I told you about. The shack's almost tumbling down, so that nobody else would live there, and I'd hate to tell you how little I pay for it. The windows are boarded up, but I like that all the better, since I don't want daylight for what I do. I paint in the cellar, where the inspiration is thickest, but I've other rooms furnished on the ground floor. A Sicilian owns it, and I've hired it under the name of Peters.

"Now if you're game, I'll take you there tonight. I think you'd enjoy the pictures, for as I said, I've let myself go a bit there. It's no vast tour—I sometimes do it on foot, for I don't want to attract attention with a taxi in such a place. We can take the shuttle at the South Station for Battery Street, and after that the walk isn't much."

Well, Eliot, there wasn't much for me to do after that harangue but to keep myself from running instead of walking for the first vacant cab we could sight. We changed to the elevated at the South Station, and at about twelve o'clock had climbed down the steps at Battery Street and struck along the old waterfront past Constitution Wharf. I didn't keep track of the cross streets, and can't tell you yet which it was we turned up, but I know it wasn't Greenough Lane.[26]

North End, Boston map, 1899—streets generally omitted. For details as of 1928, see p. 313, above.

26. See map of the Boston North End, p. 313, above.

Greenough Lane, looking north from Charter Street, Boston, 1990.
Photograph courtesy of Will Hart

South Station, Boston, 2017.
Photograph courtesy of Donovan K. Loucks

27. This is a seventeenth-century feature, found on the Witch House of Salem (built in 1642) and the House of Seven Gables (ca. 1660). It was largely supplanted by the gambrel roof.

The Witch House of Salem,
Massachusetts, 2013.
Photograph courtesy of Donovan K. Loucks

A gambrel roof ("Harvard House," 1677).

28. Will Murray suggested Foster Court in 1984 ("In Pickman's Footsteps," *Crypt of Cthulhu* 28 [Yuletide 1984], 27–32). Robert D. Marten, in "The Pickman Models," *Lovecraft Studies* 44 (2004),

Foster Court, Foster Street, Boston, 2017.
Photograph courtesy of Donovan K. Loucks

The House of Seven Gables, 2015.
Photograph courtesy of Donovan K. Loucks

When we did turn, it was to climb through the deserted length of the oldest and dirtiest alley I ever saw in my life, with crumbling-looking gables, broken small-paned windows, and archaic chimneys that stood out half-disintegrated against the moonlit sky. I don't believe there were three houses in sight that hadn't been standing in Cotton Mather's time—certainly I glimpsed at least two with an overhang, and once I thought I saw a peaked roof-line of the almost forgotten pre-gambrel type, though antiquarians tell us there are none left in Boston.[27]

From that alley, which had a dim light, we turned to the left into an equally silent and still narrower alley with no light at all; and in a minute made what I think was an obtuse-angled bend toward the right in the dark. Not long after this Pickman produced a flashlight and revealed an antediluvian ten-panelled door that looked damnably worm-eaten.[28] Unlocking it, he ushered me into a barren hallway with what was once splendid dark-oak panelling—simple, of course, but thrillingly suggestive of the times of Andros and Phipps[29] and the Witchcraft. Then he took me through a door on the left, lighted an oil lamp, and told me to make myself at home.

Now, Eliot, I'm what the man in the street would call fairly "hard-boiled," but I'll confess that what I saw on the walls of that room gave me a bad turn. They were his pictures, you know—the ones he couldn't paint or even shew in Newbury Street—and he was right when he said he had "let himself go." Here—have another drink—I need one anyhow!

There's no use in my trying to tell you what they were like, because the awful, the blasphemous horror and the unbelievable loathsomeness and moral foetor came from simple touches quite beyond the power of words to classify. There was none of the exotic technique you see in Sidney Sime, none of the trans-Saturnian landscapes and lunar fungi that Clark Ashton Smith[30] uses to freeze the blood. The backgrounds were mostly old churchyards, deep woods, cliffs by the sea, brick tunnels, ancient panelled rooms, or simple vaults of masonry. Copp's Hill Burying Ground, which could not be many blocks away from this very house, was a favourite scene.

The madness and monstrosity lay in the figures in the foreground—for Pickman's morbid art was preëminently one of daemoniac portraiture. These figures were seldom completely human, but often approached humanity in varying degree. Most of the bodies, while roughly bipedal, had a forward slumping, and a vaguely canine cast. The texture of the majority was a kind of unpleasant rubberiness. Ugh! I can see them now! Their occupations—well, don't ask me to be too precise. They were usually feeding—I won't say on what. They were sometimes shewn in groups in cemeteries or underground passages, and often appeared to be in battle over their prey—or rather, their treasure-trove. And what damnable expressiveness Pickman sometimes gave the sightless faces of this charnel booty! Occasionally the things were shewn leaping through open windows at night, or squatting on the chests of sleepers, worrying at their throats. One canvas shewed a ring of them baying about a hanged witch on Gallows Hill, whose dead face held a close kinship to theirs.

But don't get the idea that it was all this hideous business of theme and setting which struck me faint. I'm not a three-year-old kid, and I'd seen much like this before. It was the *faces*, Eliot, those accursed *faces*, that leered and slavered out of the canvas with the very breath of life! By God, man, I verily believe they *were* alive! That nauseous wizard had waked the fires of hell in pigment, and his brush had been a nightmare-spawning wand. Give me that decanter, Eliot!

There was one thing called "The Lesson"—heaven pity me,

42–80, identifies this as Foster Place, close by Foster Court. See map, p. 313, above.

29. As noted in "The Shunned House," pp. 213–48, note 43, above, Sir Edmund Andros was the royal governor of the Dominion of New England, which included the Massachusetts Bay Colony (1686 to 1689); Sir William Phipps was governor of the Province of Massachusetts Bay (the reorganized territory) from 1692 to 1695.

30. Smith (1893–1961), who won renown as a fantasy and science fiction writer as well as an artist, became HPL's friend in 1923 and, by 1924, was one of the few whom HPL regarded as a "social equal" (Letter to Frank Belknap Long, February 20, 1924, *Selected Letters*, I, 315). (The others mentioned by HPL were James F. Morton and Rheinhart Kleiner—presumably Long was included in the select group as well.) Smith illustrated "The Lurking Fear" (see pp. 121–49, above).

31. The phrase "I'm middle-aged and decently sophisticated, and I guess you saw enough of me in France to know" appears here in the original manuscript of the story, in HPL's typescript, and in the 1927 *Weird Tales* publication; however, Lovecraft provided a revised text for a reprint in *Weird Tales* 28, no. 4 (November 1936) and deleted the phrase. See H. P. Lovecraft, *Collected Fiction: A Variorum Edition*, ed. S. T. Joshi (New York: Hippocampus Press, 2015), vol. 2, 56, 66. The narrator undoubtedly refers to service in the U.S. Army in France during the Great War. By 1918, over one million U.S. troops were stationed in France, and about half took part in front-line combat. About 50,000 U.S. soldiers were killed in combat; over 190,000 U.S. soldiers were wounded (Edward M. Coffman, *The War to End All Wars: The American Military Experience in World War I* [Lexington: University Press of Kentucky, 1968], 363).

that I ever saw it! Listen—can you fancy a squatting circle of nameless dog-like things in a churchyard teaching a small child how to feed like themselves? The price of a changeling, I suppose—you know the old myth about how the weird people leave their spawn in cradles in exchange for the human babes they steal. Pickman was shewing what happens to those stolen babes—how they grow up—and then I began to see a hideous relationship in the faces of the human and non-human figures. He was, in all his gradations of morbidity between the frankly non-human and the degradedly human, establishing a sardonic linkage and evolution. The dog-things were developed from mortals!

And no sooner had I wondered what he made of their own young as left with mankind in the form of changelings, than my eye caught a picture embodying that very thought. It was that of an ancient Puritan interior—a heavily beamed room with lattice windows, a settle, and clumsy seventeenth-century furniture, with the family sitting about while the father read from the Scriptures. Every face but one shewed nobility and reverence, but that one reflected the mockery of the pit. It was that of a young man in years, and no doubt belonged to a supposed son of that pious father, but in essence it was the kin of the unclean things. It was their changeling—and in a spirit of supreme irony Pickman had given the features a very perceptible resemblance to his own.

By this time Pickman had lighted a lamp in an adjoining room and was politely holding open the door for me; asking me if I would care to see his "modern studies." I hadn't been able to give him much of my opinions—I was too speechless with fright and loathing—but I think he fully understood and felt highly complimented. And now I want to assure you again, Eliot, that I'm no mollycoddle to scream at anything which shews a bit of departure from the usual.[31] I'm not easily knocked out. Remember, too, that I'd just about recovered my wind and gotten used to those frightful pictures which turned colonial New England into a kind of annex of hell. Well, in spite of all this, that next room forced a real scream out of me, and I had to clutch at the doorway to keep from keeling over. The other chamber had shewn a pack of ghouls and witches overrunning the world of our forefathers, but this one brought the horror right into our own daily life!

Gad, how that man could paint! There was a study called

"Subway Accident," in which a flock of the vile things were clambering up from some unknown catacomb through a crack in the floor of the Boylston Street subway and attacking a crowd of people on the platform. Another shewed a dance on Copp's Hill among the tombs with the background of today. Then there were any number of cellar views, with monsters creeping in through holes and rifts in the masonry and grinning as they squatted behind barrels or furnaces and waited for their first victim to descend the stairs.

One disgusting canvas seemed to depict a vast cross-section of Beacon Hill, with ant-like armies of the mephitic monsters squeezing themselves through burrows that honeycombed the ground. Dances in the modern cemeteries were freely pictured, and another conception somehow shocked me more than all the rest—a scene in an unknown vault, where scores of the beasts crowded about one who held a well-known Boston guide-book and was evidently reading aloud. All were pointing to a certain passage, and every face seemed so distorted with epileptic and reverberant laughter that I almost thought I heard the fiendish echoes. The title of the picture was, "Holmes, Lowell, and Longfellow Lie Buried in Mount Auburn."[32]

As I gradually steadied myself and got readjusted to this second room of deviltry and morbidity, I began to analyse some of the points in my sickening loathing. In the first place, I said

32. The joke is that Oliver Wendell Holmes, James Russell Lowell, and Henry Wadsworth Longfellow (incidentally, the founders, in 1857, of the *Atlantic Monthly*) were all buried in the Mount Auburn Cemetery in Cambridge, but the ghouls have dug them up for consumption!

Mount Auburn Cemetery, Cambridge, Massachusetts—headstones of Holmes, Lowell, and Longfellow, 2017.
Photographs courtesy of Donovan K. Loucks

Boylston Street Station, Boston, 2017.
Photograph courtesy of Donovan K. Loucks

33. Kieran Setiya writes, "I can think of no better description of his creator. ... In Pickman we have Lovecraft's ideal artist—sincere, brilliant, apocalyptic—and it is a tribute to his triumph as an author of cosmic horror that his descriptions of the ghoul-changeling are so readily applicable to himself" ("Two Notes on Lovecraft," 16).

to myself, these things repelled because of the utter inhumanity and callous cruelty they shewed in Pickman. The fellow must be a relentless enemy of all mankind to take such glee in the torture of brain and flesh and the degradation of the mortal tenement. In the second place, they terrified because of their very greatness. Their art was the art that convinced—when we saw the pictures we saw the daemons themselves and were afraid of them. And the queer part was, that Pickman got none of his power from the use of selectiveness or bizarrerie. Nothing was blurred, distorted, or conventionalised; outlines were sharp and lifelike, and details were almost painfully defined. And the faces!

It was not any mere artist's interpretation that we saw; it was pandemonium itself, crystal clear in stark objectivity. That was it, by heaven! The man was not a fantaisiste or romanticist at all— he did not even try to give us the churning, prismatic ephemera of dreams, but coldly and sardonically reflected some stable, mechanistic, and well-established horror-world which he saw fully, brilliantly, squarely, and unfalteringly.[33] God knows what that world can have been, or where he ever glimpsed the blasphemous shapes that loped and trotted and crawled through it; but whatever the baffling source of his images, one thing was plain. Pickman was in every sense—in conception and in execution—a thorough, painstaking, and almost scientific *realist*.

My host was now leading the way down cellar to his actual studio, and I braced myself for some hellish effects among the unfinished canvases. As we reached the bottom of the damp stairs he turned his flashlight to a corner of the large open space at hand, revealing the circular brick curb of what was evidently a great well in the earthen floor. We walked nearer, and I saw that it must be five feet across, with walls a good foot thick and some six inches above the ground level—solid work of the seventeenth century, or I was much mistaken. That, Pickman said, was the kind of thing he had been talking about—an aperture of the network of tunnels that used to undermine the hill. I noticed idly that it did not seem to be bricked up, and that a heavy disc of wood formed the apparent cover. Thinking of the things this well must have been connected with if Pickman's wild hints had not been mere rhetoric, I shivered slightly; then turned to follow him up a step and through a narrow door into a room of fair size, provided with a wooden floor and furnished as a studio. An acetylene gas outfit gave the light necessary for work.

The unfinished pictures on easels or propped against the walls were as ghastly as the finished ones upstairs, and shewed the painstaking methods of the artist. Scenes were blocked out with extreme care, and pencilled guide lines told of the minute exactitude which Pickman used in getting the right perspective and proportions. The man was great—I say it even now, knowing as much as I do. A large camera on a table excited my notice, and Pickman told me that he used it in taking scenes for backgrounds, so that he might paint them from photographs in the studio instead of carting his outfit around the town for this or that view. He thought a photograph quite as good as an actual scene or model for sustained work, and declared he employed them regularly.

There was something very disturbing about the nauseous sketches and half-finished monstrosities that leered around from every side of the room, and when Pickman suddenly unveiled a huge canvas on the side away from the light I could not for my life keep back a loud scream—the second I had emitted that night. It echoed and re-echoed through the dim vaultings of that ancient and nitrous cellar, and I had to choke back a flood of reaction that threatened to burst out as hysterical laughter. Merciful Creator, Eliot, but I don't know how much was real and how much was feverish fancy. It doesn't seem to me that earth can hold a dream like that!

It was a colossal and nameless blasphemy with glaring red eyes, and it held in bony claws a thing that had been a man, gnawing at the head as a child nibbles at a stick of candy. Its position was a kind of crouch, and as one looked one felt that at any moment it might drop its present prey and seek a juicier morsel. But damn it all, it wasn't even the fiendish subject that made it such an immortal fountain-head of all panic—not that, nor the dog face with its pointed ears, bloodshot eyes, flat nose, and drooling lips. It wasn't the scaly claws nor the mould-caked body nor the half-hooved feet—none of these, though any one of them might well have driven an excitable man to madness.

It was the technique, Eliot—the cursed, the impious, the unnatural technique! As I am a living being, I never elsewhere saw the actual breath of life so fused into a canvas. The monster was there—it glared and gnawed and gnawed and glared—and I knew that only a suspension of Nature's laws could ever let a man paint a thing like that without a model—without some glimpse of the nether world which no mortal unsold to the fiend has ever had.

Pinned with a thumb-tack to a vacant part of the canvas was a piece of paper now badly curled up—probably, I thought, a photograph from which Pickman meant to paint a background as hideous as the nightmare it was to enhance. I reached out to uncurl and look at it, when suddenly I saw Pickman start as if shot. He had been listening with peculiar intensity ever since my shocked scream had waked unaccustomed echoes in the dark cellar, and now he seemed struck with a fright which, though not comparable to my own, had in it more of the physical than of the spiritual. He drew a revolver and motioned me to silence, then stepped out into the main cellar and closed the door behind him.

I think I was paralysed for an instant. Imitating Pickman's listening, I fancied I heard a faint scurrying sound somewhere, and a series of squeals or bleats in a direction I couldn't determine. I thought of huge rats and shuddered. Then there came a subdued sort of clatter which somehow set me all in gooseflesh—a furtive, groping kind of clatter, though I can't attempt to convey what I mean in words. It was like heavy wood falling on stone or brick—wood on brick—what did that make me think of?

It came again, and louder. There was a vibration as if the wood had fallen farther than it had fallen before. After that followed a sharp grating noise, a shouted gibberish from Pickman, and the deafening discharge of all six chambers of a revolver, fired spectacularly as a lion-tamer might fire in the air for effect. A muffled squeal or squawk, and a thud. Then more wood and brick grating, a pause, and the opening of the door—at which I'll confess I started violently. Pickman reappeared with his smoking weapon, cursing the bloated rats that infested the ancient well.

"The deuce knows what they eat, Thurber," he grinned, "for those archaic tunnels touched graveyard and witch-den and sea-coast. But whatever it is, they must have run short, for they were devilish anxious to get out. Your yelling stirred them up, I fancy. Better be cautious in these old places—our rodent friends are the one drawback, though I sometimes think they're a positive asset by way of atmosphere and colour."

Well, Eliot, that was the end of the night's adventure. Pickman had promised to shew me the place, and heaven knows he had done it. He led me out of that tangle of alleys in another direction, it seems, for when we sighted a lamp post we were in a half-familiar street with monotonous rows of mingled tenement blocks and old houses. Charter Street, it turned out to be, but I was too flustered to notice just where we hit it. We were too late for the elevated, and walked back downtown through Hanover Street. I remember that walk. We switched from Tremont up Beacon, and Pickman left me at the corner of Joy, where I turned off. I never spoke to him again.

Why did I drop him? Don't be impatient. Wait till I ring for coffee. We've had enough of the other stuff, but I for one need something. No—it wasn't the paintings I saw in that place; though I'll swear they were enough to get him ostracised in nine-tenths of the homes and clubs of Boston, and I guess you won't wonder now why I have to steer clear of subways and cellars. It was—something I found in my coat the next morning. You know, the curled-up paper tacked to that frightful canvas in the cellar; the thing I thought was a photograph of some scene he meant to use as a background for that monster. That last scare had come while I was reaching to uncurl it, and it seems I had vacantly crumpled it into my pocket. But here's the coffee—take it black, Eliot, if you're wise.

Yes, that paper was the reason I dropped Pickman; Richard Upton Pickman, the greatest artist I have ever known—and the foulest being that ever leaped the bounds of life into the pits of myth and madness. Eliot—old Reid was right. He wasn't strictly human. Either he was born in strange shadow, or he'd found a way to unlock the forbidden gate. It's all the same now, for he's gone—back into the fabulous darkness he loved to haunt. Here, let's have the chandelier going.

Don't ask me to explain or even conjecture about what I burned. Don't ask me, either, what lay behind that mole-like scrambling Pickman was so keen to pass off as rats. There are secrets, you know, which might have come down from old Salem times, and Cotton Mather tells even stranger things. You know how damned lifelike Pickman's paintings were—how we all wondered where he got those faces.

Well—that paper wasn't a photograph of any background, after all. What it shewed was simply the monstrous being he was painting on that awful canvas. It was the model he was using—and its background was merely the wall of the cellar studio in minute detail. But by God, Eliot, *it was a photograph from life.*

"He had painted a monstrous being on that awful canvas."
Weird Tales (October 1927) (artist: Hugh Rankin)

The Dream-Quest of Unknown Kadath[1]

Written between October 1926 and January 1927 and unpublished during Lovecraft's lifetime, this novella was apparently meant only as an experiment in long-form fiction, predating The Case of Charles Dexter Ward *(written a few months later) and* At the Mountains of Madness *(1931). It incorporates many Dunsanian elements, with intimations of William Beckford's* Vathek *and Lovecraft's own Cthulhu Mythos, into an adventure that might well have appeared in* Boy's Own Magazine. *Randolph Carter, who is said to stand in for HPL in other stories, ultimately finds solace, not in the dreamland through which he travels but in memories of his own home.*

Three times Randolph Carter[2] dreamed of the marvellous city, and three times was he snatched away while still he paused on the high terrace above it. All golden and lovely it blazed in the sunset, with walls, temples, colonnades, and arched bridges of veined marble, silver-basined fountains of prismatic spray in broad squares and perfumed gardens, and wide streets marching between delicate trees and blossom-laden urns and ivory statues in gleaming rows; while on steep northward slopes climbed tiers of red roofs and old peaked gables harbouring little lanes of grassy cobbles. It was a fever of the gods; a fanfare of supernal trumpets and a clash of immortal cymbals. Mystery hung about it as clouds about a fabulous unvisited mountain; and as Carter stood breathless and expectant on that balustraded parapet there swept up to him the poignancy and suspense of almost-vanished memory, the pain of lost things, and the maddening need to place again what once had an awesome and momentous place.

He knew that for him its meaning must once have been supreme; though in what cycle or incarnation he had known it, or whether in dream or in waking, he could not tell. Vaguely it

1. Written during late 1926 and early 1927, this long story did not appear in print until 1943, long after Lovecraft's death, in the Arkham House collection *Beyond the Wall of Sleep*. The title was selected by the editors of that volume from these variants found in the manuscript: *The Dream-Quest of Randolph Carter, A Pilgrim in Dreamland, A Dreamland Quest/Pilgrimage, The Seeking of Dreamland's Gods, Past the Gate of Deeper Slumber, In the Gulfs of Dream, A Seeker in Gulphs of Dream, The Quest of the Gods on Kadath,* and *The Seeking of Unknown Kadath*. HPL called it "a picaresque chronicle of impossible adventure in dreamland, composed under no illusion of professional publication" (Letter to William Blanch Talman, December 19, 1926, *Selected Letters, 1925–1929,* ed. August Derleth and Donald Wandrei [Sauk City, WI: Arkham House, 1968], 95; hereafter *Selected Letters,* II). "Picaresque," derived from the Spanish *picaro,* a rogue, is usually applied to the

adventures of a rough, somewhat dishonest, but appealing hero—not a very good description of Carter. The manuscript of *Dream-Quest* was never revised by HPL or submitted anywhere for publication. It was eventually typed by R. H. Barlow.

2. Carter appeared previously in "The Statement of Randolph Carter" (written in 1919, in the previous volume, pp. 11–17) and "The Unnamable" (1923, also in the previous volume, pp. 114–22); he would appear again in "The Silver Key" (1926, also in the previous volume, pp. 158–70).

3. "Immanence" suggests that something of the divine is inherent in the material world.

4. Marble—"marmoreal flights" are marble staircases.

5. Trekkies and even casual fans of the television show *Star Trek* (1966–69, rerun endlessly) will note the similarity to the phrase used by Captain James T. Kirk (William Shatner) in his voice-over narrative that is part of the show's opening credits of: "Space: the final frontier. These are the voyages of the starship *Enterprise*. Its five-year mission: to explore strange new worlds, to seek out new life and new civilizations, to boldly go where no man has gone before." "No man" was later altered in films and spinoffs to "no one" to be gender- and species-neutral. Of course, the phrase did not originate with Lovecraft; St. Patrick, for example, in his *Confessio*, claimed to have traveled where "no one had been before" (*ubi nemo ultra erat*) to baptize his fold, ordain clergy, and serve Communion.

6. Usually spelled "pschent" (from the Greek ψχεντ), the double crown worn by the ancient kings of Egypt.

called up glimpses of a far, forgotten first youth, when wonder and pleasure lay in all the mystery of days, and dawn and dusk alike strode forth prophetick to the eager sound of lutes and song; unclosing faery gates toward further and surprising marvels. But each night as he stood on that high marble terrace with the curious urns and carven rail and looked off over that hushed sunset city of beauty and unearthly immanence,[3] he felt the bondage of dream's tyrannous gods; for in no wise could he leave that lofty spot, or descend the wide marmoreal[4] flights flung endlessly down to where those streets of elder witchery lay outspread and beckoning.

When for the third time he awaked with those flights still undescended and those hushed sunset streets still untraversed, he prayed long and earnestly to the hidden gods of dream that brood capricious above the clouds on unknown Kadath, in the cold waste where no man treads. But the gods made no answer and shewed no relenting, nor did they give any favouring sign when he prayed to them in dream, and invoked them sacrificially through the bearded priests Nasht and Kaman-Thah, whose cavern-temple with its pillar of flame lies not far from the gates of the waking world. It seemed, however, that his prayers must have been adversely heard, for after even the first of them he ceased wholly to behold the marvellous city; as if his three glimpses from afar had been mere accidents or oversights, and against some hidden plan or wish of the gods.

At length, sick with longing for those glittering sunset streets and cryptical hill lanes among ancient tiled roofs, nor able sleeping or waking to drive them from his mind, Carter resolved to go with bold entreaty whither no man had gone before,[5] and dare the icy deserts through the dark to where unknown Kadath, veiled in cloud and crowned with unimagined stars, holds secret and nocturnal the onyx castle of the Great Ones.

In light slumber he descended the seventy steps to the cavern of flame and talked of this design to the bearded priests Nasht and Kaman-Thah. And the priests shook their pshent-bearing[6] heads and vowed it would be the death of his soul. They pointed out that the Great Ones had shewn already their wish, and that it is not agreeable to them to be harassed by insistent pleas. They reminded him, too, that not only had no man ever been

Map of Dreamland, by Jason Thompson (reproduced with permission).

to unknown Kadath, but no man had ever suspected in what part of space it may lie; whether it be in the dreamlands around our world, or in those surrounding some unguessed companion of Fomalhaut[7] or Aldebaran.[8] If in our dreamland, it might conceivably be reached; but only three fully human souls since time began had ever crossed and re-crossed the black impious gulfs to other dreamlands, and of that three two had come back quite mad. There were, in such voyages, incalculable local dangers; as well as that shocking final peril which glibbers[9] unmentionably outside the ordered universe, where no dreams reach; that last amorphous blight of nethermost confusion which blasphemes and bubbles at the centre of all infinity—the boundless daemon-sultan Azathoth,[10] whose name no lips dare speak aloud, and who gnaws hungrily in inconceivable, unlighted chambers beyond time amidst the muffled, maddening beating of vile drums and the thin, monotonous whine of accursed flutes; to which detest-

7. The alpha star of the constellation *Piscis Austrinisis*, the Southern Fish, south of Capricorn and Aquarius. Fomalhaut, from the Arabic for "the fish's mouth," has been sited in other constellations: the second-century astronomer Ptolemy assigned it its own constellation, and others made it part of Aquarius.

8. See "Polaris," pp. 15–19, note 10, above.

9. "Glibber" is not found in the *Oxford English Dictionary* or elsewhere and might be thought to be a slip of the pen for "gibber," to utter rapidly and inarticulately. S. T. Joshi confirms in the Variorum Edition that the word "glibber" is used by HPL here and elsewhere

in *Dream-Quest* (and nowhere else—he instead uses "gibber"), but exactly what Lovecraft intended this neologism to mean is unclear. "Glibbering" seems to signify some mode of communication with ghouls and other denizens of the dreamland.

10. This deity appears in many tales by HPL. In "The Whisperer in Darkness," in the previous volume, pp. 388–456, it is described as a "monstrous nuclear chaos beyond angled space."

11. Another frequently mentioned figure—see "Nyarlathotep," in the previous volume, pp. 30–34.

12. The passage is perhaps deliberately evocative of the beginning of Dante's *Inferno* (Henry Wadsworth Longfellow translation, 1867): "Midway upon the journey of our life / I found myself within a forest dark, / For the straightforward pathway had been lost." For a discussion of the gates of dreamland, see "The Silver Key," in the previous volume, 158–70, note 3. The gates of the dreaming are depicted quite beautifully in the second issue of Neil Gaiman's *The Sandman*.

13. See "Celephaïs," pp. 71–77, above.

able pounding and piping dance slowly, awkwardly, and absurdly the gigantic ultimate gods, the blind, voiceless, tenebrous, mindless Other Gods whose soul and messenger is the crawling chaos Nyarlathotep.[11]

Of these things was Carter warned by the priests Nasht and Kaman-Thah in the cavern of flame, but still he resolved to find the gods on unknown Kadath in the cold waste, wherever that might be, and to win from them the sight and remembrance and shelter of the marvellous sunset city. He knew that his journey would be strange and long, and that the Great Ones would be against it; but being old in the land of dream he counted on many useful memories and devices to aid him. So asking a farewell blessing of the priests and thinking shrewdly on his course, he boldly descended the seven hundred steps to the Gate of Deeper Slumber and set out through the enchanted wood.[12]

In the tunnels of that twisted wood, whose low prodigious oaks twine groping boughs and shine dim with the phosphorescence of strange fungi, dwell the furtive and secretive zoogs; who know many obscure secrets of the dream-world and a few of the waking world, since the wood at two places touches the lands of men, though it would be disastrous to say where. Certain unexplained rumours, events, and vanishments occur among men where the zoogs have access, and it is well that they cannot travel far outside the world of dream. But over the nearer parts of the dream-world they pass freely, flitting small and brown and unseen and bearing back piquant tales to beguile the hours around their hearths in the forest they love. Most of them live in burrows, but some inhabit the trunks of the great trees; and although they live mostly on fungi it is muttered that they have also a slight taste for meat, either physical or spiritual, for certainly many dreamers have entered that wood who have not come out. Carter, however, had no fear; for he was an old dreamer and had learnt their fluttering language and made many a treaty with them; having found through their help the splendid city of Celephaïs[13] in Ooth-Nargai beyond the Tanarian Hills, where reigns half the year the great King Kuranes, a man he had known by another name in life. Kuranes was the one soul who had been to the star-gulfs and returned free from madness.

Threading now the low phosphorescent aisles between those

gigantic trunks, Carter made fluttering sounds in the manner of the zoogs, and listened now and then for responses. He remembered one particular village of the creatures near the centre of the wood, where a circle of great mossy stones in what was once a clearing tells of older and more terrible dwellers long forgotten, and toward this spot he hastened. He traced his way by the grotesque fungi, which always seem better nourished as one approaches the dread circle where elder beings danced and sacrificed. Finally the greater light of those thicker fungi revealed a sinister green and grey vastness pushing up through the roof of the forest and out of sight. This was the nearest of the great ring of stones, and Carter knew he was close to the zoog village. Renewing his fluttering sound, he waited patiently; and was at length rewarded by an impression of many eyes watching him. It was the zoogs, for one sees their weird eyes long before one can discern their small, slippery brown outlines.

Out they swarmed, from hidden burrow and honeycombed tree, till the whole dim-litten region was alive with them. Some of the wilder ones brushed Carter unpleasantly, and one even nipped loathsomely at his ear; but these lawless spirits were soon restrained by their elders. The Council of Sages, recognising the visitor, offered a gourd of fermented sap from a haunted tree unlike the others, which had grown from a seed dropt down by someone on the moon; and as Carter drank it ceremoniously a very strange colloquy began. The zoogs did not, unfortunately, know where the peak of Kadath lies, nor could they even say whether the cold waste is in our dream-world or in another. Rumours of the Great Ones came equally from all points; and one might only say that they were likelier to be seen on high mountain peaks than in valleys, since on such peaks they dance reminiscently when the moon is above and the clouds beneath.

Then one very ancient zoog recalled a thing unheard-of by the others; and said that in Ulthar, beyond the river Skai, there still lingered the last copy of those inconceivably old Pnakotic Manuscripts made by waking men in forgotten boreal kingdoms and borne into the land of dreams when the hairy cannibal Gnophkehs overcame many-templed Olathoë and slew all the heroes of the land of Lomar. Those manuscripts, he said, told much of the gods; and besides, in Ulthar there were men who had seen the

14. The tale of his ascent is "The Other Gods," pp. 106–10, above.

15. The details of the "Elder Sign," presumably used to ward off the effects of the Elder Ones (see "The Strange High House in the Mist," pp. 301–10, above), are unknown, though it is also mentioned in a similar context in HPL's story fragment "The Descendant" (1927) and in the "revision" work "The Last Test," written with Adolphe de Castro in the same year. Frederick Thomas Elworthy, in his classic study *The Evil Eye* (London: John Murray, 1895), writes: "If in past ages the hand has been looked upon as an instrument of evil when used by the malignant, much more has it been regarded as an instrument of good—the powerful protector against that special form of evil which was supposed to be flashed from one person to another, whether through the eye or the touch of malice" (234). The *mano cornuta*, or "horned hands,"is a gesture found depicted in many cultures and religions (including ancient Hindu statuary and Christian icons) as a means to ward off the "evil eye" or other bad fortune. The "hamsa" or "hamesh" hand ("khamsa" and "h'amesh" mean "five" in Arabic and Hebrew, respectively), a palm pointing downward with a thumb on each side (possibly the image of two hands, one held in front of the other), is another common symbol used to deflect the evil eye. See also David Haden's "A Note on the Elder Signs," in *Lovecraft in Historical Context: Further Essays and Notes* (self-published, 2011), 121–24.

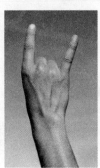

Mano cornuta, or horned hand sign.

signs of the gods, and even one old priest who had scaled a great mountain to behold them dancing by moonlight.[14] He had failed, though his companion had succeeded and perished namelessly.

So Randolph Carter thanked the zoogs, who fluttered amicably and gave him another gourd of moon-tree wine to take with him, and set out through the phosphorescent wood for the other side, where the rushing Skai flows down from the slopes of Lerion, and Hatheg and Nir and Ulthar dot the plain. Behind him, furtive and unseen, crept several of the curious zoogs; for they wished to learn what might befall him, and bear back the legend to their people. The vast oaks grew thicker as he pushed on beyond the village, and he looked sharply for a certain spot where they would thin somewhat, standing quite dead or dying among the unnaturally dense fungi and the rotting mould and mushy logs of their fallen brothers. There he would turn sharply aside, for at that spot a mighty slab of stone rests on the forest floor; and those who have dared approach it say that it bears an iron ring three feet wide. Remembering the archaic circle of great mossy rocks, and what it was possibly set up for, the zoogs do not pause near that expansive slab with its huge ring; for they realise that all which is forgotten need not necessarily be dead, and they would not like to see the slab rise slowly and deliberately.

Carter detoured at the proper place, and heard behind him the frightened fluttering of some of the more timid zoogs. He had known they would follow him, so he was not disturbed; for one grows accustomed to the anomalies of these prying creatures. It was twilight when he came to the edge of the wood, and the strengthening glow told him it was the twilight of morning. Over fertile plains rolling down to the Skai he saw the smoke of cottage chimneys, and on every hand were the hedges and ploughed fields and thatched roofs of a peaceful land. Once he stopped at a farmhouse well for a cup of water, and all the dogs barked affrightedly at the inconspicuous zoogs that crept through the grass behind. At another house, where people were stirring, he asked questions about the gods, and whether they danced often upon Lerion; but the farmer and his wife would only make the Elder Sign[15] and tell him the way to Nir and Ulthar.

At noon he walked through the one broad high street of Nir, which he had once visited and which marked his farthest

Khamsa hand.
Shutterstock.com

16. See "The Cats of Ulthar," pp. 40–43, above.

former travels in this direction; and soon afterward he came to the great stone bridge across the Skai, into whose central pier the masons had sealed a living human sacrifice when they built it thirteen-hundred years before. Once on the other side, the frequent presence of cats (who all arched their backs at the trailing zoogs) revealed the near neighbourhood of Ulthar; for in Ulthar, according to an ancient and significant law, no man may kill a cat.[16] Very pleasant were the suburbs of Ulthar, with their little green cottages and neatly fenced farms; and still pleasanter was the quaint town itself, with its old peaked roofs and overhanging upper stories and numberless chimney-pots and narrow hill streets where one can see old cobbles whenever the graceful cats afford space enough. Carter, the cats being somewhat dispersed by the half-seen zoogs, picked his way directly to the modest Temple of the Elder Ones where the priests and old records were said to be; and once within that venerable circular tower of ivied stone—which crowns Ulthar's highest hill—he sought out the patriarch Atal, who had been up the forbidden peak Hatheg-Kla in the stony desert and had come down again alive.

Atal, seated on an ivory dais in a festooned shrine at the top of the temple, was fully three centuries old; but still very keen of mind and memory. From him Carter learned many things about the gods, but mainly that they are indeed only earth's gods, ruling feebly our own dreamland and having no power or habitation elsewhere. They might, Atal said, heed a man's prayer if in good humour; but one must not think of climbing to their onyx stronghold atop Kadath in the cold waste. It was lucky that no man knew where Kadath towers, for the fruits of ascending it would be very grave. Atal's companion Barzai the Wise had been drawn screaming into the sky for climbing merely the known peak of Hatheg-Kla. With unknown Kadath, if ever found, matters would be much worse; for although earth's gods may sometimes be surpassed by a wise mortal, they are protected by the Other Gods from Outside, whom it is better not to discuss. At least twice in the world's history the Other Gods set their seal upon earth's primal granite; once in antediluvian times, as guessed from a drawing in those parts of the Pnakotic Manuscripts too ancient to be read, and once on Hatheg-Kla when Barzai the Wise tried to see earth's gods dancing by moonlight. So, Atal said, it would be much better to let all gods alone except in tactful prayers.

Carter, though disappointed by Atal's discouraging advice and by the meagre help to be found in the Pnakotic Manuscripts and the Seven Cryptical Books of Hsan, did not wholly despair. First he questioned the old priest about that marvellous sunset city seen from the railed terrace, thinking that perhaps he might find it without the gods' aid; but Atal could tell him nothing. Probably, Atal said, the place belonged to his especial dream-world and not to the general land of vision that many know; and conceivably it might be on another planet. In that case earth's gods could not guide him if they would. But this was not likely, since the stopping of the dreams shewed pretty clearly that it was something the Great Ones wished to hide from him.

Then Carter did a wicked thing, offering his guileless host so many draughts of the moon-wine which the zoogs had given him that the old man became irresponsibly talkative. Robbed of his reserve, poor Atal babbled freely of forbidden things; telling of a great image reported by travellers as carved on the solid rock of the mountain Ngranek, on the isle of Oriab in the Southern Sea, and hinting that it may be a likeness which earth's gods once wrought of their own features in the days when they danced by moonlight on that mountain. And he hiccoughed likewise that the features of that image are very strange, so that one might easily recognise them, and that they are signs of the authentic race of the gods.

Now the use of all this in finding the gods became at once apparent to Carter. It is known that in disguise the younger among the Great Ones often espouse the daughters of men, so that around the borders of the cold waste wherein stands Kadath the peasants must all bear their blood. This being so, the way to find that waste must be to see the stone face on Ngranek and mark the features; then, having noted them with care, to search for such features among living men. Where they are plainest and thickest, there must the gods dwell nearest; and whatever stony waste lies back of the villages in that place must be that wherein stands Kadath.

Much of the Great Ones might be learnt in such regions, and those with their blood might inherit little memories very useful to a seeker. They might not know their parentage, for the gods so dislike to be known among men that none can be found who has seen their faces wittingly; a thing which Carter realised even as he sought to scale Kadath. But they would have queer lofty thoughts misunderstood by their fellows, and would sing of far places and gardens so unlike any known even in dreamland that common folk would call them fools; and from all this one could perhaps learn old secrets of Kadath, or gain hints of the marvellous sunset city which the gods held secret. And more, one might in certain cases seize some well-loved child of a god as hostage; or even capture some young god himself, disguised and dwelling amongst men with a comely peasant maiden as his bride.

Atal, however, did not know how to find Ngranek on its isle of Oriab; and recommended that Carter follow the singing Skai under its bridges down to the Southern Sea; where no burgess of Ulthar has ever been, but whence the merchants come in boats or with long caravans of mules and two-wheeled carts. There is a great city there, Dylath-Leen, but in Ulthar its reputation is bad because of the black three-banked galleys that sail to it with rubies from no clearly named shore. The traders that come from those galleys to deal with the jewellers are human, or nearly so, but the rowers are never beheld; and it is not thought wholesome in Ulthar that merchants should trade with black ships from unknown places whose rowers cannot be exhibited.

By the time he had given this information Atal was very drowsy, and Carter laid him gently on a couch of inlaid ebony and gathered his long beard decorously on his chest. As he turned to go, he observed that no suppressed fluttering followed him, and wondered why the zoogs had become so lax in their curious pursuit. Then he noticed all the sleek complacent cats of Ulthar licking their chops with unusual gusto, and recalled the spitting and caterwauling he had faintly heard in lower parts of the temple while absorbed in the old priest's conversation. He recalled, too, the evilly hungry way in which an especially impudent young zoog had regarded a small black kitten in the cobbled street outside. And because he loved nothing on earth more than small black kittens, he stooped and petted the sleek cats of Ulthar as they licked their chops, and did not mourn because those inquisitive zoogs would escort him no farther.

It was sunset now, so Carter stopped at an ancient inn on a steep little street overlooking the lower town. And as he went out on the balcony of his room and gazed down at the sea of red tiled roofs and cobbled ways and the pleasant fields beyond, all mellow and magical in the slanted light, he swore that Ulthar would be a very likely place to dwell in always, were not the memory of a greater sunset city ever goading one on toward unknown perils. Then twilight fell, and the pink walls of the plastered gables turned violet and mystic, and little yellow lights floated up one by one from old lattice windows. And sweet bells pealed in the temple tower above, and the first star winked softly above the meadows across the Skai. With the night came song, and Carter nodded as the lutanists praised ancient days from beyond the filigreed balconies and tessellated courts of simple Ulthar. And there might have been sweetness even in the voices of Ulthar's many cats, but that they were mostly heavy and silent from strange feasting. Some of them stole off to those cryptical realms which are known only to cats and which villagers say are on the moon's dark side, whither the cats leap from tall housetops, but one small black kitten crept upstairs and sprang in Carter's lap

Giants' Causeway, Northern Ireland.

17. A geological formation that looks like a majestic basalt fence, on the northern coast of Northern Ireland, bordering the Antrim plateau. Tens of thousands of ruggedly elegant columns, their formation the result of a volcano that occurred sixty million years ago, are connected and form a walkway that winds in and out of grassy seaside knolls. It is referred to in *At the Mountains of Madness*, in the previous volume, pp. 457–572. Legend has it that Fionn mac Cumhaill, or Finn MacCool, a giant or a hero, depending on the source, built the causeway to facilitate combat with the giant Benandonner. MacCool is the focus of the Fenian or Ossianic cycle of Irish folklore.

to purr and play, and curled up near his feet when he lay down at last on the little couch whose pillows were stuffed with fragrant, drowsy herbs.

In the morning Carter joined a caravan of merchants bound for Dylath-Leen with the spun wool of Ulthar and the cabbages of Ulthar's busy farms. And for six days they rode with tinkling bells on the smooth road beside the Skai; stopping some nights at the inns of little quaint fishing towns, and on other nights camping under the stars while snatches of boatmen's songs came from the placid river. The country was very beautiful, with green hedges and groves and picturesque peaked cottages and octagonal windmills.

On the seventh day a blur of smoke arose on the horizon ahead, and then the tall black towers of Dylath-Leen, which is built mostly of basalt. Dylath-Leen with its thin angular towers looks in the distance like a bit of the Giants' Causeway,[17] and its streets are dark and uninviting. There are many dismal seataverns near the myriad wharves, and all the town is thronged with the strange seamen of every land on earth and of a few which are said to be not on earth. Carter questioned the oddly robed men of that city about the peak of Ngranek on the isle of Oriab, and found that they knew of it well. Ships came from Baharna on that island, one being due to return thither in only a month, and Ngranek is but two days' zebra-ride from that port. But few had seen the stone face of the god, because it is on a very difficult side of Ngranek, which overlooks only sheer crags and a valley of sinister lava. Once the gods were angered with men on that side, and spoke of the matter to the Other Gods.

It was hard to get this information from the traders and sailors in Dylath-Leen's sea-taverns, because they mostly preferred to whisper of the black galleys. One of them was due in a week with rubies from its unknown shore, and the townsfolk dreaded to see it dock. The mouths of the men who came from it to trade were too wide, and the way their turbans were humped up in two points above their foreheads was in especially bad taste. And their shoes were the shortest and queerest ever seen in the Six Kingdoms. But worst of all was the matter of the unseen rowers. Those three banks of oars moved too briskly and accurately and vigorously to be comfortable, and it was not right for a ship to stay in port for weeks while the merchants traded, yet to give no glimpse of its crew. It was not fair to the tavern-keepers of Dylath-Leen, or to the grocers and butchers, either; for not a scrap of provisions was ever sent aboard. The merchants took only gold and stout black slaves from Parg across the river. That was all they ever took, those unpleasantly featured merchants and their unseen rowers; never anything from the butchers and grocers, but only gold and the fat black men of Parg whom they bought by the pound. And the odours from those galleys which the south wind blew in from the wharves are not to be described. Only by constantly smoking strong thagweed could even the hardiest denizen of the old sea-taverns bear them. Dylath-Leen would never have tolerated the black galleys had such rubies been obtainable elsewhere, but no mine in all earth's dreamland was known to produce their like.

Of these things Dylath-Leen's cosmopolitan folk chiefly gossiped whilst Carter waited patiently for the ship from Baharna, which might bear him to the isle whereon carven Ngranek towers lofty and barren. Meanwhile he did not fail to seek through the haunts of far travellers for any tales they might have concerning Kadath in the cold waste or a marvellous city of marble walls and silver fountains seen below terraces in the sunset. Of these things, however, he learned nothing; though he once thought that a certain old slant-eyed merchant looked queerly intelligent when the cold waste was spoken of. This man was reputed to trade with the horrible stone villages on the icy desert plateau of Leng, which no healthy folk visit and whose evil fires are seen at night from afar. He was even rumoured to have dealt with that high-priest not to be described, which wears a yellow silken mask over its face and dwells all alone in a prehistoric stone monastery. That such a person might well have had nibbling traffick with such beings as may conceivably dwell in the cold waste was not to be doubted, but Carter soon found that it was no use questioning him.

Then the black galley slipped into the harbour past the basalt mole[18] and the tall lighthouse, silent and alien, and with a strange stench that the south wind drove into the town. Uneasiness rustled through the taverns along that waterfront, and after a while the dark wide-mouthed merchants with humped turbans and short feet clumped stealthily ashore to seek the bazaars of the jewellers. Carter observed them closely, and disliked them more the longer he looked at them. Then he saw them drive the stout black men of Parg up the gangplank grunting and sweating into that singular galley, and wondered in what lands—or if in any lands at all—those fat pathetic creatures might be destined to serve.

And on the third evening of that galley's stay one of the uncomfortable merchants spoke to him, smirking sinfully and hinting of what he had heard in the taverns of Carter's quest. He appeared to have knowledge too secret for public telling; and though the sound of his voice was unbearably hateful, Carter felt that the lore of so far a traveller must not be overlooked. He bade him therefore be his own guest in locked chambers above, and drew out the last of the zoogs' moon-wine to loosen his tongue. The strange merchant drank heavily, but smirked unchanged by the draught. Then he drew forth a curious bottle with wine of his own, and Carter saw that the bottle was a single hollowed ruby, grotesquely carved in patterns too fabulous to be comprehended. He offered his wine to his host, and though Carter took only the least sip, he felt the dizziness of space and the fever of unimagined jungles. All the while the guest had been smiling more and more broadly, and as Carter slipped into blankness the last thing he

18. "A massive structure, esp. of stone, serving as a pier or breakwater" (*Oxford English Dictionary*). According to the *OED*, the word is derived from the Latin "*moles*," meaning "mass."

19. This is a reference to HPL's story "The White Ship," written in 1919 and published that year in *The United Amateur*. The narrator there—though not from Kingsport—is Basil Elton, the lighthouse keeper of the "North Point light."

saw was that dark odious face convulsed with evil laughter, and something quite unspeakable where one of the two frontal puffs of that orange turban had become disarranged with the shakings of that epileptic mirth.

Carter next had consciousness amidst horrible odours beneath a tent-like awning on the deck of a ship, with the marvellous coasts of the Southern Sea flying by in unnatural swiftness. He was not chained, but three of the dark sardonic merchants stood grinning nearby, and the sight of those humps in their turbans made him almost as faint as did the stench that filtered up through the sinister hatches. He saw slip past him the glorious lands and cities of which a fellow-dreamer of earth—a lighthouse-keeper in ancient Kingsport—had often discoursed in the old days,[19] and recognised the templed terraces of Zar, abode of forgotten dreams; the spires of infamous Thalarion, that daemon-city of a thousand wonders where the eidolon Lathi reigns; the charnal gardens of Xura, land of pleasures unattained, and the twin headlands of crystal, meeting above in a resplendent arch, which guard the harbour of Sona-Nyl, blessed land of fancy.

Past all these gorgeous lands the malodorous ship flew unwholesomely, urged by the abnormal strokes of those unseen rowers below. And before the day was done Carter saw that the steersman could have no other goal than the Basalt Pillars of the West, beyond which simple folk say splendid Cathuria lies, but which wise dreamers well know are the gates of a monstrous cataract wherein the oceans of earth's dreamland drop wholly to abysmal nothingness and shoot through the empty spaces toward other worlds and other stars and the awful voids outside the ordered universe where the daemon-sultan Azathoth gnaws hungrily in chaos amid pounding and piping and the hellish dancing of the Other Gods, blind, voiceless, tenebrous, and mindless, with their soul and messenger Nyarlathotep.

Meanwhile the three sardonic merchants would give no word of their intent, though Carter well knew that they must be leagued with those who wished to hold him from his quest. It is understood in the land of dream that the Other Gods have many agents moving among men; and all these agents, whether wholly human or slightly less than human, are eager to work the will of those blind and mindless things in return for the favour of their hideous soul and messenger, the crawling chaos Nyarlathotep. So Carter inferred that the merchants of the humped turbans, hearing of his daring search for the Great Ones in their castle on Kadath, had decided to take him away and deliver him to Nyarlathothep for whatever nameless bounty might be offered for such a prize. What might be the land of those merchants, in our known universe or in the eldritch spaces outside, Carter could not guess; nor could he imagine at what hellish trysting-place they would meet the crawling chaos to give him up and claim their reward. He knew, however, that no beings as nearly human as these would dare approach the ultimate nighted throne of the daemon Azathoth in the formless central void.

At the set of sun the merchants licked their excessively wide lips and glared hungrily, and one of them went below and returned from some hidden and offensive cabin with a pot and basket of plates. Then they squatted close together beneath the awning and ate the smoking meat that was passed around. But when they gave Carter a portion, he found something very terrible in the size and shape of it; so that he turned even paler than before and cast that portion into the sea when no eye was on him. And again he thought of those unseen rowers beneath, and of the suspicious nourishment from which their far too mechanical strength was derived.

It was dark when the galley passed betwixt the Basalt Pillars of the West and the sound of the ultimate cataract swelled portentous from ahead. And the spray of that cataract rose to obscure the stars, and the deck grew damp, and the vessel reeled in the surging current of the brink. Then with a queer whistle and plunge the leap was taken, and Carter felt the terrors of nightmare as earth fell away and the great boat shot silent and comet-like into planetary space. Never before had he known what shapeless black things lurk and caper and flounder all through the aether, leering and grinning at such voyagers as may pass, and sometimes feeling about with slimy paws when some moving object excites their curiosity. These are the nameless larvae of the Other Gods, and like them are blind and without mind, and possessed of singular hungers and thirsts.

But that offensive galley did not aim as far as Carter had feared, for he soon saw that the helmsman was steering a course directly for the moon. The moon was a crescent, shining larger and larger as they approached it, and shewing its singular craters and peaks uncomfortably. The ship made for the edge, and it soon became clear that its destination was that secret and mysterious side which is always turned away from the earth, and which no fully human person, save perhaps the dreamer Snireth-Ko, has ever beheld. The close aspect of the moon as the galley drew near proved very disturbing to Carter, and he did not like the size and shape of the ruins which crumbled here and there. The dead temples on the mountains were so placed that they could have glorified no wholesome or suitable gods, and in the symmetries of the broken columns there seemed to lurk some dark and inner meaning which did not invite solution. And what the structure and proportions of the olden worshippers could have been, Carter steadily refused to conjecture.

When the ship rounded the edge, and sailed over those lands unseen by man, there appeared in the queer landscape certain signs of life, and Carter saw many low, broad, round cottages in fields of grotesque whitish fungi. He noticed that these cottages had no windows, and thought that their shape suggested the huts of Esquimaux. Then he glimpsed the oily waves of a sluggish sea, and knew that the voyage was once more to be by water—or at least through some liquid. The galley struck the surface with a peculiar sound, and the odd elastic way the waves received it was very perplexing to Carter. They now slid along at great speed, once passing and hailing another galley of kindred form, but generally seeing nothing but that curious sea and a sky that was black and star-strown even though the sun shone scorchingly in it.

There presently rose ahead the jagged hills of a leprous-looking coast, and Carter saw the thick unpleasant grey towers of a city. The way they leaned and bent, the manner in which they were clustered, and the fact that they had no windows at all, was very disturbing to the prisoner; and he bitterly mourned the folly which had made him sip the curious wine of that merchant with the humped turban. As the coast drew nearer, and the hideous stench of that city grew stronger, he saw upon the jagged hills many forests, some of whose trees he recognised as akin to that solitary moon-tree in the enchanted wood of earth, from whose sap the small brown zoogs ferment their peculiar wine.

Carter could now distinguish moving figures on the noisome wharves ahead, and the better he saw them the worse he began to fear and detest them. For they were not men at all, or even approximately men, but great greyish-white slippery things which could expand and contract at will, and whose principal shape— though it often changed—was that of a sort of toad without any eyes, but with a curiously vibrating mass of short pink tentacles on the end of its blunt, vague snout. These objects were waddling busily about the wharves, moving bales and crates and boxes with preternatural strength, and now and then hopping on or off some anchored galley with long oars in their fore paws. And now and then one would appear driving a herd of clumping slaves, which indeed were approximate human beings with wide mouths like those merchants who traded in Dylath-Leen; only these herds, being without turbans or shoes or clothing, did not seem so very human after all. Some of these slaves—the fatter ones, whom a sort of overseer would pinch experimentally—were unloaded from ships and nailed in crates which workers pushed into low warehouses or loaded on great lumbering vans.

Once a van was hitched up and driven off, and the fabulous thing which drew it was such that Carter gasped, even after having seen the other monstrosities of that hateful place. Now and then a small herd of slaves dressed and turbaned like the dark merchants would be driven aboard a galley, followed by a great crew of the slippery grey toad-things as officers, navigators, and rowers. And Carter saw that the almost-human creatures were reserved for the more ignominious kinds of servitude which required no strength, such as steering and cooking, fetching and carrying, and bargaining with men on the earth or other planets where they traded. These creatures must have been convenient on earth, for they were truly not unlike men when dressed and carefully shod and turbaned, and could haggle in the shops of men without embarrassment or curious explanations. But most of them, unless lean and ill-favoured, were unclothed and packed in crates and drawn off in lumbering lorries by fabulous things. Occasionally other beings were unloaded and crated; some very like these semi-humans, some not so similar, and some not similar at all. And he wondered if any of the poor stout black men of Parg were left to be unloaded and crated and shipped inland in those obnoxious drays.

When the galley landed at a greasy-looking quay of spongy rock a nightmare horde of toad-things wriggled out of the hatches, and two of them seized Carter and dragged him ashore. The smell and aspect of that city are beyond telling, and Carter held only scattered images of the tiled streets and black doorways and endless precipices of grey vertical walls without windows. At length he was dragged within a low doorway and made to climb infinite steps in pitch blackness. It was, apparently, all one to the toad-things whether it were light or dark. The odour of the place was intolerable, and when Carter was locked into a chamber and left alone he scarcely had strength to crawl around and ascertain its form and dimensions. It was circular, and about twenty feet across.

From then on time ceased to exist. At intervals food was pushed in, but Carter would not touch it. What his fate would be, he did not know; but he felt that he was held for the coming of that frightful soul and messenger of infinity's Other Gods, the crawling chaos Nyarlathotep. Finally, after an unguessed span of hours or days, the great stone door swung wide again and Carter was shoved down the stairs and out into the red-litten streets of that fearsome city. It was night on the moon, and all through the town were stationed slaves bearing torches.

In a destestable square a sort of procession was formed; ten of the toad-things and twenty-four almost-human torch-bearers, eleven on either side, and one each before and behind. Carter was placed in the middle of the line; five toad-things ahead and five behind, and one almost-human torch-bearer on each side of him. Certain of the toad-things produced disgustingly carven flutes of ivory and made loathsome sounds. To that hellish piping the column advanced out of the tiled streets and into nighted plains of obscene fungi, soon commencing to climb one of the lower and more gradual hills that lay behind the city. That on some frightful slope or blasphemous plateau the crawling chaos waited, Carter could not doubt; and he wished that the suspense might soon be over. The whining of those impious flutes was shocking, and he would have given worlds for some even half-normal sound; but these toad-things had no voices, and the slaves did not talk.

Then through that star-specked darkness there did come a normal sound. It rolled from the higher hills, and from all the jagged peaks around it was caught up and echoed in a swelling pandaemoniac chorus. It was the midnight yell of the cat, and Carter knew at last that the old village folk were right when they made low guesses about the cryptical realms which are known only to cats, and to which the elders among cats repair by stealth nocturnally, springing from high housetops. Verily, it is to the moon's dark side that they go to leap and gambol on the hills and converse with ancient shadows, and here amidst that column of foetid things Carter heard their homely, friendly cry, and thought of the steep roofs and warm hearths and little lighted windows of home.

Now much of the speech of cats was known to Randolph Carter, and in this far, terrible place he uttered the cry that was suitable. But that he need not have done, for even as his lips opened he heard the chorus wax and draw nearer, and saw swift shadows against the stars as small graceful shapes leaped from hill to hill in gathering legions. The call of the clan had been given, and before the foul procession had time even to be frightened a cloud of smothering fur and a phalanx of murderous claws were tidally and tempestuously upon it. The flutes stopped, and there were shrieks in the night. Dying almost-humans screamed, and cats spit and yowled and roared, but the toad-things made never a sound as their stinking green ichor oozed fatally upon that porous earth with the obscene fungi.

It was a stupendous sight while the torches lasted, and Carter had never before seen so many cats. Black, grey, and white; yellow, tiger, and mixed; common, Persian, and Manx; Thibetan, Angora, and Egyptian; all were there in the fury of battle, and there hovered over them some trace of that profound and inviolate sanctity which made their goddess great in the temples of Bubastis.[20] They would leap seven strong at the throat of an almost-human or the pink tentacled snout of a toad-thing and drag it down savagely to the fungous plain, where myriads of their fellows would surge over it and into it with the frenzied claws and teeth of a divine battle-fury. Carter had seized a torch from a

20. An ancient Egyptian city on the Nile in the delta region of lower Egypt, home to the temple of Bast. Located a few miles from the relatively populous and comparatively modern Zagazig, which was founded in the 1820s to house men hired to dig irrigation canals (barrages), Bubastis served as the capital of Egypt during the Twenty-Second and Twenty-Third Dynasties. See "The Rats in the Walls," pp. 150–74, note 61, above. Carter's appreciation here for the chaos of breeds may be seen as ironic in the context of Lovecraft's own intolerance for ethnic diversity (see, for example, "The Terrible Old Man," pp. 36–39, above).

stricken slave, but was soon overborne by the surging waves of his loyal defenders. Then he lay in the utter blackness hearing the clangour of war and the shouts of the victors, and feeling the soft paws of his friends as they rushed to and fro over him in the fray.

At last awe and exhaustion closed his eyes, and when he opened them again it was upon a strange scene. The great shining disc of the earth, thirteen times greater than that of the moon as we see it, had risen with floods of weird light over the lunar landscape; and across all those leagues of wild plateau and ragged crest there squatted one endless sea of cats in orderly array. Circle on circle they reached, and two or three leaders out of the ranks were licking his face and purring to him consolingly. Of the dead slaves and toad-things there were not many signs, but Carter thought he saw one bone a little way off in the open space between him and the beginning of the solid circles of the warriors.

Carter now spoke with the leaders in the soft language of cats, and learned that his ancient friendship with the species was well known and often spoken of in the places where cats congregate. He had not been unmarked in Ulthar when he passed through, and the sleek old cats had remembered how he petted them after they had attended to the hungry zoogs who looked evilly at a small black kitten. And they recalled, too, how he had welcomed the very little kitten who came to see him at the inn, and how he had given it a saucer of rich cream in the morning before he left. The grandfather of that very little kitten was the leader of the army now assembled, for he had seen the evil procession from a far hill and recognised the prisoner as a sworn friend of his kind on earth and in the land of dream.

A yowl now came from a farther peak, and the old leader paused abruptly in his conversation. It was one of the army's outposts, stationed on the highest of the mountains to watch the one foe which earth's cats fear; the very large and peculiar cats from Saturn, who for some reason have not been oblivious of the charm of our moon's dark side. They are leagued by treaty with the evil toad-things, and are notoriously hostile to our earthly cats; so that at this juncture a meeting would have been a somewhat grave matter.

After a brief consultation of generals, the cats rose and

assumed a closer formation, crowding protectingly around Carter and preparing to take the great leap through space back to the housetops of our earth and its dreamland. The old field-marshal advised Carter to let himself be borne along smoothly and passively in the massed ranks of furry leapers, and told him how to spring when the rest sprang and land gracefully when the rest landed. He also offered to deposit him in any spot he desired, and Carter decided on the city of Dylath-Leen whence the black galley had set out; for he wished to sail thence for Oriab and the carven crest of Ngranek, and also to warn the people of the city to have no more traffick with black galleys, if indeed that traffick could be tactfully and judiciously broken off. Then, upon a signal, the cats all leaped gracefully with their friend packed securely in their midst; while in a black cave on a far unhallowed summit of the moon-mountains still vainly waited the crawling chaos Nyarlathotep.

The leap of the cats through space was very swift; and being surrounded by his companions, Carter did not see this time the great black shapelessnesses that lurk and caper and flounder in the abyss. Before he fully realised what had happened he was back in his familiar room at the inn at Dylath-Leen, and the stealthy, friendly cats were pouring out of the window in streams. The old leader from Ulthar was the last to leave, and as Carter shook his paw he said he would be able to get home by cockcrow. When dawn came, Carter went downstairs and learned that a week had elapsed since his capture and leaving. There was still nearly a fortnight to wait for the ship bound toward Oriab, and during that time he said what he could against the black galleys and their infamous ways. Most of the townsfolk believed him; yet so fond were the jewellers of great rubies that none would wholly promise to cease trafficking with the wide-mouthed merchants. If aught of evil ever befalls Dylath-Leen through such traffick, it will not be his fault.

In about a week the desiderate ship put in by the black mole and tall lighthouse, and Carter was glad to see that she was a barque of wholesome men, with painted sides and yellow lateen sails and a grey captain in silken robes. Her cargo was the fragrant resin of Oriab's inner groves, and the delicate pottery baked by the artists of Baharna, and the strange little figures carved

21. HPL dreamed of night-gaunts at the age of five. In a letter to the artist Virgil Finlay, dated October 24, 1936 (*Selected Letters*, V, 334–35), he described them as "black, lean, rubbery things with bared, barbed tails, bat-wings, and *no faces at all*. . . . They had no voices, and their only form of real torture was their habit of tickling my stomach . . . before snatching me up and swooping away with me." Lovecraft never identified any actual person who tormented him with tickles, but HPL's artistry allowed him to master these and other childhood fears by incorporating his nightmares into his fiction. He never mentioned night-gaunts in any other story.

from Ngranek's ancient lava. For this they were paid in the wool of Ulthar and the iridescent textiles of Hatheg and the ivory that the black men carve across the river in Parg. Carter made arrangements with the captain to go to Baharna and was told that the voyage would take ten days. And during his week of waiting he talked much with that captain of Ngranek, and was told that very few had seen the carven face thereon; but that most travellers are content to learn its legends from old people and lava-gatherers and image-makers in Baharna and afterward say in their far homes that they have indeed beheld it. The captain was not even sure that any person now living had beheld that carven face, for the wrong side of Ngranek is very difficult and barren and sinister, and there are rumours of caves near the peak wherein dwell the night-gaunts.[21] But the captain did not wish to say just what a night-gaunt might be like, since such cattle are known to haunt most persistently the dreams of those who think too often of them. Then Carter asked that captain about unknown Kadath in the cold waste, and the marvellous sunset city, but of these the good man could truly tell nothing.

Carter sailed out of Dylath-Leen one early morning when the tide turned, and saw the first rays of sunrise on the thin angular towers of that dismal basalt town. And for two days they sailed eastward in sight of green coasts, and saw often the pleasant fishing towns that climbed up steeply with their red roofs and chimney-pots from old dreaming wharves and beaches where nets lay drying. But on the third day they turned sharply south where the roll of the water was stronger, and soon passed from sight of any land. On the fifth day the sailors were nervous, but the captain apologised for their fears, saying that the ship was about to pass over the weedy walls and broken columns of a sunken city too old for memory, and that when the water was clear one could see so many moving shadows in that deep place that simple folk disliked it. He admitted, moreover, that many ships had been lost in that part of the sea; having been hailed when quite close to it, but never seen again.

That night the moon was very bright, and one could see a great way down in the water. There was so little wind that the ship could not move much, and the ocean was very calm. Looking over the rail Carter saw many fathoms deep the dome of a great temple, and in front of it an avenue of unnatural sphinxes leading to what was once a public square.[22] Dolphins sported merrily in and out of the ruins, and porpoises revelled clumsily here and there, sometimes coming to the surface and leaping clear out of the sea. As the ship drifted on a little the floor of the ocean rose in hills, and one could clearly mark the lines of ancient climbing streets and the washed-down walls of myriad little houses.

Then the suburbs appeared, and finally a great lone building on a hill, of simpler architecture than the other structures, and in much better repair. It was dark and low and covered four sides of a square, with a tower at each corner, a paved court in the centre, and small curious round windows all over it. Probably it was of basalt, though weeds draped the greater part; and such was its lonely and impressive place on that far hill that it may have been a temple or monastery. Some phosphorescent fish inside it gave the small round windows an aspect of shining, and Carter did not blame the sailors much for their fears. Then by the watery moonlight he noticed an odd high monolith in the middle of that central court, and saw that something was tied to it. And when after getting a telescope from the captain's cabin he saw that that bound thing was a sailor in the silk robes of Oriab, head downward and without any eyes, he was glad that a rising breeze soon took the ship ahead to more healthy parts of the sea.

The next day they spoke[23] a ship with violet sails bound for Zar, in the land of forgotten dreams, with bulbs of strange coloured lilies for cargo. And on the evening of the eleventh day they came in sight of the isle of Oriab, with Ngranek rising jagged and snow-crowned in the distance. Oriab is a very great isle, and its port of Baharna a mighty city. The wharves of Baharna are of porphyry, and the city rises in great stone terraces behind them, having streets of steps that are frequently arched over by buildings and the bridges between buildings. There is a great canal which goes under the whole city in a tunnel with granite gates and leads to the inland lake of Yath, on whose farther shore are the vast clay-brick ruins of a primal city whose name is not remembered. As the ship drew into the harbour at evening the twin beacons Thon and Thal gleamed a welcome, and in all the million windows of Baharna's terraces mellow lights peeped out quietly and gradually as the stars peep out overhead in the dusk,

22. This is likely Atlantis of "The Temple," pp. 55–70, above.

23. "Spoke" is an archaic form of the verb used, without "with," to mean communicate with a passing vessel—for example, "the *Nautilus* spoke the *Lollipop* on Monday."

till that steep and climbing seaport became a glittering constellation hung between the stars of heaven and the reflections of those stars in the still harbour.

The captain, after landing, made Carter a guest in his own small house on the shore of Yath where the rear of the town slopes down to it; and his wife and servants brought strange toothsome foods for the traveller's delight. And in the days after that Carter asked for rumours and legends of Ngranek in all the taverns and public places where lava-gatherers and image-makers meet, but could find no one who had been up the higher slopes or seen the carven face. Ngranek was a hard mountain with only an accursed valley behind it, and besides, one could never depend on the certainty that night-gaunts are altogether fabulous.

When the captain sailed back to Dylath-Leen Carter took quarters in an ancient tavern opening on an alley of steps in the original part of the town, which is built of brick and resembles the ruins of Yath's farther shore. Here he laid his plans for the ascent of Ngranek, and correlated all that he had learned from the lava-gatherers about the roads thither. The keeper of the tavern was a very old man, and had heard so many legends that he was a great help. He even took Carter to an upper room in that ancient house and shewed him a crude picture which a traveller had scratched on the clay wall in the olden days when men were bolder and less reluctant to visit Ngranek's higher slopes. The old tavern-keeper's great-grandfather had heard from his great-grandfather that the traveller who scratched that picture had climbed Ngranek and seen the carven face, here drawing it for others to behold; but Carter had very great doubts, since the large rough features on the wall were hasty and careless, and wholly overshadowed by a crowd of little companion shapes in the worst possible taste, with horns and wings and claws and curling tails.

At last, having gained all the information he was likely to gain in the taverns and public places of Baharna, Carter hired a zebra and set out one morning on the road by Yath's shore for those inland parts wherein towers stony Ngranek. On his right were rolling hills and pleasant orchards and neat little stone farmhouses, and he was much reminded of those fertile fields that flank the Skai. By evening he was near the nameless ancient ruins on Yath's farther shore, and though old lava-gatherers had warned him not to camp there at night, he tethered his zebra to a curious pillar before a crumbling wall and laid his blanket in a sheltered corner beneath some carvings whose meaning none could decipher. Around him he wrapped another blanket, for the nights are cold in Oriab; and when upon awaking once he thought he felt the wings of some insect brushing his face he covered his head altogether and slept in peace till roused by the magah birds in distant resin groves.

The sun had just come up over the great slope whereon leagues of primal brick foundations and worn walls and occasional cracked pillars and pedestals stretched down desolate to the shore of Yath, and Carter looked about for his tethered zebra. Great was his dismay to see that docile beast stretched prostrate beside the curious pillar to which it had been tied, and still greater was he vexed on finding that the steed was quite dead, with its blood all sucked away through a singular wound in its throat. His pack had been disturbed, and several shiny knick-knacks taken away, and all around on the dusty soil were great webbed footprints for which he could not in any way account. The legends and warnings of lava-gatherers occurred to him and he thought of what had brushed his face in the night. Then he shouldered his pack and strode on toward Ngranek, though not without a shiver when he saw close to him as the highway passed through the ruins a great gaping arch low in the wall of an old temple, with steps leading down into darkness farther than he could peer.

His course now led uphill through wilder and partly wooded country, and he saw only the huts of charcoal-burners and the camps of those who gathered resin from the groves. The whole air was fragrant with balsam, and all the magah birds sang blithely as they flashed their seven colours in the sun. Near sunset he came on a new camp of lava-gatherers returning with laden sacks from Ngranek"s lower slopes; and here he also camped, listening to the songs and tales of the men, and overhearing what they whispered about a companion they had lost. He had climbed high to reach a mass of fine lava above him, and at nightfall did not return to his fellows. When they looked for him the next day they found only his turban, nor was there any sign on the crags below that he had fallen. They did not search any more, because the old men among them said it would be of no use. No one ever found what the night-gaunts took, though those beasts themselves were so uncertain as to be almost fabulous. Carter asked them if night-gaunts sucked blood and liked shiny things and left webbed footprints, but they all shook their head negatively and seemed frightened at his making such an inquiry. When he saw how taciturn they had become he asked them no more, but went to sleep in his blanket.

The next day he rose with the lava-gatherers and exchanged farewells as they rode west and he rode east on a zebra he had bought of them. Their older men gave him blessings and warnings, and told him he had better not climb too high on Ngranek, but while he thanked them heartily he was in no wise dissuaded. For still did he feel that he must find the gods on unknown Kadath, and win from them a way to that haunting and marvellous city in the sunset. By noon, after a long uphill ride, he came upon some abandoned brick villages of the hill-people who had once dwelt thus close to Ngranek and carved images from its smooth lava. Here they had dwelt till the days of the old tavern-keeper's grandfather, but about that time they felt that their presence was disliked. Their homes had crept even up the mountain's slope, and the higher they built the more people they would miss when the sun rose. At last they decided it would be better to leave altogether, since things were sometimes glimpsed in the darkness which no one could interpret favourably; so in the end all of them went down to the sea and dwelt in Baharna, inhabiting a very old quarter and teaching their sons the old art of image-making which to this day they carry on. It was from these children of the exiled hill-people that Carter had heard the best tales about Ngranek when searching through Baharna's ancient taverns.

All this time the great gaunt side of Ngranek was looming up higher and higher as Carter approached it. There were sparse trees on the lower slope, and feeble shrubs above them, and then the bare hideous rock rose spectral into the sky to mix with frost and ice and eternal snow. Carter could see the rifts and ruggedness of that sombre stone, and did not welcome the prospect of climbing it. In places there were solid streams of lava, and scoriac heaps that littered slopes and ledges. Ninety aeons ago, before even the gods had danced upon its pointed peak, that mountain had spoken with fire and roared with the voices of the inner thunders. Now it towered all silent and sinister, bearing on the hidden side that secret titan image whereof rumour told. And there were caves in that mountain, which might be empty and alone with elder darkness, or might—if legend spoke truly—hold horrors of a form not to be surmised.

The ground sloped upward to the foot of Ngranek, thinly covered with scrub oaks and ash trees, and strown with bits of rock, lava, and ancient cinder. There were the charred embers of many camps, where the lava-gatherers were wont to stop, and several rude altars which they had built either to propitiate the Great Ones or to ward off what they dreamed of in Ngranek's high passes and labyrinthine caves. At evening Carter reached the farthermost pile of embers and camped for the night, tethering his zebra to a sapling and wrapping himself well in his blanket before going to sleep. And all through the night a voonith howled distantly from the shore of some hidden pool, but Carter felt no fear of that amphibious terror, since he had been told with certainty that not one of them dares even approach the slopes of Ngranek.

In the clear sunshine of morning Carter began the long ascent, taking his zebra as far as that useful beast could go, but tying it to a stunted ash tree when the floor of the thin road become too steep. Thereafter he scrambled up alone; first through the forest with its ruins of old villages in overgrown clearings, and then over the tough grass where anaemic shrubs grew here and there. He regretted coming clear of the trees, since the slope was very precipitous and the whole thing rather dizzying. At length he began to discern all the countryside spread out beneath him whenever he looked around; the deserted huts of the image-makers, the groves of resin trees and the camps of those who gathered from them, the woods where prismatic magahs nest and sing, and even a hint very far away of the shores of Yath and of those forbidding ancient ruins whose name is forgotten. He found it best not to look around, and kept on climbing and climbing till the shrubs became very sparse and there was often nothing but the tough grass to cling to.

Then the soil became meagre, with great patches of bare rock cropping out, and now and then the nest of a condor in a crevice. Finally there was nothing at all but the bare rock, and had it not been very rough and weathered, he could scarcely have ascended farther. Knobs, ledges, and pinnacles, however, helped greatly; and it was cheering to see occasionally the sign of some lava-gatherer scratched clumsily in the friable stone, and know that wholesome human creatures had been there before him. After a certain height the presence of man was further shewn by hand-holds and foot-holds hewn where they were needed, and by little quarries and excavations where some choice vein or stream of lava had been found. In one place a narrow ledge had been chopped artificially to an especially rich deposit far to the right of the main line of ascent. Once or twice Carter dared to look around, and was almost stunned by the spread of landscape below. All the island betwixt him and the coast lay open to his sight, with Baharna's stone terraces and the smoke of its chimneys mystical in the distance. And beyond that the illimitable Southern Sea with all its curious secrets.

Thus far there had been much winding around the mountain, so that the farther and carven side was still hidden. Carter now saw a ledge running upward and to the left which seemed to head the way he wished, and this course he took in the hope that it might prove continuous. After ten minutes he saw it was indeed no cul-de-sac, but that it led steeply on in an arc which would, unless suddenly interrupted or deflected, bring him after a few hours' climbing to that unknown southern slope overlooking the desolate crags and the accursed valley of lava. As new country came into view below him he saw that it was bleaker and wilder than those seaward lands he had traversed. The mountain's side, too, was somewhat different; being here pierced by curious cracks and caves not found on the straighter route he had left. Some of these were above him and some beneath him, all opening on sheerly perpendicular cliffs and wholly unreachable by the feet of man. The air was very cold now, but so hard was the climbing that he did not mind it. Only the increasing rarity bothered him, and he thought that perhaps it was this which had turned the heads of other travellers and excited those absurd tales of night-gaunts whereby they explained the loss of such climbers as fell from these perilous paths. He was not much impressed by travellers' tales, but had a good curved scimitar in case of any trouble. All lesser thoughts were lost in the wish to see that carven face which might set him on the track of the gods atop unknown Kadath.

At last, in the fearsome iciness of upper space, he came round fully to the hidden side of Ngranek and saw in infinite gulfs below him the lesser crags and sterile abysses of lava which marked the olden wrath of the Great Ones. There was unfolded, too, a vast expanse of country to the south; but it was a desert land without fair fields or cottage chimneys, and seemed to have no ending. No trace of the sea was visible on this side, for Oriab is a great island. Black caverns and odd crevices were still numerous on the sheer vertical cliffs, but none of them was accessible to a climber. There now loomed aloft a great beetling mass which hampered the upward view, and Carter was for a moment shaken with doubt lest it prove impassable. Poised in windy insecurity miles above earth, with only space and death on one side and only slippery walls of rock on the other, he knew for a moment the fear that makes men shun Ngranek's hidden side. He could not turn round, yet the sun was already low. If there were no way aloft, the night would find him crouching there still, and the dawn would not find him at all.

But there was a way, and he saw it in due season. Only a very expert dreamer could have used those imperceptible foot-holds, yet to Carter they were sufficent. Surmounting now the outward-hanging rock, he found the slope above much easier than that below, since a great glacier's melting had left a generous space with loam and ledges. To the left a precipice dropped straight from unknown heights to unknown depths, with a cave's dark mouth just out of reach above him. Elsewhere, however, the mountain slanted back strongly, and even gave him space to lean and rest.

He felt from the chill that he must be near the snow line, and looked up to see what glittering pinnacles might be shining in that late ruddy sunlight. Surely enough, there was the snow uncounted thousands of feet above, and below it a great beetling crag like that he had just climbed; hanging there forever in bold outline, black against the white of the frozen peak. And when he saw that crag he gasped and cried out aloud, and clutched at the jagged rock in awe; for the titan bulge had not stayed as earth's dawn had shaped it, but gleamed red and stupendous in the sunset with the carved and polished features of a god.

Easter Island statues.
Shutterstock.com

24. Richard Huber notes that the description "could fit not only the images of Easter Island but Lovecraft himself" ("H. P. Lovecraft and Easter Island," *Nyctalops* 4, no. 1 [Issue 19, April 1991], 60). See "The Shadow over Innsmouth," in the previous volume, pp. 573–642, note 32. This seems a slight exaggeration—HPL's chin was not really "pointed"—but the overall resemblance is clearly there. Perhaps Lovecraft's *self*-image included a more pointed chin. Duncan Norris, in "Lovecraft and Egypt: A Closer Examination," 6, notes that the description also matches that of the heretic Pharaoh Akhenaten.

Stern and terrible shone that face that the sunset lit with fire. How vast it was no mind can ever measure, but Carter knew at once that man could never have fashioned it. It was a god chiselled by the hands of the gods, and it looked down haughty and majestic upon the seeker. Rumour had said it was strange and not to be mistaken, and Carter saw that it was indeed so; for those long narrow eyes and long-lobed ears, and that thin nose and pointed chin, all spoke of a race that is not of men but of gods.[24] He clung overawed in that lofty and perilous eyrie, even though it was this which he had expected and come to find; for there is in a god's face more of marvel than prediction can tell, and when that face is vaster than a great temple and seen looking down at sunset in the cryptic silences of that upper world from whose dark lava it was divinely hewn of old, the marvel is so strong that none may escape it.

Here, too, was the added marvel of recognition; for although he had planned to search all dreamland over for those whose like-ness to this face might mark them as the gods' children, he now knew that he need not do so. Certainly, the great face carven on that mountain was of no strange sort, but the kin of such as he had seen often in the taverns of the seaport Celephaïs which lies in Ooth-Nargai beyond the Tanarian Hills and is ruled over by that King Kuranes whom Carter once knew in waking life. Every year sailors with such a face came in dark ships from the north to trade their onyx for the carved jade and spun gold and little red singing birds of Celephaïs, and it was clear that these could be no others than the half-gods he sought. Where they dwelt, there must the cold waste lie close, and within it unknown Kadath and its onyx castle for the Great Ones. So to Celephaïs he must go, far distant from the isle of Oriab, and in such parts as would take him back to Dylath-Leen and up the Skai to the bridge by Nir, and again into the enchanted wood of the zoogs, whence the way would bend northward through the garden lands by Oukranos to the gilded spires of Thran, where he might find a galleon bound over the Cerenerian Sea.

But dusk was now thick, and the great carven face looked down even sterner in shadow. Perched on that ledge night found the seeker; and in the blackness he might neither go down nor go up, but only stand and cling and shiver in that narrow place till the day came, praying to keep awake lest sleep loose his hold and send him down the dizzy miles of air to the crags and sharp rocks of the accursed valley. The stars came out, but save for them there was only black nothingness in his eyes; nothingness leagued with death, against whose beckoning he might do no more than cling to the rocks and lean back away from an unseen brink. The last thing of earth that he saw in the gloaming was a condor soaring close to the westward precipice beside him, and darting scream-ing away when it came near the cave whose mouth yawned just out of reach.

Suddenly, without a warning sound in the dark, Carter felt his curved scimitar drawn stealthily out of his belt by some unseen hand. Then he heard it clatter down over the rocks below. And between him and the Milky Way he thought he saw a very terrible outline of something noxiously thin and horned and tailed and bat-winged. Other things, too, had begun to blot

25. The 1965 Arkham House text edited by August Derleth (in *At the Mountains of Madness and Other Novels*) gives this as "dholes," suggesting a connection to the "Doels" mentioned in "The Whisperer in Darkness," in the previous volume, pp. 388–456, but the manuscript is plainly "bholes," and S. T. Joshi corrected the text in the 1985 edition of the 1965 collection.

out patches of stars west of him, as if a flock of vague entities were flapping thickly and silently out of that inaccessible cave in the face of the precipice. Then a sort of cold rubbery arm seized his neck and something else seized his feet, and he was lifted inconsiderately up and swung about in space. Another minute and the stars were gone, and Carter knew that the night-gaunts had got him.

They bore him breathless into that cliffside cavern and through monstrous labyrinths beyond. When he struggled, as at first he did by instinct, they tickled him with deliberation. They made no sound at all themselves, and even their membraneous wings were silent. They were frightfully cold and damp and slippery, and their paws kneaded one detestably. Soon they were plunging hideously downward through inconceivable abysses in a whirling, giddying, sickening rush of dank, tomb-like air; and Carter felt that they were shooting into the ultimate vortex of shrieking and daemonic madness. He screamed again and again, but whenever he did so the black paws tickled him with greater subtlety. Then he saw a sort of grey phosphorescence about, and guessed they were coming even to that inner world of subterrene horror of which dim legends tell, and which is litten only by the pale death-fire wherewith reeks the ghoulish air and the primal mists of the pits at earth's core.

At last far below him he saw the faint lines of grey and ominous pinnacles which he knew must be the fabled Peaks of Thok. Awful and sinister they stand in the haunted dusk of sunless and eternal depths; higher than man may reckon, and guarding terrible valleys where the bholes[25] crawl and burrow nastily. But Carter preferred to look at them than at his captors, which were indeed shocking and uncouth black beings with smooth, oily, whale-like surfaces, unpleasant horns that curved inward toward each other, bat-wings whose beating made no sound, ugly prehensile paws, and barbed tails that lashed needlessly and disquietingly. And worst of all, they never spoke or laughed, and never smiled because they had no faces at all to smile with, but only a suggestive blankness where a face ought to be. All they ever did was clutch and fly and tickle; that was the way of night-gaunts.

As the band flew lower the Peaks of Thok rose grey and towering on all sides, and one saw clearly that nothing lived on that austere and impassive granite of the endless twilight. At still lower levels the death-fires in the air gave out, and one met only the primal blackness of the void save aloft where the thin peaks stood out goblin-like. Soon the peaks were very far away, and nothing about but great rushing winds with the dankness of nethermost grottoes in them. Then in the end the night-gaunts landed on a floor of unseen things which felt like layers of bones, and left Carter all alone in that black valley. To bring him thither was the duty of the night-gaunts that guard Ngranek; and this done, they flapped away silently. When Carter tried to trace their flight he found he could not, since even the Peaks of Thok had faded out of sight. There was nothing anywhere but blackness and horror and silence and bones.

Now Carter knew from a certain source that he was in the vale of Pnath,[26] where crawl and burrow the enormous bholes; but he did not know what to expect, because no one has ever seen a bhole or even guessed what such a thing may be like. Bholes are known only by dim rumour, from the rustling they make amongst mountains of bones and the slimy touch they have when they wriggle past one. They cannot be seen because they creep only in the dark. Carter did not wish to meet a bhole, so listened intently for any sound in the unknown depths of bones about him. Even in this fearsome place he had a plan and an objective, for whispers of Pnath and its approaches were not unknown to one with whom he had talked much in the old days. In brief, it seemed fairly likely that this was the spot into which all the ghouls of the waking world cast the refuse of their feastings; and that if he but had good luck he might stumble upon that mighty crag taller even than Thok's peaks which marks the edge of their domain. Showers of bones would tell him where to look, and once found he could call to a ghoul to let down a ladder; for strange to say, he had a very singular link with these terrible creatures.

A man he had known in Boston—a painter of strange pictures with a secret studio in an ancient and unhallowed alley near a graveyard[27]—had actually made friends with the ghouls and had taught him to understand the simpler part of their disgusting meeping and glibbering. This man had vanished at last, and Carter was not sure but that he might find him now, and use for the first time in dreamland that far-away English of his

26. Note that Robert Blake, the writer-narrator of "The Haunter of the Dark," in the previous volume, pp. 779–806, is the author of a tale entitled "In the Vail of Pnath." Robert M. Price suggests that this is a disguised reference to *The Dream-Quest of Unknown Kadath* ("The Works of Robert Blake," *Crypt of Cthulhu* 80 [Eastertide 1992], 31).

27. This is clearly Richard Upton Pickman, from "Pickman's Model," pp. 311–28, above; he will shortly be identified (see below).

dim waking life. In any case, he felt he could persuade a ghoul to guide him out of Pnath; and it would be better to meet a ghoul, which one can see, than a bhole, which one cannot see.

So Carter walked in the dark, and ran when he thought he heard something among the bones underfoot. Once he bumped into a stony slope, and knew it must be the base of one of Thok's peaks. Then at last he heard a monstrous rattling and clatter which reached far up in the air, and became sure he had come nigh the crag of the ghouls. He was not sure he could be heard from this valley miles below, but realised that the inner world has strange laws. As he pondered he was struck by a flying bone so heavy that it must have been a skull, and therefore realising his nearness to the fateful crag he sent up as best he might that meeping cry which is the call of the ghoul.

Sound travels slowly, so that it was some time before he heard an answering glibber. But it came at last, and before long he was told that a rope ladder would be lowered. The wait for this was very tense, since there was no telling what might not have been stirred up among those bones by his shouting. Indeed, it was not long before he actually did hear a vague rustling afar off. As this thoughtfully approached, he became more and more uncomfortable; for he did not wish to move away from the spot where the ladder would come. Finally the tension grew almost unbearable, and he was about to flee in panic when the thud of something on the newly heaped bones nearby drew his notice from the other sound. It was the ladder, and after a minute of groping he had it taut in his hands. But the other sound did not cease, and followed him even as he climbed. He had gone fully five feet from the ground when the rattling beneath waxed emphatic, and was a good ten feet up when something swayed the ladder from below. At a height which must have been fifteen or twenty feet he felt his whole side brushed by a great slippery length which grew alternately convex and concave with wriggling, and thereafter he climbed desperately to escape the unendurable nuzzling of that loathsome and overfed bhole whose form no man might see.

For hours he climbed with aching arms and blistered hands, seeing again the grey death-fire and Thok's uncomfortable pinnacles. At last he discerned above him the projecting edge of the great crag of the ghouls, whose vertical side he could not glimpse; and hours later he saw a curious face peering over it as a gargoyle peers over a parapet of Notre-Dame. This almost made him lose his hold through faintness, but a moment later he was himself again; for his vanished friend Richard Pickman had once introduced him to a ghoul, and he knew well their canine faces and slumping forms and unmentionable idiosyncrasies. So he had himself well under control when that hideous thing pulled him out of the dizzy emptiness over the edge of the crag, and did not scream at the partly consumed refuse heaped at one side or at the squatting circles of ghouls who gnawed and watched curiously.

He was now on a dim-litten plain whose sole topographical features were great boulders and the entrances of burrows. The ghouls were in general respectful, even if one did attempt to pinch him while several others eyed his leanness speculatively. Through patient glibbering he made inquiries regarding his vanished friend, and found he had become a ghoul of some prominence in abysses nearer the waking world. A greenish elderly ghoul offered to conduct him to Pickman's present habitation, so despite a natural loathing he followed the creature into a capacious burrow and crawled after him for hours in the blackness of rank mould. They emerged on a dim plain strown with singular relics of earth—old gravestones, broken urns, and grotesque fragments of monuments—and Carter realised with some emotion that he was probably nearer the waking world than at any other time since he had gone down the seven hundred steps from the cavern of flame to the Gate of Deeper Slumber.

There, on a tombstone of 1768 stolen from the Granary Burying Ground in Boston,[28] sat the ghoul which was once the artist Richard Upton Pickman. It was naked and rubbery, and had acquired so much of the ghoulish physiognomy that its human origin was already obscure. But it still remembered a little English, and was able to converse with Carter in grunts and monosyllables, helped out now and then by the glibbering of ghouls. When it learned that Carter wished to get to the enchanted wood and from there to the city Celephaïs in Ooth-Nargai beyond the Tanarian Hills, it seemed rather doubtful; for these ghouls of the waking world do no business in the graveyards of upper dreamland (leaving that to the web-footed wamps that are spawned in dead cities), and many things intervene betwixt

28. On Tremont Street (see note 45, below). It has interments dating from 1660, including Benjamin Franklin's parents, John Hancock, Paul Revere, and Samuel Adams. There is also a grave marker for the victims of the Boston Massacre.

Granary Burying Ground, Boston, 2017. Photograph courtesy of Donovan K. Loucks

29. Leng is originally identified with Tibet; however, in *At the Mountains of Madness*, it is an area of the Antarctic. This, remarks Peter Cannon (in "You Have Been in Providence, I Perceive," *Nyctalops* 2, no. 7 [March 1978], 46, note 4), "is the only major discrepancy Lovecraft allows in his work. Even then the narrator in 'At the Mountains of Madness' accounts for this confusion when he says: 'Mythologists have placed Leng in Central Asia; but the racial memory of man—or of his predecessors—is long, and it may well be that certain tales have come down from lands and mountains and temples of horror earlier than Asia and earlier than any human world we know.'"

their gulf and the enchanted wood, including the terrible kingdom of the gugs.

The gugs, hairy and gigantic, once reared stone circles in that wood and made strange sacrifices to the Other Gods and the crawling chaos Nyarlathotep, until one night an abomination of theirs reached the ears of earth's gods and they were banished to caverns below. Only a great trap-door of stone with an iron ring connects the abyss of the earth-ghouls with the enchanted wood, and this the gugs are afraid to open because of a curse. That a mortal dreamer could traverse their cavern realm and leave by that door is inconceivable; for mortal dreamers were their former food, and they have legends of the toothsomeness of such dreamers even though banishment has restricted their diet to the ghasts, those repulsive beings which die in the light, and which live in the vaults of Zin and leap on long hind legs like kangaroos.

So the ghoul that was Pickman advised Carter either to leave the abyss at Sarkomand, that deserted city in the valley below Leng[29] where black nitrous stairways guarded by winged diorite lions lead down from dreamland to the lower gulfs, or to return through a churchyard to the waking world and begin the quest anew down the seventy steps of light slumber to the cavern of flame and the seven hundred steps to the Gate of Deeper Slumber and the enchanted wood. This, however, did not suit the seeker; for he knew nothing of the way from Leng to Ooth-Nargai, and was likewise reluctant to awake lest he forget all he had so far gained in this dream. It were disastrous to his quest to forget the august and celestial faces of those seamen from the north who traded onyx in Celephaïs, and who, being the sons of gods, must point the way to the cold waste and Kadath where the Great Ones dwell.

After much persuasion the ghoul consented to guide his guest inside the great wall of the gugs' kingdom. There was one chance that Carter might be able to steal through that twilight realm of circular stone towers at an hour when the giants would be all gorged and snoring indoors, and reach the central tower with the sign of Koth upon it, which has the stairs leading up to that stone trap-door in the enchanted wood. Pickman even consented to lend three ghouls to help with a tombstone lever in raising the stone door; for of ghouls the gugs are somewhat afraid, and

Charter Street Burying Ground, Salem, Massachusetts, 2013.
Photograph courtesy of Donovan K. Loucks

30. See "The Unnamable," in the previous volume, pp. 114–22, note 3, regarding the Charter Street Burying Ground, also known as the Old Burying Point. It is the second-oldest cemetery in the United States, the oldest in Salem.

they often flee from their own colossal graveyards when they see feasting there.

He also advised Carter to disguise as a ghoul himself; shaving the beard he had allowed to grow (for ghouls have none), wallowing naked in the mould to get the correct surface, and loping in the usual slumping way, with his clothing carried in a bundle as if it were a choice morsel from a tomb. They would reach the city of the gugs—which is coterminous with the whole kingdom— through the proper burrows, emerging in a cemetery not far from the stair-containing Tower of Koth. They must beware, however, of a large cave near the cemetery; for this is the mouth of the vaults of Zin, and the vindictive ghasts are always on watch there murderously for those denizens of the upper abyss who hunt and prey on them. The ghasts try to come out when the gugs sleep, and they attack ghouls as readily as gugs, for they cannot discriminate. They are very primitive, and eat one another. The gugs have a sentry at a narrow place in the vaults of Zin, but he is often drowsy and is sometimes surprised by a party of ghasts. Though ghasts cannot live in real light, they can endure the grey twilight of the abyss for hours.

So at length Carter crawled through endless burrows with three helpful ghouls bearing the slate gravestone of Col. Nehemiah Derby, obiit 1719, from the Charter Street Burying Ground in Salem.[30] When they came again into open twilight they were in a forest of vast lichened monoliths reaching nearly as high as the eye could see and forming the modest gravestones of the gugs. On the right of the hole out of which they wriggled, and seen through aisles of monoliths, was a stupendous vista of Cyclopean round towers mounting up illimitable into the grey air of inner earth. This was the great city of the gugs, whose doorways are thirty feet high. Ghouls come here often, for a buried gug will feed a community for almost a year, and even with the added peril it is better to burrow for gugs than to bother with the graves of men. Carter now understood the occasional titan bones he had felt beneath him in the vale of Pnath.

Straight ahead, and just outside the cemetery, rose a sheer perpendicular cliff at whose base an immense and forbidding cavern yawned. This the ghouls told Carter to avoid as much as possible, since it was the entrance to the unhallowed vaults of Zin where gugs hunt ghasts in the darkness. And truly, that warning was soon well justified; for the moment a ghoul began to creep toward the towers to see if the hour of the gugs' resting had been rightly timed, there glowed in the gloom of that great cavern's mouth first one pair of yellowish-red eyes and then another, implying that the gugs were one sentry less, and that ghasts have indeed an excellent sharpness of smell. So the ghoul returned to the burrow and motioned his companions to be silent. It was best to leave the ghasts to their own devices, and there was a possibility that they might soon withdraw, since they must naturally be rather tired after coping with a gug sentry in the black vaults. After a moment something about the size of a small horse hopped out into the grey twilight, and Carter turned sick at the aspect of that scabrous and unwholesome beast, whose face is so curiously human despite the absence of a nose, a forehead, and other important particulars.

Presently three other ghasts hopped out to join their fellow, and a ghoul glibbered softly at Carter that their absence of battle-scars was a bad sign. It proved that they had not fought the gug sentry at all, but merely slipped past him as he slept, so that their strength and savagery were still unimpaired and would remain so till they had found and disposed of a victim. It was very unpleasant to see those filthy and disproportioned animals, which soon numbered about fifteen, grubbing about and making their kangaroo leaps in the grey twilight where titan towers and monoliths arose, but it was still more unpleasant when they spoke among themselves in the coughing gutturals of ghasts. And yet, horrible as they were, they were not so horrible as what presently came out of the cave after them with disconcerting suddenness.

It was a paw, fully two feet and a half across, and equipped with formidable talons. After it came another paw, and after that a great black-furred arm to which both of the paws were attached by short forearms. Then two pink eyes shone, and the head of the awakened gug sentry, large as a barrel, wobbled into view. The eyes jutted two inches from each side, shaded by bony protuberances overgrown with coarse hairs. But the head was chiefly terrible because of the mouth. That mouth had great yellow fangs and ran from the top to the bottom of the head, opening vertically instead of horizontally.

But before that unfortunate gug could emerge from the cave and rise to his full twenty feet, the vindictive ghasts were upon him. Carter feared for a moment that he would give an alarm and arouse all his kin, till a ghoul softly glibbered that gugs have no voice, but talk by means of facial expression. The battle which then ensued was truly a frightful one. From all sides the venomous ghasts rushed feverishly at the creeping gug, nipping and tearing with their muzzles, and mauling murderously with their hard pointed hooves. All the time they coughed excitedly, screaming when the great vertical mouth of the gug would occasionally bite into one of their number, so that the noise of the combat would surely have aroused the sleeping city had not the weakening of the sentry begun to transfer the action farther and farther within the cavern. As it was, the tumult soon receded altogether from sight in the blackness, with only occasional evil echoes to mark its continuance.

Then the most alert of the ghouls gave the signal for all to advance, and Carter followed the loping three out of the forest of monoliths and into the dark noisome streets of that awful city whose rounded towers of Cyclopean stone soared up beyond the sight. Silently they shambled over that rough rock pavement, hearing with disgust the abominable muffled snortings from great black doorways which marked the slumber of the gugs. Apprehensive of the ending of the rest hour, the ghouls set a somewhat rapid pace; but even so the journey was no brief one, for distances in that town of giants are on a great scale. At last, however, they came to a somewhat open space before a tower even vaster than the rest, above whose colossal doorway was fixed a monstrous symbol in bas-relief which made one shudder without knowing its meaning. This was the central tower with the sign of Koth, and those huge stone steps just visible through the dusk within were the beginning of the great flight leading to upper dreamland and the enchanted wood.

There now began a climb of interminable length in utter blackness; made almost impossible by the monstrous size of the steps, which were fashioned for gugs, and were therefore nearly a yard high. Of their number Carter could form no just esti-mate, for he soon became so worn out that the tireless and elas-tic ghouls were forced to aid him. All through the endless climb there lurked the peril of detection and pursuit; for though no gug dares lift the stone door to the forest because of the Great Ones' curse, there are no such restraints concerning the tower and the steps, and escaped ghasts are often chased even to the very top. So sharp are the ears of gugs, that the bare feet and hands of the climbers might readily be heard when the city awoke; and it would of course take but little time for the striding giants, accustomed from their ghast-hunts in the vaults of Zin to seeing without light, to overtake their smaller and slower quarry on those Cyclopean steps. It was very depressing to reflect that the silent pursuing gugs would not be heard at all, but would come very suddenly and shockingly in the dark upon the climbers. Nor could the traditional fear of gugs for ghouls be depended upon in that peculiar place where the advantages lay so heavily with the gugs. There was also some peril from the furtive and venomous ghasts, which frequently hopped up into the tower during the sleep hour of the gugs. If the gugs slept long, and the ghasts returned soon from their deed in the cavern, the scent of the climbers might easily be picked up by those loathsome and ill-disposed things; in which case it would almost be better to be eaten by a gug.

Then, after aeons of climbing, there came a cough from the darkness above; and matters assumed a very grave and unex-pected turn. It was clear that a ghast, or perhaps even more, had strayed into that tower before the coming of Carter and his guides; and it was equally clear that this peril was very close. After a breathless second the leading ghoul pushed Carter to the wall and arranged his two kinsfolk in the best possible way, with the old slate tombstone raised for a crushing blow whenever the enemy might come in sight. Ghouls can see in the dark, so the party was not as badly off as Carter would have been alone. In another moment the clatter of hooves revealed the downward hopping of at least one beast, and the slab-bearing ghouls poised their weapon for a desperate blow. Presently two yellowish-red eyes flashed into view, and the panting of the ghast became audible above its clattering. As it hopped down to the step just above the ghouls, they wielded the ancient gravestone with prodigious force, so that there was only a wheeze and a choking before the victim collapsed in a noxious heap. There seemed to be only this one animal, and after a moment of listening the ghouls tapped Carter as a signal to proceed again. As before, they were obliged to aid him; and he was glad to leave that place of carnage where the ghast's uncouth remains sprawled invisible in the blackness.

At last the ghouls brought their companion to a halt; and feeling above him, Carter realised that the great stone trap-door was reached at last. To open so vast a thing completely was not to be thought of, but the ghouls hoped to get it up just enough to slip the gravestone under as a prop, and permit Carter to escape through the crack. They themselves planned to descend again and return through the city of the gugs, since their elusiveness was great, and they did not know the way overland to spectral Sarkomand with its lion-guarded gate to the abyss.

Mighty was the straining of those three ghouls at the stone of the door above them, and Carter helped push with as much strength as he had. They judged the edge next the top of the staircase to be the right one, and to this they bent all the force of their disreputably nourished muscles. After a few moments a crack of light appeared; and Carter, to whom that task had been entrusted, slipped the end of the old gravestone in the aperture. There now ensued a mighty heaving; but progress was very slow, and they had of course to return to their first position every time they failed to turn the slab and prop the portal open.

Suddenly their desperation was magnified a thousandfold by

a sound on the steps below them. It was only the thumping and rattling of the slain ghast's hooved body as it rolled down to lower levels; but of all the possible causes of that body's dislodgment and rolling, none was in the least reassuring. Therefore, knowing the ways of gugs, the ghouls set to with something of a frenzy; and in a surprisingly short time had the door so high that they were able to hold it still whilst Carter turned the slab and left a generous opening. They now helped Carter through, letting him climb up to their rubbery shoulders and later guiding his feet as he clutched at the blessed soil of the upper dreamland outside. Another second and they were through themselves, knocking away the gravestone and closing the great trap-door while a panting became audible beneath. Because of the Great Ones' curse no gug might ever emerge from that portal, so with a deep relief and sense of repose Carter lay quietly on the thick grotesque fungi of the enchanted wood while his guides squatted near in the manner that ghouls rest.

Weird as was that enchanted wood through which he had fared so long ago, it was verily a haven and a delight after the gulfs he had now left behind. There was no living denizen about, for zoogs shun the mysterious door in fear, and Carter at once consulted with his ghouls about their future course. To return through the tower they no longer dared, and the waking world did not appeal to them when they learned that they must pass the priests Nasht and Kaman-Thah in the cavern of flame. So at length they decided to return through Sarkomand and its gate of the abyss, though of how to get there they knew nothing. Carter recalled that it lies in the valley below Leng, and recalled likewise that he had seen in Dylath-Leen a sinister, slant-eyed old merchant reputed to trade on Leng. Therefore he advised the ghouls to seek out Dylath-Leen, crossing the fields to Nir and the Skai and following the river to its mouth. This they at once resolved to do, and lost no time in loping off, since the thickening of the dusk promised a full night ahead for travel. And Carter shook the paws of those repulsive beasts, thanking them for their help and sending his gratitude to the beast which once was Pickman; but could not help sighing with pleasure when they left. For a ghoul is a ghoul, and at best an unpleasant companion for man. After that Carter sought a forest pool and cleansed himself of the mud of nether earth, thereupon reassuming the clothes he had so carefully carried.

It was now night in that redoubtable wood of monstrous trees, but because of the phosphorescence one might travel as well as by day; wherefore Carter set out upon the well-known route toward Celephaïs, in Ooth-Nargai beyond the Tanarian Hills. And as he went he thought of the zebra he had left tethered to an ash tree on Ngranek in far-away Oriab so many aeons ago, and wondered if any lava-gatherer had fed and released it. And he wondered, too, if he would ever return to Baharna and pay for the zebra that was slain by night in those ancient ruins by Yath's shore, and if the old tavern-keeper would remember him. Such were the thoughts that came to him in the air of the regained upper dreamland.

But presently his progress was halted by a sound from a very large hollow tree. He had avoided the great circle of stones, since he did not care to speak with zoogs just now; but it appeared from the singular fluttering in that huge tree that important councils were in session elsewhere. Upon drawing nearer he made out the accents of a tense and heated discussion; and before long became conscious of matters which he viewed with the greatest concern. For a war on the cats was under debate in that sovereign assembly of zoogs. It all came from the loss of the party which had sneaked after Carter to Ulthar, and which the cats had justly punished for unsuitable intentions. The matter had long rankled; and now, or within at least a month, the marshalled zoogs were about to strike the whole feline tribe in a series of surprise attacks, taking individual cats or groups of cats unawares, and giving not even the myriad cats of Ulthar a proper chance to drill and mobilise. This was the plan of the zoogs, and Carter saw that he must foil it before leaving on his mighty quest.

Very quietly therefore did Randolph Carter steal to the edge of the wood and send the cry of the cat over the starlit fields. And a great grimalkin[31] in a nearby cottage took up the burden and relayed it across leagues of rolling meadow to warriors large and small, black, grey, tiger, white, yellow, and mixed; and it echoed through Nir and beyond the Skai even into Ulthar, and Ulthar's numerous cats called in chorus and fell into a line of march. It was fortunate that the moon was not up, so that all the cats were

31. An archaic term for a cat, derived from "gray" and "Malkin," a shortened form of "Matilda." The *Oxford English Dictionary* traces its first usage in print to 1605.

on earth. Swiftly and silently leaping, they sprang from every hearth and housetop and poured in a great furry sea across the plains to the edge of the wood. Carter was there to greet them, and the sight of shapely, wholesome cats was indeed good for his eyes after the things he had seen and walked with in the abyss. He was glad to see his venerable friend and one-time rescuer at the head of Ulthar's detachment, a collar of rank around his sleek neck, and whiskers bristling at a martial angle. Better still, as a sub-lieutenant in that army was a brisk young fellow who proved to be none other than the very little kitten at the inn to whom Carter had given a saucer of rich cream on that long-vanished morning in Ulthar. He was a strapping and promising cat now, and purred as he shook hands with his friend. His grandfather said he was doing very well in the army, and that he might well expect a captaincy after one more campaign.

Carter now outlined the peril of the cat tribe, and was rewarded by deep-throated purrs of gratitude from all sides. Consulting with the generals, he prepared a plan of instant action which involved marching at once upon the zoog council and other known strongholds of zoogs; forestalling their surprise attacks and forcing them to terms before the mobilisation of their army of invasion. Thereupon without a moment's loss that great ocean of cats flooded the enchanted wood and surged around the council tree and the great stone circle. Flutterings rose to panic pitch as the enemy saw the newcomers, and there was very little resistance among the furtive and curious brown zoogs. They saw that they were beaten in advance, and turned from thoughts of vengeance to thoughts of present self-preservation.

Half the cats now seated themselves in a circular formation with the captured zoogs in the centre, leaving open a lane down which were marched the additional captives rounded up by the other cats in other parts of the wood. Terms were discussed at length, Carter acting as interpreter, and it was decided that the zoogs might remain a free tribe on condition of rendering to the cats a large annual tribute of grouse, quail, and pheasants from the less fabulous parts of their forest. Twelve young zoogs of noble families were taken as hostages to be kept in the Temple of the Cats at Ulthar, and the victors made it plain that any disappearances of cats on the borders of the zoog domain would be followed by consequences highly disastrous to zoogs. These matters disposed of, the assembled cats broke ranks and permitted the zoogs to slink off one by one to their respective homes, which they hastened to do with many a sullen backward glance.

The old cat general now offered Carter an escort through the forest to whatever border he wished to reach, deeming it likely that the zoogs would harbour dire resentment against him for the frustration of their warlike enterprise. This offer he welcomed with gratitude; not only for the safety it afforded, but because he liked the graceful companionship of cats. So in the midst of a pleasant and playful regiment, relaxed after the successful performance of its duty, Randolph Carter walked with dignity through that enchanted and phosphorescent wood of titan trees, talking of his quest with the old general and his grandson whilst others of the band indulged in fantastic gambols or chased fallen leaves that the wind drove among the fungi of the primeval floor. And the old cat said that he had heard much of unknown Kadath in the cold waste, but did not know where it was. As for the marvellous sunset city, he had not even heard of that, but would gladly relay to Carter anything he might later learn.

He gave the seeker some passwords of great value among the cats of dreamland, and commended him especially to the old chief of the cats in Celephaïs, whither he was bound. That old cat, already slightly known to Carter, was a dignified Maltese; and would prove highly influential in any transaction. It was dawn when they came to the proper edge of the wood, and Carter bade his friends a reluctant farewell. The young sub-lieutenant he had met as a small kitten would have followed him had not the old general forbidden it, but that austere patriarch insisted that the path of duty lay with the tribe and the army. So Carter set out alone over the golden fields that stretched mysterious beside a willow-fringed river, and the cats went back into the wood.

Well did the traveller know those garden lands that lie betwixt the wood of the Cerenerian Sea, and blithely did he follow the singing river Oukranos that marked his course. The sun rose higher over gentle slopes of grove and lawn, and heightened the colours of the thousand flowers that starred each knoll and dingle. A blessed haze lies upon all this region, wherein is held a little more of the sunlight than other places hold, and a

32. The kingdom is mentioned also in "The Silver Key," in the previous volume, pp. 158–70, written after *Dream-Quest* in 1926.

33. Perhaps this is the tutelary of the Oukranos River.

little more of the summer's humming music of birds and bees; so that men walk through it as through a faery place, and feel greater joy and wonder than they ever afterward remember.

By noon Carter reached the jasper terraces of Kiran which slope down to the river's edge and bear that temple of loveliness wherein the King of Ilek-Vad[32] comes from his far realm on the twilight sea once a year in a golden palanquin to pray to the god of Ourkranos[33] who sang to him in youth when he dwelt in a cottage by its banks. All of jasper is that temple, and covering an acre of ground with its walls and courts, its seven pinnacled towers, and its inner shrine where the river enters through hidden channels and the god sings softly in the night. Many times the moon hears strange music as it shines on those courts and terraces and pinnacles, but whether that music be the song of the god or the chant of the cryptical priests, none but the King of Ilek-Vad may say; for only he has entered the temple or seen the priests. Now, in the drowsiness of day, that carven and delicate fane was silent, and Carter heard only the murmur of the great stream and the hum of the birds and bees as he walked onward under an enchanted sun.

All that afternoon the pilgrim wandered on through perfumed meadows and in the lee of gentle riverward hills bearing peaceful thatched cottages and the shrines of amiable gods carven from jasper or chrysoberyl. Sometimes he walked close to the bank of Oukranos and whistled to the sprightly and iridescent fish of that crystal stream, and at other times he paused amidst the whispering rushes and gazed at the great dark wood on the farther side, whose trees came down clear to the water's edge. In former dreams he had seen quaint lumbering buopoths come shyly out of that wood to drink, but now he could not glimpse any. Once in a while he paused to watch a carnivorous fish catch a fishing bird, which it lured to the water by shewing its tempting scales in the sun, and grasped by the beak with its enormous mouth as the winged hunter sought to dart down upon it.

Toward evening he mounted a low grassy rise and saw before him flaming in the sunset the thousand gilded spires of Thran. Lofty beyond belief are the alabaster walls of that incredible city, sloping inward toward the top and wrought in one solid piece by what means no man knows, for they are more ancient than memory. Yet lofty as they are with their hundred gates and two hundred turrets, the clustered towers within, all white beneath their golden spires, are loftier still; so that men on the plain around see them soaring into the sky, sometimes shining clear, sometimes caught at the top in tangles of cloud and mist, and sometimes clouded lower down with their utmost pinnacles blazing free above the vapours. And where Thran's gates open on the river are great wharves of marble, with ornate galleons of fragrant cedar and calamander riding gently at anchor, and strange bearded sailors sitting on casks and bales with the hieroglyphs of far places. Landward beyond the walls lies the farm country, where small white cottages dream between little hills, and narrow roads with many stone bridges wind gracefully among streams and gardens.

Down through this verdant land Carter walked at evening, and saw twilight float up from the river to the marvellous golden spires of Thran. And just at the hour of dusk he came to the southern gate, and was stopped by a red-robed sentry till he had told three dreams beyond belief, and proved himself a dreamer worthy to walk up Thran's steep mysterious streets and linger in bazaars where the wares of the ornate galleons were sold. Then into that incredible city he walked; through a wall so thick that the gate was a tunnel, and thereafter amidst curved and undulant ways winding deep and narrow between the heavenward towers. Lights shone through grated and balconied windows, and the sound of lutes and pipes stole timid from inner courts where marble fountains bubbled. Carter knew his way, and edged down through darker streets to the river, where at an old sea-tavern he found the captains and seamen he had known in myriad other dreams. There he bought his passage to Celephaïs on a great green galleon, and there he stopped for the night after speaking gravely to the venerable cat of that inn, who blinked dozing before an enormous hearth and dreamed of old wars and forgotten gods.

In the morning Carter boarded the galleon bound for Celephaïs, and sat in the prow as the ropes were cast off and the long sail down to the Cerenerian Sea began. For many leagues the banks were much as they were above Thran, with now and then a curious temple rising on the farther hills toward the right, and a drowsy village on the shore, with steep red roofs and nets spread in the sun. Mindful of his search, Carter questioned all the mariners closely about those whom they had met in the taverns of Celephaïs, asking the names and ways of the strange men with long, narrow eyes, long-lobed ears, thin noses, and pointed chins who came in dark ships from the north and traded onyx for the carved jade and spun gold and little red singing birds of Celephaïs. Of these men the sailors knew not much, save that they talked but seldom and spread a kind of awe about them.

Their land, very far away, was called Inganok, and not many people cared to go thither because it was a cold twilight land, and said to be close to unpleasant Leng; although high impassable mountains towered on the side where Leng was thought to lie, so that none might say whether this evil plateau with its horrible stone villages and unmentionable monastery were really there, or whether the rumour were only a fear that timid people felt in the night when those formidable barrier peaks loomed black against a rising moon. Certainly, men reached Leng from very different oceans. Of other boundaries of Inganok those sailors had no notion, nor had they heard of the cold waste and unknown Kadath save from vague unplaced report. And of the marvellous sunset city which Carter sought they knew nothing at all. So the traveller asked no more of far things, but bided his time till he might talk with those strange men from cold and twilight Inganok who are the seed of such gods as carved their features on Ngranek.

Late in the day the galleon reached those bends of the river which traverse the perfumed jungles of Kled. Here Carter wished he might disembark, for in those tropic tangles sleep wondrous palaces of ivory, lone and unbroken, where once dwelt fabulous monarchs of a land whose name is forgotten. Spells of the Elder Ones keep those places unharmed and undecayed, for it is written that there may one day be need of them again; and elephant caravans have glimpsed them from afar by moonlight, though none dares approach them closely because of the guardians to which their wholeness is due. But the ship swept on, and dusk hushed the hum of the day, and the first stars above blinked answers to the early fireflies on the banks as that jungle fell far behind, leaving only its fragrance as a memory that it had been.

And all through the night that galleon floated on past mysteries unseen and unsuspected. Once a lookout reported fires on the hills to the east, but the sleepy captain said they had better not be looked at too much, since it was highly uncertain just who or what had lit them.

In the morning the river had broadened out greatly, and Carter saw by the houses along the banks that they were close to the vast trading city of Hlanith on the Cerenerian Sea. Here the walls are of rugged granite, and the houses peakedly fantastic with beamed and plastered gables. The men of Hlanith are more like those of the waking world than any others in dreamland; so that the city is not sought except for barter, but is prized for the solid work of its artisans. The wharves of Hlanith are of oak, and there the galleon made fast while the captain traded in the taverns. Carter also went ashore, and looked curiously upon the rutted streets where wooden ox-carts lumbered and feverish merchants cried their wares vacuously in the bazaars. The sea-taverns were all close to the wharves on cobbled lanes salt with the spray of high tides, and seemed exceedingly ancient with their low black-beamed ceilings and casements of greenish bull's-eye panes. Ancient sailors in those taverns talked much of distant ports, and told many stories of the curious men from twilight Inganok, but had little to add to what the seamen of the galleon had told. Then, at last, after much unloading and loading, the ship set sail once more over the sunset sea, and the high walls and gables of Hlanith grew less as the last golden light of day lent them a wonder and beauty beyond any that men had given them.

Two nights and two days the galleon sailed over the Cerenerian Sea, sighting no land and speaking but one other vessel. Then near sunset of the second day there loomed up ahead the snowy peak of Aran with its gingko-trees swaying on the lower slopes, and Carter knew that they were come to the land of Ooth-Nargai and the marvellous city of Celephaïs. Swiftly there came into sight the glittering minarets of that fabulous town, and the untarnished marble walls with their bronze statues, and the great stone bridge where Naraxa joins the sea. Then rose the green gentle hills behind the town, with their groves and gardens of asphodels and the small shrines and cottages upon them; and far in the background the purple ridge of the Tanarians, potent and mystical, behind which lay forbidden ways into the waking world and toward other regions of dream.

The harbour was full of painted galleys, some of which were from the marble cloud-city of Serannian, that lies in ethereal space beyond where the sea meets the sky, and some of which were from more substantial ports on the oceans of dreamland. Among these the steersman threaded his way up to the spice-fragrant wharves, where the galleon made fast in the dusk as the city's million lights began to twinkle out over the water. Ever new seemed this deathless city of vision, for here time has no power to tarnish or destroy. As it has always been is still the turquoise of Nath-Horthath, and the eighty orchid-wreathed priests are the same who builded it ten thousand years ago. Shining still is the bronze of the great gates, nor are the onyx pavements ever worn or broken. And the great bronze statues on the walls look down on merchants and camel drivers older than fable, yet without one grey hair in their forked beards.

Carter did not at once seek out the temple or the palace or the citadel, but stayed by the seaward wall among traders and sailors. And when it was too late for rumours and legends he sought out an ancient tavern he knew well, and rested with dreams of the gods on unknown Kadath whom he sought. The next day he searched all along the quays for some of the strange mariners of Inganok, but was told that none were now in port, their galley not being due from the north for full two weeks. He found, however, one Thorabonian sailor who had been to Inganok and had worked in the onyx quarries of that twilight place; and this sailor said there was certainly a desert to the north of the peopled region, which everybody seemed to fear and shun. The Thorabonian opined that this desert led around the utmost rim of impassable peaks into Leng's horrible plateau, and that this was why men feared it; though he admitted there were other vague tales of evil presences and nameless sentinels. Whether or not this could be the fabled waste wherein unknown Kadath stands he did not know; but it seemed unlikely that those presences and sentinels, if indeed they truly existed, were stationed for naught.

On the following day Carter walked up the Street of the Pillars to the turquoise temple and talked with the high-priest. Though Nath-Horthath is chiefly worshipped in Celephaïs, all

the Great Ones are mentioned in diurnal prayers; and the priest
was reasonably versed in their moods. Like Atal in distant Ulthar,
he strongly advised against any attempt to see them; declaring
that they are testy and capricious, and subject to strange protection from the mindless Other Gods from Outside, whose soul
and messenger is the crawling chaos Nyarlathotep. Their jealous
hiding of the marvellous sunset city shewed clearly that they did
not wish Carter to reach it, and it was doubtful how they would
regard a guest whose object was to see them and plead before
them. No man had ever found Kadath in the past, and it might
be just as well if none ever found it in the future. Such rumours
as were told about that onyx castle of the Great Ones were not
by any means reassuring.

Having thanked the orchid-crowned high-priest, Carter left
the temple and sought the bazaar of the sheep-butchers, where
the old chief of Celephaïs' cats dwelt sleek and contented. That
grey and dignified being was sunning himself on the onyx pavement, and extended a languid paw as his caller approached. But
when Carter repeated the passwords and introductions furnished
him by the old cat general of Ulthar, the furry patriarch became
very cordial and communicative; and told much of the secret lore
known to cats on the seaward slopes of Ooth-Nargai. Best of all,
he repeated several things told him furtively by the timid waterfront cats of Celephaïs about the men of Inganok, on whose dark
ships no cat will go.

It seems that these men have an aura not of earth about
them, though that is not the reason why no cat will sail on their
ships. The reason for this is that Inganok holds shadows which
no cat can endure, so that in all that cold twilight realm there is
never a cheering purr or a homely mew. Whether it be because of
things wafted over the impassable peaks from hypothetical Leng,
or because of things filtering down from the chilly desert to the
north, none may say; but it remains a fact that in that far land
there broods a hint of outer space which cats do not like, and to
which they are more sensitive than men. Therefore they will not
go on the dark ships that seek the basalt quays of Inganok.

The old chief of the cats also told him where to find his
friend King Kuranes, who in Carter's latter dreams had reigned
alternately in the rose-crystal Palace of the Seventy Delights at

34. The story of Kuranes is revealed in "Celephaïs," pp. 71–77, above.

Celephaïs and in the turreted cloud-castle of sky-floating Serannian. It seems that he could no more find content in those places, but had formed a mighty longing for the English cliffs and downlands of his boyhood; where in little dreaming villages England's old songs hover at evening behind lattice windows, and where grey church towers peep lovely through the verdure of distant valleys.[34] He could not go back to these things in the waking world because his body was dead; but he had done the next best thing and dreamed a small tract of such countryside in the region east of the city, where meadows roll gracefully up from the sea-cliffs to the foot of the Tanarian Hills. There he dwelt in a grey Gothic manor-house of stone looking on the sea, and tried to think it was ancient Trevor Towers, where he was born and where thirteen generations of his forefathers had first seen the light. And on the coast nearby he had built a little Cornish fishing village with steep cobbled ways, settling therein such people as had the most English faces, and seeking ever to teach them the dear remembered accents of old Cornwall fishers. And in a valley not far off he had reared a great Norman Abbey whose tower he could see from his window, placing around it in the churchyard grey stones with the names of his ancestors carved thereon, and with a moss somewhat like Old England's moss. For though Kuranes was a monarch in the land of dream, with all imagined pomps and marvels, splendours and beauties, ecstacies and delights, novelties and excitements at his command, he would gladly have resigned forever the whole of his power and luxury and freedom for one blessed day as a simple boy in that pure and quiet England, that ancient, beloved England which had moulded his being and of which he must always be immutably a part.

So when Carter bade that old grey chief of the cats adieu, he did not seek the terraced palace of rose-crystal but walked out the eastern gate and across the daisied fields toward a peaked gable which he glimpsed through the oaks of a park sloping up to the sea-cliffs. And in time he came to a great hedge and a gate with a little brick lodge, and when he rang the bell there hobbled to admit him no robed and anointed lackey of the palace, but a small stubbly old man in a smock who spoke as best he could in the quaint tones of far Cornwall. And Carter walked up the shady path between trees as near as possible to England's trees, and climbed the terraces among gardens set out as in Queen Anne's time. At the door, flanked by stone cats in the old way, he was met by a whiskered butler in suitable livery; and was presently taken to the library where Kuranes, Lord of Ooth-Nargai and the Sky around Serannian, sat pensive in a chair by the window looking on his little seacoast village and wishing that his old nurse would come in and scold him because he was not ready for that hateful lawn-party at the vicar's, with the carriage waiting and his mother nearly out of patience.

Kuranes, clad in a dressing-gown of the sort favoured by London tailors in his youth, rose eagerly to meet his guest; for the sight of an Anglo-Saxon from the waking world was very dear to him, even if it was a Saxon from Boston, Massachusetts, instead of from Cornwall. And for long they talked of old times, having much to say because both were old dreamers and well versed in the wonders of incredible places. Kuranes, indeed, had been out beyond the stars in the ultimate void, and was said to be the only one who had ever returned sane from such a voyage.

At length Carter brought up the subject of his quest, and asked of his host those questions he had asked of so many others. Kuranes did not know where Kadath was, or the marvellous sunset city; but he did know that the Great Ones were very dangerous creatures to seek out, and that the Other Gods had strange ways of protecting them from impertinent curiosity. He had learned much of the Other Gods in distant parts of space, especially in that region where form does not exist, and coloured gases study the innermost secrets. The violet gas S'ngac had told him terrible things of the crawling chaos Nyarlathotep, and had warned him never to approach the central void where the daemon-sultan Azathoth gnaws hungrily in the dark. Altogether, it was not well to meddle with the Elder Ones; and if they persistently denied all access to the marvellous sunset city, it were better not to seek that city.

Kuranes furthermore doubted whether his guest would profit aught by coming to the city even were he to gain it. He himself had dreamed and yearned long years for lovely Celephaïs and the land of Ooth-Nargai, and for the freedom and colour and high experience of life devoid of its chains, conventions, and stupidities. But now that he was come into that city and that land, and

35. This must be a lighthouse. The most famous in history was on the island of Pharos, off the coast of Alexandria, built by the architect Sostratus of Cnidus (likely commissioned by Ptolemy I Soter) in the third century BCE, at a cost of 800 talents, according to the second edition of *A Dictionary of Science, Literature and Art*, ed. William Thomas Brande (London: Longman, Brown, Green, and Longmans, 1852), 664. (For purposes of comparison, Mark Stansbury-O'Donnell, in *A History of Greek Art* [Chichester, West Sussex, UK: Wiley, 2015], 269, notes that the Parthenon cost 470 talents to build, plus 800 for the statue of Athena within, for a total of 1270 talents.) More than 500 feet tall, the Pharos lighthouse was regarded as one of the seven wonders of the ancient world; the word "pharos" became a generic term for beacon for mariners or lighthouse.

was the king thereof, he found the freedom and the vividness all too soon worn out, and monotonous for want of linkage with anything firm in his feelings and memories. He was a king in Ooth-Nargai, but found no meaning therein, and drooped always for the old familiar things of England that had shaped his youth. All his kingdom would he give for the sound of Cornish church bells over the downs, and all the thousand minarets of Celephaïs for the steep homely roofs of the village near his home. So he told his guest that the unknown sunset city might not hold quite the content he sought, and that perhaps it had better remain a glorious and half-remembered dream. For he had visited Carter often in the old waking days, and knew well the lovely New England slopes that had given him birth.

At the last, he was very certain, the seeker would long only for the early remembered scenes; the glow of Beacon Hill at evening, the tall steeples and winding hill streets of quaint Kingsport, the hoary gambrel roofs of ancient and witch-haunted Arkham, and the blessed miles of meads and valleys where stone walls rambled and white farmhouse gables peeped out from bowers of verdure. These things he told Randolph Carter, but still the seeker held to his purpose. And in the end they parted each with his own conviction, and Carter went back through the bronze gate into Celephaïs and down the Street of the Pillars to the old sea-wall, where he talked more with the mariners of far parts and waited for the dark ship from cold and twilight Inganok, whose strange-faced sailors and onyx-traders had in them the blood of the Great Ones.

One starlight evening when the Pharos[35] shone splendid over the harbour the longed-for ship put in, and strange-faced sailors and traders appeared one by one and group by group in the ancient taverns along the sea-wall. It was very exciting to see again those living faces so like the godlike features on Ngranek, but Carter did not hasten to speak with the silent seamen. He did not know how much of pride and secrecy and dim supernal memory might fill those children of the Great Ones, and was sure it would not be wise to tell them of his quest or ask too closely of that cold desert stretching north of their twilight land. They talked little with the other folk in those ancient sea-taverns; but would gather in groups in remote corners and sing among themselves the haunting airs of unknown places, or chant long tales to one another in accents alien to the rest of dreamland. And so rare and moving were those airs and tales, that one might guess their wonders from the faces of those who listened, even though the words came to common ears only as strange cadence and obscure melody.

For a week the strange seamen lingered in the taverns and traded in the bazaars of Celephaïs, and before they sailed Carter had taken passage on their dark ship, telling them that he was an old onyx-miner and wishful to work in their quarries. That ship was very lovely and cunningly wrought, being of teakwood with ebony fittings and traceries of gold, and the cabin in which the traveller lodged had hangings of silk and velvet. One morning at the turn of the tide the sails were raised and the anchor lifted, and as Carter stood on the high stern he saw the sunrise-blazing walls and bronze statues and golden minarets of ageless Celephaïs sink into the distance, and the snowy peak of Mount Aran grow smaller and smaller. By noon there was nothing in sight save the gentle blue of the Cerenerian Sea, with one painted galley afar off bound for that cloud-hung realm of Serannian where the sea meets the sky.

And night came with gorgeous stars, and the dark ship steered for Charles' Wain and the Little Bear as they swung slowly round the pole. And the sailors sang strange songs of unknown places, and then stole off one by one to the forecastle while the wistful watchers murmured old chants and leaned over the rail to glimpse the luminous fish playing in bowers beneath the sea. Carter went to sleep at midnight, and rose in the glow of a young morning, marking that the sun seemed farther south than was its wont. And all through that second day he made progress in knowing the men of the ship, getting them little by little to talk of their cold twilight land, of their exquisite onyx city, and of their fear of the high and impassable peaks beyond which Leng was said to be. They told him how sorry they were that no cats would stay in the land of Inganok, and how they thought the hidden nearness of Leng was to blame for it. Only of the stony desert to the north they would not talk. There was something disquieting about that desert, and it was thought expedient not to admit its existence.

On later days they talked of the quarries in which Carter said he was going to work. There were many of them, for all the city of Inganok was builded of onyx, whilst great polished blocks of it were traded in Rinar, Ogrothan, and Celephaïs, and at home with the merchants of Thraa, Ilarnek, and Kadatheron, for the beautiful wares of those fabulous ports. And far to the north, almost in that cold desert whose existence the men of Inganok did not care to admit, there was an unused quarry greater than all the rest; from which had been hewn in forgotten times such prodigious lumps and blocks that the sight of their chiselled vacancies struck terror to all who beheld. Who had mined those incredible blocks, and whither they had been transported, no man might say; but it was thought best not to trouble that quarry, around which such inhuman memories might conceivably cling. So it was left all alone in the twilight, with only the raven and the rumoured shantak-bird to brood on its immensities. When Carter heard of this quarry he was moved to deep thought, for he knew from old tales that the Great Ones' castle atop unknown Kadath is of onyx.

Each day the sun wheeled lower and lower in the sky, and the mists overhead grew thicker and thicker. And in two weeks there was not any sunlight at all, but only a weird grey twilight shining through a dome of eternal cloud by day, and a cold starless phosphorescence from the under side of that cloud by night. On the twentieth day a great jagged rock in the sea was sighted from afar, the first land glimpsed since Aran's snowy peak had dwindled behind the ship. Carter asked the captain the name of that rock, but was told that it had no name and had never been sought by any vessel because of the sounds that came from it at night. And when, after dark, a dull and ceaseless howling arose from that jagged granite place, the traveller was glad that no stop had been made, and that the rock had no name. The seamen prayed and chanted till the noise was out of earshot, and Carter dreamed terrible dreams within dreams in the small hours.

Two mornings after that there loomed far ahead and to the east a line of great grey peaks whose tops were lost in the changeless clouds of that twilight world. And at the sight of them the sailors sang glad songs, and some knelt down on the deck to pray; so that Carter knew they were come to the land of Inganok and would soon be moored to the basalt quays of the great town bearing that land's name. Toward noon a dark coast-line appeared, and before three o'clock there stood out against the north the bulbous domes and fantastic spires of the onyx city. Rare and curious did that archaic city rise above its walls and quays, all of delicate black with scrolls, flutings, and arabesques of inlaid gold. Tall and many-windowed were the houses, and carved on every side with flowers and patterns whose dark symmetries dazzled the eye with a beauty more poignant than light. Some ended in swelling domes that tapered to a point, others in terraced pyramids whereon rose clustered minarets displaying every phase of strangeness and imagination. The walls were low, and pierced by frequent gates, each under a great arch rising high above the general level and capped by the head of a god chiselled with that same skill displayed in the monstrous face on distant Ngranek. On a hill in the centre rose a sixteen-angled tower greater than all the rest and bearing a high pinnacled belfry resting on a flattened dome. This, the seamen said, was the Temple of the Elder Ones, and was ruled by an old high-priest sad with inner secrets.

At intervals the clang of a strange bell shivered over the onyx city, answered each time by a peal of mystic music made up of horns, viols, and chanting voices. And from a row of tripods on a gallery round the high dome of the temple there burst flares of flame at certain moments; for the priests and people of that city were wise in the primal mysteries, and faithful in keeping the rhythms of the Great Ones as set forth in scrolls older than the Pnakotic Manuscripts. As the ship rode past the great basalt breakwater into the harbour the lesser noises of the city grew manifest, and Carter saw the slaves, sailors, and merchants on the docks. The sailors and merchants were of the strange-faced race of the gods, but the slaves were squat, slant-eyed folk said by rumour to have drifted somehow across or around the impassable peaks from valleys beyond Leng. The wharves reached wide outside the city wall and bore upon them all manner of merchandise from the galleys anchored there, while at one end were great piles of onyx both carved and uncarved awaiting shipment to the far markets of Rinar, Ogrothan, and Celephaïs.

It was not yet evening when the dark ship anchored beside a jutting quay of stone, and all the sailors and traders filed ashore and through the arched gate into the city. The streets of that city were paved with onyx, and some of them were wide and straight whilst others were crooked and narrow. The houses near the water were lower than the rest, and bore above their curiously arched doorways certain signs of gold said to be in honour of the respective small gods that favoured each. The captain of the ship took Carter to an old sea-tavern where flocked the mariners of quaint countries, and promised that he would next day shew him the wonders of the twilight city, and lead him to the taverns of the onyx-miners by the northern wall. And evening fell, and little bronze lamps were lighted, and the sailors in that tavern sang songs of remote places. But when from its high tower the great bell shivered over the city, and the peal of the horns and viols and voices rose cryptical in answer thereto, all ceased their songs or tales and bowed silent till the last echo died away. For there is a wonder and a strangeness on the twilight city of Inganok, and men fear to be lax in its rites lest a doom and a vengeance lurk unsuspectedly close.

Far in the shadows of that tavern Carter saw a squat form he did not like, for it was unmistakably that of the old slant-eyed merchant he had seen so long before in the taverns of Dylath-Leen, who was reputed to trade with the horrible stone villages of Leng which no healthy folk visit and whose evil fires are seen at night from afar, and even to have dealt with that high-priest not to be described, which wears a yellow silken mask over its face and dwells all alone in a prehistoric stone monastery. This man had seemed to shew a queer gleam of knowing when Carter asked the traders of Dylath-Leen about the cold waste and Kadath; and somehow his presence in dark and haunted Inganok, so close to the wonders of the north, was not a reassuring thing. He slipped wholly out of sight before Carter could speak to him, and sailors later said that he had come with a yak caravan from some point not well determined, bearing the colossal and rich-flavoured eggs of the rumoured shantak-bird to trade for the dexterous jade goblets that merchants brought from Ilarnek.

On the following morning the ship-captain led Carter through the onyx streets of Inganok, dark under their twilight sky. The inlaid doors and figured house-fronts, carven balconies and crystal-paned oriels, all gleamed with a sombre and polished loveliness; and now and then a plaza would open out with black pillars, colonnades, and the statues of curious beings both human and fabulous. Some of the vistas down long and unbending streets, or through side alleys and over bulbous domes, spires, and arabesqued roofs, were weird and beautiful beyond words; and nothing was more splendid than the massive height of the great central Temple of the Elder Ones with its sixteen carven sides, its flattened dome, and its lofty pinnacled belfry, overtopping all else, and majestic whatever its foreground. And always to the east, far beyond the city walls and the leagues of pasture land, rose the gaunt grey sides of those topless and impassable peaks across which hideous Leng was said to lie.

The captain took Carter to the mighty temple, which is set with its walled garden in a great round plaza whence the streets go as spokes from a wheel's hub. The seven arched gates of that garden, each having over it a carven face like those on the city's gates, are always open; and the people roam reverently at will down the tiled paths and through the little lanes lined with grotesque termini and the shrines of modest gods. And there are fountains, pools, and basins there to reflect the frequent blaze of the tripods on the high balcony, all of onyx and having in them small luminous fish taken by divers from the lower bowers of ocean. When the deep clang from the temple's belfry shivers over the garden and the city, and the answer of the horns and viols and voices peals out from the seven lodges by the garden gates, there issue from the seven doors of the temple long columns of masked and hooded priests in black, bearing at arm's length before them great golden bowls from which a curious steam rises. And all the seven columns strut peculiarly in single file, legs thrown far forward without bending the knees, down the walks that lead to the seven lodges, wherein they disappear and do not appear again. It is said that subterrene paths connect the lodges with the temple, and that the long files of priests return through them; nor is it unwhispered that deep flights of onyx steps go down to mysteries that are never told. But only a few are those who hint that the priests in the masked and hooded columns are not human priests.

Carter did not enter the temple, because none but the Veiled King is permitted to do that. But before he left the garden the hour of the bell came, and he heard the shivering clang deafeningly above him, and the wailing of the horns and viols and voices loud from the lodges by the gates. And down the seven great walks stalked the long files of bowl-bearing priests in their singular way, giving to the traveller a fear which human priests do not often give. When the last of them had vanished he left that garden, noting as he did so a spot on the pavement over which the bowls had passed. Even the ship-captain did not like that spot, and hurried him on toward the hill whereon the Veiled King's palace rises many-domed and marvellous.

The ways to the onyx palace are steep and narrow, all but that broad curving one where the king and his companions ride on yaks or in yak-drawn chariots. Carter and his guide climbed up an alley that was all steps, between inlaid walls bearing strange signs in gold, and under balconies and oriels whence sometimes floated soft strains of music or breaths of exotic fragrance. Always ahead loomed those titan walls, mighty buttresses, and clustered and bulbous domes for which the Veiled King's palace is famous; and at length they passed under a great black arch and emerged in the gardens of the monarch's pleasure. There Carter paused in faintness at so much of beauty; for the onyx terraces and colonnaded walks, the gay parterres and delicate flowering trees espaliered to golden lattices, the brazen urns and tripods with cunning bas-reliefs, the pedestalled and almost breathing statues of veined black marble, the basalt-bottomed lagoons and tiled fountains with luminous fish, the tiny temples of iridescent singing birds atop carven columns, the marvellous scrollwork of the great bronze gates, and the blossoming vines trained along every inch of the polished walls all joined to form a sight whose loveliness was beyond reality, and half-fabulous even in the land of dream. There it shimmered like a vision under that grey twilight sky, with the domed and fretted magnificence of the palace ahead, and the fantastic silhouette of the distant impassable peaks on the right. And ever the small birds and the fountains sang, while the perfume of rare blossoms spread like a veil over that incredible garden. No other human presence was there, and Carter was glad it was so. Then they turned and descended again the onyx alley of steps, for the palace itself no visitor may enter; and it is not well to look too long and steadily at the great central dome, since it is said to house the archaic father of all the rumoured shantak-birds, and to send out queer dreams to the curious.

After that the captain took Carter to the north quarter of the town, near the Gate of the Caravans, where are the taverns of the yak-merchants and the onyx-miners. And there, in a low-ceiled inn of quarrymen, they said farewell; for business called the captain whilst Carter was eager to talk with miners about the north. There were many men in that inn, and the traveller was not long in speaking to some of them; saying that he was an old miner of onyx, and anxious to know somewhat of Inga-nok's quarries. But all that he learnt was not much more than he knew before, for the miners were timid and evasive about the cold desert to the north and the quarry that no man visits. They had fears of fabled emissaries from around the mountains where Leng is said to lie, and of evil presences and nameless sentinels far north among the scattered rocks. And they whispered also that the rumoured shantak-birds are no wholesome things; it being indeed for the best that no man has ever truly seen one (for that fabled father of shantaks in the king's dome is fed in the dark).

The next day, saying that he wished to look over all the various mines for himself and to visit the scattered farms and quaint onyx villages of Inganok, Carter hired a yak and stuffed great leathern saddle-bags for a journey. Beyond the Gate of the Car-avans the road lay straight betwixt tilled fields, with many odd farmhouses crowned by low domes. At some of these houses the seeker stopped to ask questions; once finding a host so austere and reticent, and so full of an unplaced majesty like to that in the huge features on Ngranek, that he felt certain he had come at last upon one of the Great Ones themselves, or upon one with full nine-tenths of their blood, dwelling amongst men. And to that austere and reticent cotter he was careful to speak very well of the gods, and to praise all the blessings they had ever accorded him.

That night Carter camped in a roadside meadow beneath a great lygath-tree to which he tied his yak, and in the morning resumed his northward pilgrimage. At about ten o'clock he reached the small-domed village of Urg, where traders rest and miners tell their tales, and paused in its taverns till noon. It is here that the great caravan road turns west toward Selarn, but Carter kept on north by the quarry road. All the afternoon he followed that rising road, which was somewhat narrower than the great highway, and which now led through a region with more rocks than tilled fields. And by evening the low hills on his left had risen into sizeable black cliffs, so that he knew he was close to the mining country. All the while the great gaunt sides of the impassable mountains towered afar off at his right, and the farther he went, the worse tales he heard of them from the scattered farmers and traders and drivers of lumbering onyx-carts along the way.

On the second night he camped in the shadow of a large black crag, tethering his yak to a stake driven in the ground. He observed the greater phosphorescence of the clouds at this northerly point, and more than once thought he saw dark shapes outlined against them. And on the third morning he came in sight of the first onyx quarry, and greeted the men who there laboured with picks and chisels. Before evening he had passed eleven quarries; the land being here given over altogether to onyx cliffs and boulders, with no vegetation at all, but only great rocky fragments scattered about a floor of black earth, with the grey impassable peaks always rising gaunt and sinister on his right. The third night he spent in a camp of quarry men whose flickering fires cast weird reflections on the polished cliffs to the west. And they sang many songs and told many tales, shewing such strange knowledge of the olden days and the habits of gods that Carter could see they held many latent memories of their sires the Great Ones. They asked him whither he went, and cautioned him not to go too far to the north; but he replied that he was seeking new cliffs of onyx, and would take no more risks than were common among prospectors. In the morning he bade them adieu and rode on into the darkening north, where they had warned him he would find the feared and unvisited quarry whence hands older than men's hands had wrenched prodigious blocks. But he did not like it when, turning back to wave a last farewell, he thought he saw approaching the camp that squat and evasive old merchant with slanting eyes, whose conjectured traffick with Leng was the gossip of distant Dylath-Leen.

After two more quarries the inhabited part of Inganok seemed to end, and the road narrowed to a steeply rising yak-path among forbidding black cliffs. Always on the right towered the gaunt and distant peaks, and as Carter climbed farther and farther into this untraversed realm he found it grew darker and colder. Soon he perceived that there were no prints of feet or hooves on the black path beneath, and realised that he was indeed come into strange and deserted ways of elder time. Once in a while a raven would croak far overhead, and now and then a flapping behind some vast rock would make him think uncomfortably of the rumoured shantak-bird. But in the main he was alone with his shaggy steed, and it troubled him to observe that this excellent yak became more and more reluctant to advance, and more and more disposed to snort affrightedly at any small noise along the route.

The path now contracted between sable and glistening walls, and began to display an even greater steepness than before. It was a bad footing, and the yak often slipped on the stony fragments strown thickly about. In two hours Carter saw ahead a definite crest, beyond which was nothing but dull grey sky, and blessed the prospect of a level or downward course. To reach this crest, however, was no easy task; for the way had grown nearly perpendicular, and was perilous with loose black gravel and small stones. Eventually Carter dismounted and led his dubious yak; pulling very hard when the animal balked or stumbled, and keeping his own footing as best he might. Then suddenly he came to the top and saw beyond, and gasped at what he saw.

The path indeed led straight ahead and slightly down, with the same lines of high natural walls as before; but on the left hand there opened out a monstrous space, vast acres in extent, where some archaic power had riven and rent the native cliffs of onyx in the form of a giants' quarry. Far back into the solid precipice ran that Cyclopean gouge, and deep down within earth's bowels its lower delvings yawned. It was no quarry of man, and the concave sides were scarred with great squares yards wide which told of the size of the blocks once hewn by nameless hands and chisels. High over its jagged rim huge ravens flapped and croaked, and vague whirrings in the unseen depths told of bats or urhags or less mentionable presences haunting the endless blackness. There Carter stood in the narrow way amidst the twilight with the rocky path sloping down before him; tall onyx cliffs on his right that led on as far as he could see, and tall cliffs on the left chopped off just ahead to make that terrible and unearthly quarry.

All at once the yak uttered a cry and burst from his control, leaping past him and darting on in a panic till it vanished down the narrow slope toward the north. Stones kicked by its flying hooves fell over the brink of the quarry and lost themselves in the dark without any sound of striking bottom; but Carter ignored the perils of that scanty path as he raced breathlessly after the flying steed. Soon the left-hand cliffs resumed their course, making the way once more a narrow lane; and still the traveller leaped on after the yak whose great wide prints told of its desperate flight.

Once he thought he heard the hoofbeats of the frightened beast, and doubled his speed from this encouragement. He was covering miles, and little by little the way was broadening in front till he knew he must soon emerge on the cold and dreaded desert to the north. The gaunt grey flanks of the distant impassable peaks were again visible above the right-hand crags, and ahead were the rocks and boulders of an open space which was clearly a foretaste of the dark and limitless plain. And once more those hoofbeats sounded in his ears, plainer than before, but this time giving terror instead of encouragement because he realised that they were not the frightened hoofbeats of his fleeing yak. These beats were ruthless and purposeful, and they were behind him.

Carter's pursuit of the yak became now a flight from an unseen thing, for though he dared not glance over his shoulder he felt that the presence behind him could be nothing wholesome or mentionable. His yak must have heard or felt it first, and he did not like to ask himself whether it had followed him from the haunts of men or had floundered up out of that black quarry pit. Meanwhile the cliffs had been left behind, so that the oncoming night fell over a great waste of sand and spectral rocks wherein all paths were lost. He could not see the hoofprints of his yak, but always from behind him there came that detestable clopping; mingled now and then with what he fancied were titanic flappings and whirrings. That he was losing ground seemed unhappily clear to him, and he knew he was hopelessly lost in this broken and blasted desert of meaningless rocks and untravelled sands. Only those remote and impassable peaks on the right gave him any sense of direction, and even they were less clear as the grey twilight waned and the sickly phosphorescence of the clouds took its place.

Then dim and misty in the darkling north before him he

glimpsed a terrible thing. He had thought it for some moments a range of black mountains, but now he saw it was something more. The phosphorescence of the brooding clouds shewed it plainly, and even silhouetted parts of it as low vapours glowed behind. How distant it was he could not tell, but it must have been very far. It was thousands of feet high, stretching in a great concave arc from the grey impassable peaks to the unimagined westward spaces, and had once indeed been a ridge of mighty onyx hills. But now those hills were hills no more, for some hand greater than man's had touched them. Silent they squatted there atop the world like wolves or ghouls, crowned with clouds and mists and guarding the secrets of the north forever. All in a great half circle they squatted, those dog-like mountains carven into monstrous watching statues, and their right hands were raised in menace against mankind.

It was only the flickering light of the clouds that made their mitred double heads seem to move, but as Carter stumbled on he saw arise from their shadowy laps great forms whose motions were no delusion. Winged and whirring, those forms grew larger each moment, and the traveller knew his stumbling was at an end. They were not any birds or bats known elsewhere on earth or in dreamland, for they were larger than elephants and had heads like a horse's. Carter knew that they must be the shantak-birds of ill rumour, and wondered no more what evil guardians and nameless sentinels made men avoid the boreal rock desert. And as he stopped in final resignation he dared at last to look behind him; where indeed was trotting the squat slant-eyed trader of evil legend, grinning astride a lean yak and leading on a noxious horde of leering shantaks to whose wings still clung the rime and nitre of the nether pits.

Trapped though he was by fabulous and hippocephalic[36] winged nightmares that pressed around in great unholy circles, Randolph Carter did not lose consciousness. Lofty and horrible those titan gargoyles towered above him, while the slant-eyed merchant leaped down from his yak and stood grinning before the captive. Then the man motioned Carter to mount one of the repugnant shantaks, helping him up as his judgment struggled with his loathing. It was hard work ascending, for the shantak-bird has scales instead of feathers, and those scales are very slip-

36. Having a horse head. Robert M. Price points out, in "Lucian's *True Story* and Lovecraft's *Dream-Quest*," *Crypt of Cthulhu* 83 (Eastertide 1993), that Lucian reported in his second-century CE parody *A True Story* that he also saw horse-bird creatures on his journey to the city of dreams, vultures with three heads that carried men on their backs that Lucian refers to as "Horse-vultures" (26).

pery. Once he was seated, the slant-eyed man hopped up behind him, leaving the lean yak to be led away northward toward the ring of carven mountains by one of the incredible bird colossi.

There now followed a hideous whirl through frigid space, endlessly up and eastward toward the gaunt grey flanks of those impassable mountains beyond which Leng was said to lie. Far above the clouds they flew, till at last there lay beneath them those fabled summits which the folk of Inganok have never seen, and which lie always in high vortices of gleaming mist. Carter beheld them very plainly as they passed below, and saw upon their topmost peaks strange caves which made him think of those on Ngranek; but he did not question his captor about these things when he noticed that both the man and the horse-headed shantak appeared oddly fearful of them, hurrying past nervously and shewing great tension until they were left far in the rear.

The shantak now flew lower, revealing beneath the canopy of cloud a grey barren plain whereon at great distances shone little feeble fires. As they descended there appeared at intervals lone huts of granite and bleak stone villages whose tiny windows glowed with pallid light. And there came from those huts and villages a shrill droning of pipes and a nauseous rattle of crotala which proved at once that Inganok's people are right in their geographick rumours. For travellers have heard such sounds before, and know that they float only from that cold desert plateau which healthy folk never visit; that haunted place of evil and mystery which is Leng.

Around the feeble fires dark forms were dancing, and Carter was curious as to what manner of beings they might be; for no healthy folk have ever been to Leng, and the place is known only by its fires and stone huts as seen from afar. Very slowly and awkwardly did those forms leap, and with an insane twisting and bending not good to behold; so that Carter did not wonder at the monstrous evil imputed to them by vague legend, or the fear in which all dreamland holds their abhorrent frozen plateau. As the shantak flew lower, the repulsiveness of the dancers became tinged with a certain hellish familiarity; and the prisoner kept straining his eyes and racking his memory for clues to where he had seen such creatures before.

They leaped as though they had hooves instead of feet, and

seemed to wear a sort of wig or headpiece with small horns. Of other clothing they had none, but most of them were quite furry. Behind they had dwarfish tails, and when they glanced upward he saw the excessive width of their mouths. Then he knew what they were, and that they did not wear any wigs or headpieces after all. For the cryptic folk of Leng were of one race with the uncomfortable merchants of the black galleys that traded rubies at Dylath-Leen; those not quite human merchants who are the slaves of the monstrous moon-things! They were indeed the same dark folk who had shanghaied Carter on their noisome galley so long ago, and whose kith he had seen driven in herds about the unclean wharves of that accursed lunar city, with the leaner ones toiling and the fatter ones taken away in crates for other needs of their polypous and amorphous masters. Now he saw where such ambiguous creatures came from, and shuddered at the thought that Leng must be known to these formless abominations from the moon.

But the shantak flew on past the fires and the stone huts and the less than human dancers, and soared over sterile hills of grey granite and dim wastes of rock and ice and snow. Day came, and the phosphorescence of low clouds gave place to the misty twilight of that northern world, and still the vile bird winged meaningly through the cold and silence. At times the slant-eyed man talked with his steed in a hateful and guttural language, and the shantak would answer with tittering tones that rasped like the scratching of ground glass. All this while the land was getting higher, and finally they came to a windswept table-land which seemed the very roof of a blasted and tenantless world. There, all alone in the hush and the dusk and the cold, rose the uncouth stones of a squat windowless building, around which a circle of crude monoliths stood. In all this arrangement there was nothing human, and Carter surmised from old tales that he was indeed come to that most dreadful and legendary of all places, the remote and prehistoric monastery wherein dwells uncompanioned the high-priest not to be described, which wears a yellow silken mask over its face and prays to the Other Gods and their crawling chaos Nyarlathotep.

The loathsome bird now settled to the ground, and the slant-eyed man hopped down and helped his captive alight. Of the purpose of his seizure Carter now felt very sure; for clearly the slant-eyed merchant was an agent of the darker powers, eager to drag before his masters a mortal whose presumption had aimed at the finding of unknown Kadath and the saying of a prayer before the faces of the Great Ones in their onyx castle. It seemed likely that this merchant had caused his former capture by the slaves of the moon-things in Dylath-Leen, and that he now meant to do what the rescuing cats had baffled; taking the victim to some dread rendezvous with monstrous Nyarlathotep and telling with what boldness the seeking of unknown Kadath had been tried. Leng and the cold waste north of Inganok must be close to the Other Gods, and there the passes to Kadath are well guarded.

The slant-eyed man was small, but the great hippocephalic bird was there to see he was obeyed; so Carter followed where he led, and passed within the circle of standing rocks and into the low arched doorway of that windowless stone monastery. There were no lights inside, but the evil merchant lit a small clay lamp bearing morbid bas-reliefs and prodded his prisoner on through mazes of narrow winding corridors. On the walls of the corridors were painted frightful scenes older than history, and in a style unknown to the archaeologists of earth. After countless aeons their pigments were brilliant still, for the cold and dryness of hideous Leng keep alive many primal things. Carter saw them fleetingly in the rays of that dim and moving lamp, and shuddered at the tale they told.

Through those archaic frescoes Leng's annals stalked; and the horned, hooved, and wide-mouthed almost-humans danced evilly amidst forgotten cities. There were scenes of old wars, wherein Leng's almost-humans fought with the bloated purple spiders of the neighbouring vales; and there were scenes also of the coming of the black galleys from the moon, and of the submission of Leng's people to the polypous and amorphous blasphemies that hopped and floundered and wriggled out of them. Those slippery greyish-white blasphemies they worshipped as gods, nor ever complained when scores of their best and fatted males were taken away in the black galleys. The monstrous moonbeasts made their camp on a jagged isle in the sea, and Carter could tell from the frescoes that this was none other than the lone nameless rock he had seen when sailing to Inganok; that grey accursed rock which

Inganok's seamen shun, and from which vile howlings reverberate all through the night.

And in those frescoes was shewn the great seaport and capital of the almost-humans; proud and pillared betwixt the cliffs and the basalt wharves, and wondrous with high fanes and carven places. Great gardens and columned streets led from the cliffs and from each of the six sphinx-crowned gates to a vast central plaza, and in that plaza was a pair of winged colossal lions guarding the top of a subterrene staircase. Again and again were those huge winged lions shewn, their mighty flanks of diorite glistening in the grey twilight of the day and the cloudy phosphorescence of the night. And as Carter stumbled past their frequent and repeated pictures it came to him at last what indeed they were, and what city it was that the almost-humans had ruled so anciently before the coming of the black galleys. There could be no mistake, for the legends of dreamland are generous and profuse. Indubitably that primal city was no less a place than storied Sarkomand, whose ruins had bleached for a million years before the first true human saw the light, and whose twin titan lions guard eternally the steps that lead down from dreamland to the Great Abyss.

Other views shewed the gaunt grey peaks dividing Leng from Inganok, and the monstrous shantak-birds that build nests on the ledges half way up. And they shewed likewise the curious caves near the very topmost pinnacles, and how even the boldest of the shantaks fly screaming away from them. Carter had seen those caves when he passed over them, and had noticed their likeness to the caves on Ngranek. Now he knew that the likeness was more than a chance one, for in these pictures were shewn their fearsome denizens; and those bat-wings, curving horns, barbed tails, prehensile paws, and rubbery bodies were not strange to him. He had met those silent, flitting, and clutching creatures before; those mindless guardians of the Great Abyss whom even the Great Ones fear, and who own not Nyarlathotep but hoary Nodens as their lord.[37] For they were the dreaded night-gaunts, who never laugh or smile because they have no faces, and who flop unendingly in the dark betwixt the Vale of Pnath and the passes to the outer world.

The slant-eyed merchant had now prodded Carter into a great

37. Nodens is first mentioned in "The Strange High House in the Mist," pp. 301–10, in the text accompanying note 13, above.

domed space whose walls were carved in shocking bas-reliefs, and whose centre held a gaping circular pit surrounded by six malignly stained stone altars in a ring. There was no light in this vast and evil-smelling crypt, and the small lamp of the sinister merchant shone so feebly that one could grasp details only little by little. At the farther end was a high stone dais reached by five steps; and there on a golden throne sat a lumpish figure robed in yellow silk figured with red and having a yellow silken mask over its face. To this being the slant-eyed man made certain signs with his hands, and the lurker in the dark replied by raising a disgustingly carven flute of ivory in silk-covered paws and blowing certain loathsome sounds from beneath its flowing yellow mask. This colloquy went on for some time, and to Carter there was something sickeningly familiar in the sound of that flute and the stench of the malodorous place. It made him think of a frightful red-litten city and of the revolting procession that once filed through it; of that, and of an awful climb through lunar countryside beyond, before the rescuing rush of earth's friendly cats. He knew that the creature on the dais was without doubt the high-priest not to be described, of which legend whispers such fiendish and abnormal possibilities, but he feared to think just what that abhorred high-priest might be.

Then the figured silk slipped a trifle from one of the greyish-white paws, and Carter knew what the noisome high-priest was. And in that hideous second stark fear drove him to something his reason would never have dared to attempt, for in all his shaken consciousness there was room only for one frantic will to escape from what squatted on that golden throne. He knew that hopeless labyrinths of stone lay betwixt him and the cold table-land outside, and that even on that table-land the noxious shantak still waited; yet in spite of all this there was in his mind only the instant need to get away from that wriggling, silk-robed monstrosity.

The slant-eyed man had set his curious lamp upon one of the high and wickedly stained altar-stones by the pit, and had moved forward somewhat to talk to the high-priest with his hands. Carter, hitherto wholly passive, now gave that man a terrific push with all the wild strength of fear, so that the victim toppled at once into that gaping well which rumour holds to reach down to the hellish Vaults of Zin where gugs hunt ghasts in the dark. In almost the same second he seized the lamp from the altar and darted out into the frescoed labyrinths, racing this way and that as chance determined and trying not to think of the stealthy padding of shapeless paws on the stones behind him, or of the silent wrigglings and crawlings which must be going on back there in lightless corridors.

After a few moments he regretted his thoughtless haste, and wished he had tried to follow backward the frescoes he had passed on the way in. True, they were so confused and duplicated that they could not have done him much good, but he wished none the less he had made the attempt. Those he now saw were even more horrible than those he had seen then, and he knew he was not in the corridors leading outside. In time he became quite sure he was not followed, and slackened his pace somewhat; but scarce had he breathed in half relief when a new peril beset him. His lamp was waning, and he would soon be in pitch blackness with no means of sight or guidance.

When the light was all gone he groped slowly in the dark, and prayed to the Great Ones for such help as they might afford. At times he felt the stone floor sloping up or down, and once he stumbled over a step for which no reason seemed to exist. The farther he went the damper it seemed to be, and when he was able to feel a junction or the mouth of a side passage he always chose the way which sloped downward the least. He believed, though, that his general course was down; and the vault-like smell and incrustations on the greasy walls and floor alike warned him he was burrowing deep in Leng's unwholesome table-land. But there was not any warning of the thing which came at last; only the thing itself with its terror and shock and breath-taking chaos. One moment he was groping slowly over the slippery floor of an almost level place, and the next he was shooting dizzily downward in the dark through a burrow which must have been well-nigh vertical.

Of the length of that hideous sliding he could never be sure, but it seemed to take hours of delirious nausea and ecstatic frenzy. Then he realised he was still, with the phosphorescent clouds of a northern night shining sickly above him. All around were crumbling walls and broken columns, and the pavement on which he lay was pierced by straggling grass and wrenched asunder by frequent shrubs and roots. Behind him a basalt cliff rose topless and perpendicular; its dark side sculptured into repellent scenes, and pierced by an arched and carven entrance to the inner blacknesses out of which he had come. Ahead stretched double rows of pillars, and the fragments and pedestals of pillars, that spoke of a broad and bygone street; and from the urns and basins along the way he knew it had been a great street of gardens. Far off at its end the pillars spread to mark a vast round plaza, and in that open circle there loomed gigantic under the lurid night clouds a pair of monstrous things. Huge winged lions of diorite they were, with blackness and shadow between them. Full twenty feet they reared their grotesque and unbroken heads, and snarled derisive on the ruins around them. And Carter knew right well what they must be, for legend tells of only one such twain. They were the changeless guardians of the Great Abyss, and these dark ruins were in truth primordial Sarkomand.

Carter's first act was to close and barricade the archway in the cliff with fallen blocks and odd debris that lay around. He wished no follower from Leng's hateful monastery, for along the way ahead would lurk enough of other dangers. Of how to get from Sarkomand to the peopled parts of dreamland he knew nothing at all; nor could he gain much by descending to the grottoes of the ghouls, since he knew they were no better informed than he. The three ghouls which had helped him through the city of gugs to the outer world had not known how to reach Sarkomand in their journey back, but had planned to ask old traders in Dylath-Leen. He did not like to think of going again to the subterrene world of gugs and risking once more that hellish tower of Koth with its Cyclopean steps leading to the enchanted wood, yet he felt he might have to try this course if all else failed. Over Leng's plateau past the lone monastery he dared not go unaided; for the high-priest's emissaries must be many, while at the journey's end there would no doubt be the shantaks and perhaps other things to deal with. If he could get a boat he might sail back to Inganok past the jagged and hideous rock in the sea, for the primal frescoes in the monastery labyrinth had shewn that this frightful place lies not far from Sarkomand's basalt quays. But to find a boat in this aeon-deserted city was no probable thing, and it did not appear likely that he could ever make one.

Such were the thoughts of Randolph Carter when a new impression began beating upon his mind. All this while there had stretched before him the great corpse-like width of fabled Sarkomand with its black broken pillars and crumbling sphinx-crowned gates and titan stones and monstrous winged lions against the sickly glow of those luminous night clouds. Now he saw far ahead and on the right a glow that no clouds could account for, and knew he was not alone in the silence of that dead city. The glow rose and fell fitfully, flickering with a green-ish tinge which did not reassure the watcher. And when he crept closer, down the littered street and through some narrow gaps between tumbled walls, he perceived that it was a campfire near the wharves with many vague forms clustered darkly around it, and a lethal odour hanging heavily over all. Beyond was the oily lapping of the harbour water with a great ship riding at anchor, and Carter paused in stark terror when he saw that the ship was indeed one of the dreaded black galleys from the moon.

Then, just as he was about to creep back from that destestable flame, he saw a stirring among the vague dark forms and heard a peculiar and unmistakable sound. It was the frightened meeping of a ghoul, and in a moment it had swelled to a veritable chorus of anguish. Secure as he was in the shadow of monstrous ruins, Carter allowed his curiosity to conquer his fear, and crept forward again instead of retreating. Once in crossing an open street he wriggled worm-like on his stomach, and in another place he had to rise to his feet to avoid making a noise among heaps of fallen marble. But always he succeeded in avoiding discovery, so that in a short time he had found a spot behind a titan pillar whence he could watch the whole green-litten scene of action. There, around a hideous fire fed by the obnoxious stems of lunar fungi, there squatted a stinking circle of the toad-like moonbeasts and their almost-human slaves. Some of these slaves were heating curious iron spears in the leaping flames, and at intervals apply-ing their white-hot points to three tightly trussed prisoners that lay writhing before the leaders of the party. From the motions of their tentacles Carter could see that the blunt-snouted moonbeasts were enjoying the spectacle hugely, and vast was his horror when he suddenly recognised the frantic meeping and knew that the tortured ghouls were none other than the faithful trio which had guided him safely from the abyss and had thereafter set out from the enchanted wood to find Sarkomand and the gate to their native deeps.

The number of malodorous moonbeasts about that greenish fire was very great, and Carter saw that he could do nothing now to save his former allies. Of how the ghouls had been captured he could not guess; but fancied that the grey toad-like blasphemies had heard them inquire in Dylath-Leen concerning the way to Sarkomand and had not wished them to approach so closely the hateful plateau of Leng and the high-priest not to be described. For a moment he pondered on what he ought to do, and recalled how near he was to the gate of the ghouls' black kingdom. Clearly it was wisest to creep east to the plaza of twin lions and descend at once to the gulf, where assuredly he would meet no horrors worse than those above, and where he might soon find ghouls eager to rescue their brethren and perhaps to wipe out the moon-beasts from the black galley. It occurred to him that the portal, like other gates to the abyss, might be guarded by flocks of night-gaunts; but he did not fear these faceless creatures now. He had learned that they are bound by solemn treaties with the ghouls, and the ghoul which was Pickman had taught him how to glibber a password they understood.

So Carter began another silent crawl through the ruins, edging slowly toward the great central plaza and the winged lions. It was ticklish work, but the moonbeasts were pleasantly busy and did not hear the slight noises which he twice made by accident among the scattered stones. At last he reached the open space and picked his way among the stunted trees and briers that had grown up therein. The gigantic lions loomed terrible above him in the sickly glow of the phosphorescent night clouds, but he manfully persisted toward them and presently crept round to their faces, knowing it was on that side he would find the mighty darkness which they guard. Ten feet apart crouched the mocking-faced beasts of diorite, brooding on Cyclopean pedestals whose sides were chiselled into fearsome bas-reliefs. Betwixt them was a tiled court with a central space which had once been railed with balusters of onyx. Midway in this space a black well opened, and Carter soon saw that he had indeed reached the yawning gulf whose crusted and mouldy stone steps lead down to the crypts of nightmare.

Terrible is the memory of that dark descent, in which hours wore themselves away whilst Carter wound sightlessly round and round down a fathomless spiral of steep and slippery stairs. So worn and narrow were the steps, and so greasy with the ooze of inner earth, that the climber never quite knew when to expect a breathless fall and hurtling down to the ultimate pits; and he was likewise uncertain just when or how the guardian night-gaunts would suddenly pounce upon him, if indeed there were any stationed in this primeval passage. All about him was a stifling odour of nether gulfs, and he felt that the air of these choking depths was not made for mankind. In time he became very numb and somnolent, moving more from automatic impulse than from reasoned will; nor did he realise any change when he stopped moving altogether as something quietly seized him from behind. He was flying very rapidly through the air before a malevolent tickling told him that the rubbery night-gaunts had performed their duty.

Awaked to the fact that he was in the cold, damp clutch of the faceless flutterers, Carter remembered the password of the ghouls and glibbered it as loudly as he could amidst the wind and chaos of flight. Mindless though night-gaunts are said to be, the effect was instantaneous; for all tickling stopped at once, and the creatures hastened to shift their captive to a more comfortable position. Thus encouraged, Carter ventured some explanations; telling of the seizure and torture of three ghouls by the moon-beasts, and of the need of assembling a party to rescue them. The night-gaunts, though inarticulate, seemed to understand what was said; and shewed greater haste and purpose in their flight. Suddenly the dense blackness gave place to the grey twilight of inner earth, and there opened up ahead one of those flat sterile plains on which ghouls love to squat and gnaw. Scattered tomb-stones and osseous fragments told of the denizens of that place; and as Carter gave a loud meep of urgent summons, a score of burrows emptied forth their leathery, dog-like tenants. The night-gaunts now flew low and set their passenger upon his feet, after-

38. Carter thus allies with an unlikely assemblage of species. Maurice Lévy, confused by this sudden and seemingly incongruous alliance, thought it evidence of "some spectacular mutations in the author's repugnances," an apparent "changing [of] attitude" that is "not explained by chronology." (See Maurice Lévy, *Lovecraft: A Study in the Fantastic*, trans. S. T. Joshi [Detroit: Wayne State University Press, 1988], 104.) But as Robert M. Price observes, in "Randolph Carter, Warlord of Mars," *Tekeli-li* 1 (Spring 1991), 37, Carter's macabre underworld alliances correspond "quite nicely" to the alien alliances forged by Carter's doppelgänger, John Carter, whose adventures on Mars are recorded by Edgar Rice Burroughs—"not to mention," Gavin Callaghan adds, "to Tarzan's routine alliances with the subhuman baboons, elephants, and other beasts of the jungle" ("A Reprehensible Habit: H. P. Lovecraft and the Munsey Magazines," 72).

ward withdrawing a little and forming a hunched semicircle on the ground while the ghouls greeted the newcomer.

Carter glibbered his message rapidly and explicitly to the grotesque company, and four of them at once departed through different burrows to spread the news to others and gather such troops as might be available for the rescue. After a long wait a ghoul of some importance appeared, and made significant signs to the night-gaunts, causing two of the latter to fly off into the dark. Thereafter there were constant accessions to the hunched flock of night-gaunts on the plain, till at length the slimy soil was fairly black with them. Meanwhile fresh ghouls crawled out of the burrows one by one, all glibbering excitedly and forming in crude battle array not far from the huddled night-gaunts. In time there appeared that proud and influential ghoul which was once the artist Richard Pickman of Boston, and to him Carter glibbered a very full account of what had occurred. The erstwhile Pickman, surprised to greet his ancient friend again, seemed very much impressed, and held a conference with other chiefs a little apart from the growing throng.

Finally, after scanning the ranks with care, the assembled chiefs all meeped in unison and began glibbering orders to the crowds of ghouls and night-gaunts.[38] A large detachment of the horned flyers vanished at once, while the rest grouped themselves two by two on their knees with extended fore legs, awaiting the approach of the ghouls one by one. As each ghoul reached the pair of night-gaunts to which he was assigned, he was taken up and borne away into the blackness; till at last the whole throng had vanished save for Carter, Pickman, and the other chiefs, and a few pairs of night-gaunts. Pickman explained that night-gaunts are the advance guard and battle steeds of the ghouls, and that the army was issuing forth to Sarkomand to deal with the moon-beasts. Then Carter and the ghoulish chiefs approached the waiting bearers and were taken up by the damp, slippery paws. Another moment and all were whirling in wind and darkness; endlessly up, up, up to the gate of the winged lions and the spectral ruins of primal Sarkomand.

When, after a great interval, Carter saw again the sickly light of Sarkomand's nocturnal sky, it was to behold the great central plaza swarming with militant ghouls and night-gaunts. Day, he felt sure, must be almost due; but so strong was the army that no surprise of the enemy would be needed. The greenish flare near the wharves still glimmered faintly, though the absence of ghoulish meeping shewed that the torture of the prisoners was over for the nonce. Softly glibbering directions to their steeds, and to the flock of riderless night-gaunts ahead, the ghouls presently rose in wide whirring columns and swept on over the bleak ruins toward the evil flame. Carter was now beside Pickman in the front rank of ghouls, and saw as they approached the noisome camp that the moonbeasts were totally unprepared. The three prisoners lay bound and inert beside the fire, while their toad-like captors slumped drowsily about in no certain order. The almost-human slaves were asleep, even the sentinels shirking a duty which in this realm must have seemed to them merely perfunctory.

The final swoop of the night-gaunts and mounted ghouls was very sudden, each of the greyish toad-like blasphemies and their almost-human slaves being seized by a group of night-gaunts before a sound was made. The moonbeasts, of course, were voiceless; and even the slaves had little chance to scream before rubbery paws choked them into silence. Horrible were the writhings of those great jellyish abnormalities as the sardonic night-gaunts clutched them, but nothing availed against the strength of those black prehensile talons. When a moonbeast writhed too violently, a night-gaunt would seize and pull its quivering pink tentacles; which seemed to hurt so much that the victim would cease its struggles. Carter expected to see much slaughter, but found that the ghouls were far subtler in their plans. They glibbered certain simple orders to the night-gaunts which held the captives, trusting the rest to instinct; and soon the hapless creatures were borne silently away into the Great Abyss, to be distributed impartially amongst the bholes, gugs, ghasts, and other dwellers in darkness whose modes of nourishment are not painless to their chosen victims. Meanwhile the three bound ghouls had been released and consoled by their conquering kinsfolk, whilst various parties searched the neighbourhood for possible remaining moonbeasts, and boarded the evil-smelling black galley at the wharf to make sure that nothing had escaped the general defeat. Surely enough, the capture had been thorough; for not a sign of further life could the victors detect. Carter, anxious to preserve a means of access to the rest of dreamland, urged them not to sink the anchored galley; and this request was freely granted out of gratitude for his act in reporting the plight of the captured trio. On the ship were found some very curious objects and decorations, some of which Carter cast at once into the sea.

Ghouls and night-gaunts now formed themselves in separate groups, the former questioning their rescued fellows anent past happenings. It appeared that the three had followed Carter's directions and proceeded from the enchanted wood to Dylath-Leen by way of Nir and the Skai, stealing human clothes at a lonely farmhouse and loping as closely as possible in the fashion of a man's walk. In Dylath-Leen's taverns their grotesque ways and faces had aroused much comment; but they had persisted in asking the way to Sarkomand until at last an old traveller was able to tell them. Then they knew that only a ship for Lelag-Leng would serve their purpose, and prepared to wait patiently for such a vessel.

But evil spies had doubtless reported much; for shortly a black galley put into port, and the wide-mouthed ruby merchants invited the ghouls to drink with them in a tavern. Wine was produced from one of those sinister bottles grotesquely carven from a single ruby, and after that the ghouls found themselves prisoners on the black galley as Carter had once found himself. This time, however, the unseen rowers steered not for the moon but for antique Sarkomand; bent evidently on taking their captives before the high-priest not to be described. They had touched at the jagged rock in the northern sea which Inganok's mariners shun, and the ghouls had there seen for the first time the real masters of the ship; being sickened despite their own callousness by such extremes of malign shapelessness and fearsome odour. There, too, were witnessed the nameless pastimes of the toad-like resident garrison—such pastimes as give rise to the night-howlings which men fear. After that had come the landing at ruined Sarkomand and the beginning of the tortures, whose continuance the present rescue had prevented.

Future plans were next discussed, the three rescued ghouls suggesting a raid on the jagged rock and the extermination of the toad-like garrison there. To this, however, the night-gaunts objected; since the prospect of flying over water did not please them. Most of the ghouls favoured the design, but were at a loss how to follow it without the help of the winged night-gaunts. Thereupon Carter, seeing that they could not navigate the anchored galley, offered to teach them the use of the great banks of oars; to which proposal they eagerly assented. Grey day had now come, and under that leaden northern sky a picked detachment of ghouls filed into the noisome ship and took their seats on the rowers' benches. Carter found them fairly apt at learning, and before night had risked several experimental trips around the harbour. Not till three days later, however, did he deem it safe to attempt the voyage of conquest. Then, the rowers trained and the night-gaunts safely stowed in the forecastle, the party set sail at last; Pickman and the other chiefs gathering on deck and discussing modes of approach and procedure.

On the very first night the howlings from the rock were heard. Such was their timbre that all the galley's crew shook visibly; but most of all trembled the three rescued ghouls who knew precisely what those howlings meant. It was not thought best to attempt an attack by night, so the ship lay to under the phosphorescent clouds to wait for the dawn of a greyish day. When the light was ample and the howlings still the rowers resumed their strokes, and the galley drew closer and closer to that jagged rock whose granite pinnacles clawed fantastically at the dull sky. The sides of the rock were very steep; but on ledges here and there could be seen the bulging walls of queer windowless dwellings, and the low railings guarding travelled high roads. No ship of men had ever come so near the place, or at least, had never come so near and departed again; but Carter and the ghouls were void of fear and kept inflexibly on, rounding the eastern face of the rock and seeking the wharves which the rescued trio described as being on the southern side within a harbour formed of steep headlands.

The headlands were prolongations of the island proper, and came so closely together that only one ship at a time might pass between them. There seemed to be no watchers on the outside, so the galley was steered boldly through the flume-like strait and into the stagnant foetid harbour beyond. Here, however, all was bustle and activity; with several ships lying at anchor along a forbidding stone quay, and scores of almost-human slaves and moonbeasts by the waterfront handling crates and boxes or driving nameless and fabulous horrors hitched to lumbering lorries. There was a small stone town hewn out of the vertical cliff above the wharves, with the start of a winding road that spiralled out of sight toward higher ledges of the rock. Of what lay inside that prodigious peak of granite none might say, but the things one saw on the outside were far from encouraging.

At sight of the oncoming galley the crowds on the wharves displayed much eagerness; those with eyes staring intently, and those without eyes wriggling their pink tentacles expectantly. They did not, of course, realise that the black ship had changed hands; for ghouls look much like the horned and hooved almost-humans, and the night-gaunts were all out of sight below. By this time the leaders had fully formed a plan; which was to loose the night-gaunts as soon as the wharf was touched, and then to sail directly away, leaving matters wholly to the instincts of those almost mindless creatures. Marooned on the rock, the horned flyers would first of all seize whatever living things they found there, and afterward, quite helpless to think except in terms of the homing instinct, would forget their fear of water and fly swiftly back to the abyss; bearing their noisome prey to appropriate destinations in the dark, from which not much would emerge alive.

The ghoul that was Pickman now went below and gave the night-gaunts their simple instructions, while the ship drew very near to the ominous and malodorous wharves. Presently a fresh stir rose along the waterfront, and Carter saw that the motions of the galley had begun to excite suspicion. Evidently the steersman was not making for the right dock, and probably the watchers had noticed the difference between the hideous ghouls and the almost-human slaves whose places they were taking. Some silent alarm must have been given, for almost at once a horde of the mephitic moonbeasts began to pour from the little black doorways of the windowless houses and down the winding road at the right. A rain of curious javelins struck the galley as the prow hit the wharf, felling two ghouls and slightly wounding another; but at this point all the hatches were thrown open to emit a black cloud of whirring night-gaunts which swarmed over the town like a flock of horned and Cyclopean bats.

The jellyish moonbeasts had procured a great pole and were trying to push off the invading ship, but when the night-gaunts struck them they thought of such things no more. It was a very terrible spectacle to see those faceless and rubbery ticklers at their pastime, and tremendously impressive to watch the dense cloud of them spreading through the town and up the winding roadway to the reaches above. Sometimes a group of the black flutterers would drop a toad-like prisoner from aloft by mistake, and the manner in which the victim would burst was highly offensive to the sight and smell. When the last of the night-gaunts had left the galley the ghoulish leaders glibbered an order of withdrawal, and the rowers pulled quietly out of the harbour between the grey headlands while still the town was a chaos of battle and conquest.

The Pickman ghoul allowed several hours for the night-gaunts to make up their rudimentary minds and overcome their fear of flying over the sea, and kept the galley standing about a mile off the jagged rock while he waited and dressed the wounds of the injured men. Night fell, and the grey twilight gave place to the sickly phosphorescence of low clouds, and all the while the leaders watched the high peaks of that accursed rock for signs of the night-gaunts' flight. Toward morning a black speck was seen hovering timidly over the topmost pinnacle, and shortly afterward the speck had become a swarm. Just before daybreak the swarm seemed to scatter, and within a quarter of an hour it had vanished wholly in the distance toward the northeast. Once or twice something seemed to fall from the thinning swarm into the sea; but Carter did not worry, since he knew from observation that the toad-like moonbeasts cannot swim. At length, when the ghouls were satisfied that all the night-gaunts had left for Sarkomand and the Great Abyss with their doomed burdens, the galley put back into the harbour betwixt the grey headlands; and all the hideous company landed and roamed curiously over the denuded rock with its towers and eyries and fortresses chiselled from the solid stone.

Frightful were the secrets uncovered in those evil and windowless crypts; for the remnants of unfinished pastimes were many, and in various stages of departure from their primal state. Carter put out of the way certain things which were after a fashion alive, and fled precipitately from a few other things about which he could not be very positive. The stench-filled houses were furnished mostly with grotesque stools and benches carven from moon-trees, and were painted inside with nameless and frantic designs. Countless weapons, implements, and ornaments lay about; including some large idols of solid ruby depicting singular beings not found on the earth. These latter did not, despite their material, invite either appropriation or long inspection; and Carter took the trouble to hammer five of them into very small pieces. The scattered spears and javelins he collected, and with Pickman's approval distributed among the ghouls. Such devices were new to the dog-like lopers, but their relative simplicity made them easy to master after a few concise hints.

The upper parts of the rock held more temples than private homes, and in numerous hewn chambers were found terrible carven altars and doubtfully stained fonts and shrines for the worship of things more monstrous than the mild gods atop Kadath. From the rear of one great temple stretched a low black passage which Carter followed far into the rock with a torch till he came to a lightless domed hall of vast proportions, whose vaultings were covered with daemoniac carvings and in whose centre yawned a foul and bottomless well like that in the hideous monastery of Leng where broods alone the high-priest not to be described. On the distant shadowy side, beyond the noisome well, he thought he discerned a small door of strangely wrought bronze; but for some reason he felt an unaccountable dread of opening it or even approaching it, and hastened back through the cavern to his unlovely allies as they shambled about with an ease and abandon he could scarcely feel. The ghouls had observed the unfinished pastimes of the moonbeasts, and had profited in their fashion. They had also found a hogshead of potent moon-wine, and were rolling it down to the wharves for removal and later use in diplomatic dealings, though the rescued trio, remembering its effect on them in Dylath-Leen, had warned their company to taste none of it. Of rubies from lunar mines there was a great store, both rough and polished, in one of the vaults near the water; but when the ghouls found they were not good to eat they lost all interest in them. Carter did not try to carry any away, since he knew too much about those which had mined them.

Suddenly there came an excited meeping from the sentries on the wharves, and all the loathsome foragers turned from their tasks to stare seaward and cluster round the waterfront. Betwixt the grey headlands a fresh black galley was rapidly advancing, and it could be but a moment before the almost-humans on deck would perceive the invasion of the town and give the alarm to the monstrous things below. Fortunately the ghouls still bore the spears and javelins which Carter had distributed amongst them; and at his command, sustained by the being that was Pickman, they now formed a line of battle and prepared to prevent the landing of the ship. Presently a burst of excitement on the galley told of the crew's discovery of the changed state of things, and the instant stoppage of the vessel proved that the superior numbers of the ghouls had been noted and taken into account. After a moment of hesitation the newcomers silently turned and passed out between the headlands again, but not for an instant did the ghouls imagine that the conflict was averted. Either the dark ship would seek reinforcements, or the crew would try to land elsewhere on the island; hence a party of scouts was at once sent up toward the pinnacle to see what the enemy's course would be.

In a very few minutes a ghoul returned breathless to say that the moonbeasts and almost-humans were landing on the outside of the more easterly of the rugged grey headlands, and ascending by hidden paths and ledges which a goat could scarcely tread in safety. Almost immediately afterward the galley was sighted again through the flume-like strait, but only for a second. Then, a few moments later, a second messenger panted down from aloft to say that another party was landing on the other headland; both being much more numerous than the size of the galley would seem to allow for. The ship itself, moving slowly with only one sparsely manned tier of oars, soon hove in sight betwixt the cliffs, and lay to in the foetid harbour as if to watch the coming fray and stand by for any possible use.

By this time Carter and Pickman had divided the ghouls into three parties, one to meet each of the two invading columns and one to remain in the town. The first two at once scrambled up the rocks in their respective directions, while the third was subdivided into a land party and a sea party. The sea party, commanded by Carter, boarded the anchored galley and rowed out to meet the undermanned galley of the newcomers; whereat the latter retreated through the strait to the open sea. Carter did not at once pursue it, for he knew he might be needed more acutely near the town.

Meanwhile the frightful detachments of the moonbeasts and almost-humans had lumbered up to the top of the headlands and were shockingly silhouetted on either side against the grey twilight sky. The thin hellish flutes of the invaders had now begun to whine, and the general effect of those hybrid, half-amorphous processions was as nauseating as the actual odour given off by the toad-like lunar blasphemies. Then the two parties of the ghouls swarmed into sight and joined the silhouetted panorama. Javelins began to fly from both sides, and the swelling meeps of the ghouls and the bestial howls of the almost-humans gradually joined the hellish whine of the flutes to form a frantick and indescribable chaos of daemon cacophony. Now and then bodies fell from the narrow ridges of the headlands into the sea outside or the harbour inside, in the latter case being sucked quickly under by certain submarine lurkers whose presence was indicated only by prodigious bubbles.

For half an hour this dual battle raged in the sky, till upon the west cliff the invaders were completely annihilated. On the east cliff, however, where the leader of the moonbeast party appeared to be present, the ghouls had not fared so well; and were slowly retreating to the slopes of the pinnacle proper. Pickman had quickly ordered reinforcements for this front from the party in the town, and these had helped greatly in the earlier stages of the combat. Then, when the western battle was over, the victorious survivors hastened across to the aid of their hard-pressed fellows; turning the tide and forcing the invaders back again along the narrow ridge of the headland. The almost-humans were by this time all slain, but the last of the toad-like horrors fought desperately with the great spears clutched in their powerful and disgusting paws. The time for javelins was now nearly past, and the fight became a hand-to-hand contest of what few spearmen could meet upon that narrow ridge.

As fury and recklessness increased, the number falling into the sea became very great. Those striking the harbour met nameless extinction from the unseen bubblers, but of those striking the open sea some were able to swim to the foot of the cliffs and land on tidal rocks, while the hovering galley of the enemy rescued several moonbeasts. The cliffs were unscalable except where the monsters had debarked, so that none of the ghouls on the rocks could rejoin their battle-line. Some were killed by javelins from the hostile galley or from the moonbeasts above, but a few survived to be rescued. When the security of the land parties seemed assured, Carter's galley sallied forth between the headlands and drove the hostile ship far out to sea; pausing to rescue such ghouls as were on the rocks or still swimming in the ocean. Several moonbeasts washed on rocks or reefs were speedily put out of the way.

Finally, the moonbeasts' galley being safely in the distance and the invading land army concentrated in one place, Carter landed a considerable force on the eastern headland in the enemy's rear; after which the fight was short-lived indeed. Attacked from both sides, the noisome flounderers were rapidly cut to pieces or pushed into the sea, till by evening the ghoulish chiefs agreed that the island was again clear of them. The hostile galley, meanwhile, had disappeared; and it was decided that the evil jagged rock had better be evacuated before any overwhelming horde of lunar horrors might be assembled and brought against the victors.

So by night Pickman and Carter assembled all the ghouls and counted them with care, finding that over a fourth had been lost in the day's battles. The wounded were placed on bunks in the galley, for Pickman always discouraged the old ghoulish custom of killing and eating one's own wounded, and the able-bodied troops were assigned to the oars or to such other places as they might most usefully fill. Under the low phosphorescent clouds of night the galley sailed, and Carter was not sorry to be departing from that island of unwholesome secrets, whose lightless domed hall with its bottomless well and repellent bronze door lingered restlessly in his fancy. Dawn found the ship in sight of Sarkomand's ruined quays of basalt, where a few night-gaunt sentries still waited, squatting like black horned gargoyles on the broken columns and crumbling sphinxes of that fearful city which lived and died before the years of man.

The ghouls made camp amongst the fallen stones of Sarkomand, despatching a messenger for enough night-gaunts to serve them as steeds. Pickman and the other chiefs were effusive in their gratitude for the aid Carter had lent them; and Carter now began to feel that his plans were indeed maturing well, and that he would be able to command the help of these fearsome allies not only in quitting this part of dreamland, but in pursuing his ultimate quest for the gods atop unknown Kadath, and the marvellous sunset city they so strangely withheld from his slumbers. Accordingly he spoke of these things to the ghoulish leaders; telling what he knew of the cold waste wherein Kadath stands and of the monstrous shantaks and the mountains carven into double-headed images which guard it. He spoke of the fear of shantaks for night-gaunts, and of how the vast hippocephalic birds fly screaming from the black burrows high up on the gaunt grey peaks that divide Inganok from hateful Leng. He spoke, too, of the things he had learnt concerning night-gaunts from the frescoes in the windowless monastery of the high-priest not to be described; how even the Great Ones fear them, and how their ruler is not the crawling chaos Nyarlathotep at all, but hoary and immemorial Nodens, Lord of the Great Abyss.

All these things Carter glibbered to the assembled ghouls, and presently outlined that request which he had in mind, and which he did not think extravagant considering the services he had so lately rendered the rubbery, dog-like lopers. He wished very much, he said, for the services of enough night-gaunts to bear him safely through the air past the realm of shantaks and carven mountains, and up into the cold waste beyond the returning tracks of any other mortal. He desired to fly to the onyx castle atop unknown Kadath in the cold waste to plead with the Great Ones for the sunset city they denied him, and felt sure that the night-gaunts could take him thither without trouble; high above the perils of the plain, and over the hideous double heads of those carven sentinel mountains that squat eternally in the grey dusk. For the horned and faceless creatures there could be no danger from aught of earth, since the Great Ones themselves dread them. And even were unexpected things to come from the Other Gods, who are prone to oversee the affairs of earth's milder gods, the night-gaunts need not fear; for the outer hells are indifferent matters to such silent and slippery flyers as own not Nyarlathotep for their master, but bow only to potent and archaic Nodens.

A flock of ten or fifteen night-gaunts, Carter glibbered, would surely be enough to keep any combination of shantaks at a distance; though perhaps it might be well to have some ghouls in the party to manage the creatures, their ways being better known to their ghoulish allies than to men. The party could land him at some convenient point within whatever walls that fabulous onyx citadel might have, waiting in the shadows for his return or his signal whilst he ventured inside the castle to give prayer to the gods of earth. If any ghouls chose to escort him into the throne-room of the Great Ones, he would be thankful, for their presence would add weight and importance to his plea. He would not, however, insist upon this but merely wished transportation to and from the castle atop unknown Kadath; the final journey being either to the marvellous sunset city itself, in case the gods proved favourable, or back to the earthward Gate of Deeper Slumber in the enchanted wood in case his prayers were fruitless.

Whilst Carter was speaking all the ghouls listened with great attention, and as the moments advanced the sky became black with clouds of those night-gaunts for which messengers had been sent. The winged horrors settled in a semicircle around the ghoulish army, waiting respectfully as the dog-like chieftains considered the wish of the earthly traveller. The ghoul that was Pickman glibbered gravely with its fellows, and in the end Carter was offered far more than he had at most expected. As he had aided the ghouls in their conquest of the moonbeasts, so would they aid him in his daring voyage to realms whence none had ever returned; lending him not merely a few of their allied night-gaunts, but their entire army as they encamped, veteran fighting ghouls and newly assembled night-gaunts alike, save only a small garrison for the captured black galley and such spoils as had come from the jagged rock in the sea. They would set out through the air whenever he might wish, and once arrived on Kadath a suitable train of ghouls would attend him in state as he placed his petition before earth's gods in their onyx castle.

Moved by a gratitude and satisfaction beyond words, Carter made plans with the ghoulish leaders for his audacious voyage. The army would fly high, they decided, over hideous Leng with its nameless monastery and wicked stone villages; stopping only at the vast grey peaks to confer with the shantak-frightening night-gaunts whose burrows honeycombed their summits. They would then, according to what advice they might receive from those denizens, choose their final course; approaching unknown Kadath either through the desert of carven mountains north of Inganok, or through the more northerly reaches of repulsive Leng itself. Dog-like and soulless as they are, the ghouls and the night-gaunts had no dread of what those untrodden deserts might reveal; nor did they feel any deterring awe at the thought of Kadath towering lone with its onyx castle of mystery.

About midday the ghouls and night-gaunts prepared for flight, each ghoul selecting a suitable pair of horned steeds to bear him. Carter was placed well up toward the head of the column beside Pickman, and in front of the whole a double line of riderless night-gaunts was provided as a vanguard. At a brisk meep from Pickman the whole shocking army rose in a nightmare cloud above the broken columns and crumbling sphinxes of primordial Sarkomand; higher and higher, till even the great basalt cliff behind the town was cleared, and the cold, sterile table-land of Leng's outskirts laid open to sight. Still higher flew the black host, till even this table-land grew small beneath them; and as they worked northward over the windswept plateau of horror Carter saw once again with a shudder the circle of crude monoliths and the squat windowless building which he knew held that frightful silken-masked blasphemy from whose clutches he had so narrowly escaped. This time no descent was made as the army swept bat-like over the sterile landscape, passing the feeble fires of the unwholesome stone villages at a great altitude, and pausing not at all to mark the morbid twistings of the hooved, horned almost-humans that dance and pipe eternally therein. Once they saw a shantak-bird flying low over the plain, but when it saw them it screamed noxiously and flapped off to the north in grotesque panic.

At dusk they reached the jagged grey peaks that form the barrier of Inganok, and hovered about those strange caves near the summits which Carter recalled as so frightful to the shantaks. At the insistent meeping of the ghoulish leaders there issued forth from each lofty burrow a stream of horned black flyers; with which the ghouls and the night-gaunts of the party conferred at length by means of ugly gestures. It soon became clear that the best course would be that over the cold waste north of Inganok, for Leng's northward reaches are full of unseen pitfalls that even the night-gaunts dislike; abysmal influences centreing in certain white hemispherical buildings on curious knolls, which common folklore associates unpleasantly with the Other Gods and their crawling chaos Nyarlathotep.

Of Kadath the flutterers of the peaks knew almost nothing, save that there must be some mighty marvel toward the north, over which the shantaks and the carven mountains stand guard. They hinted at rumoured abnormalities of proportion in those trackless leagues beyond, and recalled vague whispers of a realm where night broods eternally; but of definite data they had nothing to give. So Carter and his party thanked them kindly; and, crossing the topmost granite pinnacles to the skies of Inganok, dropped below the level of the phosphorescent night clouds and beheld in the distance those terrible squatting gargoyles that were mountains till some titan hand carved fright into their virgin rock.

There they squatted, in a hellish half-circle, their legs on the desert sand and their mitres piercing the luminous clouds; sinister, wolf-like, and double-headed, with faces of fury and right hands raised, dully and malignly watching the rim of man's world and guarding with horror the reaches of a cold northern world that is not man's. From their hideous laps rose evil shantaks of elephantine bulk, but these all fled with insane titters as the vanguard of night-gaunts was sighted in the misty sky. Northward above those gargoyle mountains the army flew, and over leagues of dim desert where never a landmark rose. Less and less luminous grew the clouds, till at length Carter could see only blackness around him; but never did the winged steeds falter, bred as they were in earth's blackest crypts, and seeing not with any eyes, but with the whole dank surface of their slippery forms. On and on they flew, past winds of dubious scent and sounds of dubious import; ever in thickest darkness, and covering such prodigious spaces that Carter wondered whether or not they could still be within earth's dreamland.

Then suddenly the clouds thinned and the stars shone spectrally above. All below was still black, but those pallid beacons in the sky seemed alive with a meaning and directiveness they had

39. A grouping of stars, smaller than a constellation.

never possessed elsewhere. It was not that the figures of the constellations were different, but that the same familiar shapes now revealed a significance they had formerly failed to make plain. Everything focussed toward the north; every curve and asterism[39] of the glittering sky became part of a vast design whose function was to hurry first the eye and then the whole observer to some secret and terrible goal of convergence beyond the frozen waste that stretched endlessly ahead. Carter looked toward the east where the great ridge of barrier peaks had towered along all the length of Inganok, and saw against the stars a jagged silhouette which told of its continued presence. It was more broken now, with yawning clefts and fantastically erratic pinnacles; and Carter studied closely the suggestive turns and inclinations of that grotesque outline, which seemed to share with the stars some subtle northward urge.

They were flying past at a tremendous speed, so that the watcher had to strain hard to catch details; when all at once he beheld just above the line of the topmost peaks a dark and moving object against the stars, whose course exactly paralleled that of his own bizarre party. The ghouls had likewise glimpsed it, for he heard their low glibbering all about him, and for a moment he fancied the object was a gigantic shantak, of a size vastly greater than that of the average specimen. Soon, however, he saw that this theory would not hold; for the shape of the thing above the mountains was not that of any hippocephalic bird. Its outline against the stars, necessarily vague as it was, resembled rather some huge mitred head or pair of heads infinitely magnified; and its rapid bobbing flight through the sky seemed most peculiarly a wingless one. Carter could not tell which side of the mountains it was on, but soon perceived that it had parts below the parts he had first seen, since it blotted out all the stars in places where the ridge was deeply cleft.

Then came a wide gap in the range, where the hideous reaches of transmontane Leng were joined to the cold waste on this side by a low pass through which the stars shone wanly. Carter watched this gap with intense care, knowing that he might see outlined against the sky beyond it the lower parts of the vast thing that flew undulantly above the pinnacles. The object had now floated ahead a trifle, and every eye of the party was fixed on the rift where it would presently appear in full-length silhouette. Gradually the huge thing above the peaks neared the gap, slightly slackening its speed as if conscious of having outdistanced the ghoulish army. For another minute suspense was keen, and then the brief instant of full silhouette and revelation came; bringing to the lips of the ghouls an awed and half-choked meep of cosmic fear, and to the soul of the traveller a chill that has never wholly left it. For the mammoth bobbing shape that overtopped the ridge was only a head—a mitred double head—and below it in terrible vastness loped the frightful swollen body that bore it; the mountain-high monstrosity that walked in stealth and silence; the hyaena-like distortion of a giant anthropoid shape that trotted blackly against the sky, its repulsive pair of cone-capped heads reaching half way to the zenith.

Carter did not lose consciousness or even scream aloud, for he was an old dreamer; but he looked behind him in horror and shuddered when he saw that there were other monstrous heads silhouetted above the level of the peaks, bobbing along stealthily after the first one. And straight in the rear were three of the mighty mountain shapes seen full against the southern stars, tiptoeing wolf-like and lumberingly, their tall mitres nodding thousands of feet in the air. The carven mountains, then, had not stayed squatting in that rigid semicircle north of Inganok with right hands uplifted. They had duties to perform, and were not remiss. But it was horrible that they never spoke, and never even made a sound in walking.

Meanwhile the ghoul that was Pickman had glibbered an order to the night-gaunts, and the whole army soared higher into the air. Up toward the stars the grotesque column shot, till nothing stood out any longer against the sky; neither the grey granite ridge that was still nor the carven and mitred mountains that walked. All was blackness beneath as the fluttering legions surged northward amidst rushing winds and invisible laughter in the aether, and never a shantak or less mentionable entity rose from the haunted wastes to pursue them. The farther they went, the faster they flew, till soon their dizzying speed seemed to pass that of a rifle ball and approach that of a planet in its orbit. Carter wondered how with such speed the earth could still stretch beneath them, but knew that in the land of dream dimensions have strange properties. That they were in a realm of eternal night he felt certain, and he fancied that the constellations overhead had subtly emphasised their northward focus; gathering themselves up as it were to cast the flying army into the void of the boreal pole, as the folds of a bag are gathered up to cast out the last bits of substance therein.

Then he noticed with terror that the wings of the night-gaunts were not flapping any more. The horned and faceless steeds had folded their membraneous appendages, and were resting quite passive in the chaos of wind that whirled and chuckled as it bore them on. A force not of earth had seized on the army, and ghouls and night-gaunts alike were powerless before a current which pulled madly and relentlessly into the north whence no mortal had ever returned. At length a lone pallid light was seen on the skyline ahead, thereafter rising steadily as they approached, and having beneath it a black mass that blotted out the stars. Carter saw that it must be some beacon on a mountain, for only a mountain could rise so vast as seen from so prodigious a height in the air.

Higher and higher rose the light and the blackness beneath it, till half the northern sky was obscured by the rugged conical mass. Lofty as the army was, that pale and sinister beacon rose above it, towering monstrous over all peaks and concernments of earth, and tasting the atomless aether where the cryptical moon and the mad planets reel. No mountain known of man was that which loomed before them. The high clouds far below were but a fringe for its foothills. The gasping dizziness of topmost air was but a girdle for its loins. Scornful and spectral climbed that bridge betwixt earth and heaven, black in eternal night, and crowned with a pshent of unknown stars whose awful and significant outline grew every moment clearer. Ghouls meeped in wonder as they saw it, and Carter shivered in fear lest all the hurtling army be dashed to pieces on the unyielding onyx of that Cyclopean cliff.

Higher and higher rose the light, till it mingled with the loftiest orbs of the zenith and winked down at the flyers with lurid mockery. All the north beneath it was blackness now; dread, stony blackness from infinite depths to infinite heights, with only that pale winking beacon perched unreachably at the top of all vision. Carter studied the light more closely, and saw at last what lines its inky background made against the stars. There were towers on that titan mountaintop; horrible domed towers in noxious and incalculable tiers and clusters beyond any dreamable workmanship of man; battlements and terraces of wonder and menace, all limned tiny and black and distant against the starry pshent that glowed malevolently at the uppermost rim of sight. Capping that most measureless of mountains was a castle beyond all mortal thought, and in it glowed the daemon-light. Then Randolph Carter knew that his quest was done, and that he saw above him the goal of all forbidden steps and audacious visions; the fabulous, the incredible home of the Great Ones atop unknown Kadath.

Even as he realised this thing, Carter noticed a change in the course of the helplessly wind-sucked party. They were rising abruptly now, and it was plain that the focus of their flight was the onyx castle where the pale light shone. So close was the great black mountain that its sides sped by them dizzily as they shot upward, and in the darkness they could discern nothing upon it. Vaster and vaster loomed the tenebrous towers of the nighted castle above, and Carter could see that it was well-nigh blasphemous in its immensity. Well might its stones have been quarried by nameless workmen in that horrible gulf rent out of the rock in the hill pass north of Inganok, for such was its size that a man on its threshold stood even as an ant on the steps of earth's loftiest fortress. The pshent of unknown stars above the myriad domed turrets glowed with a sallow, sickly flare, so that a kind of twilight hung about the murky walls of slippery onyx. The pallid beacon was now seen to be a single shining window high up in one of the loftiest towers, and as the helpless army neared the top of the mountain Carter thought he detected unpleasant shadows flitting across the feebly luminous expanse. It was a strangely arched window, of a design wholly alien to earth.

The solid rock now gave place to the giant foundations of the monstrous castle, and it seemed that the speed of the party was somewhat abated. Vast walls shot up, and there was a glimpse of a great gate through which the voyagers were swept. All was night in the titan courtyard, and then came the deeper blackness of inmost things as a huge arched portal engulfed the column.

Vortices of cold wind surged dankly through sightless labyrinths of onyx, and Carter could never tell what Cyclopean stairs and corridors lay silent along the route of his endless aërial twisting. Always upward led the terrible plunge in darkness, and never a sound, touch, or glimpse broke the dense pall of mystery. Large as the army of ghouls and night-gaunts was, it was lost in the prodigious voids of that more than earthly castle. And when at last there suddenly dawned around him the lurid light of that single tower room whose lofty window had served as a beacon, it took Carter long to discern the far walls and high, distant ceiling, and to realise that he was indeed not again in the boundless air outside.

Randolph Carter had hoped to come into the throne-room of the Great Ones with poise and dignity, flanked and followed by impressive lines of ghouls in ceremonial order, and offering his prayer as a free and potent master among dreamers. He had known that the Great Ones themselves are not beyond a mortal's power to cope with, and had trusted to luck that the Other Gods and their crawling chaos Nyarlathotep would not happen to come to their aid at the crucial moment, as they had so often done before when men sought out earth's gods in their home or on their mountains. And with his hideous escort he had half hoped to defy even the Other Gods if need were, knowing as he did that ghouls have no masters, and that night-gaunts own not Nyarlathotep but only archaick Nodens for their lord. But now he saw that supernal Kadath in its cold waste is indeed girt with dark wonders and nameless sentinels, and that the Other Gods are of a surety vigilant in guarding the mild, feeble gods of earth. Void as they are of lordship over ghouls and night-gaunts, the mindless, shapeless blasphemies of outer space can yet control them when they must; so that it was not in state as a free and potent master of dreamers that Randolph Carter came into the Great Ones' throne-room with his ghouls. Swept and herded by nightmare tempests from the stars, and dogged by unseen horrors of the northern waste, all that army floated captive and helpless in the lurid light, dropping numbly to the onyx floor when by some voiceless order the winds of fright dissolved.

Before no golden dais had Randolph Carter come, nor was there any august circle of crowned and haloed beings with narrow

eyes, long-lobed ears, thin nose, and pointed chin whose kinship to the carven face on Ngranek might stamp them as those
to whom a dreamer might pray. Save for that one tower room
the onyx castle atop Kadath was dark, and the masters were not
there. Carter had come to unknown Kadath in the cold waste,
but he had not found the gods. Yet still the lurid light glowed
in that one tower room whose size was so little less than that
of all outdoors, and whose distant walls and roof were so nearly
lost to sight in thin, curling mists. Earth's gods were not there,
it was true, but of subtler and less visible presences there could
be no lack. Where the mild gods are absent, the Other Gods
are not unrepresented; and certainly, the onyx castle of castles
was far from tenantless. In what outrageous form or forms terror
would next reveal itself, Carter could by no means imagine. He
felt that his visit had been expected, and wondered how close a
watch had all along been kept upon him by the crawling chaos
Nyarlathotep. It is Nyarlathotep, horror of infinite shapes and
dread soul and messenger of the Other Gods, that the fungous
moonbeasts serve; and Carter thought of the black galley that
had vanished when the tide of battle turned against the toad-like
abnormalities on the jagged rock in the sea.

Reflecting upon these things, he was staggering to his feet in
the midst of his nightmare company when there rang without
warning through that pale-litten and limitless chamber the hideous blast of a daemon trumpet. Three times pealed that frightful brazen scream, and when the echoes of the third blast had
died chucklingly away Randolph Carter saw that he was alone.
Whither, why, and how the ghouls and night-gaunts had been
snatched from sight was not for him to divine. He knew only
that he was suddenly alone, and that whatever unseen powers
lurked mockingly around him were no powers of earth's friendly
dreamland. Presently from the chamber's uttermost reaches a new
sound came. This, too, was a rhythmic trumpeting; but of a kind
far removed from the three raucous blasts which had dissolved
his grisly cohorts. In this low fanfare echoed all the wonder and
melody of ethereal dream; exotic vistas of unimagined loveliness floating from each strange chord and subtly alien cadence.
Odours of incense came to match the golden notes; and overhead
a great light dawned, its colours changing in cycles unknown to

40. Peter Cannon points out the very similar figure of Eblis, the goal of the protagonist's search, at the conclusion of William Beckford's *Vathek, an Arabian Tale* (1786): "His person was that of a young man, whose noble and regular features seemed to have been tarnished by malignant vapours. . . . His flowing hair retained some resemblance to that of an angel of light" ("The Influence of *Vathek* on H. P. Lovecraft's *The Dream-Quest of Unknown Kadath*," in *H. P. Lovecraft: Four Decades of Criticism*, ed. S. T. Joshi [Athens: Ohio University Press, 1980], 156). Cannon finds a number of other similarities, and points out that HPL wrote to August Derleth in early December 1926 that *Vathek* was in his mind at the time of writing *The Dream-Quest of Unknown Kadath* (*Selected Letters, 1929–1931*, ed. August Derleth and Donald Wandrei [Sauk City, WI: Arkham House, 1969], 94; hereafter *Selected Letters*, III).

41. According to the *Oxford English Dictionary*, an obscure word meaning "a goatish desire" or "lustful."

earth's spectrum, and following the song of the trumpets in weird symphonic harmonies. Torches flared in the distance, and the beat of drums throbbed nearer amidst waves of tense expectancy.

Out of the thinning mists and the cloud of strange incense filed twin columns of giant black slaves with loin-cloths of iridescent silk. Upon their heads were strapped vast helmet-like torches of glittering metal, from which the fragrance of obscure balsams spread in fumous spirals. In their right hands were crystal wands whose tips were carven into leering chimaeras, while their left hands grasped long, thin silver trumpets which they blew in turn. Armlets and anklets of gold they had, and between each pair of anklets stretched a golden chain that held its wearer to a sober gait. That they were true black men of earth's dreamland was at once apparent, but it seemed less likely that their rites and costumes were wholly things of our earth. Ten feet from Carter the columns stopped, and as they did so each trumpet flew abruptly to its bearer's thick lips. Wild and ecstatic was the blast that followed, and wilder still the cry that chorused just after from dark throats somehow made shrill by strange artifice.

Then down the wide lane betwixt the two columns a lone figure strode; a tall, slim figure with the young face of an antique Pharaoh, gay with prismatic robes and crowned with a golden pshent that glowed with inherent light.[40] Close up to Carter strode that regal figure; whose proud carriage and swart features had in them the fascination of a dark god or fallen archangel, and around whose eyes there lurked the languid sparkle of caprious[41] humour. It spoke, and in its mellow tones there rippled the mild music of Lethean streams.

"Randolph Carter," said the voice, "you have come to see the Great Ones whom it is unlawful for men to see. Watchers have spoken of this thing, and the Other Gods have grunted as they rolled and tumbled mindlessly to the sound of thin flutes in the black ultimate void where broods the daemon-sultan whose name no lips dare speak aloud.

"When Barzai the Wise climbed Hatheg-Kla to see the Great Ones dance and howl above the clouds in the moonlight he never returned. The Other Gods were there, and they did what was expected. Zenig of Aphorat sought to reach unknown Kadath in the cold waste, and his skull is now set in a ring on the little finger of one whom I need not name.

"But you, Randolph Carter, have braved all things of earth's dreamland, and burn still with the flame of quest. You came not as one curious, but as one seeking his due, nor have you failed ever in reverence toward the mild gods of earth. Yet have these gods kept you from the marvellous sunset city of your dreams, and wholly through their own small covetousness; for verily, they craved the weird loveliness of that which your fancy had fashioned, and vowed that henceforward no other spot should be their abode.

"They are gone from their castle on unknown Kadath to dwell in your marvellous city. All through its palaces of veined marble they revel by day, and when the sun sets they go out in the perfumed gardens and watch the golden glory on temples and colonnades, arched bridges and silver-basined fountains, and wide streets with blossom-laden urns and ivory statues in gleaming rows. And when night comes they climb tall terraces in the dew, and sit on carved benches of porphyry scanning the stars, or lean over pale balustrades to gaze at the town's steep northward slopes, where one by one the little windows in old peaked gables shine softly out with the calm yellow light of homely candles.

"The gods love your marvellous city, and walk no more in the ways of the gods. They have forgotten the high places of earth, and the mountains that knew their youth. The earth has no longer any gods that are gods, and only the Other Ones from outer space hold sway on unremembered Kadath. Far away in a valley of your own childhood, Randolph Carter, play the heedless Great Ones. You have dreamed too well, O wise arch-dreamer, for you have drawn dream's gods away from the world of all men's visions to that which is wholly yours; having builded out of your boyhood's small fancies a city more lovely than all the phantoms that have gone before.

"It is not well that earth's gods leave their thrones for the spider to spin on, and their realm for the Others to sway in the dark manner of Others. Fain would the powers from outside bring chaos and horror to you, Randolph Carter, who are the cause of

42. Note that in the universe of *The Dream-Quest of Unknown Kadath*, Marblehead exists as a location separate from Kingsport; Marblehead is not mentioned in any other story.

43. HPL, ever dreaming of Rome and its civic values, would have treasured the claim that the city of Providence "built like Rome upon its seven hills, . . . is not excelled by any other city in the United States for residence and business purposes" (Society of Architectural Historians, 1895, quoted in Robert H. Waugh's *A Monster of Voices: Speaking for H. P. Lovecraft*, 267).

their upsetting, but that they know it is by you alone that the gods may be sent back to their world. In that half-waking dream-land which is yours, no power of uttermost night may pursue; and only you can send the selfish Great Ones gently out of your marvellous sunset city, back through the northern twilight to their wonted place atop unknown Kadath in the cold waste.

"So, Randolph Carter, in the name of the Other Gods I spare you and charge you to serve my will. I charge you to seek that sunset city which is yours, and to send thence the drowsy truant gods for whom the dream-world waits. Not hard to find is that roseal fever of the gods, that fanfare of supernal trumpets and clash of immortal cymbals, that mystery whose place and meaning have haunted you through the halls of waking and the gulfs of dreaming, and tormented you with hints of vanished memory and the pain of lost things awesome and momentous. Not hard to find is that symbol and relic of your days of wonder, for truly, it is but the stable and eternal gem wherein all that wonder sparkles crystallised to light your evening path. Behold! It is not over unknown seas but back over well-known years that your quest must go; back to the bright strange things of infancy and the quick sun-drenched glimpses of magic that old scenes brought to wide young eyes.

"For know you, that your gold and marble city of wonder is only the sum of what you have seen and loved in youth. It is the glory of Boston's hillside roofs and western windows aflame with sunset; of the flower-fragrant Common and the great dome on the hill and the tangle of gables and chimneys in the violet valley where the many-bridged Charles flows drowsily. These things you saw, Randolph Carter, when your nurse first wheeled you out in the springtime, and they will be the last things you will ever see with eyes of memory and of love. And there is antique Salem with its brooding years, and spectral Marblehead[42] scaling its rocky precipices into past centuries, and the glory of Salem's towers and spires seen afar from Marblehead's pastures across the harbour against the setting sun.

"There is Providence, quaint and lordly on its seven hills over the blue harbour,[43] with terraces of green leading up to steeples and citadels of living antiquity, and Newport climbing wraith-like from its dreaming breakwater. Arkham is there, with its moss-grown gambrel roofs and the rocky rolling meadows behind it; and antediluvian Kingsport hoary with stacked chimneys and deserted quays and overhanging gables, and the marvel of high cliffs and the milky-misted ocean with tolling buoys beyond.

Portsmouth Harbor, 1917.

"Cool vales in Concord, cobbled lanes in Portsmouth, twilight bends of rustic New-Hampshire roads where giant elms half hide white farmhouse walls and creaking well-sweeps. Gloucester's salt wharves and Truro's windy willows. Vistas of distant steepled towns and hills beyond hills along the North Shore, hushed stony slopes and low ivied cottages in the lee of huge boulders in Rhode-Island's back country. Scent of the sea and fragrance of the fields; spell of the dark woods and joy of the orchards and gardens at dawn. These, Randolph Carter, are your city; for they are yourself. New-England bore you, and into your soul she poured a liquid loveliness which cannot die. This loveliness, moulded, crystallised, and polished by years of memory and dreaming, is your terraced wonder of elusive sunsets; and to find that marble parapet with curious urns and carven rail, and descend at last those endless balustraded steps to the city of broad squares and prismatic fountains, you need only to turn back to the thoughts and visions of your wistful boyhood.

"Look! through that window shine the stars of eternal night. Even now they are shining above the scenes you have known and cherished, drinking of their charm that they may shine more lovely over the gardens of dream. There is Antares[44]—he is winking at this moment over the roofs of Tremont Street,[45] and you could see him from your window on Beacon Hill. Out beyond those stars yawn the gulfs from whence my mindless masters have sent me. Some day you too may traverse them, but if you are wise you will beware such folly; for of those mortals who have been and returned, only one preserves a mind unshattered by the pounding, clawing horrors of the void. Terrors and blasphemies gnaw at one another for space, and there is more evil in the lesser ones than in the greater; even as you know from the

44. The alpha component for the *brightest* star in the constellation Scorpio, the Scorpion, the name signifying, according to *Allen*, the rival of or equivalent of Mars (likely because of the color resemblance).

45. A major thoroughfare in Boston, the eastern edge of Boston Common. HPL's parents were married at St. Paul's Episcopal Church on Tremont Street in 1889. The "three mountains" for which the street is named are Beacon Hill; Cotton Hill, now Pemberton Square; and Mount Whoredom (see Tony Horwitz, "The True Story of the Battle of Bunker Hill," *Smithsonian*, May 2013, and David McCullough, *1776* [New York: Simon & Schuster, 2005]; McCullough refers to Mount Whoredom as Boston's red-light district, 27). The name Mount Whoredom is said to have been

Tremont Street, Boston, 1923.

bestowed by British cartographers— a reference to a hill frequented in the mid-eighteenth century by soldiers near Woolwich, outside London. It became Mount Vernon after the Revolution. Most of Boston's hills have been erased by progress; see Rebecca Beatrice Brooks, "History of the Boston Landfill Project: How Boston Lost Its Hills," August 2, 2011, History of Massachusetts Blog, http://historyofmassachusetts .org/how-boston-lost-its-hills/.

46. See *The Case of Charles Dexter Ward*, in the previous volume, pp. 171–309, note 117.

deeds of those who sought to deliver you into my hands, whilst I myself harboured no wish to shatter you, and would indeed have helped you hither long ago had I not been elsewhere busy, and certain that you would yourself find the way. Shun, then, the outer hells, and stick to the calm, lovely things of your youth. Seek out your marvellous city and drive thence the recreant Great Ones, sending them back gently to those scenes which are of their own youth, and which wait uneasy for their return.

"Easier even than the way of dim memory is the way I will prepare for you. See! There comes hither a monstrous shantak, led by a slave who for your peace of mind had best keep invisible. Mount and be ready—there! Yogash the black will help you on the scaly horror. Steer for that brightest star just south of the zenith—it is Vega,[46] and in two hours will be just above the terrace of your sunset city. Steer for it only till you hear a far-off singing in the high aether. Higher than that lurks madness, so rein your shantak when the first note lures. Look then back to earth, and you will see shining the deathless altar-flame of Ired-Naa from the sacred roof of a temple. That temple is in your desiderate sunset city, so steer for it before you heed the singing and are lost.

"When you draw nigh the city steer for the same high parapet whence of old you scanned the outspread glory, prodding the shantak till he cry aloud. That cry the Great Ones will hear and know as they sit on their perfumed terraces, and there will come upon them such a homesickness that all of your city's wonders will not console them for the absence of Kadath's grim castle and the pshent of eternal stars that crowns it.

"Then must you land amongst them with the shantak, and let them see and touch that noisome and hippocephalic bird; meanwhile discoursing to them of unknown Kadath, which you will so lately have left, and telling them how its boundless halls are lonely and unlighted, where of old they used to leap and revel in supernal radiance. And the shantak will talk to them in the manner of shantaks, but it will have no powers of persuasion beyond the recalling of elder days.

"Over and over must you speak to the wandering Great Ones of their home and youth, till at last they will weep and ask to be shewn the returning path they have forgotten. Thereat can you loose the waiting shantak, sending him skyward with the homing cry of his kind; hearing which the Great Ones will prance and jump with antique mirth, and forthwith stride after the loathly bird in the fashion of gods, through the deep gulfs of heaven to Kadath's familiar towers and domes.

"Then will the marvellous sunset city be yours to cherish and inhabit forever, and once more will earth's gods rule the dreams of men from their accustomed seat. Go now—the casement is open and the stars await outside. Already your shantak wheezes and titters with impatience. Steer for Vega through the night, but turn when the singing sounds. Forget not this warning, lest horrors unthinkable suck you into the gulf of shrieking and ululant madness. Remember the Other Gods; they are great and mindless and terrible, and lurk in the outer voids. They are good gods to shun.

"*Hei! Aa-shanta 'nygh!* You are off! Send back earth's gods to their haunts on unknown Kadath, and pray to all space that you may never meet me in my thousand other forms. Farewell, Randolph Carter, and beware; *for I am Nyarlathotep, the Crawling Chaos!*"

And Randolph Carter, gasping and dizzy on his hideous shantak, shot screamingly into space toward the cold blue glare of boreal Vega; looking but once behind him at the clustered and chaotic turrets of the onyx nightmare wherein still glowed the lone lurid light of that window above the air and the clouds of earth's dreamland. Great polypous horrors slid darkly past, and unseen bat-wings beat multitudinous around him, but still he clung to the unwholesome mane of that loathly and hippocephalic scaled bird. The stars danced mockingly, almost shifting now and then to form pale signs of doom that one might wonder one had not seen and feared before; and ever the winds of aether howled of vague blackness and loneliness beyond the cosmos.

Then through the glittering vault ahead there fell a hush of portent, and all the winds and horrors slunk away as night things slink away before the dawn. Trembling in waves that golden wisps of nebula made weirdly visible, there rose a timid hint of far-off melody, droning in faint chords that our own universe of stars knows not. And as that music grew, the shantak raised its ears and plunged ahead, and Carter likewise bent to catch each lovely strain. It was a song, but not the song of any voice. Night and the spheres sang it, and it was old when space and Nyarlathotep and the Other Gods were born.

Faster flew the shantak, and lower bent the rider, drunk with the marvels of strange gulfs, and whirling in the crystal coils of outer magic. Then came too late the warning of the evil one, the sardonic caution of the daemon legate who had bidden the seeker beware the madness of that song. Only to taunt had Nyarlathotep marked out the way to safety and the marvellous sunset city; only to mock had that black messenger revealed the secret of those truant gods whose steps he could so easily lead back at will. For madness and the void's wild vengeance are Nyarlathotep's only gifts to the presumptuous; and frantick though the rider strove to turn his disgusting steed, that leering, tittering shantak coursed on impetuous and relentless, flapping its great slippery wings in malignant joy, and headed for those unhallowed pits whither no dreams reach; that last amorphous blight of nethermost confusion where bubbles and blasphemes at infinity's centre the mindless daemon-sultan Azathoth, whose name no lips dare speak aloud.

Unswerving and obedient to the foul legate's orders, that hellish bird plunged onward through shoals of shapeless lurkers and caperers in darkness, and vacuous herds of drifting entities that pawed and groped and groped and pawed; the nameless larvae of the Other Gods, that are like them blind and without mind, and possessed of singular hungers and thirsts.

Onward unswerving and relentless, and tittering hilariously to watch the chuckling and hysterics into which the siren song of night and the spheres had turned, that eldritch scaly monster bore its helpless rider; hurtling and shooting, cleaving the uttermost rim and spanning the outermost abysses; leaving behind the stars and the realms of matter, and darting meteor-like through stark formlessness toward those inconceivable, unlighted chambers beyond Time wherein black Azathoth gnaws shapeless and ravenous amidst the muffled, maddening beat of vile drums and the thin, monotonous whine of accursed flutes.

Onward—onward—through the screaming, cackling, and blackly populous gulfs—and then from some dim blessed distance there came an image and a thought to Randolph Carter the doomed. Too well had Nyarlathotep planned his mocking and his tantalising, for he had brought up that which no gusts of icy terror could quite efface. Home—New England—Beacon Hill—the waking world.

"For know you, that your gold and marble city of wonder is only the sum of what you have seen and loved in youth . . . the glory of Boston's hillside roofs and western windows aflame with sunset; of the flower-fragrant Common and the great dome on the hill and the tangle of gables and chimneys in the violet valley where the many-bridged Charles flows drowsily . . . this loveliness, moulded, crystallised, and polished by years of memory and dreaming, is your terraced wonder of elusive sunsets; and to find that marble parapet with curious urns and carven rail, and descend at last those endless balustraded steps to the city of broad squares and prismatic fountains, you need only to turn back to the thoughts and visions of your wistful boyhood."

Onward—onward—dizzily onward to ultimate doom through the blackness where sightless feelers pawed and slimy snouts jostled and nameless things tittered and tittered and tittered. But the image and the thought had come, and Randolph Carter knew clearly that he was dreaming and only dreaming, and that somewhere in the background the world of waking and the city of his infancy still lay. Words came again—"You need only turn back to the thoughts and visions of your wistful boyhood." Turn—turn—blackness on every side, but Randolph Carter could turn.

Thick though the rushing nightmare that clutched his senses, Randolph Carter could turn and move. He could move, and if he chose he could leap off the evil shantak that bore him hurtlingly doomward at the orders of Nyarlathotep. He could leap off and dare those depths of night that yawned interminably down, those depths of fear whose terrors yet could not exceed the nameless doom that lurked waiting at chaos' core. He could turn and move and leap—he could—he would—he would—

Off that vast hippocephalic abomination leaped the doomed and desperate dreamer, and down through endless voids of sentient blackness he fell. Aeons reeled, universes died and were born again, stars became nebulae and nebulae became stars, and still Randolph Carter fell through those endless voids of sentient blackness.

Then in the slow creeping course of eternity the utmost cycle of the cosmos churned itself into another futile completion, and

47. A "kalpa" is a cycle of history in Hindu mythology—traditionally, a day of Brahma, 4.3 billion years long.

all things became again as they were unreckoned kalpas[47] before. Matter and light were born anew as space once had known them; and comets, suns, and worlds sprang flaming into life, though nothing survived to tell that they had been and gone, been and gone, always and always, back to no first beginning.

And there was a firmament again, and a wind, and a glare of purple light in the eyes of the falling dreamer. There were gods and presences and wills; beauty and evil, and the shrieking of noxious night robbed of its prey. For through the unknown ultimate cycle had lived a thought and a vision of a dreamer's boyhood, and now there were re-made a waking world and an old cherished city to body and to justify these things. Out of the void S'ngac the violet gas had pointed the way, and archaic Nodens was bellowing his guidance from unhinted deeps.

Stars swelled to dawns, and dawns burst into fountains of gold, carmine, and purple, and still the dreamer fell. Cries rent the aether as ribbons of light beat back the fiends from outside. And hoary Nodens raised a howl of triumph when Nyarlathotep, close on his quarry, stopped baffled by a glare that seared his formless hunting-horrors to grey dust. Randolph Carter had indeed descended at last the wide marmoreal flights to his marvellous city, for he was come again to the fair New England world that had wrought him.

So to the organ chords of morning's myriad whistles, and dawn's blaze thrown dazzling through purple panes by the great gold dome of the State House on the hill, Randolph Carter leaped shoutingly awake within his Boston room. Birds sang in hidden gardens and the perfume of trellised vines came wistful from arbours his grandfather had reared. Beauty and light glowed from classic mantel and carven cornice and walls grotesquely figured, while a sleek black cat rose yawning from hearthside sleep that his master's start and shriek had disturbed. And vast infinities away, past the Gate of Deeper Slumber and the enchanted wood and the garden lands and the Cerenerian Sea and the twilight reaches of Inganok, the crawling chaos Nyarlathotep strode brooding into the onyx castle atop unknown Kadath in the cold waste, and taunted insolently the mild gods of earth whom he had snatched abruptly from their scented revels in the marvellous sunset city.

Appendix 1

OUTLINE OF THE LIFE AND CAREER OF
HOWARD PHILLIPS LOVECRAFT[1]

1890   Born in Providence, Rhode Island, the only child of Winfield Scott and Sarah Susan Phillips Lovecraft.

1893   HPL's father is committed to Butler Hospital in Providence.

1898   HPL's father dies in Butler Hospital. HPL lives with his mother's family, attends public schools.

1904   HPL's maternal grandfather, with whom he and his mother lived, dies; HPL and his mother move to apartment as finances decline.

1906   Begins astronomy column for *Pawtuxet Valley Gleaner*.

1908   Has nervous breakdown, drops out of high school.

1912   Publishes verse in *Providence Evening Bulletin*.

1914   Joins United Amateur Press Association.

1917   Volunteers for Rhode Island National Guard but is rejected after his mother intervenes. Writes "The Tomb" and "Dagon."

1919   Mother institutionalized at Butler Hospital. Hears Lord Dunsany lecture.

1920   Begins correspondence with the nineteen-year-old Frank Belknap Long, later a prolific horror writer on his own.

1921   Mother dies. Meets Sonia Greene at amateur press convention in Boston. Writes "The Outsider" and "The Music of Erich Zann."

1922   Visits New York City, Marblehead. Begins correspondence with pulp writer/artist Clark Ashton Smith.

1923   First stories sold to *Weird Tales* ("Dagon," "Arthur Jermyn," "Cats of Ulthar," "The Hound," and "Statement of Randolph Carter," in a single sale).

1924   Marries Sonia Greene, moves to New York City; turns down editorship of *Weird Tales*.

---

1. Based on Peter Cannon's *H. P. Lovecraft*.

1925   Sonia moves to Cincinnati to run her business, leaving Lovecraft in a boardinghouse in the Red Hook area of Brooklyn. Writes "The Horror at Red Hook," "He."

1926   Moves back to Providence, sharing a residence at 10–12 Barnes Street with aunt Lillian D. Clark. Commences correspondence with August Derleth. Writes "Cool Air," "The Call of Cthulhu," "The Silver Key," "Pickman's Model."

1927   Finishes *The Dream-Quest of Unknown Kadath*; writes *The Case of Charles Dexter Ward* and "The Colour Out of Space."

1928   Briefly reunited with Sonia in New York City but they do not reside together. Travels through Vermont and Massachusetts.

1929   Divorces Sonia, though final papers not filed.

1930   Begins correspondence with Robert E. Howard.

1931   Travels to Florida. Writes *At the Mountains of Madness*, "The Shadow over Innsmouth."

1932   Lillian D. Clark dies. Writes "The Dreams in the Witch House."

1933   Moves in with aunt Annie E. P. Gamwell. Writes "The Thing on the Doorstep."

1934–35 Extended stays in Florida. Writes "The Shadow Out of Time," "The Haunter of the Dark."

1936   Begins experiencing severe stomach pains. "The Shadow over Innsmouth" is published in book form by a small press.

1937   Dies March 15 in Providence of cancer of the intestine.

        Derleth and Donald Wandrei begin to assemble materials for an anthology of Lovecraft's fiction.

1939   Derleth and Wandrei form Arkham House, publish *The Outsider and Others*.

1943   Arkham House publishes a second Lovecraft collection, *Beyond the Wall of Sleep*.

Appendix 2

THE FICTION OF H. P. LOVECRAFT,
IN ORDER OF WRITING[1]

TITLE	DATE WRITTEN (OR COMPLETED)	DATE FIRST PUBLISHED
"The Little Glass Bottle"	ca. 1897	1959
"The Mystery of the Grave-Yard"	ca. 1898	1959
"The Secret Cave"	ca. 1898	1959
"The Beast in the Cave"	April 21, 1905	June 1918
"The Alchemist"	1908	November 1916
"The Tomb"	June 1917	March 1922
"Dagon"	July 1917	November 1919
"A Reminiscence of Dr. Samuel Johnson"	Summer or Fall 1917 (?)	November 1917
"Polaris"	May (?) 1918	December 1920
"Memory"	1919 (?)	June 1919
"Beyond the Wall of Sleep"	April–May 1919	October 1919
"Old Bugs"	Summer 1919	1959
"The Transition of Juan Romero"	September 16, 1919	1944
"The White Ship"	November 1919	November 1919
"The Doom That Came to Sarnath"	December 3, 1919	June 1920

1. Based on *H. P. Lovecraft: A Comprehensive Bibliography*, by S. T. Joshi. The list omits fiction that Lovecraft wrote in collaboration with other authors, known as the "revisions." No definitive study has yet been made of the extent of Lovecraft's efforts on these works, and while some may be seen as almost wholly his writing, he may have only given minimal editorial assistance with others.

TITLE	DATE WRITTEN (OR COMPLETED)	DATE FIRST PUBLISHED
"The Statement of Randolph Carter"	December 1919	May 1920
"The Street"	Late 1919	December 1920
"The Terrible Old Man"	January 28, 1920	July 1921
"The Tree"	January–June 1920	October 1921
"The Cats of Ulthar"	June 15, 1920	November 1920
"Facts concerning the Late Arthur Jermyn and His Family"	June–November 1920	March, June 1921
"The Temple"	June–November 1920	September 1925
"Celephaïs"	November 1920	May 1922
"From Beyond"	November 16, 1920	June 1934
"Ex Oblivione"	Probably 1920 or 1921	March 1921
"Nyarlathotep"	December 1920	January 1921
"The Picture in the House"	December 12, 1920	July 1919
"The Nameless City"	January 1921	November 1921
"The Quest of Iranon"	February 28, 1921	July–August 1935
"The Moon-Bog"	March 1921	June 1926
"The Outsider"	March–August 1921	April 1926
"The Other Gods"	August 14, 1921	November 1933
"The Music of Erich Zann"	December 1921 (?)	March 1922
"The Mysterious Ship"	December 1921	1959
"Hypnos"	March 1922	May 1923
"Herbert West—Reanimator"	September 1921–mid-1922	February–March, April, May, June, & July 1922
"Azathoth" (fragment)	June 1922	1938
"What the Moon Brings"	June 5, 1922	May 1923
"The Unnamable"	September 1922	July 1925
"The Hound"	September–October 1922	February 1924
"The Lurking Fear"	November 1922	January, February, March, & April 1923

TITLE	DATE WRITTEN (OR COMPLETED)	DATE FIRST PUBLISHED
"The Rats in the Walls"	August–September 1923	March 1924
"The Festival"	Late 1923	January 1925
"Under the Pyramids"	February–March 1924	May, June, & July 1924
"The Shunned House"	October 1924	1928
"The Horror at Red Hook"	August 1–2, 1925	January 1927
"He"	August 11, 1925	September 1926
"Cool Air"	February 1926 (?)	March 1928
"In the Vault"	September 18, 1925	November 1925
"The Call of Cthulhu"	Summer 1926	February 1928
"The Silver Key"	Fall 1926	January 1929
"The Strange High House in the Mist"	November 9, 1926	October 1931
"Pickman's Model"	Late 1926	October 1927
The Dream-Quest of Unknown Kadath	Autumn 1926 (?)–January 1, 1927	1943
"The Descendants" (fragment)	Early 1927	1938
The Case of Charles Dexter Ward	January–March 1, 1927	May, July 1941
"The Colour Out of Space"	March 1927	September 1927
"History of the *Necronomicon*"	Late 1927	November 1937
"Ibid"	1928 (?)	January 1938
"The Dunwich Horror"	Summer 1928	April 1929
"The Whisperer in Darkness"	February 24–September 26, 1930	August 1931
At the Mountains of Madness	January to March 22, 1931	February 1936
"The Shadow over Innsmouth"	November–December 3, 1931	1936
"The Dreams in the Witch House"	January–February 28, 1932	July 1933
"The Thing on the Doorstep"	August 21–24, 1933	January 1937
"The Evil Clergyman" (dream account)	Before October 22, 1933	April 1939
"The Book" (fragment)	Late 1933 (?)	1938
"The Shadow Out of Time"	November 1934–February 1935	June 1936

TITLE	DATE WRITTEN (OR COMPLETED)	DATE FIRST PUBLISHED
"The Haunter of the Dark"	November 1935	December 1936
"Sweet Ermengarde; or, The Heart of a Country Girl"	Unknown (1919–25)	1943
"Of Evill Sorceries Done in New-England, of Daemons in No Humane Shape" (fragment)	Unknown	1945

Appendix 3

THE "RED HOOK" INCANTATION

Gerry de la Ree, the publisher of *The Occult Lovecraft* (Saddle River, NJ: 1975), includes in that pamphlet the following material purportedly written by HPL "from [de la Ree's] personal collection." S. T. Joshi speculates that the material is from a letter from HPL to Wilfred B. Talman but has been unable to verify that source. HPL reportedly wrote:

"About that incantation from 'Red Hook'—it is actually a relic of ancient rituals, and is mentioned in more than one history of magic, so that I can hardly sign it in such a way as to indicate authorship. I don't wonder that a Latin teacher was stumped by that Hebraised-Hellenistic incantation, for it is a piece of late-ancient or mediæval illiteracy which probably has no straightforward or syntactical sense anyway! E. B. Taylor [*sic*], the well-known anthropologist, calls it 'an illustration of magical scholarship in its lowest stage.'[1] When I wrote 'Red Hook' in 1925 I thought this formula was Alexandrian in origin, but later reading makes me inclined to place it in the Middle Ages. It was first used, no doubt, by Jewish Cabalists, and later adopted by European magicians generally. I am no scholar—knowing sadly little Greek and no Hebrew at all—hence can't pretend to give a real translation. I merely took it as I found it in a history of magic (where there was no attempt to translate either this or any other formula) and tried to get as good a notion as I could of the principle words—recalling my meagre and long-ago Greek course and relying on Dr. William Smith's Bible dictionary for Hebraic lore. The result was something like this:

---

1. As noted above, HPL copied the incantation from the article on "Magic" in the *Encyclopaedia Britannica* (9th ed.), written by Edward Burnett Tylor, LLD., DCL, FRS, Keeper of the University Museum, Oxford. Tylor ascribes it to "an early Christian writer." Armen Alexanyan, in "Some Philological Observations on 'The Horror at Red Hook,'" *Lovecraft Annual* 17 (2017), 37–40, identifies this author as the third-century CE theologian Hippolytus of Rome (37).

'O Lord God Deliverer; Lord-Messenger of Hosts; Thou-art-a-mighty god-forever; Magically fourfold assemblage; And anointed one, together and in succession!'

"But I don't fancy this is accurate; for as I have said, I am no savant and the incantation is a decadent ungrammatical and misspelled piece of crudeness which would baffle even the wisest. The magazine version,[2] I believe, is misprinted slightly, but here is the correct reading:

HEL * HELOYM * SOTHER * EMMANUEL * SABAOTH * AGLA
* TETRAGRAMMATON * AGYROS * THOES * ISCHYROS
* ATHANATOS * JEHOVA * VA * ADDONAI * SADAY *
HOMOVSION * MESSIAS * ESCHEREHEYE *

"Taking the words one by one:

"*Hel* is clearly the Hebrew *el*, meaning Lord or Deity. Illiterate translations always take liberties with aspirates.

"*Heloym*, by the same token, is *Elohim*, the Hebrew word for deity in its less tribal and more generalized sense.

"*Sother* is simply bad Greek for *Soter*, meaning *Deliverer*.

"*Emmanuel* is Hebrew for God-with-us, usually applied to the prophesied future incarnation of deity in the Old Testament, whose fulfillment Christ is assumed to be.

"*Sabaoth* is an Hellenised form of the Hebrew *Tsebaoth*, meaning hosts found in the scriptures in the *Lord God of Hosts*. It was a favourite word with mediæval occultists and with them probably came to signify *hosts* or *armies* of elimental spirits. I have often wondered if this, rather than *Sabbath* (day of rest)[,] is not really the parent-word for the term *sabbat* (*Witches Sabbath*) applied to the hideous secret orgies of the witch-cult followers. Surely a word signifying *throngs* is much more appropriate for the obscene convocations of May-Eve and Halloween than is a word signifying a weekly *rest period*.

"*Agla* is a frequent word among occultists, being often engraved on the wands and

---

2. HPL means the January 1927 issue of *Weird Tales*, which used "EMMANVEL" and "OTHEOS" and "ADONAL * SADY." Most editions, including those edited by S. T. Joshi, use the words "OTHEOS" and "ADONAI" and use the Greek spelling of "EMMANVEL."

knives of magicians. It is formed of the first letters of the Hebrew words composing the sentence 'Thou art a mighty god forever.'[3]

"*Tetragrammaton* is a Greek term of magical configuration identified with a certain cabalistic diagram (fig. 1).[4] It represents a mystical symbolization of the four elements—air, water, earth, and fire, and is used for evoking their elemental spirits—respectively, the sylphs, undines, gnomes, and salamanders. There are four generally recognized magical diagrams which recur repeatedly in occult rites. The other three are the triangle (equilateral—fig. 2), sign of the Trinity or mystical threefoldness of things; the double triangle or Sign of Solomon (fig. 3), representing the Macrocosm or Entire Universe; and the all-potent pentagram (fig. 4), or five-pointed star, which represents the star of Bethlehem and is the greatest of all conjuring forces.[5] With one point up, the

3. AGLA (אגלא) is an acronym for *Atah Gibor Le-olam Adonai*, which means, as HPL states, "Thou, oh Lord, are mighty forever." The acronym is found in many kabbalist texts and is here incorporated in a German monograph at the center of the word "GOTT" ("God") in *Der Spiegel der Kunst und Natur*, plate 1, by Stephan Michelspacher (Augsburg, 1615).

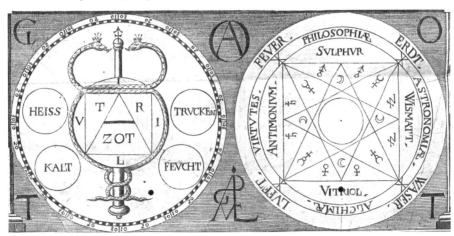

4. HPL may be correct, but more importantly, the word—from the Greek Τετραγράμματον, meaning "(consisting) of four letters"—is used to denote the four-letter name of God, יהוה, Yahweh or, mistranslated, Jehova. Thus in context here, it is simply another invocation of God by name. The diagrams HPL refers to were probably those first printed in the eighteenth century CE and included the English word "Tetragrammaton," spelled out as such.

5. Pythagoras suggested the star or pentagram signified the five elements that made up man (Earth, Wind, Fire, Water, and Spirit), and the star was drawn to coincide with the head, two arms, and two legs of a man: Renaissance ritual magicians borrowed the symbol to represent a human being. Eliphas Lévi (1810–1875), whose birth name was Alphonse Louis Constant and whose pen name was, in his mind, a Hebrew translation of the first two of those names, wrote:

Pentagram is the sign of Christ and an aid to White Magic. With two points up it is the Sign of Satan and the Black Magicians' ally. But this is a digression.

Figure 1.

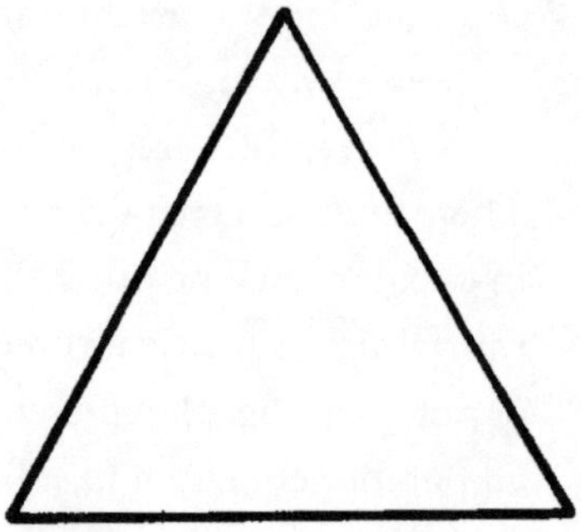

Figure 2.

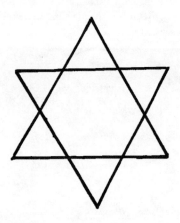

Figure 3.

Figure 4.

The pentagram expresses the mind's domination over the elements, and it is by this sign that we bind the demons of the air, the spirits of fire, the specters of water, and the ghosts of earth. It is the star of the Magi, the burning star of the Gnostic schools, the sign of intellectual omnipotence and autocracy.

Its complete comprehension is the key of two worlds—it is absolute natural philosophy and natural science. Its use, however, is most dangerous to operators who do not completely and perfectly understand it . . .

All mysteries of magic, all symbols of the gnosis, all figures of occultism, all kabbalistic keys of prophecy, are resumed in the sign of the pentagram; which Paracelsus proclaims to be the greatest and most potent of all. It is indeed the sign of the absolute and universal synthesis. (*Mysteries of Magic*, trans. A. E. Waite, 1886, 189–91)

"*Agyros* is probably a misspelling of the Greek *agris*—an *assembly*.[6]

"*Othoes* is probably an even worse misspelling of the Greek *Othneios*, meaning *Strange*.

"*Ischyros* is good Greek meaning *mighty*.

"*Athanatos* is also good Greek and means *immortal*.

"*Jehova* is the common modern pronunciation of the Hebrew *Yahweh* meaning the supreme and awe-inspiring tribal god whose name was too terrible to be pronounced save by a high priest once a year.

"*Va?* I give up. Can't make head nor tail of it![7]

"*Adonai* is the Hebrew alternative word for *Yahweh*—used commonly because the familiar use of the real god-name was forbidden.

"*Saday* is another term beyond me, although I have seen it repeatedly in the many ancient formulæ which I have copied from different sources as colour-touches for future tales.[8]

"*Homovsion* is probably a decadent variant or compound involving the Greek *Homov*—together.[9]

"*Messias* is the Hebrew *anointed*, and under the more common form *Messiah* is a frequent term for Christ.

---

6. Or a misspelling of ἀγοραῖς (agorais), meaning "in the marketplaces" or "in the public streets."

7. "Va" is a Hebrew prefix indicating past tense, as in "Jehova, previously known as Adonai." Armen Alexanyan, in "Some Philological Observations on 'The Horror at Red Hook,'" states that "VA" is "a common Semitic conjunction word meaning 'and'" (40).

8. *The Exhaustive Concordance of the Bible: Showing Every Word of the Text of the Common English Version of the Canonical Books, and Every Occurrence of Each Word in Regular Order: Together with a Comparative Concordance of the Authorized and Revised Versions, Including the American Variations; Also Brief Dictionaries of the Hebrew and Greek Words of the Original, with References to the English Words* (1890) by James Strong (known as *Strong's Concordance*) defines the Hebrew word "*saday*" as meaning "land" or "field." The anonymous blogger Dr. Chris Heard, who blogged under the name Icosahedrophilia (now offline) disputed this: "*Saday*, however, is no mystery at all to a Hebraist; it undoubtedly reflects the Hebrew word "*shaddai*," usually translated 'almighty' in modern English Bibles, as in the compound divine name *El Shaddai* or 'God Almighty.'"

9. According to the *Catholic Encyclopedia*, "*homoousion*" is a Greek word from *homos*, same, and *ousia*, essence, expressing the divinity of Jesus, the doctrine that the Son is of the same substance as the Divinity.

"*Eschereheye* stumps me again—it being only a guess of mine that the barbaric word involves the Greek meaning *in a line* or *in a row*.[10]

"And that is all I can make of the thing! However, it looks just as impressive in a story as if it meant something in particular—which no doubt it did to the naïve wizards and Cabalists of the Dark Ages."

---

10. Dr. Chris Heard, who blogged anonymously at Icosahedrophilia (see above, note 8), writes, "Lovecraft went astray on ESCHEREHEYE by seeking a Greek precursor, when Hebrew holds the real key. In a famous scene in the Hebrew Bible, Moses asks for God's name, and God responds, 'I am what I am.' Quite apart from the images of Popeye that always intrude when I hear this statement, the Hebrew phrase is pronounced *ehyeh asher ehyeh*. ESCHEREHEYE in Lovecraft's incantation seems pretty clearly to derive from the last two words of this phrase, run together, and if translated into English would mean 'what I am' (or 'what I AM' if you're trying to be pious)." Thus the phrase is, in the view of Armen Alexanyan, "a variant of Tetragrammaton that is used in some cabbalistic practices concerning the use of God's name" ("Some Philological Observations on 'The Horror at Red Hook,'" 40).

Appendix 4

A COMPLEAT LOVECRAFT GAZETTEER

PLACE-NAME[1]	DESCRIPTION	SOURCE
1761 Colony House, Providence, Rhode Island	On Charles Dexter Ward's regular walking route	*The Case of Charles Dexter Ward*
1773 Market House, Market Square, South Main Street, Providence, Rhode Island	On Charles Dexter Ward's regular walking route	*The Case of Charles Dexter Ward*
Abu Roash, Egypt	A site of pyramids near Gizeh	"Under the Pyramids"
Adams Street, Innsmouth, Massachusetts	Mentioned	"The Shadow over Innsmouth"
Adare, Antarctica	Mentioned	*At the Mountains of Madness*
Adirondack Mountains, New York	Site of small village sought by Charles Dexter Ward	*The Case of Charles Dexter Ward*
Admiralty Range, Antarctica	Mentioned	*At the Mountains of Madness*
Africa	Mentioned	"The Cats of Ulthar," "Facts concerning the Late Arthur Jermyn and His Family"
Ai	A river in Mnar	"The Doom That Came to Sarnath," "The Quest of Iranon"
Aira	A fair city, perhaps imaginary	"The Quest of Iranon"
Aix, France	To where the remains of Ibid where removed	"Ibid"
Akurion	A rock in the lake between Sarnath and Ib	"The Doom That Came to Sarnath"

1. The table does not list every appearance of the place-names Egypt, England, New England, New York, Arkham, Providence, and Boston, or of the Miskatonic River or Miskatonic University, which are too numerous to include. However, it does include all of HPL's stories, including those that do not appear in either volume of *The New Annotated H. P. Lovecraft.*

PLACE-NAME	DESCRIPTION	SOURCE
Albany, New York	Alienists from Albany examined Joe Slater; home of friend of Jan Martense; residence of Petrus van Schaack	"Beyond the Wall of Sleep," "The Lurking Fear," "Ibid"
Alexandria, Egypt	Where the Australia boat would depart from	"Under the Pyramids"
Alsace region, France	Home of a crewman on the U-29	"The Temple"
Amasa Field, Providence, Rhode Island	Hole dug there	*The Case of Charles Dexter Ward*
America	Purported birthplace of the narrator	"A Reminiscence of Dr. Samuel Johnson"
American Cosmograph Theatre, Cairo, Egypt	Houdini played there	"Under the Pyramids"
Anchester, England	Near Exham Priory	"The Rats in the Walls"
Angell Street, Providence, Rhode Island	Archer Harris built a home there	"The Shunned House"
Antarctic Circle, Antarctica	Mentioned	*At the Mountains of Madness*
Antarctic Range, Antarctica	Mentioned	*At the Mountains of Madness*
Antarctica	Mentioned as a temporary home of the Shining Trapezohedron	"The Haunter of the Dark"
Aphorat	Home of Zenig, another seeker	*The Dream-Quest of Unknown Kadath*
Appleton, Wisconsin	Home of Trever family	"Old Bugs"
Arabia (Araby)	Location of the "nameless city"; source of prehistoric books and clay tablets read by Randolph Carter	"The Nameless City," "The Silver Key"
Arabiscus, Cappodocia	Home of Maurice	"Ibid"
Aran, Mount	Near Celephaïs	"Celephaïs," *The Dream-Quest of Unknown Kadath*
Arcturus, red worlds of	Potential residence of interstellar traveler occupying Joe Slater	"Beyond the Wall of Sleep"
Arizona deserts, United States	Mentioned	*At the Mountains of Madness*
Arkham	Mentioned (first mention anywhere)	"The Picture in the House"
Arkham Sanitarium, Arkham, Massachusetts	Edward Derby was shot there	"Dreams in the Witch House"

PLACE-NAME	DESCRIPTION	SOURCE
Art Club, Boston, Massachusetts	Formerly frequented by Thurber	"Pickman's Model"
Asbury M. E. Church, Arkham, Massachusetts	Home parish of youthful grocery worker	"The Shadow over Innsmouth"
Asia	Mentioned as stripped by Constantine	*At the Mountains of Madness*
Asia, forgotten cities in	Mentioned	"The Picture in the House"
Asia, Prehistoric	Potential residence of interstellar traveler occupying Joe Slater	"Beyond the Wall of Sleep"
Athenaeum, Providence, Rhode Island	Narrator of "The Shunned House" walked by there; frequented by Charles Dexter Ward	"The Shunned House," *The Case of Charles Dexter Ward*
Athens, Greece	Where Musides's Pallas stood	"The Tree," "Ibid"
Athol, Massachusetts	On the route to Greenfield	"The Whisperer in Darkness"
Atlantic Avenue, Brooklyn, New York	Mentioned	"The Horror at Red Hook"
Atlantic City, New Jersey	To where Mrs. Ward retired	*The Case of Charles Dexter Ward*
Atlantis	With which the Lieutenant-Commander identifies the underwater city; mentioned in other stories	"The Temple," "The Strange High House in the Mist," *At the Mountains of Madness*, "Shadow Out of Time," "The Descendant"
Auckland	Home port of two-masted schooner *Emma*	"The Call of Cthulhu"
Augusta, Maine	Derby drove through there on his way back to Arkham	"Dreams in the Witch House"
Australia	For which Houdini was bound	"Under the Pyramids"
Australia Museum, Sydney, Australia	Home of Cthulhu statue. Referred to as on College Street (it is) and Hyde Park (it is across from the Park).	"The Call of Cthulhu"
Ayer, Massachusetts	On the route to Greenfield	"The Whisperer in Darkness"
Aylesbury Pike, Massachusetts	North central Massachusetts, just beyond Dean's Corners	"The Dunwich Horror"
Aylesbury, Massachusetts	Mentioned (near Dunwich)	"The Dunwich Horror"
Bab-el-Azab, Cairo, Egypt	Houdini visited there	"Under the Pyramids"

PLACE-NAME	DESCRIPTION	SOURCE
Babson Street, Innsmouth, Massachusetts	Mentioned	"The Shadow over Innsmouth"
Babylon	Mentioned	"The Nameless City," "The Festival," "The Call of Cthulhu"
Back Bay, Boston, Massachusetts	Mentioned	"Pickman's Model"
Back Street, Kingsport, Massachusetts	Route to family home	"The Festival"
Back Street, Providence, Rhode Island	Renamed Benefit Street; the Shunned House stood there	"The Shunned House"
Baharna	The port city of Oriab	*The Dream-Quest of Unknown Kadath*
Ballylough, Ireland	Peasants there warned about Kilderry castle	"The Moon-Bog"
Ballylough Abbey, Ireland	Destroyed by Cromwell's soldiers	"Ibid"
Bank Street, Innsmouth, Massachusetts	Mentioned	"The Shadow over Innsmouth"
Banof	A valley distant but visible from Olathoë	"Polaris"
Baptist Church, Innsmouth, Massachusetts	Mentioned	"The Shadow over Innsmouth"
Barcelona, Spain	Home port of the scow *Fortaleza*	*The Case of Charles Dexter Ward*
Barnes Street, Providence, Rhode Island	Where the father of Charles Dexter Ward was staying	*The Case of Charles Dexter Ward*
Basalt Pillars of the West	A monument in dreamland marking a monstrous cataract	*The Dream-Quest of Unknown Kadath*
Bates Street, Innsmouth, Massachusetts	Mentioned	"The Shadow over Innsmouth"
Battery Street, Boston, Massachusetts	Mentioned	"Pickman's Model"
Bayside, New York	Home of Suydam's fiancée	"The Horror at Red Hook"
Beacon Hill, Boston, Massachusetts	Mentioned	*The Dream-Quest of Unknown Kadath*

PLACE-NAME	DESCRIPTION	SOURCE
Beacon Street, Boston, Massachusetts	Mentioned	"Pickman's Model"
Beardmore Glacier, Antarctica	Base nearby	*At the Mountains of Madness*
Bellows Falls, Vermont	Walter Brown loafed there	"The Whisperer in Darkness"
Belloy-en-Santerre, France	Where Randolph Carter was wounded in the Great War	"The Silver Key"
Bellview, Virginia (?)	A plantation in the southern U.S., location unknown, home to the gentleman-adventurer Francis Harley	"The Rats in the Walls"
Benefit Street, Providence, Rhode Island	Poe walked there	"The Shunned House"
Benevolent Street, Providence, Rhode Island	Home of Crawford Tillinghast; part of Charles Dexter Ward's regular walking route	"From Beyond," *The Case of Charles Dexter Ward*
Berlin, Germany	Mentioned	"The Temple"
Bethlehem, Palestine	Mentioned	"The Festival"
Bibliothèque Nationale, Paris, France	Research conducted there by Charles Dexter Ward	*The Case of Charles Dexter Ward*
Biddeford, Maine	Derby drove through there on his way back to Arkham	"Dreams in the Witch House"
Bienville Street, New Orleans, Louisiana	Home of Inspector John R. Legrasse	"The Call of Cthulhu"
Big Cypress Swamp	Near cemetery	"Statement of Randolph Carter"
Biltmore Hotel, Providence, Rhode Island	Mentioned	*The Case of Charles Dexter Ward*
Bishop House, Dunwich, Massachusetts	South of the village	"The Dunwich Horror"
Bishop's Brook, Dunwich, Massachusetts	Mentioned	"The Dunwich Horror"
Bnazic Desert	In the land of Mnar, a source of camels	"The Doom That Came to Sarnath," "The Quest of Iranon"
Boardman Street, Haverhill, Massachusetts	Peaslee's family home, near Golden Hill	"Shadow Out of Time"
Bolton, Massachusetts	"Factory" town nearby Arkham	"Herbert West—Reanimator"

PLACE-NAME	DESCRIPTION	SOURCE
Bolton, Massachusetts	Home of Walter Delapore (possibly a different Bolton)	"The Rats in the Walls"
Borough Hall, Brooklyn, New York	Mentioned	"The Horror at Red Hook"
Boston Museum of Fine Arts, Boston, Massachusetts	Refused a Pickman painting	"Pickman's Model"
Boston Public Library, Copley Square, Boston, Massachusetts	Research conducted there by Charles Dexter Ward	*The Case of Charles Dexter Ward*
Boston Stone, Boston, Massachusetts	The purported center of Boston, mentioned	*The Case of Charles Dexter Ward*
Boston, Massachusetts	Possible home of narrator of "The Picture in the House," identified by old man from his accent; also, home of Joel Manton, Francis Wayland Thurston, Zenas Low, Randolph Carter, and where Herbert West obtained supplies and made his reputation as a "celebrated surgical specialist." Joseph Curwen imported goods from Boston.	"The Picture in the House," "Herbert West—Reanimator," "The Unnamable," "The Call of Cthulhu," "The Shunned House," "The Silver Key," *The Dream-Quest of Unknown Kadath*, *The Case of Charles Dexter Ward*
Boylston Street subway, Boston, Massachusetts	Depicted by Pickman	"Pickman's Model"
Brattleboro, Vermont	Walter Brown loafed there	"The Whisperer in Darkness"
Brick Church, New York, New York	Steeple is visible	"He"
Bristol Highlands, Rhode Island	Where the Olneys relocated	"The Strange High House in the Mist"
Broad Street, Innsmouth, Massachusetts	Mentioned	"The Shadow over Innsmouth"
Broad Street, Providence, Rhode Island	Mentioned	*The Case of Charles Dexter Ward*
Brown University, Providence, Rhode Island	On the faculty of which was Prof. George Gammell Angell; the narrator of "The Shunned House" obtains weapons there	"The Call of Cthulhu," "The Shunned House"
Budd Land, Antarctica	Mentioned	*At the Mountains of Madness*
Bullion Street, Providence, Rhode Island	On Charles Dexter Ward's regular walking route	*The Case of Charles Dexter Ward*

PLACE-NAME	DESCRIPTION	SOURCE
Butler Street (police) Station, Brooklyn, New York	Malone stationed there	"The Horror at Red Hook"
Cactus Mountains	Somewhere in the southwestern U.S.	"The Transition of Juan Romero"
Caerleon, England	Roman ruins, mentioned	*The Case of Charles Dexter Ward*
Cairo Museum, Cairo, Egypt	Mentioned	"Under the Pyramids"
Cairo, Egypt	Where Houdini stayed in Egypt	"Under the Pyramids"
California	Home of theosophist colony which responded to the call	"The Call of Cthulhu"
Callao, Peru	Destination of two-masted schooner *Emma*	"The Call of Cthulhu"
Camorin	A place of fragrant groves in Cathuria	"The White Ship"
Campbell's Tomb, Gizeh, Egypt	Mentioned	"Under the Pyramids"
Canton, Ohio	Allegedly the home of an asylum where the narrator's uncle resided	"The Shadow over Innsmouth"
Cape Ann, Massachusetts	Mentioned	"The Shadow over Innsmouth"
Cape Cod, Massachusetts	Mentioned as the home of a colony of Fiji Islanders	"The Shadow over Innsmouth"
Cape Verde Islands, Africa	Source of many worshippers	"The Call of Cthulhu"
Capella	Outshone by nova	"Beyond the Wall of Sleep"
Carcassonne, France	Mentioned	"He"
Carfax, Virginia	The Delapore family home	"The Rats in the Walls"
Cathuria	Mentioned as "splendid"	*The Dream-Quest of Unknown Kadath*
Cathuria	Land of Hope	"The White Ship"
Catskill Mountains	Home to Joe Slater	"Beyond the Wall of Sleep"
Caude, France	A village somewhere in France, original home of the Roulets	"The Shunned House"
The Causeway, Kingsport, Massachusetts	Steps leading up the cliffs near Kingsport	"The Strange High House in the Mist"
Celephaïs	A city in the valley of Ooth-Nargai	"Celephaïs," *The Dream-Quest of Unknown Kadath*

PLACE-NAME	DESCRIPTION	SOURCE
Cent Street, Providence, Rhode Island	On Charles Dexter Ward's regular walking route	*The Case of Charles Dexter Ward*
Central Hill, Kingsport, Massachusetts	Location of hospital near old churchyard[2]	"The Festival," "The Strange High House in the Mist"
Central Square Station, Boston, Massachusetts	Mentioned by Danforth	*At the Mountains of Madness*
Central Station (police), Providence, Rhode Island	Where Patrolman William J. Monahan was stationed	"The Haunter of the Dark"
Cerenerian Sea	On which lies Celephaïs	"Celephaïs," *The Dream-Quest of Unknown Kadath*
Chaldea	Mentioned	"The Nameless City"
Chapman farmhouse, Arkham, Massachusetts	Laboratory of Herbert West	"Herbert West—Reanimator"
Chapman's Brook, Massachusetts	On the "blasted heath" near Arkham	"The Colour Out of Space"
Charlestown, Boston, Massachusetts	Location of White Star pier from which Charles Dexter Ward sailed	*The Case of Charles Dexter Ward*
Charter Street Burying Ground, Salem, Massachusetts	Tombstone stolen from there appears in dreamland	*The Dream-Quest of Unknown Kadath*
Cheapside, Providence, Rhode Island	A district, mentioned	"The Shunned House"
Chepachet, Rhode Island	Near Pascoag, mentioned	"The Horror at Red Hook"
Chesuncook, Maine	Where Edward Derby visited	"Dreams in the Witch House"
Chicago, Illinois	Where Sir Alfred Jermyn and a gorilla wrestled; home of Ernest B. Aspinwall, Esq.	"Facts concerning the Late Arthur Jermyn and His Family," "The Silver Key"
Chicago, Illinois	Home of Angarola	"Pickman's Model"
China	Mentioned	"The Call of Cthulhu"
Christchurch Cemetery, Arkham, Massachusetts	Potential source of bodies for Herbert West	"Herbert West—Reanimator"
Church Street, Arkham, Massachusetts	A cafeteria is located there	"Dreams in the Witch House"
Church Street, Innsmouth, Massachusetts	Mentioned	"The Shadow over Innsmouth"

2. Its name, the Congregational Hospital, is revealed in "The Silver Key."

PLACE-NAME	DESCRIPTION	SOURCE
Church, Deacon Snow's, Providence, Rhode Island	Church to which Curwen defected	*The Case of Charles Dexter Ward*
Church, Dr. Cotton's, Providence, Rhode Island	Congregationalist church attended by Curwen[3]	*The Case of Charles Dexter Ward*
Circle Court, Kingsport, Massachusetts	Route to family home	"The Festival"
Circle Social Club	On the Street	"The Street"
Circular Quay, Sydney Cove, Sydney, Australia	Steam yacht *Alert* is in commercial use there	"The Call of Cthulhu"
City Hall, Providence, Rhode Island	Frequented by Charles Dexter Ward	*The Case of Charles Dexter Ward*
Clare Market, London, England	Where a copy of the *Necronomicon* was bought	"The Descendant"
Clark's Corners, Massachusetts	Near the Nahum Gardner home	"The Colour Out of Space"
Clinton Street, Brooklyn, New York	Boundary of Red Hook	"The Horror at Red Hook"
Coin Street, Providence, Rhode Island	On Charles Dexter Ward's regular walking route	*The Case of Charles Dexter Ward*
Cold Spring Glen, Massachusetts	Mentioned (near Dunwich)	"The Dunwich Horror"
College Hill, Providence, Rhode Island	Mentioned	"The Shunned House," *The Case of Charles Dexter Ward*, "The Haunter of the Dark"
College Street, Providence, Rhode Island	Mentioned	"The Haunter of the Dark"
Cologne, France	Where Coleridge found a thousand odours	"Old Bugs"
Colony House, Providence, Rhode Island	Burned down and rebuilt with funds from Curwen	*The Case of Charles Dexter Ward*
Commercial House, Arkham, Massachusetts	Mentioned	"Herbert West—Reanimator"
Commoriom, Hyperborea	Compared to ancient city on Antarctic plateau	*At the Mountains of Madness*

3. Later the First Unitarian Church of Providence.

PLACE-NAME	DESCRIPTION	SOURCE
Conanicut Island, Rhode Island	Site of Dr. Waite's private hospital in which Charles Dexter Ward was incarcerated	*The Case of Charles Dexter Ward*
Concord, Massachusetts	On the route to Greenfield	*The Dream-Quest of Unknown Kadath*, "The Whisperer in Darkness"
Cone Mountain, New York	Mentioned, near Tempest Mountain	"The Lurking Fear"
Congdon Street, Providence, Rhode Island	Along which Charles Dexter Ward was wheeled as a babe	*The Case of Charles Dexter Ward*
Congo Region, Africa	Mentioned as subject of Pigafetta's *Regnum Congo*; explored by Sir Wade Jermyn	"The Picture in the House," "Facts concerning the Late Arthur Jermyn and His Family"
Congo River, Africa	M. Verhaeran was a Belgian agent at a trading-post on the river	"Facts concerning the Late Arthur Jermyn and His Family"
Congregational Church, Dunwich Village, Massachusetts	Mentioned	"The Dunwich Horror"
Congregational Church, Innsmouth, Massachusetts	Mentioned	"The Shadow over Innsmouth"
Congregational Church, Providence, Rhode Island	Founded by Joseph Curwen *inter alia*	*The Case of Charles Dexter Ward*
Congregational Hospital, Kingsport, Massachusetts	Mentioned	"The Strange High House in the Mist," "The Silver Key"
Connecticut River, New England	Mentioned	"The Whisperer in Darkness"
Constantinopolis	Mentioned	"Ibid"
Constitution Wharf, Boston, Massachusetts	Pickman and Thurber walk by it	"Pickman's Model"
Copp's Hill Burying Ground, Boston, Massachusetts	One of Pickman's favorite settings	"Pickman's Model"
Copp's Hill, Boston, Massachusetts	Site of a mill	"Pickman's Model"
Corinth	Where Kalos's Hermes stood	"The Tree," "Ibid"
Cornwall, England	Lady Margaret Trevor was from there	"The Rats in the Walls," *The Dream-Quest of Unknown Kadath*
County Meath, Ireland	Where Denys Baerry was lost	"The Moon-Bog"

PLACE-NAME	DESCRIPTION	SOURCE
Court Street, Brooklyn, New York	Boundary of Red Hook	"The Horror at Red Hook"
Crane Street, Arkham, Massachusetts	Near campus of Miskatonic University; Peaslee lived there	"Herbert West—Reanimator," "Shadow Out of Time"
Cranston Street Armoury, Providence, Rhode Island	Narrator obtained weapons there	"The Shunned House"
Crete, Minoan	Mentioned	*At the Mountains of Madness*
Crown Coffee House, Providence, Rhode Island	Mentioned	*The Case of Charles Dexter Ward*
Crowninshield place, Old, High Street, Arkham, Massachusetts	Where Asenath and Edward Derby settled	"Dreams in the Witch House"
Cunard Pier, Manhattan, New York	From which the Suydams' ocean liner departed	"The Horror at Red Hook"
Cydathria	A city in Mnar, a source of spices	"The Doom That Came to Sarnath," "The Quest of Iranon"
Dahshur, Egypt	A site of pyramids near Gizeh	"Under the Pyramids"
Dampier Street, Pilbarra, Western Australia, Australia	Peaslee received a message from an engineer there	"Shadow Out of Time"
Danvers State Hospital, Danvers, Massachusetts	Mentioned	"The Shadow over Innsmouth," "Pickman's Model," *The Dream-Quest of Unknown Kadath*
Dark Mountain, Vermont	Near Townshend and the old Akeley place	"The Whisperer in Darkness"
Darling Harbour, Sydney, Australia	Destination of *Vigilant*	"The Call of Cthulhu"
De Grey River, Western Australia, Australia	On the way to the dig	"Shadow Out of Time"
Dean's Corners, Massachusetts	Near Dunwich	"The Dunwich Horror"
Devil Reef, outside Innsmouth Harbour, Massachusetts	Home of the Deep Ones	"The Shadow over Innsmouth"
Devil's Hop Yard, Dunwich, Massachusetts	A bleak, blasted hillside	"The Dunwich Horror"
Devonshire, England	Actual birthplace of narrator	"A Reminiscence of Dr. Samuel Johnson"

PLACE-NAME	DESCRIPTION	SOURCE
Dexter, Gregory, Lot of, Olney Street, Providence, Rhode Island	Next to lot of Joseph Curwen	*The Case of Charles Dexter Ward*
Dime Street, Providence, Rhode Island	On Charles Dexter Ward's regular walking route	*The Case of Charles Dexter Ward*
Dollar Street, Providence, Rhode Island	On Charles Dexter Ward's regular walking route	*The Case of Charles Dexter Ward*
Dothur	A source of oil (in Mnar?)	"The Doom That Came to Sarnath"
Doubloon Street, Providence, Rhode Island	Location of Curwen's warehouse	*The Case of Charles Dexter Ward*
Drinen	In the East	"The Quest of Iranon"
Dry Gulch	A town near the Norton Mine	"The Transition of Juan Romero"
Dublin University, Dublin, Ireland	Alma mater of Malone	"The Horror at Red Hook"
Dunedin, New Zealand	Home of steam yacht *Alert*	"The Call of Cthulhu"
Dunwich, Massachusetts	Evidently in north-central Massachusetts	"The Dunwich Horror"
Dylath-Leen	A seaport of ill repute	*The Dream-Quest of Unknown Kadath*
East Greenwich, Rhode Island	Home of the Roulets	"The Shunned House"
East High School, Massachusetts	Of which Joel Manton is principal[4]	"The Unnamable"
East Side District, Providence, Rhode Island	Archer Harris moved there	"The Shunned House"
Easter Island	Mentioned	"The Shadow over Innsmouth"
The Egeberg, Oslo, Norway	Mountain near Johansen's home	"The Call of Cthulhu"
Egypt	Potential residence of interstellar traveler occupying Joe Slater, source of Nyarlathotep	"Beyond the Wall of Sleep," "Nyarlathotep," *At the Mountains of Madness*

4. There is an "East Boston High School," but although Manton is "born and bred" in Boston, the story takes place in Arkham, and there is no indication that either he or the narrator is merely visiting there. Therefore, "East High School" is likely in Arkham.

PLACE-NAME	DESCRIPTION	SOURCE
Eiffel Tower, Paris, France	Mentioned	"Under the Pyramids"
Eighth Avenue, New York, New York	From where a seedy loafer was hired	"Cool Air"
El Dorado	Mentioned	"He"
Eliot Street, Innsmouth, Massachusetts	Mentioned	"The Shadow over Innsmouth"
Elizabethtown, New Jersey	Hometown of Phebe Hetfield	"The Shunned House"
Elm Mountain, near Arkham, Massachusetts	On which Randolph Carter's car was found	"The Silver Key"
Elmwood Avenue, Providence, Rhode Island	Mentioned	*The Case of Charles Dexter Ward*
Empire Street, Providence, Rhode Island	Mentioned	*The Case of Charles Dexter Ward*
England	Home of narrator	"The Hound"
Erebus, Mount, Antarctica	Mentioned	*At the Mountains of Madness*
Essex County, Massachusetts	In which Innsmouth is located	"The Shadow over Innsmouth"
Essex Institute, Salem, Massachusetts	Research conducted there by Charles Dexter Ward	*The Case of Charles Dexter Ward*
Everest, Mount	Mentioned	"The Nameless City"
Exeter, Rhode Island	Dealt with vampires	"The Shunned House"
Exham Priory, England	Restored home of the Delapore family	"The Rats in the Walls"
Ezbekiyeh Garden, Cairo, Egypt	Houdini visited there	"Under the Pyramids"
Fall Street, Innsmouth, Massachusetts	Mentioned	"The Shadow over Innsmouth"
Federal Hill, Providence, Rhode Island	Site of the Starry Wisdom Church	"The Haunter of the Dark"
Federal Street, Innsmouth, Massachusetts	Mentioned	"The Shadow over Innsmouth"
Fiji Islands	Mentioned	"The Shadow over Innsmouth"
First Baptist Church, Providence, Rhode Island	On Charles Dexter Ward's regular walking route	*The Case of Charles Dexter Ward*

PLACE-NAME	DESCRIPTION	SOURCE
First Church of Christ, Scientist, Prospect and Meeting Street, Providence, Rhode Island	On Charles Dexter Ward's regular walking route	*The Case of Charles Dexter Ward*
Fish Street Bridge, Innsmouth, Massachusetts	In ruins	"The Shadow over Innsmouth"
Fitchburg, Massachusetts	Mentioned	"The Whisperer in Darkness"
Flanders, Belgium	Where narrator served in 1915	"Herbert West—Reanimator"
Flatbush, Brooklyn, New York	District where Suydam lived	"The Horror at Red Hook"
Fleur-de-Lys Building, 7 Thomas Street, Providence, Rhode Island	Home of Thomas Wilcox	"The Call of Cthulhu"
Florida	Upton's father moved there for his health	"Dreams in the Witch House"
Fowler, Goody, farmhouse, Arkham, Massachusetts	Mentioned	"The Silver Key"
France	Home of Charles Le Sorcier	"The Alchemist"
Frankfort, Germany	Location of publisher of Pigafetta's *Regnum Congo*	"The Picture in the House"
Franklin Island, Antarctica	Mentioned	*At the Mountains of Madness*
Fraunces Tavern Museum, New York, New York	Home of some Rhode Island colonial correspondence regarding Joseph Curwen	*The Case of Charles Dexter Ward*
Fredericksburg, Virginia	Welcome Harris died in battle there	"The Shunned House"
Frying-Pan and Fish, near the New Coffee-House, Providence, Rhode Island	Shop kept by Clark and Nightingale	*The Case of Charles Dexter Ward*
Fujiyama, Mount, Japan	Mentioned	*At the Mountains of Madness*
Gainesville (Florida?)	Near cemetery	"Statement of Randolph Carter"
Gallows Hill, Boston, Massachusetts	Mentioned	"Pickman's Model"
Garden of the Gods, Colorado	Mentioned	*At the Mountains of Madness*
Gare Central, Cairo, Egypt	Where Houdini arrived in Cairo	"Under the Pyramids"
Garrison Street, Arkham, Massachusetts	Mentioned	"Dreams in the Witch House"

PLACE-NAME	DESCRIPTION	SOURCE
Gate of the Caravans	Outside the port of Inganok	*The Dream-Quest of Unknown Kadath*
Gate of Deeper Slumber, Dreamland	The entry point	*The Dream-Quest of Unknown Kadath*
Gaul	Mentioned	"Ibid"
George Street, Providence, Rhode Island	Part of Charles Dexter Ward's regular walking route	*The Case of Charles Dexter Ward*
George Street, Providence, Rhode Island	Home of Melville F. Peters, Esq.	*The Case of Charles Dexter Ward*
Germantown, Pennsylvania	Man hailing from there put on a "clever mechanical spectacle" in Providence	*The Case of Charles Dexter Ward*
Ghizereh, Egypt	An island in Cairo, visited by Houdini	"Under the Pyramids"
Giants' Causeway, Northern Ireland	Mentioned	*The Dream-Quest of Unknown Kadath, At the Mountains of Madness*
Gilman House, Innsmouth, Massachusetts	The principal hotel	"The Shadow over Innsmouth"
Gizeh, Egypt	Visited by Houdini	"Under the Pyramids"
Gloucester, Massachusetts	Mentioned	*The Dream-Quest of Unknown Kadath*
Gold Street, Providence, Rhode Island	On Charles Dexter Ward's regular walking route	*The Case of Charles Dexter Ward*
Golden Ball Inn, Providence, Rhode Island	On Charles Dexter Ward's regular walking route	*The Case of Charles Dexter Ward*
Gothenburg Dock, Oslo, Norway	Place of Johansen's death	"The Call of Cthulhu"
Governor's Island, New York	Across the water from Red Hook	"The Horror at Red Hook"
Gowanus, Brooklyn, New York	Mentioned	"The Horror at Red Hook"
Graham Land, Antarctica	Mentioned	*At the Mountains of Madness*
Granary Burying Ground, Boston, Massachusetts	Tombstone stolen from there appears in dreamland	*The Dream-Quest of Unknown Kadath*
Grand Cairo, Egypt	Point of departure of the scow *Fortaleza* on its voyage to Providence	*The Case of Charles Dexter Ward*

PLACE-NAME	DESCRIPTION	SOURCE
Gray's Inn, London, England	Where a screamer lives	"The Descendant"
Great Abyss	Near Sarkomand	*The Dream-Quest of Unknown Kadath*
Great Bridge, Providence, Rhode Island	On Charles Dexter Ward's regular walking route	"The Shunned House," *The Case of Charles Dexter Ward*
Great Pyramid, Egypt	Mentioned	"The Outsider"
Great Russell Street, London, England	Where Charles Dexter Ward lodged	*The Case of Charles Dexter Ward*
Greece	Mentioned as stripped by Constantine	*At the Mountains of Madness*
Green Bay, Wisconsin	Ibid's relics relocated there	"Ibid"
Green Lane, Kingsport, Massachusetts	Location of family home	"The Festival"
Green River, Kentucky	Communicated with the water of the cave	"The Beast in the Cave"
Greenfield, Massachusetts	Station at which Wilmarth arrived	"The Whisperer in Darkness"
Greenland	Mentioned	"The Call of Cthulhu"
Greenough Lane, Boston, Massachusetts	Definitely not the location of Pickman's studio	"Pickman's Model"
Greenwich, Manhattan, New York	Where "he" lived	"He"
Greenwood Cemetery, Brooklyn, New York	Where the Suydams are buried	"The Horror at Red Hook"
Guilder Street, Providence, Rhode Island	On Charles Dexter Ward's regular walking route	*The Case of Charles Dexter Ward*
Guinea	Home of a "loathsome black woman" who cared for Sir Wade Jermyn's son, Philip	"Facts concerning the Late Arthur Jermyn and His Family"
Hacker's Hall, Providence, Rhode Island	Where Curwen made a speech	*The Case of Charles Dexter Ward*
Hadath	By the Nile	"The Outsider"
Haiti (Hayti)	Where voodoo orgies multiplied in response to the call	"The Call of Cthulhu"
Hali, Lake of	Carcosa is on its banks	"The Whisperer in Darkness"

PLACE-NAME	DESCRIPTION	SOURCE
Hall School, Kingsport, Massachusetts	Attended by Asenath Waite	"Dreams in the Witch House"
Hammond's Drug Store, Newburyport, Massachusetts	In front of which the bus stops	"The Shadow over Innsmouth"
Hangman's Brook, Massachusetts	Near Arkham	"Dreams in the Witch House"
Hanwell Insane Asylum, England	Home of Walter Delapore	"The Rats in the Walls"
Harlem (Brooklyn, New York)	Mentioned	"Herbert West—Reanimator"
Harrow School, Harrow on the Hill, Middlesex, England	Mentioned	"The Descendant"
Harvard Square Station, Cambridge, Massachusetts	Mentioned by Danforth	*At the Mountains of Madness*
Harvard University, Cambridge, Massachusetts	Upton attended school there	"Dreams in the Witch House"
Hatheg	A town near Ulthar	"The Cats of Ulthar," "The Other Gods," *The Dream-Quest of Unknown Kadath*
Hatheg-Kla	A mountain	"The Other Gods," "The Strange High House in the Mist"
Havana	Source of Curwen's sailors	*The Case of Charles Dexter Ward*
Haverhill, Massachusetts	Home of Walter Gilman	"Dreams in the Witch House"
Heliopolis, Africa	Mentioned	"Under the Pyramids"
Hexham, England	Roman ruins, mentioned	*The Case of Charles Dexter Ward*
Himalaya Mountains, Tibet	Mentioned	"The Whisperer in Darkness," *At the Mountains of Madness*
Historical Society, Providence, Rhode Island	Frequented by Charles Dexter Ward	*The Case of Charles Dexter Ward*
Histrionick Academy of Mr. Douglass, King Street, Providence, Rhode Island	Mentioned	*The Case of Charles Dexter Ward*
Hlanith	A trading city on the Cerenerian Sea	*The Dream-Quest of Unknown Kadath*
Hobart, Tasmania	Route of the *Arkham* to the Antarctic	*At the Mountains of Madness*

PLACE-NAME	DESCRIPTION	SOURCE
Hogton, Vermont	Home of Sweet Ermengarde	"Sweet Ermengarde"
Holland, Churchyard in	Scene of tomb-robbing	"The Hound"
Hooper's Pond, Massachusetts	Outside Kingsport, on the way to the pinnacle	"The Strange High House in the Mist"
Hope Street, Providence, Rhode Island	Mentioned	"The Shunned House"
Hope Valley, near Providence, Rhode Island	Truck hijacked there	*The Case of Charles Dexter Ward*
Hopkins Street, Providence, Rhode Island	Narrator walked there	"The Shunned House"
Hungary	Where Justin Geoffrey visited	"Dreams in the Witch House"
Huntingdon, Cambridgeshire, England	A madhouse where Sir Wade Jermyn was confined	"Facts concerning the Late Arthur Jermyn and His Family"
Ib	A city in Mnar, mentioned in "The Nameless City" and compared to the city on the Antarctic plateau	"The Doom That Came to Sarnath," "The Nameless City," *At the Mountains of Madness*
Iceland	Mentioned	"The Call of Cthulhu"
Ilarnek	A city in Mnar, on the Ai River	"The Doom That Came to Sarnath," "The Quest of Iranon," *The Dream-Quest of Unknown Kadath*
Ilek-Vad	A town of turrets atop cliffs of glass, in dreamland	"The Silver Key," *The Dream-Quest of Unknown Kadath*
Illinois	Home of narrator's parents	"Herbert West—Reanimator"
Implan	A city in Mnar, a source of young goats	"The Doom That Came to Sarnath"
India	Source of Warren's book and later source of prehistoric books and clay tablets read by Randolph Carter	"Statement of Randolph Carter," "The Silver Key"
Indian Ocean	Mentioned	*At the Mountains of Madness*
Indies	Source of goods imported by Joseph Curwen	*The Case of Charles Dexter Ward*
Industrial Trust Beacon, Providence, Rhode Island	Visible to Blake	"The Haunter of the Dark"
Inganok	A port in dreamland	*The Dream-Quest of Unknown Kadath*

PLACE-NAME	DESCRIPTION	SOURCE
Innsmouth Harbour, Innsmouth, Massachusetts	Location of Devil Reef	"The Shadow over Innsmouth"
Innsmouth, England	A seaside town where Kuranes died	"Celephaïs"
Innsmouth, Massachusetts	Central location of tale	"The Shadow over Innsmouth"
Ipswich, Massachusetts	Mentioned	"The Shadow over Innsmouth"
Ireland, West of	Full of wild rumour and legendry in response to the call	"The Call of Cthulhu"
Irem	Lost city of the Arabian peninsula	"The Nameless City"
Jackson, Steven, school, opposite Court-House Parade, Providence, Rhode Island	Eliza Tillinghast attended	*The Case of Charles Dexter Ward*
James	A river near Carfax in Virginia	"The Rats in the Walls"
Jaren	Onyx-walled city on the Xari River	"The Quest of Iranon"
Jenckes Street, Providence, Rhode Island	Part of Charles Dexter Ward's regular walking route	*The Case of Charles Dexter Ward*
Jermyn House, Suffolk, England	Home of the Jermyn family	"Facts concerning the Late Arthur Jermyn and His Family"
Jerusalem, Israel	Mentioned	*The Case of Charles Dexter Ward*
Jewel Lake	Near the Norton Mine	"The Transition of Juan Romero"
Joanna Spring, Western Australia, Australia	100 miles southeast of the dig	"Shadow Out of Time"
John Carter Library, Brown University, Providence, Rhode Island	Frequented by Charles Dexter Ward	*The Case of Charles Dexter Ward*
John Hay Library, Brown University, Providence, Rhode Island	Frequented by Charles Dexter Ward	*The Case of Charles Dexter Ward*
Johns Hopkins University, Baltimore, Maryland	Awarded Henry Armitage a Litt.D.	"The Dunwich Horror"
Judge Durfee House, 49 Benefit Street, Providence, Rhode Island	On Charles Dexter Ward's regular walking route	*The Case of Charles Dexter Ward*
Jupiter, fourth moon of	Potential residence of interstellar traveler occupying Joe Slater	"Beyond the Wall of Sleep"

PLACE-NAME	DESCRIPTION	SOURCE
Kadath	Evidently a peak or peninsula in dreamland	"The Other Gods," "The Strange High House in the Mist," *The Dream-Quest of Unknown Kadath*, "The Dunwich Horror"
Kadatheron	A city in Mnar, on the river Ai	"The Doom That Came to Sarnath," "The Quest of Iranon," *The Dream-Quest of Unknown Kadath*
Kadiphonek	A peak, with the plateau of Sarkis between	"Polaris"
Kaiser Wilhelm Land, Antarctica	Mentioned	*At the Mountains of Madness*
Kaliri country, Congo Region, Africa	Explored by Sir Arthur Jermyn	"Facts concerning the Late Arthur Jermyn and His Family"
Karthian Hills	Near Teloth	"The Quest of Iranon"
Keene, New Hampshire	Mentioned	"The Whisperer in Darkness"
Kendall Station, Boston, Massachusetts	Mentioned by Danforth	*At the Mountains of Madness*
Kent, England	A manor-house there was the site of drug use	"Hypnos"
Kiel, Germany	Where the U-29 was bound	"The Temple"
Kilderry, Ireland	Denys Barry purchased a castle there	"The Moon-Bog"
King's Church, Providence, Rhode Island	Mentioned	*The Case of Charles Dexter Ward*
Kingsport Harbour, Massachusetts	Where the narrator is found	"The Festival"
Kingsport Head, Massachusetts	Site of powerful wireless station	*At the Mountains of Madness*, "The Shadow over Innsmouth"
Kingsport, Massachusetts	Location of "The Festival," home of the Terrible Old Man, and place of the strange high house	"The Festival," "The Terrible Old Man," "The Strange High House in the Mist," *The Dream-Quest of Unknown Kadath*
Kingstown, Rhode Island[5]	Source of stock for Curwen farm	*The Case of Charles Dexter Ward*

5. In the eighteenth century, Kingstown was divided into North Kingstown, South Kingstown, and Exeter.

PLACE-NAME	DESCRIPTION	SOURCE
Kiran	Houses a temple of the god of Outkranos	*The Dream-Quest of Unknown Kadath*
Kish, Mesopotamia	Mentioned	*At the Mountains of Madness*
Klausenberg, Transylvania	Charles Dexter Ward stopped there	*The Case of Charles Dexter Ward*
Kled	A region of perfumed jungles	"The Silver Key," *The Dream-Quest of Unknown Kadath*
Kleinstrasse, Altstadt, Prague, Vienna	Home of Simon Orne	*The Case of Charles Dexter Ward*
Knapp Street, Milwaukee, Wisconsin	Site of Robert Blake's home	"The Haunter of the Dark"
Knight's Head tavern, Suffolk, England	Near Jermyn House and the "headquarters" of Sir Wade Jermyn	"Facts concerning the Late Arthur Jermyn and His Family"
Knox Land, Antarctica	Mentioned	*At the Mountains of Madness*
Kra	A stream, with tiny falls, in Aira	"The Quest of Iranon"
Kurdistan	Source of many Red Hook immigrants	"The Horror at Red Hook"
Lafayette Street, Innsmouth, Massachusetts	Mentioned	"The Shadow over Innsmouth"
Lake Mendota, Wisconsin	Tribes there held Ibid's relics	"Ibid"
Lake Michigan, America	Tribes there held Ibid's relics	"Ibid"
Lake Winnebago, Wisconsin	Tribes there held Ibid's relics	"Ibid"
Lawrence College, Appleton, Wisconsin	Alma mater of Alfred Trever	"Old Bugs"
Le Tellier's, Dover-Street, Soho, London, England	Meeting place of the Literary Club	"A Reminiscence of Dr. Samuel Johnson"
Lefferts Corner, New York	Nearest village to Tempest Mountain	"The Lurking Fear"
Lemuria	Mentioned and temporary home of the Shining Trapezohedron	*At the Mountains of Madness*, "The Haunter of the Dark"
Leng	A stone monastery lies there on its cold desert plateau in Central Asia	"The Hound," "Celephaïs," *The Dream-Quest of Unknown Kadath*, At the Mountains of Madness*
Lerion	A land	"The Other Gods," *The Dream-Quest of Unknown Kadath*
Liberty Café	On the Street	"The Street"

PLACE-NAME	DESCRIPTION	SOURCE
Libyan Desert, Africa	Seen by Houdini	"Under the Pyramids"
Limoges, France	Site of the Black Prince's massacre	*The Case of Charles Dexter Ward*
Liranian desert	Mentioned	"The Quest of Iranon"
Liverpool, England	Destination of the *Victory*; Charles Dexter Ward sailed there	"The Temple," *The Case of Charles Dexter Ward*
Lomar	A land in the far north	"Polaris," "The Quest of Iranon," "The Other Gods," *The Dream-Quest of Unknown Kadath*
London, England	Source of copy of Pigafetta's *Regnum Congo* owned by old man; a port for other travelers and imports; where Walter Delapore obtained some of his furnishings; home of Kuranes. The narrator of "A Reminiscence of Dr. Samuel Johnson" moved there; the narrator of "Hypnos" had a studio there.	"The Picture in the House," "The Hound," "Celephaïs," "The Call of Cthulhu," "The Rats in the Walls," "He," *The Case of Charles Dexter Ward*
Lower Green River, Massachusetts	On the route to Innsmouth from Newburyport	"The Shadow over Innsmouth"
Luitpold Land, Antarctica	Mentioned	*At the Mountains of Madness*
Lydia	To where the repute of Kalos and Musides spread	"The Tree"
Lyons, France	Place of publication of *Dæmonolatreia* of Remigius	"The Festival"
Machu Picchu, Andes	Mentioned	*At the Mountains of Madness*
Main Street, Innsmouth, Massachusetts	Mentioned	"The Shadow over Innsmouth"
Mammoth Cave, Kentucky	Home of the Beast	"The Beast in the Cave"
Mansion House, Providence, Rhode Island	The renamed Golden Ball Inn, mentioned	"The Shunned House"
Manuxet River, Massachusetts	Mentioned	"The Shadow over Innsmouth"
Maple Hill, New York	Mentioned, near Tempest Mountain	"The Lurking Fear"
Marblehead, Massachusetts	Mentioned	*The Dream-Quest of Unknown Kadath*
Market House, Kingsport, Massachusetts	Near family home	"The Festival"

PLACE-NAME	DESCRIPTION	SOURCE
Market Parade, Providence, Rhode Island	Restored by Curwen	*The Case of Charles Dexter Ward*
Marseilles, France	Departure port of the *Malwa*	"Under the Pyramids"
Marsh Street, Innsmouth, Massachusetts	Mentioned	"The Shadow over Innsmouth"
Martense Street, Flatbush, Brooklyn, New York	Suydam's home was set back from it	"The Horror at Red Hook"
Martin Street, Innsmouth, Massachusetts	Mentioned	"The Shadow over Innsmouth"
Martinique	Source of Curwen's sailors	*The Case of Charles Dexter Ward*
Masonic Hall, former, now Esoteric Order of Dagon, Innsmouth, Massachusetts	Mentioned	"The Shadow over Innsmouth"
Massachusetts	The business life of which absorbed Walter Delapore	"The Rats in the Walls"
Maumee, Ohio	Suburb of Toledo, mentioned	"The Shadow over Innsmouth"
McMurdo Sound, Antarctica	Mentioned	*At the Mountains of Madness*
Meadow Hill, Arkham, Massachusetts	Mentioned; where a post-rider saw something strange	"Herbert West—Reanimator," "The Unnamable," "Colour Out of Space," "Dreams in the Witch House"
Meeting Street, Providence, Rhode Island	In older times, Gaol Street and King Street, part of Charles Dexter Ward's regular walking route	*The Case of Charles Dexter Ward*
Memorial Hall, Providence, Rhode Island	Mentioned	"The Haunter of the Dark"
Memphis, Egypt	Mentioned	"The Nameless City," "The Festival," "Under the Pyramids"
Mena House Hotel, Gizeh, Egypt	Houdini passed by there	"Under the Pyramids"
Meroë	Mentioned	"The Cats of Ulthar"
Meroë, Egypt	Mentioned	"The Nameless City"
Mile-End Cove, Providence, Rhode Island	Joseph Curwen purchased wharfage nearby	*The Case of Charles Dexter Ward*
Milwaukee on the Menominee River, Wisconsin	Site of a trading post	"Ibid"

PLACE-NAME	DESCRIPTION	SOURCE
Miskatonic University, Arkham, Massachusetts	Mentioned	"Herbert West—Reanimator"
Miskatonic Valley	Narrator is traveling through the Valley (first mention anywhere)	"The Picture in the House"
Mitre Tavern, London, England	Where the narrator first met Dr. Samuel Johnson	"A Reminiscence of Dr. Samuel Johnson"
Mnar	A land	"The Doom That Came to Sarnath," "The Nameless City"
Mont Saint-Michel, France	Mentioned	"Pickman's Model"
Montpelier, Vermont	Mentioned	"The Whisperer in Darkness"
Moses Brown School, Providence, Rhode Island	Which Charles Dexter Ward attended	*The Case of Charles Dexter Ward*
Mount Auburn Cemetery, Cambridge, Massachusetts	Depicted by Pickman	"Pickman's Model"
Mount Mænalus, Acadia (Arcadia)	Where the Tree stood and fauns danced	"The Tree," "The Moon-Bog"
Mouski, The, Cairo, Egypt	Houdini passed through	"Under the Pyramids"
Mtal	A shore town in Mnar	"The Doom That Came to Sarnath"
Nameless City, Arabian Desert	Compared to ancient city on Antarctic plateau	"The Nameless City," *At the Mountains of Madness*
Namquit Point, near Providence, Rhode Island	Where the scow *Fortaleza* stopped to have some cargo removed	*The Case of Charles Dexter Ward*
Nansen, Mount, Antarctica	Base nearby	*At the Mountains of Madness*
Narath	A city of carven gates and domes of chalcedony, in dreamland	"The Silver Key"
Naraxa	A river near Celephaïs	"Celephaïs," *The Dream-Quest of Unknown Kadath*
Nareil	An island in the Middle Ocean	"The Doom That Came to Sarnath"
Narg	A grotto-born river in Cathuria	"The White Ship"
Narragansett Bay, near Providence, Rhode Island	Home of the Roulets and dairymen and horse-breeders; where Dr. Dexter threw an object	"The Shunned House," *The Case of Charles Dexter Ward*, "The Haunter of the Dark"
Narthos	A valley near Narthos	"The Quest of Iranon"

PLACE-NAME	DESCRIPTION	SOURCE
Nath-Horthath, Temple of	In Ooth-Nargai	"Celephaïs"
Neapolis, Greece	To where the repute of Kalos and Musides spread	"The Tree"
Neb	Mentioned	"The Outsider"
Neck, Pawtuxet, Rhode Island	A cape near Providence, location of home of John Merritt	*The Case of Charles Dexter Ward*
Nephren-Ka, Catacombs of	Mentioned	"The Outsider"
Neustadt, Prague, Czechoslovakia	Research conducted there by Charles Dexter Ward	*The Case of Charles Dexter Ward*
New Amsterdam, New York	Home of Gerrit Martense	"The Lurking Fear"
New Church Green, Innsmouth, Massachusetts	Site of Order of Dagon Hall	"The Shadow over Innsmouth"
New France, Canada	Destination of troops quartered temporarily in Providence	*The Case of Charles Dexter Ward*
New Hampshire	Mentioned	"The Whisperer in Darkness"
New London, Connecticut	Charles Dexter Ward journeyed there to do research	*The Case of Charles Dexter Ward*
New York University, New York, New York	Galpin was dismissed from there	"Old Bugs"
New York, New York	Home port of the *Victory*; here Levantines rioted in response to the call; source of goods imported by Joseph Curwen	"The Temple," "The Call of Cthulhu," *The Case of Charles Dexter Ward*, "Dreams in the Witch House"
Newburyport Historical Society, High Street, Newburyport, Massachusetts	Where the narrator did research	"The Shadow over Innsmouth"
Newburyport Public Library, Newburyport, Massachusetts	Mentioned	"The Shadow over Innsmouth"
Newburyport, Massachusetts	Beginning of narrator's bus trip	"The Shadow over Innsmouth"
Newfane, Vermont	Walter Brown loafed there	"The Whisperer in Darkness"
Newport, Rhode Island	Hometown of Maria Robbins; source of goods imported by Joseph Curwen	"The Shunned House," *The Case of Charles Dexter Ward*
Ngranek	Mountain on which the face of the gods appears	"The Other Gods"
Ngranek	A mountain in dreamland, on the island of Oriab	*The Dream-Quest of Unknown Kadath*

PLACE-NAME	DESCRIPTION	SOURCE
Nile Bridge, Cairo, Egypt	Crossed by Houdini	"Under the Pyramids"
Nile River	Mentioned	"The Nameless City"
Nile Valley, Egypt	Visited by Houdini	"Under the Pyramids"
Nir	A burgess near to Hatheg	"The Cats of Ulthar," "The Other Gods," *The Dream-Quest of Unknown Kadath*
Nis	A grinning chasm	"The Lurking Fear"
Nis, Valley of	Through which runs the river Than	"Memory"
Nithra	A river that flows through Aira	"The Quest of Iranon"
Nooseneck Hill, Rhode Island	The district from which Ann White came	"The Shunned House"
North Burial Ground, Providence, Rhode Island	Disturbance there	"The Shunned House," *The Case of Charles Dexter Ward*
North End, Boston, Massachusetts	Where Pickman took a studio	"Pickman's Model"
North Kingstown, Rhode Island	Ann White's hometown	"The Shunned House"
North Main Street, Salem, Massachusetts	Location of Dexter's home	"Ibid"
North Point, Kingsport, Massachusetts	Site of lighthouse kept by Basil Elton[6]	"The White Ship"
North Station, Boston, Massachusetts	Peaslee received a telephone call from there	"The Whisperer in Darkness," "Shadow Out of Time"
Northam Keep, England	Home of the Baron of Northam	"The Descendant"
Northfield, Massachusetts	Mentioned	"The Whisperer in Darkness"
Norton Mine	A celebrated gold mine somewhere in the southwestern U.S.	"The Transition of Juan Romero"
Noton	A peak, with the plateau of Sarkis between	"Polaris"
Notre-Dame Cathedral, Paris, France	Mentioned for its gargoyles	"Pickman's Model," *The Dream-Quest of Unknown Kadath*
Oberlin College, Oberlin, Ohio	Where the narrator attended	"The Shadow over Innsmouth"

6. The city in which the lighthouse is found is mentioned only in The *Dream-Quest of Unknown Kadath*.

PLACE-NAME	DESCRIPTION	SOURCE
Ograthon	Mercantile center, mentioned	*The Dream-Quest of Unknown Kadath*
Olathoë	A marble city in Lomar, compared to the ancient city on the Antarctic plateau	"Polaris," "The Quest of Iranon," *The Dream-Quest of Unknown Kadath, At the Mountains of Madness*
Old Carter place, near Arkham, Massachusetts	Visited	"The Silver Key"
Olney Court, Stamper's Hill, Providence, Rhode Island	Site of a "very old house" built and occupied at one time by Joseph Curwen	*The Case of Charles Dexter Ward*
Olney Street, Salem, Massachusetts	Location of Dexter's home	"Ibid"
Onga country, Congo Region, Africa	Explored by Sir Arthur Jermyn	"Facts concerning the Late Arthur Jermyn and His Family"
Oonai	A city of lutes and dancing, beyond the Karthia Hills	"The Quest of Iranon"
Ooth-Nargai	Mentioned	"Celephaïs," *The Dream-Quest of Unknown Kadath*
Ophir	Mentioned	"The Cats of Ulthar"
Orange Point, Kingsport, Massachusetts	Narrator falls over cliffs there	"The Festival"
Oriab	An island in the Southern Sea of dreamland	*The Dream-Quest of Unknown Kadath*
Orion's Sword (constellation)	Potential residence of interstellar traveler occupying Joe Slater	"Beyond the Wall of Sleep"
Orne's Gangway, Arkham, Massachusetts	Where a strange kidnapping took place	"Dreams in the Witch House"
Osborn's general store, Dunwich, Massachusetts	Mentioned	"The Dunwich Horror"
Oslo, Norway	Original home of Second Mate Gustaf Johansen	"The Call of Cthulhu"
Otaheite (Tahiti)	Near Captain Obed Marsh's destination	"The Shadow over Innsmouth"
Ottawa, Canada	Place of enlistment of West	"Herbert West—Reanimator"
Oukranos	A river, on the banks of which lies Thran, in dreamland	"The Silver Key," *The Dream-Quest of Unknown Kadath*

PLACE-NAME	DESCRIPTION	SOURCE
Oxford University, Oxford, England	Attended by Sir Arthur Jermyn	"Facts concerning the Late Arthur Jermyn and His Family," "He"
Oxford University, Oxford, England	Mentioned	"The Descendant"
Oxus	River in central Asia, mentioned	"The Nameless City"
Packet Street, Providence, Rhode Island	On Charles Dexter Ward's regular walking route	*The Case of Charles Dexter Ward*
Paine Street, Innsmouth, Massachusetts	Mentioned	"The Shadow over Innsmouth"
Palace of the Seventy Delights, Celephaïs	Kuranes's palace	*The Dream-Quest of Unknown Kadath*
Palmyra, Syria	Sculptures mentioned	*At the Mountains of Madness*
Panama Canal, Panama	Route of the *Arkham* to the Antarctic	*At the Mountains of Madness*
Panton, Vermont	The station-agent hails from there	"The Shadow over Innsmouth"
Pardon Tillinghast's Wharf, Town Street, Providence, Rhode Island	Where Etienne Roulet was employed	"The Shunned House"
Parg	Home of black slaves	*The Dream-Quest of Unknown Kadath*
Paris, France	Mentioned	"He," "The Call of Cthulhu," "The Shunned House"
Park Avenue, New York, New York	Where Galpin's fiancée lived	"Old Bugs"
Park Street Station, Boston, Massachusetts	Mentioned by Danforth	*At the Mountains of Madness*
Parker Place, Brooklyn, New York	Site of Suydam's basement flat	"The Horror at Red Hook"
Parker River, Massachusetts	On the route to Innsmouth from Newburyport	"The Shadow over Innsmouth"
Parry Mountains, Antarctica	Mentioned	*At the Mountains of Madness*
Parsloe's, St. James's Street, Soho, London, England	Meeting place of the Literary Club	"A Reminiscence of Dr. Samuel Johnson"
Pascoag, Rhode Island	Malone relocated there	"The Horror at Red Hook"
Passumpsic River, Vermont	In Caledonia County above Lyndonville	"The Whisperer in Darkness"

PLACE-NAME	DESCRIPTION	SOURCE
Paterson, New Jersey	Which Thurston visits	"The Call of Cthulhu"
Pawcatuck River, Rhode Island	Charles Dexter Ward crossed on his way home	*The Case of Charles Dexter Ward*
Pawtucket West Road, Providence, Rhode Island	Site of the North Burial Ground	"The Shunned House"
Pawtuxet Road, Providence, Rhode Island	Location of Joseph Curwen's farm	*The Case of Charles Dexter Ward*
Pawtuxet, Rhode Island	Source of gossip about Charles Dexter Ward	*The Case of Charles Dexter Ward*
Peabody Avenue Bridge, Arkham, Massachusetts	A bridge over the Miskatonic River	"Dreams in the Witch House"
Peck Valley Cemetery, Peck Valley	Where George Birch locked himself up	"In the Vault"
Perry Street, Greenwich, Manhattan, New York	Near where "he" lived	"He"
Perth, Australia	Dr. E. M. Boyle was from there	"Shadow Out of Time"
Petrovitch's Bakery	On the Street	"The Street"
Philippines	Where tribes became bothersome in response to the call	"The Call of Cthulhu"
Phoenix Park, Dublin, Ireland	Birthplace of Malone	"The Horror at Red Hook"
Phrygia	Mentioned	"The Rats in the Walls"
Placentia	Where Ibid was born	"Ibid"
Plateau of Sarkis	Site of Olathoë	"Polaris"
Plum Island, Massachusetts	Visible from the road from Newburyport to Innsmouth	"The Shadow over Innsmouth"
Pnath	A valley between the Peaks of Thok	*The Dream-Quest of Unknown Kadath*
Ponape, Caroline Islands	Mentioned	"The Shadow over Innsmouth"
Pond Street, Bolton, Massachusetts	Location of a home of Herbert West	"Herbert West—Reanimator"
Port Royal	Source of Curwen's sailors	*The Case of Charles Dexter Ward*
Port Said, Egypt	Arrival port of the Malwa	"Under the Pyramids"
Portland, Maine	Derby drove through there on his way back to Arkham	"Dreams in the Witch House"

PLACE-NAME	DESCRIPTION	SOURCE
Portsmouth, New Hampshire	Mentioned	*The Dream-Quest of Unknown Kadath*
Post Office Square, Providence, Rhode Island	Mentioned	*The Case of Charles Dexter Ward*
Potter's field, Arkham, Massachusetts	Potential source of bodies for Herbert West	"Herbert West—Reanimator"
Power Street, Providence, Rhode Island	Part of Charles Dexter Ward's regular walking route	*The Case of Charles Dexter Ward*
Power's Lane Hill, Providence, Rhode Island	Home of Captain Tillinghast	*The Case of Charles Dexter Ward*
Presbyterian Lane, Providence, Rhode Island	Where Peleg Harris lived	"The Shunned House"
Prince Street, Boston, Massachusetts	Near Pickman's studio	"Pickman's Model"
Prince's, Sackville Street, London, England	Meeting place of the Literary Club	"A Reminiscence of Dr. Samuel Johnson"
Princeton University, Princeton, New Jersey	On the faculty of which was Professor William Channing Webb	"The Call of Cthulhu"
Prospect Street, Providence, Rhode Island	In which is located the family home of Charles Dexter Ward	*The Case of Charles Dexter Ward*
Prospect Terrace, Providence, Rhode Island	Frequented by Charles Dexter Ward's nurses when he was a child	*The Case of Charles Dexter Ward*
Providence Art Club, Thomas Street, Providence, Rhode Island	Critical of Thomas Wilcox's work	"The Call of Cthulhu"
Providence River, Providence, Rhode Island	Fumes mistakenly attributed to waste dumped there	"The Shunned House"
Providence, Rhode Island	Home of Charles Dexter Ward	*The Case of Charles Dexter Ward*
Prussia	Home of the Lieutenant-Commander of the U-29	"The Temple"
Psi Delta House, Providence, Rhode Island	Students there saw Blake	"The Haunter of the Dark"
Ptolemais, Catacombs of	Mentioned	"The Picture in the House"
Public Library, Providence, Rhode Island	Frequented by Charles Dexter Ward	*The Case of Charles Dexter Ward*
Pyramid, Great, Gizeh, Egypt	Where the adventure took place	"Under the Pyramids"

PLACE-NAME	DESCRIPTION	SOURCE
Pyramid, Second, Gizeh, Egypt	Mentioned	"Under the Pyramids"
Pyramid, Third, Gizeh, Egypt	Mentioned	"Under the Pyramids"
Pyramids of Gizeh, Egypt	Visited by Houdini	"Under the Pyramids"
Queen Alexandra Range, Antarctica	West of base	*At the Mountains of Madness*
Queen Mary Land, Antarctica	Mentioned	*At the Mountains of Madness*
R'lyeh	A great city of stone houses, sunken beneath the waves	"The Call of Cthulhu"
R'yleh	Compared to ancient city on plateau	*At the Mountains of Madness*
Rakus, Transylvania	Home of Baron Ferenczy	*The Case of Charles Dexter Ward*
Ravenna, Italy	Where Ibid was interred	"Ibid"
Red Hook, Brooklyn, New York	District where Malone patrolled	"The Horror at Red Hook"
Reformed Church, Flatbush, Brooklyn, New York	Center of the district	"The Horror at Red Hook"
Rehoboth, Massachusetts	A servant at "the shunned house" came from there; also the home of Dr. Jabez Bowen	"The Shunned House," *The Case of Charles Dexter Ward*
Reservoir Avenue, Providence, Rhode Island	Mentioned	*The Case of Charles Dexter Ward*
Rhine, ruined castles on	Mentioned	"The Picture in the House"
Rhineland, Prussia	Home of several crewmen on the *U-29*	"The Temple"
Rhode Island School of Design, Thomas Street, Providence, Rhode Island	Place of study of Thomas Wilcox	"The Call of Cthulhu"
Rhodes-on-the-Pawtuxet, Rhode Island	Home of resort, frequented by Charles Dexter Ward	*The Case of Charles Dexter Ward*
Richmond, Virginia	Defended by Walter Delapore's father	"The Rats in the Walls"
Rifkin School of Modern Economics	On the Street	"The Street"
Rinar	Mercantile center, mentioned	*The Dream-Quest of Unknown Kadath*

PLACE-NAME	DESCRIPTION	SOURCE
River Street, Innsmouth, Massachusetts	Mentioned	"The Shadow over Innsmouth"
Riverpoint, Pawtuxet Valley, Rhode Island	Site of cotton mills	*The Case of Charles Dexter Ward*
Rochambeau Avenue, Providence, Rhode Island	Truck fled	*The Case of Charles Dexter Ward*
Rokol	A principality in Mnar	"The Doom That Came to Sarnath"
Rome, Italy	Mentioned	"The Nameless City," "The Rats in the Walls," "Ibid"
Ross Island, Antarctica	Mentioned	*At the Mountains of Madness*
Ross Sea, Antarctica	Mentioned	*At the Mountains of Madness*
Rotterdam, Holland	A waystation on the narrator's journey to the churchyard from which he stole an amulet	"The Hound"
Round Mountain, Massachusetts	Purportedly near Dunwich but actually in southern Massachusetts	"The Dunwich Horror"
Rowley, Massachusetts	Mentioned	"The Shadow over Innsmouth"
Royal Society, Sydney, Australia	Mentioned	"The Call of Cthulhu"
Rue d'Auseil	A street in an unknown city	"The Music of Erich Zann"
Rue St.-Jacques, Paris, France	Where Charles Dexter Ward lodged	*The Case of Charles Dexter Ward*
Saco, Maine	Derby drove through there on his way back to Arkham	"Dreams in the Witch House"
Salem, Massachusetts	Old man's friend Ebenezer was on a Salem merchantman. Mentioned as home of Edmund Carter, ancestor of Randolph Carter. Original home of Joseph Curwen. Ibid's relics were removed there.	"The Picture in the House," *The Case of Charles Dexter Ward*, "The Silver Key," "The Dunwich Horror," "Pickman's Model," *The Dream-Quest of Unknown Kadath*, "Ibid"
Saltonstall Street, Arkham, Massachusetts	Home of Upton	"Dreams in the Witch House"
Samarkand	Mentioned	"He"
Samoa	Route of the *Arkham* to the Antarctic	*At the Mountains of Madness*
San Diego, California	Henry Akeley's son lived there	"The Whisperer in Darkness"

PLACE-NAME	DESCRIPTION	SOURCE
San Francisco	Location of narrator's hospital; port of departure for Thurston's sail to New Zealand	"Dagon," "The Call of Cthulhu"
Saratoga, New York	Where John Burgoyne was defeated in the American War	"A Reminiscence of Dr. Samuel Johnson"
Sarkomand	Deserted city below Leng	*The Dream-Quest of Unknown Kadath*
Sarnath	Mentioned	"The Nameless City"
Sarnath	A city in Mnar, near the city of Ib	"The Doom That Came to Sarnath"
Saturn	Home of very large and peculiar cats	*The Dream-Quest of Unknown Kadath*
Sayles Tavern, Pawtuxet, Rhode Island	Mentioned	*The Case of Charles Dexter Ward*
Sefton Asylum, Sefton, Massachusetts	Fifty miles from Boston, near Arkham	"Herbert West—Reanimator"
Selarn	On the great caravan road	*The Dream-Quest of Unknown Kadath*
Sentinel Hill, Dunwich, Massachusetts	Mentioned	"The Dunwich Horror"
Serranian	The pink marble city of the clouds	"Celephaïs," *The Dream-Quest of Unknown Kadath*
Shari Mohammed Ali, Cairo, Egypt	Houdini passed through	"Under the Pyramids"
Sharia-el-Haram, Gizeh, Egypt	A road on which Houdini traveled	"Under the Pyramids"
Sheehan's Pool Room, Chicago, Illinois	Where the story takes place	"Old Bugs"
Shepherd's Hotel, Cairo, Egypt	Houdini stayed there	"Under the Pyramids"
Shepley Library, Benefit Street, Providence, Rhode Island	Frequented by Charles Dexter Ward	*The Case of Charles Dexter Ward*
Ship Street, Kingsport, Massachusetts	The back gate of the home of the Terrible Old Man is on this street; Granny Orne lived there	"The Terrible Old Man," "The Strange High House in the Mist"
Siberia	Mentioned	*At the Mountains of Madness*
Sidrak	A mountain near Teloth	"The Quest of Iranon"

PLACE-NAME	DESCRIPTION	SOURCE
Sign of Shakespear's Head, 21 Meeting Street, Providence, Rhode Island	On Charles Dexter Ward's regular walking route	*The Case of Charles Dexter Ward*
Sign of the Boy and Book, Providence, Rhode Island	Customer of Curwen	*The Case of Charles Dexter Ward*
Sign of the Elephant, Cheapside, Providence, Rhode Island	Shop kept by James Green	*The Case of Charles Dexter Ward*
Sign of the Golden Eagle, across the Bridge, Providence, Rhode Island	Shop kept by the Russells	*The Case of Charles Dexter Ward*
Sign of the Unicorn and Mortar, Providence, Rhode Island	Across the Great Bridge; apothecary shop operated by Dr. Jabez Bowen	*The Case of Charles Dexter Ward*
Silver Street, Providence, Rhode Island	On Charles Dexter Ward's regular walking route	*The Case of Charles Dexter Ward*
Sinara	A mountain near the Zuro River	"The Quest of Iranon"
Skai	A river in dreamland, beyond Ulthar	"The Cats of Ulthar," "The Silver Key," "The Other Gods," "The Strange High House in the Mist," *The Dream-Quest of Unknown Kadath*
Snake Tomb, Petra	Mentioned	*At the Mountains of Madness*
Sona-Nyl	Land of Fancy	"The White Ship," *The Dream-Quest of Unknown Kadath*
South America	Home of newspaper carrying letter with dire predictions	"The Call of Cthulhu"
South Londonderry, Vermont	Walter Brown loafed there	"The Whisperer in Darkness"
South Main Street, Providence, Rhode Island	Part of Charles Dexter Ward's regular walking route	*The Case of Charles Dexter Ward*
South Pacific Ocean	From which the moon was ripped	*At the Mountains of Madness*
South Station, Boston, Massachusetts	Subway station mentioned by Danforth	*At the Mountains of Madness*
South Station, Boston, Massachusetts	Elevated station, mentioned	"Pickman's Model"
South Street, Innsmouth, Massachusetts	Mentioned	"The Shadow over Innsmouth"

PLACE-NAME	DESCRIPTION	SOURCE
South Water Street, Providence, Rhode Island	Part of Charles Dexter Ward's regular walking route	*The Case of Charles Dexter Ward*
Southern Sea	In dreamland	*The Dream-Quest of Unknown Kadath*
Sovereign Street, Providence, Rhode Island	On Charles Dexter Ward's regular walking route	*The Case of Charles Dexter Ward*
Spirito Santo Church, Providence, Rhode Island	The pastor of which was Father Merluzzo	"The Haunter of the Dark"
Spitzbergen	Peaslee traveled north of here	"Shadow Out of Time"
Spoleto, Italy	Mentioned	"Ibid"
St. Eloi, Flanders, Belgium	Location of West's field hospital	"Herbert West—Reanimator"
St. Eustatius	Source of Curwen's sailors	*The Case of Charles Dexter Ward*
St. John's Church, Hidden churchyard, Providence, Rhode Island	On Charles Dexter Ward's regular walking route	"The Shunned House," *The Case of Charles Dexter Ward*
St. Louis, Missouri	Home of Robert Leavitt; host to the 1908 meeting of the American Archaeological Society	"Herbert West—Reanimator," "The Call of Cthulhu"
St. Mary's Hospital, Arkham, Massachusetts	Place of hospitalization of narrator; the narrator of "The Unnamable" and Joel Manton recuperate there as well	"The Festival," "The Unnamable"
St. Paul's Chapel, New York, New York	Steeple is visible	"He"
St. Stanislaus' Church, Arkham, Massachusetts	Parish of Father Iwanicki	"Dreams in the Witch House"
State House, Boston, Massachusetts	Mentioned	*The Dream-Quest of Unknown Kadath*
State House, Providence, Rhode Island	Frequented by Charles Dexter Ward	*The Case of Charles Dexter Ward*
State Street, Newburyport, Massachusetts	Site of a pawnshop in 1873	"The Shadow over Innsmouth"
Stonehenge, England	Mentioned	"The Rats in the Walls"
Street of the Pillars, Celephaïs	Carter walked along it	"Celephaïs," *The Dream-Quest of Unknown Kadath*

PLACE-NAME	DESCRIPTION	SOURCE
Suez Canal, Egypt	Visited by Houdini; the *Lexington* passed through	"Under the Pyramids," "Shadow Out of Time"
Suffolk, England	Mentioned	"Shadow Out of Time"
Suken-Nahhasin, Cairo, Egypt	A bazaar of coppersmiths, visited by Houdini	"Under the Pyramids"
Sultan Hassan, Mosque of, Cairo, Egypt	Houdini visited there	"Under the Pyramids"
Sumner's Pond, Arkham, Massachusetts	Mentioned	"Herbert West—Reanimator"
Surrey Downs, England	Mentioned	"Celephaïs"
Sussex, England	Home of Sir Geoffrey Hyde	"The Tomb"
Swan Point Cemetery, Providence, Rhode Island	Mentioned. HPL is buried there.	*The Case of Charles Dexter Ward*
Sydney University, Sydney, Australia	Mentioned	"The Call of Cthulhu"
Sydney, Australia	Mentioned	"The Call of Cthulhu"
Syracuse, Sicily	The Tyrant wanted a statue	"The Tree"
Tanarian Hills	Celephaïs lay beyond these	"Celephaïs" and *The Dream-Quest of Unknown Kadath*
Tartarus	Mentioned	"Herbert West—Reanimator"
Tau Omega Fraternity, Providence, Rhode Island	One of its members saw the events	"The Haunter of the Dark"
Tegea, Greece	Where Kalos and Musides resided	"The Tree"
Teloth	A granite city	"The Quest of Iranon"
Tempest Mountain, Catskills, New York	The site of paranormal activity	"The Lurking Fear"
Temple of the Cats, Ulthar	Mentioned	*The Dream-Quest of Unknown Kadath*
Temple of the Elder Ones, Ulthar	Carter visits there	*The Dream-Quest of Unknown Kadath*
Temple of the Sphinx, Gizeh, Egypt	Houdini was held prisoner there	"Under the Pyramids"
Terror, Mount, Antarctica	Mentioned	*At the Mountains of Madness*

PLACE-NAME	DESCRIPTION	SOURCE
Thalarion	The City of a Thousand Wonders	"The White Ship," *The Dream-Quest of Unknown Kadath*
Than River	Runs through the valley of Nis	"Memory"
Thapnen watchtower, Olathoë	Where the narrator was sent	"Polaris"
The Thatched House, St. James's Street, Soho, London, England	Meetingplace of the Literary Club	"A Reminiscence of Dr. Samuel Johnson"
Thayer Street, Providence, Rhode Island	Offices of Dr. Tobey, physician caring for Thomas Wilcox	"The Call of Cthulhu"
The Troad, Anatolia, Turkey	Where Sir William Brinton made his reputation	"The Rats in the Walls"
Thebes	Where Tutankhamen was crowned	"Under the Pyramids"
Thok, Peaks of	Fabled	*The Dream-Quest of Unknown Kadath*
Thon and Thal	The beacons of Baharna	*The Dream-Quest of Unknown Kadath*
Thorabonia	A region in dreamland	*The Dream-Quest of Unknown Kadath*
Thraa	A city in Mnar, on the Ai River	"The Doom That Came to Sarnath," "The Quest of Iranon," *The Dream-Quest of Unknown Kadath*
Thran	A city of spires on the banks of the Oukranos, in dreamland	"The Silver Key." *The Dream-Quest of Unknown Kadath*
Thurai	A mountain	"The Other Gods"
Toledo, Ohio	Home of narrator	"The Shadow over Innsmouth"
Totten Land, Antarctica	Mentioned	*At the Mountains of Madness*
Tower of Koth	A stairway to a part of dreamland	*The Dream-Quest of Unknown Kadath*
Town Street, Providence, Rhode Island	Part of Charles Dexter Ward's regular walking route	"The Shunned House," *The Case of Charles Dexter Ward*
Townshend, Vermont	In Windham County, home of Henry Akeley	"The Whisperer in Darkness"
Transylvania	Home of Mr. H	*The Case of Charles Dexter Ward*

PLACE-NAME	DESCRIPTION	SOURCE
Tremont Street, Boston, Massachusetts	Mentioned	*The Dream-Quest of Unknown Kadath*
Trevor Towers, Innsmouth, England	Kuranes's body was found in the rocks here	"Celephaïs," *The Dream-Quest of Unknown Kadath*
Trinity Church, New York, New York	Steeple is visible	"He"
Tropic of Capricorn	Peaslee thought he was near there	"Shadow Out of Time"
Truro, Massachusetts	Mentioned	*The Dream-Quest of Unknown Kadath*
Tulane University, New Orleans, Louisiana	Mentioned	"The Call of Cthulhu"
Turk's-Head Tavern, Gerrard Street, Soho, London, England	Meetingplace of the Literary Club	"A Reminiscence of Dr. Samuel Johnson"
Tyre	Mentioned	"The Call of Cthulhu"
Ulthar	A town beyond the Skai River	"The Cats of Ulthar" "The Silver Key" "The Other Gods," "The Strange High House in the Mist," *The Dream-Quest of Unknown Kadath*
University of Buenos Aires, Buenos Aires, Argentina	Mentioned as repository of *Necronomicon* (Buenos Ayres)	"The Dunwich Horror"
University of Vermont, Burlington, Vermont	Henry Akeley was on the faculty there	"The Whisperer in Darkness"
University of Wisconsin, Madison, Wisconsin	Galpin's alma mater	"Old Bugs"
Urg	Small-domed village	*The Dream-Quest of Unknown Kadath*
Uzuldaroum, Hyperborea	Compared to ancient city on Antarctic plateau	*At the Mountains of Madness*
Valley of Kings, Luxor, Egypt	Mentioned	"Cool Air"
Valparaiso, Chile	Port of departure of *Vigilant*	"The Call of Cthulhu"
Valusia	Compared to ancient city on Antarctic plateau; temporary home of the Shining Trapezohedron	*At the Mountains of Madness*, "Shadow Out of Time," "The Haunter of the Dark"

PLACE-NAME	DESCRIPTION	SOURCE
Victoria Embankment, London, England	Narrator walks there	"The Hound"
Victoria Land, Antarctica	Mentioned	*At the Mountains of Madness*
Vienna, Austria	Charles Dexter Ward passed through	*The Case of Charles Dexter Ward*
Waltham, Massachusetts	On the route to Greenfield	"The Whisperer in Darkness"
Wantastiquet Mountain, New Hampshire	Mentioned	"The Whisperer in Darkness"
Washington Street Station, Boston, Massachusetts	Mentioned by Danforth	*At the Mountains of Madness*
Washington Street, Innsmouth, Massachusetts	Mentioned	"The Shadow over Innsmouth"
Water Street, Innsmouth, Massachusetts	Mentioned	"The Shadow over Innsmouth"
Water Street, Kingsport, Massachusetts	Where lies the home of the Terrible Old Man	"The Terrible Old Man"
Waterman Street, Providence, Rhode Island	Home of family of Thomas Wilcox	"The Call of Cthulhu"
Weddell Sea, Antarctica	Mentioned	*At the Mountains of Madness*
West Fourteenth Street, New York, New York	Narrator lived in a boardinghouse here	"Cool Air"
West River, Vermont	In Windham County beyond Newfane, mentioned	"The Whisperer in Darkness"
West Street, Auckland, New Zealand	Home of Second Mate Gustaf Johansen	"The Call of Cthulhu"
Western Australia	Mentioned	"Shadow Out of Time"
Westminster Street, Providence, Rhode Island	William Harris built a home there	"The Shunned House"
Weybosset Street, Providence, Rhode Island	Mentioned	*The Case of Charles Dexter Ward*
Wheaton Street, Providence, Rhode Island	A boundary of the lot on which the shunned house stood	"The Shunned House"
Widener Library, Harvard University, Cambridge, Massachusetts	Research conducted there by Charles Dexter Ward; Wilbur Whateley tries to borrow the *Necronomicon* from the library	*The Case of Charles Dexter Ward*, "The Dunwich Horror"

PLACE-NAME	DESCRIPTION	SOURCE
Wilhelmshaven, Germany	The U-29 hoped to reach there	"The Temple"
Williams Street, Providence, Rhode Island	Home of Prof. George Gammell Angell; part of Ward's regular walking route	"The Call of Cthulhu," *The Case of Charles Dexter Ward*
Winchendon, Massachusetts	Mentioned	"The Whisperer in Darkness"
Winooski River, Vermont	Mentioned	"The Whisperer in Darkness"
Witch House, Arkham, Massachusetts	The locus of strange events	"Dreams in the Witch House"
Woonsocket, Rhode Island	Malone's specialist was located there	"The Horror at Red Hook"
Xari	A frigid river	"The Quest of Iranon"
Xura	Land of Pleasures Unattained	"The White Ship," *The Dream-Quest of Unknown Kadath*
Y.M.C.A., Newburyport, Massachusetts	Where the narrator stayed	"The Shadow over Innsmouth"
Y'ha-nthlei	A many-columned city under the sea, near Innsmouth	"The Shadow over Innsmouth"
Yath	A lake or river where the captain of Carter's ship lived	*The Dream-Quest of Unknown Kadath*
Yorkshire, England	Home of Ward butler	*The Case of Charles Dexter Ward*
Yucatán, Mexico	Where a bottle with the tale of "The Temple" was found	"The Temple"
Yuggoth	A planet	"The Whisperer in Darkness"
Zakarion	A dream city	"Ex Oblivione"
Zar	A land from which the White Ship sailed; abode of forgotten dreams	"The White Ship," *The Dream-Quest of Unknown Kadath*
Zin	Vaults of the ghasts	*The Dream-Quest of Unknown Kadath*
Zion Research Library, Brookline, Massachusetts	Research conducted there by Charles Dexter Ward	*The Case of Charles Dexter Ward*
Zobna	A city in Lomar	"Polaris"
Zoölogical Gardens, Cairo, Egypt	Passed by Houdini	"Under the Pyramids"
Zuro	A sluggish river	"The Quest of Iranon"

Acknowledgments

It's been a pleasure to dive back into the works of HPL, and my plunge was aided by many people. Lovecraftians embraced the first volume of my *New Annotated H. P. Lovecraft* and were very supportive of this volume in early stages. Special thanks to S. T. Joshi, Stefan Dziemianowicz, Peter Cannon, Jason Eckhardt, the late Wilum Pugmire, Jason Thompson, Ian Ensign, Will Hart, and especially Donovan Loucks, who worked overtime on getting high-quality photos! Victor LaValle wrote an introduction that surpassed my hopes, and I value his friendship. Thanks as well to my agent, Don Maass, who dealt with the usual business issues, and my attorney, Jonathan Kirsch, who helped with rights. Bob Weil and Marie Pantojan of Liveright were thoughtful editors, and the Liveright/W. W. Norton team, including Anna Oler, Don Rifkin, Gabriel Kachuck, Steve Attardo, and Jo Anne Metsch—as usual—made this book far more beautiful than I could have imagined. Janet Byrne devoted hundreds of hours to editing and additional research, and the final product reflects her devotion. This is our fifth book together, and each one is far better for her attention. Megan Beatie and I have now worked together for fifteen years, and her wisdom about publicity (and her friendship and enthusiasm) is always valued. I'm always grateful for the support of my writer friends Cornelia Funke, Neil Gaiman, Nancy Holder, Laurie R. King, Nicholas Meyer, Lisa Morton, Bonnie MacBird, and Peter Straub, and my long-time Sherlockian pals Mike Whelan, Steve Rothman, Andy Peck, and Jerry Margolin are constant cheerleaders. My family is always understanding of my disappearances as I indulge in research and writing. Finally, without my wife, Sharon, none of my writing would ever get done. She has always been, and remains, "the woman."

Works Cited

Airaksinen, Timo. *The Philosophy of H. P. Lovecraft: The Route to Horror.* New York: Peter Lang Publishing, Inc., 1999.

Atsma, Bert. "Living on Borrowed Time (A Biologist Looks at 'M. Valdemar' and 'Cool Air')." *Crypt of Cthulhu* 4 (Eastertide 1982), 11–13.

Baring-Gould, Sabine. *Curious Myths of the Middle Ages,* Second Series. London, Oxford, and Cambridge: Rivingtons, 1868.

Bell, Michael E. *Food for the Dead: On the Trail of New England's Vampires.* Middletown, CT: Wesleyan University Press, 2001.

Blackmore, Leigh, "Some Notes on Lovecraft's 'The Transition of Juan Romero.'" *Lovecraft Annual* 3 (2009), 147–68.

Blosser, Fred. "The Sign of the Magna Mater." *Crypt of Cthulhu* 97 (Hallowmas 1997), 25–27.

Buchanan, Carl. "'The Music of Erich Zann': A Psychological Interpretation (or Two)." In *A Century Less a Dream: Selected Criticism on H. P. Lovecraft,* edited by Scott Connors, 224–29. Holikong, PA: Wildside Press, 2002.

——— . "'The Terrible Old Man': A Myth of the Devouring Father." *Lovecraft Studies* 15 (Fall 1987), 19–31.

Burleson, Donald R. *H. P. Lovecraft: A Critical Study.* Westport, CT: Greenwood Press, 1983.

——— . "'The Terrible Old Man': A Deconstruction." *Lovecraft Studies* 15 (Fall 1987), 65–68.

Burleson, Mollie. "The Outsider: A Woman?" *Lovecraft Studies* 22/23 (Fall 1990), 22–23.

Callaghan, Gavin. "Elementary, My Dear Lovecraft: H. P. Lovecraft and Sherlock Holmes." *Lovecraft Annual* 6 (2012), 198–228.

——— . "A Reprehensible Habit: H. P. Lovecraft and the Munsey Magazines." In *Lovecraft and Influence: His Predecessors and Successors,* edited by Robert H. Waugh, 69–82. Lanham, Toronto, and Plymouth, UK: The Scarecrow Press, Inc., 2013.

Cannon, Peter. *H. P. Lovecraft.* Twayne's United States Authors Series. Boston: Twayne, 1989.

——— . "The Influence of *Vathek* on H. P. Lovecraft's *The Dream-Quest of Unknown Kadath.*" In *H. P. Lovecraft: Four Decades of Criticism,* edited by S. T. Joshi, 153–57. Athens: Ohio University Press, 1980.

————. "Lovecraft's Old Men." *Nyctalops* 3, no. 2 (March 1981), 13–14.

————. "You Have Been in Providence, I Perceive." *Nyctalops* 2, no. 7 (March 1978), 45–46.

Cisco, Michael. "The Shadow over 'The Lurking Fear.'" *Lovecraft Annual* 6 (2012), 43–53.

Clore, Dan. *Weird Words: A Lovecraftian Lexicon.* New York: Hippocampus Press, 2009.

Coffman, Edward M. *The War to End All Wars: The American Military Experience in World War I.* Lexington: University Press of Kentucky, 1998.

Dendle, Peter. "Patristic Demonology and Lovecraft's 'From Beyond.'" *Journal of the Fantastic in the Arts* 8, no. 3 (1997), 281–93.

Elmslie, W. A. "The Orthography of African Names and the Principles of Nomenclature." *Scottish Geographical Magazine* 7, no. 7 (July 1891), 370–75.

Elworthy, Frederick Thomas. *The Evil Eye.* London: John Murray, 1895. Reprinted, New York: Bell Publishing Company, 1989.

Fiske, John. *Myths and Myth-Makers: Old Tales and Superstitions Interpreted by Comparative Mythology.* Cambridge, MA: Riverside Press, 1902.

Frenschkowski, Marco. "Nodens—Metamorphosis of a Deity." *Crypt of Cthulhu* 87 (Lammas 1994), 3–8 and 18.

Fulwiler, William. "Reflections on 'The Outsider.'" *Lovecraft Studies* 1, no. 2 (Spring 1980), 3–4.

Graves, Robert. *The White Goddess: A Historical Grammar of Poetic Myth.* Amended and enlarged ed. New York: Farrar, Straus and Giroux, 1966.

Haden, David. "The Annotated 'The Lurking Fear.'" In *Lovecraft in Historical Context: A Fifth Collection,* 36–81. Self-published, 2014.

————. "The Nature of the New York Streets." In *Walking with Cthulhu: H. P. Lovecraft as Psychogeographer, New York City 1924–26,* 52–71. Self-published, 2011.

————. "A Note on the Elder Signs." In *Lovecraft in Historical Context: Further Essays and Notes,* 121–24. Self-published, 2011.

————. "Of Rats and Legions: H. P. Lovecraft in Northumbria." In *Lovecraft in Historical Context: Fourth Collection,* 109–24. Self-published, 2013.

————. "'The Rats in the Walls': Otherness and British Culture." In *Lovecraft in Historical Context: Essays,* 32–37. Self-published, 2010.

Harner, Michael. "The Enigma of Aztec Sacrifice." *Natural History* 86, no. 4 (April 1977), 46–51.

Hassig, Ross. *Aztec Warfare: Imperial Expansion and Political Control.* Norman: University of Oklahoma Press, 1988.

Hazel, Faye Ringel. "Some Strange New England Mortuary Practices: Lovecraft Was Right." *Lovecraft Studies* 29 (Fall 1993), 13–18.

Hitz, John Kipling. "Lovecraft and the Whitman Memoir." *Lovecraft Studies* 37 (Fall 1997), 15–17.

Humphreys, Brian. "Who or What Was Iranon?" *Lovecraft Studies* 25 (Fall 1991), 10–13.

Joshi, S. T. "Attis and Cybele." *Crypt of Cthulhu* 72 (Roodmas 1990), 6–8.

———. *H. P. Lovecraft: The Decline of the West.* Berkeley Heights, NJ: Wildside Press, 1990.

———. *I Am Providence: The Life and Times of H. P. Lovecraft.* New York: Hippocampus Press, 2010.

———. *Lovecraft's Library: A Catalogue (Revised and Enlarged).* New York: Hippocampus Press, 2002.

———. "Topical References in Lovecraft," *Primal Sources: Essays on H. P. Lovecraft,* 126–44. New York: Hippocampus Press, 2003.

———. "What Happens in 'Arthur Jermyn.'" In *Primal Sources: Essays on H. P. Lovecraft,* 159–61. New York: Hippocampus Press, 2003.

Kimball, Gertrude S. *Providence in Colonial Times.* Boston and New York: Houghton Mifflin Company, 1912.

Lane, Joel. "The Master of Masks." *Nyctalops* 4, no. 1 (April 1991), 62–67.

Lenoir, Andrew. "Dead Lies Dreaming: Lovecraft and the Other Side of Modernity." *Lovecraftian Proceedings: Papers from NecronomiCon Providence: 2013,* no. 1, 53–72.

Lévi, Eliphas. *The Mysteries of Magic: A Digest of the Writings of Eliphas Lévi.* Translated and edited by Arthur Edward Waite. London: George Redway, 1886.

Livesey, T. R. "Lovecraft and the Ray-Gun." *Lovecraft Annual* (2009), 3–9.

Lovecraft, H. P. *The Call of Cthulhu and Other Weird Stories.* Edited by S. T. Joshi. New York: Penguin, 1999.

———. *The Dreams in the Witch House and Other Weird Stories.* Edited by S. T. Joshi. New York: Penguin, 2004.

———. *Lord of a Visible World: An Autobiography in Letters.* Edited by S. T. Joshi and David E. Schultz. Athens: Ohio University Press (2000).

———. *Selected Letters, 1911–1924.* Edited by August Derleth and Donald Wandrei. Sauk City, WI: Arkham House, 1965. (*Selected Letters,* I.)

———. *Selected Letters, 1925–1929.* Edited by August Derleth and Donald Wandrei. Sauk City, WI: Arkham House, 1968. (*Selected Letters,* II.)

———. *Selected Letters, 1929–1931.* Edited by August Derleth and Donald Wandrei. Sauk City, WI: Arkham House, 1969. (*Selected Letters,* III.)

———. *Selected Letters, 1932–1934.* Edited by August Derleth and James Turner. Sauk City, WI: Arkham House, 1971. (*Selected Letters,* IV.)

———. *Selected Letters, 1934–1937.* Edited by August Derleth and James Turner. Sauk City, WI: Arkham House, 1976. (*Selected Letters,* V.)

———. "Some Notes on Interplanetary Fiction." *Californian* 3, no. 3 (Winter 1935), 39–42.

———. "Supernatural Horror in Literature," *Dagon and Other Macabre Tales.* Corrected seventh printing. Edited by S. T. Joshi. Sauk City, WI: Arkham House Publishers, Inc., 1965.

Mariconda, Steven J. "Curious Myths of the Middle Ages and 'The Rats in the Walls.'" In *On the Emergence of "Cthulhu" & Other Observations*, 53–55. West Warwick, RI: Necronomicon Press, 1995.

Marten, Robert D. "The Pickman Models." *Lovecraft Studies* 44 (2004), 42–80.

Melton, J. Gordon. *The Vampire Book*. Detroit and London: Visible Ink Press, 1999.

McCabe, Joseph. *Morals in the Arab-Persian Civilization*. Big Blue Books B-488. *History of Human Morals*, vol. 6, edited by E. Haldeman-Julius. Girard, KS: Haldeman-Julius Company, 1930.

Monteleone, Paul. "The Inner Significance of 'The Outsider.'" *Lovecraft Studies* 35 (Fall 1996), 9–21.

Mosig, Dirk W. "An Analytic Interpretation: The Outsider, Allegory of the Psyche." *The Miskatonic*, EOD 7 (August 1974). Reprinted in *The Miskatonic: The Lovecraft Centenary Edition*, 128–33. Glenview, IL: The Moshassuck Press, 1991.

———. "A Note on *The Occult Lovecraft*." *The Miskatonic*, EOD 11 (August 1975). Reprinted in *The Miskatonic: The Lovecraft Centenary Edition*. Glenview, Il: The Moshassuck Press, 1991, 210–11.

———. "Toward a Greater Appreciation of H. P. Lovecraft: The Analytic Approach." *The Miskatonic*, EOD 1 (June 1973). Reprinted in *The Miskatonic: Lovecraft Centenary Edition*. Glenview, IL: The Moshassuck Press, 1991, 2–14.

Murray, Will. "Behind the Mask of Nyarlathotep." *Lovecraft Studies* 25 (Fall 1991), 25–29.

———. "Lovecraft's Ghouls." *Crypt of Cthulhu* 14 (St. John's Eve 1983), 8–9, 27.

———. "In Pickman's Footsteps." *Crypt of Cthulhu* 28 (Yuletide 1984), 27–32.

———. "A Probable Source for the Drinking Song from 'The Tomb.'" *Lovecraft Studies* 15 (Fall 1987), 77–80.

Neff, William. Letter to *Lovecraft Studies* 22/23 (Fall 1990), 66–67.

Nolan, Liam, and John E. Nolan. *Secret Victory: Ireland and the War at Sea, 1914–1918*. Blackrock, Ireland: Mercier Press Ltd., 2009.

Parry-Jones, William Ll. *The Trade in Lunacy: A Study of Private Madhouses in England in the Eighteenth and Nineteenth Centuries*. London: Routledge, 1972; repr. 2013.

Pierson, Robert E. "High House, Shunned House and a Silver Key." *Nyctalops* 3, no. 2 (March 1981), 5–9.

Poe, Edgar Allan. *Complete Poems*, vol. 1 of *Complete Works*. Edited by Thomas Ollive Mabbott. Cambridge, MA: Harvard University Press, 1978.

Price, Robert M. "Erich Zann and the Rue d'Auseil." *Lovecraft Studies* 22/23 (Fall 1990), 13–14.

———. "Lovecraft's Concept of Blasphemy." *Crypt of Cthulhu* 1 (Hallowmas 1981), 3–15.

———. "Lucian's *True Story* and Lovecraft's *Dream-Quest*." *Crypt of Cthulhu* 83 (Eastertide 1993), 27–28.

———. "Two Biblical Curiosities in Lovecraft." *Lovecraft Studies* 16 (Spring 1988), 12–13, 18.

————. "The Works of Robert Blake." *Crypt of Cthulhu* 80 (Eastertide 1992), 30–32.

Rössler, Eberhard. *The U-Boat: The Evolution and Technical History of German Submarines.* Translated by Harold Erenberg. Annapolis, MD: Naval Institute Press, 1989.

Schafer, Jacqueline C. "H. P. Lovecraft: Aspiring Materialist." *Nyctalops* 4, no. 1 (April 1991), 52–59.

Schweitzer, Darrell. *The Dream Quest of H. P. Lovecraft.* San Bernardino, CA: The Borgo Press, 1976.

Setiya, Kieran. "Two Notes on Lovecraft." *Lovecraft Studies* 26 (Spring 1992), 14–16.

Shaw, Ian. *Oxford History of Ancient Egypt.* Oxford: Oxford University Press, 2000.

Shreffler, Philip A. *The H. P. Lovecraft Companion.* Westport, CT, and London: Greenwood Press, 1977.

Skinner, Charles M. *Myths and Legends of Our Own Land.* 4th ed. New York and Philadelphia: J. B. Lippincott & Co., 1896.

Stetson, George R. "The Animistic Vampire in New England." *The American Anthropologist* 9, no. 1 (January 1896), 1–13.

Sweet, Frank H. "Callum's Cot'in—A Plantation Idyl." *The Craftsman* 11 (October 1906–March 1907), 712–27.

Ticknor, Caroline. *Poe's Helen.* New York: Charles Scribner's Sons, 1916.

Watkins, Alfred. *Early British Trackways: Moats, Mounds, Camps and Sites.* Hereford, UK: The Watkins Meter Company, 1922.

Waugh, Robert H. "Dr. Margaret Murray and H. P. Lovecraft: The Witch-Cult in New England." *Lovecraft Studies* 31 (Fall 1994), 2–9.

————. "Documents, Creatures, and History in H. P. Lovecraft." *Lovecraft Studies* 25 (Fall 1991), 2–10.

————. "Lovecraft's Rats and Doyle's Hound: A Study in Reason and Madness." *Lovecraft Annual* 7 (2013), 60–75.

————. *The Monster in the Mirror: Looking for H. P. Lovecraft.* New York: Hippocampus Press, 2006.

————. *A Monster of Voices: Speaking for H. P. Lovecraft.* New York: Hippocampus Press, 2011.

Wetzel, George T. "The Cthulhu Mythos: A Study." In *H. P. Lovecraft: Four Decades of Criticism,* edited by S. T. Joshi, 79–95. Athens: Ohio University Press, 1980.